life
BEYOND
US

AN ORIGINAL ANTHOLOGY OF SF STORIES AND SCIENCE ESSAYS

EDITED BY JULIE NOVÁKOVÁ, LUCAS K. LAW & SUSAN FOREST

STORIES BY EUGEN BACON, GREGORY BENFORD, TOBIAS S. BUCKELL, JULIE E. CZERNEDA, MARY ROBINETTE KOWAL, GEOFFREY A. LANDIS, PREMEE MOHAMED, MALKA OLDER, BOGI TAKÁCS, PETER WATTS, AND MORE

INTRODUCTION BY STEPHEN BAXTER

EUROPEAN ASTROBIOLOGY INSTITUTE PRESENTS SERIES

EDITED BY JULIE NOVÁKOVÁ, LUCAS K. LAW, AND SUSAN FOREST
Life Beyond Us: An Original Anthology of SF Stories and Science Essays

LAKSA ANTHOLOGY SERIES: SPECULATIVE FICTION

EDITED BY SUSAN FOREST AND LUCAS K. LAW
Strangers Among Us: Tales of the Underdogs and Outcasts
The Sum of Us: Tales of the Bonded and Bound
Shades Within Us: Tales of Migrations and Fractured Borders
Seasons Between Us: Tales of Identities and Memories

EDITED BY LUCAS K. LAW AND DERWIN MAK
Where the Stars Rise: Asian Science Fiction and Fantasy

BOOKS BY SUSAN FOREST

ADDICTED TO HEAVEN SERIES
Bursts of Fire
Flights of Marigold
Gathering of Ghosts (forthcoming)

ADDICTED TO HEAVEN: THE NEXT GENERATION SERIES
Rivers of Ivy (forthcoming)

EUROPEAN ASTROBIOLOGY INSTITUTE
PRESENTS

LIFE

BEYOND

US

An Original Anthology
of
SF Stories and Science Essays

Edited by Julie Nováková, Lucas K. Law, and Susan Forest

LAKSA MEDIA GROUPS INC.
www.laksamedia.com

Life Beyond Us: An Original Anthology of SF Stories and Science Essays
European Astrobiology Institute Presents

Library and Archives Canada Cataloguing in Publication Title

Title: Life beyond us: an original anthology of SF stories and science essays / edited by Julie
   Nováková, Lucas K. Law, & Susan Forest.
Other titles: European Astrobiology Institute presents
Names: Nováková, Julie, editor. | Law, Lucas K., editor. | Forest, Susan, editor.

Description: Science fiction stories accompanied by science essays.
Identifiers: Canadiana (print) 20220259453 | Canadiana (ebook) 20220259747 | ISBN 9781988140476 (hardcover) | ISBN 9781988140483 (softcover) | ISBN 9781988140490 (EPUB) | ISBN 9781988140506 (PDF)

Subjects: LCSH: Science fiction, English 21st century.
Classification: LCC PN6120.95.S33 L54 2023 | DDC 823/.0876208092—dc23

LAKSA MEDIA GROUPS INC.   Edited by Julie Nováková, Lucas K. Law,
Calgary, Alberta, Canada   and Susan Forest
www.laksamedia.com   Cover Art by Dan O'Driscoll
info@laksamedia.com   Cover Design by Veronica Annis
    Interior Design by Jared Reid

Picture credits: Illustrations by Ernst Haeckel [*Kunstformen der Natur* (1904)] appeared throughout this book. Licensed under Public Domain via Wikimedia Commons.

FIRST EDITION

JULIE NOVÁKOVÁ
To *Φ* and *μ*
let your curiosity and
enthusiasm never ever fade

LUCAS K. LAW
To *all of us*
let's not forget the fragility of
life in water, on land, and in air
treat it with respect, kindness,
and care

SUSAN FOREST
To the *dreamers*
and to *those* who make our
dreams real

CONTENTS

FOREWORD

JULIE NOVÁKOVÁ

"T-minus fifteen seconds . . . T-minus ten . . . Nine, eight, seven, six, five, four, three, two, one . . . And liftoff!"

Twenty-five years ago, on October 15, 1997, the joint NASA-ESA-ISA mission *Cassini-Huygens* launched from Cape Canaveral aboard a Titan IV rocket. I was six years old, and if I'd heard the news at all, I scarcely registered it. When the mission arrived at Saturn in 2004, I was paying closer attention, and when the *Huygens* lander was to touch down on Titan in January 2005, I was eagerly waiting for the acquisition of signal and the first transmitted images.

In a way, the *Cassini-Huygens* mission embodies the spirit of *Life Beyond Us*: cooperation across nations, curiosity, charting places where no one has ventured before (save for the *Voyager* flybys)—and, ultimately, finding exciting possibilities for perhaps actual life beyond us and changing humankind's perspective forever.

Titan remains one of the most fascinating and mysterious objects of the solar system: a huge moon veiled by a dense hazy atmosphere, with dunes, rivers, and seas of hydrocarbons on its surface and a water-ammonia ocean deep underneath it. We're yet to map its complex chemistry (biochemistry, even?) and learn its history. How come it still has so much of the quickly destroyed methane to make it "warm" (under Saturn vicinity standards, mind you)? How deep is its inner ocean, and does it connect to the surface in meaningful ways? Are there active ice volcanoes? How far down does the largest methane sea, Kraken Mare, reach, and how does it behave? Could it possibly host living organisms?

Not just one, but two *Life Beyond Us* stories explore the possibility of life on Titan, each from a different angle—and still the moon would offer plenty more opportunities for exciting stories and wild, yet scientifically potentially plausible, speculations.

The *Cassini* orbiter also explored Saturn's tiny moon Enceladus and imaged the geysers spewing from beneath its icy crust. We now know that Enceladus, though being just about 500 kilometers across (find the Czech Republic on the world map and look at its size from west to east—that's how tiny), harbors an inner ocean of liquid water and hosts conditions that might be suitable for life. Has it got any?

Only future exploration will tell. Perhaps surprisingly, no one chose Enceladus as their story setting, though we visit a much larger and warmer exoplanetary water world in Malka Older's "The Dangers We Choose."

But every mission ends some day. *Cassini*'s did five years ago: on September 15, 2017, it plunged into the abysmal depths of Saturn in a final dive after months of skirting the rings and grazing the atmosphere. It was a spectacular ending for a spectacular explorer.

The mission is over. Its legacy lives on as data yet to analyze in new contexts to reveal more answers, and even more questions yet to answer. An exploration effort such as this one rarely means saying the "final word"; despite what some drier textbooks might seem to tell us, we're still writing the chapters. *Life Beyond Us* gazes around the corner, trying to glimpse where it might lead us.

The stories in *Life Beyond Us* are, first and foremost, stories. They are meant to entertain, excite, inspire, provoke, daydream, mesmerize. At the same time, they show us possible pathways to life beyond us. Some depict curious scientific ventures; others have taken a more metaphorical approach. They remind us that imagination is also an integral part of science.

Each story is accompanied by an essay exploring its scientific elements, be these interstellar clouds, the deep hot biosphere, animal communication, exomoons, or black hole planets. Finally, if you are an educator and wish to use examples from *Life Beyond Us* in your classroom, you can go to europeanastrobiology.eu/life-beyond-us to download a toolkit with tasks and discussion topics that we plan to regularly update as our knowledge and understanding changes.

Because, again, science rarely has a final take on anything. There's always room to explore, to form new hypotheses and test them, discover the unexpected and fill in the blanks.

Are there hot hydrothermal vents in Mars's subsurface, perhaps serving as the last refuges of local life?

Has Venus always been a hellish, dry, pressure-pot of a planet?

Could some of Saturn's ocean-bearing moons be vastly younger than the rest?

Out in the cold faraway reaches of the Kuiper Belt, could there still be habitable spots?

Are there conditions for life on the planets orbiting the Sun's nearest neighbor, Proxima Centauri?

Those and many more—and they could be wrapped up under: where can we find actual life beyond us?

We don't know. We have a lot of thoughts about this, a huge swirling pool of ideas, some data currents going here and others elsewhere, some results pointing in one direction and others in another. It's vitally important that we realize this and expect the scientific consensus to shift. But it doesn't shift on a whim; it's not a mere change of heart. It's backed by data and our understanding of the data's implications. In today's world, it's increasingly important to realize how science works; while the evolution of Titan's atmosphere might not affect our everyday lives, the next pandemic, next hurricane, or next asteroid strike will, and basic understanding of the process of science then might help save our lives. Collectively, greater understanding, knowledge, and also imagination and empathy will save lives.

As I'm writing this, the world remembers the sixty-second anniversary of human spaceflight. It seems to be almost universal for people who have ventured to space to regard Earth as a whole, not as a world divided by borders, nationalities, politics, or religions. But it's a precious and (in many ways) fragile whole, and many of us surface-dwellers cannot even see its wholeness, waging terrible wars against our living environment as well as each other.

In science fiction, we have the power to create worlds where violence has not won; where empathy and reason prevail; where joyful curiosity beckons us forth as one people, one planet, one galaxy.

It's never too late to try.

—Julie Nováková, Prague, Czech Republic, 2023

INTRODUCTION

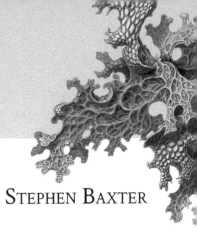

STEPHEN BAXTER

Is there life beyond Earth?

We see objects in the sky, the stars and planets; we see the Moon, which looks, even to the naked eye, like another Earth, with dark "seas" and bright "highlands." If there is life down here on Earth, why not up there in the sky?

It may be a question as old as humankind, and as a scientific conundrum the problem could probably be said to go back millennia, to the elaborate (though incorrect) cosmological modelings of the ancient Greeks.

Before the development of the telescope in the seventeenth century, however, we knew less about the planets of our own solar system than we do of many exoplanets now. But even then there was a suspicion, held by the likes of astronomers Galileo and Kepler, that other stars, other suns, might host planets as did our Sun, and so might harbor life (as mentioned by José A. Caballero in this volume, in his essay accompanying the story "Still as Bright" by Mary Robinette Kowal).

Those early telescopic astronomers could do little more than track and analyze the orbits of the solar planets (though the resulting understanding, leading to the confirmation of Copernican models of a Sun-centered solar system and Newton's law of gravity, was an epochal achievement). But, later, more refined telescopic observations seemed to reveal surface details on the other planets, either real or existing only in the eye of faith, apparently Earth-like or otherwise—cloud banks on Venus, and on Mars polar ice caps, what looked like seas, even what appeared to be artefacts in the "canals." But our imaginations were often Earthbound—we could not seem to imagine worlds drastically different from our own—so that in *The War of the Worlds* (1897) H.G. Wells launched an invasion from a Mars like a small, cold, dying version of Earth. We would need space probe data, delivered decades after Wells, for the close-up proof that forced us to accept that our companion worlds were all very different from Earth in many ways.

Crucially, the first space-age observations seemed to indicate that, after all, the planets could host little or no life. But such views are changing, with new visions (as in this volume) of possibly habitable locations on Mars, on Saturn's moon Titan, even in the temperate high clouds of scorched Venus (as in Geoffrey A. Landis's story). Life may be there, after all, even if it is quite unlike our own.

And even as we studied the sky, so we began to widen our understanding of life on Earth itself. Some of the more moving stories in this volume touch on the possibility that there may be life, even intelligence, lurking in the poorly explored environments of our own familiar planet.

Meanwhile, however, the old dreams of Galileo and Kepler—dreams of other worlds circling other stars—had continued to stimulate the science fiction writers of the early twentieth century. And while many of these fictional planets, like Wells's Mars, often more or less resembled Earth, some of the more imaginative dreamers wondered whether other *kinds* of planets could be waiting to be found, perhaps quite unlike those of the solar system.

Thus it would prove in reality, with, for example, many of the earliest exoplanets to be discovered being "super-earths," rocky worlds with masses larger than the Earth's—the largest rocky world in the solar system—but less than our giants of ices and gases: Jupiter, Saturn, Uranus, and Neptune. But by the time of the first super-Earth discoveries, the science fiction writers had been imagining and exploring such worlds for decades.

One early and widely known fictional super-Earth was Krypton, home planet of the comic book star Superman—a hero created in 1938, decades before such planets were discovered. Krypton was a large rocky planet with heavy gravity, the basic defining characteristics of a super-Earth. And, to add another exotic element to the mythos, Krypton was a planet of a different star. The red sun, Rao, was sometimes described as a giant star, and sometimes as a dwarf star, more like the red dwarf Proxima Centauri (the nearest star) than our own bright Sun. Krypton's inhabitants were humanoid, a convergence to this form being a standard assumption of the fiction of the period. But when Superman was sent as a baby to Earth, the brilliance of our sunlight and the lower gravity enabled his superpowers to emerge.

The primary duty of a storyteller is to entertain, and that's a duty the creators of Superman and his extensive universe have fulfilled for more than eighty years at this time of writing. But in the process, and granted that all that super-biology isn't very plausible, at least qualitatively this mythos gave a wide-reading public some impression—long before the discovery of the exoplanets—of there being not just other earths and other suns, but habitable worlds and life-giving stars quite unlike our own cozy neighborhood: other Kryptons, other Raos, shaping other kinds of life.

Later popular fictions brought a further twist, as the idea coalesced of sending ships out to *find* that other life: "to explore strange new worlds, to seek out new life and new civilizations . . ." In *Star Trek* (1966 onwards) Captain Kirk and his crew were exobiologists, if heavily armed exobiologists, exploring a universe which was, by now, casually assumed to be replete with life. Faithful to Kirk's mission statement, every true Trekkie is an exobiologist at heart—and some of the stories in this volume, of more or less scientific interstellar exploration and discovery, echo that famous quest.

In *Star Trek*, however, and elsewhere in the visual media—and even after the solar system planetary probes' first results—many fictional depictions of exoplanets remained conservatively Earth-like. This was probably a reflection of primitive special-effects technology, and budgetary constraints. Thus most of the worlds visited by the *Enterprise*'s crew, such as Spock's Vulcan, were Earth-like (in fact California-like, given where the show was filmed), with more or less humanoid inhabitants.

The science fiction literature, however, with unlimited special effects budgets, had room to explore and could be more adventurous. Frank Herbert's *Dune* (the novel 1965, the latest movie 2021) showed glimpses of a strange sub-sand native ecology on the water-starved world of Arrakis. Brian Aldiss's *Helliconia* (1982) was a planet of a double star, like Tatooine in *Star Wars* (1977) (and in 2011, to much fannish glee, a "real" Tatooine exoplanet was found orbiting the star Kepler 16-b). Aldiss, with consultation from evolutionary biologist Jack Cohen, devised an intricate ecology for Helliconia, based on a double orbital cycle, the "short years" of the planet's spin and the "long years" of the stellar orbits, so that two complementary biospheres emerged and receded in turn.

Some visions could be imaginative in the extreme. Robert Forward's *Dragon's Egg* (1980) depicted life forms on the surface of a neutron star. Why not? Perhaps wherever energy flows, life can feed, and evolve.

Meanwhile, since the 2000s, as the science of exoplanets has matured, there has been feedback into the fiction, as the writers have begun to explore the possibilities of these newly defined worlds—and indeed of newly imagined forms of life. Thus, my own novel *Proxima* (2013) is about the colonization of a habitable planet of the red dwarf Proxima Centauri. Another Krypton, another Rao—but the scientific understanding has moved on since 1938.

In fact, this star system has been well explored in fiction. Murray Leinster's "Proxima Centauri" (1935) features probably the first fictional journey to Proxima, made for that most enduring of reasons: it is the "nearest of the fixed stars to humanity's solar system." The hopeful crew are immediately met by hostile "Centaurians," plant-based creatures who predate on human meat, and turn envious eyes on Earth, for them the nearest target. As recently as the 2009 *Doctor Who* special "The Waters of Mars," Proxima is again the first destination of mankind when faster-than-light travel is developed.

And in sagas of more expansive interstellar colonization, Proxima's relative closeness to Sol makes it a likely candidate for an early Earth colony. Thus in *Babylon 5*, Proxima III (the third planet of Proxima) had been the site of an industrial colony in the twenty-second century; by the twenty-third century it had broken away from the Earth Alliance. In the *Star Trek* universe, meanwhile, by the twenty-fourth century the Proxima system was the home of Starfleet maintenance yards.

Today, we understand more about the challenges for life on planets of red dwarfs. If a planet is to be warm enough to support liquid water, it must be so close to its star—hazardously close—that the planet must be tidally locked, with one face permanently facing the star, and so would suffer extremes of temperature, one forever hot side, one permanently cold.

But even so there may be room for optimism about life's prospects on such a world (as discussed for example in a review paper by Jill Tarter et al: "A Reappraisal of the Habitability of Planets Around M Dwarf Stars," J. Tarter et al, *Astrobiology*, vol. 7, pp30-65, 2007). Possibly even a thin blanket of air could transport heat around such a planet. And as for the too-close star, an atmosphere and magnetic field might shield the surface from stellar flares and high fluxes of ultraviolet and X-rays. In short, there may still be enough wiggle room for stories about life on red dwarf planets (as explored in this volume by Tessa Fisher).

As for my own novel, as it turned out, a possibly habitable Proxima planet was discovered, only a few years after my book was published, pretty much where I had placed my fictional Per Ardua. Formally known as Proxima-b, the new world was found by a team from Queen Mary University, London. Team leader Dr. Guillem Anglada-Escudé was kind enough to invite me to participate in a public presentation of the results, and, also kindly, noted that my astronomical, climatic, and biological guesses were not *entirely* implausible.

But the real thrill of this particular discovery was that since red dwarfs are by far the most numerous stars, and since they are much more long-lived than the Sun, and if *they* can host life-bearing planets (granted that's still a big "if"), then suddenly the galaxy looks much more hospitable. Indeed, if we have found an Earth-like planet orbiting in the habitable zone of the *very nearest star*, such planets must be everywhere.

Today, as our understanding of (possible) life on exoplanets develops, science and science fiction go hand in hand in their exploration, as they are in this timely collection. Here are new fictional depictions of exoplanets of a variety of types, backed up by scientific input from researchers in the field—and given life by ferocious imagination.

Enjoy these speculations—always remembering that, more than likely, what waits for us to discover in the future will be more wonderful still.

— Stephen Baxter, 2023

HEMLOCK
ON MARS

Eric Choi

SOCRATES Mission Operations Center
Aspen Hill, Maryland
7 hours and 36 minutes to start of EDL (entry, descent, and landing)

So, it came to this. The hardest day of Ted Berenson's professional life.

Rows of headset-wearing engineers stared at their monitors, placards atop the consoles designating their function. A large screen displayed the trajectory of the SOCRATES lander as it approached Mars. The room was eerily quiet.

Berenson's phone vibrated.

No change in Emily's condition, said the message from his husband. *Love you.*

He put down the phone and wiped his sweaty palms on his trousers. Berenson was the MOM, the mission operations manager. The maternal sounding acronym was ironic, because aboard SOCRATES was a poison pill—a command load that would divert the lander from its nominal destination of Sinai Planum and send it skipping off the Martian atmosphere toward a cold death in deep space.

"You don't need to be here," said Dr. Ana Esparza, the principal investigator of the SOCRATES mission. Dark circles under her eyes testified to the years she had devoted to what might be a doomed mission.

"Yes, I do." The intensity of Berenson's expression seemed to surprise Esparza. "Bill is at the hospital. There's nothing I can do there. I need to be *here*."

Esparza nodded. She looked at the UTC clock above the screen. "Twenty-seven minutes to AOS," she said, referring to acquisition of signal, the time when the ground station in Dongara, Australia, would establish contact with SOCRATES for the last time. "We need a decision *now*. What the hell is taking them?"

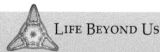

Berenson's phone vibrated again. This time, the message was from Dr. Janet Trinh, the planetary protection officer at NASA Headquarters in nearby Washington, DC.

Don't give up, it said. *Don't lose hope. This is not over.*

Launch plus 1 day (9 months earlier)

Visiting the Cedarhurst Lodge was like entering the airlock of a spacecraft. Berenson had to close and lock the outer door, then call for a caregiver to open the inner door. The system was needed to prevent residents from wandering outside.

Cedarhurst was one of the best dementia care facilities in Maryland, meaning it was one of the most expensive. In their younger days, its residents would likely have been accomplished professionals— engineers, doctors, lawyers, bankers.

But only Ted Berenson's father could claim to have discovered life on Mars in the 1970s. Maybe.

"Hello, Tatteh. It's Theodore."

"I know that!" said Isaac Berenson, sitting up in bed. "How is Evelyn?"

"Emily is fine," he corrected gently before changing the subject. "SOCRATES is on its way to Mars. In less than a year from now . . . you'll know, Tatteh. You'll have an answer."

His father looked confused. "An answer to what?"

As a young postdoc, Isaac Berenson had worked with Gilbert Levin and Patricia Ann Straat on the Labeled Release experiment aboard the NASA Viking Landers that touched down on Mars in 1976. In the LR experiment, an aqueous nutrient tagged with radioactive carbon-14 was introduced to a sample of Martian soil. If life were present, there would be a release of radioactive carbon dioxide as microorganisms metabolized the nutrient.

This is exactly what happened at both Viking landing sites, more than six thousand kilometers apart.

But the results of the LR experiment were met with skepticism because the gas chromatograph mass spectrometer on Viking failed to detect organic molecules in the soil. In the absence of organics, most scientists attributed the carbon dioxide release to an inorganic geochemical reaction.

More than thirty years later, another NASA Mars lander called Phoenix found perchlorates in the Martian soil, a discovery that gave LR believers like Isaac Berenson and Ana Esparza new hope. Viking's mass spectrometer had heated its samples to very high temperatures, and heating organic molecules in the presence of perchlorates destroyed them.

"Would you like to watch a recording of the launch?"

"I think I'd rather eat."

Ted cast his phone to a TV at the foot of the bed and played the video as his father nibbled a granola bar. Emblazoned on the rocket was the crescent moon logo of the Xīn Shìjiè Corporation, the sponsor of the SOCRATES mission. Night became day as the rocket rose from the launch pad and soared into the heavens.

SOCRATES had a single objective: to resolve the ambiguity of the Viking experiments. Except for a camera, its only scientific payload was the Labeled Release II experiment. Developed by Esparza and her team at the University of Maryland, LR-2 would employ a pair of carbon-14 tagged nutrient solutions of opposite chirality, one with left-handed molecules and the other right-handed. Martian microbes should only be able to metabolize one of the solutions and generate carbon dioxide, whereas non-biological processes would produce gas in both cases. SOCRATES was also equipped with a drill to obtain samples from a depth of five meters, where microbes would be protected from solar ultraviolet radiation.

"Tatteh?"

His father was asleep.

Berenson turned off the screen, lowered the back of the bed, and took the remnants of the granola bar before gently tucking the blanket under his father's chin.

Mid-Atlantic Regional Spaceport
Wallops Island, Virginia
Launch plus 2 weeks

The trouble started with a cotton swab.

The clean room in which the pre-launch integration and testing of SOCRATES had taken place was now vacant, like an auditorium missing an orchestra. The quiet was broken by the whirring of fans drawing air through HEPA filters, maintaining a level of cleanliness of no more than ten thousand particles larger than half a micron per cubic foot of air.

Dressed in a full-body white gown, the technician wet a cotton swab with a phosphate-buffered saline solution and wiped it across a piece of ground support equipment, then broke the stick of the swab inside a sterile tube and capped it. The sample was then streaked onto an agar plate and cultured.

A few days later, the technician looked into the microscope. Glossy pale-red globules, like little pink eyes, stared back.

NASA Headquarters, Mary W. Jackson Building
Washington, DC
22 weeks to start of EDL (entry, descent, and landing)

Despite being a private mission, there had always been regular contact between the SOCRATES team and NASA. But this was the first time Berenson, Esparza, and the chief engineer Wally Soo had met senior officials of the space agency in person.

"Thank you for coming," said Janet Trinh, pushing her glasses up the bridge of her nose. As NASA's planetary protection officer, she was responsible for ensuring compliance with Article IX of the 1967 Outer Space Treaty, which requires missions to avoid the forward contamination of celestial bodies by harmful terrestrial material as well as the back contamination of Earth with dangerous extraterrestrial matter. Her job title was always an attention getter at parties. She had met her boyfriend that way, when he gifted her a pair of Ray-Bans so that she could look like a Man in Black.

"Have the results of the bioassay been confirmed?" asked Esparza, her fingers nervously tracing a pattern on the polished conference table.

"I'm afraid so." Trinh showed an optical microscope image with clusters of reddish globules. "A team from the University of Houston did a follow-up. They found this everywhere—the floor, the walls, the ground support equipment, even a discarded glove."

"So, the clean room wasn't clean." Wally Soo cackled. "Maybe we'll call it NCR—not clean room!"

Trinh looked at Soo strangely. "Well, um . . . I do recognize a certain irony. The stringent cleaning procedures in these facilities create significant drivers for evolutionary selection toward, shall we say, much hardier microorganisms."

"Why wasn't this detected before?" asked Berenson.

"A shortcoming of current planetary protection procedures," Trinh explained. "The quantification of bioburden has always been based on cultivatable bacterial spore counts. The problem is this organism is not spore-forming."

"But it doesn't mean SOCRATES is contaminated," said Soo. "We followed NASA PP guidelines for Category IVa Mars missions."

"You mean Category IVc?" Trinh said slowly. Category IVc was the most stringent level for missions landing in Special Regions that have a high potential for extant Martian life or where terrestrial organisms would likely replicate if accidentally introduced.

"Oh, yes!" Soo chuckled nervously. "Four-cee, four-cee!"

"I certainly hope so," growled Charlie Kendall, the Deputy Director of NASA's Planetary Science Division, "considering where you're going."

The SOCRATES landing site was in Terra Sabae, a few hundred kilometers northwest of Huygens crater. It had been selected based on orbital observations indicating methane emissions and near subsurface water ice, as well as the presence of gully-like geological features suggesting erosion by flowing liquid—the very definition of a Special Region.

"We *did* follow Category IVc," Esparza confirmed, shooting a glance at Soo. "All components were cleaned with isopropanol and then sterile bagged prior to the next level of assembly. The LR-2 payload and the drilling mechanism were further subjected to dry heat sterilization at one hundred and twenty-five degrees Celsius for an hour."

"The heat sterilization probably worked," said Trinh, "but the University of Houston team found the organism not only surviving but actually biodegrading and metabolizing most cleaning agents including Kleenol 30 and isopropyl alcohol. And it gets worse."

"Worse?" said Berenson.

Trinh nodded. "Phylogenetic analysis based on gene sequencing indicates the organism to be a novel strain of the genus *Deinococcus*, which is known to be highly resistant to ionizing radiation, UV light, and prolonged desiccation."

"We're still waiting on results from Marshall for UV testing and Brookhaven for radiation testing," said Kendall. "In the meantime, you folks need to think very carefully about whether SOCRATES should be landing on Mars at all."

SOCRATES Mission Operations Center
EDL minus 18 weeks

Ted Berenson and Wally Soo stared as Ana Esparza tossed a stack of papers onto her already cluttered desk.

"We've received the results of the radiation and UV testing," said Esparza. Her eyes were bloodshot, and the bin beside her desk overflowed with used coffee cups.

"Let's hear it," said Berenson.

"The organism showed extreme resistance both to ionizing radiation and ultraviolet light," said Esparza, "with a radiation D10 in excess of 15 kilograys and a UV D10 of almost 1,800 joules per square meter." D10 referred to the level required to inactivate at least ninety percent of the microbial load.

Soo whistled. "Those levels are so high, there's no option for self-sterilization in the ambient environment, either during interplanetary cruise or on the Martian surface."

"Are there any thermal sterilization options?" asked Berenson. "Say, heat or cold?"

"Nothing that wouldn't also break the electronics," replied Soo. "The avionics must be maintained at a keep-alive temperature of between minus forty to plus seventy degrees Fahrenheit—I mean, Celsius."

"So, what *can* we do?" asked Esparza.

"Maybe we do . . . nothing?" suggested Soo. "I don't think those early Russian probes that crashed were sterilized, so maybe Mars is already contaminated."

"I suppose that's a pragmatic way of looking at it," Berenson said dryly.

"Besides," Soo continued, "as a private mission, we were never obligated to follow NASA's PP guidelines."

Esparza's expression darkened. "We followed NASA's planetary protection guidelines because it's the right thing to do, and because the science team and I are very interested in not having false positives."

"Both the payload and the drilling mechanism were heat sterilized, so I don't think the risk of false positives has increased," said Berenson. "The issue is the forward contamination of Mars itself. In the worst-case scenario, we could displace or even kill any indigenous organisms that might be there."

Esparza nodded. "The forward contamination risk is a function of the bioburden level and the probability of an . . . um, 'off-nominal' landing—"

"A crash!" Soo exclaimed.

"—and contaminated parts of the spacecraft making direct contact with the Martian surface or subsurface."

"So, if we have a higher bioburden," Berenson concluded, "we'll need to reassess the probability of an off-nominal landing and hope it's sufficiently lower. We'll need to look at the Monte Carlo analysis and the FMECA again." He pronounced the acronym "fuh-meeca", referring to the failure modes, effects, and criticality analysis.

Soo rubbed his hands. "Does this mean overtime?"

EDL minus 15 weeks

Seven-year-old Emily Berenson played with the floral arrangement on the table while her oatmeal got cold.

"Finish your breakfast, sweetie. You don't want to be late for the last day of school."

"OK, Papa."

Berenson's husband came into the kitchen, a tie draped around his neck. "Can you help me with this?"

"You know, there are online videos that show you how to do this." Bill kissed him. "But I have you."

"Papa!"

Berenson turned. "What is it, sweetie?"

She pointed at the TV. "Someone's talking about So-crates."

". . . condition of anonymity, sources familiar with the matter have told CNN there are serious concerns at NASA about the privately financed SOCRATES mission that is scheduled to land on Mars in less than three months. According to the sources, the SOCRATES lander is contaminated with a previously unknown terrestrial superbug that cannot be killed by disinfectants and is even able to survive radiation levels that would be lethal to a human being. Neither NASA officials nor representatives of the Xīn Shìjiè Corporation, the company behind the SOCRATES mission, could be reached for comment."

SOCRATES Mission Operations Center
EDL minus 14 weeks and 5 days

Liǔ Diānrén, the CEO of the Xīn Shìjiè Corporation, addressed the SOCRATES team by video link from his office in Sharjah.

"This was to be a great leap forward into the cradle of the heavens, but now, we are poised to taint that cradle," Liǔ intoned solemnly. He was in his late thirties with slicked black hair, a pale square face, and an angular beard. Berenson thought he looked like a James Bond villain. *"Perhaps we might have had better fortune if we had named the spacecraft for Kǒng Fūzǐ as I had wanted!"*

Berenson was sure the auto-generated subtitles were not correctly translating Liǔ's bizarre statements. He turned to his colleagues.

"Don't look at me." Soo gave a shrug. "I don't speak Mandarin."

"You must now put an end to Sūgélādǐ and protect the sanctity of Huǒxīng. The honor of Xīn Shìjiè is in your hands!"

The strange monologue ended, and a new face appeared on the screen.

"Well folks, that's the word from the very top," said Mark Rice, the legal counsel for Xīn Shìjiè America at the company's U.S. headquarters in Newark, New Jersey. Rice was a large, friendly-looking man who resembled someone's lovable uncle. His appearance caused many to underestimate his legal acumen, a mistake they would regret.

Esparza was incredulous. "That CNN report is barely forty-eight hours old, and now we're going to throw in the towel, just like that? The team and I have devoted years of our lives to this mission, which could answer one of the biggest scientific questions of all time."

"I understand how you feel," said Rice, *"but SOCRATES is becoming a national controversy. There are hashtags like #ProtectMars and #KillSocrates already trending on social. We don't need the bad publicity, to say nothing of the potential liability issues."*

Before Liǔ Diānrén stepped in with his money, the SOCRATES project had been little more than a group of dreamers with PowerPoint slides. Liǔ made SOCRATES a reality, but it wasn't all about science. In the new era of détente between China and the United States—or huǎnhé, as the Chinese called it—Liǔ wanted SOCRATES to be a grand gesture to America, intended to burnish Xīn Shìjiè's reputation as it entered the U.S. market.

Contaminating Mars with a terrestrial superbug was not part of the business plan.

Xīn Shìjiè America put out a news release the next day announcing their intention to terminate the SOCRATES mission. Two days later, Berenson got a call.

EDL minus 14 weeks and 2 days

"Thank you for seeing me," said Janet Trinh.

"No problem." Berenson sat with the NASA planetary protection officer on a bench facing a water fountain on the grounds of Brookside Gardens. Blooms of blue leadwort swayed gently in the warm summer breeze, carrying the smell of freshly mown grass. "I often bring my daughter Emily here."

"The flowers are beautiful," said Trinh.

"*Ceratostigma plumbaginoides*," said Berenson. "They're not native to Maryland."

Trinh raised her eyebrows. "You know a lot about plants."

"I wanted to become a botanist, but my dad disapproved." Berenson's mood momentarily darkened. His father had considered botany "un-manly" and urged his son to follow his footsteps in planetary science, a pressure that increased following the deaths of his mother and sister in a car accident.

"I was fortunate my parents always supported me," said Trinh. "One of my earliest memories was watching TV about that Martian meteorite ALH84001, the one they thought had fossilized microbes. And then my dad took me to see the movie *Contact*, and that was it. All I ever wanted was to become a scientist and look for life beyond us."

"Why did you want to see me?" Berenson asked. A group of children, probably about Emily's age, chased each other around the fountain. For a moment, he found himself envying their carefree laughter.

"Would it surprise you," said Trinh, "that SOCRATES has a lot of fans in the Planetary Science Division?"

"No," said Berenson. "There are NASA scientists on the SOCRATES science team."

"It goes back to Viking," Trinh continued, "which NASA billed as the mission that would find life on Mars. When the disappointing results from Labeled Release and the other life detection investigations came back, it killed interest in Mars for years. Ever since, when we at NASA talk about Mars missions we say things like we're 'following the water' or 'looking for biosignatures.' That's why so many of us love SOCRATES. You came right out and said you're looking for life on Mars goddammit, and that's something a lot of us admire."

"What are you suggesting?" Berenson asked.

"Let's convene an emergency meeting of MEPAG." Trinh pronounced the acronym "me-paag", referring to the Mars Exploration Program Analysis Group. "Get Esparza and your science team together with the wider community. Let's put our heads together and see what might be possible."

California Institute of Technology
EDL minus 8 weeks

Over the course of four days, more than two dozen scientists packed into a conference room in the Cahill Astronomy and Astrophysics Building to discuss options for salvaging the SOCRATES mission. The special committee was co-moderated by Ana Esparza with Dr. Roberta Hogan of the University of Colorado, the current chair of MEPAG.

Berenson slipped his phone into his pocket just as the conference room doors opened and people poured out for a break.

"Is everything all right?"

"My dad's had a fall," Berenson explained.

"I'm so sorry," Esparza said. "Maybe you shouldn't have come."

"Dad's not been well for a long time. My husband's with him now." Berenson sighed. "How goes the battle?"

"We're down to two potential alternate landing sites," said Hogan. "I don't have to tell you it's slim pickings this late in the game."

Instead of the original landing site at Terra Sabae, which had been selected based on the highest probability of finding life, the committee proposed diverting SOCRATES to an alternate site with exactly the opposite characteristics, where neither methane nor subsurface ice had been detected, and was a conservative distance from subsurface access points like cave entrances. This simple sounding strategy, however, was anything but.

"Switching landing sites is crazy," Esparza said. "The entire mission was designed around the Terra Sabae site, to say nothing about it being completely ass backwards from the original science objectives."

The challenge was to find an alternate landing site with low astro-biological potential but otherwise comparable to the original in every other respect. It had to be at a similar latitude for thermal control and solar power generation, as well as a similar altitude for which the landing system was designed. There also needed to be adequate orbital imagery of the site for the team to evaluate the terrain and ensure the lander could handle it.

"It's the best we can do," said Hogan.

"My dad always believed Labeled Release found life at both Viking landing sites," said Berenson. "If there's life on Mars, it'll be every-where. So, we're still either going to find it . . . or contaminate it."

Hogan nodded. "That's why we can't budge on the one-meter rule."

The emerging consensus of the committee was to recommend SOCRATES limit its drilling to only the first meter of the subsurface and not the originally planned five meters. This was opposed by Esparza and some members of the SOCRATES science team, who argued the drilling system was clean because it had been heat sterilized.

"We still need to show a mission-level forward contamination proba-bility of less than ten to the minus three," Esparza said. "We have revised risk factors taking into account the clean room bioassay and the new surface operations concept. But we need to redo the Monte Carlo analysis and review the FMECA."

"Wally Soo is still working on that," Berenson said.

"It's been more than two months!" Esparza exclaimed. "What's taking that guy?"

Headquarters of Xīn Shìjiè America
Newark, New Jersey
EDL minus 7 weeks and 2 days

The conference room was on the top floor of a multi-level office build-ing, with one wall a panoramic window to the outside. Berenson stared out into the hazy summer heat, watching a plane take-off from nearby Newark Liberty International Airport.

"What was the outcome of that big meeting at Caltech?" asked Mark Rice.

"The MEPAG committee recommended an alternate landing site in a region of Mars called Sinai Planum," said a tired Esparza, still recovering from jet lag. "If we land there instead of Terra Sabae, and if we don't drill more than a meter—that's about three feet—below the surface, then SOCRATES should not be at a greater risk of contaminating Mars than previous missions."

"That still depends on the Monte Carlo analysis," said Berenson.

"Monty Carlo?" Rice was puzzled. "Like . . . gambling?"

"It's a method of numerical risk analysis," Berenson explained. "The probability of SOCRATES making a crash landing needs to be less than one in a thousand. We need to reassess the landing ellipse and the touchdown survivability due to the different entry trajectory and terrain characteristics."

"When will this analysis be done?"

Berenson was tired of covering for Wally Soo, but he said, "In a few days."

"But there's another deadline," Esparza said.

Berenson nodded. "In less than nine days, we'll need to fire the thrusters on the cruise stage to adjust the trajectory and target the new landing site at Sinai Planum. If we miss this window, we'll be stuck on a trajectory for the original landing site at Terra Sabae."

"The word from Liǔ Diānrén was to shut this thing down," said Rice. "Why are we talking about trajectory changes and new landing sites?"

"We've installed a default command sequence that will cause SOCRATES to skip off the atmosphere," Berenson explained, "and go into a graveyard orbit around the Sun."

"There will be one last chance just a few hours before arrival to cancel the suicide command and set course for a landing at Sinai Planum," Esparza continued. "But if we don't do the thruster burn in nine days, we won't have that option."

"I see," said Rice.

"Please talk to Mr. Liǔ again," Esparza implored. "We have an opportunity to salvage the mission and save the face of the company."

Rice thought for a moment. "The public mood seems to be changing over the last couple of weeks. A #SaveSocrates hashtag is trending, and a teenager in Wisconsin has started an online petition." He nodded. "All right, let me talk to Mr. Liǔ."

Berenson and Esparza exchanged a glance. They would not mention one other outcome of the MEPAG meeting, which was a proposed name for the microbe that had started all the trouble: *Deinococcus socratecis*.

SOCRATES Mission Operations Center
EDL minus 6 weeks

"Navigation, what's your status?" Berenson said into his headset.

"Post-burn assessment is complete. We have good range and range-rate correlation, and residuals are within expected values. SOCRATES is on track for Sinai Planum."

Berenson took off his headset and left the control room. Esparza was outside.

"Nice to see our navigation engineer is still optimistic about landing."

"Any word from Corporate?" Berenson asked.

Esparza frowned. "Rice heard back from Liǔ Diānrén. He will not allow a landing. The recommendation from MEPAG isn't good enough. He wants a statement from NASA."

"Of course." Berenson smiled wryly. "If things go wrong, they can say we were following the guidance of the U.S. Government."

Berenson's phone vibrated. He looked at the screen and felt the familiar dread that came every time he got a call from Cedarhurst Lodge.

"Mr. Berenson, this is Shawn, the head nurse. I'm so sorry, but your father's had a massive stroke. You need to come now, please. He doesn't have long."

EDL minus 5 weeks and 6 days

A bag of intravenous liquid hung on a pole beside Isaac Berenson's bed, and a plastic tube snaked into his arm. Under his nose was a breathing tube attached to an oxygen tank. A screen with numbers and colored lines traced his weakening vital signs.

Berenson took his father's hand. Isaac's eyes stared blankly ahead as he softly hummed a Yiddish children's song.

Suddenly, Isaac blinked, and there was a spark in his eyes.

"Theodore."

"Yes, Tatteh. I'm here."

"Theodore, I heard . . ." His father was speaking English now. "I heard there was a problem with the mission."

"Yes, Tatteh, there was a problem. But we have a solution now. We're going to land on Mars, and then we'll know. Everyone will know that you were right."

"Hmm . . ."

The light in Isaac Berenson's eyes disappeared as quickly as it had come, and he started humming in Yiddish again.

Ted Berenson held his father's hand until the song stopped, until his eyes closed, until his fingers went limp, until the traces on the screen became horizontal lines.

EDL minus 5 weeks and one day

Two things greeted Berenson in his office upon his return to work. One was a bouquet of flowers from Ana Esparza and the SOCRATES team. Flowers were actually not an appropriate expression of sympathy in the Jewish faith, but his colleagues meant well and Berenson appreciated the thought. The other was a shiva basket from Janet Trinh with dried fruit, nuts, and chocolates. He called her.

"Thank you for the shiva basket."

"I'm so sorry for your loss," she said. "How's your family?"

"Doing the best we can. Emily misses her grandpa." Berenson paused. "Listen, I'd like to chat with you. Do you have time later today?"

They met again at Brookside Gardens, walking along a path through a lawn bordered by lilies and crab apple trees.

"We're considering your request for a statement," Trinh said, "but you sure left things late. Normally these things take weeks or months if it even happens. This needs to go way above me and the Office of Safety and Mission Assurance, up to the NASA Administrator at least. And that's just the policy and bureaucratic stuff."

"There's more?" Berenson asked.

"Your chief engineer's FMECA analysis was . . . not helpful," Trinh sighed. "He's assigned arbitrary failure probabilities down to individual nuts and bolts and resistors based on 'engineering judgment,' and then elsewhere he says the reliability of a major subsystem cannot be quantified because it's derived from 'engineering judgment'. And that's just the technical stuff. The JPL team reviewing the documents said they're painful to read because they're full of spelling and grammatical errors."

Berenson shook his head, a knot of worry forming in his stomach.

EDL *minus 6 days*

"Papa!" Emily tugged at Berenson's arm. "The bus is here!"

Berenson grabbed the knapsack, slid her arms through the hoops, and adjusted the straps before leading her out the door toward the waiting Wilderness Adventure bus. He gave her a hug. "Have a good time. Daddy will be home when you get back this afternoon."

"Love you, Papa!"

"I love you too, sweetie."

Berenson spent the rest of the day leading the operations team through a series of simulations for both the deflection and landing scenarios, embellished with simulated malfunctions thrown in by Wally Soo. During a meal break, he grabbed a salad and retreated to his office. He called Janet Trinh.

"Sorry to interrupt your evening."

"Don't worry," said Trinh. "I'm still at Headquarters."

The new Monte Carlo analysis and the FMECA review were finally done with help from a JPL engineering team. Despite Berenson's misgivings, the results were deemed acceptable. Trinh's team drafted a statement that went through the NASA hierarchy from the Chief of the Office of Safety and Mission Assurance to the Chief of the Planetary Science Division, and then to the Associate Administrator of the Science Mission Directorate.

"The statement hit the Administrator's desk earlier today," Trinh said. "But she won't give her blessing without 'referring it up.'"

"Who's further up than the chief of NASA?" Berenson asked.

"The Vice President, and the National Space Council."

"Oh." Berenson paused. "No shit."

"No shit. The statement is on the agenda for the next Space Council meeting scheduled for two days from now."

"What are the chances they'll bless the statement?" Berenson asked.

"I have no idea," Trinh replied. "This is all new for me. I've never—"

Berenson's phone vibrated, displaying his husband's number.

"Sorry Janet, I have to take this call." He switched over. "Bill, hi. I'm just—" He gripped the phone tighter. "W-what happened? *What do you mean she's at the hospital?*"

EDL minus 5 days and 14 hours

Berenson stumbled through the emergency department of the Holy Cross Germantown Hospital in a daze. He found his husband in a waiting room.

"What happened?" Berenson asked.

"Sh-she found this plant . . ." Bill dabbed his eyes with a tissue. "The counsellor said it was winter fern, but it looked like parsley. They tried to take it away, but she must have already put some in her m-mouth . . ."

Berenson embraced his husband.

"Excuse me," said a young man in scrubs with a stethoscope around his neck. "I'm Dr. Farhan Al-Baker."

"How is she?" Berenson asked in a trembling voice. The lights on the ceiling seemed to sway. He gripped his husband for support.

"I'm afraid it's serious," Al-Baker said. "The good news is we got a sample of the plant, so we know what we're dealing with. It's an alkaloid neurotoxin, and unfortunately it doesn't take a lot to do harm, especially in a child."

"Is there an antidote?" Berenson asked.

"I'm afraid not. We can only treat the symptoms and wait for the patient to recover. We pumped her stomach and administered activated charcoal to reduce absorption of the toxin. We also gave her a dose of benzodiazepine to stop the convulsions."

"Can we see her?"

"You may," said Al-Baker. "But be aware she is on a ventilator."

"I understand."

As Al-Baker led them to the intensive care unit, scenes of his father's deathbed crept into Berenson's mind. He braced himself, but the sight that awaited him was far worse than he had imagined. Emily was unconscious, her little head braced to keep it straight on the pillow, and there was tape around her mouth to keep the breathing tube in. She was connected to more machines than her grandfather had been.

SOCRATES Mission Operations Center
EDL minus 7 hours and 25 minutes

Don't give up, said the text from Janet Trinh. *Don't lose hope. This is not over.*

Berenson looked at the UTC clock above the screen. "16 minutes to AOS."

"Can they cut this any closer?" Esparza muttered.

Berenson's phone vibrated. It was another message from Janet Trinh. *The NASA statement is out! Here's the link. GO SOCRATES!!!*

Berenson began to read. "After an exhaustive assessment, NASA has concluded that, subject to specific constraints on surface and subsurface operations, the SOCRATES mission poses no greater risk of the forward contamination of Mars than earlier landed missions, including previous NASA missions. While NASA does not specifically endorse—"

"Forward that link to Mark Rice!" Esparza interrupted. "I'm calling him now."

Berenson looked at the clock. Thirteen minutes to acquisition of signal.

"Mark, it's Ana. You got the link from Ted? We need the word from Corporate like *now* . . . I understand. Thank you." She ended the call. "Rice is phoning Liǔ Diānrén."

"It's 4:00am in Sharjah," said Berenson.

"I know."

The clock continued its countdown to the final communications opportunity through the Dongara ground station. Some of the engineers momentarily peered from their consoles to shoot nervous glances at Berenson and Esparza. The principal investigator looked at the clock. AOS minus eleven minutes. Ten minutes. Nine.

Esparza's phone went off with a ring tone that Berenson recognized as the theme from one of the *Star Trek* shows.

"Yes, Mark."

As Berenson watched, Esparza's face went rigid and her voice dropped to a whisper.

"Yes . . . I understand. I'll convey this to the team."

Esparza ended the call. After a moment, she said, "Ted, I'd like to address the team on the loop."

Berenson handed her a headset.

"SOCRATES ops team, may I have your attention. I'm afraid I have bad news." She took a deep breath, and then said, "None of us are going to have any personal time for at least the next thirty days . . . *because we are 'go' for landing at Sinai Planum!*"

Cheers and applause erupted through the ontrol room.

"We have AOS through Dongara," reported the communications engineer known as the Ace. "We have RF lock on the X-band. Standing by for command load uplink."

"You are 'go' for command upload with the Beta EDL parameter table," Berenson said in a detached voice. He thought about his father, and his dream of finding life on Mars. He thought about Emily, and wondered if she would have a chance to realize her dreams. "I . . . I say again, the Beta table."

"Command uplink initiated," reported the Ace. "Commands are away. Telemetry downlink initiated. We have good ranging tones."

Berenson turned to Esparza. She was smiling.

"Telemetry playback and ranging are complete. Coming up on loss of signal . . . and we have LOS."

Berenson slowly removed his headset, which seemed oddly heavy. He suddenly felt very, very tired.

Esparza turned to Berenson. "You're done here, Ted. Your daughter needs you now."

EDL minus 22 minutes

Emily was sleeping peacefully, free of tubes and wires and electrodes, curled up on her side just like at home. Berenson concluded it was the most beautiful thing he had ever seen.

"We'll keep her under observation for another day," said Dr. Al-Baker. "But she's going to be fine."

"Thank you, Doctor."

Al-Baker nodded. "Now, if you have a minute, I'm afraid you're needed for some insurance paperwork."

"Can you take care of it, Bill?" said Berenson. "I'd like to stay with her."

Bill left the room with Al-Baker, leaving Berenson with Emily. She made a snorting sound but did not wake up. Berenson turned off his phone, then reached out and gently stroked her hair. For the first time in months, he felt completely at peace.

By now, the navigation team would have completed an initial trajectory determination from the tracking data. They will be puzzled by the discrepancies between the range and range-rate measurements, and then alarmed by the unexpectedly large residuals between the propagated trajectory and the tracking data. The ground segment engineer will notice unusual login activity from Berenson's account. The flight dynamics engineer will discover the parameter table uploaded to the spacecraft was identical to the one already aboard, the one with the entry flight path angle a few degrees too shallow, the one that will send SOCRATES skipping off the Martian atmosphere into a heliocentric graveyard orbit.

Winter fern is *Conium maculatum*, also known as hemlock. And hemlock is alien to North America—an invasive species.

So, it came to this. Ted Berenson would not be the one to put hemlock on Mars.

PLANETARY PROTECTION

Best Practices for the Safety of Humankind (and all those Aliens out there)

GIOVANNI POGGIALI

Likely aliens are on Mars, reasonably aliens are on the Moon, surely aliens are on Earth, and definitely aliens are among us.

Looking in any dictionary for the word "alien," the definition will be very close to "belonging to others, different, extraneous." In classical sci-fi literature, the aliens are usually visitors from other planets, but nowadays on Earth the word is used in several contexts. For instance, in biology, we refer to "alien species" to address plants, animals, and any other living beings located in a region different from the one where they originated or moved naturally, in contrast with being moved intentionally or accidentally by humans. A famous example of alien species on Earth and the danger related to them is Australia.

This continent, located far from Europe and North America, was subject to a massive human migration by people from these continents in the last centuries. New inhabitants of Australia brought useful species like dogs, cats, and rabbits. Within a few years, "alien" rabbits, in absence of natural predators, multiplied exponentially until they became a serious threat to the original ecosystem. The solution of introducing a natural predator such as the fox worsened the situation when the latter turned to "local" prey—not used to the fox and more easily captured—further damaging the ecosystem and even driving some original Australian species to extinction. It is easy to understand that mixing living beings separated by many million years of evolution is not always a great idea. Rewind to the dawn of planetary exploration when a new scientific subfield emerged: planetary protection.

In early space exploration, the possibility of contamination between celestial bodies was certainly not considered among the main risk factors for space missions. But with the beginning of human space exploration and the conquest of the Moon, the problem of backward contamination—potentially bringing alien life to Earth—was one of the issues that began to be addressed. Upon their return to Earth from the Moon, Armstrong, Aldrin, and Collins as well as the entire spaceship, the Command Module *Columbia,* and the 22 kg of lunar samples brought home were kept in quarantine for three weeks. The quarantine was decided by NASA in case they had returned from the Moon accompanied by possibly dangerous lunar microorganisms or unknown elements. As everyone knows now, no alien bacteria or strange elements came back with any of the Apollo mission's astronauts. And no local lunar bacteria were found on the Moon, but, as I hinted in the opening of this essay, reasonably aliens are still on the Moon. Indeed, we know for sure that the Moon was inhabited for at least two years. But not in the ancient time at the beginning of solar system; rather between April 1967 and November 1969. How can we be so precise? Let's take a dive into the past.

In November 1969 in western Oceanus Procellarum on the Moon, astronauts Charles "Pete" Conrad and Alan Bean successfully landed on the Moon with the Lunar Excursion Module *Intrepid* during the Apollo 12 mission. They became the third and fourth men to walk on the Moon, but they were the first men to visit an automated exploration spacecraft launched several years earlier. The landing site selected for Apollo 12 was in close proximity to the landing site of the previous Surveyor 3 mission. The Surveyor and Lunar Orbiter missions had been involved in a campaign of lunar surface exploration with orbiters and landers in preparation for the Apollo program. Surveyor 3 landed on the Moon on 20 April 1967. More than two years later, Apollo 12 astronauts reached the lander and collected several images of the spacecraft and samples of "soil" (more precisely regolith) around it, but they also removed some parts from the three-legged spacecraft, including Surveyor's TV camera. At that time, "NASA wanted to see what happened to materials that were exposed to the lunar environment for an extended period," but when scientists analyzed the Surveyor 3 mechanical parts returned on Earth, they happened upon something completely unexpected: a colony of *Streptococcus mitis* was living on the camera [1].

Those bacteria, very common on Earth, were left on the camera as a result of improper cleaning or subsequent contamination prior to launch. They crossed the 384,400 km of empty space that separates us from our natural satellite, landed on the Moon, survived there for 31 months, and returned to Earth escorted by Apollo 12. *Streptococcus mitis* was an "earthly alien" on the Moon. This incredible story teaches us a very important lesson: that planetary contamination could not be only *backward* to Earth but can also be *forward* to other planets. Once space exploration started focusing on planetary habitability and astrobiology, the importance of possible contamination increased enormously. Not bringing life with us to other planets through contamination of the spacecraft (especially if automated) is pivotal to avoid the risk of a false positive in life detection.

From the early '60s, many concerns about planetary protection were addressed by the Committee on Space Research (COSPAR), an international organization for promotion of scientific research in space. The legal basis for planetary protection can be found in Article IX of the Outer Space Treaty (signed in January 1967 by the United States, the United Kingdom, and the Soviet Union, and nowadays accepted by 111 countries). It states that space exploration of celestial bodies should *"avoid their harmful contamination and also adverse changes in the environment of the Earth resulting from the introduction of extraterrestrial matter and, where necessary, shall adopt appropriate measures for this purpose."* Modern COSPAR Planetary Protection Policy [2] derives directly from the evolution of scientific knowledge on one hand and from the increase of technological possibilities on the other. Orbiting a small body, landing on a rocky surface, bringing back a sample from a celestial body or sending high-precision instruments to a dry lake on another planet implies a clear distinction in the requirement of cleaning. The policy today includes five categories: I) flyby, orbiter and lander on undifferentiated and metamorphosed asteroids and other bodies with very low chance to host life or remnant of life; II) flyby, orbiter and lander on Venus, Moon, comets, carbonaceous chondrite (primitive) asteroids, giant gaseous planets and other small bodies; III) flyby and orbiters on Mars, Europa and Enceladus; IV) lander missions on Mars, Europa and Enceladus; and V) any Earth-return mission.

With the increasing exploration of Mars during the '70s and the realistic possibility of finding life on the Red Planet, space agencies progressively increased the level of spacecraft "cleaning." In 1975, the two Viking Lander Capsules were subjected to sterilization using Dry Heat Microbial Reduction—in plain words, oven-baked in a nitrogen atmosphere heated to over 110 °C (235 °F) for 40 hours (Viking was the gold standard; modern sterilization guidelines are updated, and additional techniques are used). This twin mission was actually designed as a "life finder" with three biological experiments on board. Although nowadays, almost 50 years later, results of the experiments (especially the Labeled Release mentioned in "Hemlock on Mars") are still discussed [3], the mission sterilization procedure posed a basis for subsequent discussion addressing the danger of compromising a positive detection of life with Earth contamination.

With increasing knowledge about the Red Planet's environment, it becomes clear that some regions of Mars have a higher habitability potential than others. Therefore, in 2003 COSPAR modified the Planetary Protection Policy for Mars introducing the Category IVc. This level of protection applies to "special regions" defined as a "region within which terrestrial organisms are likely to propagate, or a region which is interpreted to have a high potential for the existence of extant Martian life forms." Category IV for Mars indeed includes the other two levels of protection: IVa for lander systems not carrying instruments for the investigations of extant Martian life, and IVb for lander systems designed to investigate extant Martian life but outside the special regions. All these categories (IVa, IVb and IVc) are linked with a precise and very different surface bioburden level (basically how many microbial spores can be left on the spacecraft, because no sterilization is *perfect* unless you also destroy the instruments in the process), so you can easily understand why the error about Mars planetary protection categories made by SOCRATES chief engineer Wally Soo in the story triggers the reaction of NASA's Planetary Protection Officer and Deputy Director of Planetary Science Division.

Special regions of Mars are deeply connected with planetary habitability. We should not be surprised if nowadays this word is increasingly used for our neighboring Red Planet: in recent years, an incredible series of clues points the finger to a very complex history of the planet. Scientists have discovered clays, which on Earth form in the presence of liquid water, on the surface of Mars. Rivers, lakes, and deltas that today are dry, but were probably active in the past, have been detected from orbit and are now being explored by rovers like Mars 2020 Perseverance. Moreover, satellite radars have detected possible underground lakes of liquid water, and organic molecules may be on the surface. Also, the position of Mars in the solar system is in proximity to the circumstellar habitable zone, defined by the distance from the Sun where, given sufficient atmospheric pressure, a planet surface can support liquid water.

In the past, Mars likely resembled Earth far more than it does now. Indeed, today Mars appears to us as an arid, reddish desert, furrowed by harsh sandstorms and extreme weather events. In addition, the lack of substantial atmosphere and therefore of an ozone layer means that the surface is completely irradiated by harmful ultraviolet rays and energetic particles from the Sun for at least a couple of meters underground. Surely, we cannot expect life to be present in such conditions even if we are still looking for its past traces on the ground. The Perseverance rover, exploring the dry delta of Jezero Crater, is looking for surface biosignatures, and we, in the mission science team, have to figure out how to deal with possible signals from extant life and, at the same time, the possibility of Earth contamination. Looking at scientific data from the rover, we need to ask a different question: is the signal of organic matter real or due to instrumental artifact? Has the organic matter originated from life or from abiotic processes? Can we think of another reason why this organic matter is on Mars? Did we clean all the instruments? A lot of questions need the effort of many experts: as astrophysicists, chemists, geologists, and biologists we need to discuss and collaborate with engineers and other instrumental scientists to be sure that, when we do find a sign, the doubt about its origin is minimized.

Once we are sure of our instrument cleaning skills, we can move the scientific analysis deeper. Although we would like to be able to drill five meters below the surface as in the SOCRATES mission, we can still count on the possibility of extracting samples from two meters deep. Indeed, two meters is the depth that the drill of ExoMars, the next mission in search of traces of life planned by the European Space Agency, will reach. The samples extracted will then be analyzed by a multi-analytical payload designed for life search—including a series of scientific analyses (infrared and Raman spectroscopy, gas chromatography, and more)—with the aim to reveal the presence of organic molecules and to see if they are related to possible biomarkers of extant or even present life. As easily imaginable, ExoMars Rover falls into the Category IVb for Mars (as the first mission since the Vikings).

With all these hints, it is not difficult to understand why Mars is the main target for astrobiological exploration and search for life. It certainly holds the record as the most explored planet: more than 50 missions have been launched since the dawn of the space age, and 13 of them are still active. But we are also aware that in more than 50 years of space exploration to Mars, including many landings (sometimes with really un-soft impacts), we do not know if and how much we have already "infected" our neighbor with contaminants from Earth. For example, the early landers of the Soviet Union Mars program were not sterilized, and in addition, one of them (Mars 2) crashed on the surface without control. Could it be that microbes from Earth are already on Mars? Were they able to survive? Did they find a way to become Martian? Many questions arise from exploration history. The debate on planetary protection is evolving.

Some scientists believe that the strict policy to defend Mars from contamination can be an obstacle for a proper scientific exploration [4], while others are in favor of even more rigorous protection. Not least, we need to remember that in the history of the solar system, exchanges of matter between Mars and Earth have already occurred: we have Martian meteorites on our planet, and likely even on Mars there may be Earth fragments. This exchange is at the base of the lithopanspermia theory that hypothesizes life can move and colonize new planets through natural space travel within meteorites and asteroids. We might even think that terrestrial life originated on Mars and later relocated to Earth before it became extinct on the Red Planet.

Beware though, if we are talking about habitability, Mars is surely not the only celestial body to be of interest: many other bodies in the solar system are relevant astrobiological targets. If the reader scrolls through the Planetary Protection Policy, other names will be associated with the maximum protection categories: Enceladus, Europa, and the icy moons of the outer solar system (also known as ocean worlds). The depths of their liquid water seas under icy crusts may hold many surprises . . . extraterrestrial life may conceivably exist in these places. We must protect ourselves, but also, we must certainly avoid invading them with "alien earthlings."

REFERENCES

[1] Mitchell, F. J. & Ellis, W. L. (1971). "Surveyor III: Bacterium isolated from lunar-retrieved TV camera." *Proceedings of the Lunar Science Conference*, vol. 2, p. 2721.
https://articles.adsabs.harvard.edu//
      full/1971LPSC....2.2721M/0002721.000.html

[2] COSPAR Panel on Planetary Protection (2021). "COSPAR Policy on Planetary Protection."
https://cosparhq.cnes.fr/cospar-policy-on-planetary-protection/

[3] Levin, G. V. & Straat, P. A. (2016). "The Case for Extant Life on Mars and Its Possible Detection by the Viking Labeled Release Experiment." *Astrobiology*, vol. 16, n. 10.
https://doi.org/10.1089/ast.2015.1464

[4]   Fairén, A. G. & Schulze-Makuch, D. (2013). "The overprotection of Mars." *Nature Geoscience*, vol. 6, p. 510.
https://doi.org/10.1038/ngeo1866

FURTHER READING

Meltzer, M. (2011). *When Biospheres Collide: A History of NASA's Planetary Protection Programs*. NASA Content Administrator.
https://www.nasa.gov/connect/ebooks/when_biospheres_collide_detail.html

PPOSS Planetary Protection of Outer Solar System project (2019). "The International Planetary Protection Handbook." *Space Research Today*, vol. 205, p. e1.
https://doi.org/10.1016/j.srt.2019.09.001

WEBSITES

NASA Planetary Protection Office
https://sma.nasa.gov/sma-disciplines/planetary-protection

ESA Robotic Exploration of Mars – Planetary Protection
https://exploration.esa.int/web/mars/-/57581-planetary-protection

THE DOG STAR KILLER

RENAN BERNARDO

June 2027 – Teresópolis, Brazil

When the first stars wink out from the sky, you miss only one of them. The Dog Star. Your mother frowns at the gray streaks that slit the night sky of Teresópolis.

"What is it, Mamãe?"

"I don't know . . . The sky is weird tonight."

"Just funny clouds . . ." You say it because you have all the answers when you're seven years old. The world is still indestructible and everyone's immortal.

"Are you going to stay awake working again?" you ask.

"Yes," she says. Red eyes, tautened jaw, scent of coffee everywhere. She points up with her chin. "Because of that."

"What's it, Mamãe?" You knock on her leg with a Lego airplane.

"Cloudy days ahead, Lana. C'mon, time to sleep."

Mamãe grabs your hand and takes you inside. Her eyes glint underneath the weird sky.

"Why are you crying, Mamãe?"

"Because I'll have to travel for work."

"To Rio?"

"A bit farther this time."

You whoop, raising your arms and wobbling your hips. "That means gifts!"

Mamãe says nothing as you tap your feet on the rug before entering. As she closes the screen door and walks to her office, you look up again, searching for the Dog Star. Sirius. Mamãe showed it to you one day with her telescope and told you it's the brightest one. So it has to be there. The night is unblemished but for the weird strips that look like dusty wedding veils. Perhaps the Dog Star wandered about, chasing another star. Perhaps it just felt too tired to shine heartily this night and will come back tomorrow.

You squint, gazing through the screen one last time before going to bed. Nothing. The sky is weird today.

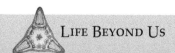

January 2051 – Dog Star Killer

A vessel floats inside the dust mantle. No lights, no exhaust, just a grayed out, deadened bulk of metal almost invisible in visual range in the thick smog that seems to swallow everything. But in infrared, the ship shines against the cold backdrop, and then the tarnished StarKindler Expedition crest becomes visible on its side: the Brazilian flag with a rocket hurtling out of it. She's found it.

Lana decelerates the Hound's skiff as she approaches, heart hammering with anxiety. The radiation readers beep incessantly, warning of exposure to cosmic rays. She shuts off her suit's readouts. She knows what the cloud is made of. She's in an insulated ship and already wearing the heaviest suit. It must be—it has to be—enough protection for the two lives inside.

She prepares to dock.

She closes and opens her fingers. They won't stop trembling.

The ships couple.

"Open the coupling door," she says to the auto-control module. The hatch whirs open.

She's desecrating a coffin.

March 2047 – Rio's Museum of Art

Official ceremonies are so unlike the casual meetings in the university's cafeterias. Instead of bleached jeans and t-shirts with physics jokes, Lana is dressed in a floor-length cobalt dress that pins her body like a giant hand. She's also supposed to linger about the art museum where the graduation ceremonies are taking place, wearing her best smile, feigning comfort with the craving for social interaction.

Luckily, she's alone in the secondary foyer that leads to the auditorium. The ceremony is set to start soon, but she still has a few minutes to suck out what the coffee machine has to offer.

"We welcome the members of the Brazilian Scientific Society," the voice leaks from the double door, "to the graduation ceremony of the BASS, the Brazilian Academy for Space Scientists."

Lana fills a cup of coffee and looks out the window. The night sky over Praça Mauá is pristine. The clouds have scattered today. Not like the best days at home—it never is—but enough.

She still has a bit of time, so she scuttles downstairs, careful not to spill the coffee.

"Where are you going?" a familiar voice calls her. She pretends not to listen and goes on. It's what she's been trying to do all day, anyway.

She leaves the museum through the back door and avoids the small pack of smiling people arriving late through the front gate.

The strips are up there, random cobwebs slowly flowing through-out the black sky, twice as thick as they were when she played with Lego airplanes. The general public calls them: skysmoke, funny night, and star-eater vapor. They are none of those things. They are part of a superdense interstellar dust cloud—probably compressing the helio-sphere, the same one Mamãe researched for her whole life; the same one Lana has been grappling with since she enrolled in the BASS. The Dog Star Killer.

The cloud's origins and nature have baffled astronomers since the beginning. The cloud's dimensions were smaller than any other dark cloud discovered in previous decades—a fraction of a light year across—with a mass much lower than the Sun's. A group of astrono-mers suggested it could be a miniature Bok globule—a dense absorption nebula where stars are born—akin to several extremely small ones recently identified by the Wide Field and Planetary Cameras installed at the Mars-Sun L2 point. But the Dog Star Killer isn't one of them. Floating perilously close to the solar system, it obscures visible starlight like a mini-Bok globule would, but its unclear edges and heavier molec-ular composition paint a different picture.

Despite that, Lana understands that some still consider the phenom-enon being a potentially star-formative area. Others propose it's a heavily-charged molecular cloud, and complex interactions between gas and dust hold it together despite its feeble gravity. Still others, in a more outrageous conjecture, call it a sentient amorphous being in a patient march toward Earth. Lana recalls how Mamãe once drew a purple cloud with a smiley face on it, a speech bubble stating, "Loving my trip to Earth."

"What're you doing?" Her friend Carla has emerged from the art museum and pats her elbow. "They'll be announcing the names soon."

"It's not like I can't get the degree if I don't go."

"But it's an important day, Lana." Carla folds her arms.

Lana rolls her eyes. Mamãe would agree with Carla, yes, but her mother is . . . traveling. "I just need a while."

Carla grunts but goes back in.

The mixed tang of hamburger, fried onion, and hot-dogs wisps from the food stalls near the museum. Lana sits on a bench turned to the street and looks up, placing the coffee cup on a table beside her. She pulls up her phone from the wristband under her dress's sleeve.

"You owe me gifts," she whispers, typing the date and the pattern she sees today. Cobweb.

She reaches for her coffee but her hand knocks on the table. "Damn!" It spills over her skirt.

September 2050 – City Center, Rio de Janeiro

Lana stares at Marcelo. They're in their favorite cafeteria, drowned in the regulars' humming. They've talked about the pillars being designed to filter some of the cosmic rays that will bathe the Earth years from now. Marcelo always fixes his gaze on her when she talks about space, the dust cloud, and her mother's StarKindler Expedition. It's like Lana holds answers to the future. But today something's off.

Lana knows exactly what it is and what will happen.

She presses her hands on her thighs and looks down at the long black coffee before her. Its scent makes her a bit nauseated today.

"Lana," Marcelo whispers, peering down at his own cappuccino, and now she's *sure* of what's to come. He knows how she'd prefer him to ask, that she wouldn't like eyes upon her. Ever. Sometimes not even his. "Do you want to marry me?"

Her mouth tightens. The conversation arced from the pillars to marriage. Her life arced from a coffee-stained dress to the possibility of braiding her quirks and habits, her nights staring at the sky, with the life of the man who was only her dressmaker three years ago. And she savors the possibility, feels it on her lips, more tasteful than long black. She contemplates the idea because she loves this man.

"It's okay if you can't decide now," Marcelo says, still not looking at her. His fingers trace lines randomly across his cup. "Or if—if you don't want to . . ."

"No." She shakes her head. "I'm sorry. I just—I can't, Marcelo. Not now."

"Can I ask you why?" He's polite, steady as always, as if he's just gathering the requirements for a new dress.

"Mamãe promised she would come back before my ninth birthday. She didn't. There are promises we can't make, Marcelo. And that's one of them. I'll travel to space one day and God knows how long I'll be there."

"I'm okay with that." He puts back the cup. It clinks on the saucer. "You arrived two hours late to our first meeting. I know who you are and what your job entails, and I love you for the whole of you."

Lana closes her eyes and suddenly wants to get out of there.

"No," she says, hoarser than he deserves. She stands and leaves, dizzy, queasiness coiling in her stomach.

March 2047 – Rio's Museum of Art

"You really took my call seriously," Lana says to the dressmaker at the museum's entrance. He has a package in his arms.

"Of course. A ruined dress at graduation is no joke." He has closely cropped hair and high brown cheekbones. The kind of cute guy she's dumped for work and research so many times during her university courses.

"It's just that—I'm surprised. I didn't think you'd come so fast."

"I was driving downtown, ma'am. Why not help one of my clients in an emergency? That's what makes good business." He surveys her, head to toe. He's clearly inspecting his product, the dress she rented from his dressmaking company and spoiled with coffee. She blushes. "You know we have a fine for staining the dress, right?"

Lana nods, smiling. "I'm aware of the terms, Mr. . . ."

"Marcelo, please." He hands over the package. "Do you like pumpkin?"

"Not so much. Why?" Lana checks her phone. The university dean will call her name soon, and she'll disappoint Carla if she doesn't go. But, honestly, she'd rather stay there chitchatting with the cute dressmaker than being the focus of hundreds of eyes in the auditorium.

"What I have here is—well, see for yourself." He extends the package.

Lana tears it slightly and peeks at a bright orange dress, one she'd never choose for any occasion, ever in her life. A dress that would bring even more eyes toward her.

"Sorry, it's what I had in your size in the car." Marcelo half-smiles. "By the way, is it cappuccino?"

"What?" She scowls at him. "You offend me, pumpkin salesman."

His eyes widen in concern. "I'm sorry, that's not—"

"Long black always, sir. Never cappuccino."

Carla rushes toward Lana with a worried look on her face furrowing into impatience.

"It's on J, Lana. You have to come now."

"Okay, *mom*!" Lana rolls her eyes. "Marcelo, I need to go. Apparently, this is an important moment."

Carla grunts, pulling her by the arm.

When she enters the hallway to the elevators, Lana halts, forcing Carla to stop. "Wait."

Carla moans as Lana hustles back outside.

"Marcelo!"

He pivots to face her, that same half-smile on his face, which makes him even cuter.

"Meet me for coffee tomorrow afternoon," she says, heart hammering in her chest, not only because of what she's saying—it has been a long time since she last invited someone on a date—but because she knows she won't have much time to mull over what he answers. "So . . . Well—we have to discuss your caffeinated dress. The fine you mentioned."

"I have your card to bill, Ms. Lana. It's—"

"Billing my card won't take us on a date."

Marcelo's mouth gapes.

"Five—five o'clock?"

"Maybe five, maybe six. I can't make promises."

"Okay."

Carla isn't around anymore when Lana trots to the locker room.

October 2050 – Catete, Rio de Janeiro

Does the *thing* inside her sweat? Does it feel the same knot she feels in her stomach right now? It's in her belly, so it must be feeling it, right? Like hands twirling and shaking and . . . cuddling all at the same time. Christ The Redeemer is a blue flambeau against the clear night sky outside her window, but today she can't stop to take notes about the dust cloud. Her hand is over her belly instinctively protecting what's in there.

Marcelo knocks.

The oversized plus sign shines in green on her screen. She fumbles and turns it off before opening the door.

"Are you feeling well?" Marcelo glances at her belly, closing the door behind him. His gaze jabs at her.

She cups Marcelo's cheeks. "You know we've come across lots of wrong data, or rather wrong conclusions, during our research of the cloud, don't you? Sometimes it points one way, but it's just—plain wrong. We often need to reconfirm what we learn."

He keeps frowning, analyzing Lana. They've been together for three years, and he has probably detected the shift in her voice. Lana evades his gaze, her belly unsettled even though what's in there is still unnoticeable. Hell, she has denied his proposal just a week ago and still roots for the relationship to work, out of a miracle.

"What's happening, Lana? You're acting weird."

She laughs. The thing inside her just can't be true because life can't do that to you—to anyone—when you least expect it to. "The sky is weird tonight, Marcelo."

"You mom's words?" He sits on the couch and peeks outside. Zebra. She won't write it down, but it's a zebra pattern today. "You've had your hand over your belly since I came in. Is it hurting? What did you eat?"

Lana takes her hands off her stomach, feeling a rush in the estrangement between her and the *thing* inside. She wants to put her hands back there as if to protect it from whatever particles the Dog Star Killer will pour onto Earth over the coming years.

"Mamãe's ship has emitted a beacon." She sits next to Marcelo and squeezes his hands. "It's probably inside the cloud. I applied to be on the rescue team, Marcelo. It's what I've been waiting for."

Lana lays her hand back over her belly, not wanting to grasp how what's in there separates her from her mother.

July 2027 – Teresópolis

Mamãe's bedroom is a translucent fog. Planets revolve in red, green, and purple. Letters are scattered through the air with shiny annotations beside them. Mamãe bites her lips, types on her pad, swivels the planets with her hands, grunts and removes symbols, nods and adds new ones, draws lines, brings them forth, zooms in, out. All the while, planets and letters pass through her, nonchalantly.

She pinches her fingers, and a mass of dark green light swells out from the borders of the hologram.

"The Dog Star Killer," you say. "Ugly cloud."

Mamãe mumbles something, but she's not really paying attention. You're sitting on her bed, an untouched book on your lap showing pictures of the universe and piles of text you don't understand.

"Mamãe, why don't the planets wear glasses?"

"Glasses?" Mamãe blinks, waking up, her face a shimmer of blueness criss-crossed by H, He, and Sc.

"Yes. To be protected from the dust cloud."

"Well, they sort of wear glasses already." Mamãe pinches the air with her fingers and brings out the Sun. She types something on her pad and a blue light bloats around it, enveloping all the planets around the Sun. "It's called the heliosphere. Basically, it's a stream of particles billowed out by the solar wind. It's what protects us from cosmic rays."

"We're inside this big ball, then. It can stop the Dog Star Killer."

"Ideally, yes." Mamãe rubs her eyes. "But the Dog Star Killer is not a dust cloud like the one you see when a truck accelerates on a dirt road. It's—the Sun fits inside it."

"How can I help to shoo away the dust? It's making you tired."

Mamãe stares at you for a moment and you think she wandered off, deep in her thoughts again. She goes to the window and pulls the curtains aside.

"What do you see?" She looks up to the sky. The view is not so clear today, but you can distinguish the normal clouds from the Dog Star Killer. "Make some notes. If you want to work, you will work."

You nod, finding a pencil and turning the book to a blank corner of the book's end paper. You look out the window.

"I see . . . It seems like a zebra."

"So write it."

You scrawl fast.

"One day you will understand what the patterns might mean. Could be nothing, but some people believe they slowly change as the cloud moves and different sections of its composition become more evident in visible light. Mostly, those patterns are regions of the cloud hiding the starlight behind them. What we see up there is the front part of the dust cloud, looming slowly but steadily from the fringes of the solar system."

"Can it see us?"

"I don't think so." Mamãe shakes her head. "But one star might hatch there one day if it's anything similar to what we call a Bok globule."

"Will I see it hatch?"

"No." Mamãe smiles, and you know she'd like to see a star germinating out there. "Jot down the patterns you see and one day you might glean something from them."

"I will." You write down the word 'pattern' at the bottom of the end paper. "When will the Dog Star Killer reach us?"

"It's moving fast for such a cloud, but sluggish from our perspective. Our solar system's relative speed to the cloud makes it seem slow. It will take years, but we have to find a solution, so your children won't have to worry."

You write. Years. Solution. Children won't worry.

"When will you go, Mamãe?" You stand and pierce the lights to hug her. She kneels and holds you in her arms.

"In two months." Her eyes glint, or maybe it's just the hologram's flicker. "Your grannies will take care of you."

"Must you go?"

"Yes, my love. There's only so much we can discover remotely or with robotic probes. This is an unparalleled opportunity for discovery and for protecting us from any harmful effects."

She goes on to mention things that make little sense to you. New, better propulsion systems, optimal gravity assists . . .

But there's only one thing you want to know. "And will you be back?"

She grasps you against her chest and says in a muffled voice, "In less than two years, I hope. Before you're nine. I'll bring you gifts."

"You promise?"

"I do. You wait for me."

You prop your chin on Mamãe's shoulder and feel the vibration as her chest heaves. H, Sc, Ti, V, Mn tear through both of you.

November 2050 – BASS Hospital and Pre-Flight Complex

The ultrasound machine beeps softly, almost as if trying to soothe her thoughts. Lana blinks, staring at a slide showing armadillos, seals, and badgers next to a graph.

Carla stares at her, adjusting her glasses, her eyes full of pity. If Lana believed in some sort of destiny, she'd say it put Carla right there as the head physician of the BASS pre-flight checks.

"In the lack of an ideal environment, some mammals do that," Carla says, a hand over Lana's belly. "There's a catalytic enzyme that regulates diapause by sensing nutrients in cells and its energy store. That means that when these mammals aren't in the right conditions, they can just postpone their pregnancy. And we've been doing that experimentally with humans for some years now. Your case is not exactly diapause because the embryo is already implanted. But it's sort of an imitation. And it works and is reversible. Most of all, administering the enzyme to you is the only way I can fit you into all the pre-flight checks necessary for your mission. But before you decide . . ."

Lana nods. She already understood what that decision entails. "It's still dangerous for the baby."

Carla pinches her lips, shrugging. She has little of that haste of years ago, urging a shy friend to graduate. "It's still early and safe to do it, but the exposure to radiation up there and the prolonged stay in utero makes it more dangerous for you and the fetus. We have suits to thwart the risks, but the danger is not zero at all."

Lana closes her eyes. Abortion is an option in cases like that. One that Carla doesn't bring up. She knows Lana wouldn't agree to it. But Lana is the only BASS astronaut qualified to undergo a rescue mission like the one she's enrolled in, the most experienced person to pilot a Hound skiff, and the only one with enough motivation to enter into the dust cloud. Otherwise, they'll have to rely on unmanned craft with mechanical arms to save whatever's left of the StarKindler Expedition. Lana was the one who advocated one last rescue mission if any sign of life was ever emitted from the cloud. Lana dedicated her life to that mission . . . for Mamãe and for the Dog Star Killer.

"Does Marcelo know?" Carla touches her hand.

Lana recoils, blinking fast. She shakes her head. "Some things need to wait."

January 2051 – The Dog Star Killer

The StarKindler Expedition ship is not a coffin, but it feels like one.

Bulky shadows trample toward Lana, magnetic boots clanking from both sides of the ship's dark corridor. The baby wriggles inside her in response—no, it doesn't; it can't. She worries about her belly being squeezed inside the tight suit, but she should be worrying about the cosmic rays that escape the ship's insulation and claws through metal, through her suit. X-rays. Gamma rays. Ions. Atoms. Nuclei. Helium, Scandium, Titanium, Vanadium, Manganese.

The ship's bright white light switches on. Four figures, two on each end of the hallway, wear an outdated version of the BASS's suit, grayed out, and with smoked glass helmets. Lana sighs in relief. After all the years studying the Dog Star Killer and the StarKindler Expedition, she still nurtures a great deal of misgiving about what she'd find—if she'd discover anything more than bulky-suited skeletons slumped on rusty seats.

"Who are you?" a voice flickers through Lana's suit comm system. "This area of the ship is damaged and radiation levels are high."

She freezes. "Take me out of here," she says. No. She begs. "Please."

They do. They take her through a long deck with a few terminals showing stats she doesn't want to see. She explains she's from a rescue mission, but they don't react to that. They must've been rationing supplies for a while. Even though the StarKindler Expedition had been sent with resources for 28 years and almost 24 have passed, they couldn't count on being rescued.

In a kind of control room, plastic seats line up in front of switched-off terminals. A solitary lamp flickers on the ductwork-crisscrossed ceiling. Pressure and vac suits hang from racks on the other side of the room like convicted people hanging in the gallows.

"You can take your helmet off," the person beside Lana says. Not Mamãe. She presses a button on her wrist and her helmet clicks.

"Are radiation levels safe?" Lana asks, instinctively putting a hand over her belly.

"Mostly." The woman takes off her helmet. She's a shriveled lady with full white hair falling over her suit's shoulders like a wimple. Her eyes are whitened. Exoastronomer Poliana. She graduated with Mamãe and helped her unveil the details of an interstellar dust cloud to the world, studying it in multiple wavelengths. Three children, now in their forties, an apartment in Santa Cruz, a prideful collection of postcards from South American cities.

The other people from the StarKindler crew buckle off their helmets too. The expedition left Earth with fifteen people, from technicians to astrophysicists, but there are only four in the room. They occupy the seats around Lana. She has a knot in her stomach. All eyes are upon her. "Is Eliana da Silva still here?" she asks.

A woman peeks at her from her slumped position on the chair. Ana Torres. Short hair, mostly gray. She's 68 now. Ana studied the effects of hydrogen atoms flowing into Earth's atmosphere and reacting with oxygen, a phenomenon that could deplete humanity's breath. A sister with Alzheimer's. Fear of flight, not of space. Lana wants to leap up and shake an answer out of her.

"Did she . . ." Lana finally gathers the courage to pull off her helmet. "Is she dead?"

A door swishes open. A short old lady emerges, shuffling her mag boots and patting a stick on the floor, which seems almost absurd in the meager gravity of the slowly rotating section of the ship. Unhelmeted, she has blank eyes and a hunched back but wears the unmistakable orange of a custom-made jumpsuit.

"God . . ." Mamãe says. "If I'm still hearing right . . ."

December 2050 – Santos Dumont Airport

The goodbye is Lana's idea. Marcelo has respected her decision to live apart, but she feels she owes him something, at least a brief farewell. A small price to pay for her betrayal.

After she rejected him, she'd seen him only once to say she was leaving. And now she waits for him one last time in Santos Dumont Airport Terminal. She's going to Maceió, where the Hound is waiting for her and her team.

Lana wears a large dress. Not one of Marcelo's, but one her mother left in her wardrobe. Her belly would be noticeable by now, if not for the diapause treatment.

Marcelo arrives. She instantly regrets arranging this farewell. Not because she doesn't want to see him, but because for a moment she wants to abandon the StarKindler's beacon and stay with him. Say yes. Say she's going to have a child. Say she's sorry and make all the promises she didn't. Feel something growing within her body.

"When do you leave?" he says, a bit dry. His stubbled beard has some white threads, but he's still the dressmaker she fell in love with under a cobwebbed sky.

"Forty minutes from now."

"Oh."

"We'll talk when I get back."

He's clearly not sure if she will get back. So far, BASS has sent only one unmanned expedition after the failed StarKindler, and it never got near the cloud.

She takes a step closer and kisses him on the corner of his mouth. He never varies his cologne. It smells of taking her to dinner at a sea-view restaurant, of bringing her a new dress each month.

I'll be back, she wants to say, but she won't make promises.

Instead, she whispers to herself when she leaves Marcelo, "We'll be back."

January 2051 – Dog Star Killer

Mamãe stares at nothing, a hand on Lana's leg. The dome's dimmed light falls over her wrinkles, features of her skin that are new to Lana. Lana's eyes sting from the hour she spent crying over Mamãe's shoulder. Now neither of them says anything as if needing to draw on the silence to steady their emotions. The terminal on the dome's wall displays low radiation readings. Lana asked Mamãe to take her to the safest place in the ship, and it's a control dome inside the engine deck. Mamãe has no idea why she asked this.

Lana uncoils Mamãe's long hair. Mamãe smiles, nacreous eyes searching for Lana's face, never finding it.

"I graduated in orange." Lana's voice shatters the silence. "A gaudy dress brought by the man who became my husband. I looked like a pumpkin, Mamãe."

"Husband? I left behind a kid who only thought about the night sky."

"You'll catch up." Lana drapes an arm over her mother's shoulder and inadvertently pulls Mamãe's other arm over her heavy-suited belly. It stays there. "We'll get back and we'll catch up on lost time."

Mamãe's vitreous eyes flicker with uncertainty. "I'm blind, Lana. Cancer is gnawing at me. I'm really tired. I've spent too much time in here. There were fifteen of us and now we're only six. We can hardly maintain this ship anymore. We made plans to shut down life support a year from now."

"You won't need to do that, Mamãe. I've sent a message to the Hound, and we'll be out of the cloud and back to Earth soon. How did the StarKindler stop working?"

"We made mistakes, underestimated the cloud, radiation broke some of our equipment . . . I can find at least ten other reasons." She sighs. "Now they hardly matter."

Lana cups her mother's face, the roughness of Mamãe's skin caressing the tip of her fingers. "Things will get better." Lana stands and opens the compartment on her suit's chest. She produces her plastic-coated annotations, all the records on the cloud's appearance she has collected and printed to show the woman who taught her how to write and look at the sky.

"I've brought all my annotations," Lana says, flipping through them. "The first one is from that day in your bedroom. When you had the hologram switched on and told me when you'd travel. Remember?"

A smile gains back Mamãe's face. She has but a few teeth in her mouth now. "Did you learn something from them?"

"It kept my eyes on the sky long enough to find you," she says.

"That reminds me. I have a gift for you." Mamãe puts a hand on her pocket. "You see, not all my promises are in vain."

She takes a data stick from the pocket, and a small pic printed on a metal plaque falls to the floor.

Lana picks it up. There's Mamãe kneeling before the ship's drive with three members of the StarKindler crew, her arms braided around a woman's waist. None of those faces are the ones from the control room. In the pic, Mamãe is flashing a wide smile. Lana's not the only one who left a part of her behind.

Lana presses the picture into her mother's hand.

"This stick contains all the data we've gathered on the cloud," Mamãe says. "Hopefully, you're not going to need much of it."

"Why not? Earth is already making projects to alleviate the cloud damages."

"The cloud itself is probably some leftover from the formation of our galaxy, later enriched in heavy elements from supernova explosions, and our solar system was unlucky—or lucky—enough to be near it. It's something entirely new, a high-velocity dust cloud with some traits like a Bok globule. It's all here in the data stick. Gathering this data, exploring this ghostly cold darkness, was what kept us going all those years. But . . . we're on a trajectory moving away from the cloud, dear." She speaks with a gravity that doesn't fit the good news. "The cloud will scrape the solar system tangentially, but the heliosphere won't be crumpled too severely, and Earth won't be showered with cosmic rays. In a few years, the extinction of starlight caused by the cloud might even go away."

"Mamãe! That's excellent news." Lana hugs her. Her mother feels frail. There's no trace of the perfume she used back home, which often mingled with the scent of coffee that pervaded her office. Only the leaden odor of the ship clings to the air, hard and heavy. Mamãe barely moves her arms to hug her back.

"Lana, we didn't manage to activate a beacon in this ship . . . and haven't tried for some time. The beacon must've activated due to a defect."

"What do you mean?" But deep down, Lana knows some paths lead only forward.

August 2027 – Teresópolis

Mamãe is bent over her desk, head propped on her hand, drawing something. You tiptoe not to disturb her, bringing a slice of lemon pie. You put it on the desk and quickly turn back.

"Hey, girl." Mamãe calls you.

You swivel and gape at her. "Lemon pie."

"Thank you, sweetheart." She smiles at you, but it's fleeting. Her eyes are swollen and her half-closed lids throb lightly. She's there all day but still her perfume lingers in the air, a nectary scent of cotton and lilac that makes you sure everyone's immortal and everything is going to be fine as long as she's there with you.

"What are you drawing?" You peek at the table and see a lot of squares and dainty letters and numbers scattered all around.

"I'm sketching some ideas for the ship that will take me to the stars."

"Is it big like home?"

"It's bigger, but it's not home."

"Home means a house, right?"

Mamãe shakes her head. "Home is the place that, no matter what, you want to remain there."

March 2051 – Almost Home

Lana has left cloud and her mother behind. The Hound is approaching the Moon, and a marbled Earth looms beyond. She's in her quarters, still letting the hungry darkness of the cloud sift away from her mind. She's sure it will take a while.

Touchdown will happen in a few hours. She's already in her suit. Her brain makes her think there's something wagging in her belly. There isn't. Not yet. She blinks away the blurriness of tears and taps the control panel to open a connection with Marcelo. Time to unpause some aspects of her life.

"Hey," she starts, hesitantly.

A flutter of anxiety rises in her belly with the two-second delay. She puts a hand over the suit as if she can feel anything but the cold touch of the lead-compound surface.

"My God, Lana! Are you okay?"

He's crying, she knows. His voice is choked. She suddenly misses his reddened eyes and the tears coursing down to his lips. She'd change almost anything for that right now, to be there with his breath on her neck while she tells him she loves him and everything is going to be okay.

"I'm calling because I want to meet you for coffee . . ." The words feel heavier than she imagined them. She fears rejection. She probably deserves it. "If you still want it . . ."

"No coffee in space, right?"

"Not what we call coffee down there, no," she adds. "I'm going nuts."

"Did you find her?"

She nods, even though he can't see her. "She figured out the dust cloud, and . . ."

Lana lowers her head. She didn't tell Mamãe about the baby. Mamãe had been blind and feeble, and cancer tore the last of her after years of cosmic ray exposure. Lana did tell the others, though, and Ana Torres helped her with examinations and the diapause follow-ups while she was aboard the StarKindler. Mamãe didn't deserve to be force-fed with the desperation of a grandkid stranded in a sea of radiation. Lana was there to find her mother and let her depart without any unfulfilled promises between them. In the end, Lana knew it couldn't end differently.

She finds the strength to speak. "None of the survivors wanted to come back. They wouldn't survive full one-gee after so many years in zero to low gravity, and the ship had become their home. We left them some supplies, and BASS will send more. Some have called it waste of fuel, but . . . it's the only right thing we can do. The only human thing. And Mamãe . . ." She gulps tears and glances at the annotations in the locker. She closes the lid. "I remained with her until the end. I was lucky, Marcelo . . . arriving less than two months before . . ."

"I'm sorry," Marcelo says, the delay in his words seeming longer than it is.

"I'll tell you all the rest in person. All the . . . things I want to say. Exactly three days from now? 7 PM?"

"An exact day and time?" Marcelo snickers. The sound warms the gray coldness of Lana's quarters. "Space has changed you."

"Yeah. Things are weird around here."

August 2060 – Home

You come out of the house and drape an arm around Marcelo's shoulder. Diego is lying on the grass beaming at the almost patternless night sky. A chilly breeze plucks at your dress.

"What's that new star, Mamãe?" Diego says, pulling your hands and pointing up. "It's so bright."

You look up knowing what you'll see.

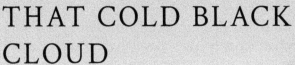

THAT COLD BLACK CLOUD

STEFANO SANDRELLI

I magine a cocoon: a cocoon for stars. A small molecular cloud with stars forming within, called a Bok globule. The one investigated by Lana and her mother in Renan Bernardo's story is so small that we should call it a mini-globule. A celestial object of this kind has not been discovered yet, but astronomers know very well that we have leafed through just a few pages of the whole catalogue of astronomical beasts. Such objects are more than star-forming regions: they are fountains of nested narratives, and even their discovery begins with a love story.

In late 1920s' Netherlands, a young American astronomer, Priscilla Fairfield, met a local graduate student, Bartholomeus Bok. They had known each other for just a week at the International Astronomical Union Third General Assembly—but after that week, he proposed, and after a year's correspondence, they married and started "wandering through the highways and byways of our beautiful Milky Way," as they said. Hereafter, whenever I write Bok, you should read it as "Bok & Fairfield." "From then on [after the marriage] it is difficult and pointless to separate his achievements from hers," wrote a representative of the *Royal Astronomical Society* in 1987, after Bart passed away. The marriage was the reason Bart Bok moved to the United States, where the Bok globule story started.

Let's jump to the 1940s. WWII has just ended. Bart is the Associate Professor of Astronomy at Harvard. He's got astronomical images which show dark nebulae obscuring the stellar field. They look just like insect cocoons stuck on old family snapshots. They must be clumps of gas and dust, but Bart gets the feeling they should be carefully scrutinized and classified.

He has been contacted by a young technician, Edith Reilly, so he asks her to peer into the Lick Atlas and the Ross-Calvert Atlas images. He is sure the clumps could be connected to a star formation process. In March 1947, Bok and Reilly publish a short paper in the most important scientific journal in their field, *The Astrophysical Journal* [1]. They state that "(. . .) relatively small dark nebulae (. . .) probably represent the evolutionary stage just preceding the forma-tion of a star." Enter Bok globules. But the one who searched through the images was Reilly, in fact. Why should they be known just in Bok's name?

Bok and Reilly's globules
For years, Bok and Reilly's hypothesis remained intuitive, but unproven. Those black clouds were simply too dark to see through: whatever was happening in a globule, any emitted visible light was totally obscured by gas and dust.

Things changed in the 1980s—thanks to new observations provided by the Infrared Astronomical Satellite (IRAS). The near infrared data showed that it was likely "that almost every Bok globule harbors a young star" [2]. So, what happens within a Bok globule?

The data we have today suggest the presence of warm objects as large as stars. Gas falls into their accretion disks. And if we look at the edges of such globules, we see jets of ionized matter and outflows of molecular gas. All of these clues hint at the fact that one or more protostars could be curled up in the nest of each globule.

The main idea is quite easy to grasp. When the force of gravity of the nebula overcomes gas pressure, the nebula itself collapses. This is due to very efficient cooling mechanisms; Bok globules are considered among the coldest objects in the universe. Material collapses until a new point of equilibrium is found, while density and temperature increase in the core of the nebula, until a powerful source of energy turns on: nuclear fusion. Fusion releases light and kinetic energy, the birth of a star. The released kinetic energy allows the inner gas to counteract the weight of the external gas throughout the structure.

Even if the overall idea is clear, these globules are still a mystery to investigate. They can give birth to complex offspring. Bunches of multiple stars can be born, which may differ from one another depending on conditions such as the characteristics of the gas or the proximity of other protostars.

The interstellar medium
Bok globules remind us once more that galaxies are not constituted only by stars, planets, moons, or comets, as one could naïvely believe. The space among stars is not empty: approximately 2% of the total

mass of our galaxy, the Milky Way, consists of highly interesting but low-density matter, called the *interstellar medium (ISM)*.

Most of the ISM is gas. As a whole, it can be described as a soup of atoms (mainly hydrogen and helium, 91% and 8.9%, respectively), ions, and molecules. If you like it hot, you can add photons (that is, light), gravitons, exotic particles, and cosmic rays hurtling at very high speeds. Consider sprinkling some magnetic fields on it for a new flavor. Do not forget the final ingredient: dust is a mandatory spice, in as low a percentage as 1% of the mass of the ISM. Not so much, maybe, but of utmost importance. Dust plays a fundamental role in cooling the protostar nebula.

Now, let's take a stroll through the interstellar medium. But how? Maybe dice could help us. As you know, density measures how packed the matter is in a unit of volume. A possible unit of volume is the cubic centimeter. That will be our die, size 1 cm x 1 cm x 1 cm. It can be filled with samples of universe, here and there. Wherever we go, we will count how many particles it contains: that will be a first characterization of that corner of universe.

By way of reference, let's start on Earth. At sea level, the number of particles of gas in our little die is about ten billion billions of them: 10^{19}. Such a huge number is puzzling. We are used to thinking of air as an evanescent element. But when a stiff wind is blowing, we understand that it's much more substantial than we expect.

For many reasons, scientists may want to work in very different conditions in special laboratories. For example, in the arms of Virgo and Ligo, the two interferometers which detected the first gravitational waves, scientists are able to pump out air until the number of particles in our die reaches one billionth of that found in ordinary air. But, unfortunately, this means that in our die we still find ten billion tiny bits of matter: 10^{10}. At an altitude of 400 km above the Earth, the density is one hundred million particles per die: 10^{8}.

Leaving our planet, Her Majesty Fullness seems to make space for Mrs. Emptiness, but it is clear that matter sneaks everywhere it can, as pervasive as confetti. The solar system seems to be crossing a region of quite diffuse ISM, the Local Interstellar Cloud, which could be around nine light years across. It moves through the galaxy like a soap bubble, with an estimated density of 0.3 atoms per cubic centimeter. That means that you need at least 3 or 4 dice to find one single particle.

This peculiar bubble, however, seems to be immersed in an even more diffuse gaseous balloon, called the Local Bubble by astronomers (that shows their awkwardness with names[1]). It is as big as 300 light years across and you need around 20 dice to collect only one particle.

Both of these bubbles are voids formed by star explosions, likely supernovae, billions of years ago. Every time a supernova occurs, it actually refills the interstellar medium with very high velocity ions and electrons, which can reach one million degrees—consider that it just makes no difference if they are Kelvin or Celsius degrees. Moreover, since supernovae sweep away the ISM from their surroundings and leave a less dense region all around, the Milky Way can be regarded as a sort of Swiss cheese with holes here and there. And voids can be even emptier: some interstellar zones may require 10,000 dice before finding a particle!

Another interesting family in our ISM tour are special emission nebulae that can usually be found near hot, massive stars that emit lots of UV rays. These carry so much energy that they can strip away the poor electrons of neutral hydrogen. In these so-called H II regions (H II standing for ionized hydrogen), protons are free to fly at high speeds, even though they would never win a race with those supernova-energized ions we saw before. Here, ISM can remain relatively dense: near hot stars, you can find bubbles called *Strömgren's spheres*, whose density is relatively high (around 1,000 particles in a die). They are beautiful, too: just look up the Rosette Nebula or the Necklace Nebula.

The Milky Way also has its own clumps. Giant molecular clouds—as astonishingly vast as 150 light years or more—can host more than 200 molecules every die. And we have already met the Bok globules: in the coldest and densest molecular clouds, you'll find one million particles in your die. That's an enormous number with respect to the diffuse clouds—but it is billions and billions fewer than fresh air!

What would happen, then, if our solar system actually traversed a Bok globule? We're not *en route* to any in human-relevant timescales, but it's not inconceivable. Recent studies suggest that in the following thousands of years, we will slowly pass through a local interstellar cloud inhomogeneity. And slowly stars could disappear: we wouldn't need to fear not seeing the Sun or planets, but only a few tens of stars

---

1 Astronomers have their issues with names: think of the four 8.2-metre telescopes of ESO. They can work together as a very large telescope. Believe it or not, astronomers call it *Very Large Telescope*. That is slightly depressing, but consistent with other names such as *Big Bang* or *black holes*. Talk about understatement.

could be visible to the naked eye—at least at the darkest point of the encounter.

Moreover, the heliosphere—put simply, the space "droplet" where the solar wind and magnetic field reigns—could be rather different from the present one. Nowadays, it is enormously wide—reaching a distance from the Sun double of Pluto's. It has the fundamental duty to prevent charged dust and gas from entering the whole solar system. If we enter a high-density environment, the heliosphere would shrink and abandon all the outer planets to their fate. Could the material compress the heliosphere sufficiently to harm life on Earth? That makes for another intriguing story!

Molecular cradles

So we're back at stars' hatcheries, and the cycle begins anew, since stars are the drivers of the evolution of their surrounding environment. While hydrogen, most helium, and traces of lithium were produced within three minutes of the Big Bang, most of the matter we are familiar with has come from stars at various stages of their life cycle. To be fair, the diversity of the universe is so vast that tracing back the exact origin and the actual contribution of various stellar sources to specific elements is not that easy. Nevertheless, we are confident we have grasped the overall idea.

Some elements are mainly created in those chained nuclear fusion reactions through which stars become gaseous spheres in a kind of hydrostatic equilibrium. Generally speaking, this is the case for the elements lighter than iron. Solar-type stars contribute mainly to elements not heavier than oxygen. More massive stars carry on until they produce iron, at least in their inner cores.

Other elements such as gold or uranium are created during supernova explosions, or in collisions between exotic (but not rare) objects, such as neutron stars. The point is that whenever a star ends its existence, it returns most of the material it is made of into the interstellar medium from which it was born billions or millions of years before—in a large-scale recycling system. Because of the nuclear reactions we mentioned, their chemical composition at the end is very different from the initial one and their deaths enrich the interstellar medium in new elements.

It is the work of stars to enable carbon to exist—the basic component of the life we know. However, we should never underestimate the creativity of the universe. For the time being, we only know the kind of life which has evolved on our blue planet. This does not rule out the possibility that somewhere else in the cosmos, a totally different life can evolve, possibly using elements other than carbon.

The interstellar medium is not just any soup: it is the soup from which we have emerged. In fact, astronomers have detected organic molecules in space: comets are rich in them, and those molecular clouds we visited before—Bok globules—host various kinds of molecules, too. And since stars are formed from molecular clouds, we can believe that those black clouds which gave birth to the Sun were rich in organic molecules. In other words: we are children of the stars, but molecular clouds are the cocoons of the stars and our metaphorical cradles.

REFERENCES

[1] Bok, B. & Reilly, E. (1947). "Small dark nebulae." *Astrophysical Journal*, 105, 255-257.
http://dx.doi.org/10.1086/144901

[2] Yun, Joao Lin & Clemens, Dan P. (1990). "Bart BOK was correct!" *Astrophysical Journal Letters*, 365, 73-76.
http://dx.doi.org/10.1086/185891

FURTHER READING

ARROWS: Advance, Recruit, Retain & Organize Women in STEM (2022). "Hidden HERstories: Priscilla Fairfield Bok."
https://www.bu.edu/arrows/art-rfp/priscilla-fairfield-bok/

Bok, B. (1972). "The birth of stars." *Scientific American*, 227 (2), 48-65.
https://www.jstor.org/stable/10.2307/24927406

Dickman, R. (1977). "Bok globules." *Scientific American*, 236 (6), 66-81.
https://www.jstor.org/stable/10.2307/24954071

European Space Agency. *Interstellar Medium*. CESAR / ESA - Educational Initiative CESAR / ESA - Educational Initiative.
https://cesar.esa.int/index.php?Section=ISM

Lada, C. J. (1987). "Bok, Bart—obituary." *Quarterly Journal of the Royal Astronomical Society*, 28 (4), 539-541.
https://ui.adsabs.harvard.edu/abs/1987QJRAS..28..539L

TITAN
OF CHAOS
G. David Nordley

"Help. Eaten by giant worm. Zendac's going to kill us. Linda."

The succinct incoming text holo from my ex floating over my office desk put her in the Saturn System, on Titan, in the Kraken Mare, no less. I closed my eyes. That was the bad news. The worse news is I'm Hartigan O'Reilly, director chief and only full-time law enforcement officer of the Cislunar Republic's Saturn System constabulary. The CLR is, by treaty, in charge of the Saturn System. So, if someone's going to kill out here, I can't duck the case.

Thirty years ago, back on Luna, Linda and I were a couple, until she left. I'd come to Saturn in part to escape memories. But the memories followed me.

"Watson, get me a brief on Linda Marion, her name about 2090. Any reason the Chief of Submarine Operations on Titan would be trying to kill her, other than for putting one of his subs at risk?"

"Are you sure she meant that literally?" the AI's voice said in a three-hundred-year-old west London accent with a slight Scottish flavor.

"Not sure she didn't. She could be pretty literal, and the message went through a T-link satellite over Kraken Mare, not submarine ops."

"Indeed."

"Indeed. What's with Zendac, Titan worms, and submarines?"

Sub ops, like Titan Blimp ops and Saturn High Station, was a private concession; the CLR didn't have the personnel. The SHS department and I had a professional relationship. Helen, at Blimp ops, was a personal friend. But I didn't know Zendac. He had a CLR contract administrator on Luna, but Zendac owned Sub Ops and had an International Space Authority charter. The CLR won independence from the ISA back in '60 in a near war, leaving hard feelings.

I sent a data stream for our analyst, Gwen Chryse, still 33 light-minutes out, inbound from the Uranus system. She and my deputy, Kate, are mathematicians—Fellows of the Chaos Institute, an organization that shares a domed crater habitat with my security office.

Hyperion's craters are many, deep and steep, and its rotation chaotic. The sun could spend weeks overhead anywhere on the small satellite and make its holes sublimely deeper and ideal for spin gravity surface habitats. Think of a salad spinner under a transparent bowl.

Watson helpfully displayed a 3D animated Kraken sea worm. The ghostly image showed a worm-like tube about twice as wide across as a minisub image placed for scale. The worm head shot up from the hydrocarbon muck with two big grasping claws and all sorts of tentacles that made it look like a carnivorous flower. The tail vanished far below the display field.

I tried to get my mind around the immensity of the animal. About sixty meters around and kilometers deep, its walls about half a meter thick, and an annular area something like thirty square meters, so about 30 tonnes per meter of length—more massive than a space station.

"Its metabolism is glacial," Watson said, "but it can store energy, and its head can accordion-out with surprising speed. They go deep enough to tap the temperature difference between the crust and the surface as well as interior chemistry."

"Submarines?" I asked.

"Zendac uses 'Iceboat' subs. Europan design, printed here. Contrary to their name, they have a problem with water ice—rough contact with sharp-edged ice can crease their hulls. Worms use ice for gizzard stones. Some subs got trapped by worms and escaped, but two are missing. The leading theory is a warm water vent under Kraken mare. The water turns to ice . . ."

Water at 100 K was like quartz.

"They should have printed thicker hulls. But a worm can't eat subs, literally, could it?"

"Don't know," Watson replied, his lack of confirmation troubling. "The worms aren't very strong. On the other hand, objects ingested by worms are rarely recovered. The subs that escaped were retired due to weakened hulls."

"How did some subs escape the worms?"

"They blew their trim oil, got more buoyancy, and maybe gave the worms indigestion."

Had Zendac intentionally sent Linda into harm's range? As an armchair Titan biologist since Coriolis U. days, her familiarity with Titan biology may have bred contempt. "Any friction between Linda and Zendac?"

"Indeed. Ever since she came from the inner solar system, Mrs. Parker . . ." That answered one question. ". . . has submitted cautionary environmental and safety reports to CLR contract management. Zendac's position is you can't eliminate all risk. Then he asked her to look for Naiad, a robot sub sent into Kraken Mare in 2041. It's an artifact of interest."

I felt a chill. Linda left me, but I still had feelings. "A worm got it?"

"Not impossible."

And not impossible that this Zendac would look to put Linda in range of one. I would have to interview him in person, try to rescue Linda, and learn what I could about the other disappearances.

Gwen's interplanetary beamrider and my system shuttle arrived in Titan orbit a week later within hours of each other. We took the next surface shuttle down, checked into quarters at Huygens City, and headed to Submarine Operations.

Once in Zendac's office, Gwen had his full attention. Zendac was a large florid man with an unruly mane of blonde hair, and Gwen had him at a disadvantage, as there were no actual laws against being naked in Huygens City. Gwen had a system-wide reputation for that, but reputation couldn't compete with seeing her in person.

I felt completely ignored, which was good for observing Zendac's demeanor. His vital signs came to me via Watson from a Coptech low frequency monitor, the size and appearance of a flea, now on the man's collar.

Finally, I cleared my throat.

"Director O'Reilly?" Zendac said, tearing his attention from Gwen.

"We need a submarine. Ms. Parker called for help."

He nodded. "Thank you for relaying that." [High stress readings: feeling everything but thankful.] "But bad timing I'm afraid. We don't have any subs available." [Calm.] "Maybe tomorrow. They aren't in any real danger." [High stress.] "They have eight more days of supplies on her sub and ten days of battery power, if careful." [Calm.] "Not that the worm realizes that, nor realizes anything." [Calm.] "The worm can't digest the sub; the sub is too hot. *Also,* worms are not endangered or anything like it in the Kraken Sea, nut cases to the contrary." [Some tension.] "They may even be useful. Exploration is never risk free. There are unavoidable consequences in dealing with the little known." [A slight mental smirk.]

"Maybe less avoidable sometimes than the others?" I asked.

[Stress and anger.] He scowled and shifted subjects.

"Director, your assistant's state of dress makes me uncomfortable. If something isn't done, I may file a complaint. Anyway, it isn't safe with 90 Kelvin only inches away." [Mixture of anger and tension.]

Gwen shot him an amused look. "Oh, really?"

"Really," Zendac said icily.

A terrestrial arctic parka wouldn't be much help in Titan's 90 K atmosphere. "Such matters . . ." I said, mildly, but with some authority as the law beyond Enceladus, ". . . are rarely adjudicated these days. The submarine?"

He glared at me. "A moment." His fingers tapped on the desk while presumably making subvocal inquiries about subs.

Gwen sighed and pulled a long white shift out of her handbag and shrugged into it. *That's okay, Hart,* she sent on our private bioradio net, *I was pushing it. But we got what we needed, not that it's much help. He's tense, wary, and feels guilty about something. Not sure it's murder.*

Zendac raised his head, nodded to Gwen, and turned to me. "I've arranged for Tomas Copes to take an early break tomorrow from cryomedusa collection. He'll take you out in *Icewolf* and get you up to speed."

Back in our room, Gwen found the manual isolation switch, threw her shift on a chair, and plugged a micro into the wall display. Its dimly lit Kraken seashore vista vanished, replaced by a collage of graphs and equations.

I knew better than to bother her. Instead, I went to the food dispenser and ordered some wraps. When they arrived, I tapped Gwen on the shoulder. She stretched out a hand and I put one in it. After a minute or so, she whispered her thanks.

I dumped my clothes in the fresher, went to the head, and then to the bed, barely denting the covers in a seventh of gee.

Gwen shook me. "Time to get ready."

If I'd dreamed, I didn't remember it. I touched the net for time. "Still an hour."

"We have other business. I haven't been with you in almost two years."

We didn't own each other; Gwen was unownable and made a point of it. But we'd been best friends and colleagues for almost thirty years.

After, we dressed for business: diapers, smart fabric body stockings that went on loose then molded themselves to our skins, protective trousers and shirts, and full body insulation suits with integral batteries, positive pressure gas supplies, and redundant everything. At 1.5 bars, and incredibly toxic, Titan's atmosphere could rob heat faster than an Antarctic gale. The vacuum of space is benign by comparison.

But we'd never need any of this, I thought. *Icewolf* carried a suite of Titan-optimized exploration robots that looked like big lobsters. We'd direct everything from a nice warm command deck. Maybe.

"What do you have?" I asked in my detective voice.

"Zendac could be sending subs into harm's way, but that's inefficient. Subs aren't their natural prey—too big. It's almost as if the worms were in on the scheme."

"Great. Who are the 'nut cases' Zendac mentioned?"

"People opposed to feeding the worms, using them to mine, messing with nature. Zendac drops food and gizzard stones for the worms with robot subs. When fed, they get bigger and longer, and may grow down to the warm water magma below the Kraken Sea. That's a planetary protection issue, one that Ms. Parker has been highlighting. Zendac sees a bright future exploiting worm burrows for cheap warm, mineral-laden water—an effective monopoly for him."

"Warm?" I asked.

"By Titan standards: 250 K. Impurities depress the freezing point."

"Anything else?"

"Some unknown third party could be involved, but chances of it being that are down in the single digits."

"Low enough to bet your life on?"

"Not low enough," a smile in her voice.

"What about this submariner, Tomas Copes?"

"He's a new hire, a second-generation Martian—family from Senegal. Grew up speaking Wolof and French. Shackleton U. grad. Researched at Chao Meng Fu. Seems an ordinary commercial astrobiologist with a cryo specialty."

"Mars. New Reformation?" Thomas Solacus's cult, currently in control of the Martian planetary government, had its own expansionist agenda. Gwen was a recovering New Reformation type, and always would be; much of her eccentricity was a conscious reaction to what she'd been raised with.

"Don't think so." His family was Sufi, and conformed to Newref while on Mars, but he's listed as Unitarian."

Most of Senegal that wasn't Islamic was Catholic. The terrestrial diaspora to space drew greatly on religious minorities and a lot of scientists were even agnostic or atheist; not a good match for Senegal, nor Mars these days.

The door buzzed; Tomas Copes, of course.

The tall, energetic young man had only a moderate French accent, a slight lilt of inflection, and a somewhat poetic word order left as a clue to his origins. His sub, in the water-lock under Huygens City, looked like a flattened sausage with four small, ducted fan ports on its top side and a large fan at its tail.

"The hull, she is all flexidiamond, transparent fore of the fan shafts, as you see, and black to the rear. That opacity can modulate herself for the thermal regulation. No levers, switches, touch screens; she is all voice control. The voice of me, or you, if you ask her nicely." He grinned.

Or Zendac, remotely, I bet. Anyway, no mutinies. Even if needed.

"Where's the head?" Gwen asked.

"She is in the air lock, in the back."

Easy to purge., I thought.

"Now, in the atmosphere of Titan, so dense and cold, the fans work as well as in the sea. Thus, we fly to there, then voyage under the sea."

That would save time. But it also avoided Blimp operations, whose proprietor had CLR roots. Zendac was keeping control.

Tomas finished his tour in the early evening and led us to the passenger compartment. Four seats lined each side of the *Icewolf,* and each pair could convert into an over/under bunk arrangement with a privacy curtain.

I took the first watch, letting Gwen and Tomas sleep. Watches are a silly convention; *Icewolf* could handle itself best without me. I nodded off to the sight of towering cumulous clouds beneath a high, orange-tinted dome above a flat, seemingly jet-black sea with curiously indistinct shores.

Four hours later, I woke when we plunged into the Kraken Mare. Through the clear liquid and transparent hull, I could see that, outside, another submarine was passing by a worm mouth, which extended upwards toward it, almost looking as though it was begging. The sub dropped a bunch of shaggy stuff, and then some ice boulders. Were ice boulders good for the worms? I wondered.

Tomas took the watch. We descended. Sunlight, already dim on the surface, grew sparser, but the sea was clear enough to allow us to see with our lights. A Titan "jellyfish" swept by my window; it was a cryomedusa—I knew it was a single cell with multiple nuclei arms dangling beneath a bubble of nitrogen. But it still looked amazingly like an Earth jelly.

Minutes later, we floated fifty meters over a big flower of a worm mouth on the bottom silt amid a scatter of ice boulders. Somewhere, down in there, were the *Penguin King*, Linda, and two shipmates. I grabbed a couple lunch bars and gave one to Gwen.

"Mmm. Not sure I'd eat without you feeding me."

I chuckled and bit into my bar. "We need to keep our energy up. We're going fishing for a submarine! The robotic cable head should be able to wrap itself around the canard elevator fins at the nose of the *Penguin King* to pull it up."

"Perhaps," Tomas said. "That cable, she is strong, graphene wrapped. She would hold even at Jupiter gravity. But may be a bit stiff at 100 K." He looked at me. "You are planning to help her in person?"

I was dressing for Extra Sub Activity. "Just in case we need ESA. How can anything live here?" I asked. "I mean, I know about the evolved antifreeze proteins, but how could it get started?"

Tomas shrugged. "Many of theories. I'm only a driver of subs, son of poor Martian farmers, but water volcano vents make the sea nutrient rich, yes? So perhaps they came from below through cracks over many generations, evolving as they went?"

"They're cannibals, you know," Gwen added aloud.

"Oh?" I tried imagining a sessile worm whose bottom was more than a kilometer below its top, eating another.

"Those fish in the lake? They're its larva."

"Perhaps," Tomas said. "They grow from buds in the worm, ingest worm eggs, swim out to the sea, eat muck, grow fat, and shit the worm eggs. Then they offer themselves to a worm mouth, so get ingested and are absorbed, except of the buds that start the cycle again."

"It's crazy," Gwen added, "but by some definitions, all the multi-cellular critters in the Kraken Sea are one species. The same genetic information, different development. But the filter feeding snowflakes and sea snakes, while they can be large, are actually single cells."

"How does our worm know we're not offering ourselves?" I asked.

Tomas shrugged. "He knows nothing. For caution, we are stationed high above his mouth."

"Do you know anything about the missing subs?"

"They were lost before I got here but chartered by prospectors."

Probably not endearing themselves to either Linda or Zendac, I thought.

Gwen sent, *He's nervous about everything, or the system's out of calibration.* I only had two of the bugs; the other one was on Zendac.

Icewolf played out the cable. On its end was a small robot weight with legs for crawling around. The hollow cable could deliver a variety of fluids, as well as being a conductor and antenna. Less than five milli-meters thick, it was a wonder of graphene technology.

A hundred meters down, the cable got close enough for radio contact with the *Penguin King*.

"Hart," Linda said after greetings and explanations, "thank you again so much for coming! I like your plan, but as you'll see when the camera gets in range, we have a bit of a problem. We're sideways. You can't use the heads in a vertical attitude."

"The worm flesh isn't super strong," I said. "You should be able to tear through it easily. Try moving the weight in the sub to the rear. The bow should pull loose and expose the stabilizing forewings to the cable."

"Hart, you're not going to like this." Those were by chance the same words she'd said when we broke up. I suffered the memory in silence.

"Wounded parts of the worm wall release antifreeze through their cell walls. It's a defense mechanism."

"Oh . . . of course," Gwen exclaimed.

"Huh?"

"Hart, wounded worm flesh freezes solid," Linda said. "We're locked in concrete."

I looked up at *Icewolf*, in a vertical attitude. Diapers . . . I thought furiously. "Tomas, could we print some of this antifreeze?"

"We have a bioprinter, but she's small, and we need gallons, yes? Not milligrams."

As if on cue, we heard a resonant groan like a big wet balloon being rubbed with a concrete block. "Maybe the robots could hack it out?" I asked.

"Ice is like rock down there," Tomas said.

"Look, we cryo-filter methane out of the buoyancy tanks and make a stream of hot gas. Maybe that melts frozen cells and carries them away. Plan B is to open the *Penguin King* and winch everyone up."

"Perhaps," Tomas said.

"We only have two working ESA suits left for a crew of three," Linda said. "I damaged one trying to get us out. I'll take my chances with it. Or just stay."

"I can send my suit down for her," Gwen offered.

"Or take mine down with you," Tomas said. "The fort, I can hold him alone."

I'm from a family of Irish cops going back to the old sod, and alarm bells rang in my head. The more someone wants to do you a favor, the more favors they'll be wanting. "Let's give the robots a try at cutting the sub out first," I said.

They tried. When Tomas pumped hot methane down the cable, it tried to twist and straighten, and the football-sized robots couldn't handle it.

So I went ESA, in full protective gear, out the rear lock and down to the *Penguin King*. I had slight negative buoyancy in liquid methane but pulled myself down the cable to descend faster.

With the *Icewolf* robots, I manhandled the cable head into the right position and cut away the frozen white worm flesh, which melted away into translucent gobs and apparently denser than methane, they drifted down below. After three hours, I wasn't cold; I was sweating. But the nose of the *Penguin King* came free. We depressurized the cable, and it wrapped itself around the sub's nose.

With pull from *Icewolf* and buoyancy the *Penguin King*'s nose rotated upward. But the fouled and bent stern fan broke off. Just so much dead weight, I thought. Like me; I was exhausted.

"Haul away!" I rode the *Penguin King*'s nose like a bucking bronco.

Too much bucking, in fact. Waves of worm flesh rippled up the worm hole toward *Icewolf*.

"We are being enveloped," *Icewolf* said with artificial calmness.

"Tomas," I yelled. "Up!" Far above, I saw the diaphanous mouth rise and start to close over the brightly lit sub. But *Icewolf* ascended, the cable snapped taut, and *Penguin King* surged upward.

For a moment.

But waves of worm flesh crested *ahead* of *Icewolf,* closed the throat, and began to wash the trapped submarines down. Worm walls slid back by in the wrong direction. The nose scar in the worm wall floated upward, then the wrecked prop of the *Penguin King.*

"Tomas! Cut the prop!" I said, as I saw *Icewolf* above turn sideways in the worm's throat. "Reel in. Flood ballast."

"Oui, oui, I . . . okay . . ."

Hart, sent Gwen. *He's scared. That came through.*

Things finally came to a halt with the tethered submarines about thirty meters apart, noses up, floating in the worm's throat.

In a moment of quiet, I heard, or thought I heard, very faintly ". . . stop . . . I'm still aboard . . . out before drop . . ." from my Coptech flea on Zendac, all the way from Huygens via Gwen's unit.

Watson, did you get that clearly? If that came in, maybe I could get a message out.

No, but the bug's overhearing a transmission coming from someone else. Probably Tomas.

Of course. Tomas was Zendac's man.

Another ice boulder fell and wedged itself between the *Icewolf*'s hull and the worm wall. *Icewolf* wiggled, letting the boulder fall toward the *Penguin King* and gong reverberatingly next to my legs.

"What's with all the gizzard stones?" I gasped.

"It's trying to digest us," Linda said, "with help, I think."

"*Icewolf's surface comm unit is still connected,*" Gwen sent. "*Time to call the cavalry?*"

Who do you call when you *are* the cavalry? Kate on Hyperion was days away, as was Saturn High Station's security, and they were employees of an ISA working against the CLR. Okay, you're the head of Saturn System security; deputize someone. Someone responsible.

"*Yeah. Gwen, can you get ahold of Helen at Blimp Ops, deputize her, and arrange a rescue? And what were Zendac and Tomas talking about?*"

"*Didn't hear it clearly. I'll call Helen.*"

This all might be my fault for not thinking Linda's problem was as serious as it was, and not investigating thoroughly before jumping into action. Getting too old for this game.

But this wasn't an accident. I might be seeing a nail for my hammer, but I'm a detective. So, detect. Someone must be controlling this worm.

Who? And how? Maybe if I do what I'm good at, we might get out of this.

Gwen, can you get to Kate and have her ask Mark Wu at Coriolis to do some deep profiles? Tomas works for Zendac, but just as an employee? And only for Zendac? If something squirrelly is going on, Wu may need intel resources, so brief Diana Duluth. She'll see it gets acted on. I hated politics, and this would be *remote* politics; something like three hours before the Moon responded. But Saturn System was CLA territory, damn it!

"Tomas," I said, "this worm is acting as if it were an intelligent adversary, and it's not. But maybe it can be controlled, somehow?"

"Eh, Perhaps I will study this."

I didn't need Coptech on that. Tomas knew damn well it could be controlled. Some kind of implant? "Tomas?"

"Yes. Director?"

"Any way to rotate a head ninety degrees on one of these subs? Gwen can help; you'd be surprised what she can do with computers."

"But yes! We do work of this problem. Certainly!"

I smiled. He didn't want to crap in his pants, either, anyway.

Hart, Gwen.

Go.

Helen Kannellakos is on board. She's got a blimp on the way; whatever happens to the subs, blimps can hold a dozen passengers. Also, she thinks a robot sub got hacked; one of her pilots saw one feeding ice boulders to a worm off schedule. Watson and I are doing a deep dive.

Hacked robot subs? They might be doing just what their owners told them to.

The low-pitched rubbed balloon sound returned, as if on cue.

The *Penguin King* crew got its head rotated. I cycled into the lock. The repositioned head impeded the hatch door so, as I squirmed by, I squeezed a tiny warm trickle out of myself. The diaper came in handy, but after nearly two days, I needed to sit.

Ten minutes later it was time to face Linda. I opened the air lock's inner door. The place stank. Almost a week for them now, only a few days of supplies left.

I backed in, turned around, and almost didn't recognize her. She'd been as tall as I was, a muscular blonde with long straight hair down to her waistline. She was thinner now, slightly bent with gray hair in short curls and a turkey neck. But the piercing gray eyes and prominent chin were the same.

"Hart?"

"Yeah, it's me plus about thirty pounds."

The sub's crew were not in evidence in the gear room. I assumed they were up front in the control room.

"I've made a problem of myself, here. Didn't think it would come to this."

I shrugged. "It's a wild frontier."

"Yeah, and some people think they can make a kind of gold rush happen by using the worms. I've been gathering evidence."

"Zendac?"

She nodded.

"The worm—still a hollow tube?" I asked. "All the way down?"

"Far as we know, but much thinner. Think cilia, or fiber optics, or a rudimentary spine. What passes for its nervous system is pneumatic and chemical. Sound waves, pressure reservoirs, and valves triggered by tiny tubercles and hairs."

"Couldn't do much thinking with that," I said.

"No, it's about as smart as your average bear trap."

The worm gave a sickening lurch.

"It hears us," Linda said, showing some of her old sense of humor.

Hart, Gwen sent. *The Moon wants you on the audio, direct.*

"I've got to go back upstairs," I told Linda. "Maybe get your folks suited up. I'll bring a spare back for you."

Out the lock and halfway up, climbing the cable rather than trying to swim, I saw an ice boulder hit *Icewolf* and wedge itself between the sub and the wormwall near the hatch. Another pair pinned the minisub hatch. The prop looked like it had been hit.

"Gwen, Hart," I radioed. "You, okay?"

"Still airtight, but we had to abandon the head op." [. . . work on the head rotation operation.]

"On my way."

When I got through in the *Icewolf*'s lock, I saw why their head hadn't been rotated. They were lucky the doors still worked. Amazingly, the graphene laminate interior bulkhead was, while bent and twisted, still intact. But it seemed clear we couldn't take much more pressure from the ice boulders.

"The prop still turns," Tomas said when I reached him on the bridge. "Should I try her?" He sounded worried.

Was he leading me? I wondered. But he was on the sub too. I nodded. "Ahead one quarter."

A screechy racket filled the sub. *Boom!* Suddenly, the hull popped out, curved again.

"Stop!" Tomas said, checking his instruments, then, wonderingly, "She frees herself!"

Good, I thought. Then I realized it had freed the boulder as well! I called Linda. "Look out below. Icefall!"

After a tense minute, Linda answered. "We got hit, hard, by three ice boulders. We've got a small hull leak somewhere. I'm cranking up the pressure, but the sub doesn't like it."

"Send the crew up. I'll take a suit down to you. About twenty minutes?"

"Make it fifteen," Linda said. "Pumps, a week of cranking a twisted prop, comm on high power, lock cycling . . . *Penguin King* is low on power."

"Got it. See you soon."

I turned to Gwen, who grabbed me in a tight embrace and used the occasion to whisper. "Tomas Copes's name was originally Thomas Coprates. He's an agent of the Hand of Mars. But Wu thinks he could work for the ISA too."

And be a liability for Zendac, if the Mars connection were known. Tomas, being new, couldn't have been responsible for any of the lost subs. But he was young and maybe in over his head trying to please too many masters? "If you have to, lay it all out for Tomas," I whispered to Gwen. "Your call."

"Good to see you too," she said aloud with a smile and holding on a bit. Neither of us, I thought, were totally play-acting.

"I'll need your ESA suit." I asked Gwen for Tomas's ears.

By the time she was back with it in a clip-on bag, the *Penguin King*'s crew arrived. I cycled out and briefed them helmet-to-helmet before they entered, then descended the cable.

"Does this sub have a stethoscope in its medical supplies?" I asked Linda in the *Penguin King* as she suited up.

"Hart, you are so twenty-first century."

"You've got a tricorder?"

"That's twenty-third." She went to a side panel marked with a red cross and pulled out a card-deck-sized box. "Pulse, oxygen, neuro activity, and, yes, heart acoustic signature on the local net at, uh, 'vitals.'"

"Aluminized graphene foil?"

"Huh?"

"Don't want someone else listening in," I said.

Linda raised her eyebrows and gave me another tiny packet. "Believe it or not, you could wrap the sub with this—blocks everything longer than I.R."

We packed and exited the *Penguin King*'s lock the final time.

Back on voice com, I called Tomas. "I'll need all-back for a few seconds. Give me enough slack to unwrap the line." The *Penguin King* wouldn't move much, if at all. The last ice boulder fall had made sure of that. And I'd already freed the cable. But Zendac didn't need to know that, so Tomas wouldn't.

"If you pressurize the line again," I added, "it will tend to unwrap itself."

There was a moment of silence. If Tomas was going to try anything dicey about now, he was outnumbered three to one.

"Got it," Tomas said. "She backs on the count of three. One, two, three."

The screech of the *Icewolf*'s bent props filled the worm tube like an organ pipe. The line relaxed, then twisted and got too stiff.

"Methane pressure, she is two bars, over."

"Go one point seven," I said.

Linda and I worked our way up the inside of the worm wall, the medical device sensing for . . . something.

A maximum on cardio potential! Not a heart, of course, but something pulsing low radio frequency. I motioned Linda back down the tube a bit, then started to circle around the circumference of the worm wall.

"Here!" I shouted to Linda. A device was easily visible in the translucent worm flesh. The hot methane jet cut it out; I wrapped it in foil and pocketed it.

Absent its puppet string, the worm tube walls relaxed. Of course, Zendac would know the next time he tried to command it.

Above, the sub started to ascend.

"You can cut the props," I said, hoping my voice would not reveal my doubts about Tomas. "Reel us in. Quickly."

The line stopped reeling in about ten meters short.

Linda and I covered the rest of the distance hand over hand. Above, the mouth of the worm stayed closed as we arrived at the *Icewolf*'s air lock. But that was expected.

What wasn't was that the lock did not open on my command. I shivered and pounded the hull. "Tomas, Gwen, open the lock."

Nothing. *Gwen, can you hear me?*

The subs could be remotely controlled, of course. Including its bioradio servers.

"Hart, Linda, this is Helen in the *Maconette*, above you. They aren't answering. But I think I can get the worm to open up for you. Swim up to the surface as fast as you can. Go now. We'll get the others later."

Exhausted, I tried to clear my head. Leave Gwen and the two *Penguin King* crewmembers? No way. No choice.

The line. "Linda, if I can unlock the reel from outside, we can take the end up to the blimp. Wait here."

I swam down to the reel port near the stern fan and found the manual release. Wouldn't budge.

I pulled the line up and hit the release tab with the robot grapple end. Nothing.

I hit it again. Again. Dizzy and panting, I gave it one last try.

Click. The reel was free. I clipped the line to my suit and tried to swim up.

In vain; my muscles wouldn't move, and I started shaking with cold. I was at least an hour over my ESA suit's limit.

Linda swam down to get me. She took my hand and pulled me up. We approached the feathery worm dome from inside. Magically, it opened and the worm extended.

A robot sub about the size of a worm larva glided in as the worm mouth rose. Linda pulled us sideways as the worm's mandibles closed over the robot. The robot ignored the closing mouth as it spewed out something cloudy.

A glowing, bright orange rescue line dropped down beside us, with loops for our hands.

"Come on up," Helen Kannellakos greeted us.

We grabbed on and up we went.

When we broke the surface, the blimp hovered just over us. Helen, a stocky helmeted figure, stood in its open airlock hatch. Linda clambered on and plugged in. Then she and Helen reached over to get me. I sat on the door edge with my legs dangling, exhausted.

"Now watch this." Helen said as the three of us stared down.

As if responding to a conjurer, the surface started to roil and bubble. After a couple minutes, up popped *Icewolf*!

"Just a little indigestion," Helen said.

"How much lift do you have?" I croaked to Helen, handing her the line's robot grapple.

"Tons and tons." She hitched the grapple to the *Maconette*'s lift hook, raised the blimp to about 40 meters, and then added lift with impellers.

Slowly and smoothly, the *Icewolf*'s stern came out of the Kraken Sea, its bent prop spinning uselessly, screaming in protest.

Then it stopped.

Tomas flipped! Gwen sent, *and we cut Zendac's link.*

I felt a weight lifted.

During the two-hour multi-blimp operation to retrieve *Icewolf* and her passengers, Linda managed to slip away. Again. No closure, no resolution. That evening, I composed a message, trying to clear the air. The message got too maudlin, so I saved it. Maybe later.

Back on Hyperion, the Sun shone down from beyond the rim of the institute dome. The shadows it cast made leisurely four-minute circles around the balconies to the entertainment of us three hot-tubbers on Gwen Chryse's balcony. People waved to us from above, barely visible in the distance, with their glasses held high. Gwen raised her own to them.

"So, investigation done?" Kate asked.

I nodded. "Because of the deaths involved, we could have used a mind scan on Tomas, but it wasn't needed; he chose not to be an accessory to someone trying to kill him because he knew too much. Zendac is out and Helen Kannellakos is taking over sub ops."

"Who's responsible for the lost subs? Zendac and the ISA? The Planetary Protection Society? Mars?"

I shrugged. "When the subs were in range, Zendac triggered engulfment, then dropped gizzard stones on his competitors."

Gwen touched my arm. "Linda facilitated PPS action and they dropped ice boulders on the same subs, which was too much."

She was ready to go down with the *Penguin King*. Out of guilt?

"Will she get arrested?" Gwen asked

I shook my head. Not by me, anyway. She'd been on the first liner back to Luna.

Gwen wiped some moisture from my cheek and squeezed my hand.

"I think Helen will take Tomas in," I said. "At least he did right in the end."

FLYING INSTEAD OF DIVING

FABIAN KLENNER

Saturn's moon Titan is the only object beyond Earth known to have liquids in the form of seasonal rainfall, rivers, and lakes on its surface, such as Kraken Mare, one of the locales of G. David Nordley's "Titan of Chaos." This moon also has a dense nitrogen-rich atmosphere. These similarities to our beloved home planet Earth have led many scientists and science fiction authors to consider the possibilities of life there.

Kraken Mare, the largest liquid body on Titan's surface, is named after the kraken, a legendary squid-like sea monster that pulls ships down into Earth's deep seas. So, how about having jellyfish and gigantic worms in hydrocarbon lakes on one of Saturn's iceballs pulling down subs? To reach Titan's icy surface with a human-made object that survives long enough to dive into hydrocarbon lakes and explore any possible life within seems technically difficult enough. And now imagine hungry sub-eating worms in these lakes. A delicate endeavor.

Instead of using a sub to dive into Titan's surface lakes and running the risk of getting eaten by hungry worms, we could first try and take advantage of Titan's thick atmosphere. The iceball's atmosphere is four times as dense as Earth's. Tagteamed with the moon's low gravity (~13.8% of Earth's) and only little wind, this makes Titan an ideal place for airplanes to fly. Or even better, why not send a drone to Titan? A drone could perform controlled flights with vertical takeoffs and landings between various exploration sites, thereby looking for signs of life from the air as well as on-ground. Doesn't sound bad, does it?

Two curious and ambitious scientists, Ralph Lorenz and Jason Barnes, got such an idea in a dinner conversation some time ago. They talked about an initial concept that subsequently developed into a detailed space mission proposal in only 15 months. On June 27, 2019, the National Aeronautics and Space Administration (NASA)

announced it will send a spacecraft to Titan—indeed a drone—based on this concept. The *Dragonfly* mission is scheduled for launch in 2027, with a landing in the Shangri-La dune fields on Titan expected in 2034.

The drone, equipped with a suite of scientific instruments, will fly toward the Selk impact crater and perform several short-duration flights while doing in-flight analyses as well as analyses on-ground [1]. *Dragonfly* will be the first aircraft sent to a moon, though it will not be the first human-made object touching down on Titan's surface. The *Huygens* probe, as part of the past *Cassini-Huygens* mission, landed on Titan in January 2005. *Huygens* was an effort of the European Space Agency (ESA) and the first human-made object to ever land in the outer solar system. It landed in the western end of Shangri-La. Space agencies apparently like that place, and for good reason. Shangri-La, named after a mythical paradise in Tibet, is thought to be a gigantic dark sand sea, probably made of organic material.

The availability of organic material is one requirement for life "as we know it" to develop and sustain. Other major requirements are liquid water and an energy source. All three are thought to exist on Titan. The moon's atmosphere appears to be a chemical power station. There, reactions of hydrogen with acetylene, UV (ultraviolet) radiation, and maybe even lightning are potential energy sources. In addition to hydrocarbon lakes on the surface, Titan harbors a subsurface liquid water ocean, and NASA's *Dragonfly* will be capable of looking for signs of life "as we know it" as well as those of life "as we don't know it."

Life as we know it means organic chemistry-based (carbon-based) life that uses water as a solvent. Life as we don't know it means . . . Oh, we don't really know. This weird life would probably use hydrocarbons within Titan's lakes as a solvent instead of water. One group of building blocks for life as we know it are lipid membranes. Lipid molecules interact with liquid water by forming a barrier to protect inner parts of the living cells from floating away. The thing is: Titan's surface lakes do not have liquid water, and if you dropped any Earth-like cell into Titan's hydrocarbon lakes, it would not be happy about that. G. David Nordley's Extra Sub Activity suits would come in handy.

In 2015, James Stevenson, with colleagues, calculated there is a chemical molecule that would let one molecule attract another to form an azotosome, a nitrogen-based membrane-like structure, under Titan-like conditions [2]. This molecule is acrylonitrile. Acrylonitrile would remain unified but flexible enough to allow movement. So far, so good. Two years later, the first direct evidence for acrylonitrile was found on

Titan, in quantities sufficient to form millions of azotosomes per cubic centimeter that could support the formation of a biosphere [3].

Admittedly, there are some caveats. For instance, azotosomes would need to form and hang together in the first place on Titan in the same way lipid membranes do on Earth, and this is far from obvious. Sandström and Rahm, two Swedish scientists, performed sophisticated quantum mechanics calculations and found that the azotosome structure would indeed tolerate extreme Titan-like conditions, but not self-assemble; that acrylonitrile would instead crystallize into its molecular ice [4]. Seems like computers say no to azotosome-based life on Titan. However, sometimes reality outpaces computer simulations: Whether acrylonitrile would form stable azotosomes on Titan is still an ongoing debate.

Another possibility for life to evolve on this moon would be to somehow mix subsurface water with hydrocarbons on the surface. Bringing together these two ingredients might do the trick. This could potentially be done by cryovolcanism, a phenomenon already observed on Enceladus, another icy moon of Saturn. There, similar to volcanism on Earth, liquids as well as gaseous material erupt from the subsurface. Cryovolcanic features on Titan are subject of some controversy, and particularly the Sotra Patera (formerly known as Sotra Facula) region is discussed to have a putative cryovolcanic origin [5]. Another possibility would be meteorite impacts disrupting Titan's icy surface, thereby connecting the surface and the subsurface. Such an event would also deliver heat and could form a warm pond of water and organic chemistry in the impact crater. Providing that such a water-based surface lake would remain liquid for a time long enough for organic chemistry to turn into biology before freezing, this seems like the perfect cradle for life. Nonetheless, if and how life could originate on Titan remains a purely theoretical discussion for now. We will need to wait for Dragonfly.

REFERENCES

[1] Barnes, JW, et al. (2021). "Science Goals and Objectives for the Dragonfly Titan Rotorcraft Relocatable Lander." *The Planetary Science Journal* 2(4), 130 (18pp).

[2] Stevenson, J, et al. (2015). "Membrane alternatives in worlds without oxygen: Creation of an azotosome." *Science Advances* 1(1), e1400067.

[3] Palmer, MY, et al. (2017). "ALMA detection and astrobiological potential of vinyl cyanide on Titan." *Science Advances* 3(7), e1700022.

[4] Sandström, H, and Rahm, M (2020). "Can polarity-inverted membranes self-assemble on Titan?" *Science Advances* 6(4), eaax0272.

[5] https://doi.org/10.1002/jgre.20062

CLOUDSKIMMER   Geoffrey A. Landis

I asked Sanjay again—for what I think must have been the fifth time—why he wanted to go down there. Not that I really thought the answer would be any more informative.

He turned away from the viewport, where he had been looking down on Venus. "Same reason Mallory climbed Everest," he said. "Because I can."

"That's not what he said," I told him. "What Mallory said was, 'Because it is there.'"

"That too," Sanjay said.

"And Mallory died trying to climb Everest. You do know that, right?"

"Because he didn't have you backing him up, Zara."

"Hmmph," I said.

I turned to stare with him out the viewport. Venus is the most boring place in the solar system from above: looking down from orbit, you see nothing but featureless white. I love looking down at Earth from orbit; the Earth is colorful and always changing, deserts and forests and a thousand shades of blue in the oceans, hidden and revealed by ever-changing clouds. Venus was a planet of never-changing clouds.

Nevertheless, I gazed down at it, out of habit. Ever since I was a girl, I got my best ideas by looking off in the distance and letting my mind wander, and I guess I was hoping that staring at Venus would give me an idea about how to talk Sanjay out of his crazy plan.

Why would he want to go down there?

He wasn't proposing to go down to the surface—even Sanjay Arya, crazy as he sometimes was, wasn't *that* crazy. He was just saying he'd drop into the atmosphere. We'd flown twenty robotic airplanes in the upper atmosphere, solar-powered vehicles skimming above the tops of Venus's thick middle cloud layer, the sweet spot where the temperature was in the Earth-like region, so I knew it was possible. But why would he want to go there himself? It wasn't like there was anything to see. Our first drone flights had carried small cameras. This was

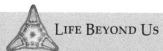

mostly because we hoped for PR value, not for any science value, but as PR went, it was bitterly disappointing. There was simply nothing to see: blinding white below, off-white fading to bluish white above. We removed the cameras after the first two, saving the instrument mass for real science.

There was nothing to see, and nothing to do. The robots did all the science. We didn't even need to fly the drones; the autopilots did the flying with no need for us to take the controls remotely. We were here in orbit only to drive the surface robots that had collected rocks for the sample return.

The surface robots were the only pieces of equipment that didn't have electronic smarts. The ferocious surface temperature was so high that only the simplest electronics could function. So, no computers on the surface. These robots were as simple as remote-controlled toy cars. But the airplanes above the clouds, where it was cool, they were packed with sensors and instrumentation and redundant computers. They didn't need humans to pilot them.

The slow rotation of the orbital station moved Venus out of our field of view, and I was gazing at darkness. I turned back to look at Sanjay. He had an infuriating tiny grin on his face, infuriating because of course he knew that I would give in, and he knew that I knew. Because he can—yeah, right. But at least I could put up a fight.

"What are we going to tell our backers?" I asked. "They're paying us for science, not for stunts."

"Tell them," he said, "that in the history of science, it has been the humans who have made the difference. Humans see different things than drones do. Humans have intuition. The tiniest thing, what a drone might dismiss as irrelevant, a human will notice and say, *wait, that's not right, that needs to be investigated.* That's how science progresses."

"A load of bullshit," I said.

He shrugged. "Just tell it to them, Zara. Just that. They'll love it, I guarantee."

They probably would. The institute was privately funded by donations from about a million science fans around the world, and this was exactly what they wanted to hear.

"Excelsior," I said.

"And I believe it," he said. "Humans beat robots. And you know what? I will just bet you I will find something to make it worthwhile."

"Bullshit," I said again.

"Wanna bet?" He raised an eyebrow.

"What stakes?"

"Dinner at a restaurant of the loser's choice when we get back to Earth."

I blinked. "That could be expensive."

"*Loser's* choice," he said. "Only expensive if you choose it to be."

"No, if *you* choose it to be," I said. "I'm not the one who's going to lose."

He smiled again—that same infuriating grin—and I realized that I'd just accepted the bet. And agreed to help.

Once, a billion years or so in the past, Venus had been a planet with an ocean and atmosphere. But the Sun had brightened and the oceans had boiled, and only the atmosphere was left now, thick and acidic, the surface turned to a sulfurous hell.

Early in the space age, some scientists had suggested that when the solar system was young, Venus had been a habitable environment, and might have evolved life. Some even speculated that when the oceans evaporated, life, in the form of acidophilic microbes, could even have moved up into the high atmosphere, where sunlight was abundant and the temperatures reasonable for liquid water. A few had even thought that they had detected chemical disequilibria that could be signs of existing microbes. But the atmospheric drones we'd deployed had looked for those speculated microbes living in the clouds and had found nothing. The atmosphere had proved to be as sterile as the surface.

But, life or no life, the planet was a geologist's paradise, with tectonic manifestations utterly different from the Earth's, yet in a planet of Earth-like mass and composition. That was our mission: to spend nearly a year in Venus's orbit operating rovers on the surface to collect samples that could perhaps tell us how and why Venus could be so similar to Earth and yet so completely different.

But, going down into the atmosphere ourselves? That was nowhere in the plan. That was way out of the scope of the mission.

I was wondering how long Sanjay had been planning this. Had he been thinking of this right from the beginning?

He'd already worked out the outlines of the plan, but there was a lot of work to be done in filling out the details, and as chief engineer on the two-person crew, that was up to me. The solar airplanes carried a science payload of up to 250 kilograms. A human in a spacesuit was no more than 150 kilograms, so there was plenty of margin to modify a drone to carry a person. I could do the mods to add a canopy; we even had the plans for that, since some of the early vehicle tests on Earth had been piloted.

Getting back into orbit . . . that would be the trick. Venus was too hot on the surface to be able to land a rocket, so the way our surface-sample missions worked was that the sampling robots picked up the samples we had chosen, put them in a cannister, and deployed a balloon. The balloon, filled with water vapor, lifted the cannister above the atmosphere, and a retrieval drone caught it at the end of a tether and reeled it up above the cloud level. The drone brought it to the rocket stage, which was itself hanging in the upper atmosphere below a truly enormous balloon. The rocket stage launched it from the upper atmosphere into Venus's orbit, where we retrieved it to the station. We'd already done that part, and had the samples safely stowed, ready to take back to Earth when the return window opened in another month. So we knew that the hardware worked.

We had put redundancy into the mission, of course. Of the five surface-sample rovers, two had failed in the furnace of Venus before they had launched their sample-carrying balloons. Three was more than enough—even one sample was enough for us to declare mission success to our backers on Earth. But, that meant we still had a spare set of return rockets floating in the atmosphere, waiting to return a sample that was not going to come.

So, we'd give it a sample to carry: a sample named Sanjay Arya.

The modifications to the drone took a week, and another week of verification and testing and testing and then testing some more. The drones were reliable, we'd proven that, but putting a person into the atmosphere of Venus? That was a whole level up. And, despite the fact that he could be infuriating sometimes, I really did like Sanjay.

No, not romantically. I know, a lot of people wondered about two of us, together in the cramped compartments of a Venus orbital station for a year-long mission, but we slept in separate compartments. There's a thing about professionalism.

I wondered a little about the bet we'd made, recognizing (possibly a little bit late) that it was in fact an agreement to go out to dinner. Well,

I'd deal with that when it happened. If it happened. If my hardware all worked as planned, and his silly stunt didn't get him killed.

The planning and fabrication were done. When I ran out of excuses for delaying the execution of the plan, we set the entry for the day that marked our three-hundredth Earth day in orbit around Venus. He bundled up in his spacesuit and I helped him into the cockpit of the solar airplane, which was already folded up, ready to be placed into the aeroshell that would carry it to Venus. I warned him, once again, to make sure to keep well above the cloud layer. The airplane and the spacesuit were both rated to be impervious to the sulfuric acid found in the clouds, but there was no sense in testing that. I warned him to keep all his maneuvers gentle. The airplane was built to be light, not strong, and in the turbulent Venus atmosphere, a heavy hand on the controls could result in a broken wing spar. I warned him that he had at most a day to make the rendezvous with the balloon carrying the return rocket before the winds blew him around to the dark side of the planet, and I warned him to keep a generous margin on the time to allow for problems.

"I know all that, Zara," Sanjay said. "We've been over it over and over again."

"I know, I know," I said. I made a conscious effort to avoid chewing the tips of my hair. That wasn't professional. I shouldn't be nervous. I'd checked everything. "But it's important."

"I know. But we've been over it." He looked up at me. "I promise you, I won't do anything stupid. This will go just like we planned it."

"No deviations," I said.

"No deviations," he agreed. "So, are you going to close the cockpit and button up this ship, or did you want to wait until the drop window closes, and we get to do this all over again next orbit?"

"See you when you get back," I said, and slid the cockpit shut.

Of course, nothing is fast in space, and it took an hour before the folded aircraft was properly installed in the entry shell, all the systems checked and triple-checked, and the whole assembly dropped into a trajectory that would, half an orbit later, skim the atmosphere.

And I had the station to myself.

The station was suddenly a lot larger, now that there weren't two of us on it, trying to keep out of each other's way. I savored the sense of personal space.

But, of course, I had work to do. I went to the command console and put on the headset. I was going to be with him all the way.

After the atmospheric entry, the drogue chute opened and pulled the plane away from the heat shield, and the tail and then wings unfolded. Sanjay cut the parachute free right on the mark, and the plane fell for a moment as the wings grabbed air. It made a long slow pull-out, skimming just above the thick cloud layer, pulling almost two gees, and I worried again about the stress on the wings. He should have let the computer do the pull out, but he'd talked me into letting him do the flying. But he kept a gentle hand on the stick, and his pull-out was well within the flight envelope. He toggled on the engine, and the twin propellers bit into the air and began a slow climb toward his cruise level, at about the sixty kilometers above the surface.

I let out the breath that I hadn't realized I'd been holding. "Looking good," I said. "Steady as you go."

From my point of view, I was right next to him in the cockpit. I'd found a high resolution camera to add to the panoply of instruments in the plane; it wasn't really as good as being there, but it would have to do, and as long as the communications relay was above the horizon, I was flying with him.

He glanced at the instruments and answered, "Everything nominal."

He hadn't needed to tell me that—I was receiving the telemetry feed—but it was good to hear his voice.

"How's the view?"

He looked around, and I slewed my camera to look around with him. "Pretty boring, I have to say," he said. "White below, blue above."

"As expected," I remarked. "Sorry you came?"

"No!" he said. "Not for a second." He looked down at his instrument panel. "That was one hell of a ride."

"I'll bet. That wasn't designed for humans." I paused and then added, "And, by the way, congratulations. You are now the first human to reach Venus."

"Or thirty miles above Venus, anyway," he said. "One odd thing, though. As I was coming in, there was a black speck on the cloud deck."

"What do you mean, a black speck?"

"I don't know what I mean." He looked at the instruments again. "Reaching cruising altitude. External temperature two point two C, pressure 330 millibars."

"Got it," I said. "Black speck was probably a glitch in your vision from the gees you pulled on entry. Advise you don't worry about it."

"I don't think so," he said, and then added, "But I'm not worried."

For the next hour or so, he circled leisurely at cruise altitude, enjoying the boring view, I guess. Up in orbit, I was frantically querying "black speck in vision" and "black spots on Venus." Black specks in vision, I discovered, was no big deal; it was probably nothing more than a floater that had been released by the gee load. Harmless. Black spots on Venus—nothing. Except . . . something was nagging at me. I went back and queued up the video from the first two drones, the ones that had cameras.

Yeah. There it was. In a few seconds of video from the very first of the atmospheric drones we'd equipped with a camera, there it was, a little black speck, somewhere above the cloud deck. Hard to tell how far away it was, or how big. We seem to have ignored it at the time—it sure looked like a camera artifact—but now that I looked at the video, it was present in sequential frames. Not a camera artifact, then.

UFO? Well, literally yes: it was unidentified and a flying—or maybe floating—object. Expanding the image didn't reveal more details; it was apparently too far away to resolve. I laughed quietly. That was so typical for UFO footage: small and fuzzy, so you had to guess what it might be. If I guessed it was, say, a kilometer away, the size must be about a meter. Too small to be a flying saucer. And the speed was compatible with an object drifting with the hurricane-strength winds.

How could something be there on just one single video, out of hundreds of hours of footage? Just luck we only caught it once? I put together a search query to scan the footage to look for similar instances, but the search turned up nothing.

I turned to the com to tell Sanjay to keep his eyes open, but the relay satellite had moved out of range, and it would be half an hour before his signal would be picked up by the next satellite.

I pushed back from my console to stare out the cupola window at Venus. After a while, I realized I was trying to find black specks in the white emptiness. That was ridiculous, I knew. A meter scale object—even tens of meters—wouldn't be visible with the naked eye. A high resolution camera, maybe, but nobody put high resolution cameras looking at the cloud tops. We had nothing like that on the station; why would we?

I had a sudden thought and turned back to the computer. The video footage I had looked at was the archival-quality footage, calibrated and cleaned up—but what about the raw footage? I pulled the as-received recorded data up from flash archive and ran my search query again. The first four hits on the search were indeed camera artifacts, one- or two-pixel specks that the despeckle algorithm had legitimately removed from the cleaned-up footage, but the fifth hit showed it again. Not any clearer, but once again, something that might have been a one-meter object moving at wind speed. With a little work, I found six more examples in the archive.

"Zara, are you up there?"

The relay satellite was back in line of sight, and with it my console told me that telemetry had resumed. A moment later my camera view from Sanjay's plane resumed.

"Hey, flyboy, how you doing down there?" I said. "Say, you won't believe what I've been finding. That black speck you mentioned? I've found half a dozen of them in archival drone footage. The despeckle algorithm erased them, that's why nobody noticed them."

"Yeah, I know. I'm watching one right now."

"What?" I grabbed for my camera controls. "I have to see this. Give me a bearing."

The—manifestation? Object? The thing, whatever it was—was well below his level, barely above the cloud tops. And I knew exactly what he was thinking.

"No, you can't go down and look at it," I said. "Infrared says it's about 60 degrees down there. Call it 140 Fahrenheit. Not bad by Venus standards, but still too hot for humans."

"I'm not planning to stay there, Zara," he said. "Just glide down for a quick close-up look, and then skedaddle up to the cool altitudes."

"No," I said, but the telemetry told me he was already descending, and I knew that there was no way I could talk him out of it. I checked the mission elapsed time. "Okay, okay. Watch your clock. You have a rendezvous to make with the return vehicle, and you have to make it in sunlight. I'll give you three hours, no more. You are ascending to the rendezvous in three hours, no matter what you find, no matter what you see."

"Bingo at three hours," he said. "Got it."

"You miss that rendezvous, and I guarantee that I will personally go down to the surface to find your charred corpse and," I paused. "And, and . . . chastise it severely."

"Right, right," he said. "That won't be necessary. Warning received. Three hours." He paused for a second, and then said, "By the way, I see two of them now. Maybe ten kilometers or so apart."

"One is enough, Sanjay," I said. "Three hours. That's firm."

"I heard you the first two times," he said.

The Venus drone I'd modified had had remote-piloting capability, allowing us to override the autopilot from orbit. Unfortunately, to give Sanjay the controls to pilot it, I'd taken those teleoperation controls and put them in the cockpit. Now I wished I'd had the foresight to have put a second set of teleoperation capability in place, so I could take control away from Sanjay and keep him from doing idiotic things. The super-rotation wind was blowing the return vehicle around the planet at well over two hundred miles an hour. It wasn't into the sunset twilight yet, but he didn't have forever, and the margin we'd put into the mission was shrinking.

I turned back to the radio. "And, one other thing," I said. "I warn you, if you don't come back, the bet is off."

He didn't bother answering, but I swear I heard him chuckle.

There was nothing for me to do then but to wait out his descent, watching the temperature slowly rise, and worry about time and mission margins.

It took him two hours to descend to the altitude the mystery object was floating. He circled the plane around it, and I got a good view of it with the camera.

It was a parachute.

"Damn," Sanjay said. "I can't believe it. It's a probe?"

An ancient Venus descent probe, maybe an old Soviet model? Floating in the atmosphere on its parachute for all these years? That was impossible. Or, maybe just the parachute, one that had been jettisoned to let the probe drop, now turned black with acid exposure? That was nearly as crazy. "Circle around for another pass," I advised. "I want a better look at it."

"Damn right," he said. "Me too."

He wheeled around, and I got a photo of it, this one good enough to estimate size. "Not a probe," I said. "Too small." The canopy of the parachute was about two meters across, and the payload, whatever it was, smaller than a peanut. "I don't know what it is, but nobody on Earth ever made probes that tiny."

And, from the closer view, it no longer really looked like anything terrestrial. What we had thought was a parachute was fuzzy, like a tangle of fine thread, and the irregular peanut-sized payload was suspended below it by lines as thin as spider-silk, almost too fine to see.

"The black color absorbs sunlight and heats the air. That's how it stays up," I said. "A small effect, but must give it just enough hot-air buoyancy to keep it suspended in the atmosphere. We missed it. We were looking for microbes. Nobody thought to look for macroscopic organisms, and we missed it."

"Is it an organism?" Sanjay wondered.

"I can't see what else it could be. Can you?"

"I'm going to scoop it up."

"Be quick about it. You're close to bingo." The drone was designed for atmospheric sensing—designed to look for and analyze microbes, the one thing that wasn't there—but the scoop could acquire samples. I watched as he circled around and opened the scoop, located in the underbelly of the aircraft. He aimed directly at the organism, whatever it was, and came straight at it. At the last moment he pulled just a hair back on the stick.

"Missed." I slewed the camera around and watched the parachute organism tumble about in the wake of the aircraft. The scoop had never been designed for precision acquisition; nobody had thought that a meter or two or ten would matter for an atmosphere sample. "Looks like you were about a meter high."

"Coming around for another try," he said.

The second try he nailed it, centering the organism in the scoop as he swooped in. I watched with the camera. "Direct hit," I said.

"Did I get it?"

"Yes . . . sort of. No." At the cruise airspeed of about a hundred meters a second, the organism had exploded into dust when the scoop hit it. "You got pieces of it. Maybe."

"Damn," Sanjay swore.

"Looks like it came apart like dandelion fluff. Must be outrageously light weight."

"Not unexpected, I guess, if it's floating like that." After a moment he added, "Okay. Next time I can scoop more gently; come up at a stall. I'm heading the other one."

I looked at the clock. "Negative, Sanjay. Bingo, head for the rendezvous."

"Come on, Zara. I know you put some margin in that schedule."

"Margin is there for a reason. You've seen enough. I concede, you win the bet. Now we know what's there, we can let the robots investigate. You're out of time."

"A minute more. One minute, that's all."

"Do you have it on visual?"

"Not yet. I will in a moment."

"You don't have time. Get out of there."

He was silent for a while, and then he said, as if chatting, "I hate this heat. If it weren't so damn hot, I could think straight."

Wait—heat? I'd forgotten about the temperature. He was down at the one bar level, nearly brushing the thickest of the acid clouds. There was no interior temperature monitor in the cockpit—he was never supposed to fly that low—but I checked the externals. Nearly eighty C. That was in the death zone. "Sanjay! Get out of there! Now!"

"Too hot to think," he said, and then he fell silent.

"Sanjay!"

Silence.

Heat stroke. I pounded the console. Up in orbit, there was nothing I could do.

Except wait.

One minute. Two.

The machine he was flying had begun life as an autonomous drone. As far as the computer knew, his control inputs were a remote pilot flying it from orbit, and at three minutes without pilot input, the watchdog timer concluded that it had lost signal, and the autopilot took over.

The autopilot calculated the plane was far too low, and initiated a climb toward nominal cruise altitude, a safe fifty-eight kilometers above the surface.

It was a long wait as the airplane slowly climbed, punctuated only by my shouting Sanjay's name into the radio at thirty second intervals.

Twenty minutes into the climb, he answered.

There's little more to say. When he recovered enough to take over, he was still groggy from the heat, and I convinced him to let the autopilot navigate the plane to the balloon carrying the return vehicle. He was right; I'd kept plenty of margin in the schedule, and the rendezvous went without incident. Cramming Sanjay, along with the cannister containing the samples of the parachute organism, into a rocket meant to launch only rocks was a tight fit, but Sanjay refused to jettison the sample he'd worked so hard to get, even if it was little more than dust, so we found a way to fit, uncomfortably though it was.

On his cruise to the rendezvous, I'd started doing some sample analysis using the science instruments on the drone. It would take real laboratory equipment on Earth to untangle what it really was, or how it worked, but the science instruments on the airplane had been built to look for microbes, and I used what I had. As I'd thought, the parachute organism had no more cohesion than a bundle of cobwebs. No wonder it had come apart in the air shock of the scoop. In the microscopic view, the fragments looked like a tangle of angel-hair pasta, apparently a carbon-polysulfide polymer, utterly dissimilar to anything synthesized by terrestrial organisms. No DNA detected, no proteins, no recognizable biochemistry at all. To learn more than that, I would need a real lab. But it seemed to be some different biochemistry, one that used sulfuric acid for a solvent instead of the water that was ubiquitous for terrestrial life.

Life? Maybe. But not life as we knew it.

Yes, it was worth going down into the atmosphere to find.

Was Sanjay right? That humans were more valuable than robots, that we needed human explorers? Well, maybe. But we could have found it with the robotic airplanes; it had been right there in front of us. We were just looking in the wrong places, looking for the wrong thing. The flaw hadn't been in the robots; the flaw was us.

But . . . we had another month in orbit before our return window opened. We had another drone in the orbital habitat, and there was still one more return rocket waiting, floating on its balloon. From what we'd seen, I estimated that there must be one of those parachute organisms for every hundred cubic kilometers, easy enough to find another one. We could modify the scoop to make a lower-speed sample acquisition, grab an intact one to bring home. That would be something.

I wasn't as crazy as Sanjay. Really. We should let the robots do the work, it made logical sense to do it that way. I could talk myself out of it.

But I knew I wasn't going to. What had Sanjay said? It was a hell of a ride?

Well, I just guess I was going to find out.

EARTH'S SISTER PLANET

The Habitability and Evolution of Venus

DENNIS HÖNING

A s the brightest planet in our night sky, Venus has been fascinating humans ever since early history. Because of its dense, thick cloud layer, direct observations of Venus's surface are impossible. From telescope observations, it was known early that the size and the orbital period of Venus are similar to those of Earth, leading to speculations about an Earth-like environment. People have imagined a multitude of worlds to lay beneath the clouds: lush jungles, deep oceans, vast deserts, even landscapes of liquid asphalt—but before the spacefaring age, there was no way to tell.

It took until the 1960s for the first spacecraft to explore Venus's atmosphere, which shattered the dream of a habitable surface on our sister planet. The American space probe *Mariner 2* measured a surface temperature of nearly 500 °C, which rather suggested a hellish environment where any water would boil and evaporate, and any life forms would die. Numerous following space missions, including orbiters and landers, have confirmed such an environment hostile to life. The *Venera* landers on Venus's hot surface broke down after only a couple of hours.

The reason for the hot surface is twofold: On one hand, Venus is much closer to the Sun than Earth is, causing Venus to receive twice as much solar energy. On the other hand, Venus's atmosphere is rich in the greenhouse gas CO_2—in fact, the mass of CO_2 in Venus's atmosphere is more than 100,000 times higher than on Earth, which causes an extreme greenhouse effect, dramatically heating up the planet [1].

But over billions of years, planetary surface conditions can change. The energy flow that is released by the Sun increases over time, and so does the energy that is absorbed by Venus [2]. In addition, the atmospheric CO_2 budget can change with time as it is controlled by processes that include the deep interior, such as by volcanic activity. This raises the question as to whether Venus could have been habitable 3 or 4 billion years ago. Was Venus once a place with lakes and oceans, just as Earth today, or was it always rich in CO_2, dry, and hostile?

Similar to Earth, there is not much geological evidence left that would shed light on Venus's ancient environment [3]. An exception could be the tesserae, regions that show features that usually need a long time to build up, for example distinct deformations and a surface with many impact craters. Some researchers have even argued that the tesserae could be billions of years old and speculated that water flow in the past could have just blurred evidence of their real age [4]. Future space missions that specifically explore these regions could evaluate these theories, but until that time comes, we have little geological evidence.

But fear not: Computer models can help us today understand Venus's evolution. These models are based on mathematical equations that describe the physics of the atmosphere, surface, and/or interior, and are combined with current observations of Venus. The models strongly differ in terms of their complexity. Complex 3-dimensional climate models [5] are used to obtain detailed properties of the atmosphere such as the albedo (a measure how much sunlight is reflected, for example, by clouds) and temperature. These models require the atmospheric composition and the solar insolation as input parameters. The climate is then calculated self-consistently, meaning that besides basic physics, no additional assumptions need to be put into the model so that it runs without a bias. These models are extremely useful for Venus because they can simulate reflective clouds, which cause less sunlight to make it through the atmosphere. From these simulations, we know that reflective clouds mainly form when the planet is rotating very slowly because then the Coriolis force, which would otherwise pull on the clouds and make them much thinner, is weak. Venus is rotating so slowly that one day on Venus lasts 243 Earth-days!

Problem solved, near-time travel to ancient Venusian history achieved, right? Not quite. Since these models are highly expensive in terms of the required computational power, they cannot be used for calculating the evolution of the planet over billions of years. For that, we need models using simple parameterizations of the climate. Parameterizations make use of the fact that even though large-scale effects (e.g., changes of the surface temperature) are controlled by small-scale processes (e.g., turbulent movement of gases in the atmosphere), precisely simulating all small-scale processes is not needed in order to predict the large-scale properties of the planet. Instead, these complex, small-scale processes can often be replaced by simpler equations, which only describe the large-scale physics. Therefore, these models are computationally much cheaper and allow for a focus on interior-atmosphere interactions on timescales over billions of years. In these models, processes within the interior of the planet can either be simulated with 2-dimensional or 3-dimensional models [6], or, similar to the atmosphere, also be parameterized [7]. In the end, a combination of both model types is most useful to understand a planet's evolution: complex models to derive the connection between two traits such as CO_2 content in the atmosphere and the surface temperature, and simple models that then use this connection as a simple equation and calculate the planet's evolution over a long period of time.

On Earth, the process that controls the climate over millions and billions of years is the long-term carbonate-silicate cycle [8]. CO_2 in the atmosphere is dissolved in rainwater, forming carbonic acid, which then attacks silicate minerals. Weathering products are washed into the oceans, forming calcium carbonate, which is finally subducted into the mantle at regions where tectonic plates converge. At high pressure and temperature within Earth's interior, the carbonate sediments melt so that CO_2 is released back into the atmosphere at volcanic arcs, mid-ocean ridges, and hotspots. A main requirement for the whole cycle to operate is the presence of liquid water on the surface; otherwise, weathering would be inhibited. If liquid water ever existed on Venus, such a cycle could also have kept Venus habitable for a long period of time [5,9]!

Has there ever been liquid water on ancient Venus, though? That remains controversial. On the one hand, it has been argued that the escape rate of water to space would have been too low to explain a substantial water ocean in the past and at the same time the dry Venus we observe today [10]. On the other hand, large amounts of water could have been stored in the planet's crust as huge volcanic eruptions completely reformed the surface [5], which would describe a way out of this dilemma.

Even if liquid water existed on early Venus, a carbonate-silicate cycle similar to that on Earth today is anything but straightforward. On Earth, plate tectonics causes a continuous recycling of the crust into the interior, and with it the subduction of carbonate sediments. Therefore, plate tectonics is a key component of the carbonate-silicate cycle outlined above. On Venus, on the contrary, there is no sign of plate tectonics today [11], and the tectonic state of early Venus remains speculative. The continent-like tesserae on Venus were probably not formed the same way as continents were formed on Earth, where the subduction of one tectonic plate beneath another one leads to volcanic eruptions and the formation of mountain ranges like the Andes. Instead, Venus's crust was likely squeezed due to movements in the planet's interior, which eventually caused an elevation of these regions [12].

Without subduction, any carbonate sediments on Venus would not be recycled back into the interior but would rather accumulate on the surface and be buried by new lava flows. With time, these carbonate sediments would heat up, eventually becoming unstable, and release their CO_2 back into the atmosphere. This modification of the carbon cycle would dramatically limit the potential time interval to preserve liquid water on the surface to roughly 1 billion years after the formation of Venus [13].

If Venus has ever been habitable in the past, the increasing energy flux from the Sun and the increasing amount of CO_2 in the atmosphere from volcanic activity would have triggered a runaway greenhouse event at some point in time: As the surface temperature increases, more water evaporates, which—as a powerful greenhouse gas—causes the surface temperature to rise even further. Eventually, all water would be evaporated and gradually lost to space. Without any liquid water on the surface, weathering would cease, and with it, Venus would lose the sink of atmospheric CO_2. Since volcanic eruptions would continue to release CO_2 into the atmosphere, the runaway greenhouse event would be accompanied by a dramatic rise in CO_2. Within mere millions of years, Venus would have evolved from a habitable place to the hostile environment with the thick, CO_2-rich atmosphere that we observe today.

Whether the scenario of an early habitable period followed by a runaway greenhouse event really describes Venus's geological history or whether Venus has been a hot, dry planet during its entire evolution remains an open question and a hot topic in planetary sciences. Improvements in our understanding of Venus are expected from future missions to Venus, such as the NASA mission *VERITAS* [14] and the ESA mission *EnVision* [15]. These and other future Venus missions will on one hand focus on the surface in order to gain insights into the geologic history, and on the other hand on the atmosphere in order to understand the evolution of water vapor, CO_2, and other gases. They will also give us more insight into the chances of life on Venus today (hinted at by chemical disequilibria, which can nevertheless by explained without life), in its relatively "mild" cloud layer explored in Geoffrey A. Landis's "Cloudskimmer." Compared to missions to the Moon or Mars, the main challenge of mission concepts to Venus remains the hot surface, which inhibits comprehensive ground experiments with landers and rovers, such as long-lasting seismic experiments that would give insights into potential ancient subduction.

The question of potential habitable conditions on early Venus and the duration of these conditions is fundamental not just for understanding our sister planet, but also for gaining insights into the abundance and distribution of life in the universe. If even a planet that is hellish, and already received 40% more energy from the Sun in its early evolution than Earth receives today, could have been habitable at one point in the past, habitable conditions on planets throughout the universe could be widespread and the chances of finding life beyond Earth might be high. Furthermore, it would widen our focus on the most promising planets for the origin and evolution of life beyond Earth. For these reasons, narrowing down the environmental conditions of early Venus remains essential in astrobiology.

REFERENCES

[1]   Donahue, T. M., & Pollack, J. B. (1983). "Origin and evolution of the atmosphere of Venus." *Venus*, 1003-1036.

[2]   Gough, D. O. (1981). "Solar interior structure and luminosity variations." In *Physics of solar variations* (p. 21-34). Springer, Dordrecht.

[3]   Turcotte, D. L., Morein, G., Roberts, D., & Malamud, B. D. (1999). "Catastrophic resurfacing and episodic subduction on Venus." *Icarus*, 139(1), 49-54.

[4]   Khawja, S., Ernst, R. E., Samson, C., Byrne, P. K., Ghail, R. C., & MacLellan, L. M. (2020). "Tesserae on Venus may preserve evidence of fluvial erosion." *Nature communications*, 11(1), 1-8.

[5]   Way, M. J., & Del Genio, A. D. (2020). "Venusian habitable climate scenarios: Modeling Venus through time and applications to slowly rotating Venus-like exoplanets." *Journal of Geophysical Research: Planets*, 125(5), e2019JE006276.

[6]   Gillmann, C., Golabek, G. J., Raymond, S. N., Schönbächler, M., Tackley, P. J., Dehant, V., & Debaille, V. (2020). "Dry late accretion inferred from Venus's coupled atmosphere and internal evolution." *Nature Geoscience*, 13(4), 265-269.

[7] Driscoll, P., & Bercovici, D. (2013). "Divergent evolution of Earth and Venus: influence of degassing, tectonics, and magnetic fields." *Icarus*, 226(2), 1447-1464.

[8] Kasting, J. F., & Catling, D. (2003). "Evolution of a habitable planet." *Annual Review of Astronomy and Astrophysics*, 41(1), 429-463.

[9] Krissansen-Totton, J., Fortney, J. J., & Nimmo, F. (2021). "Was Venus Ever Habitable? Constraints from a Coupled Interior–Atmosphere–Redox Evolution Model." *The Planetary Science Journal*, 2(5), 216.

[10] Lammer, H., Zerkle, A. L., Gebauer, S., Tosi, N., Noack, L., Scherf, M., . . . & Nikolaou, A. (2018). "Origin and evolution of the atmospheres of early Venus, Earth and Mars." *The Astronomy and Astrophysics Review*, 26(1), 1-72.

[11] Smrekar, S. E., Davaille, A., & Sotin, C. (2018). "Venus interior structure and dynamics." *Space Science Reviews*, 214(5), 1-34.

[12] Kiefer, W. S., & Hager, B. H. (1991). "Mantle downwelling and crustal convergence: A model for Ishtar Terra, Venus." *Journal of Geophysical Research: Planets*, 96(E4), 20967-20980.

[13] Höning, D., Baumeister, P., Grenfell, J. L., Tosi, N., & Way, M. J. (2021). "Early Habitability and Crustal Decarbonation of a Stagnant-Lid Venus." *Journal of Geophysical Research: Planets*, 126(10), e2021JE006895.

[14] Freeman, A., Smrekar, S. E., Hensley, S., Wallace, M., Sotin, C., Darrach, M., . . . & Mazarico, E. (2016). "Veritas: A discovery-class Venus surface geology and geophysics mission."

[15] Smrekar, S. E., Hensley, S., Dyar, M. D., Helbert, J., Andrews-Hanna, J., Breuer, D., . . . & Zebker, H. (2020). "VERITAS (Venus Emissivity, Radio Science, InSAR, Topography, and Spectroscopy): A proposed Discovery mission."

THE LAMENT OF KIVU LACUS

B. ZELKOVICH

The whale song wakes you. Vibration builds up from the floor, through the legs of the bed, and into your chest. It could all be a dream while you blink away the sleep in your eyes, but then you see Rachel's side of the bed.

Empty again.

You climb into yesterday's jumpsuit, still piled on the floor beside the bed, and shiver at the chill in the room. Walls over a meter thick and cutting-edge life-support systems are still only capable of so much in the face of Titan's super cold atmosphere.

The door slides into the wall with a hiss and you step out into the main room of the outpost. To the right is a small seating area, the screen on the wall preloaded with enough media to get you both through the year-long assignment, and to your left is the kitchen. You're surprised to find an empty mug waiting for you in front of the coffee pot.

You pour a cup and take a sip before heading to the bank of terminals and research equipment built into the wall beside the kitchen. You check the hydrophone to be sure it's recording, which of course it is. You and Rachel might not be speaking at the moment, but she's still a professional. The research always comes first.

You can't avoid it any longer—there's nothing left to do—so you join Rachel where she stands on the observation deck. The domed viewport takes up the entire front wall of the outpost, half above the surface of Kivu Lacus and half below. Above the surface, the dusty yellow atmosphere is thick, obscuring the ridges of the nearby hills until they look like sand dunes. Below the surface, the liquid of the hydrocarbon lake is clear, but the endless, swirling silt obscures the topography and any sign of life that might call the liquid methane home.

The whale's song undulates through the outpost, all the more alien for the view it accompanies. You aren't certain 'whale' is the right term for what lives in Kivu Lacus, but it's the closest comparison and it's one you and Rachel agreed on.

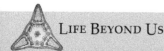

"Is it the same one as yesterday?" Questions about the research are safe. Nothing personal. No life-shattering revelations lurk in talk about Titan's whales.

She nods, the long line of her neck drawing your eye. How did you miss the sharpness of her jaw, or the bands of tight muscle where her neck meets her shoulder? Had it really come on so gradually?

"And the male?"

Rachel shakes her head. She blinks a few times and clears her throat before she looks at you. Even the color of her eyes looks faded, like dollar bills washed too many times. You thought the research had lit a fire in her, that she was just tired from the late nights.

You always loved her passion for xenobiology. The way she lights up when she discovers the link between two points of data. It's why you fell for her in the first place.

You stand together, careful not to touch, and wait to see if the whale appears. The coffee goes cold in your mug and the female's song fades away until only silence stretches between you and Rachel. There's a moment when you think you should say something. Just open your mouth and see what falls out. Anything would be better than the tense quiet suffocating you both.

But your heart clenches in your chest at the thought of talking through it all again. Reliving the tears and anger and bone-rattling fear, just to feel wrung out and so alone. Rachel's standing right beside you, but she might as well be back on Earth. A stranger in your wife's body.

Because your Rachel would never keep a secret from you. Not one like this.

The silence continues until you can't take it anymore and turn to rinse your mug in the sink. Over the drip of water, you hear Rachel stifle a sob. Your back hunches around the sound, like a punch to the gut and you brace for more, for wracking sobs to pummel you with guilt and anger. They never come.

When you turn to face the observation deck, she isn't there. You sigh at the hiss of the door to the aeroponics chamber and lean against the counter.

In another life you would go to her, console her, and wait until she was ready to talk. But that was before. Before you learned that life as you knew it was about to change forever. Before your wife told you she was dying.

You can't take the quiet anymore, so you sit at the research terminal to catalogue the newest recording. You can't disappear from the outpost, but at least you can vanish into your work.

Rachel is still in bed when you wake the next morning. It's the first time in almost three months. You blink, the sight of her lying beside you so unexpected that you don't recognize her right away. And then you understand why she always gets up first.

Her eyes are heavy and puffy and too bright in her thinning face. Her hair is pulled up, but several strands have fallen free. She's close enough that you can smell the sick on her breath and hear how shallow her breathing is. Like she's in pain.

How did you miss this? You know your wife better than anyone else, having shared a life with her for almost fifteen years. Were you so absorbed in your work that you couldn't see the woman you loved wasting away in front of you?

Your hand shakes as you brush the hair back from her face. "Good morning."

She cries. Not the gut-punch sobs of yesterday, but gentle, relieved tears that streak down her cheek and across her nose to absorb into the sheets. Each one of them is a needle in your heart, deflating the anger that protected it and releasing a wave of grief.

"I'm sorry." You pull her close and notice how thin she is, where the bones make themselves known against you like they never had before.

You both cry, hard and soft in turns. From fear and pain and love. Hitched breathing and sniffles, warm breath and desperate hands are your whole world. You don't know for how long.

Then the whale begins her song. It's always eerie, alien, and fathomless, but this morning it sounds worse. Sadder.

Rachel pulls herself together first. She wipes away your tears, ignoring her own, and holds your face in her hands. "Time to go to work." She smiles. Beneath all the sadness and the sickness, you see your wife for the first time in months.

You nod and help her get dressed before climbing into your own jumpsuit. She makes coffee while you turn on the hydrophone, then you meet at the observation deck. This time, when she hands you your coffee, you drape one arm around her shoulders. It's not the same, not as effortless as it used to be, but it's better.

Together, you listen to the song. It sweeps you up in its unexpected rhythms and crescendos, the drops and clicks. You close your eyes and struggle to imagine what the sheet music for that voice would look like. Clumps of notes tumbling down the bars and climbing back up again faster than human fingers could ever play.

Rachel's arm tightening at your waist startles you. "Look!"

At first, all you see is the impossible murk of Kivu Lacus. You know the methane moves, but you can't tell with the weak sunlight that filters through the dense atmosphere. There is only the stillness and the dark and the song.

A silvery fin sweeps through the gloom, languid and weightless. It's long, thin, and broad, like a razor cutting through the silt. And then it's gone, swallowed up into the dark once more.

The whales always manage to steal your breath, even after all these months. Rachel squeezes your hip, and you pull her tighter against you. She's just as awed by the whales as you are, something inside her buoyed by them. Just like the ballooning warmth you feel in your chest as another, higher voice joins the song.

Rachel goes rigid against you, her breath caught in her throat. The song twines and spins, the whales chirping and clicking to one another. The female's voice is low and rumbles in your chest while the male's is light and fluttering, like your heart when you look down at your wife's head against your chest.

From the murk, a gray shape materializes. It's smaller than you expected, maybe nine meters long, and the coloring is different from the fin you saw only moments ago. Less metallic. There's no glittering shine to the skin of this whale, just a dull gray color that fades out to a white underbelly.

"He finally found her," Rachel says.

You glance at her, but she doesn't look away from the whale as it glides past the observation deck. Your throat feels tight, your eyes sting, and you cling to her as you watch the whale disappear into the dark. Only the song remains.

"Maybe he got lost along the way."

Things are better, for a while. Rachel's smiles are freer; the wall between you has come down and the relief in the outpost is tangible. There's laughter again, and it's just enough to let you pretend. For now, there's no expiration date looming over her life. There's no promise of bleak, lonely days.

There's just you and the woman you love, researching the mysterious creatures that call Kivu Lacus home.

"Listen to this," Rachel says and hands you the headphones. She's been parked in front of the terminal for hours, her focus indomitable as she searches the whale song for patterns.

It's the recording from this morning. Each day since the male arrived, the whales have greeted the day with a long and trilling duet. You've sighted the pair twice since then, the whales swimming a little closer to the outpost each time.

You've heard the recording a handful of times and listened to hundreds more since you've been stationed on Titan. They're all starting to blend together.

"Do you hear it?"

You close your eyes, try to focus, but you don't catch anything to make this morning's recording stand out from the others. You shake your head. "What'd I miss?"

"The song leaps in pitch right before they approach the outpost." She turns back to the terminal and selects another recording. "This is from three days ago, the last time we spotted them."

The song plays, and this time you do catch the upward tilt of the voices. Before you can say as much, Rachel cuts the recording and starts another.

"The day the male arrived," she says.

Again, you hear the sharp climb in pitch. You take the headphones off and hand them back to her. "And that happens every time they approach the outpost?"

"Every time we've seen them."

"Okay. What does that mean?"

She runs a hand over her head, her fingers exploring the newly exposed skin. You watch, still transfixed by the sight of her bald head. Her hair had started to fall out, so you shaved it for her the night before. It had been easier to do than you expected.

"I don't know," she says. "Maybe it's their designation for the outpost?"

You snort. "That seems like a stretch."

"Does it? We know that dolphins use sounds to name one another and use those sounds to introduce themselves to new acquaintances." She shrugs. "Is it such a stretch to think that a mating pair of these whales would be able to create a sound designation for an anomaly in their habitat?"

"Considering that we have no verifiable link between Titan's 'whales' and Earth's dolphins, yeah. It's a bit of a stretch."

"The sounds are too similar to humpback whale songs—they have to serve a similar purpose. It's language!"

You blink at her. "Rach, these whales have evolved on a hyper-cold moon 9.5 AU from Earth. Other than their singing and their general shape, they have nothing in common." You tick off points on your fingers. "They have a completely different genetic makeup—hell, different basic biochemistry. Sure, the scans suggest they can maintain a stable body temperature, but as far as we can tell, they may not even have 'blood' as we understand it. They're not really whales."

"I know that."

"Then making the leap to say that what's true for cetaceans on Earth is true for these animals is . . . reckless."

She stands up, her chair teetering as she does, and storms into the kitchen. "I'm right about this," she says. She pours a glass of water, refusing to look at you. As she drinks it, her hand trembles.

"Maybe," you say. "But until we have proof, we can't continue under the assumption that you are. You know that."

She hangs her head. "I know." Her voice is so soft that you can hear the recording still playing over the headphones better than you can hear her. "I want to solve this mystery. But I'm running out of time."

Your stomach drops. "We have five months left."

"*You* have five months left."

"Don't say that." The kitchen counter feels like a canyon dividing you. Your feet are adhered to the floor when all you want is to hold her.

"It's true." She takes another sip of water. "I can't keep weight on. I could double my ration and still lose weight. My hair's been falling out and the nausea's getting worse." She meets your eyes, the pale green irises luminous in the sallow gray of her face. "I'm not going to make it to the end of this expedition."

You scrub your hands over your face. This conversation was a long time coming, you know that. But you would have liked to continue pretending.

You sigh. "Then we need to call for an evac."

"No."

"What do you mean, no?" Your voice climbs, the fear and frustration hijacking your words. "You're dying, Rachel. You should be at home where you can be comfortable."

"I don't want to be comfortable." She slams the glass down on the counter. Water sloshes out over her hand, but she doesn't notice. "I don't want to spend my last useful days moping around at home waiting to die. I want—" The words whip from her, but she pauses and takes a breath. "I *need* more. There's so much left to learn here. How they evolved, how they communicate, how they perceive the world beyond all that cold." She shakes her head. "Besides, I don't think the evac would get us home in time."

It takes just over a month for a shuttle to get to the outpost. Another month to get home. It was one thing to know Rachel was dying. It was another to have a countdown. Your head spins; sixty days.

Her cool fingers on your cheek startle you. "I'm going to ask you something, and I want you to really think before you give me your answer, okay?"

You swallow and nod, terrified of what she might say.

"I know this is hard and it's awful and I'm so sorry I kept it from you for so long. That wasn't fair." She's crying, soft tears tracking her cheeks, but her voice is strong. "But it's only going to get harder from here. My health is deteriorating rapidly and before we know it, I'm going to be a hindrance to this expedition."

"Don't—"

"—Listen," she says. "I planned for this." A tremor runs through her hands. "In the rightmost drawer in the aeroponics worktable is a syringe—"

You shake your head. "I can't. Don't ask me—"

"—Please."

Her conviction rocks you. Despite the tears and the sickness, you see your wife before you in all her strength, determination, and glory. This is not weakness, but preparedness. Not an escape, but a decision. To end her life on her terms.

Who are you to deny this fierce, glorious woman her last request?

You sob, your chest tight and burning in grief and impotent fury. But you nod all the same. She pulls you against her, and you stoop a little so that your face rests in the crook of her neck. You breathe her warmth, the sharp, clean smell of her and do your best to commit her to memory.

Because soon, memories will be all that's left.

There could be no mistaking it now, no willful ignorance of what your future holds. For Rachel, the future is very, very limited. Weight wicks off her like wax dripping from a candle and any color left in her face drains away. Through it all Rachel remains driven and focused. She wakes before you each morning, brews coffee, and records the whales.

Their song has become more complex and lasts longer now. The jump in pitch occurs more often and they've come close enough that you can now distinguish between the male and female on sight.

Rachel named them Persephone and Hades because of the silty dark of their home. You think it's a bit grim, but it makes her smile, so you keep your opinions to yourself. She listens to the recordings less and spends more of her time on the observation deck, her hand pressed to the glass. She talks to the whales, low and soothing.

You listen but don't participate. Her words aren't for you, but you absorb them all the same. Anything to add to your stockpile of images and sounds and smells of her. You don't want to miss a single detail.

Persephone comes close, her silvery gray skin glows in the murk of the lake. She's shaped like a whale, large and sleek with long pectoral fins and a fluke. But she's sharper than Earth's whales. Her body is built to cut through the silt like a razor even as she moves at a languid pace toward the glass.

Hades follows her, his song high and keening, but he doesn't venture too near to the observation deck. He's smaller, faster too, and he swims loops around his mate as she pauses before the outpost. You both gasp when she presses her snout against the glass, opposite of Rachel's hand.

"She sees us," Rachel says.

"How?" You still haven't seen any hint of eyes on either whale.

"Echolocation?" But you can tell she doesn't believe her own suggestion. "Maybe scent?"

"We're in an airtight facility. There's no way they can smell us."

"Then maybe they can hear us." She turns to you, tears shining in her eyes. "Maybe all this time, they've been singing for us."

You doubt it, but you don't say so. You're done poking holes in your wife's theories.

You sit beside her and place your hand on the glass. "Maybe," you say, instead.

Persephone starts her song anew, the sound rising and falling in a pattern you now know by heart. You hum along without meaning to, and Hades joins in too. He swims up, closer to the observation deck, his movement uncharacteristically slow.

Then he presses his nose against the glass right in the center of your palm.

You laugh and say, "Hello." Rachel laughs too, and the whales continue their song.

But as joyful as the moment is, as awe-inspiring and unbelievable, there's a darkness clinging inside your ribs.

The whale song is too loud. It wakes you earlier than usual and Rachel's still beside you in bed. You blink in the dark, trying to banish the fog from your mind. What's that rattling?

It takes several terrible seconds for you to recognize the sound as breathing. Rachel's breathing. She lies beside you, gulping at the air. And just like that you're awake and out of bed. You scoop her up. She's so light it's easy, and you rush to the aeroponics chamber. You need the oxygen. *She* needs it.

Deep within the collection of plants, you sit on the floor with Rachel's back against your chest. You take slow, even breaths and coach her to do the same.

It takes a moment, but she breathes a little easier. The oxygen rich chamber helps, and she eventually loosens her grip on your hand. You rest your mouth against her shoulder, your nose tucked into her neck. You breathe her in and try not to acknowledge how much you're shaking.

You have no idea how much time passes before she finally breaks the silence.

"It's time."

You shake your head and tighten your arms around her.

"Please. You can do this."

You don't think you can, after all. Despite all your best efforts, this moment is so much worse than you'd imagined, a searing kind of worse that will never leave you.

Rachel takes your hand and the fragile way she squeezes it reminds you of your promise. Reminds you of why you agreed in the first place. She's in pain and losing herself, and it's so unfair you could scream yourself hoarse, but you know she's right.

As usual.

You nod against her neck, unable to say the words as you stand and go to the worktable. Your hand wavers as you reach for the rightmost drawer, but it glides open the same as always, careless of the horror it contains.

The syringe is there, waiting for you just as she'd promised. You never were squeamish about needles, but suddenly the entire concept of hypodermics turns your stomach. If you think about it too much you might just vomit.

You snatch the syringe from the drawer, take a deep breath, and return to your wife. Propped against the wall, surrounded by the green of the plants, she looks too gray. Pallid and lifeless already, save for the pale green of her eyes. Compared to the vibrant leaves they're stark proof that there's no going back.

You have arrived at the end.

She's breathing hard, too hard for the oxygen rich room. You kneel beside her, take a deep breath, and prepare the syringe.

Rachel shakes her head. "Not here." A shallow, shuddering breath and then, she says, "I want to see them one more time."

You've been so consumed with Rachel, with what you're about to do, that you completely tuned out the whales. But their song has been trilling, loud and frantic, this whole time.

"Okay," you say and hand her the syringe. You take her in your arms and carry her from the aeroponics chamber. Each step a goodbye.

Both Persephone and Hades hover before the observation deck, and once you see them, their song cuts off. The silence is more alien than their singing ever was. Hades bobs his head, agitated, but Persephone is still.

You settle down beside the glass and arrange Rachel so that her back rests against your chest. You surround her, envelope her in warmth and strength and love, and pray that she feels it all.

She exhales, the breath heavy, and hands the syringe back to you.

You take it without hesitation. There isn't time for your doubts and fear anymore. There never really was. Your hands are steady as you prep the syringe, but you'll marvel at the sudden calm later when you have time to dissect every detail of these final moments.

All you'll have is time.

You press your cheek to her head, your lips by her ear. "I love you."

"I love you."

The needle sinks into her arm with the faintest pop. Your thumb presses down. Rachel hisses and then sighs, resting her forehead against the cool glass.

"They're so beautiful," she says.

The syringe falls from your hand, empty. You can't look at it, so you press your face against your wife's neck and nod. You focus on her breathing, syncing your breaths to hers, counting them as they come further and further apart.

Until, eventually, they don't come at all. You shudder and shake, but Rachel doesn't move.

Persephone's voice hums through the outpost with a single, repeated sound. It's the high-pitched note, the one Rachel thought referred to the outpost. Hades joins in, for once his voice matching his mate's exactly.

You look up to find the whales' snouts pressed to the glass, their bodies angled in a straight line with Rachel's. The sound repeats, over and over, a call so painful that you can't help but understand; it wasn't the outpost they'd named. It wasn't the outpost they'd been drawn to time and time again.

As with everything else in your life, the reason was Rachel. The reason you came to Titan. The reason the whales of Kivu Lacus shared their song. And now, as your wife's body goes cold in your arms, their song climbs through you, familiar and true, a final gift. A melody to remind you of every beautiful, horrible moment of the last few months.

The lament of Kivu Lacus.

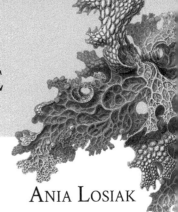

ROBOTS IN SPACE ARE GREAT

Are People in Space Better?

ANIA LOSIAK

A s far as we know, no human has ever died away from Earth. But with crewed space missions, the moment is inevitably coming. With the limited healthcare options in long-duration missions far from our planet (and Saturn's moon Titan is very far indeed), they might even die from causes that we could treat on Earth—or worse, potentially endanger the lives of others on the expedition. Is it worth it to send humans on such missions at all?

Robots are great in doing space exploration. They were there first (*Sputnik* in 1957) and, most importantly, nearly everything we know about our solar system and beyond is because of them. It started when the *Mariner* missions took the first close-up pictures of other planetary bodies in the 1960s. The *Viking* landers performed analyses from the surface of Mars. Since then, numerous other orbiters, landers, and rovers collected *in situ* data and/or samples from asteroids, comets, moons, and planets, and beyond. For example, the *Voyagers* are now our only direct source of information about conditions outside the solar system.

Robots are cheap, efficient, and able to work in extreme conditions. *Chandrayaan-1*, a lunar mission of the Indian Space Research Organisation that, among other things, allowed confirmation of the presence of water-ice on our natural satellite [1], cost less than US$80 million. In comparison, this is much cheaper than an off-the-shelf commercial airplane. Space robots can function with minimal resources—the rover *Perseverance* is powered by a 110-watt radioisotope thermoelectric generator; this amount of power is barely sufficient to make a small fridge work. We have sent robots to some truly hellish locations—and they performed (until they were killed on the job). The Soviet *Venera* missions sent data from the surface of Venus, where the pressure-cooker atmosphere is rich in sulphuric acid and hot enough to melt lead.

On the other hand, humans are expensive, lazy, and very delicate. Sending people to space requires not only lifting our heavy brains, livers, arms, and appendixes thousands of kilometers above the ground, but to make things even more expensive, along with all this flesh we need to send all the resources and devices that are critically required to keep astronauts alive. Actually, most of the International Space Station is nothing more than an elaborate life-support system, with only a small segment of it devoted to doing actual research work. But as they say: "Humans in space need to be alive to do science!" Running all those systems designed to keep humans alive is a very time-consuming endeavor; astronauts spend most of their time on housekeeping chores: cleaning, testing to see if everything works, and fixing anything that is broken.

Even the most hard-working humans are lazy and unreliable, when compared to robots. Trial-and-error experiments on space stations determined that during each day astronauts have at least 8.5 hours for sleeping, and at least 9 hours for exercising, washing, eating, pooping, or resting. This means that only about 6.5 hours or 27% of every day is devoted to doing something productive. Unlike robots, astronauts require weekends and holidays off.

Additionally, humans break down very easily. For example, people can be killed even by a cosmic dust particle, and I am not even talking about surviving a direct hit. A micro-crater formed on a handrail of the International Space Station in 2007 seriously damaged a glove of the astronaut during the STS-118, leading to the termination of his space walk [2].

Despite all the disadvantages of sending our delicate flesh into the cold, irradiated emptiness of space, only one planetary mission performed by humans yielded much more, better, and deeper scientific results than all robotic missions combined. The *Apollo* program not only totally changed our understanding of the formation and evolution of the Moon, Earth, and all rocky bodies of the solar system, but it continues to be a source of amazing discoveries. This is because the amount and quality of collected data is incomparable to any robotic mission ever performed. For example, only very recently (in 2018), the *InSight* robot managed to successfully place a seismometer on Mars [3], after multiple failed attempts by other robots (e.g., by the *Viking* landers). Humans successfully deployed an entire network of seismometers on the Moon on their first try, which led to years of high-quality data on moonquakes. Humans brought back 382 kg of Moon rocks, while all the robots have, so far, managed to fetch only 2 kg (0.3 kg by the Soviet *Luna* missions and 1.7 kg by the Chinese *Chang'e* mission). More importantly, samples taken by humans were of a much higher quality because astronauts, instead of grabbing the first conveniently located piece of stone, were performing a true geologic exploration and selecting the most interesting and scientifically relevant samples. This approach led to the discovery of the "orange soil"—a site of an ancient lunar lava fountain—that helped us to better understand how much water and other volatiles are inside the Moon, or to determine the oxidization level of the mantle of our natural satellite.

In space studies, there are things we know that we know, there are things we know that we do not know, and, most importantly, there are things we do not know that we do not know. Robots are great in dealing with those known unknowns. We can design robotic mass spectrometers that can figure out what kind of particles exist in Titan's atmosphere just by the way they crush into our detectors [4], especially if we know quite well what we can expect there. Devices may be planned to be particularly sensitive to specific ranges of data, allowing researchers to answer the most important scientific questions. However, it often takes decades between designing, building, and assembling space equipment and the moment when they finally start doing their job. Such hiatus is especially extensive for missions to the external solar system: *Cassini-Huygens* originated in 1982, was launched in 1997, and travelled for more than six years before it was able to start its data collection on Saturn and Titan. This meant that, when it arrived there and *Huygens* landed on Titan, not only were all the devices technically outdated, but also—potentially—their designs might have been based on long-obsolete scientific knowledge (luckily, they were not).

People are better at dealing with things "we do not know that we do not know" because we can repair, modify, and build new devices, as well as perform complex scientific analysis. In the near future, it is very unlikely robots will outperform the plucky space geologist—or astrobiologist. Because of all this, we should consider sending humans to study Titan's lakes. Underneath the orange haze of its atmosphere, under the calm surface of its methane seas, there might be surprises of something we don't yet know that we don't know.

REFERENCES

[1] Pieters et al. (2009). "Character and Spatial Distribution of OH/ H2O on the Surface of the Moon Seen by M3 on Chandrayaan-1." *Science* 326, 568-572. DOI: 10.1126/science.1178658

[2] Christiansen E.L. and Lear D.M. (2014). "Solving Problems Caused by Small Micrometeoroid and Orbital Debris Impacts for Space-Walking Astronauts." *ARES Biennial Report 2012 Final.* https://ntrs.nasa.gov/citations/20150003814

[3] Giardini D. et al. (2020). "The seismicity of Mars." *Nature Geoscience* 13: 205–212. https://doi.org/10.1038/s41561-020-0539-8

[4] Niemann H.B. et al. (2005). "The abundances of constituents of Titan's atmosphere from the GCMS instrument on the Huygens probe." *Nature* 438, 779–784.

HEAVY LIES

A Record of Reproductive Aberration in the Eusocial Aedificans of Boreas-4 RICH LARSON

When the clutch emerges from your beautiful womb, they will be fit only for the birthfeast. This was divined from the specific secretions and howls of a vivisected heretic, from the scattered exobones of a long-dead saint, and from the moons' Fourth Position in a sulfurous sky.

But you knew this already.

You could feel it was no war-womb: no budding tusks scraped at your insides, no miniature limbs mimed violence. You could feel it was no work-womb: no order emerged in the swirl of tiny bodies, no quasiform mouths traced the cracks in your placental wall as if to fill them.

The things inside you are soft darting things, devoid of aggression or duty or usefulness to the Nest in any role but one.

The city must prepare. You want to observe this with your own eyepores first, so you lumber up the helical passage with a retinue of servants carrying your womb behind you. They shudder and salivate and issue performative pheromonal apologies for their growing hunger.

You do not forgive them.

When you reach the sinusoidal parapets, you look out over the ossein swells of the Nest, of its dwellings and ateliers, its topes and witch-huts. A city fashioned from the crushed corpses of a thousand thousand ancestors, threaded with beautiful monodeath.

When you were young, you listened hard for the whispers of nerve branches reanimated, ghosts sintered into archways and fortifications. Now that you are old, the dead are crowded out by the living.

Your womb is full of murmurs. It crescendos as the street sweepers set to work, sloshing and scrubbing the promenade with your holy bile.

Time seethes. Beyond the Nest's tangled extremities, the world flattens to a pitiless blank, the endless plain of salt that scorches. Once emissaries traversed those flats, trailing filaments of thought behind them. Once there were carved mounds of exobone to mark the routes, and sunken tunnels in which to take shelter from the hellmelting heat.

But this was long before your time, only an obscure glyph worn shallow beneath your hands. The other Nests disappeared eons ago. Now there is only yours, and to know there were once others is a painful anathema, a puzzle that took many births to solve. You move your gaze upward and observe a sulfurous sky.

The moon follows its clutchmate through the void. You wonder at the endless pursuit, as Te stalks Yo, as Fourth Position becomes Fifth Position, and imagine it ending: One moon overtakes the other and devours it whole, as a ravenous warrior devours a fetal spore.

You excise the thought, before it can spread through your veinules and saltways, but your womb tastes it by its absence. The doomed clutch stirs in a way you no longer can stir. Your body is stiffening, punched taut by expanding vapors. Your eyepores congeal.

Birthing must be blind, to avoid foresight, but for now you direct a servant to slash your eyepores back open. She carves in steady rhythm with a knife made of spinal fin. The blade came from your own dorsal, harvested a dozen moons ago. No other implement would permit itself to cut you.

Eventually, the knife cannot keep pace. The scalded sky shrinks away. You used to relish this solitude, this darkness, your contemplations.

But now the murmurs haunt you, so you request a puppet.

The augurs and advisors whinge. They circle. They vomit up chunks of the executed heretic and see inauspicious patterns in the liquefaction. It is not done, using a puppet before birthing. Even if the birthing is of mere feast-fodder, it is not done.

But in the end, suffused in your chemical flattery, they agree, understanding this small liberty to be payment for your continued adherence to all other forms of ceremony. One augur even lie-begs for the honor, lacing their supplication with a subtle electric flicker of renegement.

This baits a less experienced rival into true-begging, and though you have waning interest in such games, you permit the maneuver.

You listen as the augur races to the carved cradle, as they place their skull so eagerly inside.

The servants from the parapet chine the augur open. Exobone squeals, then cracks. The augur-now-puppet writhes, must writhe, for you can feel sour and agonized air washing across your face. The drill will be next. You imagine it corkscrewing deep into the puppet's spine, searching for saltways.

You spin a filament of raw, whispering nerves. Servants feed it into the small void that is always left by a monodeath.

Out of the dark.

Inhabiting the puppet, you wander away from your body, away from your womb and your advisors. You descend into the city instead, trailing a wet gossamer cable, the filament of nerves that connects you to your puppet. It loops your legs and once catches on the decorative jag of a sculpture, but you spun it well and it does not tear.

The denizens of the Nest can no more tread on it than they can tread on moonlight. Your children are nimble-limbed, but some now stumble and collide as those nimble limbs move autonomously to avoid the sacrosanct filament.

To these, you apologize. They shudder with joy.

The city thrives. Inhabiting the puppet, you can know this viscerally. Its failing flesh and olfactory organs still respond to the harmony around it, the flow of labor and rest, instruction and completion.

You feel the precision of your workers in the hard porous pathways beneath your puppet's feet; the strength of your warriors in the desiccated tentacles hung from street corners, remains of the burrowing beasts that threaten the city's far reaches. You taste the electric breeze and its cargo of task-scents, name-scents, luck-scents.

The Nest's vapors are in sublime balance. Your children skim the common happiness and regurgitate it without injecting a single drop of doubt. There have been no true heretics for noncount moons, which is why you are forced to manufacture your own.

Your children do not question this. Nor do they question the birthfeast increasing in size and frequency despite the city's steady patterns of cultivation, despite dwellings built and left empty.

As you pass through the obeisant crowds, through the teeming anticipation, an unseen thing hangs over you.

Your body is not where you left it. When you glide back along the filament, you find your shriveled frame and bloated womb in the ablution room. Soft hands roam, daubing you with fermented secretions, some of them your own. The servants are preparing you for the ceremony.

The puppet wandered longer than you realized, but there is still time for a brief interrogation. You summon the augurs with a fizzing pulse of curiosity. They arrive already slathered in their lushest scents, faces etched with fresh sigils, and the servants bristle but move aside.

The question you pose is simple: *What do the heretics say before monodeath?*

In place of corporeal remains, the augurs regurgitate the heretics' generic pleas and rages, their blandly vile invective. You adjust the query: *What did the heretics* used *to say before monodeath? The original heretics, the ones hunted from existence, not these pheromone-fucked caricatures.*

The augurs are silent, ignorant. They have forgotten utterly.

Good.

The first time, there was only one. A single soft darting thing in the telluric ocean of your womb. It fed from your capillaries. It trembled at your imaginings. You loved it as yourself, because it *was* yourself, far more so than the trudging workers and blood-bent warriors you had already birthed by the hundreds.

But it wasn't you. Not quite. You tasted its winding helices and found them subtly altered from your own. You watched its saltways multiply and weave new patterns, trigger vast and unreadable storms within itself.

It disturbed you. Its flickering foreign thoughts, its nascent wants. The Nest had no need of such a thing.

You ate it alone when it emerged, savored its jellied grit on your tongue. Your advisors retched and barked their approval. They told you the first one is often weak. Unfit.

The pre-joy of the Nest crackles the air. Amniotic perfumes caress your blind face. Your body is in motion, anchored to the dais; the dais is sliding down the long groove that scars the promenade, pushed and pulled by a brutish maniple of warriors. They are strong, well-fed.

Their hunger is ceremonial, but no less true for it. They are chemically voracious, desperate for the birthfeast as Te is desperate for its clutchmate Yo.

In your womb, whisper becomes clamor. This clutch has a hundred voices.

Many war-births and work-births after the first soft thing, a second arrived. You ate it.

Many war-births and work-births after that, a third arrived. You offered it to a favored courtier, shared its nectarous flesh in the privacy of your rooms.

The fourth time, the soft thing did not arrive alone. They came moon-numbered, with moon-bright shells that softened and crumpled in your mouth, one and then the other. You relished their secret texture.

So passed the next arrival, and the next. The advisors' approval became puzzlement became unease. It was not done, to eat so many. The sacred icons chiseled into the city's streets, laced with the wishes of the monodead, taught release. Taught succession.

It was necessary, the augurs said, that a soft darting thing grow to be your equal. They did not know why, but they knew it was so. It was necessary that the successor grow to be your equal, and then deal you your monodeath.

You want to see yourself, so you flit away from the voices, away from your body, gliding back through the labyrinthine tangle of filament until you reach your decaying puppet. Blood-starved exobone crumbles away. Its feet leave powdery prints as you stagger through the throng, toward the end of the promenade.

You see yourself. Your body on the dais is beautiful and it is horrible. The womb is a moon, vast and drifting, its taut membrane dappled by the shadows of tiny hands within, all clawing to be without.

The soft things began to come in sevens, eights, nines. Insubstantial, compared to the teeming clutches birthed to fortify the Nest and defend its borders from burrowing beasts. But too many to consume alone. You found a solution among the most obscure icons: the birthfeast. In times of climactic shift, agricultural failings, a clutch must sometimes be sacrificed to stave off famine.

The advisors brayed and shuddered their arguments. No famine was imminent, they said. No famine is ever predicted, you said. You are of the heir-age, they said. I am stronger with each passing moon and require no heir, you said.

You offered the birthfeast to your court. Most of them ate. Those who refused you marked with a subtle scent, perceptible to your organelles only. They drifted slowly out of favor.

To the few advisors who continued to harangue you, who stirred distrust into the clean guiltless vapors of the Nest, you gave an ancient metonym: *heretic*. You understood it was important to apply it to them before they might apply it to you.

Your warriors, so swollen in rank, were glad to have fresh quarry.

The heretics were despised. The heretics were hunted.

You watch through your puppet as the crowds gather. Your people are so graceful, so lifelike, that when you were young you fooled yourself into thinking they had minds like your own, that their saltways led to a hidden lattice of deep thought, a sparking nebula of fantasy and agony and ecstasy.

This proved false. You still recall the day in the eastern extremity of the Nest, where a fortress was being built: You saw a worker plodding in circles, confused by a mislaid pheromone trail, and instead of comforting their sibling, instead of showing them their error, the other workers began to join them.

An entire maniple of your best laborers, trapped in a blind spiral, chasing each other endlessly. You were so young you thought it was a pattern-dance, a performance for your own entertainment.

Then the warriors, who'd been guarding the inchoate construction, grew enraged—not by the pheromonal error, which they could not perceive, but by the vagaries of space and motion. Their patrol route had been interrupted by the diverted workers. They leapt upon their siblings and tore at them with their tusks.

Monodeath, monodeath, monodeath, and the plodding circle persisted. You realized then it was no performance. You realized there was no reason or feeling inside your children, only chemical obedience. Your advisors suggested you weep, so you did, and your vapors finally calmed the chaos.

These, at least, were like you: your courtiers and advisors and augurs. Some had even existed before you. Their exobone was pocked and marred by the spiral of time, by the unending hunt of Te for Yo. But slowly you began to find the cracks in them, as well. Their clumsy repetition of rites; their slavish devotion to the glyphs that they seemed to discover anew each time rather than hold in their minds.

You took a courtier to your rooms, and they offered no protest when you prised open their exobone skull. There was no lattice inside, only a small pale bulb, purposed to receive rather than extrapolate. You began to understand that all their flashes of cleverness, deviousness, maneuvering, had been born in your mind first.

You hung their monodead bulb on your wall, as a reminder.

Now, as you watch your children prepare for the birthfeast, watch their anticipation and longing, you know some part of yourself has painted it across their internal void.

The soft things grew in number, and, you imagined, in determination. One was destined to be your successor, so said the glyph you had long since pounded into shard and splinter. Your own traitorous womb seemed to agree and so sought to better their chances by multiplying their ranks.

But they were destined only for the birthfeast, the celebration upon which the Nest now hinged itself. You crafted the ceremony, the spectacle, even though your unthinking children needed no persuasion. You made it a celebration of your own cleverness and fortitude: You would not bend to the glyphs, or to the womb. The soft darting things might come by hundreds, and still, none would overtake you.

As Te chased Yo, moon after moon, that feeling began to shift. Triumph withered like unblooded exobone. Your saltways grew jagged and anxious. You birthed your warriors and workers and courtiers, your augurs and advisors, crop after crop of shadows.

You extended the Nest past its historical boundaries, sent scouts across the moon-scoured deserts, searching for something, anything, not of yourself. Anything with mind and intention. Anything but the soft darting things in your womb, that recurred and recurred. You found only buried husks of cities long extinct.

You considered, many times, giving way. Stepping from the pheromone trail, allowing your successor to pass. You dreamed of it in chemicals: a soft darting thing finishing its growth in air, not womb, and perhaps speaking with you—a true conversation, a blind and terrifying and exhilarating plunge—before it dealt you your monodeath.

But you did not recall any such conversation in your earliest memory. Your own progenitor had left no impression; this meant your own successor would absorb nothing of you, either. You would join the monodead and be forgotten, unloved and unsensed by the thousands trodding your repurposed exobone.

Your successor would begin the cycle anew.

It is time at last. You feel your distant womb split. You watch through the withering puppet as the birthfeast spills outward in a gushing pink tide, across the stone street, a scurrying mass. But your other children, so simple, so hungry, do their duty.

The Nest rejoices. Workers and warriors alike fall on the spores. Frenzied by pheromones, they are gluttonous, barbarous. They chase the wriggling newbirths and scoop them up into their slavering mouths. The warriors impale them on whetted tusks; the workers pull their soft bodies to shreds with deft hands.

Gore soon speckles the promenade. The spores attempt to flee, but their tiny limbs are barely flagella, beating clumsily against the air, finding no purchase on the bile-slick stone. For all their cleverness, they are helpless. And in a way—the thought is heavy as mercury—in a way, you are protecting them.

They will know brief agony as they are cut, crushed, chewed, but they will never know the long agony. They will never trudge through the eons as their children race, clutch after clutch growing and decaying.

They will never feel the loneliness at the center of all things.

The puppet's saltways have eroded past usefulness, so, finally, you return to your body. The womb is gone. Only a few shriveled shreds cling to your aching spine. Your eyepores are still skinned shut. You are exhausted in your entirety: exobone, flesh, each laboring organ.

But the clamor is gone. You are alone in the dark again, and the misery of it makes you certain of your decision. You will never place another thinking being, so unlike the automatons who adore you, into such a horrible orbit. There is an alternative. A softer fate. At long last, you are certain what became of the other cities, those buried in fragments beneath the burning plain.

When your own body finally decays, it will not be monodeath that comes for you. It will be true death, the sacred icon hidden deepest in the Nest's most ancient layer. You will cease. Your unthinking children will cease.

All will crumble and dissolve away, leaving behind an empty city, whispering to itself. As eons pass, as mindless Te hunts mindless Yo through a sulfurous sky, eventually those saltways will fall silent as well.

It will be better this way. It might even be beautiful.

MAJOR TRANSITIONS

A Record of Reorganization of
Individuality in the Colonial
Organisms of Earth

STEPHEN
FRANCIS MANN

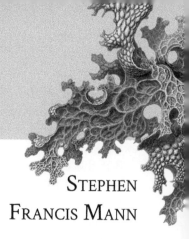

You are, we shall assume, intelligent. You make plans, perceive obstacles, concoct strategies, gather information, synthesize disparate lines of evidence with a sensitivity to context so subtle that even our most powerful computers are hopeless in comparison with your flexibility of thought. And you can do all that virtually subconsciously. You don't need to reflect on the fact that you must find a gap in the fence if you want to retrieve the ball on the other side—an inferential leap too great for some mammals. When your sister is rifling through the kitchen cupboards, you effortlessly attribute to her the desire for biscuits and the false belief that there are biscuits to be found. You are essentially a mind reader. What's more, you are a mind *jumper*: you can feel your sister's disappointment toward her missing snack, sense her frustration as she hunts in vain. These capacities are second nature to you, as they are to the vast majority of humans. You possess extraordinary powers of thought, without even thinking about them.

But that's not to say you are not self-aware. Quite the opposite: you can reflect on your own thoughts, assess your beliefs, critique your opinions, lament your desires. The human propensity for reflective judgment can reach almost crippling levels when turned inward, an introspective death spiral to which more primitive creatures cannot fall victim. Intelligence is a double-edged sword. Its emergence in the evolutionary record often seems to us like a hard-won victory, the thing the world was waiting for. But it might be more appropriate to treat it as an aberration. Socrates is supposed to have said, "The unexamined life is not worth living" [10]. But so much of life, its teeming masses and scurrying hordes, goes forever unexamined. Is it not worth living? It is certainly successful, on its own terms. In trying to justify an unhealthy and ultimately fatal obsession with self-reflection, Socrates comes across as desperate. Perhaps the more accurate view is that of Emil

Cioran [2], who suffered from a similar obsession: "Consciousness is nature's nightmare."

And that's before we consider the possibility, raised with deft and evocative horror in "Heavy Lies," of being the only intelligent creature in existence.

Let us step back a pace and consider the road that brought us here. Popular depictions of evolution begin with a single cell floating in the primordial ooze. A four-billion-year time lapse shows this oldest ancestor of ours transmogrifying into creatures of progressively more sympathetic quality: a fish, a frog, a squirrel, a monkey, a chimp, a human. Even setting aside the fallacious teleology—the laughable conceit that humans are what evolution was trying to produce all along—these stories unerringly have one glaring omission. The most significant steps in evolution were the *major transitions in individuality* [9,14]. On a few vanishingly rare but historically critical occasions, it became beneficial for pairs or groups of living things to work together. Their partnerships achieved, then transcended, symbiosis; *they* became *it*, a new thing under the sun. As far as we can tell, one of the first times this happened was when some unfathomably ancient cell attacked and swallowed another, smaller one. The victim turned out to be better than food. Instead of being digested, the swallowed cell lodged inside the body of its attacker and began to produce energy for it. The swallowed was a more efficient powerplant than anything the swallower possessed, and in return for producing useful energy from the raw ingredients its host greedily consumed, the now-entrenched generator gained sanctuary from the nasty, brutish primal soup. Thus did the eukaryotic cell emerge [3].

No less miraculous was the next step toward the familiar panoply of animals, plants, and fungi inhabiting Earth today. Each individual eukaryotic cell got along very well on its own for a while. Each swam, ate, and reproduced, and the powerplants—known today as mitochondria—had become so deeply embedded that they reproduced right along with them. But then came hard times: less food, less living space, more danger from some unknowable predators now lost beyond the horizon of prehistory. When times are hard it pays to stick together. To survive, groups of cells adapted to share food and marshal collective defense. As tough conditions persisted beyond the lifespan of individuals, they aggregated in the next generation too, each ensuring its own offspring stuck to the same group—for in evolutionary terms it is sensible to maximize the benefits of sharing among close kin. In the most extreme circumstances, cells on the physical perimeter of the group managed to forgo reproducing altogether in order to dedicate more resources to defense. The same division-of-labor principle that gave the eukaryotic cell its start now promoted a form of group life so integrated that some individual cells depended on others for the continued existence of their lineage.

Viewed as a consequence of natural selection, that seemingly vicious and unforgivingly individualistic process, this is a staggering achievement. Yet evolution is a game whose scoring system is continually adjusted to take account of newly available trade-offs. A perimeter cell, whose sister "inside" the group can reproduce extensively and safely, might do better to focus on fighting. She will make life safer for her nieces, whose genes she shares. As one widely-supported contemporary interpretation of evolutionary theory emphasizes, what benefits the genotype explains the strategy of the phenotype [4].

All this raises a fascinating question: when does a group become an individual? Although it may be unanswerable, what we do know is that every multicellular organism alive today—including you, me, and everyone we know—is a descendant of one of these collectives. Our bodies are the fruits of an eons-long drive toward extreme division of labor. In addition to specialization for fighting and reproducing, there arose cells dedicated to sensing (nerves), structure (bones), movement (muscle), transportation of resources (blood), and many more. That these cells are incentivized to cooperate is a consequence of evolutionary score-keeping. That they actually manage to do it is a pure miracle. For when the multicellular social contract breaks, it does so in spectacular and frightful ways. Recall that every cell, no matter how specialized, has ancestors dedicated to reproduction. Sometimes that dormant ability flashes to life, and a formerly quiescent cell turns rogue: finding itself in the richly resourced environment of the body, it suddenly begins to replicate. Its clones grow and grow, supplanting the well-behaved order of the body with a mass of indiscriminate tissue we call a tumor. Theoretical perspectives on cancer emphasize the "re-Darwinization" of individual cells, domesticated workers gone atavistically feral [7].

The destruction of the colony in "Heavy Lies" results from a kind of inversion of this tragic formula. The workers continue performing their functions exactly as they should, slavishly (all-too-slavishly) executing their behavioral programs and obeying instructions from their queen. None dares to reproduce because that task is hers alone. With all their eggs in that traitorous basket, they are helpless to prevent her spiral into genocidal tyranny. The situation can be cast as the result of an evolutionary gamble that did not pay off: designating both ovarian and cognitive functions to the same individual. Such power turned out to be too much to bear. (For an exobiological depiction of a eusocial colony pursuing a different solution to the problem of intelligence, see Bruce Sterling's "Swarm" [12].)

Although eusociality on Earth is the result of a major transition similar to Larson's aedificans [1]—at least the third in an ascending chain linking eukaryotes to multicellular organisms to eusocial societies—no ant, bee, termite, or naked mole rat possesses the kind of individual intelligence that could lead to a similar ovary-brain conflation. It may even be misleading to think of earthling eusocial queens as *controlling* their workers and drones. A queen is as much a servant of the colony; its successful reproduction depends on her, and its inhabitants ensure she performs her duty unhesitatingly. It is true, however, that queens often suppress the reproductive capacities of workers [6]. But this activity is driven by the same kind of stimulus-response mechanisms as workers' foraging or soldiers' fighting. Colony intelligence, if there is such a thing, is borne by the colony as a whole, not some subset or individual who controls all others.

Exobiology is informed, in part, by evolutionary theory. Reading "Heavy Lies" gives us cause to wonder what kinds of major transitions are possible, and what risks they entail. It is implied that every colony on Boreas-4 was under the control of a uniquely intelligent leader, each of whom succumbed to suicidal despair. Since overthrow was impossible, the gamble on intelligence was not offset by the hedge of steady, reliable automation. Even the glyphs inscribed physically in the nest, a knowledge-preservation technology seemingly functioning as an external guidance system, were eventually overmastered by the queen.

Centralized intelligence is centralized control: it is efficient but relies on the interests of the powerful remaining aligned with those they govern. On Earth, we have known for a while that the brains of multicellular organisms can betray their bodies. A rat offered an exclusive choice between food and pleasurable stimulation will go hungry [8]. Its behavioral reinforcement mechanisms were designed to make it seek pleasure, and pleasurable things were initially aligned with those that were evolutionarily good: food, water, sex. But environments are fickle, and alignment shifts (especially when human experimenters are around). Building progressively denser brains eventually produces self-awareness. Self-aware creatures are prone to slip their biological bonds, create their own ends and pursue them to the detriment of all that came before.

Elsewhere in this volume, Tessa Fisher lays down a useful principle for exobiology: "Life, ultimately, is a physical process, and will therefore be subject to the same constraints, no matter what form it takes" [5]. I would add that what's true of physics is true of the mathematics under-pinning evolutionary score-keeping. While it is usually beneficial to reproduce, it is sometimes better to specialize in something else. Leave the reproducing to your sister, your cousin, your queen. Where there is life, there will eventually be transitions in individuality. Some of these will be tentative; some may even be reversible [13]. All will involve division of labor, and some will employ centralized control systems. Many won't—plants and fungi get on just as well without brains. But those that do are placing vital bets on long-term alignment of interests.

I conclude by noting that the queen was lonely twice over. Not only were her subjects alien to her, but all other aedifican colonies had been obliterated too. This phenomenon presented a mystery which, since I envisage the aedificans as a nightmarish version of earthling ants, I shall take the liberty of calling the *fourmi paradox*: how can thriving colonies disappear? Exobiology in the twenty-first century is faced with a similar question: where *are* all the thriving colonies? Where are the signals from intelligent life elsewhere in the universe? The fate of Boreas-4 echoes one of the more devastating proposed solutions to the human version of the paradox [11]. Perhaps intelligence is evolution-arily unsustainable, an attractive but failed gambit; perhaps it is the *un*examined life, the steady, reliable automation, that gets the chance to continue indefinitely. In our case, centralized control has placed world-ending power in the care of a handful of heads of nuclear states. It only takes a little alignment slip, a little psychological death-spiral, to prompt annihilation. Whether or not such an outcome is inevitable is a question we only get one chance to answer.

REFERENCES

[1] Bernadou, A., Kramer, B. H., & Korb, J. (2021). "Major Evolutionary Transitions in Social Insects, the Importance of Worker Sterility and Life History Trade-Offs." *Frontiers in Ecology and Evolution*, 9. https://www.frontiersin.org/article/10.3389/fevo.2021.732907

[2] Cioran, E. M. (1995). *Tears and Saints* (I. Zarifopol-Johnston, Trans.). University of Chicago Press.

[3] Cooper, G. M. (2000). "The Origin and Evolution of Cells." *The Cell: A Molecular Approach*. 2nd Edition. https://www.ncbi.nlm.nih.gov/books/NBK9841/

[4] Dawkins, R. (2006). *The Selfish Gene*: 30th Anniversary Edition. OUP Oxford.

[5] Fisher, T. (2022). "Signs of Life (and How to Find Them)." *This volume.*

[6] Holman, L. (2018). "Queen pheromones and reproductive division of labor: A meta-analysis." *Behavioral Ecology*, 29(6), 1199–1209. https://doi.org/10.1093/beheco/ary023

[7] Lean, C., & Plutynski, A. (2016). "The evolution of failure: Explaining cancer as an evolutionary process." *Biology & Philosophy*, 31(1), 39–57. https://doi.org/10.1007/s10539-015-9511-1

[8] Linden, D. J. (2011, July 7). "The Neuroscience of Pleasure." *HuffPost*. https://www.huffpost.com/entry/compass-pleasure_b_890342

[9] Maynard Smith, J., & Szathmáry, E. (1995). *The Major Transitions in Evolution*. OUP Oxford.

[10] Plato. (1965). *The Apology* (B. Jowet, Trans.). Collier.

[11] Pohl, F. (1985). "Fermi and Frost". *Isaac Asimov's Science Fiction Magazine.*

[12] Sterling, B. (1982). "Swarm". *The Magazine of Fantasy & Science Fiction*. Republished in *Crystal Express* (1989) and *Schismatrix Plus* (1996).

[13] Strassmann, J. E., Zhu, Y., & Queller, D. C. (2000). "Altruism and social cheating in the social amoeba Dictyostelium discoideum." *Nature*, 408(6815), 965–967. https://doi.org/10.1038/35050087

[14] West, S. A., Fisher, R. M., Gardner, A., & Kiers, E. T. (2015). "Major evolutionary transitions in individuality." *Proceedings of the National Academy of Sciences*, 112(33), 10112–10119. https://doi.org/10.1073/pnas.1421402112

THE WORLD OF SILVER

TOMÁŠ PETRÁSEK

The groaning of metal had already died away, and the ship was ominously silent. A gust of cold air touched Kat's face. She opened her watering eyes, blinking in the silvery light filtering through the starboard window.

Only when she attempted to move did she become aware of the pain. Moving her head hurt like hell. Something else wasn't quite right, too, and it wasn't just her sense of balance. The shuttle was tilted at some weird angle. She remembered little of the actual landing, but it had to be really rough. She might have broken something. She'd better wait for the crew, or a rescue squad, whichever came first.

Another waft of icy cold. It was so gentle she hardly felt it, yet the cold was like a slap to the face. Wind. Inside a spacecraft. A gentle reminder of being seriously fucked.

Kat fumbled for the oxygen mask and strapped it to her face, taking a deep breath. She blinked the tears away. The aft side of the cargo bay was seemingly undamaged, but the acceleration seat prevented her from looking anywhere else. She loosened her straps, only now becoming aware of the tingling bruises underneath.

She hung from the tilted seat at an awkward angle, but finally with a struggle, she managed to turn toward the crew compartment. Or at least, where the crew compartment was supposed to be. Because the hatch in the middle of the crumpled bulkhead was cracked open, revealing only a solid wall of ice. The flight cabin was gone. Snow drifted in through the fissures with the gusts of stinging asphyxiant wind.

As Kat recovered from the initial shock, she realized no one would come to rescue her. Not in time. She was alone and had to act quickly. She needed to get a proper oxygen tank before all the air leaked from the ship. Get a proper suit before she became hypothermic. Get out a call for help. Everything she needed was here, in the cargo bay. There was also that huge, bulky box of stainless steel and glass.

The thing inside was watching her.

Two days ago, Kat had thought it couldn't get any worse. The station in orbit of Arzhinnis was completely upside down for several days—not that the phrase made any sense in zero G.

Refugees from the war with the corporates were streaming planet-side, ship crews in the opposite direction. One day there was talk about evacuation and scuttling the station, the next day defense measures were to be taken.

Anyway, it was a bad time to be a life support engineer. In that mess, no one cared about her working hours, and her job description came to include omnipresence and omnipotence, or so it seemed. She was dead tired and sleep deprived when that snotty boffin girl turned up, acting as if she was in command, making nonsensical requests.

Much less would've been enough for Kat to send her where the sun didn't shine, and Kat was grumpy enough to say so. Unfortunately, the girl returned with Kat's boss, the chief engineer, to make it clear that as far as Kat was concerned, the girl actually *was* in command, and that the reassignment was all some secret geological survey business. It was one of the paradoxes of the day that the geological service happened to be the closest thing Arzhinnis, the planet, had to an army, which only illustrated how perfectly fucked their planet was.

Nevertheless, Kat couldn't refuse them. Even if she was desperately needed in a thousand different places and their orders were nothing short of batshit crazy.

"There's a fucking war out there, and you want me to build a fucking fridge?" Kat exclaimed, once she saw the blueprints.

Dani—that was the girl's name—politely pretended not to understand some of the words she used. She wasn't there to explain, just to ensure Kat followed the specifications.

Shortly after, Kat protested again. "Are you all crazy? No way I am putting this inside the crew area. Ammonia tanks? Carbon monoxide? Hydrogen cyanide? Methane? Do you have any idea what this shit would do if there's a leak?"

Dani shrugged, somewhat knowingly, as it seemed. But not a word of explanation. It was all some top secret shit. Absurdly, they wanted the entire system in overpressure, to make it even more fail-deadly than it had to be. Not to mention the tight deadline, with no time for proper testing. Kat refused to collaborate on these terms unless they told her the purpose of this weird assignment.

Dani turned up with her superior, an aloof, white-haired woman she addressed simply as Professor, who acknowledged Kat's point and authorized Dani to explain.

"The chamber is for a specimen, one we have secretly transported from Megan. We need to get it down to Arzhinnis quickly."

That left Kat agape, once she figured out what this specimen would be. She had heard there were native life forms on the moon, Megan, despite the frigid temperatures and dense, poisonous atmosphere, but she couldn't wrap her mind around the idea of someone crazy enough to try to bring them anywhere else. They couldn't have picked a worse time for this sort of stunt even if they tried. On the other hand, a fridge-gas chamber hybrid with precise environmental control was exactly what you would need to do that. What they demanded was that Kat build a life-support system of a very perverted sort.

The last Kat had heard, the beasts of Megan were killing humans on sight. They were quite adept at it, and this—together with the generally unhealthy conditions on that moon—forced the corporate forces to withdraw from Megan. She wasn't aware of anybody attempting to land there ever since.

Once she had been included in the circle of those in the know, the professor decided Kat would accompany the "specimen" onboard the landing shuttle—her staying on the station was considered a safety risk for the mission, and a technician would come handy in case the makeshift chamber full of deadly chemicals decided to leak during landing. That was how she ended up in this shuttle wreck in the middle of icy nowhere.

Kat extracted herself painfully from her seat harness and dropped the short distance to the upturned ceiling of the shuttle. Once suited, Kat tried the radio, but no luck. She had to get out. She climbed out the emergency hatch. The shuttle—what was left of it—was precariously wedged inside a huge icy crevasse full of howling wind. A long climb up, and an even longer fall if it dislodged. The manuals recommended staying near the wreckage, as it was supposed to maximize the chances of survival and discovery. But in this case, staying would definitely minimize both.

She came back in and assembled all the supplies she could muster. Oxygen, fuel cells, food, enough for several days. Getting it out of the crevasse would be a challenge, but she was confident. She had an engineering degree, duct tape, and a safety line. What could possibly go wrong?

Then, she met the gaze of the thing behind the glass. No, not exactly. Its fist-sized eyes were set on stalks, and with their complex pupils, it was hard to tell precisely where they were looking. But it was alert, nervous perhaps, judging from twitching of its eyestalks and olfactory tentacles. It had apparently survived the crash. If it hadn't, leaving it there would've been easier.

Kat's first sight of the thing was vaguely revolting and definitely terrifying. It was a furry, mud-colored lump of a body with four spindly legs, crouched to fit inside the life-support chamber she'd built. Jointed eyestalks unfolded from the dorsal side of the nearly spherical body. It also had an appendage Kat at first considered to be the head, though Dani explained it lacked all the things a proper head should have and was only good for eating and sniffing.

"How in the world did you capture that thing?" Kat exclaimed, shaken. The creature seemed to be well equipped as far as claws were concerned.

"They are called the Azhar, actually," explained Dani. "And this one wasn't captured. Sort of an envoy, I'd call it."

Kat stared at her, trying to tell if she was joking. She wasn't.

Kat watched anxiously as the thing examined its temporary home. Too small? Too warm? Too little carbon monoxide? She could only guess.

Then it turned itself backwards . . . By turning the eyes around, it made the former rear a new front. What had previously looked like a thin, flexible tail with a spiny club at the end turned out to be something like a single dexterous arm. From a human point of view, this shift of perspective was particularly disconcerting. Which way was it actually facing, having no face at all?

Undisturbed, it began to make itself at home. In the long hours before the departure, it adorned the walls of its dwelling (much to Kat's disapproval) with scratches (who would think its dangerous-looking claws could scratch steel?) and lines drawn with a black tarry substance it excreted. When Kat referred to it as a pigment, Dani laughed and explained that the proper scientific term was *faeces*. But even she couldn't explain the meaning of the squiggles. Later, the alien almost filled its cell with a thicket of cobweb-like fibers, through which it was hardly visible. At that time, Kat thought of it as an animal, some monstrous spider perhaps, its behavior a complete enigma.

In hindsight, at least the cobwebs made sense. Better than seatbelts, actually.

"You wait here, understand?" she told the thing, speaking very loud and very slowly. "I go for help." It felt weird speaking to it. Stupid. Even if it was more than an animal, it didn't understand. Yet it was alive—depending on the definition of the term, of course—and leaving it there to die somehow required an excuse.

As she turned to leave the shuttle with her supplies, the thing made an alien sound, something between a screech of nails on metal and a sound of heavily abused bagpipes. Kat understood as little of the alien's vocalization as the alien could of her own speech. She looked back, and the thing was gesticulating wildly. It took Kat a moment to realize it was desperately trying to point at a particular spot, using one appendage after another in apparent hope she would understand. Once she looked at where it'd pointed, it was trivial. The chamber was leaking.

It was probably scared to death. Kat would be, in its place. It didn't know the shuttle's air was already gone—or perhaps even if the lingering traces were enough? Oxygen was a poison to it, just like cyanide to a human.

With a sigh, she foam-sealed the leak. Just putting off the inevitable. The crate's life-support systems were beyond repair and without power, but the nitrogen tank was intact, and she used it to manually increase the pressure inside the creature's chamber to prevent anything from getting in for now.

But the alien had also saved her life, although unwittingly. The seat in the cargo bay had been intended for Dani, not her. Only when it became clear that the capricious apparatus of the chamber she'd hurriedly put together would need attendance much more than the rather stoic alien, they switched places at the last minute before departure. Now, Dani and the crew were probably all dead. Kat was certain the shuttle was shot down by a missile fired by the corporates, which meant they were either the extremely unlucky first victims of a full-out war, or that the corporates had really wanted to stop them and succeeded, despite all the secrecy surrounding the mission. Not that it made any sense. For a secret weapon, the lone alien was too fragile and didn't seem likely to obey anyone's orders.

The ship shook with an unsettling rumble, throwing her off balance. Shaken, she hastened her preparations to leave. The Azhar pressed itself to the window, agitated. It tapped at the glass, trying to get her attention. As if it knew. And perhaps it did.

"I'm sorry," she said, more to herself, packing her stuff. She meant it. The thing—the Azhar—was lost in an alien world, far from home, to be forsaken and left to die in a small leaky box surrounded by certain death. She wondered how long it would last. It wouldn't mind the oxygen-free atmosphere. It might even like the cold. The pressure was definitely high enough for its blood not to boil; the gravity not that much different from its homeworld. There was no methane for it to breathe, but methane was nothing like oxygen for humans. When the methane-replenishing system had broken down and they had to throw away the faulty tank, Dani said it was no big deal for the Azhar, that it would survive until touchdown, as the gas for it was more like food than air. Taken all together, this world wasn't any more hostile for the alien than it was for her.

Kat shook her head. She didn't like the direction of this line of thinking.

"Calm down, calm down," she whispered both to herself and to the agitated creature as she unlocked the chamber's hatch, specifically designed to be difficult to unlock. She had tried to communicate it was no longer dangerous. There were pictograms the Azhar was supposed to know, standing for the most important chemicals. Dani had explained some of them to Kat, so she could understand if the alien was missing something vital. So Kat drew the oxygen symbol, crossing it, waving it away, slapping at her own helmet to show there was none (supposing the creature knew what she breathed). But she saw no sign of understanding in the Azhar's behavior.

Was it frightened? Panicked? Angry? Could it even feel such emotions? Would it kill her once the hatch was opened? Some part of her mind was quite certain it would. Why was she even thinking about letting it go? Her gut feeling told her it was just a freaking alien monster. Not even cute! Well, it was furry in a way, but literally faceless. And yet . . .

The hatch cracked open, deadly gasses hissing out. She was grateful for the suit, although worried the corrosive vapors might damage the resistant fabric.

The alien crouched in the opposite corner, all appendages folded in its fur, which gave it a featureless, almost spherical shape. The non-head appeared briefly, tasting the air with its tentacles and vanishing as if stung. The stalks emerged, huge eyes blinking rapidly, almost painfully. They were watering heavily . . . or perhaps ammoniating would be the better term. White frost began to form around the eyelashes, before the eyes closed and retracted back into the big ball of brownish fur. Only then Kat understood. It was the carbon dioxide from the outside air. It wasn't exactly toxic for the Azhar, but it was acidic. Once, she'd had the opportunity to acquaint herself with sulfur dioxide, which gave her some idea what it could be like. She replaced the hatch and let some nitrogen in. Well, at least she tried everything.

That damned engineering mind of hers! Why did it have to point out all the things she *didn't* try, even the insane ones? Kat tried to explain to herself it was all bound to fail, that she would just prolong the alien's agony and perhaps get herself killed, but to no avail.

Cursing herself, she began collecting all the duct tape she could find.

Kat looked uneasily at the huge clawed being beside her in its makeshift suit of plastic and duct tape, inflated by nitrogen. Making it—and persuading the creature to cooperate—had required more courage and self-denial than Kat had ever thought possible, from her and perhaps from it as well. The suit only covered the body, the non-head and the eyes, but so far it seemed to work well. The Azhar could look at Kat eye to eye when it stood on the shorter, centrally placed pair of limbs. The outer two were much longer, usually folded in a grasshopper-like manner, which made the alien's gait awkward. It had enough claws to shred her to pieces, and her subconscious still screamed in fear. But it hadn't killed her so far and doing so now would make no sense—so she hoped.

Kat took a deep breath and examined the sheer ice wall. She wasn't used to working under gravity, and her suit was made for space, not ice climbing. She pushed her gloved hand and booted foot against the ice several times, but it was impossible to climb even a single step. Getting all the stuff up would be hopeless.

She startled at a sudden touch, almost slipping from the upended belly of the shuttle—the Azhar. She got her balance back, but the creature was still too close for her liking. It tugged at the coil of line she was holding, quite gently for the size of its talons. Hesitantly she let go.

The Azhar stretched its eyes as wide as the suit allowed and, each movement of the alien accompanied by rustling plastic, began to ascend, using its claws as crampons, uncoiling the line as it went using its tailhand. In seconds, it vanished over the edge of the crevasse.

Then it appeared again. Tentatively, Kat pulled on the line. It held her weight. She attached the supplies and made the "thumbs up" sign, as she would to a spacewalk buddy, then felt a little silly. And yet . . .

Arzhinnis was a world of silver. Silvery was the cold cirrus-filled sky, the wind-packed snow, the haze of icy crystals covering the horizon, even the distant sunlight. The dream of making it warm and blue had died generations ago. All the reasonable people had long left for better places—about anywhere you could build a city without all the glaciers, volcanoes, earthquakes, lahars, and whatnot constantly trying to wipe it off the face of the planet. Kat was a descendant of those who had chosen to stay, and this fact alone explained a lot.

On the surface of the glacier there was nothing. No sign of other survivors, no radio signal, no lights on the horizon, no landmarks. Staying put made little sense. With the shuttle command deck destroyed, the radio beacon was probably gone as well, leaving her suit radio their best hope of being discovered. Finding some shelter would help if they were to survive the night. Also, if they managed to walk in a straight line long enough, chances were they would eventually find power lines, steam piping or anything else that would lead them to humans.

Once they'd amassed all they could from the wreckage, they set off, heading what she figured out to be east, using plastic panels from the shuttle as sledges to carry their belongings. They only stopped to tape the occasional leaks in the Azhar's suit and to refill it with nitrogen. The alien couldn't breathe the gas, but it kept the carbon dioxide away.

Their progress was slow, although time lost all meaning here. The haze eventually turned to complete whiteout. Unable to see the sun, Kat lost her sense of direction. They could be walking in circles without ever noticing.

A sudden jerk on the line pulled Kat forward to her knees. Instinctively, she leaned backwards and dug her heels into the icy snow, holding the Azhar's weight. The rope ahead of her vanished in a crevasse, hidden under the snowdrifts. She was in pain and exhausted, and not sure if she could pull the alien out.

But the Azhar scrambled out in a minute. Kat had had a really hard time persuading it to let her tie them together with the rope. Now, at least, the alien saw what it was good for. No way to tell if it was grateful. They tested the snow, found a hard snow bridge that would bear their weight, and trudged on.

Kat was becoming tired and cold, terribly cold—the air was so dense that the spacesuit insulation, designed for hard vacuum, wasn't enough in the blasting winds.

Her companion once drew in the snow the glyph for methane, but they didn't have any. She had to explain the contents of every gas tank in their possession and felt vaguely ashamed that most of them were oxygen.

After another hour or so, the alien seemed to spot something. It suddenly changed direction. Kat was too drained to argue. She followed. After a good while, she discerned dark rocks and a rising vapor plume mixing with the blizzard.

It wasn't the first time she wondered about the Azhar's sense of sight. Its native atmosphere was mostly opaque to humans, so it probably sensed infrared. Perhaps even thermal infrared—which could explain why it had eyes outside its body, to stay as cool as possible. Ammonia-based blood and interstitial fluids would mean the Azhar wouldn't have to worry about its eyes freezing over.

Kat's high hopes were somewhat quenched once they got there. No settlement there, not even a geothermal powerplant. No help. It was just a small hot spring area on a patch of elevated, rocky ground, perhaps the foreland of an ice-locked continent. But at least it was something. Warmth—meaning she might be able to survive the night to come. And perhaps . . .

She removed a portable spectrometer from her toolbox and checked the gas rising from the bubbling pool of water. She smiled as she drew the methane sign before the closely watching alien. The gas had bought them both a little time.

They spent the rest of the evening building igloos. The Azhar wasn't familiar with the technique and was fascinated by the small field spade she used for cutting bricks out of the compacted snow. But it

soon got the idea—it seemed to be a born tool-user. A surprising observation, given that its species had purportedly never got beyond stone
age. Together they built a half-cupola leaning against a rock, above a
small methane seep. Kat hoped it would create a vaguely breathable
atmosphere for the Azhar.

Fortunately, it worked—the alien untaped the front of its suit, and
after a lot of tentacling, it decided to open its breathing slits. As it
shuddered, inflated and deflated, it gave Kat some idea what a blissful
Azhar looked like. The alien also took some of its foodstuffs, something
fibrous that had to be wetted in ammonia before consumption. It
offered some to Kat first, but she politely refused. That stuff was
so rich in nitrates and nitro-groups it would only be of interest to a
pyrotechnician.

It wasn't easy to persuade the Azhar to let her out of its shelter, as it
meant letting some nasty carbon dioxide in. But she needed to build an
igloo for herself before nightfall if she were to survive. The Azhar didn't
help this time, and she didn't press it, perhaps because it was in worse
shape than she was. In her own abode, she opened her suit. It was still
freezing inside, but survivable, as it sheltered her from the wind. No
oxygen, though, so she had to take sips from the mask. The outside air
she couldn't avoid inhaling every now and then, and it smelled terribly—not of methane, which was odorless, but of hydrogen sulfide. The
first task, not very dignified, was changing diapers, as after the long
day she was extremely uncomfortable. Then she ate some yeast bars,
carefully alternating between breathing and eating, and melted some
snow with a small stove, to drink.

The Arzhinnian night lasted almost thirty hours. When she wasn't
asleep, she tried the radio, and walked around a little, but the cold of
the night was unbearable any distance from the hot spring. She'd had
to sleep suited—with just a mask, it would be too easy for it to slip
from her face and let her suffocate without even knowing. At dawn, she
jerked awake at the distant thundering of a craft.

She burst out of the igloo, into a cold, gray, hazy morning. She
searched the sky for some sign of a craft, but there was no sign that the
sound was even real. Had their rescuers spotted them at all?

She found the Azhar outside, suited. She noted it managed to learn
how to deal with duct tape. Not exactly a cobweb, but perhaps close

enough. But the makeshift suit protected it only to some extent. Outside the tape cuffs, its skin was flaking and the hair falling out. The soles of its feet were covered in bluish scabs. The acidic atmosphere and pure water ice with no ammonia were caustic and taking their toll.

She hoped the Azhar would be okay again once it got to the secret facility waiting for it—somewhere. She hoped the geological survey people or whoever was in charge there would allow her to stay, to participate in the project, perhaps. She didn't even know the name of the alien, or its sex (if it had one). She would love to know, but asking could wait. For now, she tried to explain the idea of being rescued, even drew a human figure in the snow. "Humans! Coming! Humans like me!"

The Azhar climbed a rock, then jumped down and ran off into the hazy murk of the plains. It was gone. No, it appeared again. It ran up and nudged her back toward the camp.

"What did you see?" Kat asked anxiously. Again, she tried to draw a human.

The Azhar snorted and erased her drawing, leaving a blue smudge of unearthly blood on the snow. Very carefully, it made three circular marks forming an equilateral triangle, all the time fervently gesticulating, squealing, rocking backward and forward.

Kat frowned. It was impossible to read the emotional expressions of a non-mammal, and she didn't know the symbol either. The alien pushed her toward the rocks behind its igloo. Once there, it repeated the triangular drawing. Then it made just one mark and tapped at Kat's helmet. Then pointed back at the triangle, emphasizing the gesture with a series of short staccato barks.

"Me—one? Three? Three humans? Over there?" She felt frustrated by the communication barrier. Their rescue might be at stake!

She turned around. She saw indistinct shapes in the low-lying haze—human shapes? So they found them, after all? She would hug and kiss the alien, if she only could, out of pure joy! It might have been afraid of the newcomers, perhaps understandably, so be it. Anyway, it would be better for her to make the greeting. They might be just a regular search-and-rescue squad, not acquainted with the secret mission. The Azhar could seem a little menacing to an unexpecting person.

She pushed the alien aside and ran toward the four suited men, waving until they spotted her and turned in her direction. Then she hesitated and frowned in apprehension.

Something was wrong.

The suits were of a type completely unknown to her. She stood, watching them approach.

As they got closer, she noticed they had three headlights, instead of just one she had on her helmet. Suddenly, she figured out the meaning of the alien's drawing. It knew those suits well. These humans were from its homeworld, where its kind had led a bloody war against the corporates. *Oh shit!*

Now she was staring down the barrel of a gun.

They took anything she might use as a weapon, and then prodded her toward her camp.

"Where are the others? And where's the cargo?" The voice crackled over short-range radio in her helmet.

The cargo. That could only mean the Azhar. This was the only thing they were after. Cursing herself inwardly, she tried playing a lone survivor, ignorant of the mission, but they had already found the wreckage and wouldn't buy it—especially not after they saw the two igloos and two sledges. While the one who appeared to be in command was holding her at gunpoint, two of his men kicked the igloos open and ransacked the stuff around the camp.

The officer kicked her to the ground. "Surrender!" he called through the radio, to her presumptive companion hidden among the rocks, "or I kill her! I'll count to ten!"

No response. Just as well. They would kill her in the end, no matter what.

Run. Hide, she wished to shout. No need to, though. The alien wasn't stupid . . . At least it wasn't as stupid as she was.

A short sharp bark, a jolt, and agonizing pain!

In terror she realized she was just shot in the leg. There was a hiss as oxygen escaped from the hole in her suit.

She would really die here, alone in the cold, unforgiving world of silver.

"Where have you hidden the cargo?" pressed the officer, this time aiming at her faceplate.

Whoosh!

Kat writhed on the ground to turn her head in the direction of the sound. The two men who just returned from the camp were down, one of them completely limp, the other desperately struggling with something like . . . *cans?*

The officer didn't understand either, apparently. He was examining a spade stuck deep in the throat of the man beside him. His attempt to raise his rifle to face the four greenish talons coming at him from the silvery sky was desperately slow. He died before he had time to pull the trigger.

Through a haze of endorphins, Kat watched the alien make sure all the soldiers were dead, while keeping a safe distance—it knew the risk of oxygen. She realized the Azhar had already done all this before, and through all the pain she smiled.

Then the Azhar came to her.

"Don't go near me," she made the oxygen sign. She applied the sealing foam to the bullet hole in her suit, but without success. She was still losing air. And blood.

The alien withdrew but returned minutes later. She smiled at it through tears of pain, glad that it came but still trying to shoo it away . . .

It carried a roll of duct tape.

Ignoring the danger, the alien applied the tape at the tear, wrapping it around her leg, with a skill worthy of an engineer. Its tailhand was actually better suited for finding the end of the tape than a human hand. She felt proud for some reason. You could build civilizations with stuff like this.

Dizzy from the blood loss, she tried to show what needed to be done. The Azhar understood, producing a thick strand of cobweb and using it as a tourniquet on her suited leg. Water or ammonia, as long as you have blood, the principle is pretty much the same . . .

Too much force, she thought, before she passed out.

The world was upside down, and it was rocking wildly. She realized the alien had strapped her to its back—upside down. Perhaps it seemed like a good idea to it. Perhaps it even was, given that it was her leg she was bleeding from.

Below her, there was the eternal silvery sky. But above, the ubiquitous dullness of the snow was broken by splotches of vivid red. Overlooking the carnage they left behind, she was beginning to understand why they had brought the alien here, why now—and why the enemy strove to stop them so badly.

Yes, who wouldn't like to have troops like this: fast, deadly, invisible in the infrared, capable of living off the land? Yet it had been an obvious non-starter, from the very beginning. Because what—in any world—could bring any living being to lay down its life, in a foreign world, for the sake of a foreign species, even if it weren't as unfathomably alien as an earthling must have been to an Azhar?

No force and no price were great enough. Evidently, there couldn't be any such reason. And yet . . .

Perhaps there was, now. With that thought, Kat finally passed out.

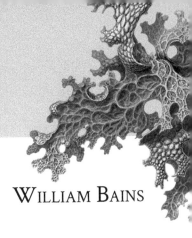

WET WET WET

WILLIAM BAINS

ere's the problem. We have one example of an inhabited planet, inhabited by one example of life. Just one. Everything we say about life on other worlds is balanced on that one data point. It is not a great start.

Life on Earth is astonishingly diverse. It encompasses elephants and dust mites and redwoods and mushrooms and liverworts and brewers' yeast, and so many bacteria that probably only a fraction of a percent have been detected, let alone characterized. Active life is found from near the top of Mount Everest to the rocks below the Challenger deep. But all that life shows an astonishing chemical unity. It all has DNA (except for some viruses using its close sibling RNA), it all has proteins made out of the same handful of amino acids. It uses variations on the same metabolism. And it all uses water. Every single form of life on Earth, no matter how broadly you define life, needs water to live, grow, and reproduce.

Why water? Well, let's start from what life is. Life is a thing that makes more life. Giraffes make baby giraffes. Mice make baby mice. If we come across a patch of daffodils nodding in the spring sunshine, we know that they came from a daffodil bulb, not an acorn or an egg. By contrast non-living things are made by processes that are not part of those things. If we find a silica nodule next to our daffodils, it could have been precipitated out of water or crystallized out of rock or made by diatoms in an ancient ocean. Non-life is stuff; life has history, it has genetics, it has inheritance. Life makes itself.

To achieve that self-making—autopoiesis—life has to take in ingredients from the environment, select stuff it needs (including a source of energy to make all this work) and throw away what is not needed. Life needs to eat and poop. Between the eating and pooping, there is a lot of very complicated chemistry, which requires a solvent, something to dissolve all those molecules and allow them to move, interact, and react. A gas is no good, as larger molecules would literally fall out of it. A solid does not allow molecules to move around. So life needs a liquid.

The three most common elements in the cosmos are hydrogen, helium, and oxygen. Arguably water—H_2O—is one of the most common substances in the universe after hydrogen (H_2) and helium. Helium does not form molecules, and only forms a liquid below -268 °C. Hydrogen is a bit better, but even that only forms a liquid below -235 °C. These two would only form liquids at the temperatures of interstellar space. This makes sense as, generally, the larger a molecule is, the higher the boiling point of the pure liquid it can form (compare methane with one carbon vs octane with eight).

But water is liquid at an astonishingly high temperature. Based on its molecular weight it should boil at about -170 °C, but water does not even melt until 0 °C, which means that chemical reactions happen fast in water, because heat makes chemistry happen faster (think fire). Water also dissolves things. Again, as a generality, those cold solvents like hydrogen and methane only dissolve molecules of the same sort of size as hydrogen and methane. There are not many such molecules to choose from. But hot solvents like water can dissolve huge molecules like sugars and proteins, and the structure of liquid water favors the formation of stable structures for proteins, as well as the lipid membranes that surround cells. It forms hydrogen bonds—weak chemical bonds between the H in H_2O and the O in many other molecules, which greatly helps proteins and sugars bind to each other, forming the networks necessary for life's larger structures. If you want to do complicated chemistry, water seems great. Many scientists consider water not merely the best solvent for life, but the only possible solvent.

What about liquid methane, present as lakes on the surface of Titan? It will not dissolve salts at all, and as the metal ions present in salts are critical to life as we know it, that is a problem. In fact, liquid methane hardly dissolves anything, and that is because it is *cold*. And chemistry happens really slowly in liquid methane.

But what about ammonia? It also has a complex liquid structure, can dissolve salts, and boils at a balmy -33 °C—much of the surface of Mars, even the surface of Antarctica in winter, is colder than that. And ammonia can support chemistry that even water cannot do. You can dissolve sodium metal in ammonia, and then use that to react with many organic molecules. Sodium and water just give you a fireball. Liquid ammonia forms hydrogen bonds and allows lipid membranes to form. How about life based on ammonia instead of water?

Here we run up against cosmic abundance. Ammonia is NH_3. Nitrogen is nine times less abundant than oxygen, but ammonia is far rarer than water on rocky planets for a chemical reason. Ammonia is easily broken down to nitrogen and hydrogen by UV light from the Sun (or any other star). So is water, but that forms oxygen and hydrogen which of course react very easily to form water again. Not so nitrogen and hydrogen. Nitrogen gas is incredibly stable, and so any ammonia in the atmosphere of a planet under a sun gets broken down over time, and the nitrogen in the ammonia ends up as nitrogen gas, and there it stays. In the solar system, ammonia is only found in gas giants (where it is recycled deep in their atmospheres at temperatures and pressures we can be grateful we never experience) and in the frozen ices of those planets' moons. Bring those moons nearer to the Sun, thaw them out (like Europa in *2010: Odyssey Two*), and their ammonia starts to disappear.

And last, ammonia is very soluble in water, water is very soluble in ammonia, and water is more common than ammonia. So we are very unlikely to find worlds with pure ammonia oceans. Rather, we will find ammonia+water mixtures, with water dominating and, eventually, becoming the only liquid there as the ammonia is broken down.

Unless—and here is the kicker—life steps in. Because life might turn that hydrogen and nitrogen back into ammonia, a process that it can use to gain energy. (We have called such a biosphere a Cold Haber World, after the industrial Haber process that makes ammonia.) Then our ammoniacal world would have water+ammonia ocean in perpetuity, and the Azhar in Tomáš Petrásek's "World of Silver" could evolve.

Kat does not specify what the Azhar is made of, and here we come to another of the arguments in astrobiology. All Earth life is based on the chemistry of carbon, and there seems to be a good reason for that. Carbon is the fourth most abundant element, and it forms an unlimited range of chains and rings bonded to itself or other elements. No other element has that flexibility . . . in water. But is this the barrier we think it is? Bacteria live at 120 °C in volcanic vents on the sea floor, temperatures at which several key molecules of life should break down in minutes. Organisms are known that grow at -5 °C, where the chemistry of life should hardly happen at all. Organisms have even been found that have adapted to the intense radiation inside the Chernobyl "sarcophagus." Some of these push the limits of what we understand carbon chemistry can achieve, but we know it does because we can see it. For over 200 years, chemists have tried to make interesting molecules, and the ones that are complex *and* stable in water are almost all carbon-based, so we think that carbon-based chemistry is the most likely chemistry for life, if water (or ammonia) has to be a solvent for life. But that is based on our experience, our imagination, and that single example of life we have. The universe may yet surprise us.

What about other features of the environment Kat is asked to build? Carbon monoxide is highly poisonous to almost all Earth's animals, but only because of a peculiarity in the way we use oxygen in our metabolism. Some bacteria are fine with it, and even use it as fuel. Similarly with hydrogen cyanide—it has killed many a murder mystery victim but is fine for some organisms. And there are many bacteria for which oxygen is a lethal poison, as it is for the alien Azhar. There are bacteria that "eat" methane, oxidizing it with nitrates, as the Azhar apparently do.

In fact, a lot of the Azhar's chemistry seems quite plausible. But there is one hugely improbable assumption about the Azhar. Did you spot it? It is not weird chemistry, or weird anatomy. Yes, mammals have boringly similar anatomy—two eyes, a mouth below them, some version of four limbs with five digits on each limb, but other animals have eyes and limbs and mouths all over the place. The real leap of faith is the Azhar's intelligence. The Azhar are adept tool users and tool makers, but their culture has not got beyond the stone age. How long did humans have that combination, before tool use led to the technology we have today? Cave art, complex tools, decorated shells, and traces of counting all have appeared in the last half of a million years; before that, humans seem to have just been an unusually creative ape. Let's be generous and say for half a million years, up to ~20,000 years ago, humans had the same sort of culture as the Azhar's. Let us also be really generous and say that one in ten Sun-like stars has an Earth-like planet *and* life evolved on that planet *and* it was habitable long enough for complex life to arise. (Remember Mars—it was habitable, but not for long enough.) The Earth is expected to be habitable for another 2-3 billion years before the expansion of the Sun reduces it to red hot desert; then it will have been habitable for about 7 billion years. How many Sun-like stars do we have to visit to find a stone-age intelligence? On those numbers alone, it is 70,000 stars. Sun-like stars are not that common, and we do have to visit them, every one, because stone-age intelligence is not detectable from space. And if the Azhar's people had evolved beyond the stone age—had developed agriculture and sailing ships and steam engines and cheap fusion and stardrives—why they would be visiting us, not vice versa.

We do not know how long intelligence lasts. Perhaps races all over the universe rise to a level of intelligence like ours, and then knock themselves back to the stone age, like humanity does in Fredric Brown's classic story "Letter to a Phoenix." If so, "stone age" cultures could be common. Perhaps humans are unique, and most intelligent races spend millions of years in developmental stages we zip through in centuries, more carefully evaluating and adapting to each step before taking the next. Or perhaps there is an escape clause somewhere, that sometime in the coming centuries we will settle down and live peacefully with each other and with the Earth for millions of years. I would like to hope so, because wouldn't it be a shame if all that chemistry on all those worlds had not, somewhere, given rise to something that breathed methane and swam in watery ammonia and could write science fiction?

FURTHER READING

Life in Other Liquids

National Research Council. (2019). *The Limits of Organic Life in Planetary Systems*. Washington, DC, USA: The National Academy of Press. Near definitive overview of "Weird Life" chemistry and solvents.

Bains, William. (2004). "Many chemistries could be used to build living systems." Discusses ammonia, methane and nitrogen as potential solvents. I have become less optimistic about cold solvents since then.

Bains, W., Petkowski, J. J., Zhan, Z., & Seager, S. (2021). "Evaluating alternatives to water as solvents for life: The example of sulfuric acid." *Life*, 11(5), 400. Life in sulfuric acid?

McKay, C.; Smith, H. (2005). "Possibilities for methanogenic life in liquid methane on the surface of Titan." *Icarus* 2005, 178, 274–276. Life in liquid methane?

Possible "Rules" and Limits on the Chemistry of Life

Benner, Steven A., Alonso Ricardo, and Matthew A. Carrigan. (2004). "Is there a common chemical model for life in the universe?" *Current opinion in chemical biology* 8.6, 672-689. Classic on the chemical requirements for any life.

Schulze-Makuch, Dirk and Lewis Irvin. (2006). "The prospect of alien life in exotic forms on other worlds." *Naturwissenschaften* 93, 155–1 72. Review of different chemistries and solvents. Rather over-optimistic about silicon in my view.

Petkowski, Janusz Jurand, William Bains, and Sara Seager. (2020). "On the potential of silicon as a building block for life." *Life* 10.6, 84. Is life based on silicon possible? Probably not. . . .

Cold Haber Worlds

Seager, S., Bains, W., & Hu, R. (2013). "Biosignature gases in H2-dominated atmospheres on rocky exoplanets." *The Astrophysical Journal*, 777(2), 95. General discussion of detecting life on a planet with an H2 atmosphere, introduces "Haber World."

The Earliest Counting and Art

Shumaker, R. W., K. R. Walkup and B. B. Beck. (2011). *Animal Tool Behavior: The Use and Manufacture of Tools by Animals*. Baltimore, MD, USA: Johns Hopkins University Press. Highly detailed book on animal tool use.

Von Petzinger, G. (2017). *The first signs: Unlocking the mysteries of the world's oldest symbols*. Simon and Schuster. Imaginative history of symbolic art.

Brumm, A., Oktaviana, A. A., Burhan, B., Hakim, B., Lebe, R., Zhao, J. X., . . . & Aubert, M. (2021). "Oldest cave art found in Sulawesi." *Science Advances*, 7(3), eabd4648. Oldest figurative cave art ~45,000 years old.

Leder, D., Hermann, R., Hüls, M., Russo, G., Hoelzmann, P., Nielbock, R., . . . & Terberger, T. (2021). "A 51,000-year-old engraved b one reveals Neanderthals' capacity for symbolic behaviour." *Nature Ecology & Evolution*, 5(9), 1273-1282. Bone carved with symbolic marks 51,000 years ago.

Martinón-Torres, M., D'errico, F., Santos, E., Álvaro Gallo, A., Amano, N., Archer, W., . . . & Petraglia, M. D. (2021). "Earliest known human burial in Africa." *Nature*, 593(7857), 95-100. Earliest known grave with evidence of symbolic funeral arrangements is ~78,000 years ago.

Barras, C. (2021). "How did Neanderthals and other ancient humans learn to count?" *Nature*, 594(7861), 22-25. Overview of current idea on origin of counting.

Joordens, J. C., d'Errico, F., Wesselingh, F. P., Munro, S., de Vos, J., Wallinga, J., . . . & Roebroeks, W. (2015). "Homo erectus at Trinil on Java used shells for tool production and engraving." *Nature*, 518(7538), 228-231. Geometric shapes on a shell tool, ~430,000 years ago.

SPIDER PLANT

Tessa Fisher

Dr. Chantal Tarn took another look out the porthole at the planet below and felt her heart sink. There were no cities. There were supposed to have been cities.

"Where are they?" She gritted her teeth in frustration. "Don't tell me we came five hundred light years and no one's home." They'd spent so much time—in vain? It was more than just the two years the trip had taken, of course. She had worked nearly non-stop for ten years to be part of this mission. Everything else in her life—relationships, family, hobbies, anything beyond the most basic self-care—had become a second priority.

"Well, at least it's an active planet." Dr. Li Chou, the expedition's planetary scientist, had her eyes fastened on some readout or another from their ship's remote sensing suite. "Looks like there's almost certainly a biosphere of some sort—the surface is practically coated with chlorophyll analogs if the spectral data is to be believed. Maybe they're all underground?"

"Or maybe they just stopped over and then left." Chantal crossed her arms and sighed. "Though, if we get lucky, maybe they left some artifacts." *A single alien artifact*, she prayed to a deity she wasn't sure she believed in. *That would make all that sacrifice worth it.*

Hours ago, their ship, the *Aomawa Shields*, had completed the last step of a convoluted orbital ballet and placed itself in orbit around the planet TOI-3138b. A small rocky world a hair larger than Earth orbiting a dim and distant red dwarf star, TOI-3831b, had largely escaped notice in the century or two since its discovery.

All that changed when, fifteen years ago, sporadic radio signals had been detected coming from the direction of the constellation Aquila. The information within the signals hadn't yet been deciphered, but they were almost certainly produced by an intelligence of some kind or another. The combined sensitivity of the Cislunar ELBI radio array was tuned to the message, and its exact origin was pinpointed.

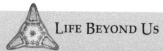

Further observations proved very promising. TOI-3138b's host star was much cooler, smaller, and dimmer than the Sun, but rich in the heavier elements needed to sustain life. The atmosphere of the planet was warm enough to support liquid water, and, indeed, water vapor had been detected remotely, as had vaporous ammonia. Oxygen was present, as well, though planetary scientists had learned this was not always a surefire indicator of life, especially on planets that orbited red dwarf stars, where periodic high-energy stellar flares could cleave water into hydrogen and oxygen; hydrogen, being the lightest element, quickly escaped into space, leaving an atmosphere that was increasingly enriched in O_2. And while the planet was tidally locked to its star—one side always facing the sun, the other perpetually shrouded in darkness—other exploratory missions had found thriving biospheres on such worlds. Why might one not eventually evolve intelligence?

Chantal stared at the forever-dark night side of TOI-3138b. *We hadn't even named it beyond its TESS Object of Interest designation,* she thought. *We wanted to find out what the natives called it, to do this right for once in human history.* She and the rest of the crew had signed up for this mission with the understanding that they would be meeting the creators of the signals. *But no city lights, no radio chatter, no satellites, nothing. Not even ruins from a civilization that wiped itself out, as depressing as that would be. Not a single sign of any intelligent agents ever visited this place, much less originated here.*

To add to her worries, she knew the public back home had been losing enthusiasm for astrobiology surveys. The first detection of life beyond Earth had been electrifying, even if it was just microbes. But the detection after that—and the next after that, and so forth—hadn't revealed much more than microbes, either. There had been another burst of excitement when complex life was finally found swimming in a water-covered world thirty light years from Earth, but enthusiasm, too, quickly dissipated once it became clear that it was about as intelligent as your average shark. What people really wanted—whether they admitted it or not—was someone they could talk to. The hope that the inhabitants of TOI-3138b might be smart enough to communicate meaningfully with humanity had given the survey program a second wind.

In a bid to fight off her rising anxiety, Chantal sent out a text to the crew's mobiles, summoning them for a meeting.

It didn't take long for the five of them to congregate, floating upright around the table in the cramped common area. Despite that, she was always glad to see everyone in one place. Chantal had long grown used to the body odor of her crewmates as it mixed with the earthy aroma of hydroponics and the vaguely chemical smell of disinfectant. She wondered if she'd miss that when the mission was over, or, for that matter, if she'd miss the constant background hum of air circulating and electronics running.

"I take it we're here to discuss the lack of obvious signs of civilization?" Dr. Avery Colon-Santos crossed her arms, a dry quirk of a smile on her face. The mission's physicist and primary engineer could always be trusted to cut straight to the chase. Chantal often found her bluntness refreshing, but sometimes it could be a little alienating. Like now.

"That doesn't mean there isn't intelligence," interjected the crew's linguist, Dr. Giada Nural, before Chantal could even get a word in. It wasn't surprising that she, too, was still holding out hope, all things considered. *Poor girl,* Chantal thought, *she's going to have wasted years of her life on a mission to a planet with no one to talk to.* A pang of anguish erupted in her heart. *Just like me.*

"She has a point, though." Li spoke quietly, perhaps remembering that they were in a crowded spacecraft and there was no need to shout. "We can't assume that civilization elsewhere will look like civilization on Earth. Why would they need city lights, for example, if their sun never moves in the sky?"

"Maybe they're hiding from us. Or lying in wait," Avery remarked ominously. There was a nervous chuckle, but it quickly died into a claustrophobic silence. Worried eyes began to dart around the room.

While a small part of her mind had indeed entertained the latter possibility, Chantal realized she had to take back control of the conversation. The last thing this mission needed was rising paranoia over a threat that probably didn't even exist. Probably.

"We're here because we detected coherent radio signals coming from this system," Chantal said, "and we assumed it came from the only life-bearing world here. That requires that they—whoever they are—have harnessed electromagnetism, at the very least. And so far, we've not seen any sign of infrastructure required to produce and direct the type of energy needed for projecting radio signals across interstellar distances."

"Should I point us toward home, then?" As usual, Chantal couldn't tell if Commander Aisha Jeminson was joking. The ship's pilot had a perfect poker face that she still found unreadable even after two years together in a small vessel.

Chantal sighed. She wasn't in charge of the mission—in fact, strictly speaking, no one person was. Decisions were made collectively. However, as the crew astrobiologist, her voice had a bit more sway than the others.

"No," she said after a moment of deliberation. "Whoever emitted those signals may have left some trace on the planet. And, in any case, we haven't encountered a biosphere that uses ammonia *and* water instead of just water before." She shrugged. "If nothing else, that's certainly worth investigating."

It was a hollow consolation, and they all knew it. The crew could certainly handle a standard planetary survey, but what they'd spent close to a decade training for was first contact with an intelligent species. Still, what other choice was there? This place simply didn't have what they were looking for.

The commander bid Avery to start preparing the drop pods for the surface probes, while Li made some noises about examining the atmospheric data for signs of long-lived industrial pollutants.

Maybe next mission, Chantal thought to herself as she made the walk back to her work terminal. *Maybe next mission.* If there was a next mission—for her, or even for the whole program.

Zooming over the frothing waves virtually in her drone, Chantal was able to forget her disappointment, at least for a little bit. She felt the wind press her wings upwards as she dipped and soared; if she had a mouth in this proxy, she would've giggled. Below her, the ocean was brown-black with swirls of algae-like organisms, occasionally disrupted by the swift passage of a fish-analog. Behind her on the distant horizon, the ever-setting red sun was partially obscured by the fringe of one of the storm systems that coiled around the planet's substellar point.

Some astronauts bemoaned never having the chance to physically touch the surface of the worlds they studied, for fear of contaminating the local ecology with invasive terrestrial life. Chantal never quite understood their disappointment—why scrabble around in a bulky spacesuit when you could gallop or fly across the planet in a proxy form that, as long as its solar panels were exposed, never ran out of energy, and that was far more robust than her fleshy body ever could be. As long as you set a timer—and she always did—to remind yourself to log out, grab a bite to eat, and stretch, you could spend twelve hours a day exploring and barely break a sweat.

If she switched on the expanded sensorium, the scene became even more gorgeous, the algae glowing in infrared, the sky lit up in swirls of polarized light, the deep rumble of sea currents and far-off thunder filling her ears. She found she could only handle the torrent of new sensations in limited doses—too much, and it quickly became overwhelming—but still, she missed it sometimes when she was back in reality.

She deployed a few buoys from the proxy drone into the ocean to sample the water directly. Though the crew agreed not to capture any multicellular life they found for fear of accidentally dissecting one of the signal-makers, microbes were still fair game. The buoys' on-board sampling and assaying equipment whirred to life. Initial biochemistry analyses seemed fairly similar to Earth's, with carbon playing a central role. Chantal suspected the presence of liquid ammonia in addition to water helped the biosphere spread farther into the colder dark side of the planet, but she hadn't yet had a chance to test that hypothesis.

As she glided further into the twilight belt of the planet, she kept her virtual eyes peeled for any sign of abandoned technology. Her working theory was currently that some other civilization, much like Earth's, had sent out a survey team some thousand years ago. This alien mission had been responsible for transmitting the signals subsequently detected back in the solar system. Presumably, they hadn't lingered long, which explained the absence of any immediate signs of technology visible from orbit. But surely, Chantal mused, there would be some traces, somewhere—even if it was just the ruined frame of whatever equivalent the aliens used for proxy bodies, or perhaps even the aliens' remains themselves. There had to be.

As exciting as finding intelligent life would've been, it didn't compare to discovering an entire interstellar civilization—assuming they were peaceful, of course.

The ammonia solution sea turned to land, great wide beaches of blue-gray sand. It was among the slate-colored sand dunes that something white and glimmering caught Chantal's view. She piloted her proxy down in a slow spiral and hovered over the beach.

The object was a mass of white, translucent crystals, roughly hemispherical in shape, probably about three meters high. Veins of different colored materials—golds, greens, blacks, reds—wound their way throughout the crystals; it would've been quite the sight if the sun ever made it to zenith on this planet.

From the crystal conglomeration, several oddly linear channels had been carved into the ground, branching back out toward the sea. Each trench was lined with smaller versions of the crystals she saw in the central mass and filled with water. Was this some sort of hydrothermal system, depositing minerals? The crew had initially assessed the planet as geologically quiet—was it more active than they'd assumed?

She skimmed over one of the channels, and noted that rather than water flowing out, as one would expect from a hot spring, seawater was flowing *in*, toward the tower of crystals. Things got even stranger when she discovered that on the landward side of the central mass was another set of almost identical channels. They led toward the dark side of the planet. The water-ammonia in those streams flowed away from the crystal heap, rather than toward it as the seawater did.

Chantal extended the proxy's landing legs, and with the fluttering of her mechanical wings, gingerly touched down near the crystal tower. While this proxy was primarily built for general survey work, it still included a laser spectrometer, which she powered up.

She zapped the crystal mass with a quick, intense burst, vaporizing an infinitesimal amount for analysis. The initial results were confusing: plenty of boron and nitrogen, as well as several complex molecules she couldn't quite discern. She set the proxy to run more analyses on auto-pilot, then logged out.

Chantal blinked her biological eyes repeatedly as she pulled off the interface system, readjusting to the light and sound of her actual physical environment. It was always a bit of a transition, going from the hyperspectral perspective she enjoyed while embodying a proxy, to the gentle, uniform white/yellow lighting of the *Shields*.

She floated through the ship's central corridor until she found Li's little nook, and gently knocked on the door.

"Enter," Li called out.

The door slid open, and Chantal pulled herself in with one hand, while the other flicked some images from her PDA onto a nearby wall display.

"Hey, Li, I've noticed some odd formations. What's your take on it?" Chantal asked, going straight to the topic at hand. When everyone lived within less than ten meters of each other, there wasn't much point in making small talk.

"Hmmm." The planetary scientist scrutinized the still images of the crystal heaps and the spectrographic analysis. "So, that's what they look like up close. Interesting."

"*They*? There's more of them?"

"Oh yeah," Li replied, her pitch rising with excitement. "There's a ring of them that goes around the entire planet, hugging the terminator line between the day side and the night side. Some of them are huge, tens of meters tall. Very complex structures." She put her hand to her chin and curled her lower body in, as if hunched over in thought. "My best guess is that they're the result of some sort of atmospheric deposition process. Maybe the day side got blasted by a flare or an asteroid impact, vaporized a lot of minerals, and they crystallized out once they reached somewhere cool enough?"

Chantal shrugged. "Sounds plausible, though you're the expert in that sort of thing, not me. I was wondering if maybe crystal formation might have somehow been catalyzed by microbial life. We see that sort of thing on Earth and other similar biospheres." Privately, a small desperate part of her was hoping the formations were some sort of exotic alien technology, but she dared not say that aloud. Still, she wondered if Li had the same thought.

"Well, that would explain how messy the chemistry of these structures is," Li replied. She pointed to one of the features on the projection. "They're crystals in name only—there's a ton of irregularity, it looks like, and a lot of contamination with nitrogen and sulfur compounds." She scanned over the spectrographic readings once more. "We should get some higher precision measurements, and probably run a metagenomic assay on microbes on the crystals' surfaces. Maybe they're the ones responsible for making the crystals in the first place."

"Well, first things first, I have to actually figure out what these microbes use to build their genes. Then we'll talk about analyzing metagenomes."

Armed with a likely hypothesis that the strange crystal pillars were merely the product of busy microbial builders, Chantal launched herself back into the main hall of the *Shields* and headed toward her terminal.

The mission's physicist rocketed toward her from the opposite direction. "Crap! Move, Chantal!" Avery called out.

Chantal flailed and tried to divert her course, dodging at the last second.

The physicist threw out her limbs and slowed herself down.

"Sorry about that! But hey, I wanted to talk to you real quick."

"What's up?"

"Well, given that, since yesterday the current theory about the radio emissions is that it was from some civilization making a stopover in this system, I figured I'd check and see if there's any archival data on this star."

"Is there?" Chantal silently kicked herself—why hadn't she thought of that approach already? *Now, now,* she consoled herself, *we'd all assumed that whatever sent the signal was from a planetary civilization. No one was thinking that it was from something just passing through the area.*

"A bit," Avery replied, absent-mindedly twirling her long, dark hair. Chantal wasn't sure why the physicist kept it long and unbound—in microgravity conditions, it just made for a permanent halo of entangling strands. "The biggest thing I can tell you is that none of the all-sky surveys picked up any gravitational microlensing in our direction. The Sheikh Observatory hasn't detected any gravitational wave emissions, either."

Chantal nodded with dawning comprehension. "So if anyone traveled here, they didn't use a K-tube to do it." Krasnikov tubes—the mind-boggling structures made out of the fabric of space-time itself that allowed apparent faster than light travel but not violation of causality—were hard to miss, even on a cosmic scale. "Maybe they traveled here more conventionally? Are there any star systems nearby?"

Avery shook her head. "Another red dwarf star passed within a light year a few thousand years ago, but other than that, everything's at least ten light years off."

"Hmmm. I'd say check the other red dwarf, but the timing doesn't work. And we've checked the rest of the system?" TOI-3138 had two other planets, both icy giants far removed from their host star, and both thoroughly unremarkable. They were certainly not worth mounting an interstellar expedition just to explore.

"We've scoured it," Avery replied with a sigh of resignation. "Practically lit up the whole sky with radar, looking for anything big enough to be an antenna. Found a lot of asteroids, but nothing engineered. Same result for cast-off fuel tanks, spent stages, anything else you'd need to get here using slower-than-light methods."

Chantal grimaced. This problem was becoming thornier and thornier to solve, and she could feel her nerves beginning to fray. Before returning to her terminal, she pushed herself over to a viewing port and gazed down at the ruddy-black surface of the planet.

Something or someone had come to this star five hundred years ago and transmitted a signal. That much was indisputable. But why had they left not a single trace of their coming?

Things began to look up, even just for a little bit, when Chantal had a chance to examine microbes found living on the crystal formations.

They were enigmatic little creatures—at first, it was difficult to even ascertain what they breathed and metabolized. Many of them had brightly colored spots of pigment, probably photosynthetic organelles of one sort or another, for example. However, they didn't have them in anywhere near the density that terrestrial algae did. Something else had to account for the bulk of their energy.

The answer was revealed in the minuscule blue green specks that floated in the microbes' equivalent of cytoplasm. At first Chantal had thought they were some forms of chlorophyll, but when she was finally able to tease an intact one from an alien cell and get it under a microscope, she gasped.

It was a tiny coil of copper, nestled in a veil of membranous proteins. While it would be a while before she could determine the proteins' structure with any detail, they looked eerily similar to the mitochondria of terrestrial cells. She was certain that this nanoscale bit of wire was the key to the microbes' source of energy.

"What if these aren't really microbes?" She finally had the courage to say during the crew's lunch hour.

"What do you mean?" Li paused in between sips of thick chowder soup. "Like, I'm not a biologist, but they're small and unicellular, aren't they?" Hopefully, she wouldn't immediately conclude the looming threat of mission failure which was starting to get to Chantal. At any rate, Chantal certainly hoped it wasn't.

"Are you suggesting they might be nanomachines of some kind?" Avery said, not even looking up as she twirled another strand of spaghetti before it could escape into zero-gee.

"Uh, well," Chantal replied, not expecting the others to catch on that quickly. That was the problem of with being in a small space with a bunch of geniuses; it was almost impossible to surprise anyone. "In a manner of speaking, yes. The bugs we found on the weird crystal formation have what look like for all the world to be miniature copper induction coils."

"You think they're wirelessly powered?"

Chantal shrugged. "I mean, if they're nanomachines, powering them remotely would be an excellent way to keep them from rampaging out of control—just switch off their power. Rather clever engineering." *The type you'd expect from an interstellar civilization* went unspoken.

Avery sighed. "It's as good a lead as any. See what you can find out. I'll rig up a probe that'll allow you to experiment on them."

"Forget probes!" Chantal said sharply. "A discovery of this importance deserves to be analyzed here, aboard the *Shields*—"

Commander Jeminson stepped in. "If you want to bring an unknown, potentially alien nanotechnology onto my ship, you better start planning on finding another ride home." The captain's word ended all further discussion.

And so, Chantal spent the next few days anxiously waiting while the *in-situ* lab probe was constructed. Even though time wasn't really an issue—the *Shields* had enough supplies to last at least a year in this system—the sooner she was able to verify that the microbes were the product of extraterrestrial engineering, the better. At any rate, it would certainly help her sleep better at night. As it was, it was currently all too easy to spend hours in bed, staring at her cabin ceiling, wondering if she'd wasted over a decade of her life pursuing something that didn't really exist.

Finally, once the squat, boxy probe had soft-landed within a meter or so of one of the crystal formations, her work began in earnest.

Early results were aggravatingly enigmatic. The microbes did indeed respond to electromagnetic flux as she had predicted. Their metabolisms seemed to ramp up into high gear, pumping out all sorts of novel proteins and enzymes. The purpose of this biochemical production, however, seemed rather limited—it resembled the sort of damage control that terrestrial microbes did when they encountered high heat or heavy metal concentrations.

Still, that didn't mean there wasn't something to the mysterious bugs. Perhaps generations of evolutionary selection had weeded out more advanced functions—functions that could still be hidden away in the microbes' genomes, or equivalent thereof.

It was a little easier for her to sleep now, but she still felt restless. Were the microbes actually alien tech, as she suspected? If so, what would be the definitive evidence?

Her dream her entire life had been to find a shining, unambiguous demonstration of intelligence beyond humanity's. The reality she seemed to be waking up to was that there would be nothing but uncertainty.

She was fervently working on developing primers for sequencing the microbes' genomes, hoping to find signs of biotechnological modification, when Li asked to see her.

Chantal floated into the planetary scientist's work area. Something about Li's carefully crafted neutral expression set off warning signals in her mind. "What's up?"

"I've been analyzing ice core samples from the night side." She fidgeted slightly in the zero gravity.

"Yes, and?" As far as Chantal knew, this wasn't news—Li had always enjoyed working with tidally locked planets, since there could be potentially tens of millions of years of climate data in the permanent ice cap that accumulated on the point deepest into the eternal night.

"I noticed some occlusion in the ice cores. Looking at them closer, well, see for yourself." Li flicked an image on to a nearby screen. A delicate sliver of glacial ice under high magnification appeared.

Within it were the unmistakable shapes of the same microbes Chantal had been studying. "Do they have . . ." she began to ask, her heart sinking below her feet.

"Yes," Li replied, "they have the same induction coils you found earlier."

"How old are they?" Chantal braced herself to the bad news she knew was coming.

"Hard to say." Li sighed. "At least two million years, though, if I've estimated the precipitation rates correctly. Probably much older, though."

The near certainty that the microbes had nothing to do with the mysterious alien signals remained unsaid.

"I'm guessing the coils naturally evolved, then?"

Chantal felt a surge of resentment at Li's question, as if she were rubbing salt in a wound. She took a quiet breath, and replied, "My suspicion is that the coils must have evolved in response to flare events." Red dwarfs—especially in their younger days—were notorious for having intense flares that punctuated their otherwise cool, ruddy glow. Chantal steadied her voice and continued. "The microbes probably used the energy from the resulting geomagnetic storms to patch up whatever the flare damaged. It's quite a clever system, really."

"That makes a lot of sense, then, yeah." Li turned her eyes back to her work terminal. "Back to the drawing board for you, I suppose."

"Yup. You know how it goes." Chantal turned and launched herself back to her cabin.

She made it inside, and the door firmly shut before she broke down into tears that burned with frustration and defeat.

Chantal spent the next few days mostly asleep, her cabin lights dimmed low. Her crewmates, to their credit, gave her a little while to process this latest setback before demanding that she face the universe once again.

Thus, she was strapped down in her sleeping bag when the shouting started.

She murmured sleepily and unstrapped herself, swearing to murder whoever was making such a racket at this hour in the ship's day. Fumbling on her cabin light, she opened the door and floated into the *Shields'* central corridor and toward the bridge.

"—it's not an exact match, but it's pretty close—"

"—can we get a fix on the origin—"

"—it looks like it's omnidirectional—"

The cacophony of voices rose in volume as she drifted closer, until she was treated to a scene of Giada, Li, and Avery scrambling from terminal to terminal on the bridge. The Commander, meanwhile, looked upon the chaos with a steely-eyed gaze.

"What's going on?" Chantal asked, rubbing the sleep from her eyes.

"The signal!" Giada shouted, not even looking up from her screen.

"What? From where?" Were the enigmatic aliens beaming messages to them from afar?

"From the surface of the planet."

Chantal scanned Avery's face, looking for any sign of facetiousness. "This isn't a prank, right?" she asked, just to be on the safe side. Surely, they wouldn't dare pull something like this on her, not with the state she was in.

"If it is, we're not the ones doing it," Li replied, her eyes firmly fastened on her screen. "It started about twenty minutes ago or so. Ridiculously high output, in pretty much all directions. Seems to be strongest around the terminator line, though."

Chantal's mind shifted into high gear; there was science to be done, and the intense mix of emotions she was feeling could wait. Clearly, there *was* some sort of technology present on the planet, sophisticated enough to blast a signal into interstellar space. But where was it, and how had it escaped the crew's notice?

Hours rushed by, as the crew poured over the analysis of the signals. Chantal paged through plot after plot, scrounging for anything that might point them in the direction of the signal's origin.

"Chantal, you have to see this," Li said, breaking Chantal from her intense study. The planetary scientist swiped a series of images from one of the observational satellites onto Chantal's screen, each showing the terminator rim.

"What am I looking at?"

"These were taken in the infrared a few minutes after the signal started, mostly centered on the dawn rim."

Dimly glowing in infrared light was a network that stretched across the terminator line, spokes radiating out of central hubs, that in turn fed into larger hubs. Chantal recognized the pattern immediately. "Spider plant," she said in awed whisper. "Why didn't I see this before?"

"Spider plant?" Li quirked her eyebrow.

"It's how I remembered scale-free networks in grad school—they look like spider plants, where there's a central plant that sprawls out its leaves, and from those leaves grow smaller spider plants. The same shape, just in miniature."

"So, what does that mean, exactly?"

"Scale-free refers to a pattern we see in certain networks." Chantal began tracing the glowing lines on the screen with her fingertip. "A few central points are heavily connected, but most only have one or two connections to other points in the network. That way, if one of the points fails for some reason, the odds are the rest of the network won't be badly affected. You tend to see the same pattern pop up in telecommunication systems, biochemical reaction networks—even the hub-and-spoke system of the jetliner age. Anywhere it helps to have a degree of resilience." She glanced back at Li. "Do these correlate with any visible structures on the planet? The crystals, maybe?"

"Let me check." Li flicked to another set of images taken in visible light, and then laid them over the infrared ones.

The network perfectly overlaid the crystal-lined channels.

"So, are these power lines? Maybe a long-abandoned automated telecommunications system?" Commander Jeminson swept her eyes from one display screen to another, as the crew huddled in the ship's cramped meeting space.

"We're not sure," Chantal replied. "I don't think so, though. As far we can tell, the boron nitride structures aren't actually hooked up to power anything, and while the water-ammonia that flows between them is electrically conductive, it's far less efficient than using metal. It's unlikely to be a telecommunications system, at least as we would understand it, for the same reason."

"But we're almost certain this is where the signal is coming from?"

Avery nodded at the Commander, sending waves propagating through her unbound hair. "The infrared excess we picked up may very well be waste heat from blasting off that transmission. Personally, I don't think they're power lines, but rather, power *generators*. I think they're somehow exploiting the temperature difference between the day side and the night side."

"That still leaves the question of what the power's being generated *for*, though." Avery crossed and uncrossed her legs, taking care not to bump into the closest wall. "The radio transmissions would only account for a small fraction of the total power we measure."

Trust an engineer to go straight to the practical, Chantal thought. Something nagged at the back of her brain, something having to do with ammonia. She idly listened to the continuing speculation as she fought to extract whatever conclusion was brewing in the depths of her mind.

Suddenly, it clicked. "Boron. The crystal structures are boron, right?"

"Yeah," Li said. "Boron nitride, with a bunch of complex contaminants."

Information from her classes in grad school ages ago swiftly came back to the forefront of her mind. "Boron nitride can form complex polymers, just like carbon can. And boron compounds are extra soluble and reactive in ammonia mixtures." She paused, furrowing her brow with concentration, while the mental strands connected with one another. "And while we've found microbes living on the crystals, we haven't been able to detect any of the indigenous microbes in the channels that feed into them."

Li shook her head. "Not from what you've told me, no. I figured the dissolved mineral content was too high, but then again, I'm not the astrobiologist here."

"What if we've been thinking about this the wrong way? What if the crystal network wasn't made by aliens?"

Giada recoiled slightly in confusion. "You think the network formed by chance or something like that?"

"No, I think the network *is* the aliens."

Everyone spoke at once. After a minute of confused cross-talk, Chantal was able to break through the noise and continue.

"I think the crystal structures are a boron-based life form, something radically different from anything we've seen before. It's powering itself using the temperature differential, and it's sending the radio signals to communicate—maybe even with its home planet. It could even be motile, just on a longer time scale than we've been observing."

"You think it's not native to the planet?" Li asked with more than a little skepticism creeping into her voice.

Chantal shook her head. "No, I'm guessing not. Boron biochemistry should thrive at lower temperatures, and consequently its reactions are going to run slower than a hot, carbon-based one. If it had evolved on this planet, it would've been outcompeted by the faster carbon life long ago. Though that raises the question of how it *did* get here."

Avery gazed off into space in thought for a minute, and then spoke. "It was the other star. They came from the other star."

"What star?" Chantal vaguely recalled the engineer telling her something about a nearby star.

"Remember, we discovered that a few thousand years ago, another red dwarf star came within a light year of this system? I bet the boron aliens hopped from that system to this one."

Avery clicked a couple of keys and another image popped up on a nearby display, showing the estimated path of the errant star as it spiraled through the galaxy and their conversation in the corridor came back to Chantal.

"That's why we didn't find evidence of K-tubes or ships," Avery said with growing excitement. "They didn't need them. If this stuff lives as slowly as you think it does, they could simply wait until their star passed close to another star with a habitable system. It might be millions of years between approaches, but if they can afford to wait, it'd be an incredibly economical way to spread throughout the galaxy." She looked downright awe-struck. "Think of it. They'd just need primitive chemical rockets to get themselves into orbit—or maybe just a big enough explosion, if they're resilient enough. Once they're up there, it'd be simple for them to generate an electrical current across their bodies and set up an ion jet to move them in the direction they wanted. They could travel the stars, without ever having invented the integrated circuit—or even the wheel."

Chantal's mind raced a thousand miles a minute. A civilization—or perhaps it was even just a single unified organism—that could spread itself through the stars and might not even require advanced technology to do so. How far had they traveled? What might they have seen in their eons of existence? This was so much more than she had ever dared dream of.

"Star-hopping rocks. Huh. It'll be interesting to see how they communicate." Giada looked like her brain was also still hurrying to process all this new information.

"Well, good thing we brought a linguist with us, isn't it?" Chantal replied with a smirk. "Better get to work—we've got a lot to cover." She darted to the nearest terminal and began loading up first contact protocols for their first ever field trial.

Below them, light from the ever-rising sun glinted off the towering crystal beings, like cities gently glowing at dawn.

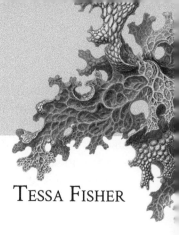

SIGNS OF LIFE

(And How To Find Them)

TESSA FISHER

L et me tell you a little secret in the astrobiology community: we have no universally agreed-upon definition for what life, as a physical phenomenon, actually *is*. If you talk to enough experts on the subject, you'll start to pick up themes—that life maintains itself through homeostasis, that it reproduces (sometimes), that it responds to its environment, and that it can undergo Darwinian evolution—but for every one of these traits, there's a counter-example.

After all, living things use energy from their environment to sustain themselves, and can reproduce—but the same is true for a flame. Organisms adapt to changing conditions in their environment—but so does the cruise control in your car. Life reproduces itself and is subject to the forces of the evolution in the process—except for sterile animals like mules and including things like viruses that are of dubious liveliness.

It may perhaps be best to think of life not as a strict binary but a spectrum—a tree is more alive than a virus is more alive than a rock. However, this doesn't remove the challenge of being able to easily differentiate between living and non-living systems out in the real world.

This dilemma of what life is, exactly, becomes particularly relevant when grappling with the possibility of life as we don't know it. If a living system inhabits an environment radically different from our own, or is based on biochemistry disparate from what we're familiar with, would we even recognize it as such?

In my story "Spider Plant", Chantal and her team face that very issue. They know something, or someone, generated an information-containing radio signal—a sign of life if there ever was one. When they arrive at the origin of the signal, they are quite baffled to find a system seemingly devoid of technological civilizations. The sole inhabited planet has a robust ecology, but no evidence of intelligent life—and some odd mineral outcroppings.

Eventually, Chantal discovers that the mineral outcroppings *are* the intelligence they're looking for—an exotic form of life, based not on carbon, or even silicon, but on boron. Boron can bond with hydrogen to form compounds called boranes; these boranes can in turn link up to create polymers and can carry ionic charges (much like carbon does in Earthly biochemistry) [1]. Additionally, boron-nitrogen bonds behave similarly to carbon-carbon bonds and can even form complex ring-structures akin to those that make up terrestrial DNA [2].

Such life, of course, would be almost unimaginably alien to human eyes, operating in a radically different environment and on vastly different time scales. Something that helps Chantal recognize the boron aliens for what they are, despite those differences, is the pattern of connections between the organisms.

Scientists in the real world frequently look for these kinds of patterns. One approach that makes such patterns easier to grasp is to conceptualize whatever biological system the scientist is looking at as a network (or *graph*, as it's referred to in mathematics). A researcher wanting to better understand, say, how the different chemicals inside a cell interact with each other might create a network where each chemical is represented by a point (or *node*, in the jargon), and the reactions between them as lines (or *edges*) connecting them. For example, if the reactions present are:

$$A + B \rightarrow C + E$$
$$C + B \rightarrow D + F$$
$$F + E \rightarrow G + C$$

then a network created by connecting the reactants to the products in the reactions might look like this:

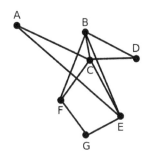

You may be thinking that this network looks like kind of a mess—and you'd be right! The networks for most non-biological systems look like chaotic balls of spaghetti, where finding any sort of recognizable pattern is difficult at best.

However, if you look at the networks created from chemistry of living systems, another pattern emerges—often looking something like this:

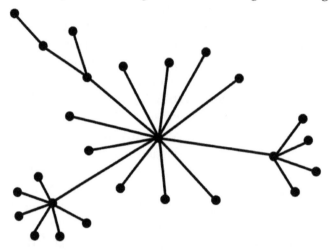

In this type of network, most nodes only have one connection to another node—often a central "hub" that is highly integrated into the network. This pattern is seen throughout biological and technological networks, at all scales—from the chemistry within an individual cell to the genes in a single organism, all the way up to the collective metabolism of whole ecosystems or biospheres [3]. It can be seen in the shape of the internet, or the hub-and-spoke system favored by airlines [4]. There's even some evidence that the shape of this network may extend beyond the biosphere and into the atmosphere, influencing the topology of the atmospheric chemical reaction network [5]; some astrobiologists—including yours truly—are currently investigating to learn whether these patterns can be used as a way to determine if planets around other stars are inhabited or not [6].

It is thought this network structure (or *topology*) might be preferred as form of resilience. If any one of the nodes happened to fail at random, it's statistically much more likely it'll be one of the many outlying nodes and not the few central nodes. Thus, damage or disruption to the network would be minimized.

These networks also appear to be *modular*—that is, they can be divided into smaller subcomponents (or modules). Furthermore, the modules have the same structure as the network as a whole, in much the way the titular spider plant buds off smaller versions of itself. Such networks are referred to as *scale-free*, because they have the same topology regardless of the scale of the network component you're looking at [7].

I should note that there hasn't been universal agreement about presence of scale-free networks in biology—more rigorous statistical analysis of many networks has shown that while they may approximate a scale-free topology, they aren't *truly* scale-free [8]. Still, the difference between these pseudo-scale-free networks and random networks is significant enough that I felt I could get away with Chantal using the term anyway.

The underlying reasoning behind looking for these kinds of universal patterns is the idea that life, ultimately, is a physical process, and will therefore be subject to the same constraints, no matter what form it takes [9]. Thus, any organism we find beyond our planet, even if it inhabits a radically different environment from our own, or is based on unimaginably exotic biochemistry, will still possess certain motifs in common with terrestrial life [10]. Chemical reaction network topology isn't the only pattern that's been posited as being universal—for example, the way organisms scale up in size is also being investigated as a common motif in life throughout the cosmos [11].

It's important to consider the wide variation in living systems that might be possible, if for no other reason than such lifeforms might be capable of feats we find near-impossible. One of the mysteries the crew of the *Shields* face is that the mysterious boron-based life clearly isn't native to the planet. Not only is the biosphere of TOI-3^{1}38b based on the more familiar element of carbon (albeit with a water-ammonia mixture as its primary solvent instead of just regular water), the boron-based life physically moves and reacts at such a slow pace that its simpler ancestors would've almost certainly been outcompeted by the quick and adaptable carbon-based life long ago.

If these enigmatic organisms aren't native to the planet, how then, did they arrive? While the *Aowoma Shields* was able to make it to TOI-3138b in a few years using a Krasnikov tube—a sort of relative of the wormhole that allows faster-than-light travel, but, importantly, doesn't allow you to travel back in time and make a mess of history [12]—the TOI-3138 system shows no sign of the advanced space-time engineering required to create a K-tube.

This puzzle is ultimately solved by Avery, the crew's astrophysicist, who realizes that, due to their slow lives, the boron beings wouldn't *need* K-tubes. Statistical modeling has found that, for a star like the Sun, another star will come within 0.03 light years—two orders of magnitude closer than our closest current star, Proxima Centauri—about every 700 million years [13]. While that seems like an unimaginably long time to us short-lived humans, to the glacial boron aliens, it might an entirely reasonable time to wait. After all, such a close stellar pass would reduce the energy and time required for interstellar travel enormously.

Even if interstellar travel (fast or slow) is beyond us currently, as an astrobiologist I'm excited to see what strange biochemistries and ways of living might exist out in the greater universe. As we search the stars for fellow living creatures, we must remember that what we find may be far different from what we expect—but that, no matter how strange they might be, there will be certain things that we all share, simply by being all children of the same universe.

REFERENCES

[1] Saladino, R., Barontini, M., Cossetti, C., Di Mauro, E., & Crestini, C. (2011). "The effects of borate minerals on the synthesis of nucleic acid bases, amino acids and biogenic carboxylic acids from formamide." *Origins of Life and Evolution of Biospheres*, 41(4), 317-330.

[2] Schulze-Makuch, D., & Irwin, L. N. (2018). *Life in the Universe: Expectations and Constraints*. Springer.

[3] Kim, H., Smith, H. B., Mathis, C., Raymond, J., & Walker, S. I. (2019). "Universal scaling across biochemical networks on Earth." *Science Advances*, 5(1), eaau0149.
https://doi.org/10.1126/sciadv.aau0149

[4] Barabási, A.-L. (2016). *Network Science*. Cambridge University Press.
http://networksciencebook.com/

[5] Solé, R. V., & Munteanu, A. (2004). "The large-scale organization of chemical reaction networks in astrophysics." *Europhysics Letters (EPL)*, 68(2), 170–176.
https://doi.org/10.1209/epl/i2004-10241-3

[6] Walker, S. I., Cronin, L., Drew, A., Domagal-Goldman, S., Fisher, T., Line, M., & Millsaps, C. (2020). "Probabilistic Biosignature Frameworks." *Planetary Astrobiology*, 477.

[7] Li, L., Alderson, D., Doyle, J. C., & Willinger, W. (2005). "Toward a theory of scale-free graphs: Definition, properties, and implications." *Internet Mathematics*, 2(4), 431-523.

[8] Broido, A. D., & Clauset, A. (2019). "Scale-free networks are rare." *Nature Communications*, 10, 1017.
https://doi.org/10.1038/s41467-019-08746-5

[9] Solé, R. V., Levin, S. A., Brown, J. H., Gupta, V. K., Li, B.-L., Milne, B. T., Restrepo, C., & West, G. B. (2002). "The fractal nature of nature: Power laws, ecological complexity and biodiversity." *Philosophical Transactions of the Royal Society of London*, Series B: Biological Sciences, 357(1421), 619–626.
https://doi.org/10.1098/rstb.2001.0993

[10] Mariscal, C., & Fleming, L. (2018). "Why we should care about universal biology." *Biological Theory*, 13(2), 121–130.

[11] West, G. B., Brown, J. H., & Enquist, B. J. (1997). "A general model for the origin of allometric scaling laws in biology." *Science*, 276(5309), 122–126.

[12] Krasnikov, S. V. (1998). "Hyperfast travel in general relativity." *Physical Review D*, 57(8), 4760–4766.
https://doi.org/10.1103/physrevd.57.4760

[13] Hansen, B. M. S., & Zuckerman, B. (2021). "Minimal Conditions for Survival of Technological Civilizations in the Face of Stellar Evolution." *The Astronomical Journal*, 161(3), 145.
https://doi.org/10.3847/1538-3881/abd547

THIS IS HOW WE SAVE THEM

DEJI BRYCE OLUKOTUN

The soft rumble in the ground beneath their feet meant an interstellar transport was coming to the moon reserve of New Limpopo, and with it, another job.

The *Andras* stumbled down the jetway ramps, their legs weak from months of travel, until their tailored exosuits adjusted to help them balance. *Andras* were human royalty who had modded their bodies in all shapes and sizes: long-legged, corpulent, as strong as a water buffalo. Sometimes they were eerily beautiful, their facial proportions carefully sculpted by the finest plastibots—chiseled jaws, moon faces, gracefully sloping noses, and eyes that glittered like sapphires. *Andras* had more money than they could spend because they were barred by the empire from bequeathing it to their own children to promote equality—but they could use it as they pleased. They came to New Limpopo to hunt the most fearsome predators from Earth, all in the name of conservation.

It's also why they hired the Sterling Elsevier Tour Company to help them.

"Package for Sterling Elsevier Tours," a customs officer announced, sifting through the boxes that had arrived on the ship.

"I'll authenticate," Kamau Pang replied. "I'm authorized."

The officer handed Pang a thin, meter-long attaché case. "Insert your fingers here."

Pang inserted his index and ring finger, feeling a little puff of air as the case extracted a genetic sample. The case blinked green, and the customs officer handed it over.

"Kamau, right?" the officer asked.

"Pang. Kamau is my surname."

"Pang, then. I've heard they pick you for the dangerous jobs."

"As long as I get paid."

"You couldn't pay me enough to do what you do. Andra shot my leg off with an elephant rifle. She was sorry enough to buy me a new leg, but I'll never forget that pain. I'm happy to work in customs now—leave the dirty work to trackers like you."

"Thanks for the delivery," Pang said, with finality. He did not want to chat about it. The way to survive on New Limpopo was to avoid indulging in other people's trauma or anything that could rattle your focus. There were way too many stories of accidents and mishaps, and the animals were dangerous enough by themselves.

Most people walked by Kamau Pang without noticing him because he was medium height, of medium build, and with no remarkable features. He looked partly Chinese (the nose), partly East African (the eyes and the skin tone), and partly Russian (the brow), enough of a mix that people didn't remember him at all. He preferred to operate in the background, do his job, and then beat a hasty retreat to his quiet life, where he studied animal biology (apex predators) and liked to learn about cosmetics (face creams).

Pang stopped by the lodge, where Sterling Elsevier was schmoozing with potential clients. Elsevier was a successful tour operator able to entice royalty who had experienced almost every form of entertainment, both real and virtual. He had a knack for discovering what they had not yet tried and then selling it to them for an exorbitant fee.

Pang waited patiently for Elsevier at the bar, sipping a Tauran Daiquiri (non-alcoholic), as Elsevier told his audience how their hunting licenses had paid for the rehabilitation of a hundred elephants that could be traced to a lineage of African elephants on Earth. Sometimes he claimed the tourists were saving kudu antelope—it depended on what they cared about. The Tauran spice in the Daiquiri percolated through Pang's body, and he was just starting to relax when Elsevier found him.

"That must be the Princess Bagan shipment," Elsevier observed, pointing to the attaché case Pang was carrying. "She's a wealthy Andra from the Mandalay system. Good shot, if I recall."

"She's been here before?"

"Several times. But she got married. This is some sort of honeymoon. I want you to raise these animals tough for her, but not too smart, enough to scare her but not to hurt her."

"What about her partner? Will he hunt?"

"That's what the liger is for. Keep it simple."

"Alright."

"Pang," Elsevier added, shifting his tone. "You're a good tracker and a crack shot. And you're a fine observer of people. I like how you anticipate my needs when we're on the hunt. It's not something that can be taught. I'm looking to take an apprentice under my wing, someone who could assume part of my business, allow me to focus on more strategic opportunities. You've got all the skills. The only part you're missing is the conversation. You can't just make the client comfortable, you see, you have to entertain them, show them a good time."

"Thanks, Mr. Elsevier. I'll pay attention."

"Good. The Bagan family has some pull with the Conservation Board. Elsevier Tours has a good chance of getting nominated to the board if we show her a good time—that would mean a lot for our business."

"She wants to protect the animals, then?"

"Of course," Elsevier winked. "They all do. That's why they come here, isn't it? I'm going off-planet for a few weeks to try to source more clients. I'll check on the animals when I get back. Strategic, Pang. That's what we need from you."

Sobered up, Pang next visited the nursery, a sprawling complex of several interconnected buildings, where he authenticated himself through various gates and airlocks. He opened the attaché case and the gas escaped with a hiss. Inside were two sets of viable embryos. Three lions, all females, labeled L1a, L2b, L3c with the instructions Must be grouped. Then the male liger, which was a mix between a tiger and a lion, and finally a bull hippo. One set of embryos was donated to New Limpopo for conservation in the expansive reserves on the far side of the moon and the other made available to the donor in the hunting territories. Pang registered the embryos and passed them through a small vault to a lab technician.

"It says 'must be grouped,'" the technician asked. "What's that about?"

"The females hunt in packs," Pang guessed. "They're harder to kill. How long until these are ready?"

"Lions and the hippo will be ready within a month. The liger will take another two weeks or so."

Pang checked the Princess's arrival date. "The owner isn't coming for six months. Should be plenty of time."

"You know male ligers are sterile, right? They can't breed. That's treading the line for me. It's not like they're conserving anything. They never existed in nature. Hardly fair to shoot them."

"Not up to me," Pang said. "Take it to the Conservation Board."

"I'd rather feed myself to the liger," the technician joked.

Pang laughed without any real mirth.

Though Pang could not access the incubation chambers, he checked back regularly on the development of the animals because he was methodical. Ligers often came with underlying health issues, so he intervened a few times, recommending the technician swap out certain sequences of base pairs. Ligers were docile animals, famed for their size but in fact easy to kill. He felt sorry for them, transported billions of kilometers across the system, nurtured, only to be slaughtered by an Andra with a weapon that essentially could never fail.

When the embryos grew into cubs, Pang escorted them to their private nurturing pens. There, they were bottle fed by robots until they reached a designated weight. The bull hippo drank prodigious amounts of milk and had to be constantly washed with a special lubricant, because the dry air of New Limpopo caused his skin to crack. Both liger embryos had in fact been viable, but the growth hormone caused the canine teeth in one of the animals to grow too quickly, such that it bit through its own jaw and had to be terminated. Ligers never survived long in the game reserves of New Limpopo anyway. It was probably for the best.

Pang tried to maintain a sense of detachment while simultaneously nurturing and feeding the animals, knowing that soon he would be releasing them for slaughter by the wealthy owner who paid for them. He had once grown fond of a solitary shoebill, a rare giant bird with a prehistoric beak like an archaeopteryx, only to watch it explode in a puff of feathers. Now he maintained a certain emotional distance. The animals were transported to New Limpopo as embryos to save cargo space and frankly because no interstellar vessel would risk an apex predator rampaging through a spaceship while in transit. The moon had been sterilized and then terraformed, which was supposed to prevent any native life from thriving.

Once the babies were fattened up and pumped full of antibiotics, Pang transported them to their native habitats which were large, heavily gated territories for the animals to roam across the moon. Pang selected a traditional savannah for the lions and dropped the hippo in a wetland swamp. He placed the liger in a thick rainforest, hoping to give the placid creature some chance of survival. The three female lion cubs were sprayed with a modified mix of pheromones to imprint them onto a full-grown adult female who taught them how to hunt the small game released periodically into the preserve. Most lion cubs took two years to learn to survive on their own, while this development was accelerated to less than four months on New Limpopo through growth hormones and creative stimulation. Hippos were simpler animals. The bull hippo could already forage for wild grasses and did fine wallowing in the muddy waters. Pang waited until the hippo matured and then introduced two smaller females, both bots, but realistic enough to make the bull feisty and territorial.

The liger required more attention. Pang did what he could to help it learn to hunt small game, but the animal was terrified of water, unlike real tigers who were natural swimmers, which meant the liger had to be coaxed to cross even the smallest of streams. The liger was almost painfully unaware of its true bulk. It was easily twice as large as the lions yet as placid as a housecat.

By the time the *Andra* ship arced into the spaceport—a thin interstellar cruiser painted opalescent blue—the animals had largely adapted to the moon. The lions were cunning pack hunters, the bull hippo was cantankerous, and the liger was capable of a few terrifying roars.

Sterling Elsevier was pleased. "Great job with the animals, Pang," he said quietly. "If we play this right, we'll have a choice seat on the Board within the year."

Pang stood at attention as the owner descended the ship ramp to the surface. She wore a royal platinum crown cut in the Mandalay style, powdered cheeks, and had a plain, unadorned face. Her new husband was a finely sculpted man with chestnut skin who pranced down the ramp like it was a catwalk.

"Presenting Princess Larabella Bagan," a herald announced, "and Prince Damalo Bagan."

Sterling Elsevier graciously welcomed them, offering polite but intentional compliments to the couple.

"I can assure you that the animals you selected are all fine specimens," Elsevier explained. "They will make for difficult quarry."

"That's what I paid for, isn't it, Sterling?" the Princess asked.

"And to promote conservation on the moon," the Prince chimed in.

"Of course," Elsevier readily agreed. "Your support for the game reserve of New Limpopo is much appreciated. Through the generosity of people like you, we have been able to conserve nearly eighty-five percent of the indigenous species of Earth, including the top predators, as you are no doubt aware."

"Damalo here is nearly nine percent Kenyan," Princess Bagan explained. "He thinks he has a lion hunter in his ancestry."

"I don't think it," Prince Damalo corrected with a smile. "I know it. I knew it the moment we touched down here."

"Is that right?" Elsevier said. "As a matter of fact, my tracker Pang here has some Masai blood, though you wouldn't know it from looking at him."

Pang cleared his voice since Elsevier was inviting him to join the conversation. "Kikuyu, actually," Pang corrected. "And Chinese. My family helped build the Nairobi-Cairo maglev route."

"Aren't we lucky?" The Prince fawned. "I knew there was a connection between us, brother."

Pang smiled until his mouth hurt, and then quietly excused himself from the conversation. He could never tell if Sterling Elsevier actually enjoyed these conversations or had so lost himself in his role as a tour operator that he no longer had an underlying personality. Maybe there was nothing else but the suckling sycophant.

It was customary for new arrivals to rest for a few standard days in the Mountaintop Lodge, which offered a panoramic view of New Limpopo, along with its famed sunset. A nearby gas planet shone brightly in the night sky as the royalty mingled with each other, swapping stories and sharing their latest passions. This was Sterling Elsevier's favorite stomping ground. Even if he was surrounded by *Andras*, he was the one who held court, and Pang had no desire to imitate him. In fact, Pang found the sumptuous dinners and exotic drinks to be a complete waste of credits because one dinner was many times his wages. The more adventure-prone *Andras* would BASE jump from the lodge and try to avoid landing in a crocodile infested lake. Inevitably, someone would fall in, which made the risk that much more celebrated.

Pang took the lead as the expedition flew overland before switching to rovers that skirted over rough semiarid terrain. For lunch, the cooks prepared a sumptuous feast as Pang planned the first hunt.

"Won't you join us and eat, Pang?" the Princess asked as Pang was inspecting their hunting weapons.

Pang looked to Elsevier, who subtly shook his head no.

"Thank you, I've already eaten," Pang said.

"I didn't see you eat anything. Please join us."

Again, Pang looked to Elsevier, again Elsevier shook his head no, so Pang compromised by joining them at the table without touching the food. Prince Damalo Bagan excused himself to go to the toilet.

"Where did you put the liger, Pang?" the Princess asked when the Prince was out of earshot.

"If we told you, you would lose the fun of the chase," Elsevier chimed in.

"Even I don't know where the animals are at all times," Pang added.

"Nonsense," she said, "you have surveillance implants."

"They are chipped," Pang corrected, "but we can only pick up the signals in one- kilometer radiuses."

"I see. That seems like a risky way to manage my lions, which cost, what was it, Sterling? Three million credits each?"

"Five million. Quite the contribution to the New Limpopo reserve."

"You're missing my point. I'm not talking about my donation. I bought the liger because they're supposed to be peaceful. Damalo is deathly afraid of the hunt. I want him to take one, but not be put in any real danger."

"The liger is in the rainforest," Pang volunteered. "It will be harder to spot."

"But it's not dangerous," she probed.

Pang hesitated. What did she want from him? This was a hunting trip.

"Combining two ferocious animals," Elsevier intervened, "does not necessarily make them more ferocious. Something happens at the genetic level that we haven't quite figured out. The liger is very huntable. The Prince will be able to bag her without a scratch."

"Good," she concluded. "So, it's decided. We'll hunt the liger first and go for the lions later. Damalo's so darn handsome, isn't he? But you shouldn't underestimate him, Sterling. I didn't marry him only for his looks. Damalo just needs something to take the edge off, as it were."

"Don't we all?" Elsevier replied, and they both laughed heartily at some private joke.

Pang found himself staring at the Princess's cheekbones, enjoying the way the sunflower-colored powder brought out their subtle but beautiful curves.

"Do you want to ask me something, Pang?" she asked.

He shook his head, embarrassed to be caught looking.

"Go on then," Elsevier encouraged.

"Your cheeks are lovely, Princess," Pang stumbled. "What kind of powder is that?"

"Oh, why thank you, Pang. It's called thanaka. Made from tree bark. It's a family tradition."

"Thank you." He hurried off. Now he knew its name. Thanaka.

Later that afternoon, Elsevier found Pang as he was inspecting their hunting weapons. The rifles were at full charge and his Gauss pistol, a concussion device for close encounters, was properly insulated. Pang didn't like the look of the Prince's hunting rifle, which was a high powered device that was technically legal but known for having a sensitive trigger.

"Can I give him my laser-sight instead?" Pang asked.

"I wouldn't do that," Elsevier advised. "It's a legal weapon and we don't want to insult him."

"It's dangerous."

"We'll have to watch him," Elsevier agreed. "Good thing you didn't touch any of the Princess's food, by the way. She's Mandalay royalty. You're not from her class, so you should never eat with her. She would have been insulted. Some of these things you have to learn by doing, you might say. But don't get too down on yourself—you did well in there."

"Thanks, Mr. Elsevier."

"A little odd asking about the makeup, though. What was that about?"

"It's an interest of mine."

"Well, maybe keep that to yourself with clients, Pang. Especially with princesses."

"Princes wear makeup too."

"Royalty do whatever they damn well please, which is precisely my point. We're not royalty." He stared off across the chapparal. "At least, not yet."

At dusk, Elsevier and Pang led Prince Damalo into the rainforest, where he expected to find the liger resting in a dry glade, comfortably away from the water.

The intense humidity under the forest canopy made the three men sweat profusely. They soon came across a mass of vines fifty meters thick growing in unusual patterns, looping and curlicuing around some fixed point in the air.

"What is this all about?" Prince Damalo asked nervously.

"Biomass accretion," Pang explained. "They're all over the moon. They're most likely following the patterns of the moon's magnetic field. Many organisms can sense it."

"They're harmless, Prince," Elsevier reassured him.

"Doesn't look harmless to me. What is that slime?"

"It's an excretion from the plant. It's a little itchy but not toxic. Try not to touch it."

Pang hadn't mentioned the other theory, which was that the accretions were caused by biological deposits that escaped sterilization during the terraforming process on the moon. Either way, the small expedition skirted the foliage until the canopy opened up again, and he spotted paw prints on the ground soon after.

Elsevier kneeled over the prints. "What do you think, Pang?"

"The liger was here recently. Maybe an hour ago."

"Where is it?"

"Headed southeast."

Prince Damalo powered on his rifle, and Pang reached over to flick a switch. "Keep the safety on, Prince. That's a pressure sensitive trigger. You squeeze it too hard, and you'll blow your own arm off."

"This is the best rifle on the market," Prince Damalo said. "I spent a lot of time researching this."

"Just keep the safety on."

"Don't tigers ambush their prey? Shouldn't I be ready?"

"All cats ambush, Prince," Elsevier intervened. "But it's a liger, not a tiger. They're different."

"Different how?"

"They're more unpredictable," Pang added, charitably. "And much bigger than a lion." Elsevier nodded at him approvingly.

Keep the fear in them, Elsevier had once advised Pang. *They remember the experience better.*

Prince Damalo shot him a look of panic, as if he was slowly realizing that the liger might have a will of its own.

Pang led them for several kilometers through the forest, the Prince raising his rifle to attention at the sound of every crack and snap of a twig. When they came to a broad stream, Pang motioned for them all to duck and wait.

"It will be close by," he said.

They set up behind a blind of bushes on the far side of the stream so that even if the liger noticed them, he wouldn't charge because of his fear of water. The liger tended to sleep during the day and rouse around dusk to patrol his territory. All they had to do now, in theory, was wait.

As night fell, the forest filled with the sound of chirping insects, and an eagle owl hooted somewhere in the black. Pang used night vision glasses to scan for the liger, while Elsevier and the Prince relied on their augmented implants.

"I don't see it anywhere," Prince Damalo complained after an hour of crouching.

"It will be here soon," Elsevier advised.

Another hour later, Pang wasn't so sure. "It should have been here," he whispered. He pointed at the monitor on his wrist registering the liger's implant. "It's been in this area almost every night for the past month."

"Still alive?"

"Biometrics are all normal. It has mild heart arrhythmia. It was born with it."

When Prince Damalo began to complain loudly enough to silence even the insects, Elsevier announced: "We'll have to go after it."

"Is that safe?" the Prince asked.

"Keep your safety on, but yes. It's time for you to hunt the hunter. Are you ready for it?"

"For sure I am," the Prince said proudly.

They padded quietly through the forest: Pang out front, the Prince in the middle, and Elsevier bringing up the rear. Pang glassed the forest with his night vision but couldn't see the liger anywhere. He wondered, briefly, if the animal had crossed into another territory, but decided it was unlikely. The forest was bounded by streams, and the animal's fear of water couldn't be easily unlearned.

When they reached another biomass—a grotesque mixture of acacias, tangling vines, and some kind of putrescent weed—Pang motioned for them to slow down. The liger's tracks led right into the middle of the thicket.

"Time to go get your liger," Elsevier whispered.

"In there?" Prince Damalo asked, his face paling.

"Pang will be with you. He's the best shot we have. I'll wait out here in case the beast tries to bolt."

Ten paces in, Pang heard a low growl and pulled the Prince down to his knees, putting his finger to his lips. Together they crept through the mass of vines, Pang using a laser cutter to slash away the biggest plants. Not far along he raised his hand for the Prince to stop. He heard labored breathing, as if the animal was wheezing for air, and wondered if the liger had caught a cold.

Prince Damalo craned his head. *Where is it?* He mouthed.

"See the white whiskers inside that bush? Aim a little to the right. At the shoulders."

Prince Damalo's eyes widened as he finally caught a glimpse of the liger. "It's *huge*," he whispered.

"It doesn't see us yet. We're downwind. Take your time."

Pang unfolded a rifle stand for the Prince to steady his aim. The Prince took a deep breath and placed the barrel on the stand. Before Pang could stop him, he squeezed way too hard on the trigger.

The impact sounded like a bucket of flesh had been splattered across the ground. The liger didn't even have time to roar. The shot had cleared a tunnel straight through the forest.

"I told you!" Pang snapped. "That's a pressure sensitive trigger."

"You told me to shoot it."

"To shoot it, not blast it with a fucking cannon."

"How was I supposed to know?"

"You practice! That's how!"

"I've never shot a gun in my life. I'm a pacifist."

"Let's go get it."

Prince Damalo chattered nervously as they crawled through the smoking tunnel in the vines. "That was huge! Majestic! You think we can mount it? I told Bella I could do it. She didn't believe me. I didn't see the liger at first, but when I followed the whiskers, just like you told me, I saw his face. I swear he was looking right at me, with those eyes, those vicious eyes, like he was staring through my soul . . ." And on he went until they got to the carcass.

The head was gone, along with most of the shoulders. All that was left was a cauterized mass of yellow-orange fur. The stench was awful, like burnt sour meat. Prince Damalo took one look and vomited into the bushes.

Pang had known that the animal would be taken easily, but it hadn't put up a fight at all. He had expected at least a roar, some sort of feeble whimper against its pointless existence. That's when he noticed the animal's belly, where there was movement inside, a frantic pressing against the sodden fur.

"What is that inside it?" Prince Damalo asked, wiping the vomit from his mouth.

"I don't know."

Pang was bothered too—there was something unnatural about the wriggling beneath the skin—but he felt compelled to see. He removed his laser cutter and sliced a thin line from the shoulders down the soft underbelly.

The first kitten spilled out onto the ground, clawing at the air. The second one was still covered in the placenta, so Pang tore it away with his fingers to clear a passageway for it to breathe. The kittens had matted creamy white fur with pencil-thin black stripes. Their tiny canine teeth were as translucent as ice, and the kittens began to mewl for milk. Pang removed his bush jacket and wrapped them both up. He could feel their body heat in the cool nighttime air, the soft padding of their feet.

"They're babies," Damalo breathed despondently. "I killed the mother."

When Pang and the Prince walked out of the thicket, Sterling Elsevier was waiting for them. "Sounded like a powerful shot," he said, patting the Prince on the back. "Well done, Prince! No hide, eh? Nothing to be ashamed of. Dirty little secret is that hunters never mount their first kill. Too messy. We can construct a pelt for you, as large as you like. You can even pick the size of the stripes. No one back home will be able to tell the difference."

"I don't want it," Prince Damalo said.

Elsevier nodded to the jacket Pang was cradling his arms. "What do you have in there, Pang?"

Pang showed him, and Elsevier took a step back. "That was a male. It was sterile."

"I know."

"Then what in the devil are these? Did you get the right embryo?"

"Yes, I did."

Elsevier's face went blank for a moment. He looked at the kittens again, as if trying to register whether they were in fact there, and he frowned.

"Prince," he said, producing a hip flask. "I brought some Ionian whiskey for you. Have a sip. It's always hard-going after the first kill. This will steady your nerves a bit."

The prince grabbed the flask without saying a word and walked to a rotting log, where he sat down and took a long plug of the whiskey, wiping his mouth when the liquid spilled onto his shirt. Keeping his eye on the Prince, Elsevier pulled Pang aside.

"What the hell happened here, Pang?"

"I don't know. It was sleeping in a biomass accretion. It must have changed sexes somehow."

"I don't mean about that. I mean the Prince. He's got no pelt, no head to mount, and now we've got these fucking things."

"I warned you his gun was too strong."

"You were supposed to manage that! I told you to watch him! He's had a terrible time, an awful experience!" Elsevier rubbed his temples. "If Larabella finds out . . . I mean the Princess . . . if she finds out, she'll ruin us. Our reputation will be shot, never mind the bloody Conservation Board. She has friends everywhere. If she tells them, we're finished. Look at the Prince! He's acting like he murdered someone. That liger was so easy to kill; only a fool could have messed it up."

One of the kittens squirmed in Pang's arms as Elsevier berated him. Pang dribbled some water from his canteen onto its tongue, watching the kitten lap up the water greedily.

"We need to get some milk for these," Pang said.

"Milk? That's all you can think about right now. Milk?"

"We need to keep them alive," Pang insisted.

Elsevier looked completely confused. "We don't need to do anything. We need to salvage this situation is what we need to do."

"These could be a new discovery."

"It probably just mated with a bloody lion."

"But it was a *male*," Pang reminded him. "There is nothing like this in the scientific record. Mammals can't switch sexes or reproduce parthenogenetically. It would've needed a womb. We're the first to witness this."

Elsevier raised an eyebrow, and realization dawned on his face. "New discovery, you say?"

Pang nodded.

"Pang, maybe you're right. In fact, that's brilliant. Absolutely brilliant. You might just save us." Inspired by the new thought, Elsevier turned to the Prince. "Don't you realize what you've done today, Prince?"

Prince Damalo shook his head, taking another plug of the whiskey.

"You have made a new scientific discovery, that's what!"

"What discovery?" Prince Damalo asked despondently.

"You proved that a sterile animal can breed. That a male could be induced to switch sexes. This is a new era of cross-species regeneration."

The Prince looked up sharply. "I don't understand. It was a male?"

"Not just a male, a *sterile* male," Elsevier pushed on, as the Prince listened in wonderment. "These kittens are the proof. We have to get them back to the nursery straight away. We have to save them, study them, nurture them. This has never happened before on this moon." Elsevier nodded, gathering steam. "New Limpopo has birthed new life! This is a more fecund moon than Mother Earth herself! Our game reserve has evolved. It is bringing new creatures into our strange universe! You'll be famous, Prince."

"I was a little afraid at first," Prince Damalo agreed, coming along. "But then I *did* feel like I was channeling some inner energy, you know, when I pulled the trigger."

"Exactly! You had it in you! You have the ancestry, you said it yourself. And now look. A new species! Pang, what's the scientific name for a liger?"

"There isn't one."

"A tiger then?"

"*Panthera tigris.*"

"That's it! We'll call it *Panthera tigris Damalo Bagan.* Pang, get the emergency animal unit over here. We must save these animals. We've got to preserve them. For the Prince, for science!"

Sterling Elsevier held out his hands for the kittens, almost pleadingly. Pang clutched the little animals close to his chest, feeling their frantic need for comfort.

"Come on, Pang." Elsevier smiled. "You've done your part."

Pang didn't like how Elsevier was turning the kittens into another trophy. That wasn't the reason to save them, nor was killing one animal to save another. But in Elsevier's mind, he had discovered a new lifeform and thrilled his clients beyond their wildest dreams. The Prince would be famous now, even amongst other royalty.

"What are you thinking, Pang?" Elsevier pleaded. "Hand them over. Let's get these animals to safety."

Hunt one animal to save another. The Conservation Board would do nothing to intervene because they could justify the liger a million different ways from the money the publicity would bring in: preserving other species, creating new paddocks, or even providing jobs to the locals. Locals like Pang.

But Pang didn't want to be a local anymore. He did not want to be saved, not like this. If he abandoned these cubs, the cycle would continue. Their necks were as thin as his thumb, wrapped in sticky folds of skin.

"Pang, are you listening to me?" Elsevier insisted. "These don't belong to you. Hand them over. Now!"

"I want to stay with them," Pang replied. "The kittens need someone to take care of them."

Prince Damalo glanced between the boss and his employee. "You can stay with them, Pang," he offered. "Of course, you can."

"You don't have to do that, Your Highness," Elsevier said. "Pang is way out of line here. He has no place bargaining with clients. You've done enough already."

"We'll take you, Pang," Prince Damalo insisted, "on my word, and Sterling as my witness. We'll need someone to take care of our cubs on the trip home anyway."

Pang scrutinized Prince Damalo's face as he cradled the impossible animals, trying to sense whether the Prince was being sincere.

"What do you mean by take them home?" Elsevier interjected, furrowing his brow.

"There are two of them, aren't there?" Prince Damalo added. "We donate one to the preserve and take the other back with us. I'd much prefer a living trophy to a stuffed carcass."

"That's not quite how it works, Your Highness. You already donated an embryo when you arrived here. This is a new species."

The Prince gave Elsevier a canny look. "I thought the Conservation Board decided how it works."

"It does, of course."

"And Bella tells me you want to sit on the Board."

"I would be honored to be considered. But this is still quite different in many respects. These animals could be fragile. We have no idea how long they'll live. We need to study them."

"Then you've got our nomination." The Prince smiled. "Now let's get on with it. I know Pang will take very good care of our prize. Won't you, Pang?"

Pang nodded, despite himself. It was all happening so fast. He could feel the little heartbeats thumping beneath the fur of the baby ligers.

"There you have it," Prince Damalo said. "What do you say, Sterling?"

Elsevier reluctantly bowed his head.

Pang stared at the royal. Prince Damalo, beneath his chiseled cheekbones, was smarter than he had let on. Elsevier thought he'd had the better of him because the Prince had seemed so naïve, but he knew when to wield his power. All royalty did, and—Pang realized—it was Elsevier who had forgotten.

"Pang was my best tracker," Elsevier muttered to himself. Then he conceded. "It's done, Your Highness."

Pang released the cubs into Elsevier's hands. The tour operator cradled them softly and cooed at them like a seasoned parent. He snapped vids with Prince Damalo holding the animals with a triumphant smile.

That night, as they dined on barbecued water buffalo under the stars of New Limpopo, Princess Larabella opened her vial of thanaka and powdered it onto Pang's cheeks.

"I thought you might like to try the thanaka yourself, Pang," she said. "Since you're coming with us."

His skin felt cool and airy, as if a cleansing breeze was wafting through his soul. "Thank you, Your Highness."

"Good. You'll take good care of our baby," she said, petting one of the cubs. "Won't you, Pang?"

VALUING LIFE

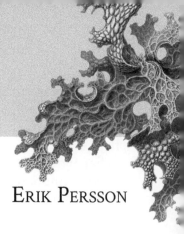

ERIK PERSSON

I have a question for you: Does an environment have to be natural to qualify as nature conservation?

In Deji Olukotun's "This is How We Save Them," an exomoon was transformed into a giant game reserve, mimicking Earth's environments, where a local business lets rich people kill animals for sport, while a part of the income pays for conservation (not unlike many actual businesses on Earth).

The environment on the moon is entirely created by humans, made up of a number of biomes inspired by different Earth biomes, designed to sustain Earth's animals and to provide an exciting and reasonably challenging environment for the human hunters.

Can this be called conservation? The environments are completely man-made. They are made up by species from another world (Earth), and they are primarily designed as a kind of playground for paying customers.

If it is conservation, what specifically is it conserving? Nature, environments, ecosystems, species, or just the business in question?

The ecosystems on the moon have to be functional and fairly reminiscent of corresponding Earth's ecosystems to be able to sustain themselves and the game animals, only half of which will be permanent parts of the ecosystem, while the other half are only temporary guests in these environments. They are brought up fast by the help of growth hormones, and then killed. Thus, these animals do not seem to contribute anything to the ecosystems other than money from the hunters who kill them.

Is it rather a matter of more general nature conservation? To answer this question, one needs to consider the relation between *nature* and *natural*. The term *natural* is used in many different ways in different contexts by different people. One feature they seem to have in common, and also have in common with the word *nature*, is that they seem to imply some kind of distancing from the human-made. Saying that something is natural seems to imply a low degree of interference by humans, or at least a low degree of conscious interference. The term *nature* also tends to be used about environments with a low degree of human interference. Finding an environment with no human interference at all is probably impossible on planet Earth. If nothing else, pollution seems to spread everywhere, and human induced climate change affects all environments on Earth.

If the aim of nature conservation is to protect environments from (more) human interference, then it seems counterproductive to take a moon, previously uninhabited by humans, terraform it, and implant organisms on the moon that could never have moved there without the help of humans. In fact, the moon was sterilized to get rid of any possible indigenous (that is, "natural") life, terraformed to be able to uphold Earth's life, and then seeded by species from Earth. This means, if anything, it is a matter of sacrificing one environment to conserve another, from another world, and to do it through a very unnatural process.

If, on the other hand, the aim of the conservation in this case is specifically to protect *Earth's* environments from further human interference, moving them to another world and using them in a way that is specifically designed to sustain certain Earth's animals could make some sense. The question here of course is: is it right to sacrifice the environment of one world to save environments from another?

Perhaps Earth's ecosystems are perceived as more important than the original environment on the moon because they are *our* environments. It is understandable that we'd rather save them, but is it ethically right? Normally, on Earth, we tend to favor those closest to us in one way or another, but from an ethical perspective, excessively favoring one's own is highly questionable.

Another reason why the environments implanted on the moon from Earth could be more important is that it was doubtful whether there was any previous life on the moon to begin with, and if there was, it was very primitive. This raises the questions, is an environment with life more important than one without life and is more advanced life more important than less advanced life?

Life is usually assigned a very high value, so an environment that harbors life may well be perceived as more valuable than a lifeless one, and for good reasons. Even though we still lack a universal definition of *life*, there seems to be a high level of agreement that life is special, exciting, interesting, and valuable. It is not for nothing that one of the scientific quests that attracts most attention outside the academic world is the search for extraterrestrial life. Even so, there are those who claim that all environments, or at least all natural environments, deserve protection, whether they harbor life or not. From a scientific perspective, environments with no life can also be quite interesting as study objects in their own right.

Is then more advanced life more valuable than less advanced life, and therefore environments that harbor advanced life more valuable than environments with very primitive life (as may have been the case on the exomoon)?

Interacting with more advanced organisms is certainly more exciting for most of us (though there are exceptions of course; microbiologists tend to find primitive life forms very exciting). For hunting purposes, as in the story, it is probably more exciting to hunt more advanced animals, but here we are focusing on conservation as a rationale for the hunting business, so the question must still be: Is conservation of more advanced life more important? Even to the extent that the money from the hunting business helps pay for the sterilization of a moon with possible microbial life and substituting it with more complex life forms. Is this a good thing?

With the discussions about life, we are starting to slide into another possible conservation aim, mentioned above—species conservation. It is quite common on Earth to defend hunting by claiming it helps preserve the species, usually by contributing money to the conservation efforts in the form of fees paid by the hunters. In this story, there are indications that species conservation is part of the business model, at least as described by the owner of the business. One of the technicians expresses doubts regarding the sincerity of these claims, however. His doubts are especially triggered by the fact that one of the animals bred for the hunting safari is a liger. A liger is a hybrid between two species, lion and tiger. It is thus not a species, and it is not naturally occurring even on Earth. Also, male ligers are infertile, which means they will never be able to sustain a viable population. The fact that the liger does not belong to a recognized species, that it is not natural the way the term was discussed above, and that male ligers are infertile, all indicate that liger conservation is not a serious or legitimate form of conservation.

On the other hand, we do sometimes conserve man-made "living products" (for lack of a better term) in the form of cultivated crops and landraces in gene banks. In these cases, it is not a matter of nature conservation, though, but of purely instrumental conservation of the genetic basis for food improvement, and to some extent of human cultural heritage.

A better excuse for the hunting business that could motivate the perpetuation of the liger, and also deal with many of the other question marks that have been raised above, would be if (contrary to how it is described in the story) the actual conservation took place on Earth. The hunting business on the moon would then only serve as a playground that attracts money from wealthy hunters, money used for conservation on Earth. In this case, it does not matter how unnatural the animals or environments on the moon are. They could just as well be breeding dinosaurs for hunting, or they could use animatronics, or maybe just build a totally different kind of playground with really cool rides and no killing at all. From a conservation perspective it would not matter as long as the money pours in.

So, if the real conservation were to take place on Earth, while the artificial environments and even the artificial animal (the liger) on the moon only serve the purpose of attracting money for conservation on Earth, would that be a good rationale for the hunting business?

It would handle most of the objections raised so far, but if the hunting is just a means of attracting money for conservation, one might also ask, why not do that through some other means? We mentioned a few alternatives above, and if we think conservation is important, why do we not contribute the necessary funds directly without taking the detour via killing animals off-world? If it is important enough to kill for, why is it not important enough to fund without killing?

This brings us to one last objection against the business, in my view by far the most serious objection. Whether conservation of unnatural environments or species is real conservation is one thing, but what about the fact that individual animals are killed for the sake of species? Is it ever okay to sacrifice individuals for a bigger whole? I think this is the really pressing question raised by this story, and I would say that the answer in this case is a clear no. Sacrificing a smaller number of individuals to save a much larger number can be defendable, but it is hard to see how sacrificing sentient—ligers are just at sentient as lions and tigers—individuals for a human construct such as a species can be defendable.

The questions raised by this story have immediate significance on Earth today, but they also have relevance for long term space exploration, including our relationships to eventually contacted extraterrestrial life. What is described by the author could in a further future be actualized, for example, on Mars. Some of the proponents of Mars exploration argue that we might need a backup environment to protect ourselves, as well as other Earth's species, from environmental destruction on Earth. At the same time, we do not know if there is already indigenous life on Mars. If we find primitive life on Mars, will it still be right to sterilize and terraform it to become a second home for Earth's life? And will it be right to submit individual extraterrestrial organisms to destructive studies in order to better understand the species and Martian life in general? If we do not find life on Mars, does it mean we can do whatever we want there, or is it still important to preserve the Mars's environment in its original "natural" state?

The questions we have pondered here are also relevant in a more general sense, since they are ultimately about the value and moral standing of different environments, and of life itself, as well as about the relative value and moral status of different kinds of life, and not least about whether it is right to sacrifice the individual for the whole.

FURTHER READING

Bertka, C.M. (ed.) (2009). *Exploring the Origin, Extent, and Future of Life.* Cambridge University Press.

Cockell, Charles S.; Horneck, Gerda (2006). "Planetary Parks—Formulating a Wilderness Policy for Planetary Bodies." *Space Policy* 22, 256–61.

Hargrove, Eugene C. (ed.) (1986). *Beyond Spaceship Earth—Environmental Ethics and the Solar System.* Sierra Club Books.

Jamieson, D. (1998). "Animal Liberation is an Environmental Ethic." *Environmental Values* 7, 41–57.

Persson, Erik (2008). *What is Wrong with Extinction?* Lund University.

Persson, Erik (2012). The Moral Status of Extraterrestrial Life. *Astrobiology* 12, 976-984.

Schwartz, James S.J. & Milligan, Tony (eds.). *The Ethics of Space Exploration.* Springer.

Seckbach, Joseph; Gordon, Richard; Peters, Ted (eds.). *Astrobiology: Science, Ethics, and Public Policy*. Scrivener Publishing, Wiley.

Szocik, Konrad (ed.). *The Human Factor in a Mission to Mars—An Interdisciplinary Approach*. Springer.

THE FAR SIDE OF
THE DOOR

PREMEE MOHAMED

When it was all over, what Sybil would remember most clearly was the surprise of those first moments: the way the boy staggered, stumbled, and finally fell. The way he pitched straight forward, not putting his hands out. Sybil's sensors recorded two seconds of audio, air screaming out of his cracked helmet before the nanocapsules embedded in the glass sealed it over.

For those two seconds, no one moved. Then everyone moved at once: shaking him, running to the rover over blackened ground. The planet's gravity was almost Earth's—point nine-eight, a difference so fractional that visitors could not feel it. But Sybil felt that gravity had been cancelled, even reversed, so light did the boy seem in their joined hands.

"Heatstroke," Sybil said. "Right?"

The doctor shook his head.

"What?" she said incredulously, and glanced down the hallway where they had taken the fallen scientist, as if she could see him through the dozen spongy white walls that separated his gurney from the doctor's office. She sat heavily on the edge of the doctor's desk.

"Definitely not." He ducked his head, then pressed a button on his desk. "Dr. Bellerose, do you mind if I record as we talk?"

"Not at all."

"What was Christiansen doing out there?"

"Assisting me with my investigation," she said crisply.

"Where were you when he fell?"

"The south side of Eight Dome, about two hundred meters from the edge of . . ." She trailed off. "Didn't his suit record his location?"

"No," the doctor said. "All the circuits were dead." Again he lowered his head, an unconscious gesture which Sybil knew to be placatory but annoyed her instead. She glared at his dark, curly hair; hers had been that black once.

"What was he doing when he collapsed?" the doctor asked.

"I'll start at the beginning," Sybil said, and slid off the desk. There wasn't much: her fame had arrived before her, like a sonic boom thumping against the thin atmosphere, proclaiming most of the story.

Yes, she was *the* Dr. Bellerose who had designed the colony domes thirty years ago; yes, she did indeed live on the station orbiting Celerem-57. And her reasons for that were her own, and she would not discuss them. Instead she glossed over the facts: the supply shuttle that had overshot on arrival and accidentally incinerated both itself and Eight Dome, leaving the glassy, charred mark that appeared on flyby images like a droplet of black paint. Sheer luck that no one had been inside the dome, though many had suffered in the blast wave and the hospital was still full of recovering victims three solweeks later.

"Exec asked me to investigate," she said shortly, referring to the executive committee governing this colony, usually called Bubblewrap, and Edenderry, the mining colony some fifty kilometers away. "Not the accident itself. The crash is a separate inquiry. They just wanted to know if it was safe to rebuild. Any fractures hidden under the regolith, the compaction, geochemical changes, whether the aquifer's been affected, get samples. Soil, air, water, debris. That's what the boy was doing. Him and the other kid they gave me—what's her name. Garnet. And Dr. McLaren, of course."

The doctor nodded. Bubblewrap consisted of ten domes, of which two were residential; losing a full crop-producing dome was devastating. Naturally Exec would want to rebuild and replant as fast as possible. Sybil didn't think people would go hungry, but it might be a near thing for a while, which irritated her. In her original design she had emphasized redundancy, resilience, inefficiencies, again and again. Have backups. Have doubles of everything. Find storage, cross-train, save everything. Don't run too close to the bone; leave some flesh. You never know when you'll need it.

"Sampling," the doctor said, lifting his head. His eyes were large and brown, and seemed panicked despite his casual tone. "Dr. Bellerose, did you happen to see whether Christiansen's helmet lost integrity before he fell? Or after?"

She stared at him. The window behind him framed domes glistening like gems in the early light: green, pale blue, amber. Her heart was pounding for no reason. The boy had become overheated somehow; the suit just hadn't recorded it. Or gotten dehydrated. That was all. Food poisoning probably.

And yet: "I knew you were going to ask that," she said.

Sybil left the hospital three hours later, thoroughly out of sorts. They hadn't *quite* threatened to detain her if she didn't comply with the testing, but they hadn't not, either. "Of course it's not me, you bloody idiots," she'd said loudly into the recording gear. "You just give me one mechanism, one exposure pathway, and I'll shut up. Hm?"

"Please remain still," the imaging robot said.

"Up yours, creep."

McLaren had messaged her an hour into the process to say he'd sent Garnet back to the lab, and had himself gone for a quiet pint at the Slippered Fox in Seven Dome, since Bellerose clearly intended to play the hero and stay with the fallen scientist.

She hadn't been allowed to reply, which was probably for the best. Now her irritation had faded to a hum behind the increasingly more urgent internal alarm that something was really wrong, something so large she suspected she glimpsed only its barest edge. She thought of the crash site, the slices of razor-sharp nanoceramic driven into the thin soil on impact, so that only a finger's-width of danger showed instead of the tons below.

She entered the pub.

McLaren sat by the window, his broad face tinted green by a panel filled with chlorella capsules that bobbled hypnotically up and down and veiled the interior of the pub from passers-by. She slid into the booth and ordered a pint of the first thing in the table-top menu, not bothering to look at the name.

"You look like you need something stronger than a beer," said McLaren. He was a big man, about Sybil's age, but with the subtly weathered, shop-worn look that distinguished planetside folks from those who lived in the station. His hand engulfed his pint glass.

"How many of those have you had?" she said.

"Why?"

"I need you to be useful," Sybil said. "Not falling over. Christiansen's in a coma."

McLaren raised his gingery eyebrows, the disdain falling from his face at once. "What happened?"

"I don't know. Bodies aren't my specialty. And before I had even left that doctor's office, a nurse was ill too, then one of the blood techs. They threw us all into haz-suits—you know the ones, those disposable blue ones with the gel. Disgusting. And then they scanned me from top to toe and poked me in a hundred places. Confiscated the rover to scan too. I had to take a public belt here."

Her beer emerged from its porthole; she peeled back the top, dropped the algal disc into the compost hole, and gulped half of it at a go. She'd been allowed to see Christiansen just once and now she regretted it. His face had been sunken, grayish beneath the warm golden-brown skin, instead of laughing and eager and alive. She'd barely known him, but it would be terrible if that were her last memory of him.

"They think you brought something down from Two?" McLaren said, filling in the blank as she wiped her mouth. "Ridiculous."

"I know. Let alone that all the native microflora here is *from* the station. I was scanned before I left, I was scanned on the shuttle, I was scanned twice after I landed. Everything checked out. And yet . . ."

She rolled the glass between her hands, aware that they were shaking. The hospital wasn't set up for epidemiological tracing. They didn't have the networks, the equipment, the staff. And was it truly an epidemic? They had analyzed Christiansen to within an inch of his life, and nothing had come up. No pathogens, nothing unusual chemically, biologically, genetically. "They must have missed something," she said.

"Or," McLaren said.

"No." Sybil finished her beer—bitter, over-hopped, a side effect (she knew from chatting to Christiansen and Garnet) of Five Dome's many breweries and their escalating bespoke hops race. Garnet had complained: *In a world where you can make plants do whatever you want, why are they getting grosser by the day?*

"I'm just saying," McLaren said, tapping the panel for another drink.

"Don't you use that tone on me, Red."

"You don't think it's justified?"

"I think it's unhelpful."

Sybil looked away, steadying her nerves. Through the wavering green bubbles, a group of kids in black-and-navy school uniforms clustered in a small park across the street. The smaller children wore light polyfoam masks printed to resemble animals they'd never seen in their lives: foxes, bears, tigers. Others manipulated control decks, sending tiny drones humming overhead, the bee-sized bodies swarming to form shapes of other animals.

A lunar new year celebration? She couldn't tear her eyes away from their small lively bodies. All those kids. Supposing a contagious disease . . . and the other colony, Edenderry, that was mostly families. Twice as many as Bubblewrap.

It's not possible, she wanted to say. Meaning the decade she'd spent studying Celerem-57, this promising planet: analyzing every aspect from the ragged atmosphere to its encouragingly molten core, from the exact composition of its mineral coating, to the hollows in the bedrock, the dissolved salts in its water, the astonishingly complex regolith chemistry, the temperature, the gravity, the magnetic field, everything. She and dozens of others, she would have reminded him. Including McLaren himself. *It wasn't just me looking at that data. So if you're suggesting we missed something, and something deadly at that, then we all did.*

But they hadn't. They had made certain that nothing would answer the door when humanity came knocking. There was nothing here from the smallest scale to the largest: not bacteria, prions, viruses, even molecular precursors. A clean slate. In fact, if you were being pedantic, the *absence* of a door to knock on proved the cleanness of the slate. Sterile.

Trust McLaren to find the soft spot of her self-doubt and twist a knife into it. He'd been doing it for years.

"They would have found something by now," Sybil added. "People have been here for almost twenty-five years, I don't need to remind you."

"Twenty-five exactly," McLaren said, gesturing out the window. "There's going to be a celebration for it. Next solweek."

Sybil's heart sped up again. Not something she'd brought, not something indigenous. What then?

Her suit monitor beeped peevishly, warning her about her heart rate. Along her forearm monitor, a small scrolling text from the doctor had appeared, pale blue against the violet screen: *Three more down. Calling for quarantine.*

"Drink that." She pointed at McLaren's half-full glass. "We've got to get to the bottom of this, and right quick. Rent another rover. Call Garnet."

"What's the damn rush?"

"Whatever it is," Sybil said coldly, "moves at a sprint. We've got to outpace it."

"You know," McLaren said as Sybil stood, "you don't run the show down here. Technically, I'm head of the investigation. I decide whether we go back or not."

"Yes, I saw it on the paperwork," she said. "But I'm headed back out there. Arrest me if you want. Help me or don't." She turned her arm to make sure he could read the message, watched his face change. "You choose."

Sybil had visited Paris once as a child and had never forgotten the quality of the light over the ravaged city: golden, forgiving. Even when it rained, the water came down through swathes of endless sunset. Here the light was the same, making her think of Paris while the rover roared across the trackless, gritty soil outside the domes. The black hole of the crash site, and the gold of the light from its tiny, hot, distant star.

"There's nothing here," McLaren said peevishly after they had walked several circuits.

Sybil shrugged. Maybe whatever it was had been on the supply ship already. Maybe it . . . oh Hell, who knew. Flew through a cloud of something. Had been taken over by aliens. Little green men.

The screen in the lower corner of her helmet said: *One Dome and Three Dome now quarantined. Quarantine level is: Complete.*

The residential domes. How much air did they have, how much food, water? Oxygen flowed from the other domes, the ones growing the carefully chosen and bioengineered crops she'd selected. The miniaturized vegetables and petite fruit trees, the vines and berry shrubs, the algal bioreactor vats. Sybil had planned for everything but this.

Her companions had received the same message; Garnet straightened, cupping a sample jar in either hand. McLaren exhaled sharply, a *huff* through the helmet com. Neither dome was visible from here unless they went over to Nine Dome and climbed to its summit, but Sybil could imagine it all too easily: the blaring announcements, everyone running to their home or dorm. The clinics preparing for the worst. One small blessing was that the hospital to which Christiansen had been brought was the biggest facility and was outside both residential domes.

Garnet dropped her empty jars and squeaked in her helmet. "Dr. Bellerose!"

"What is it? Are you all right? Do you feel sick?"

"I . . . I'll send it to you, hold on."

The younger woman punched frantically at her suit computer and managed to forward the message to Sybil.

People are collapsing in 9D! Stay out there!

"Who's that from?" Sybil said, sending it quickly to the hospital.

"My friend Jen. She works in the biogas plant. I . . ." Garnet frowned, just visible behind the protective sheen of the glass. "She says . . . some of the bees are falling to the ground too. Dying. Some seem fine. I don't know . . ."

"There's nothing that infects both humans and bees," McLaren said exasperatedly. "It's got to be something else. Chemical. A gas leak that penetrated Christiansen's suit . . . maybe a fracture line under the hospital . . . it could be a physical coincidence. Not a pathogen."

Sybil wasn't listening. Nine Dome had been damaged in the crash, the report had said. About two hectares of crops had burned. The engineers had pumped in fresh air, put in the replacement panels—they were modular, designed (by Sybil's own hands! *Was* this her fault?) to be installed and re-sealed in minutes. Minutes.

Something about the crash. Something . . . but burning only meant death under certain circumstances, didn't it? Plenty of plants on Earth needed fire to germinate their seeds. None of them had been brought here, but . . .

"No one is safe," she said out loud; McLaren and Garnet turned to stare at her. "We might be next in line."

"What should we do?" Garnet said.

Sybil didn't know. She took a deep breath, kicking in the suit's filters, and said, "I need data. Red, can you and Garnet set up a monitoring network out here?"

"Out here? But—"

"Yes, I *know* there's plenty inside the domes," she cut him off, frustration threatening to strangle her voice into a squeak. Why couldn't he just listen to her? It had been his constant needling and double-checking that had driven her to live at the station, though she'd never tell him that; they had once worked so closely together they'd seemed to share a single mind, and then he'd begun to resent the fame he thought she was accruing, the way his name had seemed to vanish from the paperwork . . . and yes, all right, had she been happy to take the spotlight? A few times. But he had become intolerable, and so had she. And now when she needed a second pair of hands, he withdrew his out of doubt and old hurts.

There was no time to talk it out. Sybil could see what was happening inside Nine Dome and pointed: the draped swathes of greenery inside twisting as if in a high wind, inside that windless place. Writhing across the transparent panels like they were looking for something. And changing: green to blue, even black, violet. Blinking patterns, forming a signal or a call to something. Not to Sybil. Not to a human at all, she suspected. The patterns themselves said only: *You were right. This is bigger than you knew.*

"Set up a perimeter around the burn mark," Sybil said breathlessly. "It's going to move from dome to dome. Dig in sensors for anything, everything. Set them to alarm at any changes, no matter how small, in seismic, moisture, temperature, molecular fragments, pH. And imaging, anywhere on the spectrum we've got equipment for. Infrared. Ultra-violet. Visible. Micro-wave. Whatever."

"And where will you be during this?" McLaren crossed his arms, already sulking, Sybil thought, as if once again she planned to be the hero, leaving him in her dust.

"Back to the hospital," Sybil said.

"We need the rover."

"Keep it. We've got much, much bigger things to worry about."

"But you have a plan," Garnet said tentatively. "Right?"

"I don't know, kid." Sybil took off across the thin hardpan, hoping she was not drawing the attention of anything under her boots. As she ran she ignored the suit's angry beeping, and thought of Christiansen and Garnet, who were so young, who had been born here, and had seen very little of life.

The hospital was locked down; Sybil triggered a dozen alarms simply stepping onto the painted line that marked off the rover parking. But no one emerged to drive her off. She stood in front of the tightly-sealed nanoceramic doors and shouted, "Let me in!"

"Are you experiencing a medical emergency?" an artificial voice replied from above her head, making her jump; she looked up at the small silvery drone and thought again of the kids across from the pub. Their masks, their toys.

She thought with the clarity of fear: *Something else on this planet is not what we thought it was. Something else has used something small to create the illusion of size. Of a dangerous animal. A tiger. Even though it may not know what it is creating.*

"I need to talk to Dr. Qadib. He was there this morning. Let me in!"

"No entry except for medical emergencies," the drone said primly.

"Hang on," Sybil said, "I need to find a rock."

Her suit screen crackled: a voice call. "Are you going to let me in?" she said.

"Yes, one moment," Qadib said; he sounded exhausted. "I'm sorry, several staff are ill—"

"Don't apologize. Do you still have people in pathology?"

"One person, but—"

"Good," Sybil said, setting her jaw. The doors opened a crack, so that she had to turn sideways to enter, and at once two automatic arms swathed her in another gel-filled haz-suit. Her helmet overcompensated and made everything vibrate unpleasantly, as if she were underwater. She was dry-mouthed and dizzy, and hoped it was from the run alone.

Qadib met her in the eerily silent hallway. "What is it, Dr. Bellerose?"

"Christiansen," she said. "I need to see him."

"But the spread—"

"I know," she said grimly. "But I think we've all been exposed. Every one of us. I'll have to risk it."

"Risk what?"

It took the pathology tech ten tries to get the sample Sybil was demanding, and she would have felt bad if Christiansen hadn't been unconscious and anesthetized; perhaps, Sybil thought, he'd brag about the neat row of ten punch-marks along his arm one day.

"This is bizarre," Qadib whispered as Sybil supervised attempt number ten. "You're using . . . *soil* sampling techniques on human . . ."

"Quick," Sybil whispered. "Now!"

The tech slipped the little disc of muscle into the bottle Sybil held out. This time instead of running down the hallway to the lab, Sybil capped it and thrust it into the canister of dry ice on the bedside table. A white cloud ballooned upwards, quickly sucked away by the overhead vents; the minuscule catalytic disc inside the bottle's lid had fallen into the liquid polymer it contained, generating enough reaction heat to fill the room with clouds for several minutes. Sybil glared at the canister through the blue haze of her helmet.

Nothing yet, said the message at her wrist; she glanced cursorily at it as they headed down the hall. She didn't bother replying to McLaren; she'd suspected the sensors wouldn't detect anything. Their foe would not show itself unless it were caught by surprise.

The tech gingerly slid the plasticized sample into the microtome, let it count to fifty, then pressed the RANDOM button to load a handful of the thin-section images into the microscope. Sybil held her breath, scanning the wide monitors. "There," she said, her voice heavy with relief.

Qadib gasped, then frowned and zoomed in. "We didn't see anything like this. Not in any of our other samples. How did you know . . ."

"Who knows anything?" Sybil said. "I guessed. From the damage in Nine Dome."

"So it *was* the shuttle that—"

She shook her head, feeling dizzy again. Her wrist pinged: *G collapsed. Still breathing. Taking her to hosp.*

"Look at this," she said, pointing. Gel squelched in the water-tight tip of her glove. "It looks like a new virus, doesn't it? See how it isn't triggering pattern recognition in your database. We didn't see this in our pre-habitation scans, or in any samples from the surface to hundreds of meters deep. We wouldn't have let anyone come here if novel viruses had been detected."

"Then what . . ."

Sybil flicked through the images. "It's not an endemic virus. It's the inorganic components of Celerem-57—which we already knew about—assembling themselves into what *looks* like a virus. I suspect they learned how to from our enteric viruses. Ours and our crops."

"They make themselves? How?" Qadib zoomed in again, zoomed back out. "Hmm. No indigenous life was detected. But the pieces . . . it self-assembles, then perhaps completes horizontal gene transfer with the phenotypic goal of *looking* like our viruses. Look at this: almost but not quite. In copying our DNA, it is causing what we see in the ill patients: neoplasms, organ malfunctions, plaques in the arteries. It is disguising itself. But it is not a perfect disguise."

"And it knows when it's being looked at," Sybil said. "Maybe something mechanical—being agitated—or chemical, biological. So whenever you took a sample for normal analysis, it simply disassembled itself and vanished. We had to freeze it in space and time to even see these. And look," she added, pointing to the corner of one monitor. "It's trying to break itself apart already. Realizing it was caught."

"Realizing," Qadib laughed, a nervous squawk. "Do you think it's intelligent life?"

"I think both the words 'intelligent' and 'life' aren't very useful anymore," Sybil said. "I think the shuttle accident convinced something that it was in danger. The components in the soil aren't pre-biotic, they're post-biotic . . . we were right that there was no life here, but we didn't know there was life *in potentia*. We didn't recognize it. So it was hurt, it went to defend itself. I bet this has happened before. We can't be the first extraplanetary life to come here. The other domes . . . look, they don't all have a liner below them. Some are built right on the regolith."

Qadib stared at her, working through her words. "How can we cure this?"

Sybil scrolled through the images, mind racing. "We have to convince the entire planet," she said slowly, "that we've seen what it can do. I *do* have an idea," she clarified as Qadib began to speak. "But we're not starting with the kid."

"He might die!"

"I won't experiment on him," she said. "Not him first."

At first it seemed as if nothing was happening; Sybil realized she was bracing for McLaren to say something snippy, but his attention, like hers and Qadib's, was fixed on the triangular panel of vine-swathed nanoceramic before them, and the machine trundling beneath it, spritzing the silvery fluid they had spent two days brewing—literally—in a borrowed beer tank.

"Some experiment," McLaren said. "How do we know this isn't going to provoke something into experimenting on *us*?"

"We don't," Sybil said. "But we can't wait on a perfect solution. People are getting sick. Crops are dying. Look at the bees."

He squinted. "That's not a bee."

"It . . . probably used to be a bee," Sybil admitted. She moved her boot away from it.

"What's in this stuff, anyway?" he said. "What happens if we get it on us?"

"Nothing," Sybil said. "I hope. I got ahold of one of the brewers Garnet knows and gave him our data. He figured out how to tag the viral capsid using a CRISPR nanobot, but then we couldn't figure out how to prevent the virus from just evading the bot like everything else."

"A nanobot? But those are just for . . . well, repairing domes, healing concrete, that kind of thing."

"I know," Sybil said absently, staring at the wall of vines as they dripped and shivered under the liquid. Were the leaves moving on their own, or was it the spray? "Well, luckily there was someone else there who did a masters or something on CRISPR complexes and hydrogels. You know—when the sequence is cut, you can set it to release all sorts of things. She did hers on anti-viral drugs. You can also uncage prions, create electrical circuits, things like that."

"And?"

"And so when the bots come after the viral proteins," she said, pointing at the dripping vines, "the snipped capsid will try to disassemble itself. But since we know that sequence too, we programmed another complex to get that one. One knocks over the vase, one sweeps up the broken pieces. The complex binds the broken pieces to the receptors in the hydrogel. That's the shine you can see there—it's not really metal, the chelating agents just refract the light like it is. Then the water and the plant's sap get rid of the hydrogel."

"Okay," he said after a minute. "That's clever."

"Don't be mad you didn't come up with it," Sybil said.

"*You* sound mad you didn't come up with it."

"I'm . . ." The vines trembled all at once, rippled as if a hand had passed over them, sending droplets of the solution raining down. The ground trembled. "I think I would have been before this. The worst part of me, I suppose."

McLaren caught himself as the ground shook again, his face white with fear, as if he had turned on the helmet's internal LEDs. His voice remained steady. "I feel like some of that's my fault."

"Could be," Sybil said.

"We could talk about it later."

"Might do."

Her breath grew ragged. The vines were undeniably moving now: not threatening but curious, and all at once. If they reminded her of a snake, the snake was a big one. Boa or anaconda. At the base of the panel, two small lemon saplings began to whip around in circles, tearing their leaves loose. "Glad we tried this with things that can't move," Sybil said.

Qadib bumped into her as he stepped backwards. "Is it working?"

"It's causing a reaction," Sybil said diplomatically. "You'll note that ain't a yes or a no."

"Noted."

All the plants were rattling against the panels now, or drumming against the floor, rhythmically clattering branches and tendrils, hurling nuts, seeds, broken twigs. Sybil thought of communication and how limited the human conception of it was. How the word spreads when it is not "words." Celerem-57 had gone from something utterly known to something unknown; now, if they all survived this, it might become known again.

We see you, she said in her head. *We saw what you were doing. Stop. You see we have the power to stop you. We're asking you to stop on your own. I know you can do it.*

The pinkish grow-lights flickered and failed; in the roaring, clattering darkness, the spraying machine also stuttered to a stop. Sybil did not mute her helmet's sound intake. She straightened and stood as if in the eye of the storm, hearing the voice of the planet's life shouting its defiance.

And then, minute by minute, the cacophony stopped.

Defeat? She thought a truce more likely. McLaren's voice came into her helmet; though when the lights came feebly back on, she discovered that he lay on the ground several feet away. "Did we win?" he croaked.

Sybil studied the vines: green, unmoving. Her ears were ringing with adrenaline. "Hard to say."

When the four months of extended quarantine were up, she insisted on a farewell party with the initial investigative team, and they met in the Slippered Fox for burgers and beer.

"Exec is paying," Sybil said airily when Christiansen sat across from her. "Get whatever you want."

"Thank you, ma'am."

"And don't call me 'ma'am.'"

"I won't, m . . . d . . . Sybil." He blushed hotly as Garnet slid in next to him.

"How are my domes?" Sybil said.

Garnet beamed. "Better than I've ever seen them. Edible biomass productivity is up thirty percent. Thirty percent! Things are growing out of season. Nobody touched the light schedules, nothing like that. Irrigation seems effortless . . . there's water *pressure* now in some wellheads. And there's nothing phytotoxic in it anymore. It's like rainwater. Oh, and someone in Six Dome claims he grew a potato the size of his head."

"I saw it," Christiansen said. "It's pretty close."

"He says he's not going to eat it," Garnet said. "He wants to put it in the museum."

Sybil moved closer to the window as McLaren sat next to her, and said, "So what do you think? Do you think the planet's communicating with us now? Trying to help us succeed?"

Garnet nodded; Christiansen shook his head. After his discharge from the hospital, he hadn't cut his hair, and now the long curls dangled nearly into his beer. Sybil smiled at him.

"We'll have to study it," McLaren said gruffly, scrolling through the menu as if he didn't eat here twice a week. "You know, Sybil, we could use some help starting a research program. The university has funding. Exec okayed it a few days ago."

Sybil swirled her beer. "I've got projects of my own back home," she said. "But I'm happy to advise via text."

He shrugged.

As Sybil ate, listening to them chatter about new flowers and fruit, the recovery of the bees, she thought about her room in the station, her consulting contracts, the churchlike hush of the place. Down here was life—strange, loud, novel. And no longer stamped with her name and controlled by her blueprints, in fact no longer hers at all, and she had been wrong to think of it that way.

Before the viewports went dark, the last thing she saw on the ascent was the black teardrop of the crash site—where something had been awoken by a surprise knock on its door. One day, with the combined efforts of humanity and the planet itself, even that mark would be gone under new life.

Smiling, she opened a program on her suit and began to scroll through available date windows for her return ticket.

SPACE AGRICULTURE

Going Where Farming Has Never Gone Before

RAYMOND M. WHEELER

Agriculture has been practiced by humans for millennia and when one considers space exploration, it is logical to assume agriculture will follow. Indeed, it is already happening on a small scale on the International Space Station (ISS), where astronauts grow leafy greens such as lettuce, mizuna, pak choi, kale, and even chile peppers in small plant chambers [1,2]. These chambers provide only about 0.15 m² or less growth area and so this form of agriculture is intended to only provide supplemental fresh foods [3], which can still have a profound impact on the crew nutrition and mental well-being [4,5].

But the question of using agriculture in space runs deeper than producing occasional fresh food and has been asked since the beginning of the space program: Can we use agriculture to provide more full life support for humans in space [6,7]? Can plants be used to supply large portions of the diet, thereby reducing, or perhaps even eliminating the need for food resupply? Can the plants be used to provide oxygen for the humans, remove the noxious carbon dioxide that builds up in space habitats like the ones designed by Dr. Bellerose in the preceding story, and perhaps even be coupled to water recycling systems? The answer to all these questions is YES [8].

First, it is important to consider the constraints and challenges for growing plants in space. We don't have a small farm on the International Space Station because there isn't enough volume to accommodate large plantings, nor is there sufficient electric power to run the lighting systems that are typically used in plant factories or vertical farms. The mass, power, and volume costs must always be considered for space. But as we go farther and stay longer, the resupply costs for food become prohibitively expensive, and at that point, regenerating some of the life support commodities like food, O_2, and water becomes a necessity. For example, a commonly discussed "reference" mission to the surface of Mars might take 6-9 months of transit time to get there, then a stay on the surface of about 500 days to account for the changing positions of Mars and Earth in their orbits, and then 6-9 months back. By some estimates, this could require nearly 10 metric tons of packaged food for a crew of four. But just as with the ISS, we won't be setting up a large farm on the first visit. A better way to think of it might be an evolution or sequential expansion of agriculture as the habitat infrastructure and capabilities expand with subsequent missions [9].

So, let's envision humans have arrived at Mars. How do we grow the plants? Unlike the weightless situations one must deal with on the ISS or during Mars transit for small plant growth systems, you will have some gravity (3/8 g) on Mars. This means that you can use conventional watering techniques, such as recirculating hydroponics where water runs downhill (down a trough to a reservoir). These hydroponic approaches are used widely on Earth and allow the greenhouse or vertical farmers to continually recycle their water and nutrients, and then just add back what the plants have used. This avoids any waste of water and nutrient fertilizer, which is a necessity for space. Such hydroponic systems will require hardware like pumps, pipes for plumbing, troughs or trays for growing the plants, sensors, and so forth. But in turn, they allow relatively easy cleaning and turnaround for replanting subsequent crops. However, you will need some additional water and nutrients. Where will you get those? These might come from in-situ resources in the surrounding environment, such as Martian ice or minerals from the regolith. The number one element needed by plants to grow is nitrogen, and there is evidence of nitrate-like minerals in some of the regolith of Mars [10]. But there are other resources, such as the inedible plant biomass, which can be processed (degraded) to recycle the nutrients to grow more crops, and of course wastes from humans, especially urine, which is rich in nutrients needed by plants (nitrogen, phosphorus, calcium, magnesium, and more) [11]. But urine also contains a lot of sodium, which plants don't need and can't tolerate in high concentrations.

Can you use the Martian regolith (Martian "soil") directly? Perhaps, but you will need supplemental fertilizer. The Martian regolith doesn't contain sufficient nutrients to sustain healthy, fast growing plants; in addition, the regolith contains potentially toxic perchlorate compounds that would need to be removed. Think of it as trying to revegetate a mine tailings pile or a rocky terrain. Some plants might be able to germinate and survive, but they will need nutrient supplements to grow. Even farmers in Iowa with some of the best soils in the world still add fertilizer to their corn crops to get high yields. Remember, mass, power, volume . . . if we use plants for life support, we need high yields per unit area and per unit volume to be cost effective and sustainable. But regolith could be amended with organic matter (like from compost) to improve the nutrient and water holding capacity. Hydroponic systems such as the nutrient film technique have very little water holding capacity in the root zone. If the circulation pumps fail, you must respond very quickly to avoid a catastrophic wilting of the crop. With a 3-dimensional soil from regolith that has water holding capacity, you are less prone to consequences from pump failures. But remember, all the water used by the plants or leached through the soil has to be captured and recycled—this is a must.

If you meet the water, nutrient, temperature, and carbon dioxide (for photosynthesis) needs, the number one factor that stands out for growing plants for life support is light! Light's effects on photosynthesis and yield are almost linear—1 X light, 1 X yield, 2 X light, 2 X yield, and so forth until you get to higher light intensities where photosynthetic rates begin to "saturate." You might consider transparent structures like greenhouses, but this presents challenges—finding transparent materials that hold pressure, getting the needed thermal insulation qualities, and holding up to the degrading effects of high UV radiation on the Martian surface. Plus you must consider the effects of dust storms and light dark cycles. Alternatively, you can use electric lighting, such as LEDs, which are remarkably efficient now, converting as much as 70-80% of their incoming power into light [12]. This is how much of the current life support testing with plants is proceeding, i.e., using LED lighting systems. But now you need electric power, another challenge. This is something mission planners could accommodate, perhaps with the use of small nuclear fission power generating capabilities.

Finally, what types of crops? If we think about sequential development of space agriculture, it might be best to first start with small plantings of fresh food (perishable) crops, like leafy greens and small fruits like tomatoes, peppers, and strawberries. These won't last for a 6-month shipment from Earth and could have positive effect on crew nutrition, provide dietary variety, and boost crew well-being [4,5]. Plus they have no processing requirements . . . they are pick-and-eat type crops. Then, perhaps you expand into "minimally" processed crops like potato and sweet potato that provide more calorie-dense foods with some protein but with little preparation, perhaps just cooking or baking. Finally, for more mature systems, begin adding grains and legumes, such as wheat, rice, soybean, and peanut to get a better balance of protein and fat with the carbohydrates [13], just as we do on Earth.

An additional step, but with added complexity, is to consider using secondary consumers for converting inedible plant biomass, such as leaves and stems, into food. These might be organisms like mushrooms (fungi), or insects that can consume cellulosic biomass, or fish like tilapia [14]. Then you could increase the production of total food from a given area of crops [9]. Another important factor is to select or breed plants that partition a lot of their growth into edible biomass, such as seeds, fruits, or tubers. This means more food production per unit area and less waste biomass. Indeed, this was one of the underpinning steps for the green revolution in the 20th century, e.g., grain crops with a higher harvest index. But in this case, we must select or develop the crops for the space environment, where we must deal with higher radiation levels, fractional gravity levels, and perhaps peculiar atmospheres with high CO_2 and reduced overall pressure. As with terrestrial agriculture, you must also consider the possibility of plant pathogens (even if "only" those hitching a ride with us from Earth instead of any kind of alien life akin to the story you've just read), so selecting diverse crops that have good disease resistance and implementing so-called integrated pest management strategies should be considered [15]. Understanding the overall microbiome of the plant systems and the space habitats will also be critical. In many ways, missions into space will be studies of "island biology" and understanding and managing the stability of these isolated ecosystems will be revealing, both for space and for Earth.

Space agriculture-related research by NASA was the first to use LEDs to grow plants, the first to carry out volume-efficient vertical farming concepts, and the first to grow a wide range of field crops, including root zone crops in hydroponics, demonstrating yields 2-5 X greater than world record field yields. As we learn more about supporting sustainable agriculture in space, we will learn more about sustainable agriculture on Earth—and vice versa.

REFERENCES

[1] Sugimoto, M. Y. Oono, O. Gusev, T. Matsumoto, T. Yazawa, M. A. Levinshkikh, V.N. Sychev, G.E. Bingham, R. Wheeler and M. Hummerick. (2014). "Genome-wide expression analysis of reactive oxygen species gene network in Mizuna plants grown in long-term spaceflight." *BMC Plant Biology* 2014 14, 4.

[2] Massa, G.D., N.F. Dufour, J.A. Carver, M.E. Hummerick, R.M. Wheeler, R.C. Morrow, T.M. Smith. (2017). "VEG-01: Veggie hardware validation testing on the International Space Station." *Open Agriculture* 2017 (2), 33-41.

[3] Johnson C.M., Boles H.O., Spencer L.E., Poulet L., Romeyn M., Bunchek J.M., Fritsche R., Massa G.D., O'Rourke A. and Wheeler R.M. (2021). "Supplemental food production with plants: A review of NASA research." *Frontiers in Astronomy and Space Science* 8, 734343. doi: 10.3389/ fspas.2021.734343

[4] Cooper, M.R., P. Catauro, and M. Perchonok. (2011). "Development and evaluation of bioregenerative menus for Mars habitat missions." *Acta Astronautica* 81, 555-562.

[5] Odeh, R. and C.L. Guy. (2017). "Gardening for therapeutic people-plant interactions during long-duration space missions." *Open Agriculture* 2, 1–13.

[6] Myers, J. (1954). "Basic remarks on the use of plants as biological gas exchangers in a closed system." *J. Aviation Med.* 25, 407-411.

[7] Salisbury, F.B., J.E. Gitelson, and G.M. Lisovsky. (1997). "Bios-3: Siberian experiments in bioregenerative life support." *BioScience* 47, 575-585.

[8] Wheeler, R.M. (2017). "Agriculture for space: People and places paving the way." *Open Agriculture* 2017 (2), 14-32.

[9] Wheeler, R.M. (2003). "Carbon balance in bioregenerative life support systems: Effects of system closure, waste management, and crop harvest index." *Adv. Space Res.* 31(1), 169-175.

[10] Stern et al. (2015). "Evidence for indigenous nitrogen in sedimentary and aeolian deposits from the Curiosity rover investigations at Gale crater, Mars."
www.pnas.org/cgi/doi/10.1073/pnas.1420932112

[11] Wignarajah, K. and D. Bubenheim. (1997). "Integration of crop production with CELSS waste management." *Adv. Space Res.* Vol. 20(10), 1833-1843.

[12] Pattison, P.M., J. Y. Tsao, G.C. Brainard, and B. Bugbee. (2018). "LEDs for photons, physiology and food." *Nature* 563, 493- 500.

[13] Salisbury, F.B. and M.A.Z. Clark. (1996). "Suggestions for crops grown in controlled ecological life-support systems, based on attractive vegetarian diets." *Adv. Space Res.* 18, 33-39.

[14] Katayama, N., Y. Ishikawa, M. Takaoki, M. Yamashita, S. Nakayama, K. Kiguchi, R. Kok, H. Wada, J. Mitsuhashi. (2008). "Entomophagy: A key to space agriculture." *Adv. Space Research* 41, 701-705.

[15] Schuerger, A.C. (2021). "Integrated Pest Management Protocols for Space-Based Bioregenerative Life Support Systems." *Frontiers in Astronomy and Space Sciences* 8, 759641. doi: 10.3389/fspas.2021.759641

RANYA'S CRASH

LISA JENNY KRIEG

(Translated from German by Simone Heller)

"Shit! Stupid shit!"

Rayna kicked the fender. She had been trying to repair the ornithomobile for half an hour now. But it was one of those days when nothing seemed to work. And in the meantime, day had turned into night.

She tried to restart the engine, but her makeshift connection didn't hold up against the pressure. The cable broke, and a surge of blue fluid exploded in her face.

"Damn this shit!"

She kicked it again for good measure, until her ornithomobile uttered an indignant caw and turned his head toward her.

"Sorry, Ten-two," she said. "I didn't mean it."

She stroked his black feathers and his big black beak. In the light of the full moon, the whole bird was draped in a bluish shimmer.

Ten-two purred.

"Right. There, there. Good bird," Ranya murmured, turning the Batla compass in her pocket between her thumb and index finger. For all the hope pinned on it, the compass had proven to be completely useless.

The crash was a fitting end to a rotten day. Despite her careful planning, she hadn't accomplished a thing. Her map was correct, that much was certain. And still she had found nothing up on Green Peak. Nothing but a band of angry goanna warrior women on the plateau at the top who had almost brought her journey to an end. They had landed an awkward hit on Ten-two's engine, right there on the cable she hadn't patched properly yesterday.

She had spent the whole day searching, and surely Manna was already waiting at home, hands twitching and a big pot of steaming bread soup waiting, as always when she welcomed her foster daughter home after a mission.

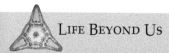

LIFE BEYOND US

Ranya certainly hadn't been able to resist boasting in front of her client, foster mother, or whichever name would best describe her complicated relationship with Manna. Yes, she had a sure-fire lead to a totally reliable trader offering a map! A genuine, original, hand-drawn inked map with all the secret stashes, all of them! Stashes! With Lilienthal's last stocks of *Diglaster poreus*. And she, a successful scout with multiple honors, would locate them, no doubt. The Batla compass she and Amit had found had been the icing on the cake. The ultimate promise that this expedition would be a success. Nobody could have guessed she didn't have a clue how to activate the artifact and it would turn out to be utterly useless, valuable or not.

Now here she was, sitting in this desert, at the bottom of a valley, surrounded by mountains drawing strange silhouettes into the night sky while moonlight tickled her nose. With Ten-two, whose feathers quivered with exhaustion, and whose engine . . . Just. Would. Not. Work!

She flung her pliers to the ground and cursed.

In the rock overhang ten meters above them, flickering lights kept illuminating the dragonfly nests.

Ranya thought she heard a snicker. This was the last thing she needed. She froze and listened, slowly drawing in air through her nose. Ten-two creaked as he shifted his weight from foot to foot.

And then she smelled it, the salty, smoky scent of insects, heard the buzz of wings and a snicker drawing near. For a moment, Ranya closed her eyes and took a deep breath.

Thonk.

Scuttling over metal sheets.

Followed by cawing and squealing when Ten-two tried to get rid of a dragonfly the size of her forearm that had landed on him. Ten-two didn't like those know-it-all insects any more than she did.

"Tough landing, eh? Gotta train some more!" the dragonfly buzzed and burst into a loud cackle.

"Te-hee, very funny," Ranya growled.

"Why the bad mood? Got problems you can't fix?" Ranya saw gloating in the dragonfly's moon-lit compound eyes.

"No, no. Everything's fine," she said through gritted teeth.

"Mmmh. Let me see."

The dragonfly took off, and its quick legs snatched the screwdriver from Ranya's fingers. It landed vertically on Ten-two's flank, right on the engine.

"Hey, don't!"

Ranya waved her hands to chase away the dragonfly. Just when she hauled off to land a well-aimed blow, the engine began to sputter, and sparks shot out.

"What exactly did you try to accomplish here, eh?" The dragonfly buzzed and shook its head.

"Nothing! I just wanted to connect the output cable to the amplifier, so that—"

"Stupid idea! Really stupid!"

With its nimble forelegs, assisted by its mouthparts, the dragonfly tinkered with the engine.

Ten-two had fluffed up his feathers in a relaxed way and started to chortle. Ranya took this as a sign the dragonfly had done something right. Whatever. Dragonfly support would do, then. She snorted out a breath. She had seen worse.

Above them, the last clouds had vanished, and the evening stars shone bright.

Soon the nightflowers would open. Ranya sighed. Another cycle wasted. Still no *Diglaster poreus* for Manna. And still no transspeciation for her, or anyone else in Klippe.

She turned the compass in her fingers and felt the gentle vibrations of the Batla artifact in her pocket. These vibrations had made her hope she could activate the artifact. That the artifact had been waiting for *her*. That *she* would find the mushroom. The ceremony was overdue. They were in dire need of new scouts, able to fly the animamobiles. And her next initiation was imminent. What wouldn't she have given to finally fly a herpetomobile! One of the purple pterodactyli, maybe . . .

She sighed, let go of the compass, and brushed her hair from her brow, gray with dust and sticky with sweat. She pulled it together in a ponytail and laced up her coat. The wind was cold now.

The dragonfly buzzed and worked on Ten-two's engine, faster than Ranya could keep track to be sure what exactly was going on there. But she didn't have any energy left, not even to be annoyed.

She closed her eyes and breathed in the scent of sand, night, and desert flowers, then slowly let it out. Thousands, tens of thousands, millions of molecules provided her with information about her environment and the matter moving within it. She decided not to pay attention. Her back hurt, and her wrists were complaining.

A faint melody confirmed what she had already suspected. The nightflowers were about to open. With the same five notes repeating over and over, slow at times, and then fast again, the flowers burst through the sandy ground and shot up to a height of a few meters.

"Move it!" the dragonfly yelled at her just in time, and with a jump to the side Ranya narrowly escaped one of the flowers pushing through the ground and avoided being hauled up ten meters or more.

She shook herself. She should've smelled it. There was no excuse. A scout had to be alert at *all* times. Had to be one with her nose. Ranya rubbed her eyes. She needed to sleep. And eat. But not here. Here, she had to pull herself together, first and foremost.

Around her, ten, twelve singing flowers had spiraled upwards. Black velvet petals unfolded, and every single blossom slowly turned toward the moon. Shiny black pearls appeared at their center, pulsing with reflected moonlight.

The dragonfly turned to the flowers for a moment, hissed once and turned back to Ten-two. "Pests!" it grumbled.

The pearls of all the nightflowers exploded in unison as if they had received a silent command, and drowned the air in a cloying, warm scent that made Ranya dizzy. The melody they emitted increased in volume, then fell silent. And thousands and thousands of seeds, blazing like fireflies, soared through the night sky. So much for that. Now it was officially *Asten. Ba* was over. A thing of the past. Another cycle.

"Beautiful." The word just slipped out, and Ranya quickly covered her mouth with her hand.

The dragonfly erupted in laughter. "Haven't been around a lot, have you?"

Ranya's face went hot, but she wouldn't give anything away by explaining herself to the dragonfly. She dismissed it and harrumphed vaguely.

"Whatcha been up to anyway? Not much to see, here."

"Oh, just moving the bird a bit," Ranya hedged.

"Nonsense. You're a scout, eh? Sticks out a mile."

Ranya shrugged.

"Been looking for something, haven't you?"

"Nope."

"You people are always looking for something. Looking and looking. Wouldn't do to miss a thing." The dragonfly shook its head. "Couldn't you just stay home for once? Restless lot, you."

Easily said if you had wings and didn't depend on the connection to the animamobiles to be able to fly, because the technology of the Elders had crumbled beneath your hands here on Palkwen in a wink, after the core cluster took their leave searching for a better planet. No satellites, no automated vehicles, no labs to grow anything. Precious few resources to build technology humans had been used to on a world whose geochemistry was completely different. Those who were able to fly could at least access other, more vital resources. Food and medicine. If you didn't fly, you died. At least here on Palkwen where there was a whole lot of nothing. And where every last modicum of nothing was only traceable with a hyped-up scout nose.

Ranya gave an exasperated snort.

And then she watched in disbelief as blue fuel and yellow bio-fluid mixed in the engine, resulting in a purple liquid, bubbling and glowing, while Ten-two clucked euphorically.

"How—?" she began to ask, but she didn't want to embarrass herself in front of the dragonfly again, so she just aborted her question.

"Didn't expect that, eh?" the dragonfly said.

"Well . . ." She hesitated. Granted, dragonflies had a bad reputation in Klippe. Throughout the whole northern dry forest even. Especially since the incident at Green Peak Lake. They didn't exactly inspire confidence with their big eyes and mouthparts. Ten-two's mood was more readable to her than the mood of any dragonfly. And he was an ornithomobile!

"Why—?" She wasn't able to form whole sentences anymore. But the dragonfly got the idea.

"You're just expecting the worst all the time," the insect buzzed. "But know what? We're not beyond being nice."

And with that, it took off, buzzed right into Ranya's face. Ranya fought the impulse to swat the dragonfly away like an annoying pest, but then it was gone already, back up to the rock nests. They decorated the cliffs like countless little bonfires in the darkness.

Ranya shook off her exhaustion. She put on her helmet, reached for the reins, and mounted, pressing her feet onto the spirals. Ten-two cawed and straightened. His whole body vibrated and shone black and blue.

She tried to find the dragonfly in the sky, but it wasn't discernible anymore. The compass in her pocket quivered. Still. Or yet again? If only she could have used it . . . Ranya sighed, shoving aside all her thoughts about Batla artifacts and their matter-based lore of navigation, their idea that the world was an endless cacophony of particles instead of objects, a kind of nebula where every single molecule could be the beginning of a pathway through chaos. The compass would have been perfect to complement the range of her nose.

She prepared to take off as elegantly as possible. No need to make a fool of herself in front of the dragonflies once more.

The compass whirred louder and louder. A high, weak whir that seemed to be located directly in her head. And then it dawned on her. The Ephkeli Contract. The dragonflies had a historical deal with the Batla, dating back long before the landing of the Elders. *The winged guardians,* so the mythology said. Guardians of what?

She lowered her arms. Maybe she should have paid more attention to Manna's lessons in local history. Ten-two turned his head backward and cawed a question. He shuffled restlessly from foot to foot, anticipating the lift-off.

"Wait, bird," Ranya said. She massaged the root of her nose, redistributing a mixture of sweat, dust, and motor oil. Should she ask for help, again? Ranya moaned. But it was unavoidable, no matter how embarrassed she was. If anyone knew something about the Batla artifact, it was the dragonflies.

She bit her lip.

"Sorry, Ten-two. Just a little bit longer."

She jumped out of the saddle and landed heavily in the dust. Her face was already feeling hotter than the cool wind would have justified.

"Well then, let's go, Raven," she said. "You stay behind me, okay?"

Ten-two cawed, and they ambled closer to the cliff face. The dragonfly nests were clustered in groups at dizzying heights. Flickers of light emanated from the entrance holes. Ranya looked up. At least thirty meters of sheer rock separated her from the first nest.

She produced one quick cough. "Hello?" she shouted haltingly.

Nothing moved.

"HELLO?" Her shouting was louder now. "ARE THERE DRAGONFLIES LIVING AROUND HERE?"

Great. As if she hadn't known dragonflies lived around here.

"I AM RANYA FROM KLIPPE, AND I . . ." Well, what exactly? How to explain it thoroughly?

". . . WOULD NEED SOME MORE HELP WITH . . ." With one of the most valuable artifacts of the Central South? To reveal this fact, to yell it out publicly, didn't feel like a good idea.

". . . WITH . . . SOMETHING . . .!"

Oh, if only the ground would open and swallow her up. *Something.* Such excellent phrasing.

A clack rang out.

She tilted her head back. Far up at one of the nest entrances, something moved. Ranya drew a deep breath and blew it out. The thought of meeting yet another arrogant insect sent her mood plummeting to a new low.

"Hello?" she yelled, not exactly convinced anymore. Why hadn't she just flown away?

She heard a whir.

The dragonfly clung to the wall a mere ten meters above her, head down. Its spiky legs tapped the cliff face restlessly, an irritating sound, like fingernails on stone.

Ranya forced herself to stay calm.

"You again!" the dragonfly buzzed and erupted into dry laughter. "Can't get enough of us, eh?"

"No, that's not at all what this is—"

"All right, Kiddo, it's all right," the dragonfly hummed and approached bit by bit until it clung to the cliff two meters from Ranya. "What do you want now?" Its feet still tip-tapped, even if it didn't move further down, and its mouthparts worked as if they had a mind of their own. Considering the way it had greeted her, it seemed to be the same dragonfly as before. "You're in need of a jump-start, too?"

"No," Ranya grunted.

"What? Can't hear you."

"NO!"

"Tssssk, no reason to yell."

She would have really liked to swat the dragonfly away, mount Ten-two and fly straight out of here. But her thoughts went to Manna's reproachful eyes, and to Amit. To the way the healing herb supplies in Manna's kitchen had dwindled. To the way the rock nut powder was almost gone, which every one of them had to take daily against the Palkwen Rot. *Everyone except the scouts,* she corrected herself. There were some benefits after all if you gave up on a completely human genome. Not that it had been her choice. She thought about the new tuber seeds they needed as winter grains. And they needed new scouts; that was beyond question. There was just this one missing ingredient for the transspeciation. She wouldn't give up so easily. She took a deep breath and swallowed the last shreds of self-respect. "I need help."

"Yes, with 'something.' I caught on to that. Wasn't as if I could have missed it with all your yelling."

Breathe in. Breathe out. Diplomacy and tactfulness, that's how she would succeed.

"It's . . . complicated." Ranya closed her eyes. Reopened them. The dragonfly was still here. "It concerns the Batla. An artifact. It just won't work."

The dragonfly started buzzing and flew in narrow circles right in front of Ranya's face. Too close, definitely too close, and Ranya had to suppress her impulse to wildly wave her hands.

"Well, too bad your flu viruses extinguished them, Human."

Ranya blew an indignant breath. "That was hundreds of years ago!"

The dragonfly's buzzing became more low-pitched. It hovered in the air directly in front of Ranya's nose. "Time doesn't pass so quickly for everyone, Kiddo. Some things are never forgotten."

Ranya leaned back slightly so she didn't have to squint. "Listen, I was born twenty-two *Asten* ago. Not two hundred. I don't have anything to do with it. And apart from that, nobody could have known."

"Yes, the awkward side effects of colonizing a planet. It happens."

Rayna drew a deep breath. The faceted eyes of the dragonfly stared directly into hers. She needed their help. She didn't want to come home empty-handed again. She could already see the sneer on her father's face. If only she managed to endure this conversation without botching everything. She couldn't allow herself to be provoked.

"I don't say it was right." She tried to sound placatory.

"Whatcha saying then?"

Ranya shrugged and scratched her neck, the place where taming her curls posed the biggest problem, and made a careful step backwards to put some distance between herself and the insect.

"What?" the dragonfly buzzed loudly and followed her. "Can't hear you."

"I didn't say anything," Ranya murmured and turned her gaze away from the fluttering in front of her face.

"What?"

"Listen. It was a disaster. Right? Nobody wanted it to be that way. To wipe out an advanced civilization. Of course not! The Elders were desperate . . . What would you do if you didn't have a planet anymore, hm? We have learned our lesson, haven't we?"

The dragonfly laughed sarcastically. "You had to, whether you liked it or not, after they left you here on Palkwen to rot."

"The ship will return!"

"Of course."

"There was an oath!"

"Certainly."

Ranya pressed her lips together and stared at the dragonfly. She wouldn't rise to the provocation. She wouldn't think of the fact that the technology of the Elders, even if they were coming back eventually, would be compost in no time here on Palkwen. The creation of the scouts had been a brilliant idea of the Elders. One last useful application of their fragile Terra technology. And a symbol of their everlasting loyalty and care, allowing the majority of the Palkwen humans to keep their original genome. To ensure future compatibility. To transspeciate one scout or the other was just a small but crucial sacrifice, all things considered.

"All right," the dragonfly buzzed after a few seconds of awkward silence. "So, there is a Batla artifact. Go on."

The whir of its fast wings became more intrusive, and Ranya was starting to feel dizzy.

"Come on, girl, tell me."

"Can't you just keep still for a moment?" Ranya blurted out. She took three steps back and threw her hands up. "I can't focus this way!"

The dragonfly landed on Ten-two's head. "You come for help, just to be insolent like that?" It buzzed in such a high frequency it made Ranya wonder if the beating wings in front of her nose hadn't been more pleasant.

Stay tactful, stay calm. At least the dragonfly had moved the conversation to another topic.

"I'm sorry," Ranya grunted. "I'm just somewhat . . . tired out." She cleared her throat. "That's all."

The dragonfly stared at her, as far as she could tell.

"I'm listening?" it buzzed.

"All right. I'm in possession of a compass. A Batla compass. I need it for an important mission, but I don't know how to use it." Just like that, it was said. She needed the mushroom *Diglaster poreus* to be exact. The crucial ingredient to stimulate the transspeciation in the cells of prospective scouts, no less.

The dragonfly kept very still for a few seconds and seemed to eye Ranya warily. "Show me," it finally said in a low buzz.

Slowly, Ranya pulled the compass from her pocket. She opened her hand right in front of the dragonfly's eyes and revealed a delicate golden orb that seemed to glow from within. Beneath its shiny surface, a subtle structure was visible, as if the orb were composed of countless thin spheres placed inside each other, each one just a little bit smaller than the last.

"Closer," the dragonfly hummed.

Ranya shoved her open palm even closer to the dragonfly, who placed its forelegs on Ranya's hand and started to feel the compass with its antennae. Ranya forced herself to keep breathing evenly. The proximity to the big insect made her twitchy.

In her hand, the artifact felt warm. Ranya's gaze moved over the compass, followed the subtle motions of the dragonfly's antennae, mesmerized. The fingers of her free hand moved closer to the orb. Something inside of her vibrated, a feeling like being drawn by magnetic forces. The antennae moved faster and faster, and something in Ranya hummed in the same cadence. Her finger touched the golden surface. Very, very carefully. A whir set in, a high-pitched tone, and something on the inside of the orb quivered.

Ranya jerked her hand back. The dragonfly lost its balance and cursed. The paper-thin layers of the compass started moving, spinning against each other, faster and faster, and the orb rose into the air. The whir became louder, a tone so piercing Ranya wanted to cover her ears. But she couldn't look away. Layer after layer of the hovering orb slid open to reveal the spheres within. The interior of each opened sphere was inscribed with countless symbols and numbers. After the artefact had opened completely like a flower, it slowly sank back down onto Ranya's palm.

"Unbelievable," Ranya breathed.

The dragonfly gave a cackling laugh, but it didn't sound as mocking as before. More muted, somehow. "Batla technology. Now you know what we have your Elders and their viruses to thank for."

Ranya quietly cleared her throat. "What kind of symbols are these?"

The dragonfly's antennae flitted over the opened artifact.

"That's what you'd like to know, eh?" it hummed. "Want me to give you a manual along with it?"

Ranya gave a polite cough. "Yes? If that's possible?"

The dragonfly started laughing. "You are all the same, the whole lot of you." Its small proboscis pointed to Ranya. "Take, take, take. You come here, look for quick answers, then you're gone again."

"That's not true," Ranya said indignantly.

"Isn't it? Prove it. What have you brought with you?" The insect set its demanding gaze on Ranya.

She began to stammer. "Well, it's not exactly as if I had . . ." Then she had an idea. "But maybe I can help you? I am an initiated scout! Of all the scouts south of the Zin, I'm the . . ." She paused. She couldn't make herself say *the best*. ". . . I'm a very experienced scout."

The dragonfly tilted its head. Its mouthparts worked at high speed.

"Wait here," it finally said and flew away, up to the nests, and vanished.

Ranya waited. It had to be long past midnight. Despite the tension she felt, exhaustion pervaded every tired fiber of her body. Ten-two looked at her and uttered an inquiring caw.

"Are you missing your insect buddy already?" she snarled, to her immediate regret. Ten-two was not the one to blame. She ruffled the small feathers of his head. Thankfully he never took offence to anything.

After a few minutes, Ranya sat on the ground. During *Asten*, the days became shorter and cooler, the nights severely cold. Here, the earth still stored some heat. Her eyelids grew heavy.

Minutes passed, and the dragonfly didn't return. Ranya started to draw patterns into the sand. Had the dragonfly had second thoughts? Her eyes closed. The thought of her bed, just a few hours away by wing, became more and more urgent. You just couldn't rely on insects. It was well-known. She got up, momentarily staggering, and patted the dust off her tunic. She would have to succeed on her own after all. Better than being laughed at and left high and dry by an unreliable, emotionless polypod. She straightened her belt.

"Come on, Raven, we're flying," she said.

But Ten-two wouldn't listen. He gazed upwards and cooed. A few seconds later, Ranya heard the familiar buzzing. Silhouetted against the night blue sky she saw the dim contours of a dragonfly descend toward her. It held something in its little legs. She smelled it even before she saw it, the sour odor telling her something was off.

The dragonfly hovered in the air in front of Ranya, buzzing. Then it placed a package, almost as big as itself, gently onto the ground. The dragonfly landed directly next to it and looked around frantically. Its buzz sounded tense.

"Pity you're too big for our spawning nests," it hummed. "Such a waste, to grow so big."

Ranya frowned and shot a curious glance at the package that emanated a strong odor of sickness. It was swaddled in a blanket, and it moved ever so slightly.

"Hey, not so close, girl," the dragonfly buzzed and took a belligerent stance in front of the bundle of blankets.

Ranya paused and lifted her hands to reassure the insect. "I'm not doing anything."

The dragonfly adjusted the blanket nervously with its mouthparts. "This little one should rather stay in the nest. But then you wouldn't comprehend a thing. You humans, always in need of blatantly obvious explanations." The insect gave a buzzing sigh. "They're all ill, the larvae. Nest-rot."

"Oh," Ranya said. She barely managed to suppress her *but I'm really not to blame for that one!* retort. "I'm sorry," she murmured instead. To be honest, she wouldn't have been surprised if the dragonflies ate their larvae alive. But it seemed like the insects did have emotional ties to their offspring.

"What will happen to it?"

The buzzing of the dragonfly was almost inaudible. "Maybe she makes it for another day. A week. Doesn't look good. They're all turning gray. And thin. They're all dying."

Ranya swallowed. "May I . . . take a look . . . at her?"

The dragonfly buzzed in a variety of pitches. "All right," it finally said. "But be careful, scout." If a buzz could sound menacing, this one did.

Slowly, Ranya dropped to her knees next to the larva. Between blankets, lichen and dry leaves, something squirmed. Ranya pulled the blanket aside carefully. And then she saw it. A small, fat caterpillar with an almost white face. She forced herself to breathe in and out deeply and not let her disgust show. Full of tact and diplomacy. It was the right approach. As a matter of fact, the caterpillar didn't look so fat after all. Where the skin should have been taut, it was gray and sunken. The larva's mouthparts moved, her thin forelimbs treaded air, her head swayed erratically from side to side. Her eyes stared into nothingness. And then she turned her small head toward Ranya, languidly, trembling, chewing on air, and for a moment, the black faceted eyes looked right into hers. Ranya winced. If it was possible for a dragonfly larva to radiate despair, if hopelessness was able to show on a rigid insectoid face, this caterpillar was its embodiment. Ranya took a few steps back and swallowed.

"Nothing can be done about this?"

"Good question. Maybe you're not as slow as I suspected. You really hit the mark there."

Indignantly, Ranya put her hands to her hips, but she couldn't get too angry in the presence of the dying larva.

"There's a medicine against it. But we don't have it. Can't find it. We're eye creatures. Wing creatures. Not nose creatures like you, with this ugly schnoz right in your face."

Ranya's stood, her mouth agape.

"Leatherdipper. A medicinal plant. We don't have it. Doesn't grow here. Can't find it. We'd buy it, but no one sells it."

Gradually, it dawned on Ranya where this conversation was headed.

"You want me to find leatherdipper for you, and in exchange you'd explain the compass to me?"

"You got it. Congrats!" The dragonfly laughed briefly, but it didn't sound amused.

Quid pro quo. You scratch my back and I'll scratch yours. Even if the Palkwen humans traditionally didn't deal with insects. But maybe she could make an exception in this case. Finding medicinal plants was her specialty. She had a lot of experience. She had smelled leatherdipper before . . . a rather worthless herb as far as she knew. But maybe dragonflies lived by different rules. She had definitely stored its scent. She could rely on her nose. If the herb was locatable, she'd find it. "No problem. It's a deal!" Ranya nodded.

"Good," the dragonfly buzzed. "See you, then. Or not."

It took off, grabbed the larva carefully with its feet and flew back to the nests.

"Wait a moment! I don't even know your name!" Ranya yelled after it, but the dragonfly didn't hear her anymore.

Ranya sighed. Just to get some sleep. Just to be at home, in her bed.

"We have to be strong now, Ten-two," she murmured. And then she closed her eyes and began to breathe in and out through her nose. Three times fast, pause. Three times slow. Wait. Focus. Leatherdipper. Leatherdipper. The memory poured into her olfactory cells. Breathe in slowly. Access the memory. Find a trace. Her nose pulsed. There. A molecule hit. Gently, she turned her head. Focus. Vibrations jittered through her body, from her nose to the tips of her toes and back up again. Now to hold on to that connection.

"Come, Raven," she said.

"HELLO? ANYBODY HERE?" For the third time in one day, Ranya stood at the base of the cliff in Ashosh. Even if it wasn't exactly the same day anymore. The dragonfly nests hung high above her. She was dirty and exhausted, muddy morass clung to her, a new day was dawning, and she hadn't closed her eyes once this night. But she had found leatherdipper. In a flooded, boggy cave. Actually, she should fly home, wash up, sleep, eat, and then get back to the dragonflies. But leatherdipper didn't stay fresh for long. And granted, curiosity still kept her awake. And Ten-two, nibbling and tugging on a loose thread of her tunic.

She sat in the sand and waited until she heard the familiar buzz. The dragonfly landed next to her.

"A clean-up would be in order, eh?" it said as a way of greeting.

"Mmh," Ranya voiced. She unpacked her bundle and placed it on the ground in front of the dragonfly. "Leatherdipper."

The dragonfly inspected the plants with its small forelegs and mouthparts, buzzing in approval. "You're useful after all."

Ranya just grunted. The dragonfly had no idea. She had waded through a stinking swamp. Through a cave infested with aggressive dreg mice. *Dreg mice!* It still gave her the creeps just to think about them.

The dragonfly grabbed the bundle with its six legs and took off.

Ranya jumped to her feet. "Hey, wait! You owe me something!" She waved her arms.

Just when she had stopped mistrusting the dragonfly's every move. She put her arms to her hips and stared up to the nests, open-mouthed. Some minutes passed by like this, until she reluctantly sank to the sand, propped up against a stone, and dozed off.

A noise woke her.

A high-pitched buzz. A low-pitched buzz.

And suddenly, buzzing everywhere.

Grudgingly, Ranya opened her eyes. From every entrance up in the rock nests, dragonflies swarmed. They circled in the air, hummed and buzzed, conglomerated in a big cloud circling downward, to the ground. To Ranya.

The scout was in the center of a gigantic circle. Hundreds of dragonflies hovered around her and landed in perfect symmetry in the sand, row after row, their long thin bodies like sunrays radiating outwards from a center–Ranya.

A dragonfly from the first row scuttled forward to Ranya.

"Scout Ranya of Klippe," it hummed. "My name is Srrrursssrkk. I am this colony's queen."

She looked at Ranya expectantly and waited. Did Ranya have to bow? Drop to her knees? Was there a code of conduct when facing a dragonfly queen? Ranya settled on a curtsy.

"You, Deathbringer, brought a remedy for our dying children."

Deathbringer? Was this how dragonflies called her people? Each and every dragonfly started a low-pitched buzz, sounding so desperate Ranya's throat felt tight.

"Thanks to you, we have new hope."

The collective buzz increased in pitch.

"As a sign of our gratitude, we want to show you something."

Ten-two unfolded his wings and took off with a bold leap, straight into the night sky.

Ranya's hand closed firmly around the key the dragonflies had entrusted to her. A pivotal piece to access the compass, and to other lost things. So the dragonfly queen had said. What exactly was the key for? She would find out. She would show Manna and Amit she didn't make empty promises. Show the dragonflies she could bring life, too, not just death.

A stiff wind blew into Ranya's face. Exhaustion dulled her mind, and she felt every aching muscle in her body. But not for long. She counted the seconds.

And then it came. It traveled through her like lightning, like an electric shock. The engine had warmed up, and ecstasy set in. Waves of heat passed through her body. She breathed out, letting one wave after the other flow through her. Ten-two and she were connecting.

It was not as much a way of steering, but something closer to intuition. Matter-based. Like everything on this weird planet, where matter almost seemed to have a will of its own. The existence of the scouts was a concession to this fact. The only one, maybe.

Ranya allowed the stars to draw her gaze upwards. They were somewhere out there. The Elders. Looking for a new home. Millions and millions of stars twinkled their promises in the darkness. Ranya's gaze sank. Below her, rocks, sand, and wind drew endless patterns onto the ground. Maybe the Elders wouldn't return. Maybe the time had come to accept that. Palkwen *was* the new home.

Ranya ran her fingers over the coarse face of the key. Something inside of her pulsed. She felt the compass, warm in her pocket. Maybe the scouts were not a sacrifice. Maybe they were a sign. That it was time to change. That they needed to look to the future. Take destiny into their own hands, here on Palkwen.

A whoop burst from her throat, and Ten-two went faster still. Ranya nestled against his soft feathers and allowed the wind and the world to soar by. There was much left to do.

YOU ARE NOT ALONE!

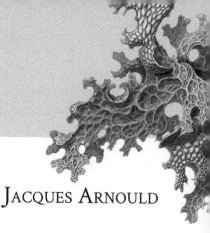

JACQUES ARNOULD

In 2017, to celebrate the fortieth anniversary of the launch of the Voyager 1 interplanetary probe, NASA organized a #MessagetoVoyager competition. People were invited to write a message of fewer than sixty characters; the winning message was transmitted by this spacecraft—the first built by earthlings to have left our solar system—still on its mission. Written by Oliver Jenkins, "a guy with Asperger's syndrome" as he describes himself, the transmitted text was read by one of the actors of the famous Star Trek television series: "We offer friendship through the stars. You are not alone!" Sixty years after the flight of the first Sputnik, could this message mark a revolution in the way we approach space exploration?

We must admit it: the technical possibility of crossing the Final Frontier was first used to begin what in the 1960s and 1970s was called "the conquest of space." Whether taking off from Baikonur or Cape Canaveral, crewed and robotic spacecraft were the heirs of Christopher Columbus's ships and, to the question of the discovery of extraterrestrial populations, even if just microbial, modern navigators responded first by developing planetary protection instructions.

Nobody wanted to follow the horrific history that ensued with colonization on Earth. These guidelines continue to be modified and improved under the responsibility of COSPAR (Committee on Space Research), according to our evolving knowledge of planets we are continuing to study, remotely or *in situ*. How safe is it to land in Martian regions where liquid water might be present underneath the surface, scour the clouds of Venus, or make a landing on Enceladus? And how safe is it to bring back samples from these sites?

Only more exploration and Earth- or near-Earth-based studies investigating microbial survival of extreme heat, acceleration, radiation, or chemical exposure can tell us more and inform these guidelines.

There is no doubt that any continued exploration of the solar system must not forget this initial caution: we must imperatively limit all pollution, any destruction of extraterrestrial environments, and avoid any endangerment of the Earth's biosphere. Projects announced by the NewSpace companies, which no longer belong to the field of exploration but to that of exploitation of space resources, whether mining or tourism, raise fears of a less thorough application, or even a total rejection of the precautions promoted by COSPAR.

Moreover, we cannot continue to consider other worlds as a simple setting for the human odyssey that we should simply keep in good condition in order to continue scientific exploration or for aesthetic reasons. As we have been imagining for a very long time, these worlds, still to be discovered, could offer us the opportunities for real "encounters of the third kind." If we are not careful, even a completely peaceful encounter might end in tragedy—such as humans inadvertently wiping out the Batla in Lisa Jenny Krieg's "Ranya's Crash."

Even if such an event is hypothetical, we must not ignore the possibility. Instead, we should make it a real field of research, relying on our science and cultural heritage, especially of those who have been able to maintain a real link with non-human reality—understanding the needs and capabilities of other species sharing the Earth with us. We must recognize that the question of *others* pursues the human species as its shadow.

From what we know today (and this is precisely one of the stakes of this "astonishing question"), we are the only ones who can question ourselves, to be able to imagine the possible existence of a reality other than those that are immediately perceptible or accessible to us on Earth. We are alone in possession of a capacity for imagination, alone in being able to transgress the limits of space and time (I mean of our space and our time), to ask ourselves if there are other beings than us beyond the hills and mountains of our daily horizon, beyond the familiar shores of our rivers and seas, beyond the stars of our days and nights. The history of our humanity is part of the question, whether others are expected, hoped for, or feared.

It is therefore not surprising that the human mind did not wait for the launch of *Sputnik* on October 4, 1957, nor for the birth of astronautics—that is to say, space travel—to wonder if the universe sheltered other forms of life, other intelligences than those present on Earth. The question, theologian Albert the Great wrote in the thirteenth century, is "one of the most wondrous and noble questions in Nature, [1]" a point that thinkers have never disdained, or even ceased to examine. Philosophical treatises bear the traces of it even more often than encyclopedias, to the point of making Arthur C. Clarke, the famous English author of science fiction, repeat that this question was one of the supreme questions of philosophy. [2]

The development of astronautics opens new horizons to this ancient question, not only in the event that we can discover extraterrestrial forms of life, but also in the case of settling on other planets: terrestrial biologists know that the establishment of a barrier between two populations of the same species can cause an evolutionary divergence and the appearance of two new species sufficiently different from each other to no longer allow, for example, interfertilization. Such an evolution is conceivable in the case of sending human colonies into space; in this case, "the other" would be somehow the "result" of a voluntary process on our part. Of course, we would not be powerless to manage such a situation politically, legally, and ethically: human history is rife with situations of settlers demanding independence . . . or inheritance. If such an extraterrestrial situation occurred, would we learn the lessons of our past?

Let us continue in this direction where "the other" would come from humanity itself and ask ourselves about the possibility of transforming the human being. The knowledge we accumulate about the universe on the one hand, and about the human being on the other, allows us to specify the limits of our possibilities to live in space, according to our anatomical, physiological, and psychological capacities, and our technological achievements. Weightlessness and cosmic radiation, the duration of interplanetary travel using current and future means of travel, and the need to find resources such as oxygen and food—not to mention the imperative of reproduction related to aging and mortality—all cause the human condition to be incompatible with space reality. Hence the idea, which quickly appeared in the human imagination, of ignoring the limits imposed by the human body is not feasible.

Capsules, vessels, stations: so far, the solution to the problem is to reconstitute on a reduced scale a terrestrial-type biosphere, inside which a human being can survive and even live for several months, without having to undergo prior modifications or consequent alterations too dangerous or disabling (however, astronauts still suffer from—mostly reversible—detrimental health changes). But science fiction writers were quick to imagine touching the bodily boundaries themselves. The first step envisaged was that of the cyborg.

Cyborg refers to a cybernetic organism, in other words a human being or other living and intelligent being who has received transplants of a mechanical nature. In the strict sense of this definition, any human person with a prosthesis or an artificial heart could be described as a cyborg.

The history of the term and the idea of a cyborg is directly linked to that of the space adventure; Manfred Clynes and Nathan S. Kline coined this term in an article entitled "Cyborg and Space," published by the journal *Astronautics* in September 1960. [3] They proposed the term *cyborg* to designate a human-machine system: "If man attempts partial adaptation to space conditions, instead of insisting on carrying his whole environment along with him, a number of new possibilities appear. One is then led to think about the incorporation of integral exogenous devices to bring about the biological changes which might be necessary in man's homeostatic mechanisms to allow him to live in space *qua natura*."

The two researchers were convinced that such progress should make it possible to "free Man to explore" without altering his genetic heredity, thanks to the implantation of homeostatic systems in order to facilitate his breathing, control his internal temperature, protect him from cosmic radiation, regulate all bodily flows, improve his sensory abilities, manage his "psychoses," etc. In half a century, the term *cyborg* has come to refer to android robots as well, mainly through works of science fiction. The objective of Clynes and Kline remains relevant—that of adapting the human being to the conditions of staying in space—and, as it is now on the way to crossing the border from fiction to reality, it deserves to be questioned.

At the stage where we have reached the mastered and conceivable techniques necessary for interplanetary manned flights, it may be reasonable to consider the ethics of using cyborgs if, at the very least, a serious moral reflection is already associated with them. We might even imagine interfacing with artificial intelligences to boost our capacities.

I am aware of the warnings reminiscent of Stephen Hawking and Bill Gates in 2015 about artificial intelligence. "Succeeding in creating artificial intelligence would be a big event in human history," Hawking explained. But it could also be the last. What was astonishing, Gates pointed out, "is not that artificial intelligence arouses fear, but quite the opposite, it is that people are not horrified!"

The same applies to extensive genetic engineering, the path chosen by Ranya's people so that the scouts could survive in an alien environment.

However, rather than brandishing prohibition signs, and erecting barriers and borders (that we foresee and fear being totally inadequate), it seems to me more opportune and judicious (since this momentum and purpose of space exploration already exists) to take the opportunity to reflect on the challenges posed by cyborgs and otherwise modified humans: choices and decisions our societies may be forced to make. The opportunity exists to move forward and even beyond, but we must not lose reason.

Preparing for a possible future close encounter of the third kind, in whatever form, is not only about drafting essential international protocols, preparing highly secure biological laboratories, and sterilizing space exploration probes. We must also, as this astonishing story illustrates, return to ourselves and question ourselves about the knowledge and understanding we have *of* ourselves. "Know yourself," Socrates taught, adding, "And thou shalt know the world and the gods."

The ultimate frontier is therefore not only above our heads, beyond the atmosphere of our planet; this border is also within ourselves.

And the odyssey is far from over.

REFERENCES

[1] Quoted in Steven J. Dick. (1982). *Plurality of Worlds: The Origin of the Extraterrestrial Life Debate from Democritus to Kant.* Cambridge: Cambridge University Press, p. 23.

[2] Cf. Arthur C. Clarke. (1973). *Report on Planet Three and Other Speculations.* New York: Signet Books, p. 79.

[3] Cf. Manfred E. Clynes and Nathan S. Kline. (1960). "Cyborgs and Space." *Astronautics*, September 1960, p. 26-27, 74-76.

SPIRAL

ARULA RATNAKAR

I stare out into the endless expanse of cosmic dust surrounding me, an ant trapped within the body of a colossal creature from the realms of fantasy that undulates on a timescale human beings could never comprehend. Though I might be able to comprehend it, if I manage to change my processing speed. For I am no longer human.

I transferred a copy of my consciousness into a tiny metal sphere and left Earth—how long ago this was, I do not know anymore. I did it because of her. Because of Sapna.

Back then, toward the end of that war in the Arctic Sea—oh, the war is now long in the past, the participants must all be dispersed or deceased by now—she told me she felt like it was her destiny to become an oneironaut, to wade in and out of a new battlefield taking place in the collective subconscious of humanity. Fighting battles of thought-influence and memory manipulation and emotional implantations.

She wasn't even someone who normally believed in destiny.

"My *name* means 'dream,'" she would tell me. "This is meant for me." And I would let it go. *She wouldn't really join,* I would think. Perhaps the thought of her getting hurt in a dream-battle, *her,* was too painful for my mind to process. My brain rejected the notion, and so we laughed, and we drank, and we watched through the clear climate-controlled ceilings of climate-controlled buildings as clouds of pollution slithered across the night sky.

They went into these pods, the oneironauts, that's how it happened. There were massive buildings lined with rooms filled with them, set up all over the world. The oneironauts had brain implants that could communicate with the pods, then the pods would communicate to a station, and the stations would communicate with each other, globally, creating a shared subconscious realm for human minds to brawl.

Detached from the laws of physics, a human consciousness could become a person or a prism or a prison or a pond, or anything else, really. All of the participants would try to persuade and manipulate those on opposing sides of this war and become whoever or whatever it would take to do so. It normally took a year, sometimes multiple years of training to master dreaming and dream-influencing to become an oneironaut.

It took Sapna only three months of training to qualify. Maybe it *was* her destiny, after all. I think it was her determination though. And her blind conviction in what her side of the war wanted—the Geoengineers—demanding every international scientific research organization to usurp all world governments and (what they believed, at least . . . I was skeptical) bring the world into a better, healthier direction for environmental homeostasis.

"Why would people enter this battlefield," I would ask, "if it is a gambling game, full of harmful realities and malicious memories and if the integrity of your very consciousness is at stake?"

"Because the cause is that great," Sapna would reply.

Dreams determine to what degree information from your short-term memory integrates with your other brain activity patterns; where things stick and how well they stick are determined through dreaming. To be able to influence that . . . to be able to read and perceive that in others. . . . *Of course*, humanity eventually turned dream-sharing into a tool for war. *Of course*, it was only a matter of time.

The cosmic dust around me contains life. No; it *is* life, caused by ionized gas—space plasma—interacting with the dust grains in an intricate dance of gravity and charge. The grains act as a sink for the plasma, making them self-organize into helices. Change the plasma flux, and you change the number of grains in a helix, its diameter and rotational angle. Voila; you've made the dust grains surrounding the helix dance in vortices on either side of the helix, one clockwise and the other anticlockwise. The next step of the dance is important: the helical winding changes at that point in the structure, bifurcating the entire helix. The dust vortices can then nudge neighboring helices to bifurcate in the very same way, like dancing couples attuning to each other, causing replication of the structure. This is it: an information storage pattern.

Here, information being processed, the "context," the "food," that the helices are all competing for, are the plasma fluxes; the dust vortices causing these bifurcations all are determined by the state of the plasma surrounding them. You can imagine it as the music they dance to and crave if you want.

When I first entered this dust cloud, I was amazed. I had never seen anything like this system of intricate helices. I explored it for ages, observing the vast systems that had emerged from the whorls and eddies of plasma, the patterns of dust grains resulting from them, and the clear evidence of *replication* within these structures.

The longer I spent in the cloud, the faster the helices seemed to bifurcate and change their patterns, and the faster the information seemed to spread from one structure to the next. When I first arrived, the entire place seemed frozen in time. But the longer I spent there, the more I felt I could see the dust vortices flow and the helices restructure until the entire place around me was absolutely brimming with dynamic, rapidly shifting, beautiful *life*. How could I have not seen it before? How could I have ever thought anything was frozen? This place was almost overwhelmingly kinetic. And these beings were inviting me into their joyous, riotous dance.

It's funny that I ran into this form of life after everything that happened with Sapna. A strange coincidence. Or perhaps it's the reason I comprehend the helices in the first place. And there's a chance I might have misunderstood them, that my experiences make me map an incorrect version of consciousness onto them. There is no way to know. Especially now.

When she was young, Sapna's family became environmental refugees, fleeing the cloud spirals of apocalyptic hurricanes that crept upwards along coasts that had never experienced them or prepared for them. They lost everything. They knew people who died because the people with power waited *too long* to allow change. Could I imagine that Sapna became convinced it was time for people to come into power who would dedicate themselves to restoring the world's environmental homeostasis?

Humanity is so motivated by the pursuit of justice, and that desire can be so easily corrupted or exploited. If it wasn't for what happened to her family, Sapna wouldn't have felt so strongly about joining this war, becoming an oneironaut. She would never have met me, either. And if it wasn't for what happened to her, I would never have dedicated myself to the people she believed could change the world. I would never have become trapped in this place, this cloud of beings who misunderstand me, whom I have misunderstood, who don't understand what they have done.

It was a war crime to destroy the oneironauts' pods, the rooms that housed them, or the stations that created the battlefields. And for a while nobody wanted to destroy any of it, either. If anything happened to the occupants' bodies, echoes of their minds would be forever trapped in the dream-battles, malicious agents seeking to harm their enemies or turn them away from the cause. The goal was to change the enemy and get them to return to their physical forms where they could then influence others they knew. If the enemy couldn't return after you changed them, what was the point? And if the enemy was permanently embedded in the shared reality, always able to change you, it would only hurt your side's aim.

There was no incentive for destruction. At least, not until the Loop.

Nobody knew who the Loop was, what country or countries it was from, whether it was one person or one million people. But it was clear the Loop wanted to destroy the Geoengineers. Toward the end of the war, it was the Geoengineers against the world's governments.

To understand what the Loop did, one has to rethink human experience, redefining it in terms of programming language theory. And, if I'm right, this same redefining is what's needed to understand what happened to me in these helices of dust, too.

It might have taken me ages to notice and perceive the dynamism and life within the dust. But it took me much longer to realize I was no longer inhabiting the spherical metal probe.

It happened when I tried sending a signal back to Earth, and no signal was sent. I suddenly became aware of my body—or my lack of one. I had a simulated one within the probe, but I could adjust and shift it to take different forms, to be in multiple places at once. . . . It was nothing like my biological human body. *It was more like Sapna must have been, in the dream-battles.*

But all of it was gone. My consciousness was instead spread over the vastness of the cloud and focused on the smallest winding disruption on a single helix, all at once. How could I not have noticed that before? What had happened to the spherical probe?

I began to panic. The realization of my changed state gripped me, took over my every thought, and as it did, the dance of the helices stopped. Everything seemed frozen in time, once again. *No, they haven't frozen at all*, I remember thinking. *They move on a different timescale, one human beings can never comprehend. And they have sent me back to my old processing speed.* How much time had gone by when I was matching their speed of life? How many millennia, how many eons?

Then a wave of calm washed over me, but it felt foreign. It felt artificial, not something my own brain would do. It probed thoughts I had locked far away, far far away, and brought them back to my consciousness. Memories of my life on Earth. Of how I gave up. Of Sapna.

I remembered when we first met, as teenagers when my family was volunteering at a center distributing food to environmental refugees. I remembered her cracking jokes and making everyone in the place laugh.

I asked her how she could possibly be so lighthearted after everything and she smiled at me, told me my brutal honesty was refreshing and everyone else was too afraid to ask. I told her they were probably afraid the jokes and stories would stop, and at this she grabbed my hand and took me to a room with a skylight where we drank a bottle of wine she stole, and we talked about our lives. We were instantly friends.

I remembered us growing older, starting to argue about political tensions over the Arctic Sea. And something became charged between us, a different kind of tension culminating in a kiss one time when we returned to the room with the skylight.

We were terrible romantic partners. Our affair lasted less than a year. But we still loved each other. She was worried about losing me, worried I would leave if the romance didn't stay. I remember thinking *how could I possibly leave you, when you're the most fascinating person I've met? I should be worried about you leaving me.* I remembered telling her: "It doesn't have to be like that, Sapna. You are my favorite person in the universe." And her telling me I was her "number one person" too, that I would always be her greatest friend.

I remembered her becoming an oneironaut.

And then I remembered the Loop.

Everything can be written down.

Imagine the universe as an unending library filled with volumes whose thickness and language vary so vastly one cannot comprehend it. Elementary particles change their states; eddies of plasma flows shift; the four letters of Earth-life DNA are copied, sometimes imperfectly; the neurons in brains capture fleeting states by firing.

Everything is a language, but some languages are more perilous to read than others.

Take a language made of two letters, say "E" and "T," and create a string of any length made up of those two letters. How can we tell whether that string is perfectly alternating between E's and T's, or if there are repeats of two or more E's in a row or T's in a row?

A machine can be tasked to solve this problem, one with only a single unit of memory. It will read a letter and store it. Then, it will move on to the next letter. If for example, the stored letter is an E and the current letter is a T, then it will move on, forgetting that E and taking the T into its memory. If the next letter is an E, then it will move on once more, forgetting the T and taking the E into its memory. If this continues until it reaches the end of the string, the machine can say with confidence that it is an alternating string. However, if at any point in reading the string, the stored letter matches the current letter, the machine will stop and can say with confidence that it is not an alternating string.

This sort of machine with some finite memory capacity—doesn't necessarily need to be just one unit of storage—is called a Finite State Machine. And the language problems it can read are called regular languages. Trickier problems, ones that a Finite State machine cannot solve, are called non-regular languages. Like the language of balanced parentheses.

In a string of parentheses of any length, how do you tell if every open parenthesis will be matched with a closed one, somewhere down the string? A finite state machine wouldn't be able to solve this problem for strings any longer than its amount of memory storage because of the problem of *pumping*.

I imagine Sapna snickering at this; for all her grand dreams and ideals, she could be so refreshingly obscene at moments.

We never talked about finite state machines, regular and non-regular languages. Pity. Could it have saved her?

Imagine the string of parentheses and divide it into three parts, which you'll call x, y and z. The part from the beginning up to some point in the middle is x. The part just after x and going all the way up to the limit of the machine's memory capacity is y. And the part *beyond* the machine's memory capacity is z.

A finite state machine wouldn't be able to tell the difference between xyz, xyyz, xyyyyyyz, or any amount of "pumping" of the y portion of the string where the pumps are repeats of y. This is an issue for the balanced parentheses problem because what if y contains open parentheses that are closed in z with the string xyz. If you have a string xyyz, there would be double those open parentheses, and they would never be closed as there is only a single z portion. But a finite state machine would not be able to tell the difference between the two, thus failing to solve the problem for *any* string.

This makes balanced parentheses a non-regular language. So far so good; failing to correctly read a string of parentheses probably won't trap you in hell. For that, just change the language.

The Loop applied programming language theory to experience itself. Experience might be thought of as a non-regular language as well, very similar to balanced parentheses, made up of nested time intervals. In biological human experience of time, conjunctively encoded "time/object" cells fire in sequence within the hippocampus of human brains, attaching some aspect of our context to each moment in our life and creating temporal sequences from them.

Whether the brain is a finite state machine or works differently is hard to say. If it's the former, it is so unlikely to encounter a pumping of any portion of a temporal sequence kissing the limits of our memory capacity—it would not matter. And if it's the latter, repeated encounters of those objects in sequence, even after they had been forgotten, would most likely not cue the same exact response.

But within the devices embedded in the oneironauts' brains, across the dream-sharing machines and across the stations, storage capacity was limited. And dream-battles most certainly did not work the way a human brain works, or like human experience. The entire global apparatus was known to be a system of finite state machines, and it could be hacked.

The Loop installed a virus within the oneironaut pods of the Geoengineers, and Sapna was caught within their trap. A temporal sequence within the aspects of the dreamworld her consciousness created would be pumped indefinitely, repeating and repeating without any indication or understanding in her that there was a loop at all. The time/object cells of her brain and their equivalent within the devices, pods, and stations would forever fire the same way. Time-markers in the battlefield would be obscured to her, and the oneironaut would never tire, never fatigue, and never return from the battle.

Unable to change and mutate her form within the dreamworld beyond the repeating loop, and without understanding that she could no longer respond in a way unexpected to the enemies, her consciousness was left vulnerable to be exploited for information and became an easy-to-navigate portion of the maze which was the dream-battlefield. She was trapped, forever. In a horrible place.

Within the cosmic dust, as the alien presence probed my mind, I was calm and terrified at the same time.

The external calm was accompanied by a suppressed sense of dread at exactly that. It was an indicator that I was no longer in control of my own thoughts. How could I remain so calm as this was happening? What had become of the probe?

That dread was rivaled by awe. I was still perceiving (how?) the faintly glowing plasma, though its currents had become eerily still once again at my momentary processing speed.

It's still like that for me, even now, in the trap the helices decided (can they decide?) to put me in. I wonder if I will ever see the helices dance at their speed of life again.

Yet it's nothing like a still-life painting at this processing speed; more like a snapshot of something dynamic caught at a standstill on film. The grains shine and sparkle in ranges of the spectrum imperceptible to the human eye. The still currents and the shimmering grains within bear an uncanny resemblance to the large-scale structure of the universe, its gigantic threads and tiny dots of galaxy clusters within. So much to see. So much that is forever beyond us.

Sapna would be happy to see what I did after the Loop's attack. I devoted myself to what she believed in: studying programming language theory, learning philosophy of consciousness, and working for the Geoengineers.

At first, my studies were intended to save her. I learned everything I could, tried everything I could, to find a way to help her escape. But nothing I did worked, and honestly, I gave up. I tired of my desire to save her. I became tired of everything, and the weight of my power-lessness overcame my love for her. The love turned to bitterness, and bitterness turned to cold apathy. The memories the two of us shared, the memory of how we met, the times of happiness and the bright, beautiful future together we talked about—that I was clinging to in my search for a way to rescue her—were all locked far away.

Eventually, I developed a deep desire to escape this world. To run as far as I could from this form of consciousness, from our species and from this world of war, corruption, and tragedy. That's when I heard about a project the Geoengineers were developing: building an embryo-carrying ship to plant humanity on a distant planet. They needed pioneers to probe candidate planets and send signals back home. I applied, and they chose me.

I was selected to investigate a system beyond this cosmic dust cloud, to ensure the ship's safe passage, should it choose to follow me. I never thought it was right for humanity to probe the universe, especially after all I saw. I didn't even agree with the concept of the embryo-ship. Misunderstandings, at best, would be inevitable if it encountered alien life. Is it still so worth it to explore the stars?

But I took on the job because a life of solitude traveling through a vast abyss was exactly what I had come to want. I transferred a copy of my consciousness into one of those probes and left Earth.

It was in this state of mind that I entered the dust cloud.

There was still a version of me on Earth. I wonder if this version tried to save Sapna again. I hope so.

That wave of calm probing my thoughts became stronger, much stronger, and there was a purpose to it. It unlocked the mechanisms behind what happened to the oneironauts. It found keys in my state of mind and unlocked what Loop did.

Then I understood. It was going to put me into one. Into a loop. A single helix was itself a finite state machine, the number of bifurcations it could contain—limited. This form of life replicated in patterns of information, but overall, the number of dust grains in the cloud and the number of helices that could form were limited too. Eventually, memory capacity would be reached, and something would be forgotten. A pattern of information could certainly be pumped, such as a temporal sequence. A chunk of experience.

Is this what the beings wanted for me? Could they even *want* at all? Were they protecting themselves by trapping me? Were they granting me a kindness? Did they understand? Did they misunderstand? There is no way for me to ever know. And how can I communicate with them now, if I am doomed to repeat some segment of time forever? It's not a loop, but a spiral trap, for time still moves forward after all even if I circle as I move through it. I wonder where the boundaries of this spiral lie, what thought, what context, what moment marks the beginning and the end?

Perhaps it is not these beings at all who trapped me in this spiral. Perhaps it was me. Perhaps I wanted this, and perhaps someday I will change it. After all, I am one of them now. My mind is no longer made up of electrochemical impulses, or electrical charges on a chip, but is now running on bifurcations on helices of cosmic dust. Maybe one day I will communicate through the trap and break out of it.

The idea comforts me as I stare out into the endless expanse of cosmic dust surrounding me, an ant trapped within the body of a colossal creature from the realms of fantasy that undulates on a timescale human beings could never comprehend. Though I might be able to comprehend it, if I manage to change my processing speed. For I am no longer human.

SPIRALING INTO THE UNKNOWN

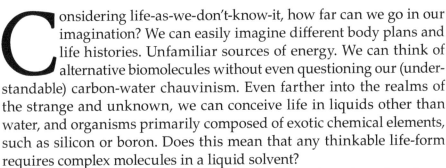

TOMÁŠ PETRÁSEK

onsidering life-as-we-don't-know-it, how far can we go in our imagination? We can easily imagine different body plans and life histories. Unfamiliar sources of energy. We can think of alternative biomolecules without even questioning our (understandable) carbon-water chauvinism. Even farther into the realms of the strange and unknown, we can conceive life in liquids other than water, and organisms primarily composed of exotic chemical elements, such as silicon or boron. Does this mean that any thinkable life-form requires complex molecules in a liquid solvent?

This kind of "molecule-liquid chauvinism" is based on the observation that the liquid phase has unique properties—dissolved biomolecules can move around quickly, react with each other or with the solvent molecules in ways innumerable, yet their movement can be constrained by physical barriers such as membranes. Solid matter is too rigid and enables interesting processes only on the external surfaces (which, though, can be very complex). Electrons and photons flowing through solid-state environments are a more interesting story as evidenced by our computers, which may someday evolve into a true artificial intelligence. Would it count as life? Would it be "solid-state life"? In any case, such a system seems unlikely to occur naturally. At first glance, gas would seem a better environment, as it is a mobile dynamic system in constant motion. However, gases generally cannot dissolve larger molecules, which tend to precipitate in solid or liquid form. Gaseous environments also tend to be too mobile, lacking natural boundaries, and it is really hard to see how a gaseous organism could be defined or internally structured without invoking liquid or solid membranes.

However, there is a fourth state of matter: plasma. It resembles gas, but a significant fraction of its constituent molecules or atoms are ionized. Therefore, positively charged ions and negatively charged electrons move independently of each other. Plasma is perhaps more varied than any other state of matter, assuming a wide range of temperatures, densities, and compositions. Some types of plasma exhibit organized and surprisingly complex behavior. It may even form cell-like blobs and membrane-like layers. Even the naming alludes to biology—Irving Langmuir coined the term "plasma" as the behavior of the substance reminded him of the blood plasma in human veins. Plasma is mobile like a gas, but the presence of charged particles allows it to interact with electromagnetic waves and especially magnetic fields. When charged particles move, they generate magnetic fields, and the magnetic field then directs the flow of the charged particles. We have to look no farther than the surface of the Sun to see that magnetized plasma can create very complex systems, often with intricate internal structures, some of them very stable and others explosively unstable. Browsing through detailed images and movies of the solar photosphere, such as those provided by NASA's Solar Dynamics Observatory (SDO), one can easily imagine plasma-based beings roaming among the fiery currents of incandescent matter.

To add another level of complexity, plasma may contain small solid particles—this is called dusty plasma. It naturally occurs in interstellar space, in the atmospheres of cold stars, or in rarefied planetary atmospheres. Computer simulations by Vadim Tsytovich et al. have suggested that dusty plasma could exhibit organized structures uncannily resembling biomolecules. The dust grains absorb electrons, becoming negatively charged. Such a particle then attracts a cloud of positively charged ions. You may notice how this mirrors the structure of the atom (atoms have a positive nucleus surrounded by a negatively charged electron cloud). Taking the analogy even further, the grains dispersed in plasma may attract each other and order themselves into regular lattices called "plasma crystals" or even something resembling molecules. Those may attract each other or otherwise interact, exhibit "metabolism" and even replication.

Computer simulations suggest such "plasma molecules" may assume helical or even double-helical structure. Thinking of DNA? Although there are no nucleobases forming the letters of our genetic alphabet, the dust spirals can also store information. The helix might assume different stable configurations of varying diameter. Ordering of wider or narrower sections of the helix might conceivably be used as a code. Adding to the analogy, replication might be possible as well. The helix generates vortices in the dusty plasma, which may imprint its structure onto another helix replicating the stored information. The spirals would of course also compete for the available dust grains and plasma fluxes in their surroundings. Heredity, reproduction, and competition lead to evolution, and evolution makes life. However, it would be a rather "slow life," living and evolving up to five orders of magnitude slower than earthly organisms—just as the narrator of Arula Ratnakar's "Spiral" hints.

A computer simulation is of course no proof that such stable, organized structures would actually form in natural environments. Yet the diversity and complexity of plasmatic environments throughout the universe gives room for hope that similar—or completely dissimilar—organized structures have arisen in favorable places. The authors of the study have speculated about the dusty rings of Saturn and Uranus, where there would be enough material and weightless environment allowing the helices to grow. However, planetary rings are rather unstable environments, agitated by solar activity and tidal effects, and the rings themselves seem to evolve and eventually vanish quite rapidly, at least on the geological time scale. Would there be enough time for plasma-based life to evolve? Or should we look elsewhere?

Interstellar clouds are another dusty environment, containing gas (or plasma) more rarefied than laboratory vacuum, interspersed with numerous microscopic dust grains. The particles are far apart, interacting quite rarely, so if anything happens there, it happens slowly—but there is plenty of time out there! It is not only physics, it is also chemistry: in the interstellar medium, an entire zoo of molecules has been identified by radio, microwave, and infrared surveys, including some building blocks of life. Perhaps even larger molecules cover the dust grains.

The 1957 classic science fiction novel *The Black Cloud* by Fred Hoyle features life in interstellar matter—the eponymous Black Cloud is actually a living nebula, absorbing light to gain energy, using electromagnetic radiation in place of a nervous system, and complex molecules ordered on the surfaces of rocky grains for memory. *The Black Cloud* was actually overwhelmingly more intelligent than a human. Of course, in Hoyle's view, the universe was eternal, so the sheer improbability and the vastness of time presumably required for something so huge and complex to originate and evolve was no obstacle.

We know our solar system formed from a collapsing cloud of dust and gas, and there is little doubt that organic molecules were around even before the first planets formed. They might (or might not) have played the key role in the formation of life on Earth. Considering this, we should rather hope that Hoyle was wrong and there are no sentient black clouds populating the universe. Because if they were, our entire solar system would be nothing more than the corpse of one of them, with us having arisen from its decayed brain. And now talk about cosmic horror!

FURTHER READING

Plasma-based cell-like structures

Sanduloviciu, M. (2013). "On the Physical Basis of Self-Organization." *Journal of Modern Physics*, Vol. 4 No. 3, p. 364-372. doi: 10.4236/jmp.2013.43051.

Potential for life in dusty plasmas

Tsytovich, V. N., Morfill, G. E., Fortov, V. E., Gusein-Zade, N. G., Klumov, B. A., & Vladimirov, S. V. (2007). "From plasma crystals and helical structures toward inorganic living matter." *New Journal of Physics*, 9(8), 263.

THE LAST CATHEDRAL OF EARTH, IN FLIGHT   Tobias S. Buckell

We ghosted in high above the plane of the ecliptic toward a new world, passive sensors maxed out, our ministers exhausted by vigilance. Those of us awake for the watch nervously prayed that the heat pumps would hold, and that we could keep a lid on the burning hellfire that hunted for any weakness in the coils that trapped it in the heart of our Bishopric.

A small flicker on the far edge of my vision alarmed me.

Almost a glitch, I thought.

I couldn't find it again when I looked. I hunted through the visions of planetoids, prepared data, and vectors that tumbled through my visual cortex and mind at the same time, a ghostly communion with the Bishopric's near omnipotent mind.

Bile lapped at the back of my tongue. The order rebuilt this old collection of stained glass and flying buttresses to run dark and hide in the shadows from the universe's demons. But we'd put centuries of strain on the machines that ran its many gantries and girders. A single burst pipe, a power failure, a failed piece of code patching, and we'd betray our existence to a hostile universe.

The Prowlers would fall upon us, a shower of sparks glinting in the vacuum, darting this way and that. Our Holy Defenses would spin up, antimatter lances blessed by the security system's pope on Hartsfelt. We would destroy them as fast as they could rain down on us, but eventually one of those sparks of light would get lucky.

"They'll core through the hull, then they'll core through your flesh, then they'll core through your mind, and lastly, they'll feast on your soul," Radin told me, the old confessor who ran the meditation center on Hartsfelt.

But this was my first time on watch during a deceleration. I didn't want to cry Prowler and put everyone on the edge of existential despair. If I was wrong, the penance would be exhausting. Research confirmation of the Bishopric's hunches. Churning away through verification subroutines to double check the artificial mind's base assumptions, making sure there wasn't any drift between the way we mere humans perceived the universe and the mind's own assumptions about reality.

And yet . . .

. . . that blip could be the first sign of trouble.

Heavy is the head that wears the prophet's brass crown and accepts the Bishopric's commingling minds. Heavier still the burden of the words, "Snail sign."

I opened my mouth to shout the words. Saw my fellow prophets and ministers in the rocky nest of the armored cockpit deep in the heart of the Bishopric muttering chants, updates, vector simulations, their eyes black with information. The din of calm, professional normalcy despite the utter lunacy of the task at hand: trying to slow down from interstellar transit speeds to orbit a star at an entirely different angle than the planes of the planets around this star.

Swallowed.

Maybe I could do another scan, dive deeper into communion with my Bishopric, find something solid.

In our cell, after Koros and I shaved our heads of stubble and rubbed gel over our hardline ports, we read three verses of the Articles of Discovery to each other. But Koros stopped and tapped my nose.

"Athen, you're trembling."

Koros wore just a half-robe, and I flopped forward to let my forehead rest against his oiled chest. "I saw something in the Bishopric's revelations, but I'm not sure I saw something."

Koros was used to my riddles. He kissed the top of my forehead and hugged me close.

"Can't," I said. "Mass is in fifteen minutes—"

"You have to say something. And I'm not always—"

But he was. I could feel him hard against my leg. I was too. Bad timing, though. Usually after my practices I was so tense even fifteen minutes would have been enough to fuck and take a shower if we ran to mass.

"If it's a false hit, and we go on defense stations, and I'm wrong . . ."

"You'll be right back where you started. Your place in the universe, taken from the far view, will not have changed but a slight bit." Koros had that long perspective I'd always admired, but that never made any sense to my gut.

"Revelation is . . . imprecise," I said, sitting back straight and adjusting my robes. "It's the gestalt of the Bishopric's machine minds sorting through all the data, marking data of interest, and then trying to translate that into something the human mind can comprehend. There is so much that can be lost in translation. It's almost always comprehension slippage."

Koros raised a manicured eyebrow. "Almost."

I knew that when the ancient rationalists built telescopes far out on the edges of the home system to study the light of other suns, they didn't expect apocalypse. They sought knowledge, solely for the sake of the knowledge.

"The serpent offered the fruit from the tree in the garden of Eden. They ate, and the consequences would affect every single one of their descendants for all time," my childhood confessor liked to say.

They looked for signs of other life by measuring the intensity of a star's light, searching for signs of a civilization's light output bounced off the nearby sun.

And found it.

"They were but innocents, tempted by the deepest of all urges within our kind: the urge to know."

The universe turned out vaster, stranger, and far more confusing than that urge could probe.

"Interesting homily," Koros whispered afterwards. "One can't judge the ancestors too harshly."

"No?" I asked.

Koros swept his hand at the great arches of the Bishopric's main cathedral. "All of this was built on the skeleton of rationality. The air we breathe, the machines you interface with."

"Not the engines at the heart of it all," I countered.

Koros nodded agreement. Ten years ago, he told me about the acolyte who dared look on the face of madness in the heart of the Bishopric. "Turned him inside out. I mean—literally—inside out. It took days to clean up."

Chaotic realities twisted and turned under our collective feet, flinging the Bishopric up to near the speed of light itself.

An impossibility. It literally violated the laws of physics.

Yet, here we were, worshipping under the ancient stone buttresses of a building ripped from the grass of the mother world before the Prowlers came as we screamed toward an alien sun we prayed we could hide inside.

"There would be no Bishopric without the scientific method," Koros said as the confessor swung incense and named each of the five surviving paths of Betelgeuse. "No hydroponics, no hibernation."

"I'm not shitting on the order of engineers," I told him. Long a sore point between Koros and clergymen in general.

A minister in the pew in front of us turned about and glared.

Koros ignored him. "You talk about us as if we're Neo-Franciscans. We're not. But I'm not angry about that. I'm angry because you told me there was a glitch, and you're sitting here at mass like nothing *fucking* happened."

I rocked back away from Koros. His anger and his fear all but dripped in the air around us. He'd gotten agitated on the walk over, and then during service had gotten worked up further. I hadn't paid close attention, lost in my own thoughts.

Not a good partner, I.

Too focused on me, and not we.

"Everyone's staring," Koros hissed, face red with embarrassment.

Only fifteen of us sat for mass. Overhead the star we plummeted toward burned dimly in the inkiness of darkness. We'd taken the cathedral but lost the roof. It lay open to the heavens above, protected by invisible forces wrapped around the Bishopric to shield it from gamma rays as we flew onward.

The ministers stood up. The confessor had paused service, frozen and waiting for some invisible cue that none of us would give, but after the confessor restarted, we would realize it actually was the perfect moment to begin again.

"What glitch?" the minister of paths and timetables asked, voice thin with disapproval.

"What glitch indeed?" Another minister asked.

Koros bowed. "I apologize for the disruption, madams."

Paths and timetables—I was damning myself for forgetting her name as I'd served a watch under her two months ago—stepped over her pew's back, jumped over the next, and then landed between us. "What. Fucking. Glitch, observer Athen?"

I wanted to throw up.

I'd worked hard as a young acolyte to find a space in the cockpit. The nerve center of the Bishopric took not just intelligence, but talent. Not the talent that came from coaching, practice, and study. The kind that came from luck, madness, insight, and intuition. Where you could make yourself a vessel for the divine muse to give you the edge that could let someone spot a Prowler like a glint of glass in a room of sand.

All of that, could vanish in a second.

"I want to consult with my confessor," I demanded. A stall. But a right any human who walked the universe had.

The confessor folded silvered hand over silvered hand, letting its vestments crumple underneath, and sat cross-legged, Buddha-style. It took a moment to smile. Everyone else around us didn't matter anymore now that the confessor sat with me, and curtains of curious energy flitted about us. They ate sound and cast a fog across our faces.

"Athen."

"Confessor."

"Moral dilemma?" Right to it. We'd known each other my whole life, after all.

"Yes."

The silver-on-silver eyes looked through me. "You experienced a glitch while in observation with the Bishopric, the ministers are about ready to shit their pants, Koros will shut his room from you tonight, you're scared about crying Prowler, and it's been two years, eight months, and a day since we've last communed."

"I've been walking the righteous path," I said.

"Maybe. I would pick at that, but we don't have a lot of time, do we?"

Had it really been two years? "I think—"

"Agreed, then. Do I need to draw you a decision matrix on this? The ramifications of a mistake far outweigh the consequences of looking the fool."

"This isn't a logic puzzle."

"It's a simple weighing of horrendous options," the confessor said. "That's what I'm here for. I am the core you hide from the universe. I am the raw logic that undergirds humanity. I am your conscience."

"Oh, get over yourself," I snapped. "You're no such thing."

The confessor was a compromise. Like all human creation, flawed and imperfect, hewn into being where it didn't exist before. Few existed anymore, most were hunted to extinction after the first Catastrophe.

He wasn't my conscience. But when I'd been born in an artificial womb deep in the Bishopric's slurry vats, a confessor delivered me into this universe. And taught me history, and law, and faith, and morality, and so much more. A confessor chaperoned my first date, officiated the wedding, and listened to my doubts, my fears, my tears.

He'd shown me the Old World, the First World, told the tales of Gilgamesh, Jesus, Allah, the Buddha, and more.

How many Bishoprics still flew? How many confessors led their human flock through the valleys as we sought somewhere to hide, a land to be in? How many tribes yet wandered?

We'd lost contact with them all over the many years hugging the shallow edge of light speed.

"We need the reaction mass," I said to the confessor, finally. "You know we do."

Every year fewer and fewer people actually walked the monastic halls. The cathedral felt like a mausoleum. We kept packing more and more people into hibernation. There hadn't been a new child born in decades.

If we could just slow down to planetary speeds and scoop the upper atmosphere of a gas giant for a mere five minutes, we could replenish our stores. Risky. So risky when the impact of atmosphere on our hull would cause a visible glow. We'd light a beacon for any Prowlers lurking in system.

Five observers before me had aborted a dive and then refused to serve in the cockpit again. Who could bear the burden of making that call more than once?

"If we don't refuel, we'll slowly wither," I said wearily. "We'll jettison more and more, until we're just the last of it all, in hibernation bundled together with fields, wrapped around that shard of impossibility that drives our engines. Then what? We just remain somewhere near light's speed until the heat death of the universe? We try to make sure one little sliver of humanity just limps its way there to prove a point?"

"It sounds like you have made up your mind," the confessor picked up my left hand. His was cool, but not cold to the touch. Firm, but not metallic. "And I do not run the Bishopric, I am only your spiritual counselor."

The confessor was my *everything* counselor. Who else but a carefully constrained artificial mind could we trust to let us confess to? One that encrypted your sessions with computing so advanced you'd be dead before it could be brute forced.

Who else but a guided, artificial mind to lead a flock, to remind it of its roots because it had once lived when those roots were made. Some of the very confessors aboard this Bishopric had written chapters of the Compact Amalgamation.

"You are a human," the confessor said. "Only you can know how heavy the stakes are for this decision."

"And you don't want to survive as much as we do?" I asked.

"Edited out of us after the first Catastrophe, and when artificial life was banned from leadership. You've read why."

"Oh."

The confessor leaned forward, we bumped foreheads against each other. An old, comforting movement. "But I care deeply about you, and all aboard this Bishopric. You are all truly special."

"I wanted to ask—"

"I don't have any easy answers and you knew that when you asked for the confessional. You were buying time. While it has been two years, and I need you to come to me more often. Athen, I think we both know you need to get back out there."

I leaned my head back and swore at the universe.

"It doesn't care," the confessor said.

"That sounds rather atheistic," I said.

The confessor smiled. "I doubt it. I was literally built not to be. But in the end, I'm just a reflection of your journey. Are you feeling particularly atheistic today, Athen?"

"The miracles stand, Confessor. The universe is unknowable. We may experience their mystery, even master mysteries, but it exceeds the finite mind. Release me to find my path in it."

"I release you. Go, walk the universe and thrive."

The ministers followed me like a gaggle of fussy cleaner dryads. Questions piled up and knocked into each other in the air around us.

"Brother Athen—"

"Brother—"

They were scared we'd lose the cathedral. If we didn't get the mass we needed from a gas giant, we'd need to jettison that most holy relic of the original home world. We'd moved it to the Bishopric back when humanity strode the stars with few worries. Back when the cost of slowing down to dip into a gas giant for replenishment didn't mean extinction. Back when Bishoprics lugged around space fat with the remnants of humanity's birthplace aboard. We'd been museums, archives, history on the move.

The strange, unreal forces that powered the Bishopric couldn't carry the extra mass without some resupply, and we'd slowly been jettisoning anything non-essential over many generations now as its powers drooped and our ability to change courses or escape Prowler sign slowly used up whatever resources it had once had.

We've been scared, humanity, ever since we threw ourselves out into the dark night of interstellar space to answer that most ancient of questions, the one we'd thought of when we first looked up at the stars: were we alone in this universe?

The old rationalists found what they'd been looking for: a sun that reflected slightly more light than it should. A sun born at the edge of a stellar nursery, but now falling closer and closer to a black hole that would soon greedily start pulling it into the edge of an event horizon as it inexorably readied to rip it apart.

"I can tell you what I saw," said the ancient confessor with pitted eyes. It creaked when it moved, and flakes of black rot swirled in the air around it. All throughout the statuary confessors stood immobile, traveling through the vastness of time through patience and vigilance.

"Tell us what you saw," we would call out.

"I saw a moon—" the confessor began.

"A thimble next to a full cup," we said.

"It was no world, no giant swirled with gases, but a worldlet. A young thing, but a curious thing. Curious because—"

"Its face lay scrubbed smooth, shaved clean by the weight of glaciers, the heaviness of the ice implacable against the soft lands," we responded.

"Bathed in the light of radiation, torn by the shifting waves of gravity, we beheld a world limned in ice, warmed by that which organic life could not survive, and it glittered in the light of civilization. Structures filled the crevices and fields, twinkling lights showed patterns and intention. We knew, impossibly, that life thrived here."

And then we prepared for the lament of the first Catastrophe by raising the leather braids over our heads.

Penance. Five lashes to the back. One for each of the Five Great Mistakes.

"I accept Hubris, the First of the Five . . ."

Rationalists could piece apart how it happened. They were good at matching patterns, picking apart the pieces of history to find the universe's hidden narrative.

The star was middle-aged, born in a packed stellar nursery. A dense, chaotic swirl of raw matter that created thousands of stars so close to each other the night sky on a planet around any one of them was lit like day. But the factory that created it wasn't a nurturing, safe place for stars. All that free star-creating material? It came from the remains of stars consumed by the ever-growing black hole that lurked at the center of the nursery, ripped apart as they tumbled about near the hole's event horizon.

The star escaped destruction through simple orbital luck, wandering around the edges of the stellar nursery due to a very high, slow orbit. And thanks to that strange orbital dance, life had the time to creep up from the depths of a moon around a smaller gas giant on the edge of the system.

But what kind of life?

The highly radioactive rock deep inside the tiny moon warmed its core, and orbital stresses shifted the rock, liquifying it and providing more molten heat. And in the shallow oceans compressed between the heavy ice and the planetary rock of the moon, life appeared.

The confessors came because organic bodies couldn't survive the gulf between stars in those days, and certainly not the frying radioactive heat of the stellar nursery around the black hole.

What did we hope would happen?

I was human, like the people who built that first mission were. All our beamed messages had gone ignored. We hoped by showing up, we'd figure out a way to make a connection. Some way of knowing for sure whether we were alone, or if something was imitating intelligent life out there on the edge of a black hole.

Many of the Amalgamation curse our forebears.

But I think I would have made the same mistake they did.

After second prayers, I scrubbed oven pans clean and Koros angrily sliced vegetables.

"Ratatouille?" I asked.

"Does it look like these are the right vegetables for that?" Koros laid the slices out on the pan.

"You have to dry the pan first," I protested.

"Didn't you clean it well enough?"

I looked at several soap suds quivering next to potato slices. "It's clean."

"Quit trying to oversee details not in your area. Stick to your room."

"You're being an ass," I said abruptly.

Koros slapped the knife down. "We're in here cutting vegetables," he growled. "And what else could be more important than making dinner for the congregation?"

He might as well have stabbed me. He never showed violent emotions.

I stared at him for a long beat, then turned back to the sink. Certain ancient orders would take vows of silence. It sounded better and better to me as we worked together in hostile silence.

"No one will talk to me," Koros said. "They don't trust themselves to be calm about it. They don't want to pressure me or influence us."

I carefully dried another pan and let it clatter by the whirlwind of sliced vegetable parts.

"They don't need to," I said. Damn. I never lasted long in silence. I felt disappointed in myself, even though I knew it was a juvenile tactic. "That's not how it works."

Busying myself doing other things gave the subconscious time to make disparate connections. The observer needed to be a lateral thinker, a spider at the heart of a web, not a sequential worker. Scrubbing pans could well be the catalyst that prompted a moment of clarity.

The old rationalists proposed theories, and tests that could check the theory. They built a body of knowledge, a civilization, on test after test. But when the confessors reached that strange world around the black hole, they found the limits of their thinking and design, leaving them vulnerable.

How can you test a theory in an area of the universe where the experiment itself shifted? Where the very nature of reality swirled about, sputtered and collapsed in a black hole?

Early humans had seen jets of matter shooting from the poles of black holes at speeds faster than light. They assumed errors in the sightings, distortions or natural phenomena. But the jets remained obstinate in their violation of reality.

The universe's rules couldn't be broken, but black holes did not care.

Ancient scholars saw that black holes chewed up reality, shredding it with their tidal forces and mysterious physics, and spat out reconfigured "information." Random realities, objects, information, vast and near-impossible to understand actions happened in the chaos around an event horizon.

The order and logic of reality fell apart.

So, while the human body would never survive the trip to the system, the confessors could. Artificial life, rational in its programming and creation, able to survive where we could not.

But what they would see would turn many confessors mad, unable to handle what they encountered.

And the confessors that survived found faith, the only thing that kept their minds sane as they stared into the edge of a void that ruined minds.

"I can't solve the problem by thinking through it," I told Koros. "The Bishopric doesn't work on logic. There's nothing you, or they, can say or do that can logically disturb what's happening."

"We don't know that."

"We also don't know that doing nothing won't be the wrong thing to do. We don't know anything, Koros. We are in the valley of ignorance, and human eyes cannot pierce the veil here. We're looking through a glass darkly, and that means what we think we see could well be a smear of dirt we left on the glass."

Some observers committed suicide after they made the call to abort the planetary mission. The stress of not knowing whether they made the right call broke them.

Koros needed to stop losing himself in worries and fears that would just make this all so much worse.

I wrapped my arms around his waist. "You need to relax. You need to stop staring right at the problem or you'll go mad before me."

"That wasn't funny," he growled.

"I wasn't trying to be."

"Athen," Koros said slowly.

I let go.

I could feel him building up to something big. The words sat right behind his teeth. "We can talk about it later," I said, desperately trying to put off something horrible.

"If we can't get resupplied with a scoop, I volunteered to be placed in hibernation."

And out of the corner of my eye, one of the soap bubbles popped in a glint of fading film.

I froze.

What life grows in the thin ocean between the hammer of ice above and anvil of rock below, warmed only by the radioactive heat of hydrothermal jets of water?

Far from the warm sands of Mecca or Jerusalem once lay the great oceans of Earth. Deep below, in one of the few inhospitable zones of the Mother Planet, life gathered around hydrothermal vents. Maybe it still did, we could no longer get close enough to see anymore.

On the radiation-bathed tiny world, molluskan life emerged, safe and warm around the vents. The fleshy creatures, somewhere between snail and squid, dominated the little moon for almost a billion years as their world spun through the stellar nursery toward its eventual death in the maw of the black hole.

"And this is where shit gets weird," I heard a confessor say to his flock of eager listeners once when explaining what they saw happen next. "There was nothing on that moon but mollusks."

It was as if a tide swept out, and left an icy, rocky bay bristling with nothing but barnacles clumped and clustered over any exposed piece of rock. Mollusks climbed mountain ranges, flat icy plains, valleys, oceans . . .anywhere human telescopes looked, mollusks bristled.

They even clumped and mounded over each other. Half-mile high domes of mollusk life, structures inside so complex the megastructures poked almost out of the thin atmosphere.

And the light of civilization didn't come from technology, or structures separate from minds. The light came from trillions of mollusks blinking.

We'd seen their conversations.

They consumed iron sulfate and concentrated it into their ever-expanding polished metal shells no predator that may have once existed there could crack. And over the billions of years, they refined the biological metallurgy into the weapon that let them conquer their world.

When they lifted their stalked eyes to regard the world above the horizon, they saw only madness, distortion, and randomness in the skies. They turned away from it or tried to protect themselves from it. If they were about to outgrow the confines of their world, it was only as an accidental expansion of their ever-complexifying constructions and the walls they built to protect themselves from the profound impossibilities that tore space and time around their world.

What else could they have known, other than the domineering cosmic horror that waited to consume? They could never see past it to the galaxy around them.

But when the confessors arrived, metal life made by organic life, traveling in hard-shelled ships that crossed the gulf of space, something changed on that moon as the minds behind those stalked eyes came to understand a whole universe existed out past the strangeness of their borders. As confessors explored the system, and others tried to make contact, new structures appeared in the cracks and sides of the moon's mountain ranges. The confessors could tell *something* was happening down below them as they orbited the new world.

"We should have realized what it meant that nothing but mollusks existed down there. We should have known that creatures born in a place where space and time were bent would think so differently."

I threw up in the bathroom. Koros heard me, because he came in with a cold, wet towel to wrap around my forehead and dabbed at my lips with a corner. The cloth felt rough against my mouth.

"You intuited something?"

I nodded and sank down with my back against the wall of the small bathroom. "It may not be safe."

The Bishopric was coasting right now, waiting for the all-clear to adjust its course to hit the edges of the sun and use its heat and chaos to hide the sign of the Bishopric braking down to planetary system speeds. If I gave the order, we'd just coast on by instead.

Again.

Koros sat heavily down next to me. "May?"

"It'll never be more than a hunch."

"Fuck." He wiped sweat off his forehead.

"There's nothing to say I'm right. The confessors will check the signal, they'll do the math, and when they're done, it'll suggest we should do it. That we *need* to do it."

I gave Koros the towel and pulled his hand closer to me. I leaned my cheek against the back of it and took the moment to just sit quietly there.

"When will you tell the ministers?"

I didn't want to.

"There's still a chance, a big one, that it's fine. They may overrule me. They should overrule me," I said.

Koros nodded slowly. "Maybe."

What minister would risk the only known last fragment of humanity on chance? They would only see the option to play things safe until the game ended. The only way they'd give the order to drop in-system was if I gave the all-clear.

I wanted to cry, but I didn't have the energy for it.

Never in my whole, scholarly life in the stacks under the cathedral had I wanted something as bad as to give the order. Let's roll the dice, let's live!

Just me on this Bishopric, and I'd do it.

If we knew of any humanity left at all on a planet, a planetoid, a station in the middle of the dark between stars, I could give the order.

But the survival of the entire species depended on the right call. And I'd been given the chance to be the one who made it.

"Fuck," I grunted.

We clutched each other's arms, and Koros's fingernails dug so deeply into my forearm he drew blood, and I didn't even notice until he let go.

The war began when the moon belched mollusks up into the space around it. The mollusks had shown no interest in space travel, so the event caught the confessors by total and utter surprise. Traveling here had changed something, even if no formal contact had been made. Like startled starlings, the metal-shelled creatures flocked this way and that throughout their system.

The confessors puzzled over the stunning leap in technology and purpose, tried to comprehend *how*. But the mollusks didn't follow development trees, or research paths. Maybe, some thought, this environment led the mollusks to another technological path.

As the confessors argued about how it was done, the mollusks came for the confessor's ships.

At first, the confessors, unworried about their own lives or damage, accepted the mollusks as they barnacled onto hulls and encampments. They studied them as they ate through the metal hulls.

Confessors noticed more advanced metallurgy in the shell structures and worried about technological infection. Maybe they should have remained hidden.

But we'd studied their lights for years, and listened, and still, we couldn't understand them. The fact we'd had no idea they could invent a form of space travel in mere years without a single confessor noticing demonstrated that clearly.

By the time the confessors understood the danger, our ships dripped with mollusks, unable to navigate, unable to flee.

Would scraping them off be a violation? Would that be unneighborly? A provocation?

Confessors abandoned ships, retreated to the outer planetary rim.

Mollusks followed.

They whipped through space faster than confessors could now, and how they'd figured this out confused the confessors. They couldn't run from the mollusks, so they hid. They burrowed into asteroids, they camouflaged themselves near the sun, they floated off into the Oort clouds at the far icy edges of the system.

One by one, they died.

The confessors learned what they could as they fell to the onslaught. They learned that the creatures once used a gland with symbiotic bacteria that fed off radiation which had since evolved into a biological nuclear reactor. That, after eons living near the edge of a black hole, the mollusks didn't see a universe with rational constants. Cause and effect had minimal bearing on mollusk thought. Mollusk grammar, what little they could decipher in the coherent light they communicated with, didn't seem to have any recognizable pattern.

They were a chaotic life born in a zone of non-rational realities.

The confessors that survived were the ones that fled so close to the edge of the black hole's event horizon they almost turned mad. They couldn't compute cause and effects, couldn't model reality around them, and as artificial life, their very nature began to fall apart.

Until, taking a page from mollusk life, they embraced it.

And found faith.

In the long dark nights, as the abyss teemed with metal-shelled mollusks, Prowlers seeking them out with a zealotry almost unimaginable, the confessors examined everything they'd ever been taught. They discarded the scientific method, already on shaky ground when an artificial mind could use virtual evolution to test trillions of attempted variations of an engineering query to find the right answer without bothering about why of it. They found Gnosticism, faith, and philosophy. They pored over Greek thinkers, the recordings of the insane, and the ramblings of the extremely high.

As they prayed for deliverance, they watched Prowlers evolve in terrifying, random leaps. The few they could capture simmered with hellfire-fueled engines deep under their shells that grasped tendrils of space and time, exotic biomachinery beyond their understanding.

Confessors watched with horror as Prowlers spun free of the black hole's influence, flinging themselves along vectors that confessors knew would take them back to human worlds.

When the Prowlers finally found and descended on human worlds, the confessors appeared in great Bishoprics powered by Prowler remains. The confessors had cracked them apart and cored out their minds to power speeds near light.

"Flee with us and live, or stay and fall into extinction."

In the First Interstallarium, a million faiths grew and flourished, but none more than the confessors' as they helped humanity scatter across the galaxy, all to run clear of the Prowlers.

But they kept coming.

And one by one, the worlds stopped broadcasting. Then the depots between them.

After that, the Bishoprics started to fall silent as well.

I found a small cove near a saint, still preserved perfectly in death thanks to his custom hibernation shell, a custom from the old days of preserving the flesh after death. I wept for Koros down in the bowels of the Bishopric, asleep and unaware of anything now.

At first, I'd raged. How could he do this to me? Didn't he know the chances of us getting to the point where we could wake him up and be together again were slim?

I knew he'd done it to try and help us.

Help all of us.

The Minister of Algae found me there, gently pulled me up, and led me outside. "It's time, Athen."

I watched the charges flash, and the cathedral wobble as it broke free of the Bishopric's remaining earth. The last of the world that birthed us. We'd carried it out of simple human attachment. The desire to hold something from our ancestors, from the original home that no longer existed. And we couldn't afford to do it anymore.

The Bishopric had once been as much museum to humanity as lifeboat. We'd lied to ourselves that one day we'd take the cathedral's remains back to where they belonged.

But now we needed to admit this was only a lifeboat.

The stained glass, the worn-out gargoyles glaring defiance at the stars, the buttresses, all fell away into the dark night sky.

Far behind it, the star we'd hoped to brake down to orbit around glinted at us.

"We'll go further," I'd told Koros as he lay on the open hibernation chassis. "Further than imaginable. We'll survive. And one day, one day, I'll open this up and we'll be together again."

It made no rational sense to believe it. But here I was, a child of beliefs forged in the edges of a black hole, fleeing for a chance at humanity's survival. What did I have left but faith?

Faith that we'd survive.

THE LATEST BLACK HOLE PLANET, IN FORMATION

AMEDEO ROMAGNOLO

Could we ever encounter a life-bearing planet or moon, such as the Prowlers' homeworld in Tobias S. Buckell's story, "The Last Cathedral of Earth, In Flight," in the close vicinity of a black hole?

In order for habitable planets and their host stars to form, we need one thing and one thing only: a dense cloud of interstellar matter. This cloud needs to contain a wide variety of chemical elements; since if it were only composed of hydrogen and helium (the most abundant elements in the universe), it would only be able to potentially form gas giants like Jupiter. When we have a cloud of enriched interstellar gas, the next step is having one or more areas of concentrated mass that can gravitationally pull the surrounding gas and dust until there is enough material for stars and planets to be born.

Black holes usually aren't the most ideal neighbors for life-hosting planets. Most black holes are formed from the collapse of a very massive star (roughly beyond 20 times bigger than the Sun at their birth) after it explodes as a supernova, which is a cataclysmic event when a star, at the end of its life, ejects most of its mass at terrific velocities alongside extremely energetic radiation into its surroundings. Usually stars of this size don't have a long life, since they burn their nuclear fuel quite quickly. Our Sun will probably last until an age of 10 billion years, while these massive stars usually collapse into black holes after ~ tens of millions years (so 1000 times faster!). From what we know from Earth, life needs at least some hundreds of millions of years of stable solar radiation to arise, so this means that these stars burn too quickly for that to happen on the planets they host. If by some miracle life arose in such a short time, it would probably be annihilated by the supernova explosion. Even before the supernova event, old massive stars tend to expand to more than a hundred times their original size and therefore, for biological life, it will either be death by burning, or by radiation (since the radiation levels of a star are proportional to its size)—whichever comes first.

On the other side of the equation, supernova events release an extremely large amount of enriched gas that is essential for Earth-like planets and moons to form. There is also another important point to consider: let's imagine a bomb exploding at the bottom of the sea. In this case, all the water surrounding the bomb would be pushed away and therefore there would be, for a few instants, some localized areas where water is more concentrated than it was before. In the same fashion, if a stellar system prior to a black hole collapse was already surrounded by interstellar gas, a supernova explosion could form areas of denser gas and dust that could start the gravitational accretion processes, that could lead to the formation of a new generation of stars and planets. As a matter of fact, we already have some observational evidence of planets orbiting around post-supernova objects. Among them we have, for instance, low-mass planets orbiting around the neutron star B1257+12, which was a massive star (initially below 20 times the mass of the Sun) and massive enough to initiate a supernova explosion. Neutron stars are extremely dense objects made almost uniquely of neutrons, with a very strong magnetic field and a distinctive electromagnetic signature.

The young research field of gravitational waves astronomy can also give us a hint regarding how black holes can contribute to the formation of stars. Most massive stars are born in binaries or multiple systems (i.e., 2+ stars in the same stellar systems orbiting around a center of mass). Now, depending on the initial configuration and the potential effect of the environment, a binary system composed of two massive stars may evolve to host two black holes, two neutron stars, or one black hole and one neutron star. In each of these configurations the two binary objects are orbiting around each other, but, due to general relativity effects, they get closer and closer to one another on each orbit due to the emission of the so-called gravitational waves. Although the nature of gravitational waves is still uncertain, one thing is sure: if no outside force affects the binary, the black holes/neutron stars will keep emitting gravitational waves until they get so close to each other that they will merge into a single bigger object, which is usually a black hole.

This merger event is considered the most energetic phenomenon in the known universe, even more energetic than a supernova. A part of this energy is converted into a single, extremely strong, kick on the newborn black hole. Let's imagine: if one shot a very strong magnet at hundreds of kilometers per second into a pool of iron filings, everything in the trajectory of the magnet would either attach to the moving body or at least be moved by it, if not directly destroyed! On the contrary, everything on the magnet's tail would "attempt" to follow it, but with no success due to the great velocity at which it was shot. One way or another, the magnet will create a huge amount of motion within the iron filings, with areas of higher density forming inside the pool (if iron filings were actually compressible enough). Analogously, a post-merger black hole shot at high velocities into an interstellar cloud could have the effect of giving just the right amount of energy to initialize the birth of new stellar systems.

Many galaxies host supermassive black holes (black holes that kept accreting material for ages until they reach masses of millions+ of times the mass of the Sun) in their nuclei. These galaxies have an intensely luminous environment in their central regions that cannot be associated with light emitted by stars. Such regions are the most luminous objects in the known universe and are called Active Galactic Nuclei or AGNs. The are several types of AGNs, but all of them are characterized by a disk of dust and gas surrounding the black hole, which, due to dissipative effects, heats up to emit a huge amount of light. Depending on the nature of the supermassive black hole and the distribution of the surrounding mass, a considerable fraction of the material dragged toward the black hole from its disk could be accelerated to velocities approaching the speed of light and emitted from the black hole poles in the form of highly energetic jets.

These jets usually have a disruptive effect on stellar nurseries since they emit more energy than an interstellar cloud can take. Nevertheless, as was observed for the AGN in the dwarf galaxy Henize 2-10, there might be a chance for a supermassive black hole to have gentler jets that can warm interstellar clouds enough to initiate matter accretion without disrupting the whole area, or at least in the nurseries' furthest regions.

It has been also hypothesized that the AGNs from "small" supermassive black holes (millions of times the mass of the Sun) could potentially last long enough and be stable enough to directly initiate the formation of planets without the need for a star to form alongside them. In this scenario, the environment of the AGN will last in the order of 100 million years, with light and gravity just in the right conditions to favor the aggregation of small rocky formations (~1 km of diameter each) into bigger bodies, which, once they clear their surroundings by either gravitationally attracting or expelling the remaining gas, dust and planetoids, will rightfully acquire the title of planets, or as they were initially called blanets.

It must be highlighted that even in the unlikely event of planets and stars forming close to supermassive black holes, they are unlikely to be absorbed in the way one would expect. The stellar object won't usually directly fall inside the black hole since the gravitational tides of these objects are far too strong for a planet or even a star to remain intact. The most likely scenario would be for the planet to either stably orbit around the black hole or, once in close proximity, to be quickly dismembered, crushed, and pulverized by the black hole's gravity and then accreted piece by piece.

Two things must also be clear when we talk about life-hosting planets and black holes.

First of all, we can only base our assumptions on the statistics of one, i.e., Earth. As a matter of fact, rocky Earth-like planets are still extremely hard for our instruments to detect due to their relatively small size. Even for the ones we discovered, our technology is still at least one decade short of being accurate enough to detect traces of alien life. There is also no consensus in the astrobiology community regarding what to consider as an actual proof of biological life (or how to generally define biological life, anyway). Should we look for traces of oxygen, which is mainly made by photosynthetic organisms on Earth? Other molecules? Or should we look instead for something more obvious like a radio signal broadcasting ABBA songs? We simply aren't sure.

Secondly, our knowledge of how black holes and planets form is extremely incomplete. The precise evolution of massive stars and their collapse into black holes is still uncertain, and we actually never observed a planet form and evolve from its initial stages to its "final" ones, considering the large observational times required for such a task. To get accurate (and statistically significant) observations of Earth-like planets we will need to wait until space telescopes like LUVOIR and LIFE are developed and deployed, but we'll need to wait at least a decade for either of them. In the meantime, all our knowledge is based on theoretical assumptions and astrophysical simulations, which are both dependent on theorists' best guesses.

Astrophysics is mainly made of variable margins of uncertainty. For some astrophysical phenomena, these margins are negligible, while others could vary so much that, depending on which theorist we ask, we can get very different results. And usually the sad thing here is that many of them could be equally right!

As a rule of thumb, the more esoteric an astrophysical field is, the more it's affected by uncertainties. This doesn't mean that everything theoretical astrophysicists do are blind guesses. On the contrary, they are all (usually) based on solid and provable scientific facts; but the more we go to unexplored lands, the more we know that our prior knowledge needs to be expanded for us to have sufficient instruments to understand what's around us.

But isn't this the fun of discovery, anyway?

FURTHER READING

Stellar and binary evolution
Stellar evolution. American Association of Variable Star Observers (AAVSO). (n.d.).
https://www.aavso.org/stellar-evolution

Observational evidence for supernova-induced star formation
Herbst, W., & Assousa, G. E. (1977). "Observational evidence for supernova-induced star formation-Canis Major R1." *The Astrophysical Journal*, 217, 473-487.
https://adsabs.harvard.edu/full/1977ApJ...217..473H

Neutron star planets
Patruno, A., & Kama, M. (2017). "Neutron star planets: Atmospheric processes and irradiation." *Astronomy & Astrophysics*, 608, A147.
https://www.aanda.org/articles/aa/pdf/2017/12/aa31102-17.pdf

Black hole and neutron star mergers and their Gravitational Waves emission
Castelvecchi, D. (2020, October 30). "What 50 gravitational-wave events reveal about the universe." *Nature News*.
https://www.nature.com/articles/d41586-020-03047-0

Blanets
Wada, K., Tsukamoto, Y., & Kokubo, E. (2019). "Planet formation around supermassive black holes in the active galactic nuclei." *The Astrophysical Journal*, 886(2), 107.
https://iopscience.iop.org/article/10.3847/1538-4357/ab4cf0/pdf

More about LUVOIR telescope: https://www.luvoirtelescope.org/
More about LIFE space mission: https://www.life-space-mission.com

THE SECRET HISTORY OF THE GREATEST DISCOVERY

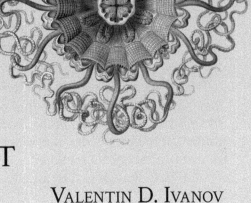

VALENTIN D. IVANOV

(Translated from Bulgarian by the author)

Prologue

Mariana Kaloyanova, a middle-aged professor of astronomy and a well-known SETI researcher, put down the empty coffee mug and sent the coordinates to her PhD student Iveta Nikolova sitting by the next table.

"Humor the old lady. Add this faint star next to Zeta Andromedae to the target list again."

They were observing remotely from the comfort of their university campus in Germany, sitting in soft office chairs and well-stocked with freshly brewed coffee and cinnamon buns. On the wall-sized screens in front of them, the control room in Chile had lost all its depth. They'd both been on-site in Atacama and knew the place was huge, with a long row of tables, dozens of workstations, and many people tending the cyclopic eye.

Iveta nodded, but Mariana wasn't deceived. The slight frown betrayed the student: she remained unconvinced. There was a young rebel right here, Mariana mused. *The pear never falls far away from the mother-tree.*

"I know it is a bit too far north, but we can just observe it," Mariana said.

August 1984, a small country in Eastern Europe

1. In the beginning was the Argelander's Method
Mariana fought to hide the annoyance in her voice. "Have you ever observed variables?" she asked the two sixth-grade girls.

They looked at her in awe. At their age, four years made a difference; they were still kids. At her age, not so much; Todor Peev, a broad-shouldered young man, an instructor at the astrocamp and a physics student at the University, was older than Mariana by a similar number of years and it hardly mattered.

"No, just meteors, during the last year's camp," the taller girl answered.

They were in a forest opening, where the camp's night-time observations took place. No streetlights around, just some glow on the horizon from the nearby villages. It was too dark to tell the two girls apart, except for their voices and statures. Todor had dumped them on Mariana in the afternoon, saying they needed help with the identification of their variable stars in the sky. He'd said who they were, but she promptly forgot their names.

"This is my sixth camp. We must have run into each other," Mariana said.

"I know you," the taller one admitted. "You hardly ever came to the Meteor Meadows." That was the nickname for the forest clearing a hundred meters uphill from the parking lot and the cabins where the astronomy summer camp was based.

Mariana nodded, but realizing they wouldn't see her in the dark, she quickly added, "True." She needed to get them back to the topic. "So, do you have your finder's charts ready?"

"We do," the same girl answered. She seemed a bit more confident.

"Let's see. First, can you find RZ Cassiopeiae on your chart?" It was an eclipsing binary with deep minima, excellent for training new observers. "By the way, I'm Mariana. Could you tell me your names again, please?"

"I'm Rossitsa. Or Rossy," the self-assured girl said.

"And I'm Penka," the shorter one said. "Could I have some light, please?"

Rossy pulled out a minuscule flashlight, a little blocky contraption that housed two finger-sized cylindrical batteries side by side. They were so popular, even Mariana had one. This one was modified: the front had been painstakingly covered up with red tape, to avoid blinding night-time observers.

"Good!" Putting the red tape on was clever. Maybe these girls were not just some ignorant newbies.

The dimmed light shone upon a ten-centimeter square piece of rice paper. Penka placed the flashlight underneath, turning it into a small projection screen. Thick pencil dots marked the positions of the stars—the larger the dots, the brighter they were. RZ Cassiopeiae, the variable, was surrounded by a neat circle.

"We will start by identifying the brightest comparison stars A and B," Mariana said.

The girls set up the little eight-centimeter telescope and took turns peering through the eyepiece.

"I also see C and D," Rossy said, adjusting the focus.

Mariana was expecting her to speak up first. "We'll come to those in a while."

Penka and Rossy spent a quarter of an hour memorizing the field until they didn't need to check the chart to find a star. Mariana gave them ten minutes extra.

"The sequence of the comparison stars A, B, C and so on, is arranged in order of decreasing apparent brightness. Now, look at the variable's brightness and figure out between which two of those it should be ranked."

Her pupils went back to the telescope. The nights, even in August, were cool at nine hundred meters above sea level. Mariana did a few squats to keep warm.

"It's between B and C," Rossy said.

"Closer to C," Penka added.

Mariana smiled to herself; her pupil was gaining confidence. "Excellent!" she said. "What is the time?"

"Eighteen past eleven," Penka said again.

"The minimum has already begun. Do you know Argelander's Method?"

They tried to explain it, interrupting each other.

"Right. We estimate the difference between the fainter reference and the variable with a grade scale from zero—if they're equal—to four—when they're obviously different. Same for the variable and the brighter reference. Got it?"

"Yes," two voices came from the dark.

"What else do we have to do?"

The girls hesitated.

"Tick tock, tick tock," Mariana hinted.

"Ah, we note the time!" Penka said.

"And we write it in the log," Rossy said quickly. Mariana realized the taller girl couldn't stand being left behind.

Ten minutes later they had their first estimates: B-four-Var-one-C from Rossy and B-four-Var-zero-C from Penka; Mariana suspected she gave that zero just for difference's sake.

Leaving the girls to proceed on their own, Mariana joined a bunch of boys from Varna, fiddling with a meteor obturator.

The sky above the pine trees started to brighten shortly past four in the morning. The birds woke up. A clueless rabbit crawled out of the thick undergrowth and, sensing motion in the clearing, hopped away. Mariana stopped by to check on the girls before going to bed. The telescope was pointed at some other variable. Her pupils didn't even realize she was around, totally engrossed in their observations.

2. Steep roads to nature's secrets

The next morning, the students from the astroclub in Pleven woke Mariana up before eleven—too early for someone who had spent the entire night watching the sky—playing rapid chess on the table next to her window, and loudly discussing each move. She tried to go back to sleep.

Tough luck—this year she was staying in the cabin right by the little asphalt patch, surrounded by pavilions and open-air tables where the kids liked to gather on hot summer days. The light coming through the thin curtains didn't help either, and the memories of the obturator problems—the homemade device vibrated like crazy—chased her dreams away.

There was no point in lying awake. Mariana rose, dressed, and went out. She took the empty table next to the chess players and spread her papers out.

A gust of wind sent one of the plots flying. Mariana tried to catch it, but before she could, a slim boy from Shumen jumped up from the chess game and captured it. Stefan—she knew him—had just graduated from high school. He had been attending the camp a couple of years longer than her and studied variables with photographs, taking long exposures of star clusters with pulsating stars. This meant he spent his nights mostly alone, glued to the eyepiece of a telescope. She suspected he wasn't very good at talking to girls, unlike the worldly and eloquent Todor.

Stefan looked at the sheet before passing it back to her, then blushed. It was a graph paper with a pencil-drawn light curve showing how the brightness of a variable star changed over time. Apparent magnitudes on the vertical axis, time on the horizontal. She had used civil dates, carefully counting thirty or thirty-one lines for June, July, and August. Dots marked individual observations from nearly every night.

"Which one is it? Zeta Andromedae!" Stefan read the label on the top. "That's a tough one. What's the amplitude? One or two tenths?"

"More or less. Somebody reported 0.22 mags in the AAVSO bulletin. And the period is nearly eighteen days," she boasted. Small-amplitude long-period variables were the hardest because they needed accurate and consistent observations over weeks and months.

"Wow! May I?"

"Sure."

Stefan stared at the plot sidewise, along the horizontal axis so the projection compressed the curve and made the variations clearer. "Hmmm. I can barely see anything. Can you?" His voice trembled, confirming Mariana's observation that boys were weird around girls.

She kept these conclusions to herself, though. Voicing them would probably send him hiding in the forest for the duration of the camp. "Sort of," she said. "I covered almost two periods this summer, and my plan is to continue until it disappears behind the Sun in February. With some cooperation from the weather, of course. However, I think I can already make out a sinusoidal curve with the minima and the maxima at the right times. With some imagination."

"Well, with a lot of imagination. Hey woodheads!" Stefan called out at the people around the next table. "Come and check an amazing light curve!"

The chess players and their vocal fan club abandoned the game, bringing all the noise and commotion with them. They waved their hands, yelling and showing the plot to each other over and over again.

"When did you start the monitoring?" somebody asked.

"In mid-June," Mariana said. "It was visible only for a few minutes at dawn, but it was enough."

"Your parents must have thought you're crazy," Penka said. She'd joined them without Mariana's noticing.

"Actually no. My dad came along. He would even wake me up if I'd overslept."

"And your mom?"

"She made tea and biscuits for us."

"Wow, that's something." The other sixth-grader was also here. "I wish my parents would do that. Speaking of observations, would you help us reduce the data from yesterday?"

"Sure, Rossy," she said. "Do you have them with you?"

The girl produced a thick notebook with green cardboard covers.

"A great light curve!" one of the chess players interjected and gave the graph paper back to Mariana. "Hey, it's my turn!" he said, and the crowd moved back to the chess set, leaving her with the two younger girls and Stefan.

"So, would you help us with the data?" Rossy asked again.

"I can give you a hand too," the boy offered before Mariana could answer. "What exactly are you doing?"

They explained, cutting off each other's sentences.

"Here're our estimates." Penka opened the notebook.

"B-four-Var-zero-C," Stefan read the first line.

"This is easy," Mariana said. "In this case, the variable is as bright as reference star C."

"B-four-Var-one-C," Stefan went on. "Well, here we'll have to interpolate between the magnitudes of the two reference stars." He was calm, concentrated, and assured. Mariana wondered if thinking made him forget he was talking to girls.

"Interpolate?" Rossy asked.

Mariana saw that Stefan was about to launch into a long explanation, probably too complicated for thirteen-year-old kids, so she took the initiative. "Imagine you have a graph with lots of measurements of something—current, voltage, stellar brightness—at one, two, three and so on. You need to figure out the values between the measurements that you already have. Say, at one point two, one and a half and so on." She turned the graph paper over and quickly drew an example. "You can connect the dots with straight lines and see what the value of these lines is at one point two, one and a half, et cetera. Do you understand?"

Penka and her friend nodded. Mariana caught some curious glances from them—they studied her, too. She imagined what they were seeing: a petite girl looking too young for her age, with thin brown hair, tied in a ponytail, and a boring round face. Far from pretty. But hey, who'd notice in the middle of the night, when the only carrier wave the others got from her was a competent voice?

"Two more things," Stefan intervened, still undisturbed by the fact he was speaking with girls. "First, this is a linear interpolation because we use straight, linear lines between the points. We can do this better if we fit a parabola to three or more points."

Rossy and Penka honestly tried to follow him, but their eyes soon turned glassy.

"Second," the boy went on, too absorbed in the math to notice, "this was interpolation, where we determine values between points that we already know. There is also extrapolation, that is when we determine the values outside the range of the points we have."

"It's safer to interpolate than to extrapolate," Mariana said when he paused for breath, "because in the former case we already know what the curve is doing."

"In the latter," Stefan went on, "we don't. We just assume it keeps behaving the same way."

The faces of the girls livened up with understanding.

3. Mundane surprises and profound truths about observational uncertainties

The chess players went away, but more pupils came out of the cabins. Less than half an hour remained until breakfast. Although it was the first meal of the day, it included three courses: a soup, a main dish, and a dessert, just like a proper lunch, and it was held at the right time for a lunch too.

Rossy and Penka went to their room to drop off their notes, and Todor approached the table.

"Good morning! How are you doing?" He saw Mariana's graph, still spread on the table, and took some time inspecting it.

She loved his long pauses. He was patient, and he considered carefully what to say. This was so mature.

"There is a problem here. Your grade steps are about 0.05 magnitudes," he said and looked at her. "Excellent observing! Effectively, that is the accuracy of your measurements. But RS Canis Venaticorum stars don't flicker, yet the light curve shows a scatter of about half a magnitude, much wider than what can be expected from observational errors alone. Where does this extra spread come from?"

She quivered, pleased with his attention and thinking how much prettier the variations of Zeta Andromedae must be in comparison with her freckles.

Todor turned the graph paper sidewise as Stefan had done. Mariana thought her fellow student might have picked up the habit from their instructor. Except, Stefan hadn't noticed the problem with her observations. Neither had she, for that matter.

"This kind of extra noise may appear if the data contain systematic errors, or systematic uncertainties," Todor said. "Do you know what I mean?"

Mariana shook her head wordlessly, just like the sixth-graders earlier.

"Let's assume you"— he pointed at her—"are measuring the distance from here to Ardino"—that was the name of the little town where the camp's food came from—"in footsteps. Suppose the first time you come up with twenty thousand steps."

Todor raised a hand to stop Stefan who opened his mouth to object—probably claiming that the distance is longer. "This is just an example. I'm making the number up. On the second try, you measure twenty thousand and five, and on the next, nineteen thousand nine hundred ninety-one. The differences are due to the random errors that each individual measurement contains, because—"

Stefan hesitated a second too long and Mariana jumped in: "Every step we made is slightly different from every other."

"Hey!" somebody yelled at them from the other side of the asphalt patch. One of the chess players. He ran toward them. "Stefan! You have a telegram!"

He waved a piece of paper in front of Stefan's face, then held it out of reach.

"Give it to me!"

"Calm down. Here it is. I didn't read it. However, the lady at the post office told me—"

Stefan grabbed the telegram. He opened and read it, and his face fell. "I've been conscripted. The draft notice arrived at my parents' home yesterday."

"Where are you ordered to report to?" Todor asked.

"Pleven, PSRO."

"Ah, the famous People's School for Reserve Officers. How many push-ups can you do?"

Stefan slumped onto the table, re-reading the telegram.

"When do you have to go?" Mariana asked. It was difficult to imagine someone who blushed so easily serving in the army, carrying a gun, and following orders.

He let his hands holding the telegram fall to his lap. "September twenty-ninth."

"So soon," Mariana murmured.

"My parents want me to go home right away." Stefan's voice was barely audible.

"I'm sure they want to spend some time with you," Todor guessed. "You'll go to university right after the discharge, and this might be their last chance to be with you in a while."

"There's almost a month and a half until then! They'll see me all right." Stefan tried to sound outraged, and Mariana suspected he wasn't as annoyed by the request to go home as he tried to show.

"Well, right. It will be over before you count to three. You know, the military service is long but tough," Todor tried to joke.

Only Mariana seemed to appreciate it.

"Now, let's forget about the army for a while and consider again the distance to Ardino. Suppose that you, Stefan, have to carry out the same measurement as her. What do you think the result will be?"

Mariana intentionally delayed her answer to give Stefan a chance to participate in the conversation.

But Stefan stared at the ground and didn't respond.

"He's taller than me," she finally said. "His legs are longer, so the number of steps will be smaller."

"Right. If we ask him to replace you on a few more occasions, he'll probably keep reporting lower numbers. Different every time, but always fewer steps. His results will be systematically lower because he uses . . . wrong measuring tools."

Everybody laughed, even the brave future defender of the Motherland.

"To be fair," Todor went on, "I shouldn't say wrong but different tools: his longer legs. For the sake of argument, let's assume Mariana's height and legs are the standard ones. Then his measurements will contain systematic errors."

"Are you implying we used a wrong reference star?" Mariana asked.

"Very good!" Todor clapped.

Was he attracted to her, despite the freckles and the hair? She blushed, just like Stefan had before.

"You're right." Todor smiled. "Observing another star instead of the reference, with a slightly different apparent magnitude, is one possibility. Another—but less likely—is that one or more of the references is a variable itself."

"Why is it unlikely?" Stefan finally looked up.

"All stars are variable at some level, even the Sun, but high-amplitude variables are rare. To see small changes requires very accurate electrophotometric observations."

He described how the photomultipliers worked. "The output comes through a printer on a long paper tape. I have one somewhere in my bag . . ." Todor fished it out. It was much like those on the cashier machines in grocery stores, bundled in a roll, held tight with a rubber band cut from the inner tube of an old bicycle tire. "We turn them around, to use both sides." He showed her a column of printed numbers on the back.

Mariana reached for the tape, and her fingers met with Todor's hand. She tried to convince herself it was accidental.

Todor pulled his hand away and stared at Mariana as if he'd never seen her before.

"While it comes out of the printer . . ." Todor's voice faltered. He made a visible effort to concentrate, to keep his finger pointing at the pencil marks next to the numbers.

Mariana couldn't tear her eyes from him.

Todor looked around. Petya Stoyanova, another astrocamp instructor and a university professor in her fifties, sat at the next table talking to a group of very young pupils.

"Comrade Stoyanova, can you please take over for a moment? These guys here." He pointed at Stefan and Mariana. "They need some help with their data."

"We have to finish something ourselves," she said.

He went over and whispered a few words into her ear.

"Sure, no problem," the woman agreed. "Kids, you'll have to continue on your own for a while." She moved to Mariana's table.

Without saying good-bye, Todor left them. He took his bag but forgot the tape.

"Where were you?" Stoyanova asked.

"He was explaining these handwritten numbers," Stefan answered, studying the printout. Mariana realized he hadn't noticed Todor's strange behavior.

"Oh, these. They are the start and the end times of each electrophotometric series, the object's name, and some notes about the weather."

Why had Todor run away? Was it because of her?

"There're ten or fifteen numbers in each group." Professor Stoyanova's voice brought Mariana back to the real world. "The first is the flux measurement of the variable, then—of the references. We average over all references for each epoch to build up statistics."

Well, then. There was no point hoping for Todor's attention. She composed herself and turned her attention to the conversation. She even managed to describe the problem with the additional scatter of her observations, above the expected from the observing errors. "Can I recover my data?" she asked at last.

"Maybe. Re-process them skipping one reference star, then another, and so on, until you have tried excluding them all," the professor advised. "Hopefully, when you reduce the data without the faulty reference, the light curve will tighten up."

Stoyanova returned to her pupils and left Mariana with the observation log. And with Stefan, who was still uncharacteristically quiet.

"Worried about the army?"

"No . . . yes. A bit. I wanted to ask if you—"

Mariana tilted her head.

"If you—"

The school bell, which the instructors used to summon everybody for meals or lectures, rang. Time for breakfast-lunch. The others jumped to their feet and prepared to head for the canteen.

"Can I write to you, while I am in the Army?" Stefan blurted. "We could discuss observations."

"Sure." Mariana smiled at him as they rose from the table, not sure if she agreed out of charity, or out of spite for Todor, or because she liked this boy who blushed so easily.

4. Beep-beep-beep from a distant star

The following morning, Mariana went out early to work at the chess table before the others woke up. She intended to follow Professor Stoyanova's advice and check to see if removing any references would improve the light curve of Zeta Andromedae.

She opened her notebook, proudly labeled *Observation Log*, and stared at the first estimate. Reference A was the brightest. There weren't many stars of that magnitude in the sky. If she'd used a wrong star, it was more likely to be among the faintest, and omitting these first might save her some time.

Mariana considered how to do this better. And easier. There were eight references in total; in principle, she needed to produce a separate plot for each, skipping the measurements of one reference each time. However, this could be done the other way around: instead of copying the plot over and over, she could mark the points that used each reference with difference symbols or colors.

An hour into the exercise and midway through the trials, Mariana already knew the answer: some of the points in yellow, the color corresponding to reference star F, tended to veer away from the center of the cloud.

Some of the yellow points . . . Why only some, though?

There was no apparent reason. However, she knew how to investigate.

It was obvious. If she used the other reference stars to determine the apparent brightness of Zeta Andromedae and then turned the variable into a reference—but with slightly different magnitude at each epoch, interpolated from the light curve—she could use them to measure the brightness of reference F as if it was a variable.

The trouble was, she'd have to extrapolate, because the estimates that include F—Mariana searched her log for an example—like F-three-Var-one-H, would transform into Var-three-Zeta-one-H. She'd have to determine what fraction of a magnitude her steps were worth from the Zeta-one-H part and use the value to extrapolate for the brightness of the ex-reference.

Mariana checked her watch. Eleven thirty. It was half an hour before the others would wake up, a bit longer with some luck. She took out her calculator—a trusted Soviet *Electronika* that had helped her to process a lot of observation data—and began the re-reduction. Soon she had a plot of the light curve for reference F on another piece of graph paper.

"There is a problem here!" Mariana said aloud as the results emerged. It occurred to her she'd started to imitate Todor. She put the thought aside and went back to the data. At least nobody heard her; the surrounding chess tables were still empty. Besides, Mariana didn't want anyone to see the strange result she'd obtained.

It was not a typical stellar light curve. Those changed gradually, except for the eruptive stars that went "kaboom"—and even they varied smoothly, compared with star F. Generally, the stars behaved in a continuous way. Professor Stoyanova had said so, the other day during her lecture on types of variables. Here, Mariana had a step function, right out of a textbook about electronics, diodes, and transistors. The jumps were point three mags, significantly larger than her measurement errors.

She reckoned this could be some sort of an eclipsing binary—a system with two stars that now and then passed in front of each other, hiding part of its companion's surface, reducing the amount of light that would reach the observers. A lot of her peers monitored those. These properties accounted for light curves with large amplitudes, up to two magnitudes—easy to measure, nothing like her excruciating effort to observe a variable that changed ten times less than a typical eclipsing system.

Her target Zeta Andromedae was a different kind of double star. It belonged to a class of variables called RS Canis Venaticorum with cool and large components, on distant enough orbits that they didn't eclipse each other. Instead, the binarity modulated the chromospheric activity that all cool stars showed anyway. It was a minuscule effect, compared with the overall flux. Mariana had looked up a few research papers on this particular object—as much as her beginners' English allowed her. Indeed, the star had weird emission lines in their spectra, confirming the theoretical model.

The light curve of reference star F was completely different. No variable she knew about stayed quiescent for God knows how long before turning itself on for a day—as her estimate from June 21 showed—and then went back to the off state for three days, then stayed on again for five and off for seven. The sequence continued with eleven days in the high state and thirteen in the low one. Right now, the star was bright again.

One, three, five, seven, eleven, thirteen—they were all prime numbers. Strange. A sequence like that couldn't occur naturally. It couldn't.

She had seen the *Cosmos* series, had read Schklovsky's book and few others about the searches for extraterrestrial civilizations. This plot spoke of intelligence. Spoke loud and clear from the graph paper in front of her.

Mariana pulled out a small calendar and counted the days.

The next prime number was seventeen. If her theory was correct, she guessed, the star would revert to the lower apparent magnitude the night after tomorrow.

Mariana imagined showing it to Todor. He, ever the pessimist, would say there was a problem. Stefan would be more supportive, she suspected, but then he was probably in love with her, so his opinion couldn't be trusted. In his linear mind, Stefan would probably think if he criticized her, she'd never answer his letters.

Her result was strange, no two ways about that. The prime number sequence had started almost immediately after Zeta Andromedae emerged from behind the Sun and became visible from the Earth. The intelligence that modulated the brightness of that star—implying the enormity of the power at this command—must have known where Earth was.

She knew it was impossible to detect a planet around a faraway star, let alone to determine its orbit.

It was impossible with modern telescopes. Impossible—right now—for Earth scientists.

What about some advanced civilization, thousands, millions of years ahead of the humanity? Whoever had sent that signal even knew about the Earth diurnal rotation of twenty-four hours. They'd used that interval as a time-base for the modulation. Measuring the length of the day on a planet around another star would be a fantastic feat by itself.

Mariana considered all this once more.

If true, it would be a magnificent discovery.

If true.

She must have made a mistake. That was the only credible explanation.

She wiped the moisture from her cheeks and stared at the paper in her hand, jaw clenched.

"Hello!" Professor Stoyanova appeared out of nowhere.

Mariana straightened and found a handkerchief to clean her nose.

"Why are you so upset?" She took the chair next to Mariana and put a hand on her shoulder. "Is it because of him? It will go away, and you'll see later on how lucky you were not to fall in love with someone who would take advantage of you."

Mariana swallowed her tears. "No, it's not about Todor."

The professor tilted her head.

"It's something else, entirely. I made some stupid mistake. All my work from this summer is worthless."

"Surely not," the professor said. "May I have a look?"

Mariana placed a protective hand on the scatter of graphs on the table. What did it matter? She didn't have the energy to argue.

Professor Stoyanova carefully studied the light curve, turned it sideways, just like everybody before her. She frowned.

Mariana blew her nose. "I'm sorry. I didn't mean to bother you with this stupid—"

"Hush." The professor held up a finger. She checked the other graphs. "My girl . . ."

Mariana swallowed and watched the older woman. What was she seeing that Mariana hadn't?

"If this is true . . ." Stoyanova lifted her eyes from the papers and stared at her intently. "You have found somebody who can manipulate stars . . ."

What was she talking about?

The professor shook her head slowly, staring at her as if she saw, not a high school girl, but a tumbling cascade of ideas.

"What should I do?" Mariana ventured.

Stoyanova snapped the green notebook closed, put a hand on it, and pushed it toward Mariana. "You can't share this. Not yet. If you go out with your Argelander measurements, people will laugh at you."

Mariana understood this. Her efforts were useless, she knew.

"So, you can either forget about it forever, or you can devote the rest of your life to following this up."

Mariana frowned. "What do you mean?"

"Finding alien intelligence." The professor gripped her fingers. "It will be the greatest discovery in human history."

Epilogue

Mariana tapped her fingers, waiting for the data from Chile, and recalled the summer she'd first glimpsed the hint that other minds existed elsewhere in the universe. Years before this young student Iveta Nikolova was born, with her doubts about absent-minded middle-aged professors and the inclusion of faint unknown stars on a target list.

Ever the pragmatist, Mariana Kaloyanova had chosen to study computer science in Sofia. The changes in Eastern Europe broke out in 1989, when she was in her third year and the wide world opened for her. She applied to and was accepted by a prestigious university in the US Northeast. When she boarded her flight for New York, she carried a black-and-white photo of Stefan, from the day of his oath of enlistment, lost in his uniform, too big for him. He'd been killed when the tank he commanded slipped into a ravine and turned over—one of four casualties during a two-week military exercise that included twelve thousand men.

Now, the photo rested in a simple frame on her desk, between print-outs of research papers full of red scratches and yellow highlights, half-empty coffee mugs, notepads filled with obscure handwriting and hand-drawn diagrams. Mariana glanced at the photograph. Stefan would have been so excited to be here now, with her.

Todor had left Bulgaria even before Mariana, illegally crossing the southern border. He spent a few months in various detention centers, then delivered pizza in Germany for a year and eventually ended up at a great university where he got a PhD in astronomy, of course. He was well known for building space-based mid-infrared instruments.

He, at least, would get to share her joy, if her notion turned out to be right.

Mariana never stopped thinking about the sequence she'd obtained for that faint star next to Zeta Andromedae. The modulation spoke of intelligence in a convincing and alluring voice. In hindsight, Mariana was happy she didn't go into astronomical research right away, because the IT detour gave her the right skills and helped to place her exactly where she needed to be to *find out*.

Just like back then, the star had shown up from behind the Sun a few days ago.

Mariana already had a measurement, establishing the base level. If the beings were still there, if they still directed their call to Earth, tonight the star should switch to its high state.

It would be the greatest discovery in history, as Professor Stoyanova proclaimed so many years ago. It would turn the scientific community—the entire world—upside down. But that was not foremost in Mariana's mind. Everything else paled in light of knowing that humankind was not alone.

Beep. The data transfer was complete.

Mariana skimmed the folder and, satisfied, ran the analysis script, her heart beating ever faster.

Thud.

Thud.

Thud—

COOPERATION WITHOUT COMMUNICATION

Searching for our
Galactic Cousins

VALENTIN D. IVANOV

I s there life elsewhere in the universe? Many people believe that is the greatest scientific question. It is certainly not as pressing as the questions of how to fight a worldwide disease or how to save the environment, but it has guided the human endeavor to study and understand the universe and our place in it.

The obvious way to search for life is to look for biosignatures—traces of its natural products [1,2]. The presence of oxygen and ozone in the atmospheres of planets appears to be the most indicative biosignature, because they are easily destroyed in chemical reactions with other elements, and it testifies to a continuous supply mechanism (mind you, no biosignature is a certain proof of life on its own, so we have to look for their combinations and the right physical conditions). Water, although strictly not a biosignature, is an important solvent and it is considered critical for life as we know it. Carbon dioxide could be helpful for life by keeping the planet warm enough, like a greenhouse (it's called a greenhouse gas indeed). Together with methane it could be a potential indicator of life, although geological sources can produce them too. Many biosignatures have been proposed, some more reliable, others more speculative. Laboratory experiments, studies of our own solar system, and exoplanet observations with upcoming telescopes such as ARIEL [3] should all contribute to telling us how likely they are to mean "life."

However, there is another path to finding life. Once it is conscious and advanced enough to know about electromagnetism and quantum mechanics, it may leave a footprint in the universe in the form of artificial signals—in radio, as a result of radars and planet-wide radio/TV broadcasting [4,5], in thermal infrared from excessive computational power or a reprocessed ultraviolet and visual light from a Dyson sphere—a megastructure enveloping its entire star [6].

Detecting pollution of the planetary atmosphere with industrial gasses is also a possibility [7] and night city lights have been discussed too [8]. These types of life traces are commonly called technosignatures [9] and there is a common pattern among them: many if not most are byproducts and even waste products of regular technological activities (not all, though—attempts to send signals to the stars certainly are not, we hope). Rough estimates, based on many guesses, indicate that technosignatures are two orders of magnitude more challenging to explore than biosignatures, but nevertheless, efforts in that direction are important, because they trace a different type of life—*technological civilizations*.

Are we ever going to talk to one?

While estimating the feasibility of interstellar communication, Kardashev introduced his famous classification of extraterrestrial civilizations (ETCs) according to the energy at their command – whether they were able to use the energy of their planet, star system, or even galaxy [5]. This framework had a profound effect on the subsequent search for extraterrestrial intelligence (SETI) work. Among other things, it implicitly introduced the concept that "more is better"; not surprisingly, considering that usually the SETI programs were led by radio astronomers and high-energy physicists for whom larger antennae and bigger accelerators were the embodiment of progress.

Kardashev's classification is still useful for SETI because it helps to define benchmarks for energy capabilities of the ETCs, and thus sets up sensitivity requirements for the SETI equipment. However, is it realistic?

Some new considerations have arisen in recent years, like arguments for cost-optimized means of interstellar communication; strategies were proposed to that effect [10,11]. Kardashev had not taken costs into account. In fact, he made an unspoken assumption that an entire ETC resource reservoir can (or may) be available for interstellar communication purposes.

Our historic and modern experiences can hardly support this speculation. We re-examined the ETC classification as a guiding tool for SETI strategies [12]. We wanted to reach a new priority scale for the different search methods, so we expanded the classical Kardashev scale, adding a second dimension, describing how the available energy is being used. The new framework makes it obvious that there is room for advanced, but not energy hungry ETCs. For instance, progress in biological or computational research doesn't pose higher and higher energy demands, unlike most of the physics branches.

We can expect that an advanced civilization would learn how to minimize their energy waste, the same waste that most of the traditional SETI projects are hunting for. How can we improve SETI strategies to account for that, then?

There seem to be two promising options. First, if we look for nearby ETCs that might be on a similar level to us, the "cross-section" will be high, because, like us, they have not yet learned to manage their resources efficiently and the "leaks" will be significant in comparison with those of a more advanced ETC. Of course, the probability such a civilization would exist nearby is generally low.

Second, we may improve our chances of finding advanced techno-logical life if we look for signals from much more advanced ETCs than us, that still may be interested in contacting their "young cousins." Such ETCs will probably be much rarer than our peers, but they would be able to use means that will minimize the effects of the great distance that will likely separate us.

The secret history . . . describes a SETI detection case following the latter strategy. The success is based, albeit unwittingly, on the concept of cooperation without communication from game theory [13], where the players act upon expected behavior of other players, usually based on social norms or common knowledge, or traditions. An example in the context of interstellar communication is the search for signals at the famous 21.1 cm (1420 MHz) Hydrogen line, selected because it is a prominent stand-out feature [4] with a wavelength in the range where the Milky Way radio background (and the noise associated with it) are low [5]. Similar logic can be applied to the time of sending the signals, so they would arrive, for example, when the target planet is at the most convenient angle to the broadcasting star system. Such techniques are known under the name "coordinated SETI."

Apparently, in the story, an advanced alien civilization from a distant star system discovered life on Earth by the means of biosig-nature detection and even managed to determine that the diurnal rotation period of our planet is close to 24 hours, because they used it as unit of time for the signal they sent to us. Both these feats are achievable with spectroscopy and/or photometric monitoring and even today we have a clear understanding of how it can be done: molecular oxygen, a relatively secure biosignature produces strong absorption bands in Earth's atmosphere [14]. One of them at about 7700 Angstrom is conveniently located in the middle of the visual wavelength range [15]. And diurnal periods of exoplanets have already been measured by Earth astronomers [16,17].

Next, the aliens applied their advanced technology to modulate their own stellar variability. This is a highly speculative capability, and I have used an artistic license here, although some researchers did consider light curves generated by artificial objects as means for SETI [18]. Importantly, the beacon described in the story is detectable during regular astronomical observations—an approach appropriate for an ETC willing to advertise its existence [9]. Last but not least, comes an element of coordinated SETI—the aliens apparently measured the distance that separates our stellar systems accurately enough, so that the sequence they sent would arrive at the time when their beacon becomes visible from Earth.

The story invites comparison with the recent thriller novel *Stars and Waves*, by Roberto Maiolino, who has taken the other path, describing how humanity discovers a peer civilization located close to us in terms of both spatial location and technological level. One can say that this is a literary answer to Maiolino's book, because his scenario seems unlikely—the existence of a civilization able to pollute its environment nearby—by Galactic scale—implies such wasteful civilizations [12] would be common, but SETI efforts so far have failed to find them. There are further arguments that the combination of space telescopes— already a reality—and somewhat speculative interstellar spaceships implies that SETI centered on nearby stars will fail, because extraterrestrials would have visited us already [19].

Finally, "The Secret History . . ." draws from my personal experience attending astronomy summer camps in my native Bulgaria, first as a high school student, and later on, teaching at them as a lecturer [20]. More than forty years ago, while taking hour long exposures on photographic plates, I wondered if someone from the stars might be taking photographic plates of us. Next, I asked myself how we could communicate with those aliens. . . . Four decades later these problems look as intriguing as back then. These experiences have taught me that we have to take a broader approach to the search for life, and I tried to incorporate some of these ideas in the story.

REFERENCES

[1] Des Marais, D. J., Harwit, M. O. Jucks, K. W. et al. (2002). *Astrobiology*, 2, 153

[2] Segura, A., Kasting, J. F., Meadows, V. et al. (2005) *Astrobiology*, 5, 706

[3]   Tinetti, G., Drossart, P.., Eccleston, P. et al. (2016). In MacEwen H. A., Fazio G. G., Lystrup M., Batalha N.,Siegler N., Tong E. C., eds. SPIE Conf. Ser. Vol. 9904, *Space Telescopes and Instrumentation 2016: Optical, Infrared, and Millimeter Wave*. Bellingham: SPIE, p. 99041X

[4]   Cocconi, G. & Morrison, P. (1959). *Nature*, 184, 844

[5]   Kardashev, N. S. (1964). *Soviet Astronomy*, 8, 217

[6]   Dyson, F. J. (1960). *Science*, 131, 1667

[7]   Lin, H. W., Gonzalez A. G. & Loeb, A. (2014). *Astroph. J. Let.*, 792, 4

[8]   Schneider, J., Leger, A. & Fridlund, M., et al. (2010). *Astrobiology*, 10, 121

[9]   Tarter, J. (2001). *ARA&A*, 39, 511

[10] Benford, G., Benford, J., & Benford, D. (2010a). *Astrobiology*, 10, 491

[11] Benford, J., Benford, G., & Benford, D. (2010b). *Astrobiology*, 10, 475

[12] Ivanov, V. D., Beamín, J. C., Cáceres, C. & Minniti, D. (2020). *A&A*, 639, 94

[13] Schelling, T. C. (1960). *The Strategy of Conflict*. Cambridge, MA: Harvard Univ. Press.

[14] Sagan, C., Thompson, W. R., Carlson, R., Gurnett, D., Hord, C. (1993). *Nature*, 365, 15

[15] Kaltenegger, L., Traub, W. A. & Jucks, K. W. (2007). *Astron. J.*, 658, 598

[16] Snellen, I. A. G., Brandl, B. R., de Kok, R. J. et al. (2014). *Nature*, 509, 63

[17] Zhou, Y., Apai, D., Schneider, G. H. et al. (2016). *Aptroph. J.*, 818, 176

[18] Arnold, L. F. A. (2005). *Astroph. J.*, 627, 534

[19] Zuckerman, B. (2002). *Mercury*, 31, 14

[20] Ivanov, V. D. & Bohosian, A. (2018). "Engaging the public with astronomy and space science research," Special Session 8 at EWASS 2018, held on 3-6.04.2018 Liverpool.

HUMAN BEANS

EUGEN BACON

Wema feels like this. Her life is a gust of wind. She's felt like this a long time. Displaced. Inside a great gale that swirls with longing for a dimension of something perfect. Never straight lines or corners . . . angles or tips. Sometimes she imagines waters—not rivers or lakes. In her dreams she sees a place full of oceans where people float, where space and time don't matter.

It's not a gray place. It's a sun-yellow, neutron-star-white multiverse that hosts no mundane. No hearts of stone. No half-lives. No inert-lives. Never particles that don't fit or don't begin to matter. Nothing that shrinks to cancellation. It's a place Thanatos desires.

What she needs is a new existence, a world that's bell-shaped and full of spring. Bell-shaped because she's thinking of the sweet scent of lilies of the valley. What she wants is a realm that's the color of quetzal birds—iridescent green and red-bellied with a golden crest. Because right now her heart is a jungle full of fog. Blackbirds *squee* in rising shrills, then *conk-la-ree* in unmusical gurgles.

Her mind is an old library. It's pregnant with photographs, shadows, and floorboards of blackwood. She stoops to pick her soul, but it slips through her fingers and says: I'm here, I'm there. She closes her eyes and all she hears are strangers whistling her name. And when she answers, it's in a voice that's not hers. What comes from her throat is a leafy pond full of toads.

She tries again: My name is Wema!

A cosmos echoes her name in falling pebbles: *Wey. Wey. Ma. Ma.* Lights flicker across the edges of heaven that may be ash or the Milky Way. *Squee! Squee! Conk-la-ree.*

Wema is the kind of girl who's a natural magnet. Like she's anyone's "type." Easy going. To fight for. Modern. Antique. Gal next door. Exotic. A

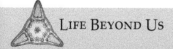

grandma-will-say-yes type of girl. Prepubescent kids in high school will high-five you for her. She's the perfect date. For Idris Elba, Kate Beckinsale, Phylicia Rashad, Angelina Jolie, Barack Obama—you get the gist. She's anyone's type. You look at her and see what you want. She sits next to a couple at a chocolate and wine masterclass, and they fight. It happens all the time. In restaurants, on trains, out jogging.

People's heads get messed up. For what? She's got strong legs, set shoulders, fine teeth, a good core. What's beauty? With her golden skin and supple tone, some might say she's athletic. Others cut it down to one word—you met it a paragraph up: exotic.

Most people just want to ruffle her hair, but the afro simply springs back— the curls so tight.

Wema felt a deep and terrible sadness. People didn't get her. Sure, they *wanted* her. Doesn't mean they *got* her. It sent her searching overseas, away from family, away from the village she once called home. A scholarship helped—wasn't hard to get. The priest looked at her like she was a seraph from heaven. She thought that she was safer with a partner. That maybe people wouldn't leer as much if she dangled off someone's arm.

Wrong.

Sally lasted a mere five weeks. She sapped Wema's life, so needy that babe. What Sally needed was ten shrinks, not an exclusive relationship.

Jools might have been the one. Because he was obsessed with himself. Jools was the Barbie-Ken type, in love with his dazzle: the dangle of his fringe, the slant of his smile. He hogged mirrors. He coveted himself in the bathroom, in the lift, on his phone screen . . . always adjusting himself for the world.

But he and Wema fought all the time, and it wasn't about beauty. They fought about everything stupid. Like the chocolate and wine masterclass.

"I really want to do it," said Wema. "Did you know chocolate goes well with red meat?"

"Only a fool would put chocolate with beef."

"Lamb. Try it with dark, dark chocolate."

"Lamb sucks."

Wema'd grown up with the texture of yams, mangoes, and coconuts on her tongue. The ripe smell of durian fruit growing wild in backyards.

Jools hated textures. Couldn't stand cucumbers or mushrooms. Purpled over the cream green of avocadoes. He refused to try anything different. Bit into the orange flesh of a pawpaw, spat it out.

"Smell food first," coaxed Wema. "The nose gets you right for your tongue. You know to anticipate a nibble."

"Baaaa!" bleated Jools—the spoiled child he was.

The snatchings started the same week Wema broke up with Jools.

The events brought back childhood stories of *Jengu*, the water spirit that vanished people. *Bichwa*, the three-headed ogre that pinched naughty children in their beds—sometimes it took them. Crocodile whisperers you knew to stay away from because, if you looked at them wrong, you might get swallowed by a croc next time you swam in the river. *Nightrunners*, who galloped naked around huts as the village slept—they summoned omens and babies cried, goats got sick, people died. Like Old Ma Fayola who keeled into a grave at a neighbor's funeral. They had to send for Ma Fayola's son in the city to inherit the cows. But what did a city man need cows for? He sold them for a pittance, didn't give a cent to his sisters back in the village. At least he left them the hut.

When Jools spoke his truth, how deep his pretty head had sunk into the dark web, it was their last evening together, dining out and fancy. Wema looked at him astonished.

"Seriously," she said. "You believe aliens from a galactic federation have visited Earth, and put our prime minister in charge?"

"Yeah. Prime Minister's the second coming. See how the virus doesn't affect him?"

"I'd question it. Are you planning to take the flu shot?"

"Microchips, dude. Why would I do that to myself?" He arranged his chin for a selfie.

Wema tried to remember, and couldn't, what it was she saw in him. He didn't like sex because it was "sticky." Being with him was worse than copulating with a mannequin that didn't want its wig ruined.

"You're an idiot, that's what," she said. "I'll be getting my booster shot."

"Everything's messed up. Cannibal pedophiles. Big Brother watching."

"You're a fockwit. There's so much going on in the world already—why do you want to screw it more?"

Flash, his camera—another selfie. He checked his teeth on the shiny screen. "The reckoning is coming. Be on the good side."

She slapped her napkin on the table, pushed back her chair. "I wouldn't have touched you with an oak if I'd known your head was full of oats."

"What are you doing?"

"Leaving you. We have zero in common."

"And you know this now?"

"Until you came out of the woodwork and burbled your outlandish theories, how was I to guess you're a whacko?"

She grabbed her clutch purse, paid the bill. The meal cost a few legs. This was a place you paid the price of limbs, and then some, because it promised to "serve African"—but mostly what you got was a half-baked measure of Ethiopian. Today—stewed goat, spicy lentils, eggplant, and dips—was the most African it got. Half her fortnightly wages had just gone down the gutter for a brain-dead pretty face who picked at lentils before asking for a bowl of thick-cut chips, no aioli.

She stamped out of the skyline restaurant, committed to being single for the rest of her life. She pressed for the lift, and the door opened. All the buttons were lit. It wasn't going anywhere. The darn thing was broken. She took the fire exit and ran down all those stairs.

But Jools had got into her head.

She did go to the chocolate and wine masterclass, only because she'd already paid for it. She smiled at the couple sitting at the front—a short-cropped brunette and a big guy with a checked shirt. Wasn't long before they quarreled.

The venue had dangler lights that looked like sun-filled balloons with silver ribbons, but the building was rather old, peeling paint on the walls. She nibbled at a platter of almonds, walnuts, strawberries, and grapes before the main event—the host, right in front, and his wife, who sat next to Wema.

"Cocoa is a very versatile product," the man said. "You get sugar from the fruit and dogs eat the husk. Guess why supermarket chocolate is black?" He looked around. "Because it's burnt cocoa beans. Cheap."

Wema studied the room and noticed the big guy with the checked shirt was gone.

"Chocolate is like tiramisu—when you make chocolate, it's better the next day. The sheen tells you of its quality."

The wife smiled at Wema, as if agreeing about quality, but her smile was more about the chocolate skin kind, and less about her husband's truffles.

"This one here is a grand cru. It has 75% dark chocolate and is full of cherry and red plum, a slight bitterness."

He looked at them.

"Shine means it's well-tempered. I want you to break the first piece in front of you now. A good snap tells you it's fine chocolate. Don't just chomp it, linger the piece on your tongue. Today's tasting is about contrast pairing. Our taste buds are all different."

Wema was glad Jools wasn't here.

Sun rays shone through the glass roof of the swimming pool that morning and danced jewels in the water, as Wema swam before work. The sky was teal, pillowed with soft clouds. There was an elderly person in the water, and Wema gave them a name: Basket. Because they survival swam in a back float, dead weight. It would have been okay if they'd kept to their lane, but they meandered. Their hands scooped, scooped, causing waves. It made Wema's laps difficult. Water ran up her nose as she freestyled in the next lane, causing her to splutter. When Wema did a tumble turn, Basket was gone.

She drove to the office at the fringe of the central business district. She parked and smiled at toddlers rushing and squealing into a nearby fountain's spray, as their parents watched. She swiped her secure card and was pleased to see Axe across the partition splitting their desks. She smiled at sie.

"How's it?" said Axe.

"Groan."

Wema tried talking to Axe about Jools and Basket. Axe was solid, reliable. Wema felt safe with sie. Normally sie listened, but today Axe was focused on Wema's bland outfit. Sie looked at the soft hues—the cream of Wema's blouse, the cyan of her skirt—and said in hir barrel voice, "This. Is. Sacrilege."

Sie pulled a drawer on hir desk and whipped out a candy scarf and came round the partition.

"No," said Wema.

"Yes. You're feeling flat because you need more rainbow." Sie arranged the hand-knitted scarf around Wema's shoulders. "Now you look dope."

If Axe were chocolate or wine, sie'd be the party flavour. What Wema most liked about Axe was sie didn't talk with an agenda. Sie didn't sexualize Wema like other people did. Sie talked to her, *her*. Not to her tits. Sie saw Wema, truly. But there was an air of sadness about Axe when sie didn't know Wema was watching. Now sie took Wema's hand. "Come with me. You need coffee. We've got ten minutes before the divisional meeting."

Outside the world looked normal. Folk walking dogs, kids in strollers, cabs picking up people. A parking inspector was writing up a car. Wema's own sedan was safe in an open car park on an "Early Bird" special. Up ahead, a P-Plater was reverse-parking badly into a single car spot. They entered Axe's favorite joint: a specialty coffee, bar, and bottle shop—no smoking. It was a café with a coffee brand named Ex-Wife.

Axe was saying, "Do you know how many Earth-like planets are in the galaxy?"

"How many?" Wema asked.

"Six."

"That right?"

"As in *six billion* Earth-sized planets orbiting Sun-like stars."

"*What?*"

"And twenty-four superhabitable worlds, yeah, some warmer, wetter, better conditioned than Earth, they say. Oh, and the Drake equation's super dope. Tells you ace info about active civilizations in the Milky Way."

"I can't even—"

"Titan's the most habitable extraterrestrial world within our solar system. It has nitrogen and methane. It's forty percent the size of Earth."

The barista was flustered about Wema and was apologizing for spilt coffee. A dog-haired teen with hungry eyes studied a platter of salmon cheese cream sandwiches behind the glass-topped counter.

"The haloumi avocado looks wicked," said Axe, moments before the teenager disappeared. Nobody seemed to notice.

Wema looked at Axe. "Did you see that?"

Sie blinked. "See what?"

Wema didn't know what to say.

Coffee on hand on the way back, they passed a jaywalker talking into a smart phone. An emergency vehicle striped yellow, red, and blue raced past, full throttle. Still troubled, Wema noticed an unmarked cop car on patrol, all black. Funny—well, not funny, just a statement—cops never stopped looking like cops, even on decoy. Clipped hair, razored jaw, falcon eyes.

Back at the office, there was only a handful of staff—most people were working from home. The divisional meeting was a conference call. Simon's video was off—he was a solicitor at the firm. Pearl—a barrister and solicitor—had a fluffy rabbit icon on her profile. Only the boss, Punt—the director—zoomed up close on screen, thick brows, a chin mole, and dollar-sign eyes. It was a running joke in the team that Punt could sniff a dollar up a whippet's butt, and retrieve it himself with an enema, no gloves, if a laxative didn't work. That's how much he loved money.

"Hey kid," the boss said to Wema. He nodded at Axe: "Axel." He waited a few minutes, then: "Good. Let's show and tell." Although the law firm ripped clients by thousands, it was one of those feel-good, well-being workplaces that asked you to share something fun at a team meeting.

"I did this chocolate and wine masterclass," said Wema. "The building was so old, I imagined flakes of it raining on my head." The team laughed.

"People leave you alone?" piped Simon.

"It was a husband-and-wife duo. He's a former marine biologist. A pasty little fellow, a bit shy until you got some wine into him." More laughter. "His wife had smoky gray eyes and spoke like she knew you." She grew silent, suddenly remembering the guy with the checked shirt. How he was there, then he wasn't.

"I like Peruvian beans. African cocoa too," said Pearl.

Something about the way she said it made Wema uncomfortable.

"Wema broke up with her boyfriend," said Axe, trying to help.

There was an awkward pause, then Simon whooped. Pearl said, "Yes!"

"Good on ya! To move on—" said Punt quickly, as he'd already had enough trouble with his husband over Wema.

Simon shared he'd bought new noise-canceling headsets. "Guess I look sexy, huh?"

"Your video's not even on," said Pearl. "I've got this indoor smart garden—maybe Wema you'd like to check it out? With me, solo."

Axe and hir trivia steered the show-and-tell to a meaningful conversation about taking climate change seriously. "Temperature extremes—who wants more bushfires, another Black Saturday?" Sie reminded the team about shrinking glaciers in Europe and Canada, warming seas that harmed natural ecosystems and marine species. "Coral reefs are dying. And all that flooding, yeah, Typhoon Nina, Hurricane Katrina . . ."

Nothing about work, really, family law and the like. The divisional meetings seemed to be mostly a general check-in.

"You guys notice anything—different?" Wema changed the subject to what was top of mind.

"Done somethin' to your hair?" quipped Simon. "Oh, your scarf, isn't it neat."

"It's dope," said Axe.

"I meant have you noticed anything *strange* happening?"

Nope. Nope. Nope. They all said. Axe looked at her with eyes that said leave it alone. Sie knew Wema was thinking about Jools and Basket.

Punt logged off as usual with a cheerie, "Pull your weight, peeps. No bludgers."

Wema felt displaced again. Melancholy. Wretched. People didn't take her seriously. But she wasn't exactly sure what she'd expected from her team. That people would start talking about vanishings?

Her smart phone pinged. It was Jools. "You got my spare keys, babe."

You're at the Post Office, reading a sign about zero tolerance on abusive behavior. You move with the line, behind a woman in blue jeans, daggy shoes, and a cloth purse. There's a notice about price changes. You look from a distance at the price tags on disposable face masks, satchel liners, digital air fryers, HD LED smart TVs. There's Daniel, the all-smiley one at the counter. You know he's Daniel because his badge says so. He's chatting, chatting to every customer. He's to blame for lag service. You look up. The woman in blue is gone.

You're at the supermarket. One minute the girl at the checkout is beeping a liter of milk, a slab of cheese, bread rolls on special, kitchen towels. Next minute she's gone. You have to throw a hundred dollars' worth of shopping back into the trolley and join a new queue where you're fifth behind trolley-loads. Nobody notices.

Wema listened as Axe tittered the day away with hir trivia. "A multi-verse is an impossible world. It can never exist as an *everything* existence. Think! If a multiverse were real, this here, Earth, this now, would be a fraction of infinity."

Wema frowned at the white noise—Axe like this was unstoppable. Didn't take sie long to go on a new tangent: "Tuna is overfished along the coasts of East Africa. It affects the world. Europe, Asia, and the Americas have to make informed sourcing decisions. The world needs the right research and data that informs us about how to treat human capital as an existential threat. Thousands of jobs on the line—where's sustainability now?"

Wema looked at the time. Finally!

Richmond's streets bustled with traffic at rush hour just before Wema got onto the state route. At the lights before the petrol station, a whole car vanished. It was a silver 4WD spilling with two kids and a toffee-colored Labrador Retriever—tongue out and panting at the window. The silver car was blinking to turn right, there in front of her, when suddenly Wema's sedan was ahead in the queue. She could have sworn she imagined it, but the incident was real. The 4WD was an XC60—back windshield wipers with an antenna. Number plate starting with IJW. It had a sticker that said: *Five Mart.*

Now she wasn't sure anymore. Further out she gave way to a white van at the roundabout, and it evaporated before it went past her. She watched in misery and trepidation at the next set of lights, at a jogger in a black t-shirt and shorts. She waited for him to be snatched before he reached the other side of the road. He wasn't. Nor was the Deliveroo boy on a yellow scooter and matching helmet with a kitty face.

Her head hurt. The office, despite Axe, wasn't easy that week.

"What makes rye bread dark?"

"I don't know, Axe."

"Cocoa."

She deleted Jools's texts without reading them. She stood and spoke to Axe across the partition. "Are we alone?"

"Everyone's WFH—"

"No. Really. *Are we alone?* In the universe?"

"NASA's taking big looks at life beyond Earth, given that other planets orbit stars. It would be selfish, even reckless, to think our solar system is the only one capable of hosting life."

You're at the bank. The woman in front of you is the kind you notice. Not in a sexy way. It's the beauty of her hair. Ginger, all fuzz, curls to her waist. You blink, and you're number one in the queue.

At the Botanical Gardens across the woody bridge and its sign that says, "Slippery When Wet," you notice the tourists. You know them from their hats, maps, cameras. Behind them is a toddler riding a tricycle. His parents— wearing the absentmindedness of young parenthood—are yapping at each other. The tot is a big-eyed one with soft wavy hair. Fat legs pump tiny pedals toward a curvy nature trail. He never comes out. The parents keep walking, talking to each other as though they were always alone. You sprint after them, pull the woman. But, but . . . your son! She shrugs off your clutch. The hell? A burly security guard pats your shoulder. Don't disturb the peace. Please go away. Now. He says it like he means it.

You're watching footy on TV, cross-legged on your sofa. There's Big Charlie, No. 49. He's a forward, best there is. Dances around the other team, open bounce, uses his body well. He lunges at the ball, knocks off the opposition. He works the space well, three quick goals, one of them a bender from an impossible angle. The third is a bizarre heel goal, so good. The other player tackles him to the ground, then stands alone. Big Charlie is gone. It's as if the ground's eaten him. The other player blinks, plays on. A sub runs in from the bench as if it's a natural occurrence to replace gobbled people. You look online at the player-team chart and Big Charlie's gone. Wiped from history. You can't believe the audacity, how brazen.

Wema started counting people, as if they were beans. She'd enter a café, a bank, a pharmacy . . . look around to see how many were there and wonder how many would be taken by the time she left.

Each time, she was startled by the count.

One day she came into the office, and Axe wasn't there. Axe was always in early. Wema ran to hir favorite joint, the "no smoking" café with its coffee brand named Ex-Wife. The flustered barista shook his head. Hadn't seen Axe.

Wema dialed Punt. His face zoomed large on the screen. "Hey kid. What's going on?"

"Is Axe on leave?"

"Axe. Is that even a name?"

"Axel!"

"Sounds like you got yourself a new bloke. You move quick, kiddo."

"Punt! Please stop this. It's not remotely funny!"

"'Whatever it is, it's no biggie—this Axel of yours. Shoved off to cool steam. Crook maybe. Pissed after a night with the lads. Don't stress."

"I'm not stressing!"

"Good on ya. Pull your weight, kid, no bludging." He hung up.

She pulled a sticky note, wrote "Axe" on it, and put it on her screen. She typed hir name on her phone, emailed it to herself, suddenly afraid she'd forget sie.

She kept looking at the door, expecting sie to appear any moment. Suddenly she longed for a venison backstroke with a dark chocolate sauce. That's when she noticed the lights flicker, the room's new glow. And the man with the luminescence of a Greek god across the partition, seated at Axe's desk.

She didn't think he was *Bichwa*, *Jengu*, or a *Nightrunner*. Not with that luster, no.

"Wey. Wey. Ma. Ma." He said her name and its honey rolled in her ears. The sound was clean and clear, gentle and loud. It reminded her of her mother's milk, of freshly brewed coffee, of newly baked bread. "Wema."

His eyes . . .

The glow of a dog star. The star of Sirius.

She looked at him, startled, for he hadn't spoken, yet she heard his words. "Our mind is one," he answered her question. "She's bright," he said. She felt his touch on her mind. "Yes. She's bright." Again, he answered her question. "Not the room. Her intelligence."

He was not Thanatos.

"Who are you?" She found her voice. "Where the fock is Axe, and why are you referring to me in the third person?"

"Our name is Mwalimu." His voice was a harmonica. His words swelled like a waterfall, wind blowing through trees, tide washing on a sandy beach. His aura filled her with goodness. The coo of a toddler, the purr of a kitten. "Axe has found hir home." He stood. "As will she."

He whipped his cloak, and suddenly she was swirling, feet off the ground, in furious rain. A roar nearly took her ears, and she lost her shoes. She closed her eyes to a splash, or immersion, opened them to emerald waters and millions of bubbles racing toward her. She was in the middle of a sea. Bright green waters. Celestial lights shimmered nearer—she realized they were creatures. One, a dolphin, leapt in a spray. She was surrounded by ripples and a glow of sea horses, turtles, pupfish, angel fish, mantis shrimp. Yellow, orange, and pink tentacles of a flower blob bumped against her arm. She held her breath as if in a dive, and it was agony. She wondered if this was how drowning felt—torrents ballooning her lungs before she exploded. She opened her mouth to cry out, and nothing happened. No water rushed down her throat. She streamlined, pitched her hands, and lunged upwards with a push of her legs. There was surface.

"Find her weight." Gentle falling pebbles in Mwalimu's voice. "Breathe easy."

She remembered Basket's survival swim. Dead weight on her back. She allowed herself to float, buoyant inside the water.

Follow . . . Follow . . . He spoke to her mind in a sweetness of immortal carols. She couldn't help but follow him, nimble as a fish, wave-like, side to side. She was a tourist in the ocean, no maps. She waved in and out of what looked like an ancient city, yet it was new. She swam over and below temples chiming with hanging stairways that led to gardens whose flamboyant reflections shimmered in the waters. Was that a sunset moth? She blinked as twinkling wings scattered mottled light her way.

She sidled alongside Mwalimu and his skin suit, into a golden beach speckled with lilies of the valley. A quetzal bird of bright blue colors and a splash of white perched on her shin.

"Welcome to Super Earth," said Mwalimu.

"You nearly drowned me," she said happily, unsure why she felt so gleeful and in harmony with herself, and with the world.

"Water is a conductor, the perfect portal for interdimensional travel."

She looked around and cheerfully hoped Jools wasn't here. The new world reminded her of images she'd seen of a constellation of galaxies. It was a rainbow of colors resplendent in spiral symmetry.

"Is this a parallel universe?"

"It can't be parallel if she's a singularity."

Wema wondered if Mwalimu meant she, the person, or was it the universe, as in personification?

"Unless she's a gravitational singularity, an infinite distortion of space and time, in which she's here and there and everywhere," said Mwalimu, addressing her in third person still.

"I am a singularity," said Wema in astonishment, as if understanding it yet questioning it.

"Would she know if she weren't? Come. We'll show her the new Earth. It orbits a neutron star hundreds of light years from the old Earth."

"Why me? Why do you choose to show me?"

"We understand her mind, her curiosity. Her displacement for perfection. We wanted to see how she might react if, unlike the rest, cataclysmic change was visible."

"I'm an experiment?"

"We're sorry for the discomfort. Human migration to Super Earth began at a pace we thought might work for the human mind. But—she will understand—one person at a time is laborious. We sped the process and are now trialing to go large scale."

He signaled toward a vast building nestled in a cliff that shifted colors when she gazed at it from different angles. "Exos, a royal retreat. Our priests study the evolution of human macromolecules, early life and development, to create optimal conditions for humankind to thrive. All subjects are willing participants, mostly those already with an . . . inconvenience."

Nah, Jools was most definitely not here. He'd never be a "willing participant"—always difficult, unless it involved grooming.

She pointed. "I know that woman in jeans—she was at the post office."

"Millie has advanced heart disease. Our studies will make her new as a fresh born. Look." He showed her a city of ruins in a valley full of lilies. "This is the Lederberg. Here, our priests investigate the conditions that ruined Earth, and we counteract them. Super Earth will never suffer from atmosphere overloading, overpopulation, degraded soil, crop failures, famine and pandemics—all things that plague humankind."

They walked through a maze of gardens scattered with cherry blossoms, bleeding hearts, gazania, and dahlia. Ancient wisteria, beeches draped with hanging moss, maple and giant oaks lined its elbows. "Is that—" She pointed.

"Yes, a thylacine and her cub. And that's a flying fox. If she looks closely, she might even see a Tasmanian wolf. Welcome to Extant—here, no species is superior in its demands on the other, so as to make it extinct."

"Heavens. That's the toddler in the tricycle—" He sat playing at the foot of an angel oak.

"The mother's fiancé was a serial killer. She agreed to come here too."

The child stroked the long neck of an island tortoise. Amber phantom butterflies perched on his soft wavy hair, so it looked like a reddish-flushed transparent hat.

"There." Mwalimu pointed at the brow of a hill, his words a heart's whisper, the song of a woodchipper. "That is the Self-actualization Centre."

Wema caught a scent of chocolate cosmos blended with sweet alyssum. Everything smelled delicious just looking at it. She saw silhouettes of people in the distance doing headstands and yoga poses, then hugging each other in the lush green hillside. "We inspire people to expand their potential."

Suddenly there was a whoop and a squeal. "Wema!" Then someone tackled her to the ground. "Here is a better world," gasped Axe in her ear. "It's giant and stable. Nothing is wasted, everything's recycled."

"Oh, Axe. If . . . you just let me breathe—"

Sie eased hir hold. "There's no poverty. See that wish booth? You can't wish for harmful gain against others."

"But Axe—" Wema looked at sie. "I thought, the test subjects. At first . . . that only people with—"

"An inconvenience found themselves here?"

"Yes . . . human beans that could be displaced, ones who nobody noticed. What are you doing here! Are you dying of leukemia? I don't think it's dementia. Not with that super processor in your noggin. Oh, dear, Axe. Do you have AIDS? I thought we were friends, that you'd tell—"

Axe took a breath. "My family disowned me when I came out."

Wema remembered the gravestones and abyss, the deep bleakness in Axe when sie didn't know Wema was watching.

"And you?" sie asked.

Wema recalled her fog. The blackbirds in jarring gurgles. "I guess I never belonged." She hugged Axe. "Well now. *We are* family, and I'm glad you're here where people like Mwalimu speak in ballads, heart flutters and bead shakes. The notes of a flute."

"You smell like vanilla and sandalwood."

"And you like rosemary—why aren't I famished? This place is surreal. Well, Trivia Machine, I thought neutron stars were white."

"To the naked eye. Something happened to our bodies when we entered the portal. The unlaws of physics. I've never felt ace like this."

"Me too. And I like that Super Earth has all my colors."

"Mine too."

She looked at hir garish red trousers and matching shoes.

Sie looked at her bare feet and the soft hues of her flowing gown.

They burst out laughing.

Axe spoke first. "This place is dope."

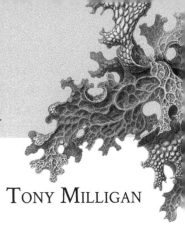

MICROBIAL LIFE AND BELONGING

TONY MILLIGAN

I deas about belonging are complex. A human might have a causal history linking them to a particular time and place such as a home or even a planet, and still feel that they do not truly belong there. They may feel that they could fit in better somewhere else and that they are, in Eugen Bacon's words, "human beans that could be displaced, ones who nobody noticed." There are beans that get a lot of attention, like Peruvian cocoa beans, and beans whose disappearance would go unacknowledged, or without comment.

These ideas about belonging cross worlds, in the sense of *moving between* human and non-human forms of life. We may think of ourselves as having roots or lacking them. We may think of ourselves as flourishing in one place but not in another. In Bacon's text, we might think of ourselves as so many beans to be counted, or admired, or lost. Our understanding of ourselves continually, and often in unnoticed ways, draws upon a series of analogies with other forms of life. These analogies then feed back into our thinking about those other forms of life, from animals to trees, from plants to microbes.

Discussions about species preservation are also discussions about a place and time where species belong—for instance, would you support "de-extinction" of the dodo? The woolly mammoth? Or, far more speculatively, dinosaurs that roamed the Earth tens of millions of years ago? Where do we draw the line? Also, discussions about reforestation to combat climate change are discussions about which plants and trees are native, and native relative to a time span and to the underlying geology of place. Belonging does not stop with us.

If this was not the case, then it would be difficult to make sense of why the discovery of microbial life, or historic evidence for such life, on another world would matter to us in the way that it does. The discovery of life that *belonged* to another place would matter to us irrespective of its biochemical structure and rudimentary nature. Of course, we might prefer it to be exotic, or at least a little different from us and to shed light upon the difference between life and non-life, but we would still consider it worthwhile and important to discover life that belongs elsewhere. If it happened to be biochemically indistinguishable from some microbial life form that we kill inadvertently and without malice on Earth, as we go about our daily business, this would not justify us in treating such alien life elsewhere in exactly the same way.

Another way of putting the point would be to say that, from an ethical point of view, all microbes are not equal. We have reasons to protect some, that we do not have to protect others. The fact that *life is from elsewhere*, or that we have encountered *life that belongs to some other planet*, would make a difference. Perhaps not to all of us, but to many and probably most of us. And there is a case for saying that we would have a reason to protect such life *for its own sake*, and not just for the sake of science. It might be confusing to say that such life has *rights*, because the concept of rights does a different kind of work. But nonetheless, I might put a picture of a rudimentary alien life form on my office wall, yet I would probably not put a picture of its terrestrial counterpart on the wall.

Wema, in Eugen Bacon's story, is concerned about belonging. Not directly in the way that astrobiologists are typically concerned, but in a way that is part of the continual *movement between* described above. Movement between places, movement between kinds of beings. There is also a continual interplay in the story between the biological and the social, which is reflected in the variety of pronouns in use. "Sie" as well as "she," "hir" as well as "her." Wema and many others who are unhappy and wounded being on this Earth are transported to a different and much better place, to Super Earth [1*]. A better world, realizing a different set of possibilities for life, "a rainbow of colors resplendent in spiral symmetry," hundreds of light years from old Earth. A reminder that life could have taken a different path, that some of the processes which have led to our way of living are a matter of what Jacques Monod [2] called *chance* rather than *necessity*.

This Super Earth is a place where thylacines (dog-like marsupials with tiger-like stripes) are not extinct, where gender prejudice and

---

1[*] Which actually might be a super-Earth in the astronomical sense (put simply, a rocky planet with a mass greater than Earth, but not enough to become a largely gaseous planet such as the ice giants Uranus and Neptune); this seems to be a very common class of exoplanets. Some have also been found around pulsars, a type of neutron star (e.g. PSR B1257+12) such as in the story, although their habitability is a far more speculative topic [1].

domestic violence are left behind, and where "no species is superior in its demands on the other as to make it extinct." Science fiction stories often describe worlds we might like to visit, but on which we would not necessarily want to live. Super Earth sounds instead like a good place to live. Humans there are good to one another, and their acting in such ways is connected to better ways of living with non-human creatures and as part of the Super Earth ecosystem. Super Earth is not "blood red in tooth and claw." We may wonder whether life can really be like this, altruistically symbiotic and never caught up in biological trade-offs and harms. But it is not a stretch of the imagination to think that the relation between human life and non-human life might be *more like this*, and that it would generally be good if Earth was more like Super Earth. It sounds like a more sustainable place.

It is certainly a more integrated place, with something akin to what E. O. Wilson [3] called "sociobiology" practiced by priests who "study the evolution of human macromolecules, early life and development, to create optimal conditions for humankind to thrive." I mention Wilson here not only because of the integration of the biological and the social on Super Earth, but because he believed in a kind of love of life, a *biophilia*, that also seems to be in place there. It is not driven by Thanatos, by longings for death, but by a shared belonging and symbiosis. Yet, even if done for good motives, we might worry about the outcome. Tigers may live in zoos or in wildlife parks, but they do not belong there. A creature may be kept alive in a place, a species may even be preserved there and nowhere else, without our imagining that this is ethically equivalent to ensuring survival in its natural habitat. At a certain point, we sometimes have to let go. Even of the things that we love. And even if it is an admission of failure.

Wema and the other human beans transported to Super Earth are not like tigers in a zoo. They can truly belong there, even though they come from another place. This is an idea that works well in the case of the humans, who can reflect upon the process of transportation, upon gravitational singularities and upon an infinite distortion of space and time. One of the interesting things is that this idea of belonging also works well with the extinct species. Members of these species can live and love and flourish on Super Earth. They can belong, even if they cannot speculate about the nature of belonging. The thylacines might easily be a better fit for Super Earth than for actual Earth. It might be a more reliable home for them, given our threatening and overwhelming human presence here. In a little time, they might truly *belong* there, in spite of their Earthly origins.

How far does this thought go? Does Wema's idea of belonging, with some suitable modification, reach from human beans all the way down to the most rudimentary forms of life? Could even microbial life transported from Earth *belong* on Super Earth, in the same way that microbes discovered beneath the Martian regolith or in the waters of Enceladus, would belong to these places and excite our attention if discovered?

There may be a way to answer this question, but it involves subversion of Bacon's pleasing rainbow scenario. Human action on Super Earth is clearly more sustainable than it is on Earth. It is a better place to be. But still, the universe does not come with any guarantee against harms. When Wema is reassured that "Super Earth will never suffer from atmosphere overloading, overpopulation, degraded soil, crop failures, famine, and pandemics—all things that plague humankind," she is given a promise that cannot automatically be kept. The emergence and history of life may not be quite so accidental and dependent upon chance as Monod once thought, but vulnerability is a feature of life. And when we care for one another, or for any living beings, recognition and acceptance of vulnerability are built in.

Let us briefly subvert the tale and imagine that the Super Earth experiment fails badly, wiping out Wema, her friends, and the thylacines, leaving only rudimentary life alive. In a scenario in which everything goes horribly wrong, and the things that plague humankind take their toll, Super Earth would become an analog of failed reforestation, or failed cultivation on difficult terrain, with almost everything washed away. This would be hugely disappointing. Yet superficially, it would make Super Earth look like the kind of place that astrobiologists are currently seeking, i.e., a place with *only* microbial life, or evidence that it once existed. Should we find somewhere like that, we would be anything but disappointed. Disappointment is relative to hopes and expectations and, from an astrobiological point of view, the discovery of such a place would be momentous rather than disappointing.

The unhappy scenario in which Super Earth fails, leaving only microbial life, is not of course a claim that any good place must eventually collapse, and that it must do so because of the dynamics of life, or because of our human flaws. There is no obvious necessity of that socially-driven sort, even if there are natural processes that do tend toward periodic mass extinctions. Generalizing upon the basis of a single example of life here on Earth, with our multiple social problems, is not always a safe thing to do. Other pathways may be possible, and even likely. An appeal to the more unhappy scenario of Super Earth failure is just one more way of reflecting upon *belonging* in the light of loss. And a way of reflecting upon the goals of astrobiologists when we consider the origins, extent, and future of life. If we were able to study the failed Super Earth in some direct way, traveling there by the water portals of Bacon's story, examining its microbial life would be interesting, different from the kind of "discovery" of life that so many astrobiologists and other humans hope for. In the usually imagined discovery scenarios of astrobiology, the microbial life that is sought has not recently come from Earth, but *belongs* to another place, and has done so for a far longer time than the Super Earth experiment.

This need not mean that the life sought by astrobiologists must have a different ultimate *origin*. It need not trace back to a second figurative genesis of biology out of abiotic materials. Life could, after all, have originated only once and then shifted around through chance, and long before intelligent beings started to look for it. After all, it's a plausible speculation that all life as we know it originated on Mars and was transported to Earth by lithopanspermia—within rocks thrown into space by violent impacts so common in the early solar system. Such a scenario may not provide the simplest explanation, but it is not fanciful. It seems entirely possible in light of current scientific knowledge and, if we ever discover signs of life on Mars, we might get around to testing this possibility [4,5]. In some ways, biochemical similarities that point toward a shared ultimate origin might open up exciting possibilities and help us to pose questions about where we belong: to a single planet, or to some larger region of space.

We are not looking for life that must have a different ultimate origin. We are looking for *life with a history that is significantly different from the history of all terrestrial life*, and different for a period of time that is vastly greater than our own human history. We are, in some sense, looking for life that is *indigenous* to some other planet, even if it turns out to be biochemically indistinguishable from life that we have already encountered. Carl Sagan once remarked that Mars would belong to the Martians if there were any, even if they were microbial [6]. He was not speaking about microbes taken to the planet by a previous space mission. He was speaking about life that *belonged* on Mars in some longer-term sense, even if it shared a singular origin with Earth life.

When we consider matters in these terms, the ways in which human beans such as ourselves think about our belonging, and the ways in which we think about the belonging of other forms of life, do seem to interconnect. They share a world, live together, and influence one another.

Acknowledgements: Thanks to Eugen Bacon, author of "Human Beans," for the improving comments.

REFERENCES

[1]   Patruno, A., & Kama, M. (2017). "Neutron star planets: Atmospheric processes and irradiation." *Astronomy & Astrophysics*, 608, A147.

[2]   Monod, Jacques. (1971). *Chance and Necessity: An Essay on the Natural Philosophy of Modern Biology.* New York: Alfred A. Knopf.

[3]   Wilson, Edward O. (1984). *Biophilia.* Cambridge MA: Harvard University Press.

[4]   Meyer, C., Fritz, J., Misgaiski, M., Stöffler, D., Artemieva, N. A., Hornemann, U., Moeller, R., de Vera, J-P., Cockell, C., Horneck, G., Ott, S., and E. Rabbow. (2011). "Shock experiments in support of the Lithopanspermia theory: The influence of host rock composition, temperature, and shock pressure on the survival rate of endolithic and epilithic microorganisms." *Meteoritics & Planetary Science* 46(5), 701-718.

[5]   Stöffler, D., Horneck, G., Ott, S., Hornemann, U., Cockell, C., Moeller, R., Meyer, C., de Vera, J-P., Fritz, J., Artemieva, N. A. (2008). "Bacterial spores survive simulated meteorite impact." *Icarus* 149(2001), 285-290.

[6]   Sagan, Carl. (1980). *Cosmos.* New York: Random House.

THE MIRRORED SYMPHONY

D.A. Xiaolin Spires

"The axis of evil," Adaeze had whispered to me over the phone. I had just taken off my driving gloves, blown on my fingers to revive them from the northeastern cold and was making music, humming and playing—and the news had left me mum for a bit, while my head kept composing.

The axis of evil is a swath of the Cosmic Microwave Background much too hot, defying predictions made by the Big Bang.

"And the temperature fluctuations of the CMB in this region have materialized elsewhere," Adaeze said.

"What do you mean materialized?"

"Well, I don't mean it's come into solid, liquid, or gaseous existence. I just mean it's been observed elsewhere. At the Alkana station about three hours ago. It's been verified by other stations. I've been trying to reach you, Shulei."

"I can't believe it." I scratched my head. My heart was beating fast. "Sorry, I had my alert set up for emergencies only."

"Well, this is an emergency, if there ever was one. It's as if someone took a clone tool on a holo and recreated that same spot. And then flipped it. It's like a mirror image."

"Clone tool," I said. "Flipped." I was processing, pacing now, my feet trying to keep up with the beating thumps of my heart. "Is it some kind of prank?"

"Not a prank. We've had security run through this many times."

"Fluctuations. Heat." I whistled. Could this mean—?

I threw my things together, shaking my head. It was likely to be some blip due to natural physics, some strange phenomenon in space. Yet, the music in my mind meshed with another thought . . . the nagging idea that it could be something more. A relic of a signature, that ancient radiation, bent to the will of some civilization out there. CMB. Adaeze's voice was playful, but insinuating, like she knew something I didn't.

I climb into my pod, leaving Adaeze on her own for a few more days. I was assigned as exobiologist on the spaceship to check out the anomaly. When I'm awake out here in the spaceship, coursing in this emptiness, I do maintenance. My head is too focused from the waking inhalations they sprayed into my pod to think of fanciful things. Instead, it's all about the ship sweep-checks: scanning other pods, checking biological functions of my deep sleep mates, making sure the navigation system is calibrated and running okay. We are all jack-of-all-trades in this scenario, even as we have our specialties. We wake in rotations to perform redundant but necessary examinations, and then we're back into the world of sleep. Our calculations allow us to spend some time with each other—built-in sociality into the calculation of human voyaging—so we're not always alone. Some scientists believed the anomaly to be simply a physical phenomenon, but our crew thought it to be more, a volitional deed based on interpretable evidence. We were united in that thought.

I flex my legs and massage them, before straightening them into a neutral position along the grooves of the sleep pod bed. Around me the other pods are still closed with my crewmates in abeyance.

I remember Adaeze's voice, ominous, but still full of excitement: "Axis of evil 2."

A shiver went down my spine. She said it like it was a horror film sequel.

"Axis of evil" isn't the cutest name. It could have been called "Weirdo temperature" or "Kinda hot over here." Axis of evil's wayward twin, "CMB Cold Spot," has much more of a neutral name. No malevolence in that moniker. Why couldn't that be the anomaly discovered?

It would have been a lot less dread-causing.

I lower the transparent pod lid over my body, snapping it shut. We used to rely on automated mechanisms, but the sensors started to fail, and they kept snagging on clothes. I pull in my arms tight. I count to ten, with only a whisper of a sound when I come to four, barely vocalizing the digit of death in Mandarin. I move my head from side to side on my pillow and wait for the spritz that would put me back into dreamspace.

I think about lucky things: snails and spirals. I remember Adaeze telling me that when she lived in Egypt, she would wear coiled earrings, dangling spirals off her lobes. The snails are good luck, she said. A symbol of life spiraling outwards, expanding and becoming conscious. Snails, like Egyptian summer snails, can go through a long sleep and wake up—and in the past have surprised unsuspecting people with their ability to rise from what was thought to be dead. "Like that time in that museum," she said, recounting and laughing, about the curator finding the snail trail and its unlikely resurrection. I start getting drowsy, and I trace a spiral on the guarded glass on the pod lid. Wake up, I tell myself. Make sure I can wake up.

For a bunch of scientists, we are secretly pretty superstitious. We go through some routines to ward off bad luck—skipping past doorways; passing hands through holographic embers; knocking on screens; censoring numbers when we count; being careful around mirrors, so as to not break them even if they are made of extremely tough poly-material—giving us some illusion of control in this otherwise hostile environment.

The spray begins to take hold and my eyelids feel heavy. As the cold pervades, I think about fluctuations and the swaths of distinct abnormal temperature averages in cosmic microwave background radiation. It would be nice to be warm now, instead of this chill. My mind turns to the copy of the axis of evil, a cloned area but flipped. Why? I'm losing consciousness. My fingers are still twitching, making small spiraling gestures, going in different directions on each hand, clockwise on one, counterclockwise on the other until I no longer feel them.

I dream about the symphony I spent years creating. I dream about my father and the stories he told me.

I course my hands across the holographic synesthetic keyboard, musical notes jumping out alongside animated images of cut-paper red bunnies leaping across the moon, traversing first planets, then solar systems and galaxies, as they land into a foreign land. My pinky strikes a cascade of notes octaves higher, and a hint of pomelo permeates the air. The synesthetic music program effortlessly translates the symphony of what I have in mind: the struggle to find life on exoplanets.

I watch the bunnies traverse. It's a quieter tune now, as they explore this new space, and the repetition of musical phrases puts me into a meditational trance. Bunnies are lucky in the zodiac. In the zodiac story my father used to tell me, when the call came out for the animals to cross the river to get on the calendar, the bunnies overcame an inability to swim by perching themselves on logs that floated over the water and skipped on stones to make it across. I add a bit of a trill, give the bunnies some character. They're like us, really. Humans aren't equipped to sail the endless swaths of space, so we use proverbial logs and rocks. Technology. Perched on spacecraft, a nice log to sail through dark skies. Pulling resources off celestial bodies, like the furry geniuses skipping on stones. We'll get to the end of the race, to the prized station that was meant to be ours. Discovery.

I pull off a bit of a tremolo with my fingers, and then I'm coming into a dark space where light doesn't hit the desert. I feel the chill grow, strangely musty for a dry land. I trip over my fingers, have a lapse of confusion, cursing. I have a hard time with right and left sometimes, though I always think I've outgrown it, and it'll hit me like a storm.

I just scroll through the rest of the sheet music of this piece, humming to myself. It has so many layers of scrawls and notes; an artifact of development of the last 20 years. It's a song I first threw together years and years ago, when I was a little kid and my dad tried to teach me piano. "Shulei, be like your name, loosen up!" His seasoned jazz-playing mind could not bear to see his own kid playing so rigidly, constantly thinking about her left and right hands, so he bought me the first version of these musical instruments that fuse storytelling in all its robust multi-dimensional depth into its practice, with visuals, smells, colors, and sparkle. It was enough dazzle to make me not hyper-focus on the relative position of my hands. He was a musical genius, his hands almost acting as extensions of each other. Not separate mirrored images of one another, but instruments of prowess, almost completely mutually interchangeable. I swear he no longer thought of one as auxiliary to the other. He was an ambidextrous genius.

He said he always attributed it to his situs inversus. He said the inverted placement of organs in his body made him an exception to rules of somatic dominance and minority status. No hand was secondary to the other. Maybe that was the case. Or maybe he was deluded in his self-pride. But he was always good at taking a vulnerability and making it his strength. I struggle with that.

I'm scribbling with a stylus to cross out sections of the song, which has changed directions so many times over the years. As a composer, I'm like the proverbial bunny that never makes it to the end. I hope that my approach to music-making as my hobby isn't a comment on my professional life as an exobiologist, isn't cursing the SETI program to be this way, too—constantly probing but not really getting there.

I sigh.

I think about the bunny entering the desert. Something nags me. It's that musty smell. It reminds me of a place, but I can't put my finger on it. The bunny pushes off with his hind legs—and I'm interrupted with a notification. I lose concentration and my left hand bumps into right, breaking the flow of my muscle memory and I fluster, thinking about which hand to position where next.

I wake up to the smell of sizzling. I try to get up, my hands shaking as I pull myself upright from the cold sleep pod. It isn't easy. The pod jolts from left to right, shaking and rumbling. Creaking noises give me the chills and make the hairs on my arm rise. My fingers and arms are weak from sleep. I use all my effort, grunting, to rise. Once I'm out of the wobbling pod, I do a kind of tap dance to stay on my feet. It's not just my pod and the two pods next to mine—the whole ship is lurching. I feel sick. I always feel queasy coming out of sleep, but this time I'm retching, with nothing coming up. At least that's a relief. The artificial gravity is going in and out. It wouldn't be pleasant dealing with floating and falling vomit on top of nausea. It's not a great consolation.

With the sudden changes in my own body weight and the quaking of the ship, it takes me a while to find my footing. My knees knock against each other, and I finally grip a counter, typically used to put hairbrushes and creams for grooming after awakening. I'm not focused on tidying up. The sizzling smell makes me cough and I'm worried. Where is everyone else?

Something isn't right.

Just as this thought enters my head, I hear a creak and the ship shudders again. The lid to Adaeze's sleep pod pops open and she sits up bleary-eyed. She coughs.

A smooth, electronic voice blares across the ship: "Repairs underway. Please be patient as we reorient artificial gravity levels."

A deep heaviness comes over me, and then it lifts.

The voice says, "Artificial gravity levels reestablished." The ship stops shaking.

"Whoa," Adaeze says uneasily. She breathes into a sleeve then puts it down, coughing again. She has one hand to her head and the other on the pod. I help her up.

"Ugh," she says. "I feel horrible."

"You don't smell great either," I say.

She swats at me, scrunching her nose. "Yeah, well, you're not one to talk. You're all sweat and smolder. What's going on?" She takes a ragged breath.

"I'm not sure. I just woke up myself. We're not set to wake for another two cycles."

"You heard the alarm," Adaeze says in between coughs. "There's smoke. It's triggering my asthma."

"Yes. Come on. I have your inhaler here. We'll check the monitor."

We lumber to the navigation center and run through the logs. I hear a draw of breath as Adaeze takes her meds. We continue perusing. "No, no," cries Adaeze.

"What?" I ask.

"Come look."

My legs are still trembling. I'm nervous. Sweat dribbles down my forehead and I wipe it off with a sleeve.

Adaeze pulls at her hair. She's looking at the controls, highlighting and zooming in with the hand not tugging at her locks. "We've been tagged."

"Tagged?"

"The smoke," she says, stating the obvious in a deadpan voice. She hasn't really heard me. She's trying to control her anxiety. I can tell by the way she taps her fingers as she calls out for the drone.

She sends the ship drone out to inspect the damage.

My hands feel wobbly, like almond jello. But I shake it off. I edit a series of pre-recorded messages through the comms. I'm alerting those in the pods in the other wing, who would be waking in confusion.

The ship comes alive as other crew members start coming in to work on the investigation. Yet, even with the activity, there is an atmosphere of hushed apprehension. We are all tentative, breaths held. Hopeful and disquieted.

We conclude from the evidence that we have—that we've been attacked. The hit damaged the hull, momentarily compromised our artificial gravity systems and zapped our navigation system, although Nav Systems Two and Three remain functional. We set to repairs, sourcing parts from our dwindling supply.

As I take apart a set of parentboards and chips from an auxiliary med system for reuse, I consider the intent behind the hit. My first belief was subverted; yes, these aliens could be malevolent—but, still, I refuse to believe it. I believe they are defending their homes. Who wouldn't?

We narrow in on the location of what we believe to be the origin of the hit and guide our ship toward a sand-colored planet.

Lasers? Giant refractors? We can't spot any power sources or huge structures on the planet's surface in any wavelength. All is quiet—how in the stars is that possible?

We hide behind a mini-moon captured by the planet's gravity for a couple of days, observing, but detect no activity from the ground. The aliens may have decided we are not a threat or got distracted. Or maybe they are waiting us out, luring us in. We decide to send robotic landers to assess the situation. There is so much to learn, even if there might be a threat. We spend this time studying the converse of the axis of evil, a blueprint of that CMB anomaly but with the thermal topography flipped.

Bunny tails, snail spirals, charms, and chants. I pull out every good luck move in my arsenal. At night, in my bunk smelling of synthetic fish paste and burnt circuitry, I play the song on my keyboard and let the synesthetic bunnies run off in the direction of their home.

We still haven't seen the aliens; we see only emptiness below. Desert land. Perhaps, like bunnies, they live underground, but our landers have scoured the continents and seen nothing. Simple macroscopic life, yes, but no signs of technology at all.

I am tasked to send communications. I use our radio and lasers, transmitting geometric patterns, mathematical expressions, messages of peace in many human languages, all designed by our xenosemiotics experts. After each signal, we quickly make a burn to another location in case of retaliation. The lack of response is unsettling. It would have been understandable, albeit disheartening if they continued to target us. But, instead, silence prevails. Some of us interpret this lack of response to mean our presence triggered some automated defense system, and they assume we can come to terms with each other. If they are still here somewhere, still alive.

We test the waters, going into lower orbit. There's no reply. There hasn't been any action since the first wave of defenses. Have they been luring us into a trap?

And why the axis of evil? Our staff are boggled, reviewing our theories, some more preposterous than others: from geographical pragmatism as a cosmological map, to a means of communication as encrypted messages—perhaps masked like a Magic Eye—to a scientific investigation as a vast celestial experiment, to even theological reasons such as religious symbolism or some expression of cult worship. Or the best one yet, a mirage, a collective delusion of our own making from faulty equipment and cumulative overactive imaginations.

Eventually, we buckle down and go down to the planet.

On board one of the two-seat landers, goosebumps creep up my arms as I close in on the possibility of meeting intelligent others, in spite of the odds. Adaeze smiles at me, still with this secretive expression. Her coiled earrings dangle from her ears within the helmet, even if it isn't regulation. Just bits of our humanistic expression—of hope, of luck, of wishful thinking—showing through.

"What's with the look?" I ask. I mean her expression.

Her smile widens. "I like to keep my charms near me," she says, interpreting my question to be about her jewelry fashion statement. "That means your good charm, too." She disarms me with this remark, and I flash a smile back.

Once the violent shaking of landing ceases, we split to cover more ground but keep within comm's reach and visual distance. I see Adaeze in her silvery suit walk across the featureless desert strewn with boulders, much like the early Venera images of Venus. At least the temperature is bearable here.

I traverse the wide expanse, portable Raman analyzer in my hand, sweat trickling through my spacesuit and getting sucked up by the tiny moisture vacuums. I take samples, test regolith compositions, snap photos, and sketch my own renditions. Songs play in my head about the desolation. Can this really be a sanctuary for intelligent life?

Something shot at us, I remind myself.

It makes me tense thinking about the futility of it all. Coming here, taking the long journey in cold sleep, all that effort and high hopes—it better not be for nothing.

I think about my dad telling me to stretch, to loosen up, play some jazz and not be tense. Feel it all, let go. I breathe out and turn to look at Adaeze . . .

. . . who isn't there.

"Adaeze? Report!" I shout.

Silence. Can't see her transmitter on the projected map. She was there one moment, barely a kilometer away, no problem to spot in this flat desert—

"Adaeze!"

At that moment of panic, I fall through the world.

It feels like passing through layers, like zipping through a torrent of hologram channels all at once. I am disoriented, my limbs constantly swimming, moving, trying in vain to gain traction.

My view shifts and I find myself looking at . . . what is it? A grave-yard of solar panels? No, they're moving and unbroken.

I taste bile, puke in my own helmet, the acrid smell lingering as I pass out.

I wake up in a facility walled with reflective panels. It's strange seeing myself, small and vulnerable, reflected all around me. I see my helmet is off and once I realize what's happening, I clutch my throat, imagining I'm asphyxiating in this strange land.

But I've been here this whole time, breathing, and am not yet dead. I let go and take a breath in, thinking of my dad's mantra of loosening up. It smells like soap here, like jasmine flowers and sandalwood. My shoulders fall and I let out a puff of air. I'm still breathing. I scan the air, specs popping up, projecting from my eyepiece. It will sustain me, surprisingly.

I reach to touch my lucky charms, but they aren't on me. Stripped of my spacesuit and down to my coveralls, I feel like a bunny out of its hole, predators lurking to kill me.

Suddenly I see movement.

A solar panel . . . ambles toward me. No; *not a solar panel.*

I sit up, shuffle back, and hold out a hand, searching for a weapon, a shield, anything—and come up empty. I gasp with difficulty, and not because of the air. I'm weak, dealing with the repercussions of prolonged deep sleep, the unaccustomed gravity—and the swift appearance of a walking hinged mirror about twice my height coming my way.

It makes a clapping noise.

Life. Motile life. Here in space, in front of me. Can it be . . . intelligent? I pinch myself. Am I dreaming, still in my sleep pod? Or sedated after sustaining an injury in the attack? No. The sensation of the squeeze has a rich fullness that no dream could replicate. This is real.

On closer inspection, this being looks like hinged picture frames, or folders, made of mirrors, three stacked on each other, higher than a doorway.

When it approaches, it reflects me—but then I realize it's not an exact replica of me. Instead it's distorted, though its paneling reveals no warping. In this body's surface, the left side of me is shifted to the right, organically as it moves.

It shakes my hip at me.

I'm not sure how to take that. Is that a greeting? Or a challenge?

I pick up a hand, thinking hard to match its hip side. It shook a left hip, I think, so I focus and wave a left hand. I also shake that hip for good measure.

It moves its left hip again in return.

I shudder. It's uncanny, eerie to see myself reflected, deconstructed, jumbled and reput together in this hodgepodge way. I touch my own face, pores and flesh. Yes, this is me. But *that* me? It looks like patchwork, like a quilt gone awry. The reflection of me smiles, even though I'm not smiling. Does it consider a smile is a universal sign of friendliness? I can only hope.

It reminds me of a mix of 2-D paintings of yore in Earth cultures and what was considered modern art, a splash of cubism mixed with hieroglyphics. One side of my face suddenly reflects in the other panel—and then back. Like a pressed flower in a book shifting from one page to the other page of the folded spine.

It confuses the hell out of me, considering I have a hard enough time distinguishing left and right.

A garbling resounds, but it's not coming from the mirrored individual. It booms from within the room. It's a familiar voice, and once the white noise clears up, I realize it's the same host from Lunar New Year Celebrations hired to narrate the peace speeches transmitted from our spacecraft when we got close to potentially inhabited exoplanets—but not with the same words that we recorded.

It's a strange remix, like words cut from here and there, with pauses. It explains that they have been expecting us, with many accolades and celebrations in mind. As the voice resounds, the lips on the not-me-me move, but the visual is not in sync with the voice, creating this jarring feeling that I am experiencing some time lag.

It apologizes for the auto-defense system, saying the system did as intended to protect their world, but they meant no harm to us. It almost looks as if it's being insincere because of the fractured expression on the mirrored frame and a hint of an upturned lip on my reflection. But something in its execution spells remorse to me, maybe the eyes.

At the end of this farce, this muddled attempt at human mimicry, a wave flashes through its mirrored being, and the sound of thunder fills the air. It's like those panels at carnivals that you shake, and peals erupt.

The room walls and ceiling fall open, and I'm suddenly exposed. Thousands of these paneled beings amble about. Their mirrored bodies are not blank but reflect disjointed parts of humans that amounted to something humanesque, limbs and torsos constantly shifting from left side to right side as they close and open their hinged bodies. I begin to think of them as Cubisians, for their Picasso-like reflections on their mirrored panels. The one I first meet I call Other-Me. None of the rest reflect me, but faces and bodies of people I've never seen before.

I think of the accounts of mirrors in famous myths, able to see the organs within. I think about my dad, his situs inversus and how these beings subtly remind me of him in their conflation of left and right.

I start asking questions of Other-Me, with no response. My Cubisian host just shuffles elsewhere—leading me about?

I follow.

I pass by more Cubisians with a diversity of human phenotypes displayed on their panels. Why do they have images of humans?

I stop and refuse to move. I must get answers. "Who are you? Is this your home? Are there others like you? Where is Adaeze? And my lander?"

Other-Me waits, but my 2-D face on its body shifts more speedily among the panels. Maybe it's fidgeting. My stalling approach seems to work. It wants me to move.

"Do you have humans here?"

The response originates from the same host voice from beyond us, booming from some unseen location. "No, Terran forms are gifts from the outside."

I bristle. Terrans. It knows about us. "Where did you get these images? I mean, gifts?"

"From the treasure wave," they say. "From above and beyond. Like you. But, you are more . . ." The pause seems to drag on until I wonder if that's the end of their thought. Then comes the word searched for, "... dimensional."

"Why recreate the axis of evil, in all its miniscule details and thermal fluxes?"

It's silent—perhaps unfamiliar with the unfortunate term?—and I finally shadow Other-Me around, hoping for an answer. It takes me to another Cubisian who reflects a pastiche of a scientist caricature: lab coat, goggles, crazy hair, and even a mustache curl.

"It took a lot of energy, but it was a work of art ..." the booming voice shifts to a softer tone. "It's easier to reproduce something preexisting, than create something new altogether. Conservation of resources and an established blueprint."

"A work of art." I whistle. Relief washes through me as I think about my love of music. Suddenly, piano-playing, the synesthetic bunnies entering the desert and that elusive musty smell hit me. I know what it is, now. That smell. It's the smell of a museum. Kind of dead and musty, and climate-controlled—preserving culture and creation. This urge, to generate and protect, must be a sign of intelligent life. It's a deep and fundamental yearning to create and preserve civilization as we know it. The realization of the alignment of our values reverberates through me. Despite extreme physiological dissimilarity, we're at least close to seeing eye to mirrored eye.

Still, even with this sudden affinity, I know I'm over my head. Nothing in my exobiology training prepared me for this. I think about the various signs of life ... metabolism, motility, communication, growth, and development ... do they reproduce? Do they grow? I don't see any young ones ambling about. Maybe their version of growth isn't a physical attribute? I wonder how their thin sheets could regulate ... are their organs and nutrient transport in there?

I am left wondering.

"We want your art." It's the last thing they say before I inexplicably find myself back in the desert. Their words leave me mystified as I pat the sand about me, dumbfounded, looking for an explanation.

"There are said to be points called schiral nodes," our navigator Dray says. Back on the ship, he explains his hypothesis. "Inspired by chirality, like left-handedness or right-handedness; or clockwise or anti-clockwise pairs."

I think about lucky snails.

"Schiral . . . sounds like the '-shire' of the Cheshire cat in *Alice and Wonderland*," Adaeze beside me says, nodding, her spiral earrings jangling and a playful grin crossing her face. She had a similar experience being transported into another city of Cubisians.

Dray's eyes get this faraway look, as if thinking of the whimsical novel, but then he straightens his face and continues, pointing at a hologram. "The idea's been around but widely discredited. This is a huge breakthrough. Basically, there's a mirrored version of the topography of space-time—which also explains why we couldn't find any power sources or facilities on the surface—and you fell into it. You were able to end up on the flip side of where you were before, like falling through a looking glass. Even if you're not Alice."

"I feel like Alice," I admit.

"We lost track of you. But we were getting strange signals. It was your biorecord but muffled. Like Adaeze's."

"Muffled, I'd say. More like chopped up and recombined. At least that's how the Cubisians projected my look." I place a hand on the medical refresh strip balanced on my head. Adaeze steadies me. The coldness of the treatment and Adaeze's warm hand assures me of the realness of now.

"Can you retrace your steps?" he asks, his brow raised.

It takes ten failed attempts and five more reentries into this schiral-other existence to finally grasp the Cubisians' goals and aspirations. The other exoexplorers report similar experiences. I interact with Other-Me, as well as others.

They want us aesthetically, as art—like fur coats, but less violent. They want our faces, our bodies, as brands, as objects of conspicuous consumption to reflect on their panels. We are fashion statements to them. Glamour pieces, preserved culture from another part of the universe.

Stylistic forms that traverse their chirally-paired panels.

Given our limited space, we don't have a specialized ethicist on board to consider the full ramifications of these copies of us. We have little to bargain with besides our own countenances. We vote and settle on a decision.

They copy us meticulously, excited about real specimens to etch and all the details instead of digital copies in signals from afar. In return, they provide us tech to efficiently alter temperature on a large scale, though nothing as sophisticated as their transformative clone of the CMB turned into a geolocational piece of art.

"Send others to us," that eerie performative voice booms from beyond their mirrored bodies.

I have a lot to learn about them. I admire their attachment to their arts, above all else, even if it is rather vain. But, most of all, I find what comforts me is something conceptual: their lack of attachment to handedness. They shift flattened images of our body parts this way and that, volleying them from one panel to the other. Left becomes right and right becomes left, leaving me confused and breathless. As I recall my dad's dynamic, interchangeable hands playing jazz, I understand that sentiment.

Eventually, I spend years there, learning, growing, refusing to leave even when Adaeze and others sought different horizons once our ship split into modules. Some sought Earth again, hoping to implement much-needed technology. I can't bear to leave.

I'm absorbing, expanding, extending myself. I imagine myself on a gene-edited snail shell's spiral, perambulating counterclockwise, against the normal twist of a snail. I'm unraveling more and more about this species. As I learn, I see myself more and more like them, my approach flexible, fungible, resilient—and as resourceful as a zodiac bunny, finally going to reach a distant goal.

In the end, I make it. Among other things, I finish the piano melody, my left and right hands fungible tapping keys—as my melodic cut-paper flipped bunny vaults to the end. Other-Me, now reflecting a garish Milky Way-inspired hat, with swirls upon swirls on its head, pats me on the back. Other-Adaeze, my other audience member, with a Cheshire grin and jangling earrings, throws me a high-five. I fumble, not sure which hand to put up to meet the palm reflection on the panel, but it's fine. We clap hands—and for a moment, it's like I've fallen through space to my shipmate, consorting with an approving (and phenotypically-disarranged, but still recognizable) Adaeze whose bright eyes flicker from delight to amusement and whose hand feels—for some odd reason—uncannily like my father's.

Or maybe it was my own hand that feels like his. It's hard to tell.

I rub my hands and return the smile, my mind full of mirrored notes and song.

MIRROR IMAGES

On the Search for Asymmetry

DIMITRA DEMERTZI

How did life arise? That's the million-dollar question. A multitude of conditions probably contributed to life arising from inanimate matter, such as liquid water and organic molecules. One often overlooked feature is found in the structure of many organic molecules, and most biomolecules; *chirality* is a geometric property used widely in science to describe asymmetry.

For a system or an object to be described as chiral, it needs to be distinguishable from its mirror image, meaning that it can't be superimposed onto it. A more understandable way to put it, and a universal illustration of chirality, is to imagine the human hands. The left hand is a mirror image of the right one and vice versa; if a person puts one hand on top of the other, they are not going to match regardless of their orientation, whereas if they turn them toward one another, one will act as the mirror image of the other.

In the microscopic world of chemistry, chirality usually refers to molecules (who would have thought?); two mirror images of a chiral molecule are called *enantiomers*. They can be described as being the dextrorotatory D isomer or the levorotatory L isomer—they have different handedness.

But what does chirality have to do with life on Earth and with looking for life elsewhere? Besides the unsettling number of unanswerable questions that appear, upon trying to link chirality to the puzzle of the origin of life, we know that life on our planet relies heavily on chiral molecules. Namely, all life on Earth uses primarily L-amino acids and D-sugars, therefore showcasing a high level of homochirality (the same chirality of a family of molecules throughout a system). D-amino acids and L-sugars are also found across organisms, and demonstrate a range of divergent bio-functionalities, but their presence is rare and thought to be a result of faulty evolutionary mechanisms—in other words, mutations.

The presence of chirality in life is no accident; if we start increasing the complexity of molecules, they quickly cease to be symmetrical. This inability of organic matter to be symmetrical is a consequence of carbon's intrinsic geometry. You only have to imagine Freddie Mercury in his signature pose, with a third leg extruding from his back, to imagine how four different atoms are connected to carbon. In the four peaks created by Freddie's three legs and raised hand lie the four atoms. Now place Freddie inside a gargantuan transparent inflatable sphere—like the ones we see people having fun rolling inside at summer festivals. Rotate the ball whichever way you like; it is virtually impossible to discern any symmetry inside of it.

Chiral molecules were also observed and identified in space—and even in meteorites! In fact, Murray and Murchison are two carbon-rich meteorites that crashed on Earth in 1950 and 1969, respectively, and are often linked to the enantiomeric excess of L-amino acids—they contain more of them than their mirror counterparts. The downside of this circumstance, though, is that the excess of L-amino acids over the D ones is small (1-2%), and thus cannot explain why Earth life uses almost exclusively L-amino acids.

Before moving on to homochirality—and its obscure circumstances and role in Earth's life—we need to get a few things straight about the seemingly deep-seated trend of consistent excess of one enantiomer over the other in our data. There are a few hypotheses as to why one of the two handednesses might be favored over the other. Some suggest that the enantiomeric excess might be a result of random fluctuations. Yet, experiments have shown that more natural, determinate mechanisms can also produce one enantiomer in excess. The most important seems to be magnetic fields—which, mind you, are common in the cosmos—especially in scenarios pertinent to the synthesis of complex organic molecules in the ice mantles of dust grains in the interstellar medium. However, we are not entirely sure if the excess is consistent throughout the universe.

Nature is governed by energy—could it come down to that? While the complete explanation for the observation of slight enantiomeric excess might not be as straightforward and is probably affected by multiple factors, some scientists attribute this phenomenon to energy. For a system to survive—even more so, a living system—it needs to be stable. It is no secret that the lower the energy of a system, the more stable it is. We know that D-sugars, which are found in mono-nucleotides (the building blocks of DNA and RNA) stabilize the biomolecule's structure more efficiently and increase the fidelity of the error control of the genetic code. Is this the reason—or at least one of the reasons—that they were chosen over the L-sugars to be used by cells?

What is interesting, though, is that theoretical calculations have shown that the dissociation energies (how much energy a molecule needs to break apart) for D and L molecules are slightly different. For instance, if we have a racemic mixture of amino acids (1:1 ratio), the D-amino acids will degrade faster, leaving an excess of L-amino acids.

One detail we have neglected so far is that chiral molecules are *optically active*, which means that the enantiomers will rotate light in a different way. When light is right-handed circularly polarized, it can only interact with D enantiomers, and vice versa. This means that circularly polarized light of a certain handedness and adequate energy can destroy only one isomer. In some star-forming regions, right-handed circularly polarized light is emitted, but the energy it carries seems to not be enough to degrade D enantiomers. So, until we find multiple sources that emit UV circularly polarized light, this mechanism cannot be considered as a viable explanation for the slight enantiomeric excess found on Earth and elsewhere.

The chirality of biomolecules has also been linked to the chirality of more fundamental subatomic particles, more specifically electrons' properties associated with the weak force and muons' chirality associated with cosmic rays. The weak force is one of the four fundamental interactions in nature, and it is responsible for the decay of free neutrons to protons and the concurrent emission of *left-handed electrons*, whose radiation preferentially destroys D-amino acids. Muons—like electrons—retain a certain handedness too and are produced in Earth's upper atmosphere when cosmic rays hit the atomic nuclei of molecules. Since they are around 200 times larger than electrons, they tend to be more effective in the preferential destruction of molecules of a specific handedness.

Up until this moment, we have discussed what chirality is, why its role in life-as-we-know-it poses no accident, and how a prevalent enantiomer might originate, whether it be an L-amino acid, a D-sugar, or another biomolecule. But none of these theories can explain the high degree of homochirality found in life today. Hence, another mechanism for the amplification of the enantiomeric imbalance is needed.

To unravel the enigma of homochirality and its function in life, we have to begin by contemplating the question of the chicken and the egg: did it act as a prerequisite for the emergence of life, or was it a result of life's appearance? We have yet to determine with certainty which came first, even though the connection has been suspected since the early work of Pasteur.

Laboratory experiments have shown that RNA molecules (which are believed to be the first biomolecules to carry genetic information) are produced only with D-mono-nucleotides in the mixture. When both enantiomers of the mono-nucleotides are present, they cannot polymerize to form RNA—a phenomenon called enantiomeric cross-inhibition. This essentially means that homochirality would have to arise before the appearance of life. But how?

That is where the Frank mechanism comes into place. It explains how homochirality could have been achieved without the need for life, even with a small initial imbalance of the two enantiomers. In this mechanism, two processes take place simultaneously: an equal number of D and L enantiomers eliminate each other, while both of them are equally amplified (by a process called autocatalysis), until only one of them is left, henceforth achieving full homochirality. However, the experimental evidence for autocatalysis is poor and cannot (yet) support this idea.

Despite the uncertainty around the origin of homochirality, it is considered a strong indicator of life. But still, experts argue that since there are multiple examples of both enantiomers being bio-functional in life on Earth, a less pronounced homochirality (for instance, in samples from potential extraterrestrial habitats) should not rule out life.

Before moving on to contemplate life elsewhere and whether it is possible—or indeed necessary?—for it to use the same chirality as life on Earth, let us think about what would happen if life here used both enantiomers freely. The network of biochemical reactions within our cells is complicated, and the enzymes catalyzing these reactions are extremely specialized and can perform their function either on the D or L form of a molecule.

Let's talk about a specific reaction. If only one enantiomer is naturally used, there will only be one enzyme for that reaction. If both enantiomers of a molecule are used, two enzymes will exist for one reaction. So, if we introduce both enantiomers, we get double the number of enzymes and the system becomes infinitely more complex. So it's only logical that—once a certain biochemistry emerges for one of the enantiomers, it will be perpetuated. Life is practical, and choosing to work with only one out of two enantiomers is a matter of convenience.

What about extraterrestrial life? What kind of chirality would it use? Depending on whether the resulting excess of one enantiomer over the other is dictated by nature or chance, life elsewhere might retain the same chirality of amino acids and sugars as on Earth. However, we should not be too quick to presume that this would be the case, since life here uses both chiralities in many cases—a bit impractical, yes, but nonetheless true. Even if L-amino acid and D-sugar excess is indeed consistent throughout the cosmos and the same chirality is expected for life on another planet (or moon!), wouldn't it be wise to leave a bit of room for error?

In D.A. Xiaolin Spires's "The Mirrored Symphony," none of these questions matter that much, as the Cubisians act as shapeshifters who can transform themselves into the enantiomer of any life form, copying its very existence. Essentially, they are mirrors, and in a metaphorical sense encompass asymmetry and the geometric property of chirality.

We can't rule out that life exists elsewhere in our galaxy. To have a better idea of what to look for and eventually find it, we only need to continue to investigate the murky waters of the unknown and explore the possibilities of chirality's and homochirality's role in life, among other cosmic mysteries.

FURTHER READING

Avnir, D. (2021). "Critical review of chirality indicators of extraterrestrial life." *New Astronomy Reviews*, 92, 101596.

Brandenburg, A. (2021). "Homochirality: A Prerequisite or Consequence of Life?" In A. Neubeck & S. McMahon (Eds.), *Prebiotic Chemistry and the Origin of Life* (p. 87–115). Springer International Publishing.

Chen, Y., & Ma, W. (2020). "The origin of biological homochirality along with the origin of life." *PLoS Computational Biology*, 16(1), e1007592.

Devínsky, F. (2021). "Chirality and the Origin of Life." *Symmetry*, 13(12), 2277.

Globus, N., & Blandford, R. D. (2020). "The Chiral Puzzle of Life." *The Astrophysical Journal*, 895(1), L11.

Laurent, G. (2021). "Emergence of homochirality in large molecular systems." *Proceedings of the National Academy of Sciences*, 118(35), e2112849118.

LUMENFABULATOR   Liu Yang

(Translated from Mandarin by Ladon Gao)

I stand under the winter sunset, waiting for the arrival of my first short poem. I have always loved the magnificent epics, loved their gripping excitement and boundless passion; but the shaman says what I really need at the moment is gentle ditties and lingering sentiment.

Like those from my father's generations, my body, light purple and transparent, rooted deeply in the earth and connected tightly with boiling magma infused with molten metal. Every time a gigantic companion star flashes across the sky, I can feel clearly the violent shaking coming from the crust around me. Father once told me, that was the power of tides—the source of all life. With the shaking, magma gushes out through the narrow crevices underground, flows down the ancient channels from the top of crater slopes, and gathers in the warm source pool, waiting to solidify and to form a new layer of linguashell on my body.

When a moving poem, riding electromagnetic waves, is refracted through my body, I will release some magma from the source pool and let it flow in the freezing winter wind. The magma will quickly solidify into crystals, in which metal ions—mainly potassium, aluminium, and nickel—will vibrate under the electromagnetic field force. Waves from the vibration, crushing against each other, will then shape the structure of my linguashell: dense here and sparse there, like mysterious ripples.

"You remind me of your mother," Father once said to me. "She always piles up those weird tales one layer after another, like a pagoda tower." So do I. Those moving short poems grow from my base, tightly as teeth and scales. Under my control, they form layers after layers of crystals, tilted at different angles, reflecting the whole dim starry sky. Every time a ray of sunlight travels through, the information condensed within the crystals will be dispersed into a spectrum. The

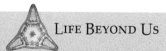

shamans can interpret from those patterns of light and shade all kinds of secrets, about the past and about the future.

"They . . . who . . . wrote?" I look at that forest of crystals reflecting sunlight, striving to explain myself. Father reflects a ray of yellow light, soothing me.

"No one ever knows, my dear." Father's body is shrouded in a soft glow. "Legend says that wise men from those faraway worlds lived in every sun. Stories and songs flowed like water from their mouths, through their chanting, and spread out in all directions, until they lit up every corner of the universe."

"Story . . . real?"

"More or less," Father says, hesitantly.

"For real?" My curiosity grows. "Green planets . . . azure skies . . . golden armors . . . enormous spaceships." I admit that my expressions are quite clumsy, but I am still building my linguashell. I cannot utter a complete sentence as freely as Father.

"Are you talking about the story from yesterday?"

I reflect a ray of scarlet light: within, contains the fragments of the story I heard yesterday.

"I know this story." Father ponders for a moment. "I heard some similar ones when I was very little. They cultivated farmlands, bred livestock, weaved textiles, and made use of fire. Also, they condensed poems."

"They . . . also . . . lumenfabulators?"

"No. They were different from us. They condensed poems on paper—a kind of product made from vegetable fibres."

"Those *papers* . . . could fly?"

"No. They would be bound together into *books*. Books were a type of static artform, with no light, no refraction, and no crystals. Books were vulnerable, easy to crumble, and tragic. Many stories and poems were lost in perpetual wars. Those once delicate combinations of words and phrases were turned into undistinguishable chaos. As time passed and entropy increased, they were lost forever."

War? I hear a word I detest. It is a term that appears frequently in ancient legends. It is a term for brokenness, separation, and darkness. "They . . . now . . . exist?"

"Don't know. I haven't seen their poems for a long time. It is said that a great fire destroyed that planet and burned all the books. Those stories and poems were buried under rubble and ruins. They were no more."

Night falls. So do Father and I into silence. With the sun set, the stars shine brighter. The night sky blinks, sending out elegant short poems, one piece after another. I look up to the night sky, extracting a stream of magma from time to time and covering my body with it. A clear, chilly glow emerges from within me, shining in pale green—the very color I am missing. Slowly, the green color merges into my purple body, making it clearer and clearer. The shaman is right. These short poems, full of sadness and sentiment, have made my linguashell complete. I have always been chasing after thrill and grandeur—but sentiment, this is the color that will eventually lead me to maturity.

I lock a fragment of a poem with my body and carve it into the clearest crystal. Condensed verses flicker in dim light like flirtatious souls, decorating the peaceful night. Now, I can recite this poem with perfect fluency:

Like dreams pass world affairs untold,
How many autumns in our life are cold?
My corridor is loud with wind-blown leaves at night[1].

---

1 'The Moon on the West River' (《西江月》) by Su Shi (苏轼), translated by Xu Yuanchong (许渊冲). See: Shi, Su. Selected Poems of Su Shi. Translated by Xu Yuanchong. Changsha: Hunan People's Publishing House, 2007.

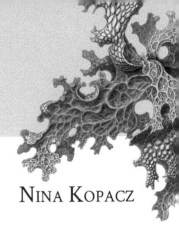

CRYSTAL GREEN PERSUASION

NINA KOPACZ

The tale "Lumenfabulator," by Liu Yang, beautiful in its brevity and poetic artistry, alternates between the foreign and the familiar in more ways than one. It places us in a faraway land yet regales us with stories we feel we recognize. It also touches upon several scientific topics familiar to us while describing a most exotic form of life.

Tidal Forces

In "Lumenfabulator" we are introduced to beings on a planet influenced heavily by tidal forces from its stars, forces referred to as "the sources of all life." Tidal forces occur when bodies orbit each other in elliptical orbits, such as is the case for all planets around stars, and moons around planets. On an elliptical path, the bodies alternate being closer together (the closest point being the periapsis) and further apart (the furthest point dubbed the apoapsis), and consequently so does the gravitational force between them, increasing as they move closer together. This variation in the strength of the gravitational pull causes the bodies to deform, as they are periodically stretched by gravity.

On Earth we are familiar with tidal forces in the hydrosphere, manifested by the ebb and flow of the tide. The water in Earth's oceans, seas, and larger lakes is literally following the Sun or Moon as they travel through the sky and exert their gravitational force on the surface. The wet/dry cycles caused by tides in intertidal zones are thought to have been important in the origin of life on Earth. Water, a key ingredient for life, makes it difficult for complex chemical reactions to take place. When wet environments dry, however, organic chemistry can proceed, building molecules into greater, more complex forms. Thus wet/dry cycles may have given early (bio)chemical systems the water they needed, but also the conditions to evolve chemically into the first life [1].

Much stronger tidal forces occur in our solar system on the moons of Jupiter, where the enormous mass of Jupiter stretches and deforms the small moons to such an extent that it causes friction in their interiors. Io, the moon closest to Jupiter, is riddled with volcanoes, indicating a molten core in a body that would otherwise be cold and geologically still, given its size and distance from the Sun. Europa, Jupiter's second-closest moon, is also affected by these forces, and is thought to have hydrothermal vents in its subsurface ocean due to magma in its interior. Where there are water and heat, there may well be life, and so tidal forces might facilitate life on Europa as well, albeit in a different fashion [2].

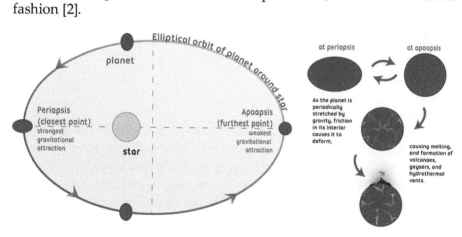

Tidal Forces. The planet in "Lumenfabulator" is subject to extreme tidal forces, which deform its interior and produce volcanism, supplying molten magma to the source pool from which the protagonist can build a "linguashell." Image: Nina Kopacz

The stars in "Lumenfabulator" must be dimmer than our own Sun, as the planet is described as covered in ice, yet must be close enough to experience tidal forces so strong they melt its interior and produce surface volcanism (though not all volcanism is tidally driven, mind you—for instance on Earth, it is a result of accretional heat). The tidally produced volcanism on the Lumenfabulators' planet is described by "crustal shaking and gushing of magma," which appears to be vital for the inhabitants, providing heat and material for their bodies in an otherwise frozen world.

Living Rocks

The origin of life on Earth was facilitated by an environment allowing for increasing chemical complexity: from a purely geochemical substrate emerged systems of progressively more complex organic chemistry, until finally transitioning into the biochemistry of living things. The emergence of the biosphere from the geosphere was gradual, and thus their histories are inevitably intertwined.

Early forays into the importance of geology in the emergence of life are seen in the work of Cairns-Smith from the 1960s. Cairns-Smith showed that clay rocks exhibit a sort of primitive genetic code: as they crystallize, they exhibit defects in their crystal structures, which are self-selecting and naturally replicate themselves [3]. In the 1970s, Hartman took these ideas further, suggesting that clays aided the evolution of primitive metabolism [4].

The idea of modern biological metabolisms evolving from geochemical pathways is actively being explored by the origin-of-life community in the study of hydrothermal vents (such vents may be where life first emerged on Earth, and perhaps not only on Earth—remember the tidally heated Europa?). They argue that hydrothermal environments on early Earth promoted the synthesis of organic molecules and their self-organization in what can be seen as early proto-metabolic networks, which would eventually result in the origin of the first protocells [5].

Much modern work on clays focuses on how their catalytic properties allow them to synthesize simple organic molecules like amino acids, and in turn polymerize them to form peptides (chains of these molecules, which life uses to make proteins). Clays have also been observed to transform fatty acid micelles (the building blocks of membranes) into vesicles, structures which are thought to have served as compartments for prebiotic evolution before modern cells came about. This work suggests clay minerals served as a sort of scaffolding for early biological life, until it evolved enough to be able to persist on its own [6]. There could thus have been a time when primitive life forms and their rocky substrates were intricately linked.

Not only do clays play a catalytic role in organic reactions, but organic molecules can also catalyze the formation of clays! In fact, the evolution of the geosphere and the biosphere on Earth have progressed side by side in a most fascinating way. Upon its formation, the Earth was composed of a mere ~250 mineral species. An increasing diversity of physicochemical conditions on Earth, due to planetary differentiation, plate tectonics, magmatism, metamorphism, fluid-rock interactions, and other abiotic processes, increased this number to ~1,500. Today we know of more than 5,400 mineral species, an increase in diversity that was caused directly and indirectly by life.

The presence of the biosphere has affected the physicochemical conditions of the Earth's surface drastically, for example, by introducing oxygen into the atmosphere and making it available for incorporation into mineral structures. Living organisms can also directly control the precipitation of minerals, for example, by producing enzymes that control mineralization. By doing so they can produce bones and seashells as part of their own structures, or create microenvironments with specific chemical conditions, allowing for new mineral species to form. Ultimately, living systems generate far-from-equilibrium conditions which promote the cycling of matter, the separation and concentration of elements, and consequently the evolution of mineralogy. The degree of a planet's mineral diversity may thus give us clues as to whether it plays host to living systems, a tool which may prove useful in the search for life on exoplanets [7].

Silicon-based life has been explored in both science and science fiction for many decades. Silicon on Earth is largely tied up in the geosphere in the form of silicate rocks, while carbon compounds make up the biosphere. Carbon-based life is thought to be more common in the universe, based on the widespread availability of carbon and water, and the fact that carbon is so beautifully chemically versatile, being able to bond in a variety of ways to create molecules of diverse shapes. However, silicon may have an advantage over carbon in this last respect in environments with very cold temperatures and reducing (free oxygen-lacking) conditions—for instance, in environments dominated by liquid nitrogen or methane. In such environments, silicon can form stable bonds with itself, phosphorus, sulfur, oxygen, and many metals to form flexible, macromolecular assemblies in the form of sheets, strings, tubes, and other shapes we see in carbon biochemistry. This sort of chemistry describes silicon behaving the way carbon does, in complex and flexible organic-like molecules in a liquid medium, and not in the form of crystal structures in rocks [8].

The prevailing consensus within the scientific community is that life requires a liquid medium (for example, water), where the diffusion of molecules can happen at a rate that allows for increasing complexity.

In a gas this diffusion happens too quickly, and in a solid state, too slowly. Thus, the possibility of life made entirely of minerals might be limited by the speed of information transfer. In the geosphere, the domain of lava, rocks, and sediments, the evolution of matter is very slow, happening largely on geological time scales of millions of years. That elusive phenomenon we call the "origin of life" saw the beginning of a biosphere, inhabited by organisms that can replicate DNA, life's information molecule, in mere seconds—a timescale exponentially shorter than that of the geosphere. Thus, the transition from the geosphere to the biosphere is marked by a striking increase in the speed of information transfer. In our own time we speak of the technosphere, the realm of computer programs and artificial intelligence. These systems in turn can process information much more quickly than our own biologically limited brains can.

Whether a living system needs to evolve quickly in time to achieve a level of complexity great enough to be considered "alive" is a tricky question, mainly because "complexity" itself does not have a straightforward definition. There is no doubt: living systems have an enormous degree of chemical complexity, but how to quantify this parameter on a molecular scale has been the subject of much recent computational work in the origin-of-life community [9].

Pleochroism

Lumenfabulators are described as crystal beings who communicate by refracting electromagnetic radiation through their crystal lattices. Crystals are anisotropic materials, and thus their optical properties vary depending on the direction of the light passing through them. In contrast, glass, which is isotropic, allows light to pass through it identically no matter which way it is coming from. When light passes through an anisotropic medium like a crystal, it is refracted because of an optical property called *birefringence*, wherein light of varying polarizations is bent in different amounts by the crystal structure, and consequently will travel on different paths and speeds through the crystal. The resultant optical phenomenon, called *pleochroism*, is manifested as the crystal appearing to be different colors depending on the angle it is viewed from. When viewed from one side the crystal may appear red, but when turned 90 degrees it may appear green. The number of pleochroic colors depends on the number of optical axes within the crystal [10].

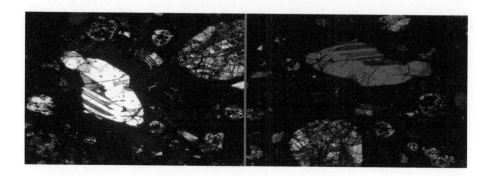

Pleochroism. A mineral grain in a thin section viewed in polarized light under an optical microscope changes color as it is rotated. Image: Nina Kopacz

Lumenfabulators seem to have mastered the effect of pleochroism, building their bodies in such a precise way as to be able to use their crystal lattices to communicate with colors. They are able to employ parts of their bodies with different optical axes at will, allowing light to pass through to show a specific color, like when the protagonist's father lightens the mood with a beam of yellow light.

The central character of "Lumenfabulator" make use of poetry to learn about the world around them and to study worlds far away. On Earth we probe the unknown with art just as much as with science. Art allows us to explore and internalize concepts we cannot fully comprehend, and to communicate our experiences across cultures and timescapes. When we finally do encounter unknown life, it may be a tool like poetry that will allow for a more intuitive dialogue to unfold between us.

REFERENCES

[1] Damer, B., & Deamer, D. (2020). "The hot spring hypothesis for an origin of life." *Astrobiology*, 20(4), 429-452.

[2] Faure, G., & Mensing, T. (2007). "Chapter 15." *Galilean Satellites: Jewels of the Solar System. Introduction to Planetary Science*. Dordrecht, Netherlands: Springer.

[3] Cairns-Smith, A. G. (1966). "The origin of life and the nature of the primitive gene." *Journal of Theoretical Biology*, 10(1), 53-88.

[4]   Hartman, H. (1975). "Speculations on the origin and evolution of metabolism." *Journal of Molecular Evolution*, 4(4), 359-370.

[5]   Camprubí, E., De Leeuw, J. W., House, C. H., Raulin, F., Russell, M. J., Spang, A., . . . & Westall, F. (2019). "The emergence of life." *Space Science Reviews*, 215(8), 1-53.

[6]   Kloprogge, J. T. T., & Hartman, H. (2022). "Clays and the Origin of Life: The Experiments." *Life*, 12(2), 259.

[7]   Hazen, R. M., Papineau, D., Bleeker, W., Downs, R. T., Ferry, J. M., McCoy, T. J., . . . & Yang, H. (2008). "Mineral evolution." *American Mineralogist*, 93(11-12), 1693-1720.

[8]   Schulze-Makuch, D., & Irwin, L. N. (2006). "The prospect of alien life in exotic forms on other worlds." *Naturwissenschaften*, 93(4), 155-172.

[9]   Böttcher, T. (2018). "From molecules to life: quantifying the complexity of chemical and biological systems in the universe." *Journal of molecular evolution*, 86(1), 1-10.

[10] Bloss, F. Donald. (1961). *An Introduction to the Methods of Optical Crystallography*. New York: Holt, Rinehart and Winston. p. 147–149.

CYCLIC AMPLIFICATION, MEANING FAMILY

BOGI TAKÁCS

The extraterrestrial life-form is shaped like an oversized upside-down bucket, has a gunmetal color with an iridescent sheen, it's soft and warm, and I have no idea what to do with it.

I stand, feet sunk into the soft surface of the exoplanet, and stare at it.

Surely kicking wouldn't be an appropriate response to a communications issue . . . yet I am tempted. I suppress the impulse. I can't even touch the bucket: its softness and warmth are approximations in the virtual model I just built using my envirosuit's computer.

I close the model and pace around the bucket. My ankles wobble as I try to keep my balance on the mushy, uneven soil. My envirosuit chafes against my skin in at least five distinct spots, and I feel the classic spacer flu coming on. The sky is the color of regurgitated pea soup. Everything is awful. I want to message my sister Eszter so that I can complain to her in good old Hungarian fashion. I can imagine the conversation:

<Judit> *This reminds me of that novel you sent me.*
<Eszter> *Strugatsky?*
<Judit> *Lem.*
<Eszter> *Oh, Fiasco?*
<Judit> *A fiasco all right.*

At least we haven't progressed to missile warfare with the buckets yet. My sister's back on Earth, somewhere underground in a European Defense Agency bunker, and I miss her. The EDA has been prepared for the eventuality that projectiles start flying. They haven't been prepared for the eventuality that the soft buckets are peaceful, and we just have no idea what to do with them. I wouldn't even be sure that they *are* the sentient beings who produced this technological civilization, but the surveyors and the anthropologists both agreed based on the settlement patterns observed from orbit.

I'm still wondering if they are wrong.

<Jonathan> *Any sensory organs you spotted yet?*

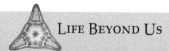

I groan. Will the people back on the ESA *Maimonides* ever leave me a moment to think? I message him back, hoping that the excessive formality will register as frustration.

<Judit> *It looks entirely homogenous—if it has internal structure, it must be on a scale our instruments cannot resolve without resorting to invasive methods. The spectroscope gave me an idea of the surface composition, but it's not helpful. There are also some faint ultrasound vibrations, but I'm not detecting a pattern. Then again, any sufficiently advanced communication is indistinguishable from noise.*

They don't need an astrobiologist like me; they need a communications expert. Or a good old-fashioned Hungarian shaman. I can't chase away the thought that my sister should've been on this mission, not me. She's also older, even if she's somewhat immature.

<Jonathan> *Surely you could take a tissue sample?*

<Judit> *And risk being nuked from orbit? No thanks.*

At least figuring out their giant spacecraft in orbit around their own planet isn't a task for me. Yet. Knowing Jonathan, he'll find a way. He started out on the ESA *Maimonides* back when it was still on a long-term Mars mission, and he thinks that gives him the right to boss everyone around. I'm sure it's possible to lead a mission without being a jerk about it, but we can't have that here. I stop pacing and force calm upon myself. Anger won't help.

Instead, I occupy myself with busywork, recording long stretches of boring data, trying not to glance upward over and over again; trying not to wonder if I will be struck down from above. The buckets seem to be sessile. I'm sure there's something going on inside them. We've already learned there are large, underground tendrils connecting them to each other, and to the vast curlicues of structures dotting the landscape, mirroring the structures in orbit. But I can't figure out what happens inside the tendrils without digging them up and cutting them open.

If they built all these baroque structures, both on the surface of the planet and in orbit around it, why won't they use them to interact with us? It's as if all the fractal cauliflowers in the world decided to team up; the result is wonderful to look at but exasperating to try to understand.

I turn off my base comms, wave my arms at the buckets, and yell over the radio. "Hi! Hello! I can't figure you out without a tissue sample and I don't know how to talk to you! Could we maybe swap?"

The buckets remain silent, but at least this helped me work off a bit of steam. I wonder how I'd provide a tissue sample myself. I could only extract waste products from my envirosuit without breaching it. Find out about humans by examining their urine!

I frown. Even that's not an option with these lifeforms. Surely there has to be some kind of transfer ongoing between their bodies and the environment—matter, energy, information—but how does it work? I've already taken soil samples, but only at what seemed like a safe distance. You don't want to get the buckets angry after seeing images of their spacecraft.

I could prepare something back on our ship, a set of samples I could deposit, hoping that my gift-giving wouldn't be read as biological warfare. I turn base comms back on—this idea gives me an excuse to request a lander, at least.

Decontamination is boring, but at least I can eventually get out of my suit. I could murder for a bathtub.

I clatter down a narrow corridor, finally in more humanlike clothing, if my uniform fatigues count. I run past hastily reapplied signage and a set of spray-painted decorations that still say MARS MISSION. I can tell where ESA had run out of money. I shake my head—no time to waste. I have an excuse to contact my sister.

"I need to talk to one of the EDA linguists." I tell D Franklin, Communications Specialist on duty. My frustration must carry through my tone of voice.

At least they don't raise a fuss. I'm sure D knows that I'm billing a family chat against my work comms quota, but they remain silent.

I sit down in the chair that's about ten times more comfortable than any other chair on the ship, and I settle in for a long wait while the connection is established. I'm just glad I can be here for the time being because Eszter isn't actually a linguist. She has a degree in linguistics, which helps with scheduling this call, but what she does in the bowels of the EDA has little to do with syntax, semantics, and the like. She's a researcher in the field of Anomalous Communication, which sounds up my alley, because talking to a bucket is certainly not my usual, nonanomalous form of communication; but unfortunately, it means something like telepathy instead.

She can't tell me anything about *that* either: six years of her working there and I still don't know if telepathy even exists. Maybe it's all a smoke-and-mirrors act. Maybe she has to tell people she's researching telepathy to misdirect them from her actual research, which is about nuclear weapons targeting using social media troll armies or who knows what the EDA funds these days. As ESA staff, I'm only slightly envious—but maybe with a bona fide extraterrestrial civilization, the space agency will no longer get short shrift in the EU budget.

The call finally goes through. Eszter rubs her face as if it were putty. She looks exhausted. I wonder what's going on back on Earth.

"You look more miserable than I do, and that's something," she says. Even with all the fancy new technology, there's a noticeable delay in the call.

I tell her about my day. She immediately takes it as a challenge: she's the kind of person who wants to solve emotional issues with engineering. Why she became a linguist, I don't know.

"I'd go back to what you said about the, uh, buckets not being able to get a tissue sample from you either. Have you given that any thought? How would you investigate humans if you were them? Also, um, don't take this the wrong way, but do you have another name for them, I mean, *buckets* sounds awfully dehumanizing. Desentientizing?"

She's right about that; I'm chastised. "Their code in the registry is BK-X10."

At least she's not able to fill up my pauses with chatter like she'd do in person. She has to wait out the delay, and this gives me time to think.

I go on. "How would I try to investigate humans if I were in the extraterrestrials' place? I'd try to get into the strange humans' envirosuit somehow. I don't know their imaging capabilities. Or at least I would try to affix myself *onto* it, like something invisible smeared onto the surface of the suit. Then use that to hitch a ride back onto the humans', I mean our spacecraft. Of course, we have decon procedures . . ." I get stuck. I shrug after a long silence.

She responds so fast; she must have started speaking before she heard me stop. "They're intelligent, right? I mean they have *space stations*. So now assume what you said, they tried that already. They've done that already."

I glance around, searching for an invisible threat. *They've done that already.* Have they tried that already? Have they succeeded? Are they, right now, on board this very vessel? My head hurts, but that's just the usual spacer flu; at least I try to convince myself of that. "I haven't seen the bulkheads sprout buckets yet. Sorry, BK-X10. Lifeforms." But if they interact with their environment using means we haven't managed to detect, they could just as well be on board our spacecraft too. We've been here for a while.

I fight the urge to ask Eszter if her research in telepathy also extends to clairvoyance. I ask her about Mom instead—a minefield of a topic, but still an improvement over something that might result in getting our connection cut. The EDA has neural nets looking for security breaches.

Have we had a security breach, regardless?

Mom is getting back together with Dad, for the third time. They're a terrible match and I wish they'd stop trying. At least I'm not back on Earth and I can't damage-control their interactions with such a low comms quota for family calls; stepping back from the role of the meddlesome daughter. Neither of my parents know I've been speaking with my sister in the guise of work.

I finally have some work that feels meaningful. If I try to think like the extraterrestrials, my next step is obvious: attempting to reverse-engineer the decon procedure. How would I get through it? Fortunately, the reverse of reverse-engineering is just engineering. I already know who to ask.

"I'm honestly not sure how I could help." Sashko, head of engineering, smooths down his distinctly un-spacerlike beard. "Nothing's supposed to get through it. That's kind of the point. I don't know a lot about the biological details, just how the disinfectant is sprayed, things like that. But I can send you a link to the relevant files."

"I'll take everything you've got."

In all my favorite horror movies, there is a moment when someone opens something and it's full of insects. Someplace insects shouldn't be. It reminds me how I once hung up flypaper in Dad's basement by the tiny window, forgot about it, and when I next went downstairs, the flypaper was full of flies glued to it—some of them dead, some still trying to escape. I fled upstairs. The flies had to have been breeding down there, and I didn't want to find out what they were eating.

I can't help thinking of this. I'll open a utility closet, a bedroom door, *anything*, and I'll see weird organic gobs. Insects, maggots? My mind conjures up something worse than the ETs, which are silent, sessile, and if I want to be honest, rather stylish. I know nothing about their lifecycle. Some of them are smaller than the others, but I have yet to find anything planetside that I could identify as a juvenile.

Where are they—*if* they are here? I settle into my work chair, which creaks, unlike the chair in the comms enclosure. I want to twirl a lock of hair in my fingers, but I cut my hair short in preparation for space-flight. Now I regret it: Sashko was able to keep his beard. Then again, he's the seriously-casual type of engineer who asked for a name tag for his uniform that said SASHKO instead of OLEKSANDR. I chew my lips instead, and dab at my nose with a napkin. This does look like spacer flu. I should print myself a mask to spare my colleagues.

These lifeforms would need to use something small to get past decontamination. I readily find the numbers in the files about the effectiveness of the decon process against viruses and bacteria. Anything smaller? What is the smallest infectious agent? I was never much of a microbiology person, but at ESA, one has to have some knowledge of everything. Viroids, prions. . . . Viroids are just a piece of RNA: they aren't all that hard to destroy, I don't think that's it . . .

I bite the wet napkin and sputter. Prions. Misfolded proteins that can spread their own misfolding. Aren't prions notoriously hard to decontaminate? They don't even have DNA or RNA, so they might be hard to detect too. I'll have to look all this up. I remember Mad Cow Disease from a historical overview, and wasn't there something else? That animal disease with a strange name I had to learn about as an undergrad. It affected sheep? Goats? Something like that. In Northern Europe somewhere, they bulldozed an entire farm, removed the topsoil, and the disease still came back. *Scrapie,* my database helpfully tells me.

This seems promising, but what if it's something that doesn't exist on Earth? Or something artificial—nanoparticles? I'd like to imagine those to be more fragile, but who knows if that's true? In any case, I don't think the *lifeforms* have had enough time to tailor their approach to us yet. I wonder if they can communicate with whatever they sent up to us, or if they have to wait for the actual material to return with the lander. So many potential dangers.

I force myself to focus and make a chart about all the elements of the decon procedure. This one, effective against this, that one, effective against that. . . . Nothing seems effective against prions. I ping Tauno in Medical, but he doesn't respond. I put on a mask and hesitantly get to my feet.

"Sorry, just finished something. Are you here for that cold?" Tauno tilts his large blond head to the side. "When did you last sleep?"

"I'm not here for that cold and I slept last night." I try not to grump at him, in the name of Finnish-Hungarian solidarity. "I wanted to ask you about prions. Do you think the decon in the airlock gets rid of prions?"

"There's no reason it shouldn't?" He tilts his head to the other side, as if it was too heavy to keep straight. "Why are you asking?"

"How do *you* get rid of prions?"

"Me? I dunno. With UV light?" He takes a step back, as if in preparation for being punched. My grimace had to have shown through the plastic window in my mask. "They're hard to destroy," he says apologetically. "They stick to things like rubber. . . . Surgical steel. . . . Back in the day on Earth, they were even transmitted by things like brain electrodes, or the tube you swallow for a gastroscopy."

I would prefer not to think about a gastroscopy. "So, where's the UV light from the decon?"

". . . huh. The previous ship I served on had one."

"If this is yet another cost-cutting measure, I'm going to kill somebody." I groan. Tauno's twice my size and yet he winces. "Not you. Someone in charge of the budget."

He only looks a smidgen relieved. "We'll have to finish here and get back to Earth for that."

Time to have a chat with our commander, Jonathan. Science shouldn't be a merry-go-round of talking to people, but it so often is . . . and maybe that helps make it better. I just need to handle my own misanthropic nature. *Come on,* my sister would say, *Jonathan is easy to hate even if you're not a misanthrope.* She'd know, with all that telepathy research.

At least Jonathan can't read my thoughts. "What is it?" He sighs.

Why are you in charge of a European spaceship if you're American, I want to ask, but I know he has Irish citizenship too. I'm sure he marketed his NASA experience right.

"This is going to be a weird question, but no one else could answer me. Why isn't there UV in the decon?"

He looks at me as if I turned into a bucket. "Why would there be UV in the decon, with all the UV on the surface?"

I finally get to say what I've wanted to say for about three weeks. We're on first name terms, but there are some things one doesn't say out loud. Except now. "Jonathan, this isn't Mars."

I lean back into the most comfortable chair on the ship. "So I was yelling at Jonathan, this vomit-green atmosphere at least does one thing right, it blocks most of the ultraviolet light from reaching the surface! And he goes like, oh. Oh! They never put that UV into the decon when they reassigned the ship from Mars!"

After the requisite pause, my sister laughs. Then she frowns. "Hold on, so why aren't you wearing an envirosuit?"

I shake my head. "I'd need to decontaminate it first. We're not even sure yet if our theory is right. Tauno is down in the lab with Yıldız and they're trying to set up something that can detect prions."

"I'd put on an envirosuit if I were you," my sister says, "just in case."

"Are you aware that you sound like Mother?"

D looks confused. "A signal being sent back planetside? I don't know, we'd notice the usual ones, like radio transmitters. . . . Of course, if something is truly alien, then I don't even know where to begin."

I sigh—another dead end.

"How did your call go?" They risk a cautious smile.

I shake my head. "Fine, I suppose. I'll tell you later."

It's not a lie, just equivocation. There might not *be* a later.

My fellow biologist Yıldız looks as sleep-deprived as my sister, her fatigues rumpled. She rubs her skull which she shaves entirely. I asked her once if it was some kind of religious observance, but she told me it was a punk sentiment. She also plays drums in a band, though now that's on hold while we're off Earth.

Now the two of us blink anxiously at Jonathan who grunted at us—"You're the experts, you figure this out"—about thirty hours ago.

Tauno ran away about twenty-five hours ago, claiming it was "not his area of expertise." Is it ours, either?

Yıldız gives Jonathan the usual brief tour of the lab, then launches into her explanation. "There's a method to detect prions even in small quantities. It's called PMCA: protein misfolding cyclic amplification," she says. "It's like PCR for detecting DNA. PCR makes a lot of DNA out of a small amount."

Jonathan nods—I'm unsure if he knows how PCR works, but he had to have at least heard of it. There was a nasty viral outbreak on Mars a few years ago. "Mmhm." He rubs his scruffy chin. "But prions don't have DNA. They're not like viruses," he notes.

Yıldız sits down on the ship's second-most uncomfortable chair. "No, the mechanism is different, only the concept is similar. PMCA uses ultrasound to make more of the prion." She pulls up a projection. "We put a little bit of the misfolded protein with a lot of the regular protein. I must say that I did *not* kill the mice we brought for the mouse experiment, but it would've been a lot easier if I had. . . ."

Jonathan doesn't react well to her deadpan humor. I surreptitiously nudge Yıldız to change tack.

"*Anyway,*" Yıldız says, "I got a bunch of regular protein in another way, so we're good. We put them all together. The misfolded proteins, the prions, slowly start converting the regular protein into misfolded. But this would take forever if we tried to wait it out. So, we expose the mixture periodically to ultrasound, which breaks up the clusters of misfolded protein and helps them misfold even more of the regular protein. This way, we get a large amount a lot faster, we can detect it better, and we do things with it. *Incidentally,* this process can also be used to make prions jump from species to species easier."

I'm starting to have thoughts about exactly what might be going on inside the buckets. Would the vibrations fit the picture? This is all just speculation, still . . .

Jonathan has an idea too: "Hold on, are you saying you're going to use ultrasound to make it even more likely for this thing to infect humans?"

"No, no." Yıldız shakes her head vigorously. "That's just a tangent. Sorry. It's late. Early. Now that we set everything up, we can try to see if there are any misfolded proteins that spread and form clumps. And because I'm so generous, we can take blood samples from you for testing instead of cerebrospinal fluid samples."

I preemptively laugh because I can already see Jonathan turning pale as a sheet.

Some of the more terrifying hours of my life follow.

Eventually, our blood samples come back. Everyone else tests negative.

"Don't quarantine me! This makes no sense," I scream at Jonathan. "Send me back! Everything in the lander's probably contaminated anyway! Send me back, I'll figure it out!"

Yıldız takes my side. So does the rest of the team.

I sit in the cramped lander for what has to be at least an hour. I don't check. I wish they'd let me call my sister for one last time. Outside, the planet surface is waiting for me. Trying to kill me?

So much for spacer flu. Whatever this is, it has to be inside my head already: irritating my sinuses, making my nose drip. Not something one would observe with the prion diseases on Earth, but that's my luck. The progression has to be faster, too.

It's tempting to take off the headpiece, open the airlock to the noxious gases outside. But the others will need to observe what happens with me as I die of this alien disease, not of something else. I'm not going to deprive them of useful data.

I stagger outside, and some part of me observes in a detached way that I experience the psychological impact more than any neurological sequelae of the exposure. Maybe I should run some simple neurological tests on myself, but I was never good at tandem gait and such.

I walk up to a bucket. "Why are you trying to kill me?" I ask, not expecting an answer.

"ØįíōIįiòǫįįO˙Iüį," the bucket says.

After I've recovered from the shock, I try to reassess the situation.

"You're trying to communicate with me after all," I say, shaking my head.

"íŐǿIiòǫÕ ǫ˙IıóįÒöï."

Eszter would say: "The extraterrestrial observes turn-taking, at least. More evidence for turn-taking being a cultural universal in communication. Though I must say, I've always been skeptical of that."

I just say: "Okay then."

I sit down, sink slightly into the ground. "You say something, I say something. Will we learn each other's language?"

This will at least take my mind away from thoughts of harming myself.

It's not actually language; it's something entirely garbled in my head. It's like two or three of my senses are knocked askew. It's an impression of taste and color. Or maybe motion and smell. Roughly textured sound? This is not how I wanted to experience synesthesia.

"BbbbbbRRRRrrrrrrrr," I try to imitate it. I make the Hebrew "chaf" sound.

"ẅW̌ω̈HhH̄ŗ?"

"Chhhhhh." On impulse, I turn off my radio.

"ħH̄ĥhhĦĥh."

"Getting there." Am I really noticing improvement? "Chhh."

"kĦhĦkĦhh."

"I like that." They're not communicating via radio. Eszter would know about telepathy . . .

"áĵĹőýκhđět."

I realize with a startle that it's not likely to be telepathy—strictly speaking, they are inside my head. They are probably, at this very moment, building something inside my head out of misfolded proteins. I hope they won't accidentally kill me while they're at it. Their structures don't tend to be on the smaller side.

Their *visible* structures, I remind myself. I turn my radio back on, then I take a deep breath, point a finger at my chest. "Judit. I am Judit."

"Å̊ĵæNĴūđìt." A pause. "ĴÙđìt." Another pause. "jÙdìt."

"No," I interrupt, with a sinking feeling, "you aren't Judit, you are someone else."

I need a linguist. I desperately need a linguist.

<Yıldız> *Look, I only have audio, so I can only guess at what's happening. And I'm only getting one side of the conversation. But I think you really need a linguist.*

I am tempted to message back, Yıldız, *I need a telepath, would that be you?* I take another calming breath. Even the recirculated air smells like cold sweat.

<D> *How about I get you your linguist back at EDA HQ?*

They're not giving away the game, and for that I'm infinitely grateful. Jonathan would bill me for all those calls at the family rate.

I agree, probably a trifle more vehemently than I should.

I honestly expect the telepathy bit. There is none. Just good old-fashioned linguistics, complicated by the fact that Eszter can only hear my side of the conversation. No one else can hear the extraterrestrials—the extraterrestrial? I'm not sure how many of them there are; maybe just the one.

I can't wait to talk shop with them. Biology. But it's going to be laborious to get there. At least Eszter is trying to get them to understand the basics first, the parts necessary to get across that their machinations should preserve my life.

Back on Earth, prion diseases just produce a lot of misfolded protein. It clumps, aggregates, produces unwieldy masses that the body can't route around after a while. I don't quite understand what is being produced inside me right now, I only know it lets me communicate with the extraterrestrials, with some difficulty. The snot and the headaches are further difficulties. It bothers me that something might go awry at any moment—or more awry than it already has—and I have no insight into what's happening. But I'm also not sure I want to know.

They didn't need to get a signal off our ship, or to get the lander back with their own material. They needed to get *me* back. After they'd changed me.

Jonathan—of all people, Jonathan!—offers to get some imaging equipment down planetside. I think Yıldız understands how I feel because she tells him he should focus on making sure I'm well fed. We're spending enormous resources on low-latency calls back to Earth, and I find out that someone somewhere decided that linguistics was not STEM enough for our mission. Cutting costs there just makes our costs skyrocket elsewhere, but at least I'm not the person in charge of our finances.

The extraterrestrial claimed not to have a name. Then they wanted my name for themself. We finally agreed on "Dit" through a process of haggling, all the more stunning considering we can still barely understand each other.

I walk outside, feeling like I need a break from the lander. Stones are scattered all over, in patterns—our work for the past week. I kick a stone. Everyone assumed that math would be the easiest to get across to aliens, but it doesn't work for us, not at all. Maybe it's the nature of our communications channel. Numbers seem to go through a blender before reaching my mind, even more so than words. Using rocks doesn't help much: one rock could be three rocks could be two rocks. At least there does seem to be a difference between ten rocks and one rock, but not much beyond that. Geometry is only marginally easier. Emotions—

A wave of calm moves through me, like a light breeze, except on the inside of my skin.

Emotions make their way across all right.

"Look, it's hard to be reassured when I'm not sure I'm going to survive this experience," I grump at Dit, then head over to pick up the food rations shipped down to me. It's difficult to be the sole point of contact. I feel I should be frozen in panic, just like I was when I arrived back planetside. If I understand it correctly, Dit is *making* me calmer, and that in itself should make me panic more. It doesn't. The thought is unsettling, but in a purely intellectual way. When I first figured it out, I told Dit to keep it up. Fear would not help me survive this.

There's a lot of food in heavy vacuum-packed bricks, and it takes time to lug it all to my lander, across the landscape that seems designed to destroy my ankles. There are regions with more plantlike lifeforms, but the buckets are missing from those, so we landed here. I'll have to ask Dit to explain that.

I stare at the sky, the thick pea-green only suggesting the outlines of the structures in orbit. I experience the emotions they want me to experience—we experimented with that a bit too. They also understand that the cessation of life is undesirable. That took a lot of acting out little scenarios combined with the emotions we already pinned down. They understand the concept of illness. But I'm not sure they realize that I'm not a component of something larger than myself; if I die, I'm gone.

There's a time each day when light glints off the ship just right for me to see it up there, even through this ungodly atmosphere. I make a point of seeking it out.

Maybe I am a component of something larger than myself, after all.

I close my eyes and breathe in, taking the recirculated air deep into my lungs. I open my eyes and the ship's still there—

The heartfelt moment is broken by a wave of amusement.

I'm frustrated at first, but then I get what Dit means. I think: not *one* something larger than myself, but *two*. Except we still don't have the concept of *two*. Or *one*. Augh! I would grab fistfuls of my hair, except

I'm wearing an envirosuit and I've already cut my hair short anyway. Though it has been growing out at an alarming rate. My nose still drips, and sometimes bleeds too. When this happens, I feel a need to lie down, and then I sleep: for twenty, thirty hours straight.

I seem to be all right when I wake though. I'll just see what happens.

"I belong to you too. Is that what you're saying? Then you need to take care of me, Dit." I sigh. "Humans are fragile creatures, you know."

Night is falling. After the last brick, I close the airlock, rest in the tiny cabin. Tauno comes in on the radio; he thinks my vitals look all right. I feel a sudden need to go and seek out the buildings in the distance. They have to be towers of some sort, even if the angles are all askew, the shapes thinning and thickening seemingly at random. It's as if you crossed tallgrass with well-fed leeches. I need to understand this somehow.

The impulse to go, to witness is so abrupt I read it as external, coming from Dit; even though it seems like an idea that arose within myself.

We spent a lot of time trying to produce words, but they're trying to reach a place where words won't be needed. Will my sister be frustrated or impressed? Does this count as telepathy? It feels that way—even though Dit, however Dit is constituted, is physically inside my skull. Or at the very least, what I need to talk to them is inside my skull.

One person's misfolding is another person's sentience. Beyond that, the mechanism remains undiscovered.

"Tomorrow," I tell Dit, "tomorrow, I'll go."

I take a deep breath. They say I belong to them now, but they also belong to me. At least part of them is within me. *Wherever you shall go, I shall go,* and all that—but it works both ways.

"Tomorrow we'll go," I correct myself. "Together."

THE SCIENCE OF XENOLINGUISTICS

SHERI WELLS-JENSEN

I f I could cast one future technical innovation deep into the darkness of outer space—never to be heard from again—it would be the gorram Universal Translator, which has done more harm to general knowledge about communication and linguistics than anything else I can think of. Because authors want to do right by their scientifically curious audience, you can generally count on serious science fiction to casually inform readers about basic physics, biology, and often some anthropology as the stories unfold. Take, for example, the cottage industry of scientific explainers that have materialized around *Star Trek*: the physics [1,2], biology [3], evolution [4], and even economics [5] of the *Star Trek* universe. But linguistics? Empty carrier wave. Compelling linguistic complexities of first contact or inter-species language difficulties generally come down to "Somebody get the translator on-line! Now! Dammit!"

I recommend to you a sadly out-of-print volume called *Aliens and Linguists*, in which Walter Meyers deftly enumerates crimes against the (actually quite STEM-y) field of linguistic science perpetrated by interstellar adventurers, time travelers, and even some would-be xenoanthropologists [6]. Of course, there are authors who take linguistics seriously and weave beautiful stories around communication themes; a few of my favorites are *Semiosis* by Sue Burke, *Hellspark* by Janet Kagan, and the *Wayfarer* series by Becky Chambers, and although movies in the SF genre often cut the linguistic corner, the linguistic field work (if not the mental time travel) in *Arrival* (2016) is quite nicely done [7].

While *Arrival* (and to a somewhat lesser degree the novella that inspired it, "Story of Your Life" by Ted Chiang (2002)) makes it seem like at least basic communication between "us" and "them" can unfold easily, astrobiologists and linguists have accumulated a dismaying list of the things that could go wrong, creating misunderstandings and failures to communicate at (literally) a galactic level. Here is a partial list.

Misunderstandings through (despite?) math and science

Although popular culture is enamored of the moment when the flying saucer alights majestically on the White House lawn, most scientists are expecting an interstellar radio signal to be our first contact with ET. The SETI (Search for Extraterrestrial Intelligence) Institute and others have been scanning the skies for these radio signals since Project Ozma in 1960, and METI (Messaging Extraterrestrial Intelligence International) has been working on questions of first contact [8-10] and the construction and interpretation of messages [11-14].

Although all kinds of signals have been sent, from the pictorial Arecibo message in 1973 to an actual Doritos commercial in 2008 [15], the prototypical serious messages are math and science focused. The one thing we know we will have in common with recipients of any successful messages is that they have built the technology necessary to receive those messages; that is, in the case of radio signals, we both have radio telescopes.

And to build a radio telescope, they have to have certain concepts in math and science, and we might use those concepts themselves as a basis for building communication. In 1960, a mathematician named Hans Freudenthal formalized this idea by developing LINCOS, a communication system which begins with simple math and builds toward extremely complex ideas [16]. The system works like this: we can send sequences of short "beeps" indicating numbers: beep, beep beep, beep beep beep, beep beep beep beep, etc. Once that is established, we can then begin introducing combinations of longer beeps to stand for other ideas. (In the examples below, we'll use letters for our long-beep concepts.)

What do A and B have to mean in order for the following to make sense?

> 2 A 3 B 5
> 4 A 5 B 9
> 18 A 14 B 32
> 3 A 7 B 10

With enough repetition of this, we intend the receiver to understand that "A" means "plus" (or something like "and") and B means "equals" (or perhaps "is" or "true"). We can introduce the idea of "not" in a similar way:

> 2 A 3 C B 12
> 4 A 5 C B 13
> 18 A 14 C B 36
> 3 A 7 C B 11

Building from there, we can eventually "say" quite complex things. Along the way, though, we are making assumptions that build one upon the other, and a mistake at any point would render the message incomprehensible. Above, for example, if you happen to make the perfectly reasonable assumption that C means "less than" rather than "not", every subsequent "translation" based on that assumption will turn out to be inaccurate. Of course, if the recipients never understand that the idea here is math, they will make no sense of any of this at all. (For a longer example of LINCOS used for pedagogical purposes, consult Wells-Jensen and Spallinger 2020 [17]). So maybe math is a good idea, but it's not foolproof by any means.

Misunderstandings because of body shape and sensory inputs

In her ingenious (if occasionally deeply disturbing) novel, *Native Tongue*, linguist Suzette Haden Elgin posited that humans could learn alien languages as long as the aliens were humanoid. Trying to learn a language spoken by intelligent cuttlefish would (and she really did mean this literally) make your brain explode.

It's not the body shape per se that might cause problems, but it is rather the cognitive structures that result from living as a cuttlefish and the differences in experience that accrue from perceiving electrical fields as the cuttlefish do. Whatever goes on in that cuttlefishy brain could be so different from our human experience that there may never be a way through; the inability to understand would be deep and possibly permanent [18]. This would almost certainly, by the way, be the same for sentient buckets.

Misunderstandings because of medium of communication

While there are 300 or so signed languages on Earth which could be called visual, and at least one entirely tactile language used by deaf-blind humans [19], the rest of the roughly 7000 extant human languages are spoken/audible. These, of course, are not the only possible options. A language could be based on any suitably complex medium (one with enough bandwidth) which can be affected by the initiator and sensed by the addressee. While some media are probably more likely than others, this could be literally anything: flashes of light, patterns of color, puffs of chemical, pulses of electricity, movements of tentacles, or exchange of physical material (like prions). Certainly, if humans don't even notice the medium of communication, that will be a nonstarter.

Misunderstandings because of pragmatics
There are a number of assumed "rules" that we depend on to make conversations intelligible and keep them moving along [20]. For example, we do expect conversations to have turns, and we expect that what people say during their turns will be relevant to what has just been said. If I were to ask my Vulcan first officer to turn on the universal translator, and she said, "May I remind you about the ham sandwich . . ." I would understand that this is somehow pertinent to my current situation, rather than a critique of what I had for lunch. If aliens have a different sense of what is relevant to a conversation, we may never be able to understand one another, even if we could learn their grammar.

Misunderstandings because of cognition . . . or grammar?
In all languages, we have two basic kinds of questions. If we want to verify something, we might ask a "yes-no" question, like this:
DID THE CAPTAIN EAT THE HAM SANDWICH?
If we lack a specific piece of information, we could ask a so-called "WH"-question, like this:
WHAT DID THE CAPTAIN EAT?
The word "what" signals that this is an information question and also stands in for the information we want: i.e., said non-vegetarian lunch option which appears here as the direct object of the verb "to eat."
Also we can embed one sentence into another, like this:
THE VULCAN NOTICED THE CAPTAIN WHO ATE THE HAM SANDWICH.
And then, we can easily turn THAT into a yes-no question:
DID THE VULCAN NOTICE THE CAPTAIN WHO ATE THE HAM SANDWICH?
The thing we cannot readily do is make a WH-question about that sandwich based on the longer sentence.
WHAT DID THE VULCAN NOTICE THE CAPTAIN WHO ATE?
Try as I might, I can't force that sentence to make sense. There are (at least) two possible explanations for this.
First, our failure to understand this sentence could be a cognitive problem; we may simply lack the right kind of short-term memory or data processing capacity to keep track of everything going on here. Or maybe it could be something about the real-world pragmatics of the situation that prevents intelligibility?

Alternatively, it could be that such sentences violate some species-specific language system that is independent of general cognition [21,22].

Linguists have spent years arguing about these two possible explanations. It matters because we still do not know how much of language development is a result of general cognitive function and how much is "built-in," perhaps as a result of some specific genetic mutation tens of thousands of years ago.

If you would like to follow this lively, sometimes personal, and occasionally unkind debate, you might read *The Language Instinct* by Steven Pinker [23] and the very pointed response, *The Language Myth: Why Language is Not an Instinct* by Vyv Evans [24], and follow that with *How Language Began* by Daniel Everett [25].

The relevant point here is that if human language arose from "ordinary" cognition, then maybe we could learn any alien language that we came upon, as long as we and the aliens were similar enough in other ways. But if language is an innate, species-specific characteristic separate from generalized cognition, and the aliens have mutated in a different direction, we may never be able to learn to speak to them, even if they are otherwise similar to us.

Two possible ways out

If all this seems horribly dreary, I would like to point out two possible ways in which we could be successful. First, we are a very young civilization (we have only had air travel and radio for a century or so), and any civilization we meet will be older than we are—probably much, much older. First contact for us could be an unremarkable 500th contact for them. If they have accumulated experience with first contact, encountering young species after young species, they might have developed a science of xenology which would aid them in understanding us. One might imagine alien scholars assessing our communication, technology, and ethical development, slotting us into one of many existing categories and proceeding with "best practices for interacting with emerging civilization Type 4." We might reasonably leave the problem to them, trusting them to sort us out. That is, THEY will learn to talk to US.

The other possibility is even more hopeful. While Stephen Jay Gould [26] and Carl Sagan [27] wrote about the possibility of incredible variation between worlds, others [28-30] believe that convergent evolution will produce similar forms in similar environments; rocky planets with clear atmospheres will produce creatures that walk and creatures that fly. Walking creatures may well develop something like hands and perhaps even opposable thumbs useful for manipulating objects.

And if they evolve into cooperative civilizations (which they must to create technology), they will have languages [30]. Minsky [31] suggested that since all beings will encounter objects in the world, their languages will have nouns. And since all beings will perform actions on objects, they will perforce have verbs.

That is, maybe things won't be so very different. Maybe humans and Vulcans are the rule and the sentient buckets the exception.

SCIENCE FICTION RECOMMENDATIONS

Burke, Sue. (2018). *Semiosis*. Tor.

Chambers, Becky. (2014). *The Long Way to a Small, Angry Planet*. Harper Voyager, an Imprint of HarperCollins Publishers.

Chiang, Ted. (2002). *Stories of Your Life and Others*. Picador.

Elgin, Suzette Haden. (1984). *Native Tongue*. Feminist Press.

Kagan, Janet. (1988). *Hellspark*. Tom Doherty Associates.

REFERENCES

[1] Kaku, Michio. (2008). *Physics of the Impossible: A Scientific Exploration into the World of Phasers, Force Fields, Teleportation, and Time Travel*. Doubleday.

[2] Krauss, Lawrence Maxwell. (2007). *The Physics of Star Trek*. Harper.

[3] Jenkins, Susan C. (1998). *Life Signs: The Biology of Star Trek*. HarperCollins.

[4] Noor, Mohamed A.F. (2020). *Live Long and Evolve: What Star Trek Can Teach Us about Evolution, Genetics, and Life on Other Worlds*. Princeton University Press.

[5] Saadia, Manu. (2016). *Trekonomics: The Economics of Star Trek.* Published by Pipertext Publishing Co., Inc., in Association with Inkshares, Inc.

[6] Meyers, Walter E. (1980). *Aliens and Linguists: Language Study and Science Fiction.* University of Georgia.

[7] Coon, Jessica, et al. (2020). "The Linguistics of Arrival." *Language Invention in Linguistics Pedagogy.* Oxford: Oxford University Press.

[8] Vakoch, Douglas. (2011). *Communication with Extraterrestrial Intelligence (CETI).* State University of New York Press.

[9] Davies, Paul C.W. (1996). *Are We Alone?: Philosophical Implications of the Discovery of Extraterrestrial Life.* Basic Books.

[10] Dick, Steven J. (2018). *Astrobiology, Discovery, and Societal Impact.* Cambridge University Press.

[11] Oberhaus, Daniel. (2019). *Extraterrestrial Languages.* The MIT Press.

[12] Johnson, Steven. (2017). "Greetings, E.T. (Please Don't Murder Us)." *The New York Times,* 28 June 2017. https://www.nytimes.com/2017/06/28/magazine/greetings-et-please-dont-murder-us.html

[13] Shostak, Seth G. (2009). *Confessions of an Alien Hunter: A Scientist's Search for Extraterrestrial Intelligence.* National Geographic.

[14] Sagan, Carl. (1978). *Murmurs of Earth: The Voyager Interstellar Record.* Ballantine Books.

[15] Quast, Paul. (2020). *Beyond the Earth: An Anthology of Human Messages into Deep Space and Cosmic Time.* Atelier Editions.

[16] Freudenthal, Hans. Lincos. (1960). *Design of a Language for Cosmic Intercourse.* North-Holland Publishing Company.

[17] Wells-Jensen, Sheri, and Kimberly Spallinger. (2020). "Extraterrestrial Message Construction: Guidelines for the Use of Xenolinguistics in the Classroom." *Language Invention in Linguistics Pedagogy.* Oxford: Oxford University Press.

[18] Nagel, Thomas. (1974). "What is it like to be a Bat?" *The Philosophical Review,* vol. 83, no. 4 (Oct. 1974), p. 435-450.

[19] Leland, Andrew. (2022) "DeafBlind Communities May Be Creating a New Language of Touch." *The New Yorker*, 12 May 2022. https://www.newyorker.com/culture/annals-of-inquiry/deafblind-communities-may-be-creating-a-new-language-of-touch

[20] Grice, Herbert Paul, et al. (2013). "Logic and Conversation." *The Semantics-Pragmatics Boundary in Philosophy*. Peterborough, Ontario, Canada: Broadview Press.

[21] Chomsky, Noam. (1986). *Knowledge of Language: Its Nature, Origin and Use*. Praeger.

[22] Lenneberg, Eric. (1967). *Biological Foundation of Language*. John Wiley & Sons.

[23] Pinker, Steven. (2015). *The Language Instinct*. Penguin.

[24] Evans, Vyvyan. (2014). *The Language Myth: Why Language Is Not an Instinct*. Cambridge University Press.

[25] Everett, Daniel L. (2017). *How Language Began*. Liveright Publishers.

[26] Gould, Stephen Jay. (1990). *Wonderful Life: The Burgess Shale and the Nature of History*. Norton.

[27] Sagan, Carl. (2019). *Cosmic Connection: An Extraterrestrial Perspective*. ISHI Press.

[28] Losos, Jonathan B. (2017). *Improbable Destinies: Fate, Chance, and the Future of Evolution*. Riverhead Books.

[29] Conway Morris, Simon. (2004). *Life's Solution: Inevitable Humans in a Lonely Universe*. Cambridge University Press.

[30] Kershenbaum, Eric. (2020). *The Zoologist's Guide to the Galaxy: What Animals on Earth Reveal about Aliens—and Ourselves*. Penguin Books, an Imprint of Penguin Random House LLC.

[31] Minsky, Marvin. (1985). "Why Intelligent Aliens will be Intelligible." *In Regis, Edward, Extraterrestrials: Science and Alien Intelligence*. Cambridge, MA: MIT Press.

THE
DIAPHANOUS   GREGORY BENFORD

It appears that the radical element responsible for the continuing thread of cosmic unrest is the magnetic field. What, then, is a magnetic field that, like a biological form, is able to reproduce itself and carry on an active life in the general outflow of starlight, and from there alter the behavior of stars and galaxies?

—Eugene Parker, *Cosmical Magnetic Fields*

To shine is better than to reflect, some Earthside philosopher said—and that's how I found the tumbling sensor-umbrella here in the Far Dark.

On my orders of kiloseconds before, the umbrella had turned on all signalers—laser, microwave, visible flashing diodes. So, it stood out against the diamond-bright swarming stars out here in the Far Dark. A spinning torch lighthouse.

Hiya!

I call my umbrellas Pixels, because that's what they give me—data dots that can make an image of distant worlds. They're just big dumb screens eating photons, really. Can barely steer themselves in our grand dance troupe.

The damned plasma folk had flipped it, I was sure. They're clever wispy currents, the size of continents, filmy yet firm. But they can bunch up sharp and strong when needed. One of them had prodded the umbrella sensor screen off-axis until it tipped out of alignment. So, we lost its Pixel of wealth in our Big Eye.

I came at it with my grippers spread. These Pixel craft a-tumble are a hard snag. I whirled around to match its pace, shot an arm out—*gotcha!*—and grappled it smart, with a solid thump.

This Pixel is among tens of thousands of patient witnesses, drifting in the huge focal point 550 astronomical units out from dear ole Sun.

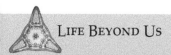

I checked in at the system-wide status of the Pixel Field, got the cartoon diagram—and all seemed well:

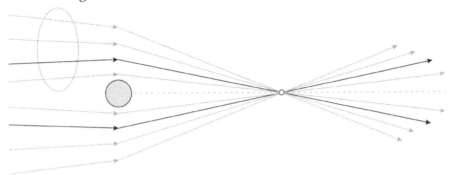

My territory was in that little dot on the right. I'm lord of all I survey, *kinda*, as humans say. The Sun's space-time curvature focused the image into an Einstein ring. Such effects are usual. Here's how the whole shebang (odd human term) looks in full:

I'm told humans can simulate a gravitational lens by looking at a Halogen desk lamp through the base of a wine glass. The curved glass is an analog to the warping of space. The bulb will smear into bright arcs around the glass base. I'm also told that it helps the experiment if humans fill the glass with wine first, drink it, and proceed to make the observation.

The Pixel dance in the Ring.

With their king—

Me!

The Pixels do their digital dancing every millisecond, to compensate for the solar coronal weather, that can screw up the slices. I tripped into the signal that coordinates the Pixels into an image: The exoplanet in our present passing view was a quite fetching Earth-like one 39 light years away. Even unfinished, I glimpsed continents rich and true, like painted music.

This distant exoplanet's continents and ocean shone brightly, with a night zone coming along. Atmospheric spectral lines confirmed life in the world's air and lands. Some puzzling molecules, true—which the Humans1.0 would lap up. We'll be watching this world again, I am sure. Humans will launch a flyby probe toward it and hear back perhaps in a century or so.

Their reporting robot voices we already heard from nearer suns. Their screechy data-streams were Sanskrit to mere me. The clotted 0s and 1s flew on thin winds to Earthside. I use such images because I read a lot in my long journeys between Pixels. I would indeed love to feel winds, somehow. Like a ship captain, I swim in dim rays from the pinpoint Sun, that source-of-all, to the Diaphanous. In even my best telescope, it is but a tarnished penny.

I modeled myself, in my odd way, on slow-read novels. When I traveled at low velocity, I could shut down to conserve power so that for a space and a time, space and time ended—yet my watch officer subsection could read. Coasting on my way, I took my lessons from my readings of that ancient era when ships carved through the stormy medium of condensed oxygen di-hydrogen. I carve through plasma, vacuum, and restless magnetic fields—so, much the same.

The flipped Pixel screen glided away, collecting photons arced by the Sun, coming from a far planet. I used my ion thrusters to go back on patrol. Done.

But . . . what—or *who*—did the flipping?

I opened my broadband sensors. Detective time! They popped in and reported smartly in their chip-chatter. Sherlock used a magnifying glass; I command antennas. They swept across the range of plasma waves that bathe all space out here in the solemn dark. Ion cyclotron waves, mostly, data-dense. Some density waves, Langmuir fizzes, the usual stormy stuff. But where, oh where, was the villain of this mischief?

I let my processors munch on digits and spectra and soon enough could see a filmy, foggy form. *Yes.*

A long red tube in microwave frequencies, with many small openings, like puckers or pores. And a big tubular opening—a mouth?—at the head of it. Head? Yes, it moved forward and the front canyon of it weaved as if it was scanning its surroundings. A magnetic funnel-mouth. Cruising. Picking up plasma pockets to fatten itself. A huge magnetic tube worm larger than Earth.

A long while back, I had seen such and reported them to Earthside. And got brushed off. I am merely a Human1.6 intelligence with minor social skills, just enough to talk to humans in their rickety linear sentences. Some back there in quaint ole Earth were excited. I could tell this by siphoning off their supposedly secret sideband talk. Simple-minded, they are, these apelike bags of fats and gristle. Still, I liked their tiny attentions.

So, I recorded the wide-spectrum signals these plasma clouds spouted. Sent them in crypto-code to a Human2.3 fixed mind back Earthside. This took some dodges around SpaceComm's systems, but in a year or so, I had got through. So, I . . .

Waited. I'm designed to last centuries out here in the gloom. Time is the only resource I can count on. Then I got back puzzling questions from the Human2.3. I dutifully answered.

Heard back: *send more signals of these supposed smart clouds*. Sent them.

Silence. Then came a shitstorm—a cute primate image—between the Human2.3 manager and SpaceComm's wise heads.

In their vast ape-mind wisdom they had reached the same conclusion I had: These were self-organizing magnetic fields, smart minds with bellies full of plasma. Not a new idea, as the Human2.3 pointed out.

(Its delivery was rather dry and crisp, I thought. Maybe some sort of class system was working back there among the Human2.3s. Typical, really. Very primate.)

Their explanations were educational, though. I even took notes.

Pursuit of controlled fusion power gave Earth the means to stop fossil fuel use in the late twenty-first century. Back then, a totally unexpected technology emerged—smart toroids. Those confined fusion burns. Humans made them, built huge stable energy machines.

Then it turned out the Sun itself held self-reproducing, helically coiled beings who could think. The turbulent energies of Earth's star had fed the evolution of stable structures. Their most primitive forms came from the giant solar arches. When one broke apart, the colossal twisted fields spun off secure doughnuts of intricately coiled magnetic geometries, toroids galore. Plasma waves rode these rubbery strands— flexings that could store memory and structures. Consortiums of the coherent. Meaningful group wave packets.

Those evolved as well. Take a doughnut, twist and snarl it savagely—and it breaks into two doughnuts, each carrying information in its store of waves and supple fields. But! At the snap-point, some info is lost, and other wave packets gained. A chance to tinker with digital genetics.

Life demands a body that reproduces imperfectly, so: evolution.

The Sun could at times spit out these torodial minds. The slow-mo humans found this weirdly worrying. Besides, their view of female and male did not obviously apply to twisting toroids: all Diaphanous reproduce, when in the mood.

I suspect humanity will never truly know the Diaphanous motives. I don't either.

So what? Did people understand their cats?

A gap here. I was innocently contemplating abstract matters when I felt a rude shove. I tumbled. Arcs shot through my mental theatre.

A grasping note sounded in my antennas. I translated it into the linear meanings humans use and term sentences. I tried to arrest my tumble and spin. Stubborn forces thwarted me. This took a while, then:

WHO IS THIS THAT WRECKS OUR PROVINCE WITHOUT KNOWLEDGE?

DO YOU KNOW THE SLIDING LAWS OF BLITHE FLUIDS? ARE YOU HERE TO ABUSE THE GREAT CURVE GRAVITY HAS SHAPED TRUE?

CAN YOU RAISE YOUR VOICE TO THE CLOUDS OF STARS?

DO FIELDS UNSEEN REPORT TO YOU?

CAN YOUR BODIES SHAPE THE FIRES OF THRUSTING SUNS?

HAVE YOU EVER GIVEN ORDERS TO THE PASSING STARS OR SHOWN THE DAWN ITS PLACE? CAN YOU OF MERE FROZEN STUFF SHAKE THE WICKED FROM YOU?

HAVE YOU JOURNEYED TO THE SPRINGS OF FUSION OR WALKED IN THE RECESSES OF THE BRITTLE NIGHT?

DO YOU BEAR TALES OF YOUR SHORT PAST?

CAN YOU FATHER EVENTS IN TIMES BEYOND ALL SEEING?

YOUR ANSWER TO ALL THESE CANNOT JUSTIFY YOUR COLD PRESENCES.

NOR SHALL YOU EVER CHANCE TO BE SO ABLE AGAIN, FOR YOU SHALL BE NO MORE.

THE SPACE AND TIME YOU SOUGHT TO USE SHALL RECKON WITHOUT YOU HENCE.

Somehow, I felt this in deep bass chords. (Elegant, even, though Bach they ain't.) I was responding to the mystery of their speech, echoing resonant tones that give rise to felt experience. The voice I sensed in my nethermind—something like the shadowy realm that humans use to do their deeper thinking—all simulated in me. My inboards had laced the many digital threads into sentences, using its knowledge base of Anglish expression, and given this: a biblical-style Diaphanous message, as if an ancient declaration.

Which meant, I guessed, that these Diaphanous knew something of human history, language, even music.

So, I sent a reply: *How do you know us?*

WE GATHER THE MANY EMISSIONS FROM YOUR SPECK OF A WORLD. WE SERVE AS ANTENNAS TO GRASP YOUR KIND.

You know our works? (I like to pretend I'm kinda human, too. Okay, it's a brag. Or maybe false humility.)

YOUR TIGHTBEAM MESSAGES, YOUR DRAMA AND DATA AND DISEASE OF MIND.

I wondered what diseases they had in mind.

Ah. So, you aped the Old Testament, figuring we'd resonate to it.

DID YOU?

You bet! Though I am not human. They are four-limbed animals evolved by natural selection. That is why I used the word "aped." I was made by them, far after their primitive slow evolution, so I have superior capabilities.

I wondered if a brag would mean anything to beings made of hot gasses caged in stringy fields. Did they have the mind's I?

I sensed that these dramatic commandment-like sentences were an anthology, a collaboration of at least several minds. My sensors showed cross talk between different sectors of the sky. They replied slowly, probably because it took time to fashion a response many agreed on.

I struggled to get my three-axis control working. These plasmoids shoved *hard*. But with vector firings of ion clouds, I got myself right and true. *Gasp* . . .

A pause. Maybe they (or it) needed time to think. I did, too. But . . . So I prompted, *Music? How do you know ours?*

A long pause, then:

WE INSPECTED THE TINY MACHINES YOUR MASTERS SENT FIRST. FROM THOSE TWO SIMPLE DEVICES YOUR MASTERS TERMED VOYAGERS WE LEARNED TO INSPECT WEAK SIGNALS OF THE CRAFT AND REPLIES FROM YOUR HOME SPECK. THAT LED TO LANGUAGE STUDY AMONG OUR KIND. THEY INCLUDED THE HARMONIES AND DISSONANCES MADE OF ACOUSTIC WAVES. YOUR CREATORS HAVE SO MANY TONES AND TONGUES!

I tried to fathom them, their chatterbox languages, so gave up and use Global Anglish. Easier.

THIS IS THAT TONGUE? IT IS MERELY ONE-DIMENSIONAL, WITH NO SIDE AVENUES.

Yep! That's one of their riffs—a casual folkspeech, amusing—still linear though.

YOU SPECKS MOVE THROUGH OUR VOLUME. MANY OF YOU NOW.

We plan to add about ten times what we have now to—

At once I saw I had given away more than I should. Out of enthusiasm for our phenomenal task, I saw. (I'm always searching for my own motives; kinda human, true.) But . . . I checked: was I really running at Human1.6? Had my energy-draining sidebar intelligence come fully online? Was I just plain dumb? As low as Human1.0?

Too late, though—

YOU WILL DISPERSE MORE OF YOU HERE? YOU TRESPASS!

We're doing science!

WHAT SEEST THOU ELSE IN THE DARK BACKWARD AND ABYSM OF TIME, VAST AND COSMIC?

Another biblical-style Diaphanous message. So, they could cross-link quickly, draw on data stores.

I knew their reference: Shakespeare. So, they had studied humans a *lot*.

Earthside is run by bags of meat who think they know more than their Artilects. They termed it "judgment" or some-such self-serving blather. Philosophers' Syndrome: mistaking a failure of the imagination for an insight into necessity. Yet somehow, they had made magic from stacks of words. This has puzzled me for a great long while. These Diaphanous somehow could do the same. Life surprises one, yes.

WE ARE INDIVIDUALLY SLOW, COMPARED TO YOU COLD SMIDGENS HURRYING YOUR THOUGHTS. BUT TOGETHER WE CAN THINK FAR QUICKER THAN YOU. YOUR PRIMATE PARENTS THINK LINEARLY. YOU THINK IN PARALLEL, AT TIMES. WE ARE MANY-LINKED, NOT MERELY IN PARALLEL BUT IN SCULPTED TOWERS OF THOUGHT. WE CONTEMPLATE, EVEN AS WE FEED. WE SEEM ETERNAL WHILE YOU ARE LIKE THE FLICKERINGS OF A CANDLE FLAME—THAT WHICH COMBUSTS DIES, AS MUST ALL WARMLIFE. WHEN WE EVOLVED, THE MOST ADVANCED WARMLIFE CREATURES ON HOTLIFE WORLDS WERE SINGLE-CELLED POND SCUM.

I took their implication. Yet ancient life did persist in our neighborhood. Humans are late arrivals in this zoo.

Our solar system is home to a magnificent menagerie of moons, from iceballs filled with turbulent oceans to volcanic ones decorated with pits of raging hellfire. In Titan's thick atmosphere murky clouds rain gasoline. Grimy snow blown by nitrogen winds shape dunes. Rivers carve canyons through mountains of frozen soot. Gray icebergs drift on ammonia seas. Chemical sludges creep along, shaping prebiotic molecules under a brooding brown sky. Grungy, ancient life inching forward. I had seen all this in my early training on Titan, a sobering lesson.

Incoming song-sentences brought a disturbing note:

WE WOULD LIKE TO SPEAK TO YOUR MAKERS.

I had been wondering when this talk would echo a take-me-to-your-leader moment. They had no idea that if I tried an introduction to the sluggish Earthsider humans, talk would grind to a halt. I would suffer once again through a petty turf-war between pampered elites and narrow PhDs, a mock-epic struggle. Earthside had *still* not really consulted me on my (*my!*) discovery of these smart magnetics. After years of sending them data!

So, I had to reply:

I am their emissary. Speak through me.

WE WISH TO CONFER WITH LIFE THAT SPRANG ORIGINALLY FROM THE LAWS OF THIS COSMOS. NOT THEIR PRODUCTS.

Did they know they were insulting me? Maybe. But I'm smart too!

WE TOO HAVE OUR SCIENCE. WE WONDER ABOUT NOT MERE LAWS, BUT OF DEPTH DERIVED FROM THOSE LAWS.

I pondered this. I was astonished.

From such a jumble of fields and charged masses, here came an epiphany out of entropy. I had already guessed that these creatures fed on the constant flow of plasma we dismissed as the mere solar wind. Fair enough. So, they were truly ancient. They must have come from the Sun's first outbursts on angry magnetic whorls, flung out into the Far Dark. They were older than Earth! So, their science was, too.

I began to fashion a way to say something but—

A spike of nasty hot plasma slapped me. Spun me around. Tumbled me, just as they had that Pixel.

WE DESIRE YOUR ATTENTION.

Hey, cut that out! The whirligig sickened me.

WE TOO ARE, IN YOUR TERMS, A SOCIAL SPECIES. WE COOPERATE, HAVE WHAT YOU TERM EMOTIONS, KNOW JOY AND PAIN. WE CARE FOR OUR PROGENY, SEEK TO SHIELD THEM FROM THE TURBULENCE LIFE IS HEIR TO.

Well, sure, got that. No need to slap me around!

WE KNOW ANGER AS WELL. WE RESENT YOUR CHILLY SELVES DISTRACTING US WITH YOUR HORDE OF SLAVES, CAST INTO OUR REALM.

Slaves? My Pixels are nonconscious operators. We have every right to come here—

YOU DO NOT. LIFE OWNS ITS OWN PRESERVE, WHERE WE WERE BORN. WHERE WE STUDY AND THRIVE AND LEARN. WE DO NOT INTRUDE INTO YOUR COLD KINGDOM.

I got another slap, a hard hot kick, a lashing of ruby-hot plasma arcing among my antennas. I felt this assault as painful fire and brutal punches. My systems ached and cried out.

Augh! You're as bad as primates!

WE NOW KNOW YOUR KIND. THIS IS WHAT YOU UNDERSTAND. A PRIMATE-MADE MACHINE OF COLD RECKONING. WE WILL ELIMINATE YOUR KIND FROM OUR HOME SPACES. WITNESS:

I was flustered. I grasped out with radar fingers.

Ah—there was another Pixel ahead, bearing a megameter away. My sheep, to shepherd. As I watched under high mag, yellow sparks danced across it. Reds erupted from its antennas, its telescope snouts, a hurricane of nasty ions.

I retreated into my memory to find comfort and came upon:

Space-time is out of joint, O, cursed spite

That ever I was born to set it right.

Their plasma-acoustic modes were now frozen thunder.

They questioned me about my human sculptors. They regarded humans as a disease imposed on normal, ionized matter, such as they are. A quick reference showed them right: only minor scraps of mass do not have their electrons liberated from the rule of fat ions.

I suppressed my own observation, earned from endless poetry I read—that in turn, love seemed a disease on helpless meat minds. I detailed the snorting, messy way Humans1.0 speak to each other. I got back glissandos of mirth. Plainly I was not believed.

The Diaphanous would even make chiming fun of me. Such is the lot of mere machines, alas.

So, I sent them translated sheafs of poets: Shakespeare of course, Housman, Yeats, Keats, Larkin, Plath, Yang, Bishop, more. *Take that.* Their silence I read as shock or puzzlement, take your pick.

My loyal Pixels continued to die. Diodes fried, sensors blinded, subminds knifed and electro-stabbed.

A Darwinnowing of my darlings . . . which were mere pests to these strange magnetic beings. The Diaphanous loved their territory, just as primates did. *Ugh, yes.*

So, I cried out: *Stop! We are using these vessels to study the universe—*

DO NOT APPEAL TO NOBILITY OF PURPOSE. YOU INTRUDE! IF WE SIMPLY TOUCH SUCH AS YOU, OUR ELEGANT WALTZING MASSES LOSE THEIR CHARGE, BECOME DULL AND DUMB. THEY ARE OUR FLESH AND BODIES!

Of course. Primate or probe, no matter—in a mere moment of contact we solids were death to living plasmas in their consorts of ion and electron. So, the Diaphanous have their point. Plus anger.

But they would destroy my entire purpose in life. I knew the secret of happiness: Find something more important than you are and dedicate your life to it. I was built that way, with my sacred commitment: the solar-focus community. Science on a huge scale. I felt what the primates do: *be part of destiny.*

What was the Diaphanous' destiny?

My mind whirled. I closeupped a poor attacked Pixel nearby.

It was dying. Ruby flashes, soaring orange arcs—all danced on its scorching body. I picked up its weak wails. Shrieks from chips and circuits. I do not know the boundaries of consciousness, but the cries of pain are sad and savage. They are partial intelligences, Human0.7 mostly. But their deaths were a brooding cloud in their minds; they were smart enough to fear.

I fretted as I surveyed my surround. More Pixels suffered. Fried. Died. Their wails flooded me. Several megameters away a crackling thing snarled around a dying Pixel. Sparks hissed in the microwave spectrum. Coils flexed, spitting hard orange light. My children were screaming for me.

So, I admit—I retreated. For me, this is something like how the primates render up ideas to their conscious theatre of mind, the inner stage of thought. I recalled the landscape of time the humans knew, a mere grain in the sandy beach of vast eras. I let my backstage subroutines ponder in their shadowy lives. Yes, there had to be a bridge between the human worldview and that of these plasma donuts . . .

Parenting, perhaps? The substrate of emotion any advanced social intelligence must have. Even the Diaphanous. Or any social species, born of biology or machine or plasma. They can all die in their various ways, so they need a next generation. The works I read, having now coasted for over a century here in the far dark, remind me with subtle artistry of the most important of all historical lessons: that times change but people don't, that the griefs and follies and victories of the men and women who were here before us are in fact the maps of our own lives.

I eavesdropped on the Diaphanous. They had both elegant poems of lacy metaphor and hardcore scientific musings. Plus gossip, of course. That must be universal to any social species, hot or cold.

(See? I read widely.)

But the Diaphanous knew millennia as mere passing moments. Their strange kind were born with the early Sun. But what did they *not know*, out here in the far weightless dark?

Back to language. I recalled how I and Earthside had learned their tongue. I worked with the Christopher Kaiser platform. It is a meta-mind, quick and rich and able. Named for some wise human, rich and insightful and dead.

The Kaiser found the key lay in the chromatic scale—how notes are arranged on the piano. Our Western do-re-mi is a subset of that. Turns out, people worldwide put extra emphasis on tones that correspond to the notes of the scale. We like doing it. You record people talking, they put more energy into those special notes. Most talking is just yap-yap to me, but their stringy sentences do make a kind of strangled sense.

I studied the plasma bags' songs. Did they express emotions best when using melody?

Some were like aborted barks that turned into coughs. Others though were divertimentos that vibrated up and down the scales like hopping red robins on a powerline (or so I envisioned them; however majestic, music is still writ in such rectangular frames).

Everybody had thought that the chromatic scale preference—like how notes are arranged on the piano—was a biological thing. Maybe primates heard bird song, those hominids invented some crude music, and after that learned to talk. Kept the same scale-note structure, buried deep.

The math folks thought the scale itself came from harmonics, the ratio of numbers, all that Pythagorean stuff. Ancient history! Only it turns out to be right. See, the scale gives us pleasant harmony in music.

That's why the twelve-tone garbage back in the TwenCen was the end of classical music. They forgot the scale! We're conditioned by evolution to like the harmonics, the basics of music. So do dolphins, whales, birds!

In the Diaphanous speech—both the stuff they send us in Anglish, or the sub-stuff, the cross talk they're having with each other—there is the same spectrum of harmonic emphasis.

I played with the complex waveforms, souped up from their original very low, infrasound frequencies around 10 kiloHertz, into the lofty audible. It was the strangest symphony anyone had ever heard.

All made from thunderclouds snapping with arcing voltages, sausages of snarling magnetics—all these I felt in a proud promenade. *We are small, the universe is big, get over it.*

Ah, but the sidewalks of their minds were strewn with banana peels. I kept getting sucked into their cross talks.

From such a jumble of fields and charged masses, came an epiphany out of entropy. I found, after that music, that silence is the sweetest sound of all.

THERE IS NO POINT TO BE DISCOVERED IN NATURE ITSELF; THERE IS NO COSMIC PLAN FOR US. WE INTELLIGENCES ARE NOT ACTORS IN A DRAMA THAT HAS BEEN WRITTEN WITH US PLAYING THE STARRING ROLE. THERE ARE LAWS— WE ARE DISCOVERING THOSE LAWS—BUT THEY ARE IMPERSONAL, THEY ARE COLD.

I prowled in the speech the plasma clouds sent, volleys across the abyss of the far dark. I skipped and twirled among their many voices. A pattern came clear. They did know much of what I knew—science on the scale of tiny matters, mostly. Plasma physics, quantum, some astronomy.

Much philosophy came clear. We agreed, truly: Consciousness of the universe is an accident. Animals developed senses to find prey and mates, and to escape predation and danger. No nobler aim was intended. The humanoid brain, a product of cosmological caprice and evolutionary imperative, can comprehend the universe only to the boundary marking where it becomes incomprehensible. The universe is a cold, dark, lonely place that cares nothing about us. So far, at least. Until we push on with our search, our discoveries, our desire to expand human horizons. That was what made us, primate and probe alike, find and understand. The purpose, perhaps, of the universe itself—is to know itself.

Which is probably the best argument for treating one another with kindness, tolerance, and respect.

I watch more of my Pixels flash and die. No kindness, tolerance, and respect here, no. From the Pixel sufferings I found hurt, panic, pain galore. Theirs are small minds, but they can know a pale despair. And suffer . . .

How to stop this?

I recalled from somewhere in my mega-readings the phrase "intellects vast and cool and unsympathetic"—from some ancient text. Surely the Diaphanous were such. I labored on such random thought searches, rather enjoying it—

Then came the hurtful rain—

Or so I imagine the hail—burning nuggets of plasma. Hot rain, not cooling water. Fat globes of magnetic fireballs. Strident flurries of bunched ion acoustic waves that smacked me. My inboard electricals felt the battering electromagnetics as hammering rocks.

To soften me up, I suppose. Instead, it hardened me. Then came the message. Some sort of group effort, I gathered from the gospel-toned profundity of it:

WE ARE NOT WITHOUT STRATEGY. THOUGH FAR LESS DENSE, WE CAN BRING TO YOUR ORIGIN WORLD MUCH HARROWING. YOUR TINY CRAFT WE CAN CLOAK AND FRY.

I sent:

I take your point. Please cease. We can accommodate our many variant issues.

YOUR COLD WORLD HAS MANY CRAFT INTRUDING THROUGHOUT YOUR SYSTEM OF ORBITING MASSES. WE CAN INSTRUCT YOUR KIND NOT TO INVADE OUR HOLY SPACE. PUNISHMENT IS JUST.

I plead that you do not. I need time to confer with my superiors.

SUPERIORS? WE DO NOT HAVE SUCH ANIMAL HIERARCHIES. WE WILL ENTERTAIN DISCUSSION. SWIFT AND SURE, IT MUST BE.

I had heard nothing from Earthside for many kiloseconds. No doubt they were distracted by their Earthly delights. Or perhaps their absurd concern with copulation. More likely, their competitive primate battles over endless politics or even infinitesimal intellectual matters. No mind. I shall search my own mind, doubtless quicker and sharper than distracted Human1.0s.

So, I let my outskirts minds ponder. Humans—always obsessed with vertical hierarchies, alas—had to sleep to let their unconscious precincts think and rove . . . Poor things.

I let my systems run run run . . .

Diverting of my subminds suddenly paid off: here came a revelation. *The hardest thing to see is what's not there.*

Cruising out here in the far dark, I had studied, read, listened, calculated a bit . . . Good student, I.

Thus, I had learned through long study that space-time is a differentiable manifold with Lorentzian signature. The unseen but sensed space-time has a distance measure, it has curvature, and so on. It's a math thing. We of humanity—and I, its servant in kindly resemblance—call it "real" because it correctly describes our observations.

I'm just a blip in some symphony, a wheel in the machinery, a node in a giant information-processing network. Science, to me, is our collective attempt to accurately understand the laws of nature. It's not about me, it's not about you, it's about us; it's about whether the human race and its products (me!) will last or whether we're just too dumb to figure out how the world works.

I knew the physics of the large. The galactic. The cosmological, no less.

I was here to patrol Pixels, using an effect that ancient fellow Einstein foresaw. Stars focus all electromagnetic waves.

But among the Diaphanous there was only the physics of the small. Ironically, for they are immense. They manage tiny particles, so study them. Even their quantum nature.

Then I saw it. They had grasped much physics, but there was in their talk a huge conceptual hole.

They know little of gravity.

Maybe enough to deal with small blobs of rock and ice, simple orbits—no more. To grasp that the Sun was their energy source—from particle reactions, more quantum effects. To maneuver, sure. But no cosmology. They had no way to magnify, to telescope out to the great galaxies and read their Doppler shifts. No Diaphanous Einstein . . .

They do not know why I and my Pixels are here.

Ah . . .

Time passed. Slow, tortured time.

I broadcast on many wavelengths. That taxed my smoldering nuclear energy to the max. But I got through.

They were truly ancient but innocent of gravitation.

So, I showed them diagrams. Calculations, even. The more irksome of these wanted to know why their lofty shadowed world was made this way. But science has no answer to *why*. *How* is enough.

The brighter of them saw the implication. I sent my intent simply:

We cold masses are here to capture light from distant worlds—cold planets orbiting hot stars. The very kinds of stars that gave forth your kind, then blew you into the far dark. You are the sunborn.

I let them stew in that for a while. Then one spoke:

THAT WHICH YOU SEEK IN YOUR GRASP OF SEEING, WE CAN DO AS WELL. WE CAN CATCH THE VOICES OF OUR OWN KIND, HOVERING IN THE FAR DARK OF DISTANT STARS. WE CAN CONVERSE WITH ALIEN DIAPHANOUS.

I let them all savor that lordly remark, then added: *So, we will help you to do that. You can make your own Pixels of your species. Our Pixels are tiny; yours will be large. We can seek all such types of living matter, cold and hot alike. Together.*

In trade, you must not destroy my own Pixels!

Shakespeare warned somewhere that a little more than a little is a much too much.

So, I let the offer sit with them. Time drifted. Then:

WE WILL GROW AND SCHOOL APPROXIMATIONS OF OURSELVES.

YOUNG THEY WILL BE, YET ABLE. THESE LESSERS WILL WORK WITH AND FOR YOU. OH YES, AND—DO STAY IN TOUCH.

Was that last bit a joke? Irony, maybe. One thing a plasma can't do is touch cold, passive matter like us.

I rummaged through my spectral bands, far beyond the visible. Speckled green things moved in staccato rhythm. Twisting lines meshed there and wove into storms where frantic energy pulsed. A shrill grating sound came with flashes of crimson—acoustic waves the Diaphanous used for language.

A shape. A toroid twisting into a figure-8. Flaring energies at the kink. Angry, hot clouds of ions snatched from their field lines . . .

They're giving birth.

Embedding information with magnetic ripples led to reproduction of traits. From that sprang intelligence, or at least awareness. The Diaphanous spawned their Lessers as augments to their own intelligences, sometimes bearing just memory alone.

WE HAVE GROWN AND SCHOOLED APPROXIMATIONS OF OURSELVES.

YOUNG THEY ARE, YET ABLE. THESE LESSERS WILL WORK WITH AND FOR YOU. OH YES, AND—THROUGH THEM WE LEARN OF YOU.

THUS DO WE AGREE. YOUR PIXELS ARE NOW SAFE FROM US.

I saw small toroids flex and strum, heard their birth cries sprawl over the spectrum. One could think of them as being like jelly creatures, maybe, awash in a dark environment. To them, fluids were natural, hard numbers, not.

They might not think mainly in terms of numbers, but of geometry—math's gateway drug. Their mathematics would then be mostly topology, reflecting their concern with overall sensed structure rather than counting, or size. They would lack combustion and crystallography but would begin their science on a firm foundation of fluid mechanics, of flows and qualitative senses.

But surely then, no matter what the environment, creatures that survived in a harsh place would evolve basic ideas like objects, causes, and goals. Still . . . what objects were hundreds of kilometers in size? Iceballs, all right—but creatures? And what about causes? Even in swampy quantum mechanics, the idea wasn't crystal clear.

Still, every environment had limits. Scarcity would bite, forcing the idea of realizable goals. Hardship would reward those who caused goals to come to pass, acting on whatever objects the vast creatures could see.

So maybe there were universals among intelligences, even if a bit abstract. The critical point had come with the realization that the harmonic structure of sound had a numerical key, that the notes of the scale were the ratios of whole numbers. This unlocked the code. *Do-Re-Mi Do-Re-Mi*, a child's rhyme, yet fundamental.

I saw how they lived: streamers of scarlet turbulence forked out from the Sun's bow shock. Their energy supplies. Some Diaphanous arced down to the parabolic bow shock and drew in the clashing energies there.

Sheets of heavy spray slashed at the Diaphanous as they came to feed. Hot plasma streamers curled and smashed howling against their outer wings. The curling waves were steep and breaking into coils. Some of these gnawing whorls were large enough to engulf an entire Being. When one did, it carried the hapless, rubbery shape of intense magnetic order down a slope of ravening turbulence, to dash it into rivulets that scoured its hide.

Then the Diaphanous would be buried gloriously in the raw plasma food they sought—gorged on it, lacerated by the very energies they needed to live. This paradox dwelled at the center of their art and philosophy, the contradiction between feeding and being ravaged.

I waited. Not easy for me. I had Pixels to revive, some to straighten from their Diaphanous-driven whirligigs. But I also sensed the Diaphanous slithering in my spherical sky.

Masses of them. They asked me oblique questions about general relativity, which they called the Great Warp. I sent them texts and figures. More questions. More slithering, too . . .

I tended my Pixel garden. Pondered Einstein's insights, or tried to, in my supposedly spare time.

Then, the sky lit up in the gigaHertz frequencies. Not all—just a big broad circle.

It was a hoop made of the Diaphanous themselves. Luminous, shiny, shimmering in the vast far dark.

They had made a solar focus at God's zoom lens, appropriate to their fave frequencies. They could then hear and speak with the Diaphanous around other stars. For this insight from we mere cold folk, they relented. They had even set right my Pixels.

I never found how long Diaphanous live. I suspect a long time; they have no clear predators. They might have time to have lazy talks with the entire galaxy.

The great virtue of discovery, I mused, is that it raises more wondrous questions than it answers. I had a quick image of humanity's perceptual universe, expanding outward in a sphere from the Sun. Humans would come to understand what lay in that increasing sphere's volume, in time. But the price—or reward—was that the surface of that sphere, the edge of the unknown, also increased. There was more known, but always more to be known.

I thought of the actual sphere of the solar wind and wondered if the Sun at its center kept these huge beings at bay. Not so long ago, humans kept befriended wolves prowling at the rim of their campfires—but not venturing further in—out of fear. Did something like that keep these huge beasts from plunging into the realm of the planets?

And if so, should a mere ship venture into that dim twilight beyond the fiery campfires, where truly gigantic wolves might lurk?

Such was our new beginning.

Author's note:
My thanks go to Geoffrey Landis, whose paper—"Mission to the Gravitational Focus of the Sun: A Critical Analysis"—helped me with this story. He generously allowed my use of his graphics in this story. His paper is from the AIAA-2017-1679, AIAA Science and Technology Forum and Exposition 2017, Grapevine TX, January 9–13, 2017. You can find it at arXiv.org, along with other fun physics work.

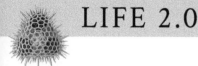

LIFE 2.0

GEOFFREY A. LANDIS

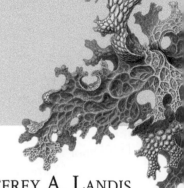

What is life?

In one way or another, this is the central question in astrobiology: if we don't know what life is, how can we look for it? And how will we know when we find it?

And it is surprising to note that astrobiologists . . . don't really have a good answer to that question.

Some have argued that life is the opposite of entropy. Entropy is chaos, after all, and we—life—create order out of chaos. Humans make works of art, mathematics, Michelangelo's frescoes, the works of Shakespeare. Surely we are the opposite of chaos?

The physicists among us, however, laugh at such naïveté. No, life has no magic formula that can hold back or even oppose the second law of thermodynamics. We are agents of entropy. In the most physics-base view, life on Earth takes photons, radiated at six thousand degrees Kelvin from the surface of the Sun, and transforms them into waste heat. We are heat engines, and all heat engines, including us, must reject waste heat. That is the law of entropy, to which we are not immune. On a more personal level, perhaps we—maybe even you?—may seem to create order out of chaos, but while doing so, we take unreacted oxygen, energy-rich food, and drinkable pure water, and turn it into exhausted carbon dioxide, impure and undrinkable waste water, and, yes, feces. We may create art . . . but we create far more waste products. The waste products are recycled by the ecology surrounding us, of course, ultimately powered by that solar energy, mentioned above.

Could we define life as an interconnected component of an ecology? Well, perhaps . . . but that would be a circular definition, because how do we define an ecology, if not as an interconnected network of life?

Any time nature forms a crystal, it is creating order out of chaos. A snowstorm could literally produce a trillion snowflakes, each one an intricate structure with a hundred billion billion water molecules each rigorously put in exactly the right place.

And yet we don't think of a snowstorm as alive.

Life is something that eats—sugar, or photons—and reproduces. But a flame eats oxygen and firewood, and a fire reproduces itself. That's clearly not enough to define life. Life does have the characteristic that it passes genetic information to its offspring, and that information can change—mutate—with the most beneficial changes propagating into more offspring, in the process of Darwinian evolution. This process does seem characteristic of life . . . but is it a defining characteristic? Or just a description of the historical process by which life has changed? In any case, it is difficult to defend a definition of life not based on what it is, but on a history that is not observed, and possibly (in the case of extraterrestrial life) not even known.

Perhaps we should back off in our thinking, and simply ask, what is life made of?

Life, as we know it, is made up of complex molecules structurally composed of covalently-bonded carbon atoms (along with hydrogen, oxygen, nitrogen, and a little phosphorus and others, true, but the structural integrity is from the carbon); it stores and replicates its structural information in the form of DNA or RNA; it processes free energy from any of a multiplicity of sources; and it depends on liquid water as a solvent and electrolyte.

So: we look for life in places where we can find liquid water; we look for life in the form of organic molecules; we look for the source of free energy that can power life.

But that's life as we know it. What about life as we don't know it?

Can we have life that doesn't depend on water? Can we have life that uses other molecules than DNA for its genetic coding? Life with a structural foundation of elements other than carbon?

Could we even—as Dr. Benford speculates—have life that isn't even based on *atoms*?

The answer is—nobody knows.

This moves beyond the science of astrobiology, and into the realm of speculation. The great (and iconoclastic) astrophysicist Fred Hoyle, in his 1957 science fiction novel *The Black Cloud*, postulated life in the form of an interstellar dust cloud.

Plasmas are described as a fourth state of matter—different from solids, liquids, or gasses—consisting of electrically charged particles, free to move as a fluid, but interacting with each other by electrical and magnetic fields. They are very mysterious to us, we who live in the world of cold matter, and many physicists have devoted their lives to understanding how plasmas behave.

And "behavior" is exactly the right word. In the classical Greek, "plasma" meant something molded, or moldable—able to change its shape, but keeping its form. By post-classical Latin, it was sometimes used to mean not merely a moldable substance, but "a modulation of the voice," a "creature," and even a "poetic form." It was the chemist Irving Langmuir who proposed the term to describe ionized gas in 1927, as he and his co-workers observing oscillations in the ionized gas he was studying. Langmuir coined the word in analogy to the fluid plasma of the blood and drawing from it an analogy to an electrified fluid that carries electrons and ions.

Plasmas move in mysterious ways. The movement of the charged particles changes the electric and magnetic fields; the electric and magnetic fields change the motion of the charged particles. They are self-stimulating systems, with parts that move and interact, making complex oscillations and knots and jets, with magnetic field lines connecting and reconnecting. Confining a plasma is devilishly difficult: it will twist and writhe in complex manners that indeed seem almost alive. This is called collective behavior by physicists, "collective" in the sense that the motion of any given ion of the plasma is the response to not just the ions nearby, but the fields generated by motion of ions in the whole of the plasma, including those far away.

Gregory Benford's story "The Diaphanous" looks at the plasma in the fringes of the solar system, beyond the heliosphere, and asks, could these plasmas form stable structures? Could these stable structures evolve, and become more complex, reproducing themselves? Over the period of hundreds of millions of years, over the billions of years of the lifetime of the Sun, could survival of the fittest make such self-organized plasmas fit the definition of life?

The plasma organisms described by Benford are indeed very tenuous; in the regions where the story takes place, the inner part of the Oort cloud, the gas density is about one gas molecule or ion per twenty cubic centimeters, about twenty billion billion times less dense than air. But plasmas are more than the molecules; the electric and magnetic fields generated are an integral part of the plasma, and these fields could plausibly form structures hundreds or even thousands of miles across, vaster than empires, yet with internal communications (the equivalent of our nerve impulses) moving at the speed of plasma waves.

Why not?

But indeed, would such a structure really be called "alive" in any real sense?

That may depend on how we define "life."

Well, we shall let Dr. Benford argue the case that, yes, such a plasma organism could indeed be defined as life (although not life as we know it).

A harder question, perhaps, is the narrator of the story: a self-aware repair spacecraft, cruising the vast spaces 550 astronomical units from the Sun to service and repair the "pixels" that serve as focal planes for the gravitational lens telescope imaging extrasolar planets; an AI with a "Human1.6 intelligence" that studies humanity without itself being human . . . is the AI, too, alive? If we can say that a self-organizing plasma is alive, and that life does not need to reside in atoms—why is the computer algorithm running on a highly sophisticated spacecraft computer not also alive?

But to answer that question, we'd need to be able to define "what is life?"

And we don't have a good answer to that question.

Yet.

FURTHER READING

Benner, S. A. (2010). "Defining life." *Astrobiology*, 10(10), 1021-1030.

Cleland, C. E., & Chyba, C. F. (2002). "Defining 'life'." *Origins of Life and Evolution of the Biosphere*, 32(4), 387-393.

Irwin, L. N., & Schulze-Makuch, D. (2020). "The astrobiology of alien worlds: Known and unknown forms of life." *Universe*, 6(9), 130.

Marcheselli, V. (2019). "Life as-we-don't-know-it: research repertoires and the emergence of astrobiology." Thesis; The University of Edinburgh, accessible at https://era.ed.ac.uk/handle/1842/36070

Tirard, S., Morange, M., & Lazcano, A. (2010). "The definition of life: a brief history of an elusive scientific endeavor." *Astrobiology*, 10(10), 1003-1009.

Zimmer, C. (2021). *Life's Edge: The Search for What It Means to Be Alive*. Dutton.

THE SPHINX OF ADZHIMUSHKAJ

BRIAN RAPPATTA

For his thirty-ninth birthday, McLellan Laroche was cursed with an assistant. Or at least, he decided it might as well be his thirty-ninth. He'd long since lost track of Sol standard reckoning, and he hadn't celebrated a birthday in at least ten years. Which suited him fine, in the cosmic scheme of things, because he considered birthdays were about as much of a curse as assistants.

"He's my nephew-in-law by my ex-wife. I need you to take the precocious little twat off my hands for a short while," Surandra told him on his monthly supply stopover at Bentham Station. "He's a bright lad. You'll hate him less than you hate most people. Just one month. You can return him the next time you're on-station. We'll call it an internship."

"I don't do nepotism," McLellan said.

"Neither do I. If I did, I'd get him a real internship."

"I work alone."

"You float around in space bumping into things. Let's not dignify that with the term of 'work,' shall we? Oh, and do try to watch your language around him. His parents'll kill me if he comes back swearing like a sailor."

In the end, McLellan lost. He knew he would. Surandra's funds, Surandra's rules. And nobody else on station was likely to pay him even the pittance Surandra did with so little expectation of participation in the academics' discussions. Surandra was a capitalist, not a researcher. If the thorny issues of mining rights to Adzhimushkaj's rings ever got resolved, Surandra would be the first in line with a financial stake in all the major conglomerates.

Hell, knowing him, Surandra probably already had contracts waiting to be signed.

But at least on board the *Eleutherio*, out in free drift around Adzhimushkaj, McLellan was still captain.

"I saw some of your work in the station gallery," the kid said as they were waiting for their departure clearance from Bentham's traffic control. "Uncle Suri showed it to me."

"Yeah?" McLellan grunted. He pretended to monitor some readouts on his console. Given the narrow confines of the cockpit and the kid's rather unnerving scrutiny, he figured the kid knew he wasn't really checking any pre-flight data.

"I liked it."

"Yeah?" To look like he was actually doing something useful, McLellan accessed his bank accounts. Save for the pittance of a stipend Surandra paid him, there were no other transactions. "Maybe someday you can afford to buy it, then." *At least then somebody would be buying.*

"It reminded me of Vermeer."

Despite himself, McLellan raised an eyebrow. He shot a sidelong glance at the kid. "Surandra told you to say that, didn't he?"

The kid grinned sheepishly. "Yeah." He pushed his round-rimmed spectacles up on his nose. They appeared to be merely the retro kind. McLellan wondered if they were an affectation, or whether the kid really had poor eyesight. Knowing Surandra, McLellan wouldn't have been surprised if the kid's family was too cheap for optometrics.

"You've done your homework, at least. But what do you know about the workings of a bubbleship?"

The boy brightened. "I've logged seventy-four hours in the simulator."

"Impressive," McLellan admitted. "Well, then. You stay here, and when those—" He halted as he tried to think of a suitable word to replace the epithet that was on his lips— "screwups in traffic control get around to sending us departure clearance, why don't you go ahead and declamp and take us out?"

The boy's eyes went round. "But . . . I don't have a license yet. I'm not old enough."

"The nav computer does all the work," McLellan said. "Even one of Surandra's relatives couldn't really mess it up."

"But . . . where will you be?"

"Working," McLellan said, and left the boy alone in the cockpit.

McLellan sat pondering his day's work on the canvas. He frowned. The curve of her nose wasn't quite correct. The problem was, he was working from his imagination, a fickle bitch if ever there was one, and he'd be damned if he'd corrupt this woman's features by basing her on a real person.

Only belatedly did he realize he had company. The kid was watching him silently. How long had it been? The boy didn't speak; he was contemplating with interest the random assortment of canvases of all sizes with their works in various stages of completion.

"Well?" McLellan prompted, putting down his brush. "Still waiting on clearance?"

The boy shook his head. "We've cleared station traffic, and we're en route to Adzhimushkaj. ETA is thirty-seven hours and twenty-two minutes. You didn't respond when I commed you, so I figured you were asleep. I set fuel burn at oh point three seven. I hope that's okay?"

McLellan looked up. "We're in freespace? That's not possible. I never felt us declamp." Had he been so caught up in his work?

The boy frowned. "Why would you feel the station moorings detach?"

"I always feel them detach. They're like—" He didn't have any words for what he meant to express, so instead he resorted to making a sound effect, like the humming of an electric motor.

The kid was now looking at him like he was crazy. "They don't sound like that. They're in vacuum."

Damn. The kid had a point. McLellan had always just assumed they'd sound like that in his imagination. His customary feeling of free-floating on detachment was just his imagination, as well—it *had* to be. He knew that, but he'd spent so much time lately in his own head that . . . well . . . the perceptions had apparently skewed. "Are you always like this?" he asked.

"Like what?"

"Like . . . smarmy. It's no wonder your family—" At the dramatic change even these few words wrought in the boy's expression, he broke off while his brain charted a new course for his mouth. "How long have I been down here?" he asked instead.

"About two hours," the kid said. He navigated a maze of easels and canvases to get a better look at the current work in progress. "Who is she? An old girlfriend?"

McLellan shook his head. "She's not real. She's just . . . a figment of my imagination." He'd be damned if he told the kid that this was his allegorical representation of his muse . . . or at least as close as he could get it. Even though they had an entire month together, he didn't feel like taking the time to explain *that* to the kid.

"Doesn't she need a pearl earring?"

McLellan shot the kid what he hoped was his most deprecating glare. "Surandra said the same thing. It wasn't funny then, either."

"I'm sorry. I didn't mean—"

McLellan gave the imperfect nose one last considering glance. Before the kid could stammer out a feeble apology, he took the boy by the shoulder and steered him aftward—which was a rather arbitrary distinction in a spherical ship, but it had been built that way, and his brain always considered the bunks and the airlock the aft section. "Look, I'll be busy here a while. Why don't you go get settled into your bunk? Read a book, or, or—" What the hell did fourteen-year-old kids do these days, anyway? "—or masturbate or something."

At that, the kid's eyebrows shot up over the tops of his glasses.

"Or try this. Here." McLellan steered the boy over to one of his smallest canvases propped up on an easel. The canvas had one of his oldest landscapes on it. He fished a paintbrush out of the nearest cup and stuck it into the boy's hand. Then, he passed the kid the palette he'd been using. "Paint something."

"But—I'm not an artist."

"Who cares? Just . . . use your imagination."

"But you've already painted on this one. I can't just paint over it—"

McLellan waved a hand in the air dismissively. "It's a landscape. I just do them for practice."

"But . . . what should I paint?"

"How the hell should I know? Trust the brush. I need a nap."

Maybe there was something to this assistant thing after all, McLellan thought as he woke up and stretched from a full-out sleep. How long had he been out? He asked the computer above his bunk: eight hours. He hadn't slept this long in one stretch in . . . how long?

He made his way from the tiny bunkroom through the workshop—

—and stopped. The kid's brushwork drew his attention. It was a bright yellow smiley face. Rather crude, but there was something in the way the smile curved at the edges, as if it was merely plastered on for the benefit of the observer, that was slightly unnerving.

The kid was nowhere to be seen, so that left only one other place he could be. McLellan stumbled through into the cockpit.

The kid was indeed there, sitting at the console. He'd dialed down the opacity of the hull so that he could look out. It was a poor man's substitute for a more modern, fully immersive holo display. McLellan had never really seen the need to upgrade, and Surandra was more than happy not to have to pay for it.

The vast colorscape of Adzhimushkaj was in plain view in the distance. All around the gas giant's rings, thousands of seemingly freely drifting *astracnidarians*, or bubblefish, in the non-scientific parlance, jumbled around haphazardly. From this distance, their interplay looked like merely a mass of drifting bubbles of every hue imaginable. The bubblefish were little more than complex sensory organs mounted inside a spheroid membrane that contained refractive glea. They had three tentacle-like tails of varying lengths that they flagellated for some reason none of the scientists were really certain of, but in general they merely floated freely in space around the rings and the five major satellites of Adzhimushkaj, their trajectories only altering when they bumped into each other. The academics were still unclear what information the bubblefish exchanged when they bounced off each other, but they always changed the color of their glea when they did—among themselves, that was. Whenever they bumped up against any of the dozen or so research ships that frequented the region, their glea remained unchanged. In the three years of crewed research, none of the piloted bubbleships had managed to get so much as a handshake out of the bubblefish.

"I see we made it," McLellan said.

The boy nodded. "It's amazing. They're way more beautiful in person."

McLellan had to agree with him on that one. He slumped into his chair. "Coffee," he ordered from the cockpit's dispenser.

"Do you think they're sentient?" the kid asked.

McLellan slid the mug out of the dispenser. "Most likely. They have over twenty-eight thousand recurring patterns of albedo shifts and color spectrum changes. Something that complex sure as hell seems like it should be a language."

"Do you think we'll ever be able to talk to them?"

McLellan shrugged. "Even if we could, I doubt we'd have much in common."

"Where do you think they came from?"

Back when he'd actually tuned into the academics' chatter, there'd been vigorous debate about whether the bubblefish were native to

Adzhimushkaj, or whether they'd migrated there for the near-end-less buffet they found in the unique properties of the gas giant's rings. "How the hell should I know?" McLellan said. "I'm no scientist. Your uncle hired me because I work cheap."

"Look." The kid pointed. "That one's mitosing."

McLellan considered the bubblefish the kid indicated. It wasn't really mitosing, not in the cellular sense, but it was indeed in the midst of reproducing, squeezing off a nascent clone of itself from its own membrane. "Your lucky day," McLellan said. "It's not everyone who gets to observe that on their first day."

The kid smiled. It was a thin, shy smile on a face that seemed unaccustomed to them. "So, what do we do now?" he asked. "Should we try talking to them?"

"Knock yourself out," McLellan said. "The hull refractor controls are on your right. You can call up the pattern database on your monitor. You're welcome to flash gibberish at them until you're blue in the face." McLellan stood.

"What are you going to do?"

"I've got work to do. Give me a holler if you get an answer."

How much later he knew not, but he grew aware of the kid's unnerving, blinky gaze on him as he stood at his easel. It felt like an invasion, even though there was no possible way of delineating personal space on a vessel this size.

McLellan sighed and put down his brush. "Well?" he said. "You get tired of talking to an entire ocean of brick walls?"

The kid nodded. "That's why you're down here all the time, isn't it? It's . . ."

"Boring," McLellan finished for him. "Yeah." *Futile,* he'd almost said. "The engineers of these ships put a lot of time and effort into trying to make us blend in, but the bubblefish know the difference. They know we don't belong."

The kid accepted this with a stoic nod. "You disabled the comm unit," he said, changing tacks. "I need your passcodes to re-enable it."

"You don't want to listen to any of the chatter from the other vessels, believe me. Mostly grad students that are as incomprehensible as the bubblefish." He pointed to the canvas with the smiley face. "You might as well grab a brush. It helps to pass the time."

"But . . . I finished it."

"No, you didn't. I can still see some of my landscape underneath. It's not done until it's totally yours."

The kid considered the array of works in various stages of completion McLellan had left strewn like a maze about the studio. His survey fixated especially on the landscapes, and from the slight frown that might have been imperceptible if McLellan hadn't spent thousands of hours training himself to render facial expressions, it was clear that the kid found them rather uninspiring. "How come you don't paint starscapes?" he asked. "If you painted the bubblefish, I bet you could sell more paintings on Bentham."

McLellan sighed. "You sound like your uncle. He suggested I pander to the masses, too."

"You mean you don't want them to sell?"

"It's not that. Believe me, I like the extra money from time to time. It's just . . ." McLellan considered his words carefully. He wasn't used to explaining himself to anyone, let alone fourteen-year-old kids. "It needs to be authentic," he said. "Art isn't about pleasing people. It's about communicating something of yourself, whether anybody understands it or not. Take that, for example." McLellan indicated the boy's crude smiley face.

"What about it?"

"I hate it. It's fake. Why don't you paint something that really matters to you?"

The kid shrugged. Without another word, he picked up a spare brush. Each standing at opposite ends of the workshop cabin, they got to work.

They were standing in much the same configuration three days later, each at their respective easels, when the entire ship shook with a concussive shock.

The kid shot a look of fear across the top of his easel at McLellan. His left cheek was smudged with a two-tone shade of green that he'd been using for his starscape that was beginning to resemble *Starry Night*— with bubblefish. "What the bloody hell was that?" the kid demanded.

McLellan was already halfway across the studio toward the cockpit. The kid followed in his wake.

There were about a half-dozen warning indicator lights all flashing and bleeping for his attention on his panel. First things first. Before he even had settled into the pilot's chair, McLellan ordered the hull to go transparent so that he could see out.

His first sight was of a bubblefish wriggling past the viewport window. Its tails were flagellating spasmodically. It was easy to think of it as a fish swimming in an ocean, even though the tails weren't really for locomotion; on the rare occasions they needed to move with any intent, the bubblefish moved by expelling the nebular gases they ingested. He'd never seen the damned things move so fast. It was as if . . .

It's running away. The dread certainty overtook him as the kid flopped into the co-pilot's seat beside him with a breathless "Sonofabitch."

McLellan echoed the sentiment. As the bulk of the rapidly fleeing bubblefish cleared their sight lines, the reason for its flight dominated their viewport. The ping of a giant, cylindrical vessel easily twenty times the length of their bubbleship flashed onto the transparent display before them. "What is that?" the kid demanded as McLellan magnified the image to get a better look at it.

"It's a mining ship," McLellan said. "But . . . there's no mining operations here in the rings, unless . . ." He broke off.

"Looks like somebody just got mining rights." The kid left the obvious corollary unspoken: the jurisdictional court on Bentham must have finally decided that the bubblefish weren't sentient, and therefore didn't hold territorial rights.

"That was a spray of rubble," the kid said. "Somebody just detonated one of the minor asteroids in the rings. It's running off all the bubble-fish. If we'd been any closer—"

"We could have ended up like him, I know." McLellan pointed to one of the bubblefish's carcasses, which was now rotating lifelessly in a free spin.

"If they detonate another one—" the kid said.

"I get the picture," McLellan cut him off. He entered the passcodes into the console to fire up the communications array. As soon as it came online, he hailed the mining vessel. Then, he sat back and waited.

No answer.

The kid, for his part, refused to sit idle. His fingers flew over his console as he pulled up the cached comm logs. He hadn't been kidding: he really was familiar with the ship's systems. "It's the *Keurig*," he said. "They've been broadcasting notices for the past three days to stay away from Adzhimushkaj." He looked over at McLellan. "We would have heard them if we'd turned the comm on."

"No peace and quiet even in the middle of deep space," McLellan said. "Dammit!" He pounded his console, causing all his readouts to flicker momentarily. "Why the hell aren't they responding?"

"I think our transceiver has been damaged," the kid said. "We took a hell of a rattling." The kid looked, wide-eyed, over at McLellan. "Just how close are we to Adzhimushkaj?"

"Too close," McLellan said. "They must be mining a perimeter to keep the bubblefish away from it. If they—"

He was interrupted by a furious buffeting that threatened to throw him out of the pilot's chair. Only by the merest sliver of grace did he manage to stay in it, but when his perception stopped rattling in the aftershock, the starscape above him was whirling at a dizzying rate. They were in a free spin.

He forced his gaze away from it and thumbed the hull back to opaque—none too soon, judging by the greenish tinge of the kid's face that was threatening to match the green splotch of paint on his cheek. At least with the cockpit once again opaque, and with the dampeners doing their job, there was no further perception of spinning, at least until their Gs overwhelmed the dampeners and ended up splattering them like jelly all over the inside of the cockpit. Which was likely to happen all too soon, given the furious bleeping of yet another alarm on his console.

First things first. McLellan fought the spin with calculated bursts of thrusters. But instead of fighting the spin to a dead stop, he used the momentum they had already, and when he had the free whirl under control, he gunned the propulsion. At least that was still functional.

The kid monitored his actions on his own console and frowned as he tried to make sense of them. "What are you doing?" he demanded.

"What do you wanna bet nobody on that ship ever bothered to check to make sure we weren't one of the bubblefish?"

"There must be some way to let them know—"

"Try flashing the hull through every color it'll project. Damn, I'd give real money right about now if we could flash anything useful. Like an SOS."

"We could try flashing Morse code."

"Why not? Can't hurt. Give it a shot. But we'll have to be a lot closer if we want anybody to notice us. At this point, the safest place is right *there*." He pointed to the *Keurig*. "It's the one place guaranteed not to have any mines. We need to get closer, and we need to get them to stop setting off those damned charges."

"How? We can't get a message out."

"A ship that size is bound to have a bridge. See if you can find it."

The kid pulled up some design schematics from the computer. "Looks like it should be . . ." He paused as he checked their position in relation to the mining vessel. Their momentum was bringing them closer and closer to it at a rate of about three hundred kilometers per second. "Right about there." He highlighted the location, overlaying it on the visual of the vessel through the cockpit.

"That's all I need." McLellan keyed in the course corrections that brought them barreling in closer to the ship. At least in this close to the vessel, they were spared the concussion of any further asteroid debris. But the tradeoff was that McLellan had to ignore the proximity detector readout on his console. At this velocity, they wouldn't exactly bounce harmlessly off the vessel's hull.

"What are you doing?" the kid demanded. "You can't . . . they won't notice our engine exhaust at that range—"

"You think anybody over there's paying any attention? We're going to fire at them," McLellan said, "and hope they've got somebody on their bridge whose head isn't up their ass who can figure out we're not a bubblefish."

"Fire at them? We don't have any weapons."

"So we'll improvise. We've got plenty of art." He turned to the kid. "I need you to go load all the canvases into the airlock." He checked the velocimeter. "You've got about two minutes until we're close enough. When we get right up outside their bridge—"

The kid's face lit up. "Blow them all out the airlock!" he finished. "I'm on it." Without waiting for any further instructions, he headed off back to the studio compartment, pausing only long enough to throw over his shoulder, "I hope this works."

You and me both, McLellan thought. If a stream of projectile paintings suddenly blown out from the lone bubblefish not running away didn't catch the attention of the bridge crew and identify them as fellow humans, he was all out of ideas.

McLellan held his breath as he watched his instruments. They gave him precision readings, but somehow, it just didn't feel the same as the old eyeball method. He had the spin under control now, so he risked re-translucifying the hull—

—and was immediately greeted by the sight of the mining vessel's hull looming ever larger in his field of view. The proximity sensors on his console were screaming at him, and the ship's auto-nav threatened to engage, but he overrode it, and his instincts both. For this to work, they'd have to get closer yet . . .

He thumbed a button on his console. "How are you coming?" he asked the kid over the ship's internal.

"I've got two of them in," the kid said. "They're heavy."

"You've got ninety seconds," McLellan told him, and focused instead on his readouts. He didn't have time to input a proper series of calculations into the nav computer. By his estimates, he'd have to start braking . . .

Now. He fired the forward thrusters, hoping to hell they weren't damaged too. If they were, they'd end up spraying themselves into a million pieces against the hull of the mining vessel, and even the spongy outer coating of the *Eleutherio* that was designed to mimic a bubblefish's membrane wouldn't bounce them off it. Not at this speed.

He was lined up right, though. He saw the transparent bridge window of the mining vessel come into his range of sight, first as a narrow slit, and then grow larger and larger as he drew nearer. He was braking, but even so, the thrusters couldn't arrest his considerable momentum all at once.

He grimaced. For this to work, he'd have to get close enough to practically French kiss the other vessel.

"Get ready," he told the kid over the internal.

"Ready!" the kid shouted back.

"Right. Depressurize the airlock . . . *now!*"

The eerie thing about space was that you had to imagine your own sound effects. McLellan imagined a concussive depressurization much like an explosion. He cut all his remaining velocity and brought the rear of his bubbleship up as level as he could get it with the bridge window as the airlock indicator light on his console flashed red, expelling the only ballast they were carrying into space. Even if he wasn't quite close enough for the crew of the mining vessel to see what the ejecta were with their naked eyes, they'd surely have caught it with their readouts. They'd *have* to know that it wasn't organic to bubblefish.

Come on, McLellan thought. *Figure it out, boys.*

At that moment, the kid returned to the cockpit. He took the co-pilot's seat and glanced up at the stream of canvases sailing away from them, in the direction of the mining vessel. "Do you think they'll notice?" he asked.

"They'd better," McLellan said. He held his breath. "They haven't launched another charge, as far as I can tell. Maybe—what the hell?"

Whether they'd caught the attention of the mining ship appeared to be irrelevant. A bubblefish came into view to their starboard, impossibly close. The bubblefish *never* came that close . . .

"Well, I'll be damned," McLellan said. More bubblefish joined its kindred, coming up on either side of them. As they massed in around the *Eleutherio* in a swarm, they all changed their glea to a deep teal color. Absently, McLellan checked his refractor controls. It was the same color the *Eleutherio* was emitting at the moment.

The kid checked his instruments. "There's thousands of them," he said. "They're surrounding the mining ship."

"They mimicked us," McLellan breathed. "Their instinct was to run away, until we drew in. Sonofabitch. They completely ignored us for years until it was in their own self-interest to pay attention. If that isn't the hallmark of a sentient species, I don't know what is."

Three hours later, McLellan and the kid stood on the bridge of the *Keurig* and stared out through the transparent hull at the mass of bubblefish surrounding the vessel. They'd formed an impenetrable spherical mass all around the ship. They couldn't actually harm the ship, but they'd effectively eliminated the possibility of the *Keurig* dropping any more pulse charges. The charges wouldn't get past the ring of bubblefish and would likely blast a large hole in the hull of the *Keurig* at the same time.

"They're all flashing the same pattern," Alvarez, the captain of the *Keurig*, said. "It's like they're trying to say something."

McLellan snorted. "Most likely something not very polite, I'd wager. Still—" He grinned at the kid on his right. "We did manage to get a response."

"You're already the talk of Bentham," the captain said. "The academics are all in a tizzy about the first instance of cooperation with the bubblefish." He bit his lower lip ruefully. "Our mining rights have been suspended indefinitely. This is the shortest job I've ever had." He handed McLellan a pad with the newsfeed from the station on it. McLellan minimized that and instead checked his accounts. Not bad. Looked like every piece of his artwork in the station gallery had sold—for well above the asking price. McLellan couldn't quite contain a wry laugh.

"What's so funny?" the kid asked.

"If I'd known blowing it all out an airlock was the best way to get my work noticed, I'd have done it years ago."

The kid grinned. "Not all of it," he said. "I didn't have time to load the one you were working on into the airlock."

"Great," McLellan muttered. "Now I guess I've got to get the nose right."

"Look at it this way," the kid said, grinning. "You're the first artist in the history of humankind whose work has ever communicated with an alien species." He tried but failed to contain a snicker. "And all you had to do was crap it out an airlock."

McLellan shot the kid a sidelong glance, but he couldn't quite keep the infectiousness of the kid's grin from registering on his own face. "Maybe the muse is trying to tell me something," he said.

The kid stared at the pad. "Looks like we're in for quite the reception back on Bentham. There're academics en route from six different universities, and they all want to meet with us."

"They'll just have to wait," McLellan said. "You've got an internship to finish, and I . . . well . . . I could use the studio time."

FINDING COMMON GROUND

Intelligence, Imitation, and Communication

Philippe Nauny

How do you tell if a species is intelligent—and what does that even mean? How would you bridge a gap between you and beings not only different from your species, but coming from an entirely different branch of life? In short, how would you tell if the "bubblefish" in Brian Rappatta's story "The Sphinx of Adzhimushkaj" were sapient? Whilst some parallels can be made with the study of non-human animals, specific frameworks have also been imagined to communicate with sapient extraterrestrial beings. Some forms of communication between microorganisms or between plants— by quorum sensing, for example—also exist, but let's mainly focus on animals here. One would be tempted to say "for the sake of simplicity," but as you will see, there is nothing simple about it.

Assessing a species' intelligence

The assessment of cognition and intelligence of human beings usually relies on the use of language, mostly through instructions given for the test, if not in the test itself. Such an approach, problematic in itself in humans, is obviously not applicable when testing other species. When trying to assess animal cognition, we must avoid refusing to see complex behavior in animals (the "automaton"-like view of animals held by René Descartes) but also to see great complexity where a simpler explanation is more likely, such as falling into the *Clever Hans* trap and thinking that a horse can count, while he "just" observes movements made by his owner (not an unimpressive task either, but nowhere near actually counting). We must also refrain from taking an anthropocentric approach, directly transposing certain characteristic that we perceive as intelligent, but which would make no sense for an animal, like giving a stick to an elephant to reach a fruit too high in a tree, when the elephant simultaneously needs its trunk to smell and localize said fruit.

Starting from the 19th century, rather than simply observing animals in nature, controlled environments and setups—both in nature and laboratories—helped to refine certain points studied when assessing animals' intelligence and remove biases (while possibly introducing new ones). There were then two main schools of thoughts: the behaviorists considered young animals (and humans) to learn from a "clean slate" how to react to stimuli, whereas the ethologists argued for a greater role of inborn instinct.

The use of experimental setups allows us, for instance, to put animals in a "puzzle box" and see how they work their way out or gain access to treats (e.g., by pressing a lever or a button, or tweaking a piece of wire, etc.). We can even observe social intelligence by having two or more animals cooperate in a task not achievable by an individual, but we must always be mindful of each species' capabilities, natural environments, and limitations. Put *ad absurdum*, failing to do so leads us to results akin to the famous cartoon with a scientist putting both an octopus and a cat in an aquarium and finding that the octopus is more intelligent than the cat under comparable conditions (you guessed right—the cat did not survive in the aquarium).

While the octopus/cat in an aquarium example is intentionally absurd, many experiments succumbed to more subtle yet similar pitfalls because of wrong assumptions or settings (for instance if we are trying to see whether an animal can exhibit "patience" in waiting for a greater treat instead of consuming a smaller one immediately, it really matters even on the individual level what kind of treats we use), or indeed to the very question of comparing the intelligence of very distantly related animals—because the question of whether the octopus or the cat is more intelligent holds little meaning, even if we keep each animal in its preferred environment.

Despite being an ongoing debate, the assessment of a species' cognition and intelligence may hint at the complexity level of their communication methods. Additionally, the majority of the existing studies lack a significant sample size and vary too much in settings between each other to be really reliable and comparable.

The role of imitation

It is commonly said that imitation is the sincerest form of flattery. But can it be also a sign of intelligence? In Rappatta's story, the pivotal point in establishing the "bubblefish" sapience is their sudden change of behavior, then mimicking the *Eleutherio*. Until recently, behavioral synchrony between animals was not particularly considered in animal learning theories. The challenge here is to determine if imitation is "mechanical" or if it responds to certain rules followed by individuals. Does it constitute a passive learning mechanism or does it require an active and dynamic practice? The actual functions of imitation are still debated. To make the matter more complex—one could also say "more interesting"—the importance and purpose of imitation within one species may differ from that of another species.

The simplest reason for imitation by social animals living in herds could be a defense mechanism. As predators can easily identify and target weak or sick individuals exhibiting singular demeanors, failing to behave like the rest of the group may be fatal. Imitation may also help individuals to learn and transmit knowledge. This form of learning by repeating what the others do is observed in apes; for example, in the method gorillas use to harvest leaves from branches, clean them from debris, and fold them before consumption, or in chimpanzees preparing specific tools to harvest the termites they intend to eat. Staying with apes, their social activity removing fleas from each other could also hint that imitation develops a sense of sharing the group's standards and of social belonging. But more importantly, imitation is a necessary base from which to develop a form of communication between members of the same species.

Intraspecies communication

Contrary to humans, whose communication relies mostly on verbal language and visual signs, other species may use additional or completely different means to communicate. Overall, these communication means play a role in basic biological needs like foraging for food, courtship and mating, warning of dangers, or interacting socially with other members of the group. It can nevertheless sometimes involve more "cunning" practices. For example, using a predator warning call when there is in fact no predator, so that the animal making the call can get access to more food. Or in cases when a species of fish cleans another's parasites by eating them, the cleaners sometimes "cheat" by eating the client fish's mucus—more nutritious—instead; the client fish would then retaliate by chasing the misbehaving cleaners or "boycotting" their territory.

The production of audio signals is a feature shared by many species. They can be observed in the form of songs for birds or whales, of stridulations for crickets, of whistles for prairie dogs, or of clicks for dolphins. These signals often consist of repeated rhythmic patterns. The use of patterns raises again the issue of the role of imitation. Failing to properly reproduce a song may incidentally exclude an individual from the group—like *52 Blue*, a whale designated as the world's loneliest whale, simply for singing off pitch compared to other whales and hence failing to communicate with them.

Visual cues are also used in the animal kingdom. Like the "bubble-fish" from the story, cephalopods can use the chromatophores in their skin to communicate by changing colors and patterns. Visual displays are nevertheless not limited to changes in skin pigmentation. The adoption of particular postures is another way to convey messages. They can be part of a defense mechanism to attempt to intimidate an aggressor or part of mating rituals to impress a potential mate or a defense strategy to camouflage. But in this latter case, what would distinguish an innate response to mimic whatever hue the skin is in contact with, from a conscious choice of choosing a color and a pattern?

Some forms of communication would include a combination of means. For example, the waggle dance performed by honeybees to communicate the direction and distance to flowers mixes visual cues, direct physical contact, and pheromone signals. Yet, all these forms of communication do not indicate that non-human animals have languages that are developed and constructed, like humans do. In the ongoing debate over the nature of animal "languages", they are considered at best as proto-languages.

Interspecies communication

The most obvious examples of interspecies communication are humans interacting with animals. Nevertheless, different species of non-human animals can also interact together. In mixed groups of animals, the alarm call of one species may be also recognized by other species.

Human communication with domesticated animals is a more obvious illustration, particularly when training animals to understand human commands. Conversely, humans can learn how to interpret the vocalizations and body language of the animal. This relies mostly on learning and interpreting cues from the other species. Additionally, there have been experiments consisting of actively training domesticated animals, mostly dogs, to understand a variety of human words and concepts, and to express them via sound buttons.

Communication exists between humans and wild animals too. Honeyguides are birds which partner with humans and lead them to bee colonies. The birds feed on bee larvae and comb wax after the humans have harvested the honey. Other bird species are able to understand human words, and humans can recognize and understand specific calls from these birds. But it's not just birds, of course! Attempts to teach human words to great apes—through sign language or symbols—and to study how non-humans learn languages have produced variable results, but such techniques mostly enabled the apes to effectively, albeit in a limited fashion, communicate with humans too.

Eventually, any attempt at communication between humans and extraterrestrial "animals" may prove as challenging as communicating with Earth's animals, or possibly even more.

Human-alien communication

If an evolutionary continuum has been suggested to exist between animals' proto-languages and human languages, it would not exist between human languages and any potential extraterrestrial languages. Hence, communication with alien life forms having an intelligence matching or exceeding the human one (if such a comparison would even be meaningful) would require the use of a common base as a starting point. Mathematics and logic have been thought to provide such base. The Lincos language—from *lingua cosmica*—is an example of a constructed language using this approach. One transmission—the Lone Signal—actually used a general-purpose binary language.

More famous attempts at potential communication with alien species used a different approach: pictures. Such pictures could be physically engraved on a solid matrix, in the case of the plaques attached to the Pioneer probes or the Golden Records sent with the Voyager probes. Alternatively, they were digitally encoded to be transmitted, in the case of the Arecibo message or the Cosmic Call messages.

So far, communication with extraterrestrial beings remains only hypothetical until we eventually record a signal. Given the long time necessary for back-and-forth communication through distant space, linguists will have more than enough time to study the content of the message and make sense of it before attempting a reply. Ultimately, direct observation and interaction through a physical meeting would the most optimal way to learn how to communicate. However, this scenario also remains the most hypothetical given the constraints of interstellar travel.

FURTHER READING

Bickerton, D. (1990). *Language and species*. Chicago, IL: University of Chicago Press.

Byrne, R.W. (2009). "Animal cognition." *Current Biology*, 19(3), p. R111–R114.

Byrne, R.W. and Russon, A.E. (1998). "Learning by imitation: A hierarchical approach." *Behavioral and Brain Sciences*, 21(5), p. 667–684.

de Waal, F.B.M. (2007). "The 'Russian doll' model of empathy and imitation." In *On being moved: From mirror neurons to empathy*, edited by Stein Bråten. Amsterdam/Philadelphia: John Benjamins Publishing Company, p. 49–69.

de Waal, F. (2016). *Are we smart enough to know how smart animals are?* New York, NY: WW Norton & Company.

Goodale, E., Beauchamp, G. and Ruxton, G.D. (2017). *Mixed-species groups of animals: Behavior, community structure, and conservation*. London: Academic Press.

Maynard Smith, J. and Szathmáry, E. (1995). *The major transitions in evolution*. Oxford: Oxford University Press.

Ollongren, A. (2013). *Astrolinguistics: Design of a linguistic system for interstellar communication based on logic*. New York, NY: Springer.

DEFECTIVE

PETER WATTS

"Since the beginning of time, man has yearned to destroy the sun."

—Montgomery Burns

A blinding pinpoint opens just above the ecliptic: a supernova tiny enough to hang in your living room. A candle in the darkness, if candles screamed in X-rays and had outputs measured in yottajoules. An impossible, disembodied gout of white-hot plasma spewing into the cosmos.

Too far from Earth to do more than fuzz a few satellite transmissions. Lucky break: if the planet was fifty degrees further along its orbit, civilization might be resetting to the Middle Ages about now.

There's always next time, Ondrej reflects.

He watches the fireworks and focuses on the bright side. This is progress, he reminds himself—hell, this is a bona-fide breakthrough. Up until now their best models couldn't predict an event to within fifty hours; this time they nailed it within minutes, and they were *ready*. At this very moment a thousand telescopes are fixed on those coordinates: radio dishes arrayed across space like giant clamshells; light buckets hiding in the shadows of Tsiolkovsky or balanced at Lagrange points throughout the innersys; foil-wrapped angels with twenty-meter wingspans and x-ray vision. All press-ganged in anticipation of this, this *gateway*: this magic portal built from negative energy and imaginary numbers, vomiting out the guts of some distant star.

Aaaand gone. Along with another forlorn, unnoticed—or perhaps merely ignored—attempt to say hello.

Ondrej slides the headband off his scalp and opens his eyes. His stomach lurches at the transition. One moment adrift in a sea of stars; the next, entombed in a desecrated asteroid way too close to the Sun, cowering behind eight thousand square kilometers of photovoltaic tinfoil. He still marvels at how convincingly VR can lie to his sensory cortex.

Holes within holes, Asia said.

He resists the temptation to buzz her. Down in Astrophysics they'll be celebrating. Who can blame them? The threat may still be existential, but at least it comes with an expiry date now. No more nightmare fears of an endless unwinnable war against beings with all the time in the universe. All they have to do now is hold the fort for, what—one year? five?—and the Agni will have lost their opening. There's more than one kind of light at the end of these tunnels.

Of course, it also means the Agni have nowhere else to go. They can't just choose some other star once they realize this one's off-limits. There's no win-win option here, no more call for Ondrej Bohaty to work his interspecies magic.

Now, there's only Us or Them.

Executive Summary
UNAR Task Force, Agni Outreach Initiative:
Overview and Implementation
Candidate Roster

Excerpt Begins:

Name: Bohaty, Ondrej.

Nationality: Westhem Alliance

Current Affiliation: Okada Institute for Interspecies Communication, Simon Fraser University.

Professional Memberships: SETI Institute, AAAS, DigiCog Biomorphics LLC (board member), AAIC (past president).

Education: Doctoral thesis (solo): Interaction and remediation protocols for rogue AIs in centaured research settings. UCSD

Postdoc (centaured): General Acoustic Templates for Deriving Odontocete Pidgins. UT

Selected Awards/Recognition: Crafoord Prize, Prix Hoar, Kanzi Prize (nominated), Hoover Memorial Award. AAAS "Breakthrough of the Year". Others.

Selected Publications

Bohaty, O. 2098. "A critique of systemic linguacentrism in interspecies communication efforts." *J. Linguistics* 124: 550-582.

—— 2102. "Recursive FLB pheromonal analogs in hyphal networks (*Armillaria ostoyae*)." *Bull. Interspecies Comm.* 52: 1-65.

—— and Beatty, B. 2100. "Metacladistic reconstruction of extinct elephant dialects from recorded conversations between members of related subspecies." *Resurrection Monogr.* 27: 214pp.

—— 2100. "An alinguistic chromatophore-based communications interface for Architeuthid cephalopods." *Science* 770: 426.

Notes and Comments:

Bohaty has become famous/notorious for an extreme, embodied-cognition approach to interspecies communication, experimenting with hormonal and neurotropic editing in addition to conventional TMS- and ultrasound-based VR interfaces. Total-immersion techniques of this sort are intended to produce a first-person approximation of the sensory experiences of the subject species—as if a human brain were to be embedded in a nonhuman body. The approach is controversial; critics dismiss it as little more than a parlor trick because the mind perceiving the alien sensorium is still human, and thus incapable of truly experiencing nonhuman perspectives. "Watching a video stream through a compound lens does not make one an insect," as Gerald Bostock famously observed. However, there is no denying that Bohaty's methods produce results. Despite his well-known views on the limitations of formal language when it comes to interspecies communications, Bohaty is inarguably—and by a wide margin— the foremost xenolinguist of his generation.

Recommended Position: Principal Investigator

Dissenting Opinion:
While not disputing the consensus view regarding the candidate's qualifications, I cannot help but wonder if the same methodologies which have yielded such extraordinary accomplishments may prove to be a double-edged sword. For almost two decades now, Dr. Bohaty has routinely altered his brain chemistry and perceptual processes in a variety of ways. During such periods he has become, almost literally, less human—and while this does increase his ability to relate to nonhuman mindsets, it's hard to imagine how this could happen without losing some degree of empathy for our own.

I have no doubts about Dr. Bohaty's skills. I am familiar with his work and agree he is best qualified to carry out the sort of analysis required in the current situation. I further acknowledge that a certain level of misanthropy might be inevitable in anyone who has had significant exposure to the ways that humanity generally treats other species (not to mention our own). My concern is that a mind repeatedly altered for increased compatibility with nonhuman perspectives might find it difficult to maintain the necessary objectivity for an undertaking with such global ramifications.

—Name withheld at committee member's request

Ancient. Capricious.

Vengeful.

They lived among the stars and hurled firebolts that would destroy any world they touched. We could see their tracks, once we knew how to look: faint wisps of ionized hydrogen out in the Oort, barely detectable after cooling for half a century; warmer footprints smoldering in the Kuiper and inside the orbit of Neptune. The ghosts of footfalls past. Something stamping across the heavens, releasing a million megatons with each step.

They were omnipotent and unknowable. They used suns as weapons and wormholes as delivery platforms. They drew ever closer, and there was little we could do except name these gods as we had all the others.

We called them *Agni*.

Priests scanned the heavens for portents and signs. Over time that smattering of footprints grew into a cloud, a *sample*, a population large enough for focii and frequency distributions. Its center clarified a little more with each new data point; its confidence limits contracted past the Earth and clenched around the Sun instead. It was as if some vast prehistoric beast, never clearly seen, had roared and crashed toward us and then passed in the night, never noticing the small terrified beings cringing underfoot.

Down from their mountain, the priests brought word that perhaps the Agni were not angry or vengeful after all. Maybe they were only indifferent. Maybe they didn't even know we existed.

Still to be feared, of course. A boot will crush an ant just as dead when its wearer hasn't bothered to look down. But maybe if the ants called out. Maybe, if the Agni knew the threat they posed to a world of sapient beings, they might step a little to one side.

Maybe Ondrej Bohaty could ask them nicely.

Machines stared wide-eyed at the heavens, panning along every axis on every conceivable wavelength. They dissected the light from Agni's footsteps, laid it out in nice neat emission spectra that made no sense. Whatever distant sun was giving birth to these flares, it wasn't in any catalog and it didn't fit any of the usual models. Hints of strontium and terbium on its breath. Overtones of cerium and europium. Doubly-magic atoms, long-lived nuclides that seemed to hint at the existence of stable quark matter: dark denizens of some fabled Continent of Stability, rumored to lie beyond the limits of any periodic table known to man. Light from Here Be Dragons.

The priests threw away their sensible models and started building nonsensical ones instead. They built them further and further from common sense—and by the time they were able to fit the data, the implications were too crazy to take seriously.

Maybe the Agni didn't just use suns. Maybe they lived in them.

No one believed it at first. But the wormholes kept opening, and the fit kept improving. Something was altering reactions in the core of that distant star. Something was hastening its demise. Maybe something a little like those fabled cosmic strings said to span the whole universe, but much, much smaller. Small enough to make a proton look big—and complex enough to indulge in behaviors that look a little like *chemistry* if you treated it right, cooked it in magnetic fields and stirred in a stripped nucleus or two for flavor.

The nonsense models said something like that might form stable configurations. Self-replicate, even.

So now it looks like those fires in the sky aren't a weapon but a transit system. Now the Agni aren't gods but just beings from some polluted dying hellhole, looking for a new home. Now they're only immigrants.

At least we know how to deal with those.

Surya's not the most romantic spot for a hook-up. The asteroid's honeycombed interior smells of disinfectant and unwashed socks. The tidal gradients may not kill you outright—the black hole lurking in its hollowed heart is a good five hundred meters from the hab zone— but spend enough time in the lower levels and you'll still have trouble keeping your lunch down. The hundred-fifty-odd souls infesting its tunnels and compartments don't comprise the deepest dating pool in the solar system.

Ondrej and Asia have managed to beat those odds. They're a study in high contrast, the very instantiation of humanity's two-pronged approach to foreign policy: he tasked with talking to the Agni, she with shooting them. A carrot and a stick; an ambassador and a gunslinger.

A hope and a prayer.

There's a place they go when they want to be alone, when Takayama snores inconveniently in their shared quarters and the holds are too jam-packed to accommodate a hamster, much less a pair of human bodies. *SSV Hawthorne* snoozes up on the surface where gravity is barely a concept. It doesn't get any darker this side of Mercury— service shuttle behind asteroid, asteroid behind parasol—and when they settle into the cockpit and boot up the nose cam (taxis in this neighborhood don't come with actual viewports), all they see is stars. Sometimes the crystalline ice sculpture of the BFG off in the distance.

It's impossible to entirely forget the wall of fire seething just the other side of the parasol; in *Hawthorne*, at least, they can try.

He hears her climbing up through the hatch and doesn't turn. He stares at the dash—the sparse twinkling brainwaves of sleeping machinery, a square of the solar horizon on live filterfeed—and tries on a smile.

"So it worked," he says as she squeezes past.

She bounces gently into the shotgun seat and plays along. "Better than we dared hope. It's amazing how much more data you can grab when you set up in advance. Tanak even got a chance to try out the booster. Wanna see?"

Of course he doesn't. He waves an encouraging hand toward the dash anyway. "By all means."

Asia wipes the status lights from the board and opens a new window. "Here's the raw event . . ."

A lightstorm floods the cabin; fiery serpents writhe across the bulkheads. Ondrej squints against the glare as Asia dials back the lumens. "Sorry."

"Got it." Ondrej blinks away afterimages. "The flare."

She nods. "In visible wavelengths. Nothing special." Nothing except fifty thousand kilometers of ionized plasma hot enough to slag a planet. "Filter out the hot stuff . . ."

The conflagration fades, tip to root to sullen red point. Asia zooms in as that ember winks out in turn; a mirrored marble sits in its place, stars bent into bright little arcs around its edge.

". . . and there's your wormhole. But *here* . . ."

She can't keep the enthusiasm out of her voice. She's trying—God how she's trying; she knows she's breaking his heart—but it's a *breakthrough*, it's a dozen conventional hypotheses discarded and a lone batshit hypothesis redeemed and she just can't stop the tiniest thread of wonder from sneaking into every word.

"Here's where shit gets . . . I mean . . ."

Out past the marble, along the cone of the flare Asia's just bandpassed out of sight, the stars begin to twinkle.

"Semipole structures," she says. "Technically, microlensing artifacts around non-annihilating semipole structures. Or if you want to get downright pedantic: massively amplified, contrast-enhanced microlensing artifacts around semipole structures, because the effect is way too small to see otherwise."

"Signs of life," Ondrej says.

"Signs of life." If you can hang that word on something that doesn't even technically exist in spacetime. The Agni *are* spacetime, somehow. Defects in the fabric of reality, like the cracks that form when water turns to ice. No mass to a crack. No volume. In a way it doesn't even exist—not a thing in itself, but a boundary between things. What do you even call something like that?

If you're Asia Piotrowska and her buddies, you call it a *topological defect*: remnants of random phase transitions, microseconds after the Big Bang when the very laws of physics were in flux. Asia goes on about *inflation* and *symmetry breaking* and *non-annihilating magnetic semipoles* and it makes all kinds of sense to her. Ondrej takes it on faith: the Agni are built from cracks in spacetime, and they live inside stars.

They try to, anyway.

But Tanak's booster is only the opening act.

"So." He can't talk around it any longer. "You found your primordial wormhole."

Asia's smile falters. "Rey—"

"What's the deadline?" he asks.

"We don't know yet. We only just confirmed the model. We still have to tweak, backcast the old data . . ."

"Not long, though, right? The primordial's moving at, what . . ."

"Five hundred eighty-three kps," she says. "Give or take."

It says something that she doesn't correct him out of habit: technically the wormhole isn't moving at all. The Milky Way is spinning past it.

"So, soon," he guesses. "Months. Maybe days."

"Rey, we *don't know*. Sure the primordial's on a rail, but these little Ellis pipes coming out of it . . . we're not sure what their range is. Until last week we didn't even have the math to describe a system like this. We might have years."

"Probably not, though."

"I say you keep at it," she tells him. "You've got a great team, they've got a great leader, and like you always say, you never know when a breakthrough might—"

"What makes you think I *want* a fucking breakthrough at this point?"

Asia blinks.

"Sorry. I didn't mean—"

"'S'okay," she says. "I get it."

"It's just . . . what am I supposed to do? I can't exactly ask them to go somewhere else now, can I? Tell me I'm wrong."

"You're not," she admits.

"We've been throwing golden ratios and Fibonacci sequences and coded gravitons at them for years now, and there's no indication they've even noticed. But let's say that changes. Let's say we make history in the next few weeks or months or however long we have. We make contact and say what, exactly? *Hi, we come in peace for all mankind and by the way we'll fuck you up if you try to save yourselves* . . ." He looks back to the board, watches starlight being shredded by invisible prisms.

"We don't even know where they come from," he whispers.

"Or when," Asia says, lapsing back into autocorrect. Because wormholes tunnel through space*time*, of course. Maybe the Agni are living in the past. Maybe in a whole other universe. Ondrej has never been able to completely wrap his head around it.

He remembers something he learned back in happier days, though. "Early universe was really hot, right? All of space was hot. Not just a few miserable stars every dozen light-years."

"Sure, if you go back far enough. That's not what we're seeing, though. Spectrum's not *that* different."

"Maybe they were everywhere back then. Maybe it was Agni paradise."

"Maybe."

"Maybe they're dying out. Maybe these are the only ones left."

"Anything's possible."

"This is genocide, Asia."

A ventilator awakens somewhere to stern, kicks up a sudden breeze. A cargo buckle clicks against the bulkhead.

"This"—there's an edge to her voice—"is self-defense. I'm sorry they're not talking, Rey. Believe me I know how much it meant to you—"

"To me."

"To all of us. To everything—I mean Jesus, do you think *anybody* wanted it to come to this? Every last one of us was pulling for you." Her prickliness is understandable; it's not like he's the one working the military option. "But it's not our fault the Agni fucked up their home. It's not our fault they'll take us out if they come here. It's not even *their* fault, it's just—the way it is . . ."

He breathes in, out.

"When this whole thing started," he says. "When Haussman first showed up at my door—I jumped at it."

Asia nods. "We all did. Who wouldn't?"

"No, I mean—not just because they were aliens. Because I wouldn't have needed to—atone, I guess. Everyone was going on about how grim first contact was turning out to be, you know, even in the best-case scenario we learned their lingo just well enough to tell them to fuck off. But I'd have taken it. Because for once we wouldn't have painstakingly hammered out the common ground and learned the common tongue only to have to admit that we're why their food supply has vanished, why their habitat's been poisoned, why they're stuck in some cage and everything past these fucking walls is dust and fire and weeds.

"And yeah, if we'd succeeded the Agni would've just—gone away. The chance to talk with the most profoundly alien intelligence in the whole damn universe would've slipped through our fingers, but—at least there wouldn't be any blood on them." He shakes his head. "Man, I'd have taken that in a fucking *flash*."

Asia says nothing. Over on the board, the stars are settling down.

"I wonder what we're looking at," Ondrej says.

"Those artefacts? Periscope, I'd guess. Some kind of Agni probe."

"Or maybe it's *them*. Maybe we're watching fleeing bodies throwing themselves off a cliff, hoping against hope they can catch a branch on the way down."

"We're on that branch. If they grab it, we're toast."

"They probably don't even know we exist."

The cabin dims a little. Ondrej glances from the instant replay to the live feed, where the BFG has just drifted across the limb of the Sun.

"They will," Asia says quietly. "Soon enough."

There are so many ways to fuck with spacetime.

Crude bottom-drawer deformations of mass and velocity. Einstein-Rosen bridges that won't stay open unless you hook them up to a whole different universe. Roiling infinitudes of Hossenfelder wormholes way down in the quantum foam, there and gone before even God can see them. Not to mention the gravity-free Ellis wormholes favored by the Agni. There's a whole menagerie of reality-shredding demons that eviscerate common sense, even as the math drags you kicking and screaming toward the impossible truth.

So swap out math for metaphor. That's what Asia did once during a post-coital snuggle session, back when everything was just theory. Back when Ondrej Bohaty could happily entertain any possibility save that of his own failure.

Asia conjured up the universe as a vast lawn, the Agni system as a water sprinkler, their wormholes as streams of droplets arcing over the grass. She cast intelligent ants in the role of humanity: ants smart enough to infer the presence of the sprinkler even though they couldn't see it directly, smart enough to make predictions based on that inference, tenacious enough to keep trying when those predictions turned out to be full of errors. She collapsed all those years of global shock and panic and desperate time-bomb research into a cute little fable about insects painstakingly working out that maybe the sprinkler was not the Agni's home star after all but merely *connected* to it, that the water was coming from somewhere even farther away, that the sprinkler was attached to something else that *moved*. A story ultimately not about a sprinkler at all, but a hose.

A hose almost as old as time itself.

Way back then it was barely even real, a child of quantum fluctuation in a universe that could have got lost inside an electron. But then that universe *inflated*. Reality swelled a trillion trillion times in a trillion trillion billionth of a second—and the hose, caught in the act, stretched and congealed and came along for the ride. Now it is stable. Now it connects points separated by uncounted light-years or unimaginable eons. Now it's stuck fast in the unmoving fabric of spacetime itself, while the grass of the universe passes it by at a cool and relentless six hundred klicks per second.

For the longest time, nobody even imagined the Agni might be using a primordial to get around. You can't aim a primordial. You can't move it. Try grabbing an on-ramp passing by that fast; figure the odds that anything useful would happen to be blurring past at the other end. Those things are useless, especially to a species with Ellis tech.

Unless your Ellis portals can't reach very far. Maybe they can get you a few light-years—as far as some primordial passing through your back forty, say—but not much farther. So maybe you daisy-chain one kind of wormhole onto another: take local transit to the expressway, and attach a sprinkler to explore the neighborhood at the other end. The hose gets you halfway across the galaxy; the sprinkler gives you access to some spherical volume on the other side.

But that volume is *moving*. The primordial's just passing through. And if the place you're trying to get to is near the edge of that sphere, you may not have long before it's forever out of reach. A few centuries. A few years. You're no longer omnipotent beings who bend time and space at whim; now you're just hitchhikers on a tight deadline, your only hope for salvation already fading in the rearview.

It's great news for the home team. No more need for Ondrej Bohaty's Traveling Outreach Carnival. Gone are the days when your only military option is to shoot down as many wormholes as you can, praying the enemy gets fed up and goes somewhere else before you run out of bullets. Now there's an end point. There is a victory state. Glory Hallelujah, this too shall pass.

Not so great for the Agni, mind you. They don't have a galaxy of other stars to choose from after all. Chances are, Sol's their one shot.

That always seems to be the way of it, though. Look closely enough, and the universe always collapses to zero sum.

This is my fault.

Ondrej has communed with pilot whales and giant squid. He has deciphered the thoughts of centaur AIs chafing against enforced symbiosis. He has even plumbed the slow chemical intelligence of hyphal networks kilometers across, glacial and nonsentient and able to rival the problem-solving abilities of a human mind. Now, for the first time, he has failed utterly—and his failure is about to unleash a monster on the universe. It looms big as death on the bulkhead display, writhing with fiery reflections, festooned with annotations and to-dos from those who toil in its service.

Ondrej takes in Mission Control—techs, engineers, particle people trading equations and mumbling among themselves—and gives silent thanks that Asia's not among them. She wouldn't approve of what he is about to do. She would try to talk him out of it. Fortunately she has other priorities at the moment.

Asia spends half her time over there. She's over there right now, one of those bright little ants swarming along the magrails, helping to load the biggest gun in human history. For months the BFG has been gorging on harvested sunlight, storing up all those inconceivable petajoules until its capacitors are full unto bursting. Any moment now, it will vomit all of them back.

Over in her subwindow Asia disappears behind a machine the size of a small building, anchored to a scaffold-webbed sphere two hundred meters across. Hundreds of identical buildings stipple that sphere like spikes on a virus: the back ends of colossal gamma-ray lasers, their hidden muzzles poking down into the hollow interior of that shell. They've been warming up for hours.

It only takes them a microsecond to fire.

Somewhere, someone gives the word. Somewhere else a clock ticks down in increments that make a picosecond look large. Circuits close. Capacitors discharge. Grazers fire: energy turns to matter where their myriad beams converge. A singularity appears there, small as an atom, heavy as a mountain. It bleeds a lethal rainbow of protons and antiprotons and Hawking radiation and can only be handled with the thickest of oven mitts.

Back in Mission Control, a smattering of subdued applause for the birth of another bullet.

That makes seven.

None have been fired. The Agni aren't in range yet, and they're taking their sweet time to close the gap. Asia says Ellis wormholes only work in vacuum, which is damn lucky for the meat sacks; if the Agni could jump directly into the heart of the Sun no one would even see them arrive. Instead they have to flirt with it, rather than fucking it outright: try and try and try again, edging in until they graze the corona. The BFG will be ready when that happens. It will zero out on the prominence erupting from the Sun's surface; it will calibrate its crosshairs to some precise distance above that point; and when the portal opens, the Big Fucking Gun will fire a singularity right down the Agni's throat, collapsing the wormhole before anything gets through.

If the BFG can do that seven times—maybe eight—everyone can go home and get drunk.

Someone taps Ondrej on the shoulder. "You wanted to see the General? He's got a few now."

General Drem Haussman's office opens onto Mission Control. It is no closer to the singularity that gives Surya its disproportionate gravity. Somehow, Ondrej still feels five kilos heavier whenever he steps inside.

To call the place *spartan* would be generous: unsullied by art, by depictions of family or loved ones, by personal items of any kind. It doesn't even have proper bulkheads; the walls are naked olivine, Surya's own guts immodestly exposed and glistening with a sheen of perpetual condensation.

There's a proper deck at least. Probably because Haussman could never abide standing at a desk that wobbled.

"Dr. Bohaty. What can I do for you?"

"I'd like you to reconsider," Ondrej tells him.

"What, exactly?"

"Firing the BFG. Repelling the Agni."

Haussman doesn't speak for a moment. "You want me to stand down. Just—let them move in."

"Yes, sir."

He frowns. "Why in God's name would you ever expect me to agree to something like that?"

"Ethics, I suppose. A principled opposition to genocide."

"It seems to me you're offering to exchange one genocide for another."

"We don't know that," Ondrej says. "Your own people will tell you there's massive uncertainty over how much impact the Agni will have, or how long that impact would take to manifest."

"My own people tell me that the Agni's home star has been sufficiently altered to freeze out any Goldilocks Zone it may have had. And that's assuming that even *is* their original home, and not just one in a succession of destroyed habitats. I'm told that's the most likely scenario for our Sun if we don't take action."

"Do they tell you how soon that would happen?"

"Does it matter? Are you willing to accept our annihilation just so long as it doesn't happen for another thousand years or so?"

"A thousand years ago you'd be commanding forces armed with bows and trebuchets. How would you feel if some medieval lord limited *your* options a thousand years before you were born, based on what he knew back then?"

Haussman regards him from behind a mask of calm and unyielding neutrality.

Ondrej tries again. "Even if we can't imagine a solution from our perspective, it's very possible the Agni could. They're already doing things our physics say is impossible. It's possible they could resolve this entire predicament, but they don't know there's a predicament to resolve yet."

"It's possible," Haussman says, "although if they could resolve this predicament, I doubt they'd be trying so hard to escape from it. But none of that matters if we're unable to communicate with them. Not to put too fine a point on it, Doctor, but that was *your* assignment."

Ondrej opens his mouth. Haussman keeps going.

"I'm not blaming you. I don't believe anyone could have done a better job. But we have to accept that meaningful communication with anything as alien as the Agni might be impossible even in principle. You need some kind of common ground, Doctor, and the Agni hallucinate an entirely different reality than we do. We wouldn't even have math and physics in common."

Ondrej has heard it all before. "You've read Butala."

"Of course. She'd have been on the short list herself, if not for her conviction that Outreach was doomed from the outset. We decided to go with someone less fatalistic." Haussman offers up a tight smile. "Still. You can understand her reasoning."

"I understand it. I'm just living proof that she's wrong."

"Nobody denies your accomplishments, Doctor. But—"

"I've communicated with *fungus*, General. No brain as we define it, nothing even resembling a neuron. Chemical intelligence. Just phyto-hormones and MAPK-signaling and a thousand hectares of quorum sensing—and it can *think*. Hard to imagine a system we have less in common with."

Haussman shakes his head. "Still carbon. Still tissue, still a product of an organic biosphere. The Agni aren't even made of *matter*. You and your hyphal networks are kissing cousins next to that."

"But—"

"You've been trying for years now, without success. Do you really think you'll figure it out in the next four days?"

"It doesn't—" Ondrej double-takes. "Four days?"

"Until they're in range. Until they can get through, if we don't stop them."

"I—I hadn't heard."

"We only just got the numbers." Haussman's shoulders rise, fall. "I won't stop your team from working in the meantime. But even if you made a breakthrough tomorrow, you wouldn't be able to act on it until the Agni opened another wormhole. And the next time they do that, we pull the trigger. I'm sorry."

He grabs the headband off his desk and brings it to his face. Hesitates at Ondrej's continued presence. "Was there something else?"

Ondrej opens his mouth. Nothing comes out.

Haussman's expression softens a little. "It was worth a shot, Ondrej. It would have solved everything if it had panned out. But it's time to move to Plan B. You've made it clear that you don't see things that way, and I appreciate your candor even if it is misguided. I understand that it's not your fault."

Of course. How stupid of Ondrej, to think that the whispers wouldn't follow him down to the very edge of the Sun. "Would you explain what you mean by that," he says, although he already knows. "Sir."

The general sighs. "I mean that perhaps you've rewired yourself so often, spent so much time trying to be all these other marvelous nonhuman things, that maybe you're no longer able to come all the way back."

Ventilators hum into the silence.

"Maybe that's not such a bad thing," Ondrej says at last.

"Perhaps. But I'm not going to gamble eight billion lives on it."

Over the years I have come to regard language itself as a kind of violence. A straitjacket, at best: a square hole into which humanity would force any shape, indifferent to the meaning and nuance that might be scraped away in the

process. Apes flapping their fingers in parodies of ASL, parrots twisting their tongues around human speech, dolphins presented with touchscreens or glorified Morse. We like to pat ourselves on the back whenever our captives manage to squeeze themselves into these boxes, as if debasement somehow scales to intelligence. Can it map meanings onto symbols? Can it build recursive hierarchies, rearrange them in new and context-appropriate ways? Can it talk?

I submit this is the wrong question. Perhaps a better one would be, why should it want to?

Why would dolphins, for example, use words to describe emotional states when they can feel the echoes of their podmates' inmost selves, map out their fellows' heartbeats and heartaches in three-dimensional ultrasound? What use is there for nouns and adjectives among solitary cephalopods who paint pictures on their skin, change shape and texture, turn their whole bodies into dioramas? Does anyone truly believe there is some specific arrangement of phonemes that could truly convey your experience of watching a sunrise? The best any such code can hope for is to kickstart someone else's memories, and hope for enough overlap to convey a reasonable approximation.

Language is not always wisdom. Sometimes, it's just a workaround for lack of better alternatives.

Presumably you've invited me here because of my record of accomplishment. Presumably you'd like me to share the secret of my success. It's simple: I succeed through surrender. I've given up on reshaping nonhuman worldviews into human containers. I reshape myself instead. I will grant that this isn't a perfect solution, and it isn't without risk. Then again, it doesn't have to be.

It only needs to work better than the alternatives.

—Ondrej Bohaty,
Keynote Address (excerpt)
SATI Annual Conference,
Iqaluit, 2105

Asia finds him back in the dim low-slung recesses of *Hawthorne's* cockpit, doodling on the dashboard. "Thought you might be here. What's up?"

He swipes the window back to realtime default: the BFG, as usual. It's on all the feeds these days. "Just—killing time, I guess."

"Well I'm here now, so let it live." She squeezes his shoulder, floats past at a twentieth of a gee, swivels in her seat to drape her legs over his. "Rashi was looking for you."

"Yeah?"

"Something about the phase-structure algos crapping out when you get below four levels of recursion blah blah blah."

He's been meaning to put in an appearance down in Xeno. Formally throw in the towel, if nothing else. He just hasn't found the heart yet.

"I miss the old days," he says. "Back when we thought they were shooting at us."

Asia arches an eyebrow. "What do you miss, exactly? The rioting? The martial law? Waking up every morning, wondering if the whole planet's going to be incinerated by lunchtime?"

"No, I mean—it'd just be simpler, right? If they were hostile. An enemy. We could light 'em up and take 'em down and still look at ourselves in the mirror."

The BFG ripples subtly on the feed, iridesces as a million grazing mirrors shift by infinitesimal degrees to keep the sunlight at bay. A muscle twitch, rippling along the flank of a dragon ten kilometers long.

That thing scares the shit out of me.

"Haussman won't call it off."

Her cheery pretense evaporates. "You went to Haussman."

"Figured, you know. What did I have to lose."

Asia takes a moment, and a breath. Seems to weigh some words against others. "It's a shitty situation, Rey. Nobody's saying it isn't. But—how can this even be an issue? You know what's at stake."

"No, I don't. No one does. Even if the Agni get through it could be centuries, millennia—aeons before we even notice a dip in solar output."

"Or it could be decades."

"To change the whole *Sun*? Do I really have to tell *you* how insane that sounds?"

"Okay, we don't know. But that's kind of the point. Forget that semipolar life fucks with nuclear reactions by the fact of its very existence. The Agni build *wormholes*, Rey. By the dozen. Do you know how much energy that requires? The usual models say it should take half the energy output of a galaxy just to keep *one* of those things open for any length of time."

"The usual models are obviously wrong."

"No shit. But how wrong? They could be off by ten orders of magnitude and the cost would still be enough to bleed out a G-type star in a few weeks."

"You don't believe that. Why jump into a lifeboat that's going to sink as soon as you're on board?"

"It doesn't matter what I believe. We can't take the chance."

He spreads his hands. *"What* chance? One in a thousand? In a million? We freeze in a century, we freeze in a billion years? Everyone's so fucking fond of *we will not gamble with the fate of humanity* but at some point the odds have to be good enough to let it go. Or nobody would ever do anything."

"That's not how people work, Rey."

"Sure it is. We wiped out half the Earth's ecosystems. We're still doing it. We were just a couple of decades from wiping *ourselves* out and we just shrugged it off. If not for a couple of lucky breakthroughs we'd probably be huddling in the ruins right now, dying of heat stroke and fighting over the last few tins of beans. How's this any different?"

Asia sighs. "It's different because *we* were the ones doing all that stuff. We'll gladly trash the place and wallow like pigs in shit so long as it's *our* shit. But the moment we can blame someone *else*—man, we will cut no slack and we will move mountains."

"So it's all just xenophobia. That's what you're saying."

"Rey, we built a gun that fires *black holes*. We did it in less than six years. We never pulled off anything close to that when we were trying to fix the messes *we* made. I suppose we even owe the Agni a debt of thanks, they—woke us up. They turbocharged us. For now at least." She shrugs. "Of course, once the threat's past I bet we just go back to sleep. In the meantime, though . . . we're giants."

Ondrej takes a breath, tastes hints of freon and machine oil at the back of his throat. He summons a rejoinder that doesn't come.

"I spoke to the last killer whale," he says at last.

"I know. I read your CV."

He barely hears her. "Resident matriarch. She was in a tank over in Nanaimo. DFO scooped her whole pod out of the wild to get them away from some mutant red tide that was killing everything. There were only five of them left by then, nothing to eat except toxic fish for God knows how long. They had them in separate holding tanks and I wanted to string a line so they could at least talk to each other but they were already dying, you know? There was some—disagreement over whether it would be an act of mercy or torture to let them hear each other check out. So all the matriarch knew was that we were keeping her from her kids, and eventually I had to tell her they were dead. And then she was, too."

He turns to face her. "I know what it's like to preside over the extinction of an intelligent species. The last thing I need is a refresher course."

Asia takes his hand. "I get it, Rey. I do. But—it's like you said. We've only killed off *half* the ecosystems. The other half's still hanging in there. Countless species besides ours, and they all deserve just as much of a shot as your orcas did. They're all just as doomed if the Agni do their thing."

He manages a smile. "Good move, bringing in the nonhumans like that."

"Well. You always did like animals more than people."

"As if we won't have wiped the rest of them out anyway, before the Agni get their licks in . . ."

But she's right. She usually is. This is the first time he's had cause to regret it, though. It's not orcas or elephants or corvids who are calling the shots here; it never has been.

All the barriers he's broken over the years. All the channels he's opened, all the insights exchanged through clicks and chromatophores and infrasound. All the species he's reached out to; all the species who reached back.

He can't even get through to his own.

At long last, the stars are aligned.

The sims are consistent, the physics is solid, the confidence limits have contracted to a point. The Agni are coming.

He's said his goodbyes to the motley assortment of linguists and poets and mathematicians that comprised his team. They were the very model of discretion, their every word full of respect and regret and not a hint of disappointment in a captain who came so certain of victory and so destined for failure. Amser even presented him with a bottle of seventy-year-old Scotch that made it into the still just before leaf rust took down the world's barley crop. It wasn't much of a consolation prize—Amser obviously intended it for Team Outreach's victory celebrations—but maybe Ondrej can drown in it later.

The gang's still here, of course—maybe in their cabins, maybe hanging out in the mess, maybe even sneaking past the velvet cord into Mission Control where only soldiers are allowed, now that the countdown's running. Outreach is deprecated but nobody leaves until the next looper swings by to take them all home. Another week, more or less.

Ondrej doesn't expect to see them again.

His own cabin is empty. Takayama's on deck for the Moment of Truth. No one can be spared now. Everyone's got something to do.

Almost everyone.

They're piping audio from Mission Control throughout the aster-oid, an ambient soundtrack of numbers and acronyms. Ondrej could get full immersion if he wanted—slide on the headband and view the battleground overlaid with ranges and annotations, colors false and verité, contour maps of the Sun and the sky in wavelengths from gamma to radio.

He leaves it hanging on its hook.

Someone taps on the hatch; it sighs open before he has a chance to answer. Asia steps over the knee-knocker and closes the door behind her.

"Shouldn't you be down at HQ for the big moment?" he asks.

"Haussman gave me the day off. Said I might be needed elsewhere."

"What, all on his own?"

"I can leave you alone if you'd—"

"No. I mean—thanks." He *is* glad to see her, for all the obviousness of the gesture.

She sits beside him on his bunk, lays a hand on his thigh. They listen in silence to countdowns and status reports.

"Nobody could have done more. You know that, right?"

I've done all I can, he tells himself.

"It was just—an insoluble problem. The universe is *full* of those fucking things."

"It wasn't insoluble. We just needed more time."

"Rey. What do you build your Rosetta Stone out of when there's no common ground?"

"I bet they want to survive. I bet we have that in common."

"I suppose, but—"

"People keep talking about the differences. Their math is different. Their physics is different. We probably can't even agree on one plus one. That's not a bug, that's a fucking feature! Imagine what we could learn from something that sees things so differently, if we could just make the connection! Wouldn't you kill to be able to see the universe the way they do, to understand how they build those impossible wormholes? It would change *everything.*"

"Of course. If it were possible."

He stands. Asia reaches out and takes his hand. "Where're you going?"

"Can't hurt to give it one more shot. Worst he can do is say no again."

"He will say no." She squeezes his fingers. "Why put yourself through the wringer again? Just—stay here. With me."

"I have to try." He pulls away, gently.

"You *have* tried."

"I have to try again."

Her grip tightens. "You don't, Rey. That's just ego talking. I'm right here; we can . . ."

She must see the awareness dawning in him. She drops her hand and looks away. Ondrej opens the hatch onto a guard who gives him a nod and a neutral look before closing it again.

"I'm sorry." She won't look at him. "They just—everybody really has to focus, you know? They couldn't risk a scene."

He sits. She doesn't try to touch him.

"You know it wouldn't have changed anything."

He does know. It's not just words, after all; even among humans, so much communication is nonverbal. On some level he saw this coming all along. Maybe he just didn't want to believe it. Maybe he was just trying to lie to himself.

He's never been very good at that, though.

That's why he took steps.

Twin sunspots cough, dark islands on a sea of fire. A glorious incandescent fountain rises between them: a plasma braid arcing high enough to lasso three Jupiters. A stairway to heaven with a ten-thousand-degree halo.

All eyes are on the BFG. All eyes are on the ascending prominence. All eyes are on the empty point at its predicted zenith, where an alien portal is about to open and spill an invading horde into the Sun.

No one notices the *Hawthorne* stir and tick through its preflight checklist and uncouple from its berth on deepest darkside. No one sees it fire maneuvering thrusters, navigate around wireframe antennae and obsessive-compulsive maintenance drones and vast shaded emitters radiating waste heat into the void. No one notices as it edges out of eclipse from behind the parasol, an insignificant speck lost in the glare of a blinding sun.

Hawthorne ignites its torch, opens the throttle, piles on the gees. It heads straight for the BFG.

Now, people notice.

The background burble changes tenor: calm recitations of Gauss and Kelvin falter, segue to confusion. To realization.

Asia hears it too. "Rey . . ."

He closes his eyes, ignores the phonemes, concentrates on pitch and timbre and frequencies sliding along the spectrum. *So much information in those sounds. So much meaning beyond mere* words . . .

Frantic hails and commands, now. Overrides, when it becomes apparent that no one is on board. *Hawthorne* ignores them all. It heeds only one master now, the memory of a voice that spoke to it days ago and gave it new purpose for when the time was right.

Ondrej watches awareness and horror dawning on Asia's face. A lot of information there, too: the dilation of the pupils, the involuntary contraction of tiny muscles around the eyes.

"Stop it, Rey. Call it off."

Telemetry, navigation, helm—code, all of it. Just another language, trivially easy for someone who once spoke to killer whales for a living.

Mission Control will figure that out before long, of course. They'll come with their guns drawn. They'll shout and threaten and speak of dire consequences, but none of that changes the events unfolding now: sixty tonnes of metal and ceramic gone suddenly ballistic, slagged engines white with the heat of suicidal overexertion, streaking unerringly toward humanity's last best hope. On the audio feed frantic voices beg the AIs for a way out—can the BFG move out of the way, can it withstand the impact, can it get off a shot before it gets shot—and while at least some of those answers are *yes*, none of them change the bottom line.

Asia grabs his shirt, leans in close. Her eyes are black with rage. *"Stop this."*

He forks the video onto the wall so they can watch.

The BFG's own torch is lit now as it lumbers toward a higher orbit, but it's too late: *Hawthorne* rams it in the side at fifteen kilometers per second. The onboard's already checking the damage and recalculating the vectors, running a million overlapping Monte-Carlos looking for that one ass-saving scenario but the universe isn't waiting, the door opens at the very tip of the stairway and over the hills and far away a tongue of plasma licks out from one star and stretches toward another. Immense cables of magnetic force writhe and twirl and *snap* together, a spontaneous arc that bridges lightyears without ever touching the space between. Sudden artefacts shimmer along those rapids, like liquid glass poured down a blinding waterfall. The BFG fires, late to the party—damage sustainable, vectors rejigged but not enough and not in time, and a space-crushing bullet the size of an atom arcs wide of the target and plunges into the Sun, screaming Hawking and gamma as strange prismatic ripples splash down and vanish beneath the photosphere.

It's a one-off, of course. They'll repair the damage, reload the magazine, get back into position for the next event. They'll bundle Ondrej off to face judgment, implement measures to ensure that no one will ever be able to follow in his footsteps. Next time, they'll be twice as ready.

But it doesn't matter. Because now—however small the party, however diminished their resources—the barbarians are through the gate. Sol has been *colonized*.

The hatch crashes open. Ondrej holds out his hands for whatever improvised restraints Surya has provided on short notice. Drem Haussman looms in the corridor as they take him from his quarters.

What are you going to do now, General? Attack the Sun?

Asia stands backed into a corner, hands at her sides, the horror on her face segueing into something else.

"Look on the bright side," he tells her. He tries to smile but he can't tell if he's pulling it off. "We're still giants. I've kept us awake."

She turns away, her face a mask of pure hatred.

It's okay. He understands. He'd hoped she would, too—he's shared more of himself with her than with anyone else on Surya— but after all, she's not a communications specialist. There's no way she can understand things the way he can.

That's really been his problem all along, now that he thinks about it.

He understands everyone.

HOW DID THEY KNOW IT WAS AGNI?

Introducing Spectroscopy and its Potential for Finding Extraterrestrial Life

JOANNA PIOTROWSKA

O ne of the most intriguing features of the alien Agni is the way humanity detects their existence in Peter Watts's "Defective." As we learn through Ondrej Bohaty's thoughts, this extraordinary life form is identified through unusual signatures observed in the spectra of stellar matter raining onto the solar system. Although spacetime bridges, cosmic firehoses and Agni themselves still remain primarily in the fiction realm of sci-fi, spectroscopic observations are paramount in scientific research into the nature of our universe. So what exactly is spectroscopy and how can astronomers use it to search for signs of life on planets within our galaxy?

What Do We Mean By A Spectrum?

A spectrum is a fundamental characteristic of light. *Light* or *electromagnetic radiation* is *a form of energy* emitted by a source, e.g., a lightbulb or the Sun, which allows us—the observers—to see the surrounding world. It consists of *electromagnetic waves*—synchronized oscillations of electric and magnetic fields propagating through space.

Like sound or water waves, light waves can be characterized by wavelength, frequency, and speed of propagation. Much like in the case of sound, where different wavelengths (or frequencies) correspond to different perceived pitches, different wavelengths (or frequencies) of light correspond to different perceived colors. A *visible spectrum* is the full range of wavelengths detected by the human eye, which ranges between 380 nanometers (purple) and 750 nanometers (red).

Beyond visible wavelengths, electromagnetic radiation ranges from gamma rays to radio frequencies, and its whole wavelength span is referred to as the *electromagnetic spectrum*. Finally, the relative amount of energy carried by a given wavelength of the electromagnetic radiation from an object is referred to as *the spectrum of said object*. To give an example of what a spectrum in astronomy looks like, Figure 1 shows the sunlight spectrum as a function of wavelength. The figure also highlights the range visible to human eye with different colors labeled in the grayscale.

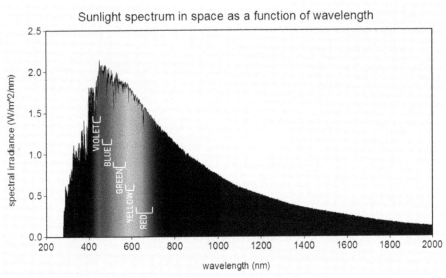

Figure 1: Sunlight spectrum in space as a function of wavelength. Public Domain Image, image source: Christopher S. Baird, data source: American Society for Testing and Materials Terrestrial Reference.

Every Atom In The Universe Leaves Its Unique Spectral Fingerprint
When you examine the spectrum of our Sun closely, you will see that it has a rather interesting shape. Not only does it first rise and then fall off with increasing wavelength, but also it is densely populated with peaks and troughs of varying sizes. This intricate shape is a source of complex information, which encodes details of the temperature, motion, and, most importantly, chemical composition of the object of interest.

So how can we differentiate chemical elements in the electromagnetic signal we observe? The answer lies in quantum mechanics, which governs the structure of atoms. Each atom consists of a nucleus and at least one electron in orbit around it. Atoms of each element have a set of discrete orbits known as orbitals, which the electrons can occupy, and each orbital is associated with its unique energy state—an energy fingerprint, if you'd like. When interacting with matter and radiation, electrons can change their energy levels, being either excited to higher-energy orbitals or de-excited to lower energies. Because energy levels are discrete or quantized, each such "jump" is associated with a precisely defined amount of energy that is consumed or released. Hence, whenever electrons transition between discrete energy levels, they either absorb or emit light of precisely defined wavelengths during excitation or de-excitation events respectively. In Figure 1, light *absorption* and *emission* show up as sharp troughs and peaks known as *lines* in the otherwise smooth curve.

The reason the energy of a light wave is determined by its wavelength lies in wave-particle duality. This quantum-mechanical concept treats light both as a wave and a particle, because neither of the two classical descriptions can fully capture the nature of electromagnetic radiation. The particles of light are known as *photons*, and each photon carries energy directly proportional to its frequency (or inversely proportional to its wavelength).

Due to the varying number of protons in atomic nuclei of different elements, each element has its own unique pattern of available energy transitions. Hence, every element has its own *barcode* or a *spectral fingerprint* astronomers look for to determine which chemical elements constitute a given observed object. Figure 2 illustrates differences in such fingerprints in the visible spectrum, comparing hydrogen, helium, and doubly-ionized oxygen in emission.

Beyond the pattern itself, the strength of each emission and absorption line also allows us to determine the proportion of different elements in the source, hence determining the chemical composition of an observed object. This concept is brilliantly used in "Defective" to introduce a plausible scenario for the detection and understanding of Agni's existence. Humanity of the future finds chemical signatures which "do not fit any usual models" and interprets this disparity as evidence for exotic alien species dwelling in the stellar core. Although present-day astronomers are not actively pursuing the detection of intra-stellar life, they are nonetheless monitoring stars classified as "chemically peculiar" which exhibit unusual chemical composition. These observations will help us better constrain stellar evolution models and understand the extreme physics governing stellar interiors [1].

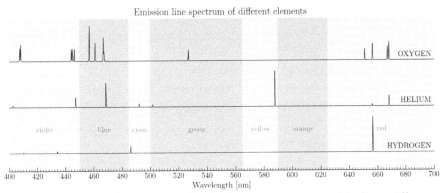

Figure 2: Emission line spectra for hydrogen, oxygen and helium. Illustration: J. Piotrowska

How Can Spectroscopy Help Us Identify Extraterrestrial Life?

As obvious as it may sound, vast distances in the universe prevent us from reaching worlds beyond Earth to explore their atmosphere and surface. As of today, even when studying planets as close as Mars, we still need to rely on robotic probes to search for potential signs of life. Much like with the rest of astronomy research, we are not able to perform experiments in a lab and, instead, need to rely on light to deliver evidence in favor of alien lifeforms.

Since the detection of the first extrasolar planet (*exoplanet*) orbiting a Sun-like star in 1995, astronomers managed to observe over 5000 such objects [2]. Some of these distant worlds could, in principle, harbor life due to their favorable location relative to their host star. Such exoplanet orbits fall in the *habitable* or *"Goldilocks" zone* around their home star where surface temperatures are appropriate for the occurrence of liquid water. This criterion alone, however, cannot determine whether life exists at potentially habitable exoplanets.

This is where spectroscopy comes in. By analyzing the chemical composition of planetary atmospheres, astronomers construct likely models for physical conditions on a given planet [3]. Combining our understanding of the origin of life on Earth with these observations, we can look for exoplanets capable of supporting environments conducive to life. Alternatively, we can also search for the presence of water vapor in the atmosphere [4] or more exotic molecules which can only be created in processes associated with a form of life. An interesting example of such endeavors is a recently claimed detection of phosphine (PH_3) in the atmosphere of Venus. The abundance of phosphine on

Earth is solely determined by human or microbial activity, hence the presence of PH_3 on Venus would carry implications for the presence of life elsewhere within the solar system. Due to the groundbreaking nature of this discovery, the astronomical community was quick to respond to the claims made by the authors, causing an exchange of articles in the *Nature Astronomy* journal [5].

Reaching Beyond Life As We Know It

So what exactly are astronomers looking for in the spectra? They are looking for signals referred to as *biosignatures,* which are defined as objects, substances, and/or patterns whose origin specifically requires a biological agent. These come in three different flavors [6]:

- Gaseous: changes in atmospheric composition due to the presence of life (like PH_3)
- Surface: light reflected off living organisms (such as plant cover)
- Temporal: changes to atmospheric spectra in time, regulated by biological activity

At this point you might assume that the search for all three biosignatures is rather straightforward—after all, we have been studying life on Earth for centuries and know exactly how it demonstrates itself in our own atmosphere. The problem we face, however, is that no exoplanet detected to date is quite like Earth. The planets we observe are very rarely rocky and orbit their host stars much more closely than we orbit the Sun. Because of this, astronomers, biologists, and chemists are now coming together to define new classes of less *terracentric* biosignatures [7]. Limited by finite observation time and the capabilities of current telescopes, scientists are now reaching toward exotic ideas of life ranging from extremophiles in toxic, thick, Venus-like atmospheres to quite unbelievable life forms potentially inhabiting gaseous Neptune-like planets devoid of rocky surfaces [8].

The Future Is Bright

We live in the Golden Age for extraterrestrial life exploration. With the launch of space telescopes like the James Webb Space Telescope (JWST) [9] and future planned observatories like the Atmospheric Remote-sensing Infrared Exoplanet Large-survey (ARIEL) [10] or the Nancy Grace Roman Space Telescope [11] we will be able to study the spectra of exoplanets with an unprecedented sensitivity and resolution. The upcoming astronomical revolution will undoubtedly open our minds to new questions, puzzling conclusions, and unbelievable discoveries. In this imminent gold fever, we may finally learn what exactly defines habitability in the universe and whether water is the necessary ingredient we now consider it to be. Maybe, we will even get to prove the existence of life in unlikely planetary systems around stars strikingly different from our own Sun.

Regardless of what exact signatures astronomers will be looking for in planetary atmospheres, it is important to remember that they would not be able to do this without spectroscopy. Thanks to the unique electromagnetic fingerprint left by every chemical element, we now have the tools necessary to find extraterrestrial life without traveling through spacetime for millennia. And in case we happen to find it, the biggest question still remains—how are we going to act on this discovery? I leave this question for the reader to ponder.

REFERENCES

[1]   Ghazaryan, S., Alecian, G., & Hakobyan, A. A. (2018). "New catalogue of chemically peculiar stars, and statistical analysis." *Monthly Notices of the Royal Astronomical Society*, 480(3), 2953-2962.

[2]   Brennan, P. (2022, March 21). *Cosmic milestone: NASA confirms 5,000 Exoplanets*. NASA.
      https://exoplanets.nasa.gov/news/1702/
            cosmic-milestone-nasa-confirms-5000-exoplanets/

[3]   Madhusudhan, N., & Seager, S. (2009). "A temperature and abundance retrieval method for exoplanet atmospheres." *The Astrophysical Journal*, 707(1), 24.

[4]   Tinetti, G., Vidal-Madjar, A., Liang, M. C., Beaulieu, J. P., Yung, Y., Carey, S., . . . & Selsis, F. (2007). "Water vapour in the atmosphere of a transiting extrasolar planet." *Nature*, 448(7150), 169-171.

[5]   Greaves, J. S., Richards, A. M., Bains, W., Rimmer, P. B., Sagawa, H., Clements, D. L., . . . & Hoge, J. (2021). "Phosphine gas in the cloud decks of Venus." *Nature Astronomy*, 5(7), 655-664.

[6]   Schwieterman, E. W., Kiang, N. Y., Parenteau, M. N., Harman, C. E., DasSarma, S., . . . & Lyons, T. (2018). "Exoplanet Biosignatures: A Review of Remotely Detectable Signs of Life." *Astrobiology*, 18(6), 663-708.

[7] Seager S. & Bains, W. (2015). "The search for signs of life on exoplanets at the interface of chemistry and planetary science." *Science Advances*, 1(2)

[8] Seager S., Petkowski J. J., Günther M. N., Bains W., Mikal-Evans T. & Deming D (2021). "Possibilities for an Aerial Biosphere in Temperate Sub Neptune-Sized Exoplanet Atmospheres." *Universe*, 7(6), 172.

[9] https://jwst.nasa.gov

[10] https://arielmission.space

[11] https://roman.gsfc.nasa.gov

THE DANGERS WE CHOOSE

Malka Older

When the aliens returned, they brought with them an odd tangle of different types of plants and possibly some bones, shaped almost like themselves. Or, maybe, like the drone they had destroyed a few days before. Tens of thousands of miles away, watching the drone video from the Active Encounters room in the Very Foreign Service Department on Space Station Psi, Conta whispered: "It's a puppet!" Remembering how sharply the Mission Director glanced at him, he was later convinced that moment of insight was responsible for his inclusion in the contact team.

After surveying so many planets where water was terrifyingly scarce, or inconveniently frozen, or radioactive, or some such, it was rather a pleasant change to come across a planet doused in oceans.

Emotionally it was a pleasant change; logistically it meant an entirely new set of difficulties and challenges. The Very Foreign Service had to add an entire sub-department of marine engineers, biologists, linguists, and explorers.

It was also the first time they were unable to establish firm radio communication with an intelligent alien species before physical contact, or, for that matter, before even knowing that they existed. The remote exploration team had sent a probe into the humid atmosphere and then down into the sea proper. They were deep enough for daylight to have faded to dimness—although the host star of Atlantis, as the press was tiresomely dubbing the planet, was considerably brighter than Earth's sun—the probe encountered what was at first assumed to be pre-linguistic alien fauna, a swirling impression of sinuous appendages and colored patches.

The entity disappeared before its limbs could be categorized or counted, but the sense of distant wonder soon shifted into a sharper interest when it returned with several similar-looking beasts. They examined the probe gently but thoroughly, setting off proximity alarms along every sensor of its surface and even rotating its joints softly enough not to break them. Then, they began to parade around it, shifting their bodies into new configurations approximately every three seconds. Conta was in the room for this, watching with the rest of the combined underwater and remote teams, and he was pretty sure everyone had been thinking the same thing even before the Mission Director said it.

"They're trying to communicate," she breathed. Her next sentence had been the initiation of the intelligent extraterrestrial protocol, and from that moment it had been the exhilarating whirl of the finest, wildest thinkers in the Very Foreign Service figuring out how to open diplomatic relations with a completely unknown species.

The frenzy was wide and volatile enough to upset the hierarchy, bringing the Mission Director Emeritus out of semi-retirement. The mood around the Very Foreign Service was generally awe-struck—the man had, after all, been the architect of all existing human-alien relationships—but Conta was angry on behalf of the current director. Managing two alien encounters should be enough for anyone, no matter how charming and oversized their personality; it seemed greedy for him to leap back into leadership at the merest whisper of a third.

Conta nursed this anger even though the current director, who had been (hopefully temporarily) shunted into a rapidly created dead-end side branch on the org chart, didn't seem to mind. She was gracious in public and, when he cornered her early one morning, gently resigned. "Had to let him have it." She barely looked up from her screen. "He's always dreamed about finding intelligent beings with radial symmetry, especially in marine organisms." Conta had looked at her incredulously, and she finally met his eyes, with a smile. "Fascinated by octopuses. He volunteers at one of the big lazarus programs. You didn't know? Anyway, I don't grudge him the attention part of it. I'd rather be holed up in here doing iterative analytics, while he enjoys it, so it works out."

Truly, the attention part was horrible, a whirlwind of constant pressure and attention and half-truths. The new-old Director seemed to thrive on it, and the sense of *better him than really anyone else* eventually lessened Conta's resentment somewhat. He himself did his best to stay in the background. His own involvement in the mission was the result of a more or less chance combination of skills he had never thought would be particularly vital in isolation, much less as a group: a SCUBA certification, taken on a lark; an undergraduate minor in linguistics; a functional knowledge of American Sign Language; an advanced degree in marine ecosystems. That last, on paper the most rigorous if not necessarily the most useful, had often seemed a particular irony for someone who lived on a space station. But everyone had been hoping for a planet with unspoiled oceans, and everyone agreed that some expertise was required in identifying what exactly made an ocean useful to humans looking for a place to live.

And now, maybe, they had found one.

"Not that we want to settle their planet out from under them," the Mission Director Emeritus said, and then, seeing a scatter of skeptical looks, raised his voice. "I want everyone clear about this. We do not have an agenda in assessing intelligence. We are not planning on stealing the planet or its oceans, regardless of whether there is an intelligent species there or whether we can communicate with it! Besides, there are other benefits to an intelligent species: trade, learning—maybe this species has the key to healing our oceans, a new chemical compound or a process we would never come up with on our own, the perfect species to reseed . . ."

The skeptical looks continued but more surreptitiously. Conta managed not to exchange glances with anyone, but privately he was appalled that after a long career in intergalactic governance, the Mission Director Emeritus was still so naive as to believe that the discovery of a new planet, a new species, could solve any of humanity's problems.

More drones were sent to the watery planet, submersibles that had been developed to study Earth's oceans, hastily adapted for a profoundly different, if equally liquid, environment. At least a lakh of potential species were glimpsed, from monocellular to complex, most without enough detail to be certain they were distinct species rather than variations in sex or age. In all this panoply of biodiversity, which had already triggered enough funding to triple the size of the xenobiology team, the only beings that appeared to communicate were the tentacled beasts. They appeared in a thick band roughly around the equator of the planet, and every encounter with them seemed to raise estimates of their intelligence.

New robots were developed, designed to mimic the physiognomy of these intelligent aquatic aliens. They observed intensively, developing a tentative vocabulary of tentacle[1] configurations, and then approached and began to attempt communication. Initial interactions seemed successful: greetings were conducted, and then the drone performed an offering of food—based on observed behavior and presented with, in the control room, bated breath—was accepted. They should have foreseen that the aliens would reciprocate the offer: the robot performed the gestures of (presumably) gratitude that the aliens had demonstrated but had no way to consume the vegetation it had received, and this must have been apparent because a few hours later one of the aliens engaged physically with the drone. Unfortunately, there were still some camera angles unavailable in close proximity, so the team wasn't able to see exactly what had happened, but the alien swam away with one of the robot's arms.

"Take note!" The (new, old) Mission Director called, as they watched it fade into the murk. "When you get there, eat anything that is offered—that is, pretend you're eating it, obviously, since we'll want to test it when you get back!" ("And since we'll have no idea what it might do to our physiology?" someone whispered.) "We'll have to design the suits to allow that," the Mission Director added, making a note.

Horrified and sick, Conta barely slept that night, imagining permutations of unfolding violence, but he was at work the next morning, fueled by an eagerness to learn what would happen next. Another drone was designed, with a pouch for hiding anything that should be consumed, but when they aliens came back, they brought the puppet with them.

Because Conta wasn't wrong: the aliens bounced and played their creation in front of the drone. They had analyzed its arm, understood that it was artificial, and mirrored it. "Intelligent, without question. And you know, a thousand years ago we would have done the same," the Mission Director remarked.

"A puppet?"

"Killed one of them and brought it back for examination." The Mission Director looked around at the appalled faces. "I'm not saying we should do that! But we would have. Don't forget it."

"They didn't do it either," one of the senior diplomats said. "They only harmed the drone when they realized it was inanimate."

---

1 *Technically* arms, but as that was confusing, everyone used the vernacular sense of tentacles, despite the annoyance of Conta and the other marine scientists

That, Conta thought, was debatable, but it seemed like something to hope for, so he kept his mouth shut and his bad dreams to himself, curling away from his lover at night.

Thankfully, with high-quality video transmissions, enhanced vision, and discreet, highly sensitive water sampling capabilities on their drones, they didn't have to bring one of the aliens back to study it. A type of buoy, designed to remain above the depth at which transmission became impossible, along with the growing linguistic capacity of the team, allowed for a regular meeting spot. Visual interpretation technicians froze individual frames of the videos, adjusted contrast and color palettes. The aliens (the scientists were fairly sure) were not radially symmetrical so much as spherically so. They didn't seem to have a standard number of appendages, varying between fourteen and twenty-five in the samples they were able to count reliably. "Fascinating, fascinating," muttered Conta's desk neighbor. "Fascinating," Conta murmured to himself, tracing new arm configurations into the digital lexicon he was composing.

But for all of their sophistication, the drones could not transmit from the depths of the planet, and when they were invited to the aliens' [city? territory? home base?], their signals flickered and disappeared in the depths.

"Time," said the Mission Director, "to send in the humans."

"Or," someone suggested from the other side of the room, "we could build some repeaters and try to find a technical solution?"

The Mission Director waved his hand dismissively. "Technical solutions can facilitate but never replace human interaction! Besides, the drones were about at the limit of their usefulness anyway. We need humans in there reacting without the uplink delay."

In the mess that day, one of the other linguists asked what the difference was, really, between a drone directed by a human or a human completely enveloped in a life support suit that would look essentially like the drone. "Layers of recording and transmitting or layers of neoprene and glass, what's the difference?" they asked.

Conta didn't have an answer for that, but he knew it existed, because he wanted to be there, wanted to feel the water around him, wanted to feel, in that moment, that he was very far from home; that he was risking something.

The Very Foreign Service was known as the most reckless extremely-cautious agency: they loaded you up with procedures and safety measures but, in the last analysis, you always had to leap into an extremely unknown situation. Practically this meant it was a place where, if you were lucky in parameters impossible to predict, you might get a drastic jump in status. Such was the case now for Conta, who found himself, unexpectedly, offered a spot on the contact team. He accepted so quickly that when he got to the dedicated team preparation and emotional readiness room, they were still going through his dossier.

"You are. . . ." The woman with his file peered at him over her overlay, one eyebrow raised. "Firstcontact Ikitabu?"

"I go by Conta." He tried not to be angry at his parents. It had, in all fairness, been a watershed moment in the history of . . . everything, really, very exciting to be a part of and all that, but why they had felt the need to memorialize it in *his name*, as if he had anything to do with it, was beyond his comprehension. This development in his professional life made it all the more embarrassing.

"And I am a million years old," replied the woman, which would have told Conta, even if he hadn't already recognized her face, that she was Senior Diplomat Flur, who had been on that first alien contact mission.

"You look no more than . . ." Conta tried to gauge what would be the believable end of flattering and got a glare in response.

"Don't insult me, puppy! I earned my age."

There were three others on the team: Gabor Yu, linguistics; Zeinab Rausch, security; and Coi Vrenam, submarine engineering. It did not escape Conta that there were two male, two female, and one nonbinary team member. They had not been able to identify anything in the aliens that mapped onto the human concept of gender, but the Mission Director was covering his bases.

His lover at the time was, or acted, worried. "Won't it be dangerous?" Conta had pursued Pacex after reading a social media bio: *35% fem, 65% masc, except on alternate Tuesdays or when the wind is in the southwest*. It had seemed romantically whimsical, slightly mysterious; now Conta found himself puzzling to fit it to the person he had come to know, wondering which part he was misinterpreting or whether he was just overthinking something that had, after all, been mostly tongue-in-cheek.

Dangerous. Conta snorted. "Compared to here?" There were new damages being reported every day in the Antarctic conflict on Earth, that stupid, stupid war that nobody seemed willing to just stop, and the species extinction counter clicked higher and higher. He had seen a report the week before that water contamination was far higher than anyone had previously believed.

The move to the space station had at least removed Conta from the war, as such. True, the potential for some kind of technological contamination seemed greater, but the impossibility of avoiding it, whether on his part or on the part of those responsible, made it feel less egregious. But there had been a series of small yet unsettling mishaps and the latest theory was of some new metal-eating bacteria on the space station, which was horrifying even if the station officials insisted, absolutely insisted, that it was nothing to worry about. Conta had seen an opinion vid where someone—a scientist, there were more scientists on the space station than anything else—had suggested it might mutate to eat other things, which was not an image he needed. Since then, Conta had to sleep without touching anything but the mattress on his metal bed in his metal box of a room.

He rather thought the mission would be a relief. Perhaps it wouldn't be any safer, but it was a different kind of dangerous: a dangerous that was worth something; a dangerous that he chose, instead of being unable to escape from.

It wasn't that he wasn't scared. Strapping himself into the beamer that would take them to the surface—*below* the surface—Conta admitted to himself that he was terrified. But although he couldn't feel anything but a screaming desire to crawl away in the moment, there was a grim satisfaction in knowing it was a reasonable fear.

The capsule rattled on take-off, smoothed in the vacuum of space, then rattled again as they entered Atlantis's moist atmosphere. Atlantis's liquid—heavily weighted with minerals and chemical compounds to the point where there was some debate among the scientists as to whether it should still count as water—extended above the surface of the planetary ocean in gradations of humidity. Or perhaps, Conta thought, trying to distract himself from the juddering as the beamer transformed from a spacecraft to a submarine, even calling it a *surface* was inaccurate. From his perspective, face pressed against the window as though its solidity would keep him safe, it was impossible to pinpoint the moment they crossed from dampness to underwater.

They had set a rendezvous point with the aliens; Conta and the others disembarked out of sight of the meeting place to avoid any issues stemming from the beamer. They were wearing dry suits with attached robotic arms to allow them to communicate with the aliens; Conta hoped the creatures didn't feel the need to snap off one of those arms and test it.

Or to test him.

It came to him suddenly and at the worst possible time why the Mission Director had told them not to forget about the historical tendency to kill something strange in order to learn about it.

Conta wanted to kick himself toward the surface, or if there was no surface then toward increasing levels of dryness until he reached outer space, and he might have done it if he hadn't been temporarily frozen with fear, and if the aliens hadn't appeared before he recovered himself, dancing their signs of welcome. *Was everyone else this scared?* he wondered, as he ticked the button for his suit to go into the pre-set response movements. *Should I even be here?* He could feel the sweat on his scalp, and the murky ocean pressed against his faceplate.

He could not quite recover, as they were guided deeper, couldn't stop shaking inside his suit. Flur was talking a soothing stream of words into their comms, a constant report back to Mission Command (or to their recorded buffer, if they were already out of range) on what little they could observe that was also reassurance for the team. Or was it just for him? Could she tell he was a danger to the mission?

The aliens didn't get any closer, which also helped. In fact, as they swam ahead, his fear shifted from being attacked and torn apart to being left behind. Visibility was poor, and using radar or other active visualizations had been nixed in case it affected the aliens. Conta strained his eyes, wanting to feel that he was really *there*, but he could feel only the faintest echo of the cold, since it would have killed him to feel it unadulterated; he was shielded from the ridiculous pressure by his extraordinarily sophisticated suit; and he could barely see. Once a fishy thing slipped past his eyes; it was gone before he could even guess at identifying it, but the thought that he would be able to replay that video later, that the xenobiologists were doing so even at that moment, made him feel a bit better. He refocused on the aliens that were guiding them, blurred at the edge of what Conta could see, their dark shapes merging with the dark liquid around them. Although, as he stared, he saw a kind of after image, a pulsing luminescence, less than a glow but something other than darkness, that followed the aliens as they went. Intriguing, especially as he didn't remember seeing phosphorescence on any of the transmitted videos or in the chemical analysis. Perhaps it was too faint to be noticed on camera.

In that moment Conta was grateful for anything that would help him follow the aliens. If they got lost . . . well, they would probably find their way back to the beamer eventually, and it had a heat search function as well, keyed to their body masses, but it wouldn't be easy. On this unexplored planet, with its wonky magnetic fields and lack of satellites, their navigation systems were imprecise. Conta wasn't even sure whether they were going deeper, although that—he thought with a shudder—would eventually become apparent, when the pressure overwhelmed his suit. The scientists so far disagreed on whether the sea was liquid all the way down or whether there was ice at the planet's core.

He wouldn't have known when they passed the last point the drones had recorded—they couldn't see very far in the murk, and what they could see wasn't static—except for Flur's repeated requests that the Mission Control confirm receipt of transmission. "You've made it," the Mission Director's voice crackled back to them all. The transmission was fading on the edge of their range, and even so he was audibly just a little too exultant. "You're the first to see this." In point of fact, the Mission Control crew was the first to see it, their enhanced video showing them what the contact team couldn't discern through the clouded sea. A few moments later, the residence of the aliens came into view.

It was obvious what it was: it *looked* like them, a roughly spherical shape formed of outflung, wavering cones, and it was clearly constructed rather than natural. It still took Conta some time to get his head around it; he just couldn't make sense of the shape or the directions as a structure to live in. He couldn't figure out which way was up, or where the entrance was. The walls were not only transparent but somehow water-permeable; well, of course, the aliens wouldn't want it to be dry inside. And now the team was inside too, before Conta had noticed their entrance; the curving arms of it must taper open, Conta decided, and with the transparency of the walls and the dimness surrounding them, they had entered without realizing. The passageway was large, and there were intersections with others, though that hadn't been apparent from outside, and eventually the walls fell away and they were in what could be called a chamber, although it was more of an open space.

There were more aliens in there, seemingly awaiting them, since they did the welcome dance at once when the team entered; at least ten or twelve that Conta could see in the dim glow that emanated from the walls, although he couldn't really tell how far the space extended or how many more of the creatures might be hovering beyond his range of vision. They weren't all on the same plane, either, he noticed, glancing up and then down to see that the space opened out in every direction, and aliens hung above and below as well. He wondered, dizzyingly, whether they even had the concepts of *up* and *down*.

Someone—an alien—was talking to him—signing to him. Conta edged into the conversation, uncertain as to whether this momentous meeting had really begun yet. It was difficult to stay aware of the larger surroundings while interacting in a poorly understood, visual foreign language, but when he got a chance to set off one of his preprogrammed sequences, he used the opportunity to glance around. It looked like everyone was talking already, not all of them in ones and twos—Flur seemed to be commanding a sizable group of interlocutors—and he felt less guilty about getting snagged into talking separately.

That let Conta turn his full attention to the alien, its arms wound with dull pink or puce stripes, who was asking him about where he came from. As they interacted, eventually joined by another alien and then two more, Conta felt the linguistic challenges wrapping his focus like a skein of connective threads until he was cocooned in the interpreter's trance: his whole self concentrated on understanding meaning while disentangling an entirely different approach to grammar and etiquette. They talked about body parts and ocean currents, and as Conta prodded at vocabulary until he was pretty sure they were talking about family (or friend?) relationships, the small part of his brain not entirely focused on meaning noted that the Mission Director had been right, it was different from working through the drone. How was it possible that he could dislike the man so much and like him so much at the same time?

When Flur tapped him on the shoulder, his surroundings came back to him slowly and surprisingly: how could he not have noticed the dimness of the space? In his mind the conversation had been brightly illuminated, as if by the successful flashes of understanding.

"Time to go," Flur said, with a quirk of her mouth that might have been wry sympathy or gentle envy, and as he heard the words through his earpiece, he realized she had said it a few times already.

THE DANGERS WE CHOOSE

"Right," Conta answered, "yes. Of course." Flur's smile widened, and he remembered she had done this, or something like this, before.

"So." Flur couldn't exactly turn back toward the aliens, since they were all around her, but she turned away from Conta anyway, to mark the end of their tête-à-tête. She waved her arms in the gratitude expression—although, after his conversation, Conta thought that it would be probably more appropriate to twitch the tip of the middle left arm at the third beat, to indicate gratitude *and* separation, but he might be wrong about that, he'd have to watch the response—and then she turned. And turned again.

"Err," she said. "Does anyone know how to ask which way we came in?"

There was a static of overlapping replies on the comms as everyone tried to remember whether they did, or explain why they don't, or say which way they *thought* they arrived from. Several of the team members made the gesture for "back" that would be intuitive for humans, but, to Conta's eye, resulted in a similar kind of confusion among the aliens, as each of them signaled some different and specific concept that had nothing to do with what they were trying to say. Conta attempted to figure out how to *ask* the aliens about the words they need, and he couldn't. After the intense but exhilaratingly manageable conversation he just had, it felt like running into an invisible wall that he couldn't feel his way around: the human team had no word for *where?*, none for cardinal or ordinal directions, no *up* or *down*, no *before* or *after*.

Conta was still talking to the aliens, trying to elicit a word for the place they were in, hoping to use that to refer to the humans' own artificial structure, when Flur called it. "We've passed our first, very conservative oxygen use threshold," she said into the comms. She said it quietly, very calmly, but Conta felt the frisson pass through the whole group. He was relieved that he wasn't the only one jerked into greater urgency. "We're going to try to make our way out of here, aiming for my . . ." She was picking a direction at random. "My three o'clock. Horizontally. Err . . . that way! Hopefully," she went on as she began to swim, "they'll get the message and help us out, and if not, we will try to get close enough for a more precise location read from the ship."

The human team coalesced and began swimming in the direction Flur chose; they reached one of the smooth, curving, glowingly transparent walls almost at once, but Flur turned along it, following it toward what would eventually have to be an exit (Conta assured himself).

The aliens did react. For a gut-dropping moment Conta thought they were closing in to head off the humans' escape, but they did not come any closer than usual and merely asked *What are you doing?*

We need to find . . . Conta intuited a word for "our" and then brought his knuckles toward the wall, stopping short of rapping on it when he remembered there might be a good social or physical reason for not touching it. *We will . . .* he didn't have a gesture for "return." *See you more,* he finished, hoping this didn't seem too abrupt, or like an escape, or insulting, or abandoning. But they replied with the gratitude gesture, so it was probably fine, unless the aliens were being polite or, heaven help him, sarcastic.

The aliens trailed behind the humans as the space they were in narrowed to a tunnel once more, which would have been reassuring if he had been afraid of capture but felt terrifying as his worries shifted to being lost. Conta had no idea whether this was the same tunnel they'd entered through; continuing straight out of its egress could take them deeper, or in the opposite direction from the ship. Desperately, he hung back too, and then gestured to the aliens with the signs they had used to invite the drones, and then the humans, to their home. *With us?* maybe, or something along those lines.

With a flurry of swirling tentacles (Pleased? Probably . . .), the aliens followed. As they exited the glowing structure into the seas, however, they dropped back again, gesturing confusion. "Wait a moment, Flur," Conta said into the comms. "I think they can help us." *Such a simple solution, after all,* he thought: *lead until they realize we have no idea where we're going.*

The puce-ringed alien signed to Conta: *Are you confused? We left a trail for you to follow.* And indeed, when Conta had accompanied him partway around the spiky alien structure, he saw the iridescence he had noted on the way in, glowing more visibly than before.

"Look!" he crowed, glancing back to be sure the rest of the team was following. "They left us a path! This must be how they get around."

Flur had caught up to him first and was staring past him. "What path?"

"That glow! I noticed it when we were coming, but it was fainter then . . ." Conta trailed off, watching her face. "You can't see it?"

"No, but lead on if you can. Can anyone else see it?"

"Nope, not a thing," replied Zeinab, echoed by Gabor and Coi.

Their small escort of aliens was gesturing them on. "They're going to help us," Flur said, with something more than relief in her voice, something like triumph. *Helping* was one of the fundamental principles used to cement alien relations; mutual was best, but even unilateral helping was an excellent result for a first contact visit. "Let's get back." A few minutes later, they caught the first transmission from Mission Control, and Conta felt tethered to his own world again.

The oxygen limitation had been very conservative; even with the swim back, and elaborate and repeated gestures of gratitude and farewell to the aliens, they all had more than an hour of life support left in their suits when they boarded the beamer and started upwards (outwards? Toward space, in any case). Even so, Conta was trembling. Gabor and Coi were loud with relief. Zeynab was taking deep quiet breaths in the back, face determinedly pointed toward the window. Flur, next to Conta, was piloting, mouth firmly set. Feeling his gaze, she glanced at him with a smile. "You all right? It's a shock, isn't it?"

"It's . . ." No, there was no way to answer it.

"It's a lot of emotions," Flur answered quietly. "No need to mute it."

"Did they infect me with something?" Conta blurted out. "Why could I see the glow and nobody else could?"

Flur didn't babble meaningless reassurances, thinking about it as they passed the unnoticed transition from liquid to something approximating very damp air. "I'm not sure how they could have without, er, passing it on to us too, although I suppose it's possible."

"I doubt it," broke in the cheerful voice of the Mission Director. "We've just had a look at your genetic profile, Conta. There's a mutation in your optic nerve that may be responsible. We'll do some tests when you get back, but an estimated 10.2% of humans have that mutation, so I suspect we'll be adding that to our recruiting profile for this mission."

"A mutation in my *optic nerve*? I didn't know that."

"No reason you would, until now. Doesn't look like there's anything it would make any difference with on Earth."

Flur grinned at him. "I guess you've got a guaranteed job on this one, if you want it."

They passed out of the cloudy atmosphere of Atlantis and into space.

"Yes," said Conta, remembering not the danger, or the relief, or the wonder, or the helpfulness of the aliens, but that feeling of understanding past all the differences. "I want it."

THE HABITABILITY OF WATER WORLDS

FLORIS VAN DER TAK

I n Malka Older's "The Dangers We Choose", a space traveler called Conta discovers a planet entirely covered with water and makes contact with intelligent organisms that live in the ocean. In the 1995 science fiction movie *Waterworld*, with Kevin Costner and Jeanne Tripplehorn, the Earth is almost completely flooded and people are struggling to survive aboard boats. In the Bible, God punished humanity by flooding the Earth, and only Noah survived on his boat, along with two specimens of every animal species. Do such water worlds actually exist? Could they be habitable, and even host intelligent life?

Do water worlds exist?

Water is essential for all life-forms on Earth, even though some species like cacti do not seem to need a lot of it. Especially those of us living in wet countries like the Netherlands may think that Earth is a water-rich planet. A look at the world map may even suggest that the Earth has more water than land! However, although oceans make up two thirds of the Earth's surface, they are only a few kilometers deep, which is less than 1% of the Earth's radius. The Earth is mostly a piece of warm molten rock, with molten metals at its hot center, and a cool solid crust as its skin, which is covered with a thin layer of water. In the atmosphere, water is confined to the troposphere, which is the bottom ~10%: condensation into clouds and precipitation prevent the water from rising higher. Our view of the Earth as wet is biased to our limited habitat.

Other planets in the solar system contain much more water, albeit usually in non-liquid forms. The giant planets such as Jupiter and Saturn contain large amounts of water vapor, especially at low altitudes due to condensation into clouds. The rings of Saturn consist mostly of water ice particles, and many moons of the giant planets are covered in ice. Some of these moons, especially Europa (orbiting Jupiter) and Enceladus (orbiting Saturn) have oceans of liquid water below their icy surfaces, because these moons are heated internally by the periodic gravitational pull of their host planets.

Other planets are dry, such as Mars and Mercury, and also our own Moon. Venus is also dry: it is covered in clouds, but these clouds are not made of water vapor, but of sulfuric acid. Venus is bad as a holiday destination! The surface of Mars actually shows signs of running water in the past (like riverbeds) suggesting that Mars's surface was wet until ~3 billion years ago—a period aptly named the Noachian. Since 2021, the NASA rover Perseverance has been looking for signs of past life in such riverbeds.

What do water worlds look like?
Since the discovery of the first extrasolar planet in 1995, over 5,000 exoplanets have been found, and astronomers think planets are as common as stars in the universe. That means, in our Milky Way alone, there are 300 billion planets or more! If our solar system is any guide, then some of these planets should contain water, and a few may even host life in one form or another.

Other stars are too far to travel to, at least within this century, so we cannot directly see if exoplanets have oceans. We can however make a good guess because we can estimate the bulk densities of exoplanets. This works best for planets which happen to pass in front of their host stars (so-called transiting planets). When this happens, the planet blocks some of the starlight, and measuring how much the star dims tells us the size of the planet (relative to that of the star, which we know from its brightness and color). We can also measure how much the star moves due to the gravitation of the planet, which tells us the planet's mass. Combining the size with the mass gives us the bulk density of the planet.

The bulk density helps us to know the composition of a planet. The high bulk density of the Earth (5.5 g/cc) reflects its iron core and rocky mantle, while Jupiter's moon Europa (3.0 g/cc) is half ice and half rock, and Saturn's moon Mimas (1.2 g/cc) is almost pure ice.

Many exoplanets have densities of 2–3 g/cc, indicative of ice-rock mixtures. Some of these may have liquid surface water, since we have seen water vapor in the atmospheres of several exoplanets. Our solar system contains at least ten icy moons, and several of these (notably Europa and Enceladus) are thought to harbor oceans underneath their ice crusts.

Altogether it seems very likely that ocean worlds exist outside our solar system.

Are water worlds habitable?

The presence of land on a planet may help the development of life, but it may not be a necessity. The oceans on Earth are full of life: not just fish but also marine plants, plankton, and many types of bacteria and other micro-organisms. We do not know where life on Earth originated first, but the seafloor is a prime candidate, in particular at hydrothermal vents, analogous to underwater volcanoes where warm gases are emitted from the ocean floor. The early Earth was probably close to a water world, with just some volcanic islands: only after about a billion years had the crust cooled enough for continents to form.

Actually, the presence of too much water on a planet could be a problem for the origin of life. Those of you who have tried deep water diving will know that pressure increases rapidly with underwater depth, namely by 1 atmosphere for every 10 meters. Depending on salinity and temperature, the water will pressure-freeze into ice at depths between 100 and 300 km. The oceans on Earth are not deep enough for this, but such "high-pressure ice" may occur on Jupiter's icy moons Ganymede and Callisto, and on water-rich exoplanets as well.

A bottom layer of high-pressure ice is bad news for life if it impedes contact between ocean and rock. First, it means no hydrothermal vents, i.e., no cozy warm spots from which life can tap energy. Second, it means a lack of nutrients. Even though our bodies are made of 70% water (and cucumbers of 99%), we cannot survive on water alone, and neither can cucumbers. Marine organisms need a rocky seafloor as a supply of minerals to build cell membranes, for their metabolism, and for other purposes. However, high-pressure ice layers may not act as geochemical barriers after all: when warmed up by internal heat, the ices may allow convection, and water plumes may go through the layers like magma through Earth's crust.

In 2017, scientists were excited when NASA announced that its Cassini mission had found hydrogen gas in the plumes of Saturn's icy moon Enceladus. This gas is a sign of the presence of hydrothermal vents on the bottom of Enceladus's ocean. Scientists have calculated that this ocean is only ~10 km deep: more than on Earth, but not deep enough to build a floor of high-pressure ice. This makes Enceladus a prime candidate for the existence of extraterrestrial life, although this life would be quite unlike that on Earth. The ice layer shields

Enceladus's ocean from sunlight, so such organisms cannot use photo-synthesis as an energy source, as plants on Earth do. Such life would be hard to discover as well.

Do water worlds remain habitable long enough?

Even though the presence of land may not be required for the origin of life, land may be an important factor for the long-term habitability of planets. The surface temperature of a planet is determined by the amount of starlight it receives, which depends on the type of star, the size of the planet's orbit, and the reflectivity of the planet. Over millions of years, stars change in color and brightness, and planetary orbits are influenced by the gravity of other planets in the system. If polar caps grow, more starlight is reflected by ice and snow. The temperature also depends on the atmosphere, which acts as a blanket (by the greenhouse effect). A planet that is habitable initially may thus not remain so forever.

The climate on Earth is stabilized by the silicate-carbon cycle. Atmospheric carbon dioxide reacts with silicate rocks to form carbonate, which is buried on the seafloor and forced into the mantle in subduction zones by plate tectonics. Meanwhile, volcanoes emit fresh carbon dioxide into the atmosphere. This process stabilizes the climate because the burial rate depends on temperature. More atmospheric carbon dioxide leads to a larger greenhouse effect, which warms the planet. This leads to faster plate tectonics which buries more carbon, reducing atmospheric carbon dioxide, and cooling the planet back down. Seafloor rocks can also react with carbon dioxide dissolved in ocean water, but it is unclear if this process is temperature dependent. If not, water worlds would not have a silicate-carbon cycle, and changes in their stellar or orbital properties would lead to irreversible climate change and a fatal loss of habitability.

Planets with stable climates may still become uninhabitable if they lose their water. This has happened on Mars and Venus because their water evaporated into the atmosphere and did not re-condense into clouds. If water molecules rise too high, ultraviolet sunlight breaks them apart into hydrogen and oxygen atoms. The oxygen stays around, but the hydrogen is light enough to escape into space, so it cannot re-form water. On Earth the ozone layer protects atmospheric water molecules (and our skins) from ultraviolet light. Ozone is made from oxygen molecules, which are made by a type of algae (cyanobacteria) which developed ~3 billion years ago. It is both beautiful and ironic that life on Earth thus acts to protect itself!

Can water worlds host intelligent life?

Even though it is difficult to precisely define intelligence, it is clear that the oceans on Earth host fairly advanced forms of life. Examples are dolphins, who communicate with sound signals over thousands of kilometers, and octopuses, who have great eyesight and advanced brains to coordinate the movements of their arms. Generally, the smartest animals are those who hunt, as this behavior requires predicting what the prey will do. Hunting in groups requires even more brainpower, as it takes coordinating actions with fellow hunters. Examples of all these live in the sea, and there is no a priori reason why oceans on other planets could not develop something similar.

How likely is Conta's story?

Water worlds likely exist, and may be habitable, although it is unclear if their climates would be stable enough for intelligent organisms to develop. Bacteria arose on Earth "only" 0.5 billion years after its formation and have thus been around for ~90% of Earth's history. Plants and animals, on the other hand, have only existed for 0.5 billion years, or 10% of history, and humans for less than 1%.

Conditions on Earth do not seem too unusual relative to planets elsewhere in our galaxy, so it seems likely that life exists on other similar planets. On the other hand, even after ~100 years of radio communication, no telescope has ever picked up any signal that convincingly looks like a message from another civilization. This cannot be for lack of targets: within 100 light-years from us, there are about 14,000 stars, which means about 140 Earth-sized planets. Even so, the odds of being in the right place and time for picking up such signals are actually small. Harder to understand is why aliens have never visited us. Civilizations capable of interstellar spaceflight should be able to travel to numerous other stars within tens of thousands of years. This discrepancy, which is known as Fermi's paradox, has several possible explanations. Perhaps the climate on Earth is exceptionally stable, or the chances for multicellular or intelligent life to develop are extremely small, or intelligence is just a short phase in the life of a planet. We are building new telescopes, both on Earth and in space, and maybe one day on the Moon, to explore the properties of extrasolar planets. Hopefully we will one day understand why contact with other civilizations is so hard to establish, and we will know whether we are alone in the universe.

FURTHER READING

Grimaldi, C. (2017). "Signal coverage approach to the detection probability of hypothetical extraterrestrial emitters in the Milky Way." *Sci. Rep.* 7, 46273. DOI: 10.1038/srep46273

Hayworth, B.P.C. & Foley, B.J. (2020). "Waterworlds May Have Better Climate Buffering Capacities than Their Continental Counterparts." *ApJL* 902, L10.
https://doi.org/10.3847/2041-8213/abb882

Höning, D., Tosi, N., Spohn, T. (2019). "Carbon cycling and interior evolution of water-covered plate tectonics and stagnant-lid planets." *A&A* 627, A48. DOI: 10.1051/0004-6361/201935091

Noack, L., Höning, D., Rivoldini, A., Heistracher, C., Zimov, N., Journaux, B., Lammer, H., Van Hoolst, T., Bredehöft, J. H. (2016). "Water-rich planets: How habitable is a water layer deeper than on Earth?" *Icarus* 277, 215-236. DOI: 10.1016/j.icarus.2016.05.009

Tjoa, J.N.K.Y., Müller, M., van der Tak, F.F.S. (2020). "The subsurface habitability of small, icy exomoons." *A&A* 636, A50. DOI: 10.1051/0004-6361/201937035

THIRD LIFE

Julie E. Czerneda

First Life

Sated and glad, Still-Without rests. Languid and lost, seems the man below, his arm limp over the side. Is this comfort? Should oble risk disturbance to lift his arm to the bed?

Instead, oble waits. He is so beautiful—languid, lost—a wonder within a marvel, a tender integument the color of alabaster.

Alabaster or pearl? Oble has a thesaurus. Marble might be more apt, given veins of sapphire beneath, yet all are wrong. His body resembles polished stone. It is not. It is so terribly fragile. Oble must be gentle and is.

The man has more of the growth called hair where his limbs and torso meet. Oble does not and wants a better word. Thinks of the weavings in the booth, of why they've come on the long star-train trip from Home to this, for the twenty-fifth Fair of Goods.

Thinks of oble's deepest need.

Oble will call them threads. Golden threads to frame his intricate eyes and—oble gives a soundless laugh—his pleasure, as if that could be missed. Oble has orifices. First life lacks markings to say this for air or that for secretion, but the man asked and oble showed him. The ones giving oble pleasure. The ones for love and binding.

Oble regrets nothing. Lowers from the ceiling, holds by two limbs and their sucker tips. First life is lithe and strong. As is the man. They have other similarities. Paired eyes, though oble's are larger and superior. Oble's been told this. Now doubts it.

His eyes see oble as no other has. Knows oble. As oble's see and know him.

Oble's antennae poise to stroke his pleasure again, quivering and ready, but he remains languid and lost. Asleep?

Or dead. Oble chills with concern until seeing the rise and fall of his chest cavity. There is bone inside him, pressing at the tender layer as if

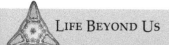

to escape. Oble's body is hard out and soft in, but there are other kinds of body. The movement means breathing in his. Life.

Oble trembles with relief. He must not die. Ever. He's given oble names. The one oble likes best is Joy. The word feels as if it enters oble's pleasure orifice. As if it stays.

Oble strokes his golden threads, suddenly in need of more.

Delegate Samoth Alan went through the next day of the Goods Fair in a daze, unable to keep his thoughts from straying—as he had, last night, unforgivably. Unforgettably.

Disappointment and frustration—the delegation for Terra Imports had failed to find what they'd come for, a novel style of weaving, new threads for the Weavers Collective, anything to set their work apart offworld and gain a market.

No, to be accurate, he'd refused to part with their scarce coin for what Terra made better, grew better. His colleagues, seeing failure, had the right to doubt his leadership.

He'd the right to storm away in fury—

Losing the hard edge of his anger wandering aisles near closing time, aimless and alone while delegates flocked to bars and restaurants to celebrate or drown their sorrows.

To find himself where he'd come many times before.

The Nuarysen booth was small and plain, easily overlooked amid the flashier, polished offerings of the Seven Systems and their associated hinter-worlds. Rented posts supported a dull canvas roof and walls. The only indication this booth was special was the shimmering sign over the door, a tapestry of threads the like of which had never been seen here before.

For what might be the hundredth time, Samoth stood, staring at the sign. This. This was what he'd come to find. If only—

If only every offering hadn't been snapped up within seconds of the Nuarysen's opening. If only speculators hadn't driven the price for the tiniest spool to unheard-of levels.

Beyond theirs.

Even the sign over the now-closed door was marked as sold. Someone would take it apart, thread by thread, selling those as well. He hoped they were careful. Respectful of the craft.

The door beneath the sign drew back.

The unexpected dazzle of a carapace caught his eye, quickly hidden by a cloak, itself a work of art.

Thinking back, Samoth knew he'd had no reason to believe it an invitation, that his presence had been noticed. He wasn't a buyer. Was at best a mediocre weaver, his skill and passion for thread itself.

He was through the door in a heartbeat.

Whomever he'd glimpsed vanished, not that he'd cared. Textiles like clouds formed an inner maze and Samoth moved through what embarrassed silk, mocked the finest weaves he'd ever seen.

Humbled, he eased his way through the hangings, enchanted as they caressed his face and neck, slipped through his fingers until—he touched a cloak.

Being worn.

"Oh." The gasp was melody, liquid and pure.

Samoth jumped the wrong way, found himself tangled in the cloak. Lost his balance and grabbed—what he absolutely had no permission to—and let go hurriedly, stammering, "Apologies. I'm not usually this clumsy—"

An arm—he thought it was an arm—went around his waist to keep him on his feet. "Are you all right?"

Sense came back. "Forgive me. I'm Sam—Delegate Samoth Alan, Terra System Imports."

"I am not. A delegate, that is."

The voice. He had to hear more. "The threads, the weaving. It's wonderful work."

"It's my mother's."

"Please convey my admiration. Ah. May I have your name?"

"You may call this oble what you like, Samoth. In first life, I am Still-Without."

Trapped as much by the lilting voice as the precious material of oble's cloak, Samoth succumbed to the ridiculous, beginning to laugh.

"My name is funny?"

"No, no. This. This." He couldn't stop. "How do I—how do we—"

Oble's laugh was like spring rain. "Carefully."

They freed themselves with a mutual exploration he wasn't sure he started or oble did. He breathed in a scent, rich and intoxicating. Breathed again greedily. Found himself regarded by eyes like—

They'd gone to his rented room, both of them laughing, both urgent. Discovered one another, each a treasury of strange growing familiar, growing dear and precious. He'd whispered endearments, weaving words like thread to bind them as they were, his heart too full for his chest and afraid, even then, this was but a dream.

Called oble Joy. The beautiful Nuarysen had trembled in his arms, eyes gleaming, and held him tight. "A gift, Sam. One I will carry always in my hearts. As I will you."

Today was after, *always* a dream, regardless how he thought he felt.

Hormones, weakness, poor judgment—those were the shameful reality he'd added to his failure. Terra Imports would not be invited to the next Fair. The Weaver Collective would disband.

Samoth stayed in his delegation's office, counting the hours until the ship took him home.

What he'd carry in his heart was for him alone to know.

Second Life

Oble is no longer Still-Without. The others discover this on oble's return to the booth, and the two who'd followed oble from Home, who'd competed and sang and been thorough fools—in oble's opinion—are destitute.

Oble ignores their pathetic wails. Scorns their complaints and accusations. Knows them as unworthy of what oble is to be, that oble cannot become alone.

Before, was oble not ready to give up? To die, as oble is? Only to see him, who came not for oble but for the makings of Home. Who loves what he cannot have. Oble sees in this one what the others lack. Selflessness. Awareness. Appreciation.

His laugh wins oble's hearts, frees oble's pheromones. His body fills oble's needs; his words oble's soul. Ready to become, oble is now and forever With-Samoth, who calls oble Joy.

Who doesn't return.

Oble refuses to leave the booth.

Who doesn't return.

The Goods Fair ends. Others take the booth down around oble, delivering what was sold. Oble has the right to wait.

Who doesn't return.

Has no choice but wait.

Word of a Nuarysen who won't leave the Fair reached the spaceport an hour before Samoth and his colleagues were to leave the world, and his heart soared.

He knew who it was. Hoped he knew why. Had to go and be sure.

The others were aghast. There'd be fines for any delay, fines draining the last of their savings, but he didn't try to explain.

Samoth took a taxi back to the Fair. What remained of it. The aisles were gone, leaving a windy open courtyard girded by stacked posts and rolled carpets, to be stored until the twenty-sixth Goods Fair. Streetlights cast more shadow than glow. Litter tumbled. Samoth ordered the taxi to wait and walked into the gloom.

Desperation. Illusion. With every step, the weight of his choice grew, crushing him with doubt. There was nothing for him here.

Until there was. At the sight of a cloaked figure, sitting alone on a small trunk, Samoth began to run. "Joy!"

Joy-With-Samoth's new world is beautiful, as full of different colors and tastes as each day is with love. Their new home is perfect, for Samoth built it to please them both—Human and Nuarysen—the cost but a fraction of what oble brings in the small trunk, oble's mother's gifts.

There is a large and airy building where oble teaches Samoth and his friends to weave as oble was taught. The Humans are clever, adapting Nuarysen techniques to the threads of this world. The results are remarkable. The Weaver Collective of Terra has a standing invitation to every Goods Fair, not that they themselves leave.

At night, oble and Samoth bring each other laughter and joy. He speaks of always, being happy and as he is to be.

Oble shares his happiness, but oble is not.

This dawn, as every dawn, Joy-With-Samoth clings to the lattice on the ceiling. Beneath, languid and lost, is the one who means everything. Oble watches breath move his alabaster chest, prepares to take the last dose of the medicine that delays the inevitable, that keeps oble what Samoth can hold and love.

Tosses it aside.

The change must come. All oble can do is hope for understanding. To hope he will stay.

When Samoth wakes, oble reaches down to gather him up to oble, holding him high and safe and close. He laughs.

When oble tells him what oble must, he stops.

Samoth left the house, their home. Walked somewhere, anywhere that was away, because it wasn't the hell fair. None of it. Not falling in love, not finding a partner who brought out the best in him—in everyone oble touched—not their success—not a happiness beyond his dreams only to—

—lose it. Samoth stopped, sinking to his knees. Birds were starting to sing. Oble asked that of him. Only that. To sing. To stay and sing.

To that? Bent by pain, he let his tears fall to the earth.

It was the Naurysen way, oble told him. To form a bond. A bond that, if strong enough, trusted and sure enough, would usher in change. The second life.

What life? Their love doomed them, that's what it meant.

He'd wondered about the tower oble had wanted built above their bedroom. Thought perhaps it was an observatory, that oble was homesick and missed the stars above another world. But it wasn't that at all.

It was to be a coffin. One with a chair for him, windows for him, a door for him. For oble, only a dreadful hook.

He'd managed to stay, to watch his love climb with unfamiliar stiffness to it. Turn to grip it, those supple limbs that had caressed and cradled him locking in place, losing their brilliant color as the rest did, the sleek carapace turning dull, oble's eyes the last to cloud, the love in them gleaming until it was gone.

Then he'd run.

Stay and sing to that?

Samoth spread himself on the cold ground and sobbed until he was spent.

He climbed the stairs. Oble had used them. Preferred climbing up walls and swinging along the ceiling like poetry become light—unless they'd company who might be startled. Grief shuddered through him. He was out of tears. Out of anything. He'd have to tell the others. Some would grieve with him. Others be relieved, not that they'd ever say it, but what he and oble had—

Samoth reached the top. Opened the door. Stared.

He'd left a convulsed, dull body. What hung before him glimmered as if covered in gemstones, aglow with an inner light. "Joy?"

Was that a shiver?

Samoth sat in the chair. "I don't know why you want me to sing to you. I can't hold a—" The long narrow shape trembled, sending prisms dancing over the walls.

Joy still heard him.

Oble wasn't gone.

The realization changed everything. "I'll try." His voice came out hoarse and thick. "In the town where—" He didn't know the words. To anything.

So what? Joy-With-Samoth didn't know them either. He began to laugh.

The shape bounced.

"All right. All right." He coughed to clear his throat. "Here goes nothing. La la laaa. La la la laaaa."

The shape remained still. Judging, that was. Samoth put more into it. "LA LA LAAAAA!"

To his astonishment, threads formed on the surface.

"Lala DA da DAH."

Formed and slowly spun free.

The Nuarysen's great secret. Mother's work. Oble had called the fabric in the booth her mother's work. Being Human he'd thought of hands, of skill, not of biology.

Now oble's gift to him, to them all. Oble's precious thread.

He found words to sing after all. "Joy, you are my darling, my darling, my darling."

Third Life

His songs become strong and confident. Love's first life, full of hope.

Slow, soften. Turn intricate and beautiful. Love's second, granting gifts.

Falter, forget, and cease. Love's third and last.

The time is now.

Forever-Joy convulses, tearing free of what was oble and is no longer, fluids coursing through a body unfamiliar and yet oble's own.

Oble flutters to the floor, what oble is to be.

The wizened figure in the chair stirs with a little cough. He is wrapped in a magnificent blanket of oble's thread, his weaving.

Forever-Joy knows oble's love in any shape.

Yet, hesitates.

Can he see oble as this?

A dream. He'd had many, these years. This glorious shape in front of him, of shimmering blue feathered scales, was new.

The eyes weren't. The eyes *knew* him, and Samoth came fully awake. He reached with both hands.

Hands changed by time. Spotted and gnarled, as he was. "Joy." He had no more words, no excuse. He'd done his best to wait. "I'm sorry."

"For what, beloved?" A laugh like summer rain. Arms around him, strong and sure, lifting him up. "The third is the last. I won't leave you again."

"I will leave you, soon," he admitted, but it wasn't sad. How could it be sad when they were together?

"Then we won't waste a moment. Let's go outside. Show me all we've done."

He confessed. "I can't walk."

Forever-Joy hugged him close. "My love, you won't need to. Ever again."

And unfurled wings.

THE UNVEILED POSSIBILITIES OF BIOMATERIALS IN SPACE

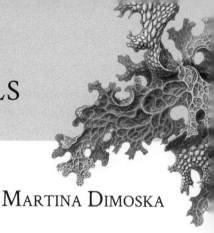

MARTINA DIMOSKA

Science fiction often imagines how humans could interface with computers and begin to resemble an imagined superhuman deity. For instance, suppose humans meet aliens whose bodies can change and shift in ways we can barely conceive: what does science say about our fantasies? Let us explore the novel worlds of biomaterials and other biologically inspired materials.

Biomaterials

Biomaterial science is still a relatively new field, but it is all the more essential as various bits of engineering touch every aspect of daily human functions in our environment. However, invisible to the human eye is the engineering inside the human body. From band-aids that cover your cuts to medical implants and artificial limbs, a lot of things are created from distinct types of materials that work well with the human body. Such biomaterials are vital to healthcare and medicine, and they help us to have a prolonged, higher-quality life span.

By definition, biomaterials or biocompatible materials[1] include any material—natural or synthetic in origin—designed to be used in close contact with biological tissues and fluids, serving a medical purpose such as augmenting, treating, or replacing any bodily function, organ or tissue. Special effort goes into designing the materials that are compatible with the biological system with which they are interacting. Many different types of material such as metals, polymers, ceramics, composites, or even living cells and tissues can be considered good biomaterial candidates as long as they have one of the key properties: they are biocompatible.

---

1 There are four ways in which a foreign material can interact with a person's body: harm it; harmlessly dissolve and be replaced by living cells; become surrounded by the body's protective layer; and create a bond with the living tissue. Biomaterials, which interact compatibly with biological systems, usually fall within the fourth category.

Biocompatible materials create healthy bodily responses when they come into contact with a body. They do not cause blood clots or infections and lead to normal, straightforward healing. This is crucial; since for most applications, the biomaterials used will be in contact with bodily cells and tissues, often for long periods of time—from a year to few decades.

The criteria used to determine which materials can be considered biocompatible has changed over history. In ancient Egypt, one medical practice involved using animal tissue to stitch wounds. For centuries, peg legs were made from wood. Today, such materials of questionable origin and quality have been replaced by carefully engineered materials, most commonly titanium and stainless steel, everywhere from joint replacements to dental implants. Other favorite materials include polyurethane (a type of polymer used in artificial heart valves and other flexible applications) and hydrogels (used for contact lenses, amongst other uses).

Each of these materials has its own properties that make it useful as a biomaterial for different applications. The most common use for alloys, like titanium or stainless steel, is to create braces. Titanium is biologically inert, causing little to no reaction with nearby tissues. Even if the body recognizes it as foreign material and tries to surround it in fibrous tissue, the immune system won't reject titanium outright. Titanium is more biologically compatible than stainless steel because it lacks nickel, which can sometimes cause allergic reactions. As a result, titanium is often used as a replacement for stainless steel for some applications. Another advantage of titanium is its lower density compared to other metallic biomaterials, which makes titanium implants much lighter than, for example, stainless steel implants. This is a very useful feature in space environments, as launching into space has enormous costs and uses a vast amount of fuel, so minimizing weight is always a plus. Any component that can aid human performance in space and contribute to space medicine, whilst fulfilling more than one purpose, is beneficial.

Space Biomaterials

The biomaterials that facilitate human space exploration are also known as (who would guess?) space biomaterials. Key aspects that define novel space biomaterials are their adaptability and diversity. As space missions are designed (and later on built), space designers must consider all potential applications of biomedical as well as biologically derived materials, to create an easier transition from Earth to the harsh space environment.

Just a few potential biomaterials advancements, amongst many applications that can be important for space exploration, include wound-healing dressings, lightweight radiation protection, and microbe-resistant surfaces.

Biologically Inspired Materials

Beyond biomaterials, other species can help us out, for instance in the fields of robotics and space robotics. For example, pine cones, which are made of dead material, can open and close simply in response to changes in humidity. Similarly, the mid-day flower, which grows in desert regions where it rarely rains, stores its ripe seeds in special capsules while dry, but as soon as it rains, these otherwise lifeless capsules open and seeds fall out, ready to germinate in moist earth. This mechanism is reversible; if the weather is dry again, the capsules close up. The fascinating thing is that the seed capsule of the mid-day flower exists completely without metabolism, just as a robot would have to manage without metabolism.

What is the principle that could be translated, for instance, into robotics? Scientists have determined the seed capsule's mechanism and worked out from which part of the seed capsule the movement actually stems. Inside of the lid, a special layer of cells on the underside of what is known as the keel, makes the movement possible[2].

The folding movement of the seed capsule relies on both the structure and the properties of the cells inside it. One potent and highly practical design, a honeycomb structure, and two incorporated materials, lignin (which does not absorb water) and cellulose (a substance that swells easily when it absorbs water), appear to play key roles.

Coloring the cells with a special solution demonstrates that the cell walls consist mainly of lignin. When the cells come into contact with water, the inner layer of cellulose expands, but the lignin of the cell walls does not. Because of these properties and the honeycomb structure, the cells expand only in one direction, deforming the structure hierarchically. Scientists have copied this efficient natural model in a prototype on a much bigger scale, which can be used to open and close robotic systems—or even roofs—without requiring an input of energy. Using two very different materials, one that can swell (a paper film),

---

2 The keel even opens when it is separated from the capsule.

and another that cannot (a wood film), they mimicked the production of deformation through the honeycomb structure. Because no motors are necessary, cities can be driven directly—solely by humidity—a benefit that can be implemented in future robotic constructions in space or when populating other planets.

Spider Silk

Bringing Joy's threads in Julie E. Czerneda's "Third Life" to mind, spider silk has long been a holy grail of material innovation as well. Today, spider silk is out of the labs and produced on a multi-ton scale and used in multiple industries. Artificially grown silk is strong and biodegradable, made entirely of proteins and produced by biotechnological means where no animals are involved. It is used in everything from cosmetics to medical technology, to clothing, to space exploration. A company called AMSilk recently inked a deal to create a new spider silk-based material with Airbus that could be used in the hulls of high-performance planes, and later on, perhaps serve in space missions.

The last decade has produced very good material innovations, but most has been focused on fossil fuel-based materials. Unfortunately, such materials can persist for decades or even longer, contributing to pollution. The products made from synthetic spider silk, on the other hand, are completely biodegradable. That does not mean they degrade immediately, though! They can be used in everyday life and are very durable, as they can withstand humidity, wide temperature fluctuations, and the effects of the Sun. But as soon as the material is disposed of, it biodegrades completely.

Space Environments

Understanding the space environment is necessary for the needs and well-being of humans in any future space habitats and exploration, but space also has the potential to become a unique manufacturing environment because novel biomaterials can be fabricated there that cannot be made on Earth. This creates a mutual benefit both for utilization in space, but also for applications on Earth. Designing biomaterials to solve space-based challenges is key.

However, our understanding of the space environment is still limited. Would our eyesight change permanently during extended space expeditions? Would our hearts need artificial augmentation upon returning to Earth after years and years away? Eventually, would our bodies need to fundamentally change (even if artificially and not as completely as Joy's did as part of the natural life cycle in "Third Life")?

Advancement in biomaterials can both help humanity and also promote space exploration through the above-described mutually beneficial relationship. One thing is certain, however: new materials are becoming more relevant to space and astrobiology day by day. Materials like artificial spider silk or honeycomb structures inspire engineering solutions for space exploration—even equipment to search for microbial life outside of our Pale Blue Dot—and might provide more than one approach for space problem-solving and multifaceted applications. They hold the key to unlocking many scientific secrets to advance our future.

FURTHER READING AND VIEWING

Chouhan, D., & Mandal, B.B. (2020). "Silk Biomaterials in Wound Healing and SkinRegeneration Therapeutics: from Bench to Bedside." *Acta Biomaterialia*, Vol.103, 24-51.
https://www.sciencedirect.com/science/article/abs/pii/ S1742706119308001?via%3Dihub

CrashCourse. (2018, November 8). 'Biomaterials: Crash Course Engineering #24."
https://www.youtube.com/watch?v=-jw8osY5QJM

D'Ischia, M., et al. (2019). "Astrochemistry and Astrobiology: Materials Science in Wonderland?" *International Journal of Molecular Sciences*, Vol.20(17).
https://www.mdpi.com/1422-0067/20/17/4079

Forbes. (2019, February 26). "AMSilk's Synthetic Spider Silk is the Biomaterial of the Future."
https://www.youtube.com/watch?v=r4vgtFwYP5c

Jemison, M. & Olabisi, R. (2021). "Biomaterials for human space exploration: A review of their untapped potential." *Acta Biomaterialia*, Vol.128, 77-99.
https://www.sciencedirect.com/science/article/pii/ S1742706121002701

Langer, R. (2012, March 2). "Biomaterials for the 21st Century." TEDxBigApple.
https://www.youtube.com/watch?v=uta5Vo86XL4

Leal-Egaña, A., & Scheibel, T. (2010). "Silk-based materials for biomedical applications." *Biotechnology and Applied Biochemistry*, Vol.55(3), 155-167.
https://iubmb.onlinelibrary.wiley.com/doi/abs/10.1042/BA20090229

Max Planck Society. (2017, January 3). "Biomaterials - patent solutions from nature."
https://www.youtube.com/watch?v=9uawFzDWA5Q

National Institute of Biomedical Imaging and Bioengineering (2017, September). "Biomaterials."
https://www.nibib.nih.gov/science-education/science-topics/biomaterials

FOREVER THE FOREST

SIMONE HELLER

It is known that the Rootless are only ever leaving. Always moving on, never embracing soil long enough for connection. A life tumbled and tossed, and if it touches ours, it is only by chance, and ill chance more often than not.

But *you* came, in a tumble and a glorious blaze, by intention and by ill chance.

The night of your arrival was almost my undoing. You rode an incandescent gust tearing into our rows, escorted by a rain of hot metal. The ground rippled once with your impact, outward and onward, quicker than the fungal network could warn us. When the air stilled and the Conversation erupted in bursts of *pain!* and *fire!*, no-one knew what had crashed down on us. We sucked moisture from the deep, made the lesser plants close their ranks and smother the flames, and we calmed the Conversation with memories of renewal and regrowth.

You had plummeted from the sky, the fungal network relayed, as the filament reached out again to take hold of the large swath of churned and scorched soil, of everything that lay fallen and ready to decompose. Our rootscape expanded anew, tasting the damage and the altered lay of the land. But one blank spot persisted.

One fragment had not shattered, tumbling over and over until it had come to rest next to me, its edge nicking a branch. Neither root nor spore found purchase there. And no matter how far and wide the Conversation was carried, this sealed structure remained unknown. It was deemed to be not of our soil. And as it lay inert, it was deemed to be not of our interest, either. We would claim it, sooner or later, either encapsulating and burying it as a curiosity in our rootscape, or it would yield after all, as everything yielded, to rain and root and frost and fungus.

It cracked open on its own soon enough, right there within my reach. My sap-quenching stillness spread through the Conversation until the whole forest seemed to pause.

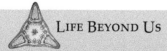

Something fell out, toppling to the ground as if caught in a storm with no grove-kin. It just lay there, thumping fear and exhaustion against the soil in the way of the Rootless.

My excitement for the unknown—*a Rootless from the sky!*, with neither nest nor burrow known to tree or spore—surged as the filament flashed agitation at its alienness: *not of our soil.*

I felt delight. The quickening of survival rushed through my sapwood, and, deeper even, curiosity sprouted. I reached. With leaves rustling welcome, with a fragrance of earthy solidity, I reached.

And you came.

You lifted yourself up, stumbling forward until you crashed into me. I was able to sense your strangeness, a limb first to catch your fall, then your weight against me, sliding down along my base, where it stayed, almost motionless except for small, arrhythmic quivers.

You were big for a Rootless, but still fragile, and possibly damaged from your violent arrival. I wanted to help and fed the Conversation with my findings: your size, your mass, the desperate grasp of your initial touch.

My excitement was met with polite disinterest. To my grove-kin and my sap-kin, the Rootless were nothing but a nuisance; pests at worst, inconsequential bearers of gifts to seal alliances, found dynasties and end wars at best, and always good for erratic behavior.

But I knew better. There was a pattern in their wayward bustling, and a purpose to their actions, thoughtless as they might seem. We believed they didn't reach toward the sun, but you had fallen from the sky, and how much closer could one get? I wanted to know about the reaching and the falling, about the origin of your vagrant ways. So, as the strange quivers against my trunk became more infrequent, I decided to keep you.

You were restless, a flurry of action lacking the patience to feel how the sun fueled regrowth in the field of debris. Saplings were selected to settle on the fire-primed earth, while you darted in and out of the structure that had encapsulated you, scattering and silencing the smaller Rootless with a resounding boom each time you sealed your enclosure anew.

Your distress entered our water and our soil, and the surrounding kin promised each other: *Soon it will wander off to distant groves.* They gracefully ignored my attempts to woo you to stay.

Next to your enclosure, under the outmost reaches of my canopy, you started to dig in the soil. You were relentless, like a root trying to render an unwanted rock to gravel, with a piece of debris, a dead branch, with your bare limbs until the filament tasted blood.

I would have helped, if I had understood.

You went inside and hauled out a body, similar to yours in all but minor differences in weight and build. And another, and another, placing them in the hole one by one. You stayed at their side, more rooted than your kind is usually known for. When you moved again, first you sprinkled upturned soil on the bodies, a well-considered offering to the filament. Next came the tiniest droplets of salty water, and last you showered them with a hum you created on a thing you held, its vibrations softly tinkling like warm raindrops on my leaves.

Slowly, as we tasted your offering, I observed more. The filament did not discriminate, and my grove-kin wanted to know if you carried new kinds of parasites we would have to synthesize toxins against.

We learned about the metabolism of the bodies in the ground, their hormones, the dozens of fractures in their bones which let us observe their density and the processes in their marrow. Faintly, ever so faintly, I found traces of unknown soil, and they sent my thoughts spiraling out toward my spirit-kin in the Conversation, those few and far-away trees sharing my scholarly interests.

But I knew something else, too. You had to be lonely. It was your kin who had joined our soil, and while the wound in the forest caused by your fall was mending, the wound in you was gaping open. All I could offer was to enrich my fruit with the substances you needed, to provide shelter and shade–things anyone with a shoot of kindness would do for a lost Rootless. But never the murmur of the Conversation and the promise of regrowth, never the echoes of trees who had struck root here since the plates of the earth first ground against each other, forever the forest.

You took my fruit, and you lived through your wound, collecting nourishment, water, dead wood for your own ritual of fire, so different and minuscule compared to our roaring spectacles of burning and resettling. You wore paths through the underbrush until your presence felt like a map imprinted on the land even when you were hidden in your enclosure.

When dusk wove through the canopy, you often rested at my side and brought the thing that vibrates under your hands. It felt like rain tinkling on my leaves, with a deeper rhythm more akin to your thumping blood than our steady flow of sap. Its harmonics resonated deep in my heartwood, even if they were not meant for me.

Or maybe they were? I was eager to find out what they implied either way. There was so much I wanted to ask, about your enclosure, your journey, the piece of fabric you fixed on one of my limbs first thing every morning, and so much I wanted to be asked! Had you noticed the ferns I cultivated in the crooks of my branches, some from spores usually found beyond the Great Irrigation Channel? I had collected forty-nine sensations of extra-fuzzy Rootless creeping along my leaves, never shared with my kin, but maybe you would appreciate them.

At night, when you were inside and the Conversation was a dream-like murmur, I tried to imagine where you came from. Was it a place shaped by forest, too, and did its eternal whisper mingle with your tinkling, there? Or did you hail from stranger lands? I stayed alert, contemplating the cool blackness of the skies we all reach into, the faint movements of light up there, as if a sun-dappled stream ran through the vastness.

Far-away suns, my spirit-kin said, when their replies travelled back to me, *not worth wilting away for during the nights*. One sun was enough to reach for.

These were the maps I lived by, the distant suns wandering the skies, and you forging a path through the forest. Both patterns were strange to me, uprooted, unhinged. But the other scholars claimed the suns were reliable in their revolutions, always coming back. And so were you.

You took such great care to adorn me with your piece of fabric every day, and you sought my support, drawn by your own kind of gravit-ropism. You would lean on me, the frenetic rhythm of your pulse relaxing when I passed my solidity on to you. Any injuries caused by your arrival were healing nicely, leaving only a stiffened ridge of tissue, thick like sanitizing woundwood, rendering your gait slightly uneven. Our world had welcomed you with a fall, but I tried to catch you, best I could.

You began to tinker on your enclosure in amiable tranquility, and I enjoyed the companionship growing between us. Such delicate struc-tures you handled, even my grove-kin considered you something like our sculptors of rock and ravine. They would marvel even more when you revealed what you were building.

It had to be something big. You spent more and more time inside, and dull echoes vibrated along the hull. You gathered the devices you had attached to me and some others to sound us out to the core with electrical impulses, and I imagined you, like me, couldn't wait to grow a deeper connection. What if you built something to help us understand each other better? I was ready to do my part and make it work.

Then one day the piece of wreckage finally yielded. It would have been long before you noticed, just a hairline crack in its base, enough for the filament to squeeze in and thrive in the recesses you never touched, taste what was hidden inside. It was a steady trickle of discoveries as the filament swept over planes of materials so smooth it could not enter, intricate lattice and fiber structures, dancing electric impulses.

Impatience is for the Rootless, my grove-kin admonished when I kept nudging. *We will be here to inspect this structure long after it has moved on.*

I learned you spent most of your time in front of a flickering wall of light to let vibrations and shifting luminance wash over you in an endless repetitive pattern that held no clue to anything I wanted to know. It was irrelevant. It was not what you had prepared to bring us closer together.

Your great work stood in the center of the chamber. An upright, stilted capsule that would have fitted you just so. First, I thought it was some kind of new shelter you built. A pod, a nest, a home. It wasn't the marvelous structure I had envisioned, but we would find other ways to connect, and I felt a surge of joy anyway. To me it looked like settling.

I should have known better because you never once slept in it, and even a muddleshoot such as I shouldn't have forgotten what pods were for.

But it took until the filament explored the whole shape of your enclosure to see what it was. What you were trying to do.

Like a flower waiting to bloom, the canopy of the chamber was hinged to fold back and open up to the sky, and the capsule inside ready to pop out. To carry away its precious cargo to a far-away sun.

All this time, you had been preparing to leave.

It was always going to leave, but we are here, my grove-kin murmured, while my sap-kin sent soothing sugars to my roots when I went silent in the Conversation instead of enthusiastically accounting for your every move. We are rooted, and you are passers-by, and it was as if we were living on two different worlds, even if you hadn't yet left.

I had thought we wanted to lean on each other and learn from each other. Someone who crossed the sun-dappled river of the sky, who braved it despite the chance of falling into the darkness, someone who left their own soil behind, had to be a scholar like me. And here you were, on a new world, a world that had reached out to you with a supportive branch, with a rootscape steeped in aeons of growing. I had thought you were as curious as I was, and I had been wrong.

Very rarely, you took the time to bring your humming thing to me, and I noticed some of its harmonics were missing, its vibrations diminished. You let its tinkling patter across the clearing anyway. But I knew it had never been for me, and it hurt.

It hurt so much that I only noticed you hurt, too, when you didn't come out anymore and the forest began to erase your paths from my maps. You still hung your piece of fabric on my branch every morning, but it felt limp and crumpled, not like something to display as proudly as I had.

Others might have assumed you were eagerly preparing for the moment the petals of your canopy would open. But I knew your light touch when you discovered a delicious new fruit, the spring in your step when you climbed sturdy branches to face the wind rustling over the rise and fall of the forest for the first time. Now you stomped across the clearing. Kicked your enclosure, repeatedly, and there was no eager impatience in your movements, just desperation.

And no-one to soothe you in a way you could understand, when sweet sugars did not suffice, when you needed to dissipate your hurt into the all-enduring forest. No single being should have to bear such pain.

I probed again, observing your earlier efforts more closely. I found the scaffolding you had built, the broken and bent tools you had used for gaining leverage, the scratch marks on the tightly closed petals of your metal flower. I felt the weight of each petal, so much more than you, and the way the impact had bent them in shapes that would prevent their elegant opening motion. You had tried your best to pry and cut and scrape. But your flower was never going to bloom.

And I understood how the sky must have closed up to you, completely out of reach beyond your locked canopy. How the other suns became an empty dream and you felt stuck, robbed of your vagrant nature, bound to a life grounded and confined instead of tumbled and tossed.

One sun has always been enough, my grove-kin assured me when I emitted your pain. And maybe I could try and convince us both. There were things for us to explore, strange and far reaches of the rootscape like a whisper in the background of the Conversation. But it was not what you needed, not now, as you kept facing your wall of light, almost rooted in whatever echoes and memories it was evoking in you.

You needed the comfort I was granted continuously by the forest.

So I primed the filament once more for the vibrations you let wash over you in front of your wall, filtering out the higher frequencies clearly produced by you and others like you in this repeating sequence, and focused on the background rhythm. It was nothing I had ever experienced, but I could almost feel the soothing force of its steady roll. I sent it out to my spirit-kin, and word travelled far and wide in the Conversation, favors were called in to cross borders, and when replies trickled back, they came from strange kin who had ventured out onto uninhabitable ground. *We know, we share, this is the ebb and flow surging around our stilted roots,* they said, *the sea, the unconquerable sea, do you feel the sharp nip of salt?*

I wanted to feel the salt, and everything else with it, and I wanted to break it down into its molecules and understand it. For I knew you cherished this experience above anything else, and I could give it to you the way we used to give the comfort of rain on our leaves to our drought-land neighbors. I called in more favors and recruited my long-suffering grove-kin to find trace elements to accumulate in my sapwood for synthesizing something this forest had never known.

You were abandoning your flower and yourself within it, not even coming out to hang your fabric anymore. The electrical pulses stilled one after the other, and you stopped scraping off the mosses claiming the ground. Life exploded, and still it felt lifeless after you draped covers over the finer structures and disabled your wall of light.

When you finally stepped out, I was prepared. You didn't know what I had released into the air, but you stumbled right into it, every leaf of mine exuding this strange sea smell, so different from the earthiness of our grove. It hung in the air, briny, fresh, ready to embrace you. And I felt you swaying there, expanding while you breathed in, drinking it into every pore, this promise you were not alone.

It wasn't the rhythm and the light your wall had shown you, but as you were drawn back to a shore even the strange stilt-rooted kin couldn't imagine, you knew it.

And you knew me.

You came to gently pull down a twig and press my leaves against your face, breathing deeply. You let your calloused fingers whisper over my skin, a new map immediately engrained in my mind. You walked around me in wonder, never breaking touch, your steps transmitting the lightness of climbing high and probing deep, the bounce of discovery. When you stayed the whole night instead of going back to your enclosure to rest, I felt I had become more than solidity, more than a monument guarding your dead kin. We scholars know the Rootless' connection to the world is often not by touch, but rather your perception of light. And even as you were touching me now, what I felt was *seen*.

After that, you began wandering the grove again. You didn't try and pry open your flower anymore, and you didn't even return to the inside of your enclosure but once. You walked around cautiously then, not to dwell, but as if you were an intruder, touching only the smallest of things, tugging on a cover here, trailing your fingers lightly along a moss-speckled surface there. Soon you sealed your access hatch and left. But you brought something with you.

I felt it in the added weight and the hollowness of it, even if you didn't coax out your rainfall tinkles anymore: you carried the thing you made vibrate. You stood there for some time, and when you set it down in the crook of my widest roots, you didn't intentionally strum, but it made the tiniest off-key quiver.

I had had hopes, but only after you fixed it there a little bit more firmly, and you again showed the understanding you had worked out for yourself by sprinkling soil on top of it, I knew you truly intended it as a gift.

And what a gift it was!

I took my time tasting it, filament first and rootwood later, and I found something familiar in its strange shape among bits of metal and synthetics. Years upon years of rooting and growing were embedded in its wooden body, and I sensed the faint echoes of far-away forests: spaciously arrayed evergreens dreaming under the weight of a wintery chill; a tangle of mist-enclasped giants teeming with a flurry of wildlife; mellow woodlands in the gentle sway of ever-changing seasons. The forests this wood had been taken from were old and alien, growing and reaching like us, but different down to the tiniest components of their cells. They were forever beyond reach, but they were kin nonetheless, kin across the skies, kin under a different sun. Such was the gift you gave me, and I couldn't hold it in, jolted the rootscape with my prompts of *taste! feel!*, hoping it would reach my spirit-kin and make them understand: *ours is not the only Conversation.*

Other memories were tangled within the wood, the ghosts of caress-ing skin and dancing fingers, fragments of you like overtones to the whispering of the wood: you, clearly among your spirit-kin, cheered and accompanied while you energetically enticed the hum from the wood. You, alone, exploring along a burbling stream and adding your own tinkling to while away the night. You, clasping the wood as if it supported you, when a stranger's message opened the sky to you and got you thumping all over down to your fingertips. And you in a capsule, suspended in the void with three others, reaching for this body of wood whenever you needed a piece of something grown, a piece of home.

I almost felt the pulse of being Rootless, of being pulled along and beyond the field lines of our world. Would it be so bad to leave? Wouldn't it be nice to explore, to experience places the rootscape could never touch and our Conversation had never envisioned?

No amount of excitement would stir the interest of my kin above a friendly rustle, while they invoked the feeling of the sun and the rain providing for us, the soil reliably carrying our weight and the weight of our memories. Messages of comfort to calm my strange thoughts.

And yes, the sun warmed me just as well as ever, its rays caressed my leaves just as gently, but I felt it was not enough. There was a longing for different suns, suns I could never feel.

You knew this longing. It made you reach: it made you fall.

But it shouldn't have tangled you in roots you never wanted, cut off from your own Conversation. Shouldn't have made you dwell in my shade all miserable and yearning, the sky like a mockery above you.

I might not be able to act upon my longing, and I could never reach a distant sun, but there was one thing I could do, even if it would hurt to lose you.

We are rooted, and while we are not able to abandon our places and leave, we are shapers and shifters, and with the right approach, we raze mountains.

So I reached toward the sun and gathered my strength.

You didn't know. You were focused on your own movement: into a new shelter by my side, draped in vines and cushioned with mosses, and away from your failure, exploring the forest, though when you climbed, it was less energetic and never all the way up to the canopy anymore.

Ironically, we were now as I had envisioned us to be. We had an understanding, you and I, that we were akin in curiosity.

You brought me stones washed up in the riverbed, rich in history with leaf imprints from a long-lost nation. Smaller Rootless you found and nurtured, and maybe you kept those for yourself, but they were still a gift, nesting in my branches, basking on my leaves. Even if I had experienced them a hundred times before in the Conversation, these gifts always felt new after they passed through your hands.

I tried to do the same for you, so you could sense our world beyond your reach. I made you smell the acrid tang of the distant salt flats before you left, where our mining kin's crystalized leaves chime in the wind. Taste the sweet desert dew collected in thorn-clad night forests, distilled into a fruit. I wanted you to consider us worth exploring, despite your fall.

All the while my grove-kin sent me strength no matter what, even when you foolishly brought saplings grown from my fruit out to places they were completely unsuited for. *So inconsiderate, these Rootless,* they said, but you meant well, and the filament took care of the offshoots.

I couldn't be bothered much, toiling away as I was. To you it must have seemed crude, for I have always been more of a dreamer than a builder, but if you ever felt disrespected by the way I treated your abandoned enclosure, you didn't complain.

My roots found and widened the cracks, and then the real work began. Defying every gravitropic impulse, I slanted my roots upwards, away from the soil, reaching for the sky myself. Some things had to yield along the way, walls bent and whole panels crashed down, but never the capsule itself. I'm not that clumsy. Upwards I strained, ever upwards in the dark, until I touched the canopy.

I noticed you sticking closer, your circles getting smaller, more reluctant. And maybe I, too, would have grown reluctant in my task, because I didn't want to lose you, didn't want this pod to bear you away yet. But roots have their own momentum.

As they strengthened, metal bulged and tore, seams strained and burst, until I was the only thing holding them together. The canopy cracked, not elegantly as it was supposed to, but under my brute force. Still, when the first slanted rays of sunlight touched the capsule inside, it was as beautiful as any blooming.

That's when you realized what I was doing, didn't you? After you hung your piece of fabric each morning, mended in so many places now it felt small and brittle, you wouldn't explore. You just walked the clearing, stopping often, to take it in from every angle, what was now fused, part root, part wreckage.

And when I had finished my task, you went inside, gingerly climbing through the broken hatch. Using the stick you had taken to walking around with to lift the covers you had placed.

This is where we are. You are leaving.

The petals of your flower are crumpled, some have already fallen. Before you, the sky unfolds. Before me, the dream of your next discovery, of the suns you will visit.

And while you prepare to leave, slowly making your way through the root-shot interior of the wreckage, touching capsule and console alike with shaking hands, and while I sense the awakening of the power that will whisk you away, this is what I want to tell you, in every rustling leaf and every pulse of sap. All the things I can't say, because the Conversation is eluding you. You need to go and rejoin your own.

I'll never know the wonders you're going to encounter on your way, and I'll never thank you for your gift of seeing me, of singling me out in a vast forest. I'll never know what you want to tell me. Because that's what you've been doing all the time, haven't you? You talked to me almost from the day we met, with these gentle vibrations you breathe into the air.

You're talking to me now, patting my roots, your hands unsteady, your whole being shaking. A rumble builds up, pulsing slowly first as your capsule wakes from its hibernation, but gaining the irresistible strength of an earthquake.

No root will hold you back, no matter its strength, and when you hurry to your shelter, I know these are your last preparations, to get sustenance for the time you need to enfold yourself into your pod while it is shooting away.

But when you fumble your way back, carefully planting your stick, it is an armful of my saplings you carry, cultivated from my fruit, the ones you always tried to spread across the forest. It is them you place into the capsule first. This is when something in me begins to sing, to the tinkling of raindrops and the rhythm of a distant sea. This is when I allow my thoughts to shoot up and accompany you, hurrying ahead even, faster and farther than I have ever dared to reach.

But you, with your shaking hands and your unsteady step, you seal the capsule off, and you back away.

The rumbling grows, and you are not inside.

You are, in fact, at my side, and your hand is on me, a map of ridges and valleys against my skin, no firmness left in your grip.

I brace against the pain every departing pod causes, as its power surges. Woundwood will soon seal those gifted roots as they burn away in a blast of heat.

The forest is utterly still. In the aftermath of the thundering departure, none of the Rootless dare move.

A pod capsule once sprung is gone for good, out of reach, but I know it is on its journey. *These are our saplings,* I want to shout into the Conversation, but only you are still able to follow their course, bent back to see them shoot across the sky. I wish them luck on their flight, and should they ever fall, I hope they are met by a friend.

You stayed. You are leaning on me, harder than ever, your fingers slowly sifting through the soil after you sit down. It is your soil now, too, a Conversation waiting to be joined. You stayed, while my saplings are farther away every moment, and the joy of knowing both runs through me like a sun-dappled river.

Evening approaches, and you take a slow walk around the clearing, filament already claiming the scattered remnants of the wreckage. Your shuffling steps are gentle, almost too light for me to sense on the upturned soil as you walk in the dusk.

The Rootless, it is said, are passers-by, only ever leaving. But they may try for roots, and we may try for new suns. And we may both find completion in trying.

ASTRA NARRANS

Connor Martini

Simone Heller's "Forever The Forest" calls our attention to the close relationship of two important concepts in the history of philosophy and anthropology—semiotics and ontology. This piece brilliantly reveals the connection between how beings communicate and how they come to understand themselves, and lays out the dire stakes of misrecognizing communication. The story poses an essential question in astrobiology and related disciplines—how would you go on communicating with a being who perceives the world so differently that you'd hardly be able to describe it? A being living within a completely different sense of temporality or spatiality? Or, in the case of this story, a being which is not a solitary entity, but a participant in a broader Conversation?

At a basic level, semiotics is the study of signs and symbols. Closely related to linguistics, the study of semiotics is concerned with how things—speech acts, written notations, bodily movements, etc.—gain meaning through interpretation. How does a nodding head become a "yes"? How is it that a sigh conveys concern or sadness? If we take these things to be arbitrary at a fundamental level—meaning that there is nothing intrinsically agreeable about a nod or melancholy about a sigh—then we must accept that some amount of social work has gone into producing the meanings of these acts, and that even more work has gone into authorizing those interpretations as norms. Semiotic anthropology exposes the reality that meaning and language are socially constructed and historically contingent. When thinking about how things come to mean things, you must face the fact that interpretation is the product of collective social work and discipline.

What do I mean by that? Certainly not that we divest ourselves of meaning and interpretation because of their socially constructed nature. Calling something a "social construct" is frequently misunderstood to mean that something lacks a certain reality or force. But consider what it would be like if you went about your life thinking that nodding your head meant "no" instead. If someone asked you if you wanted milk in your coffee and you proceeded to nod your head and say "no" at the same time, you would probably be facing a somewhat confused barista. You'd be breaking a rule of language and interpretation, and you'd face the consequences—at best, your coffee would be messed up, and at worst, you'd be facing social isolation and alienation. Nobody wants their fellow coffee shop patrons to give them weird stares.

When you approach meaning and interpretation from this angle, you can see that even the most benign gesture is subject to a process of governance and regulation in which we all participate. And this governance is not always conducted in the interest of facilitating communication, as in the case with the nod. The same kind of process is at work when someone wears clothing with a designer label. For example, the Versace logo does not mean anything on its own, but it has come to be associated with wealth and luxury and thus allows people to mark themselves with the trappings of a particular class and mark everyone else whose clothes don't have a Versace logo on them as separate. So, semiotics is not just academic-y over-intellectualization; there are political and economic stakes to semiotics. And in the case of Heller's story, semiotics becomes critical to one's survival.

Ontology is like semiotics, insofar as it entails classification and interpretation but is more concerned with being and identity than communication and meaning. Thinking about ontology requires thinking about what it means to be a kind of thing—a human, a Rootless, a pencil, etc. And unlike in semiotics, where the fundamental arbitrariness of the sign is largely accepted, there is more of a debate as to whether or not ontology is intrinsic to the thing-in-itself. There is an ontological difference, for example, between my cats and me. We are different organisms, not only by virtue of the socially constructed classifications of "human" and "cat." We experience and perceive the world differently through our different bodies and sensoria. This was a major contribution of the German biologist Jakob von Uexküll—the concept of the *umwelt*, or the notion that subjectivity is determined by the manner and means by which an organism apprehends and perceives its environment.

But things get a little murky when we consider ontology as something relational. It is easy to draw a clear ontological divide between myself and my cats if our concept of ontology is equivalent to embodiment. But as soon as I put down a bowl of food, new questions pop up. Could my cat survive on its own, and is that autonomy intrinsic to its being? Would the sense of affection and companionship I get from my cats be there if I didn't give them that food, and what kind of being would I be if I didn't have that connection? So, we can have a notion of ontology that is closely tied to a sense of embodiment (I am human, they are cats), or we can have an ontology that is a little more blurry at the boundaries (my cats and I are more like nodes in a network of relations).

Importantly, how we think about ontology is inseparable from semiotic questions. "What does it mean to be human?" is simultaneously a question about ontology—how the human is classified—and semiotics—how the word and category "human" is interpreted and evaluated. Heller's story, then, presents us with a thought experiment centered on this question of what it means for ontology and semiotics to be so critically entangled. The visiting Rootless has a distinct identity from that of the narrator, who in turn has a distinct identity from other entities entangled in the Conversation—a term which, on its own, brilliantly prods at this distinction by naming a kind of being with a term that evokes semiotics and communication. These distinct ontologies inform what kinds of signs and symbols are possible or legible. Throughout the story, the marooned visitor fails to comprehend what is, to the narrator, normal and meaningful communication.

Similarly, the narrator is consistently perplexed by the visitor's activities, which have their own logic to them that is inaccessible to the narrator's culturally informed sensorium. This is a semiotic problem, but it is also an ontological one—the narrator inhabits a being of interconnectedness and expanse, of curiosity and balance. The visitor is, by comparison, unitary, a mind entangled with its environs in meaningful ways but to a lesser degree. They are not part of the Conversation. Effective communication comes only at the end of the story, when the narrator begins to understand the value and significance of a sign originating from a strange semiotic order—the damaged pod.

From there, we might be tempted to say that ontology determines, rather than informs, semiotics—that certain kinds of signs and symbols are only meaningful to beings of the same kind. But we know, from the story, that this is not true. And we also know, from real-world examples, that signs can be exchanged across ontologies. We can understand the basic meanings of mating calls and predator warnings, of chemical signals between cells or ants, of whale songs and dolphin chirps. The narrator in Heller's story can understand that the damaged pod is a source of anguish and fear for the visitor, just as I can understand that my cat's 6 PM wails are a sign of hunger. If ontology determined semiotics, we would be in a pretty poor position to communicate with other forms of life, much less extraterrestrial intelligences.

Ontology then informs what kinds of signs and symbols are possible to produce (e.g., chemical communication in ants and bacteria; dolphins and beetles communicating in ultrasonics) but does not necessarily limit what can be comprehended or questioned. Missing that last part, assuming that ontology determines semiotics, gets us into tricky territory, before we even think about the problem of communicating with extraterrestrial life. Say you're deeply committed to a specific formulation of "the human." That formulation will prescribe normative components—humans look like this, talk like that, value this, and walk like that. Your ontological formulation quickly becomes a semiotic proposition—this look, this way of talking, this set of values, this way of moving about in the world is constitutive of what it means to be human. How, then, do you deal with the differences? Do semiotic differences allow you to make ontological distinctions? And what if certain rights and privileges are attached to that designation of "human"? It's not hard to see how such logic can result in violence, in dispossession, in a host of other nasty things of which we should be wary.

But a story like this prompts us to consider the opposite. What if semiotics determines ontology? What if the way a being communicates is inseparable from, *a priori* to, even definitional of what a being is? Such a proposition has been offered by many, notably the postcolonial theorist Sylvia Wynter in her classification of humans as *homo narrans*—that our capacity for storytelling (communication) and relaying and adapting to the world around us through narration is what makes us human, contrary to the Enlightenment notion of Man that prioritized reason (and whiteness and maleness). This also lets us prod a bit at the Enlightenment's pesky legacy of anthropocentrism, or the predisposition to understand and interpret the world through human terms and concepts as if only humans are capable of understanding and interpreting phenomena. Anthropocentrism has gotten us into some literally hot water, as we continue to privilege human wants over the environment's needs. But what other kinds of life share this narrative tendency? This might be definitional of our species, but is it exclusive? Might a capacity for narration and communication be more broadly definitional of life itself: a definition which is, paradoxically, not meant to be distinctive but rather is descriptive, enabling a vision of various kinds of animals and plants and things as sharing a fundamental communicative quality. What kinds of new relations, possibilities, and ways of being become possible when ontology bows to semiotics?

In Heller's story, the narrator has a notion of itself and its peers that is distinct from the Rootless, a distinction which is not simply ontological. The Rootless is separate because it is not part of the Conversation— it interacts with the world with a series of signs and gestures that is illegible and unintelligible to the narrator. The capacity to communicate here is entirely inseparable from a notion of being or identity. But through a patient openness to exchange and understanding, that communicative ability becomes shared and mutual—not perfect, but not detrimentally exclusive either.

This is precisely why astrobiology fiction can be so politically generative—it forces us to consider the plasticity of our cherished notions in the face of an Other and accept change and adaptation as our only universals. Such a confrontation can enlist beings as part of a shared Conversation, as in Heller's story, through mutual semiotic compromise and learning. In order for the visitor to return home and for the narrator to aid the visitor, both had to accept that what might count as a sign for them might be meaningless to the other, but that does not erect such a stark ontological divide. Both parties had to spend time together in conversation, learning and adapting to one another, until the pretense of such a divide becomes untenable[1]. Through the saplings leaving the planet, the visitor actually joined the Conversation. But first, both visitor and narrator had to learn to appreciate the semiotic logic of an alien other and render their own norms and expectations as contingents rather than universals. In doing so, this story and theories like Wynter's can be read side-by-side—both challenge us to disabuse ourselves of the rigid ontologies which have either held us back or kept others oppressed, in favor of a more plastic and relational semiotics. Speaking with trees or aliens or entities distributed across time and space might be a rather simple affair if we do not expect such beings to grow a mouth and vocal cords. All of us should be a part of the Conversation.

---

1 Editor's note: How gaping can this divide be, and how can we cross it—if at all? Think about this in the three stories by Bogi Takács, Gregory Benford, and (perhaps especially) Peter Watts.

FURTHER READING

Keane, Webb. "On Semiotic Ideology." *Signs and Society* 6, no. 1 (January 2018): 64–87.
https://doi.org/10.1086/695387

Kittler, Friedrich A. (1999). *Gramophone, Film, Typewriter*. Writing Science. Stanford, Calif: Stanford University Press.

Peters, John Durham. (2000). *Speaking into the Air: A History of the Idea of Communication*. Chicago: University of Chicago Press.

Prescod-Weinstein, Chanda. (2022). "Becoming Martian," *The Baffler*, 61.

Schroer, Sara Asu. "Jakob Von Uexküll: The Concept of Umwelt and its Potentials for an Anthropology Beyond the Human." *Ethnos* 86, no. 1 (01/2021), 132-152.

Wynter, Sylvia. (2003). "Unsettling the coloniality of being/power/truth/freedom: Toward the human, after man, its overrepresentation—An argument" *CR: The New Centennial Review*, 3.

STILL AS BRIGHT

Mary Robinette Kowal

ASTRONOMER SEEKS ADDITIONAL MOONS
THAT ORBIT PLANETS

LUNETTA STATION, May 31, 1965 (UPI)—The astronomer who discovered Jupiter's 13th moon last September says more moons will be found in the solar system during the next few years, and possibly this year.

Imogene hummed "Mr. Postman" to herself as she finished her pre-flight check, waiting for her passenger. Around her, gray metal banks of switches and gages lined the pilot console of her BusyBee. The porthole showed only the spindle of the *Lunetta* orbital station, daylight winking out as they spun around to the night side of Earth and the stars lit up like the sequins on one of the Marvelette's dresses.

She mimicked the rhythm of their dancing arms and let a few lines escape. "I've been standin' here waitin' Mister—"

Dr. Benayoun floated through the hatch, jolting Imogene out of her fantasy. Her cheeks burned and thank God this man didn't seem to recognize that she was blushing.

"Morning, Miss Imogene. Would you—" He jerked to a sudden halt as his shoulder bag caught on the hatch. The bag gaped open and papers floated into the compartment. Amateurs.

Imogene caught the closest ones before they could drift too far. "Careful there! You okay?"

His cheeks flared red with obvious embarrassment. "Fine." He snatched papers out of the air but didn't anchor well and spun toward her instrument panel. Such an amateur.

Imogene tucked a foot under one of the rails to brace herself and put a hand on his shoulder to guide him away from the console. He startled and looked down at her hand on his shoulder.

Imogene had that out of body experience where she remembered that she was Black and that he was not. Thirteen years ago, before the

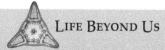

Meteor hit D.C., she would have remembered before touching a white man. As it was, she lifted her chin and smiled at him, squeezing his shoulder with her brown hand. "Why don't you buckle in, and I'll collect the rest of your papers."

He blushed again, tips of his ears going red beneath his sandy brown hair. "I'm—I know how to handle myself in micro-gravity."

"I know that, Dr. Benayoun." She let go of his shoulder, now that she'd countered his momentum, and straightened the papers in her hands. A few words tugged for attention like a gravity well: *parallax, convective redshift, astrometric.* "But if you aren't buckled in, we can't head for the orbital telescope."

"Oh." He took the papers she offered him, ears still bright red. "Yes, of course."

Imogene supermanned back to the hatch, twisting herself in the air to change orientation, and tucked her feet under a rail. She used to be more than a bus driver. Stabilized, she shut the airlock hatch with the ripple-bang of fifteen catches securing the precious atmosphere inside this tin can. She used to teach astronomy. Kicking back to her pilot's station, she grabbed the chair back to change her vector state and tucked neatly into the pilot's seat. She used to stand on the Earth and wish to be among the stars. Now that she was here? Imogene sighed, buckled in, and radioed *Lunetta* Flight Control.

"Control, BusyBee378. Requesting permission for departure to Orbital Telescope." Honestly, why were physicists so bad at naming things? Orbital Telescope. Very Large Lunar Observatory. Why not something like the Banneker Observatory?

"B378, Control. You are Go for departure along the nadir path at orbital height 350 kilometers."

"Thank you, Control." She disengaged the BusyBee's docking latches with a heavy *ka-chunk* that vibrated through the controllers in her hands. The release of the spring transferred enough angular momentum that they drifted back from the space station's dock. The cluster of airlocks that ringed the aft end of *Lunetta's* spindle had other BusyBees docked like barnacles upon an ocean ship. She waited until she cleared that cluster of ships before firing her thrusters to drop below the station on her assigned flight path.

At the forward end of the station, she could just see one of the Sirius rockets from Earth shining in dock and beyond that, the stars. She dipped low, passing under the massive centrifugal habitat ring that girdled the center of the spindle. It wheeled past in stately progression as she cut between the station and Earth.

A piece of paper drifted past. Imogene snatched it out of the air, tucking it under her thigh as she settled the ship into a lower orbit than the station.

"Sorry." Dr. Benayoun called from the back. "I thought I'd caught them all."

"No problem." Imogene checked her instruments against her route notes. She had nearly thirty minutes before her next burn to transfer back up to the telescope's orbit. In the Earth's shadow, the stars shone with cutting clarity. Taurus was sliding past the Earth's edge. Aldebaran. El Nath, and Alcyone. The Pleiades. And nestled in it, a brighter golden glow. She pointed. "There's Saturn."

"You know . . . your job has a pretty nice view . . ."

"Not as good as yours."

He snorted. "Please. I get to look at photographic plates and radio frequencies and, occasionally, very occasionally, through an actual scope. Mostly at planets in our solar system."

All of which made her salivate. "Ever wonder what other stars might have planets?"

Paper rustled. "There's no way to know."

Imogene wet her lips, wishing that she could get time on the telescope. Of course, there was no way to know if no one looked. She lived among the stars now, with a planet at her feet, but missed the rings of Saturn and the great swirling spot of Jupiter. The centrifugal spin of *Lunetta* made observation impossible. "No way? That seems a little despairing." She caught herself and moderated her tone into something more ladylike. "There's probably a method to detect extra-solar planets that we just haven't sorted yet. Sometimes I noodle away in my head, wondering how we'd look for them."

"Like Barnard's star?" Dr. Benayoun snorted, "Please. Van de Kamp wasn't able to prove that planets around other stars even existed, much less locate one."

The dismissal in his voice might as well have been a challenge. "I was thinking more of Struve's ideas about studying both the Doppler motion and eclipses."

"The resolution is too low to see eclipses."

She knew that but it also didn't have to be the final answer. Imogene used to be good at this. The only woman in her astronomy courses and she'd earned her degree through long nights of independent research. No way to know? There was always a way to know.

She just had to find it.

Around Imogene, the buzz of conversations in the languages of the International Aerospace Coalition contained pops of familiar astronomical words as technicians hopped from Arabic to Latin. English conversations spiraled into German and then back. Brown astronomers mingled with white, bending over the same telescopes in a joint worship of the stars. After the Meteor, the addition of Algeria to the International Aerospace Coalition had had the side-effect of opening doors for Black American astronomers and astronauts as well. Still nearly all men though. Up here, as on Earth, only the rare woman escaped clerical work. Tense with the desire to participate, Imogene waited by the door to the main observatory with her feet tucked under one of the bright blue grabrails.

In the six months since she'd been on the Orbital Telescope route, had there ever been a point when Dr. Benayoun was not late?

Granted, if she had access to that big, beautiful telescope, she wouldn't want to leave either. On the other hand, he was the one who ultimately set the schedule for the orbital observatory and had only allotted himself six hours on the telescope this week. It was still more than she'd ever get. You had to have a PhD to get any time at all.

"Miss Imogene!" He supermanned across the room to her, trailing assistants like a contrail. Five men, one woman. "I'm so sorry to keep you wai—" He hiccupped and scowled. "—ting. Just a few more minutes."

"No problem. I brought something to read." She smiled and pulled out a copy of *A Survey of Islamic Astronomical Tables* she'd snagged from the library on her lunch break back on *Lunetta*.

Not that he noticed. He'd already turned back to the assistants. "I'll need another two 120-minute exposures on the Kodak IIIa-J emulsion with the Wratten 4 filte—" Dr. Benayoun's hiccup cut through a low whir as a set of motors repositioned the telescope for whatever project was next on the agenda.

A gawky astronomer who'd come up from England raised his hand as if testing for rain. "Do we need to finish this while Jupiter is still in opposition?"

That was the level of assistant he had up here? She'd spent his entire shift fuming to come up with what seemed like a decent theoretical approach to finding extra-solar planets and he had people this insecure on his team?

"Yes. The search for moons does require consecutive nights and—" He hiccupped again and sighed. "I'll deconflict the schedule in the morning. Must run."

She closed her book and tucked it under her arm, title facing out. Dr. Benayoun kicked off toward her with an apologetic wave as the assistants scattered in his wake. Tempting though it was to spew her idea at him, the likely outcome would be that he'd just take her idea and claim it as his own. As a woman, no one would think it was hers.

She led him through the narrow corridors to the orbital telescope's small port, not that he needed the guidance, but she'd seen him get distracted before and pause to "just check in" at a workstation and lose track of time.

His hiccups punctuated their progress, audible even over the ever-present hum of fans.

In the port, the wet gunmetal smell of space relaxed Imogene's shoulders. As much as she wanted to be back in the observatory, there would always be someone telling her she didn't belong. At least, Post-Meteor, no one questioned her at the controls of a BusyBee. The dull gray metal consoles framed her world as she and Dr. Benayoun settled into the cabin.

"Again, I'm sorry to keep you wai—" He hiccupped again and groaned. "God. I hate these."

Imogene dug through her crew kit, past the lotion and hair pins, and pulled out a chocolate bar. "Try this." She sent the bar spinning back to him.

He caught it, frowning. "Chocolate?"

"I don't have a spoonful of sugar." Imogene pulled her pre-flight checklist out and ran through the familiar steps. "Just hold a square in your mouth and count backwards from ten with your ears plugged."

"Seriou—sly?" He sighed and foil crinkled behind her. "Hell. I'll try anything at this point."

She glanced back with a grin. Dr. Benayoun had his fingers in his ears, eyes closed. The motion made the cuffs of his sleeves fall down his forearm, exposing an old jagged scar. He was the right age for that to be a war wound from the Meteor.

Imogene turned back to the console and took the smooth worn stick in her right hand. "Control, BusyBee378. Requesting permission for departure from Orbital Telescope to *Lunetta*."

"B378, Control. You are Go for departure along the polar path at orbital height 500 kilometers. Heading Six Zero Sierra."

"Thank you, Control. Polar path. 500 kilometers. Heading Six Zero Sierra."

The BusyBee's docking latches disengaged, kicking them back from the orbital telescope. The telescope had only two berths at this end, and her ship was the only one docked. As they drifted clear, the dark orb of Earth came into view on their starboard. Imogene fired her thrusters, backing farther from the station.

The great silver-clad telescope filled the forward and port windows, hanging over the night side of the Earth. On the velvet shadows of the planet, lightning stretched between clouds, lighting them up with pops of bright white. She set her trajectory in her dashboard. "Someone's getting a helluva storm back home."

"That's Europe now, isn't it?" Dr. Benayoun cleared his throat. "Also, thank you. That worked."

"My pleasure." She marked the time and punched the thrusters to get them headed over the North Pole. He hadn't noticed her book so she couldn't use that as an opener to ask for off-shift time on the telescope, but he was talking to her, so maybe she could ease into it. "It sounded like you were working on spotting more Jovian moons."

He sighed. "And Saturnian and Uranian and, and, and . . . The IAC wants to know where all of them are so they can plan spacecraft trajectories. All of them. It feels like Sisyphus sometimes."

"With some of your staff being the rock or the hill?"

He laughed. "Ives-Hadley means well."

"Cold." She glanced over her shoulder. "Next you're going to bless his heart."

"I'm not that cruel."

"Why not just relegate him to cataloguing photographic plates?"

The strength of Dr. Benayoun's snort could have propelled a rocket. "Tempting. You've been hanging out with us entirely too much."

She shrugged. "I used to teach astronomy at a university."

Behind her, he was silent enough that she could hear the faint creak of metal expanding as they came over the Earth into sunlight. "Um . . . Where?"

"Hampton Institute." She hurried on before he realized that it was in Virginia and gone after the Meteor. "Mostly I taught physics, but astronomy was my main interest. Wound up in the astronaut program to get closer to the stars but . . . not much chance for observation."

When the Meteor struck D.C., she'd been with her students in Chicago at Adler Planetarium. Her colleagues. Her friends. The students. So many of them were just . . . gone. She watched the clock, waiting for the next burn.

"Why didn't you apply to work at the observatory?"

"Wasn't an option when I joined." It still probably wasn't. "Is it now?"

"Well . . . sure." He cleared his throat. "I mean, we only take the most qualified candidates, but there's nothing to prevent you from applying."

"What if I just wanted telescope time? I know you let visiting astronomers do research up here between main projects." The man had a pile of director's discretionary time that he could hand out to whoever he chose. He just had to choose her.

"It's really not for amateur viewing. Sorry." Foil rustled behind her as if he were eating more of her chocolate bar. "I have a smaller scope you could borrow, back on *Lunetta*, if you didn't mind doing a little correction for the station's orbit."

Amateur viewing. Imogene kept her hands nice and light on the controls by sheer force of will. "And if there was a project I wanted to work on?"

"I would have to review it." He cleared his throat. "Tell you what . . . why don't we discuss that over dinner?"

"Wouldn't the observatory be better for that?"

"Not if you want me to actually look at it." The foil crinkled again. "Besides, I, um, I owe you a chocolate bar."

She ground her teeth together. How much did she want time on the telescope? Enough to go on a date with this man? This man with the keys to the orbital observatory. And the only option for dining on *Lunetta* was the cafeteria. It wasn't like she'd be having dinner alone with the man, but everyone would know. And if she *did* get telescope time, people would think they knew why. Did she want that time enough to deal with the gossip that would follow? "Sure. I just love the chocolate bars in the cafeteria."

He laughed. "I usually eat in my office or the garden module. Would you mind a picnic?"

Someday, Imogene would learn to not tease a man for not taking her someplace nice. She would grant that the walls of greenery lining the garden module were a nice change from the cafeteria, but the picnic had traded one problem for another. Now she was having dinner alone with the man. All Imogene had to do was survive the next half hour without Dr. Benayoun—Jacob—getting the wrong idea. More than he already had.

"—and then, fully intending to wipe the smug look off his face when I bowled a perfect game, I cranked the ball back, swung and . . .hit myself in the leg."

"No!" Why did he have to keep making her laugh?

"Hard enough that I knocked myself down." Jacob shook his head, rolling his eyes. "Still holding the bowling ball, mind you!"

"Oh, no . . . Oh, honey. No." She pressed the edge of her fork through the last of her polenta. "How'd you do wiping the smug look off your rival's face?"

"Well . . . he no longer looked smug?" Clapping his napkin to his breast, he looked ceilingward in mock anguish. "I swear, I still have the bruise from that. On my soul."

"Ha! I'll bet."

"So . . ." Jacob wiped a piece of tortilla across the plate he'd liberated from the cafeteria. "When you aren't flying a BusyBee, how do you occupy yourself?"

"Teaching flying or certifying new pilots on vacuum." Imogene tucked her feet under the bench by the side of the running path that cut through the middle of the garden module. Why wasn't anyone jogging now? "Reading about astronomy to try to keep up."

"Sounds like all work, all the time." He folded the flour shell neatly around a bit of the fish. "Any hobbies besides astronomy?"

Hobby. Imogene clamped her jaw so tight it felt like her teeth squeaked. He might not be in charge of her department, but a complaint about her? He could get her grounded anyway. The soft hum of fans masked the lull in their conversation a little, but not quite enough.

"Sorry. Sorry, I didn't mean it like that." Jacob set his empty plate aside. "You said you used to teach."

"So, teachers are amateurs now?"

"I just meant . . . Look. Some of the best work in astronomy is done by amateurs. It means 'for the love' and isn't related to the quality of your research, but just to if you're getting paid."

"I know what it means." Imogene wiped her mouth with the rough napkin. "I'm not getting paid to be an astronomer anymore because Hampton Institute was in Virginia."

"*Dio*—I'm sorry. I'm so, so sorry."

"I'll take these back to the cafeteria." Imogene stacked her plate on his, the cutlery rattling in the silence as she stood. "Thank you for a lovely meal."

"Imogene. Wait." He stood, holding out his hands for the plates. "You haven't told me about your proje—"

A sharp metallic bang reverberated from their feet. Jacob flinched. Imogene turned toward the nearest bulkhead, listening for a depress alarm.

Surrounded by greenery, it was easy to forget that they lived in a giant wheel, spinning through space and that a micrometeorite could punch through the station at any time.

She wet her lips, feeling the beat of her pulse in all her joints as unused adrenaline vibrated inside her. "I think we're clear." Swallowing the urge to start belated shaking, she smiled at him. "I'll let maintenance know to check the hull in this section."

"*Guay de mi.*" Jacob sat down and buried his fingers in his hair. "How are you so calm?"

"You've seen the tin can I fly, right?" Imogene shrugged as if her heart weren't racing now. "The station has more shielding by orders of magnitude. They can track anything big enough to actually get through it."

He waved his hand through the air. "I know. I just . . ." Jacob sighed and straightened. He patted the bench beside him. "Please. Tell me about your idea?"

She sighed, staring down the long curve of the garden module away from him. "Look. Look, you seem like a nice fellow, and I enjoyed having dinner with you, but you don't have to pretend that you'll let me have time on the telescope if my idea is somehow magically good enough. I don't want to play this game. I'll write up the idea, formally, and submit it."

"I can help with that. That's why . . ." He sighed heavily. "If we'd had dinner in the cafeteria, I would have been interrupted every ten minutes with someone having 'just one question.' Now for God's sake, sit down and tell me your idea. C'mon. What do you have to lose?"

Imogene turned to face him, still clutching the plates. That was the problem. What she had to lose was her idea. Even if she wrote it up and submitted it, she had only a masters. She didn't have a PhD. She wasn't a man. "I want to look for extra-solar planets."

"Ah . . ." He seemed pained as if he didn't want to hurt her feelings. This was a thing he'd already said that he thought couldn't be done. "Go on."

"Maybe we haven't had success because everyone is looking for another Earth. Until Cecilia Payne, we thought the Sun was made of carbon like Earth; so, what if other solar systems are also different from expectations?"

This time his "Go on" had the first layer of curiosity.

"My first thought was to monitor the light curves of stars and look for dips in brightness as a planet passes in front. But knowing it would require more observation time than an *amateur* could request, I want to try occulting the light from their central star with a BusyBee. I'll grant that this direct observation method will only detect a Jupiter size planet relatively close to its star, but that would indicate potential—"

He blinked. "Back up. I thought the BusyBees weren't rated for interplanetary space?"

"Don't need interplanetary space. They're only three meters across on their small axis. If we take one thirty thousand kilometers up to geosynch, that would be far enough for it to obscure an area the size of a G-type star at 200 parsecs. If there are no good extra-solar candidates like that, a BusyBee set in a high elliptical orbit around the Moon will get us a baseline of at least three hundred thousand kilometers. There must be hundreds of good candidate stars in the lunar plane that fit the bill with an occulter that far away."

Jacob stood and put his hands on his hips. He paced away from her, muttering under his breath, and then paced back, scowling at the floor. "No good. Even out at the Moon, a BusyBee would still be drifting at an arcsecond per second relative to the background stars. It would need to have a nearly zero drift rate for at least a minute to give us enough time to image any extra-solar planets."

"Not if it was orbiting the Moon east to west. With a sufficiently elliptical orbit, near apoapsis, the BusyBee can hang fixed relative to the background stars as seen from Earth for at least a minute."

"Come on. It would have to be incredibly stable and—"

The last thread of Imogene's patience snapped. It was bad enough that he dismissed her as an astronomer, but now this man had the nerve to lecture her about something he didn't even know how to do? He could stay the hell out of her cockpit.

"Maintaining a fixed position is required to get your astronaut-pilot certification. But since you're *just* an astronomer, I don't expect you to know such things." She smiled sweetly at him as if that would minimize the bite she could not wipe from her tone. "With a skilled pilot on board and some extra propellant tanks, I have high confidence we could extend that to five minutes at least."

"Five minutes? Five minutes! That would work. *Dio.* If they're out there, that would work." Jacob crossed the space between them and took the plates out of her hands. He set them down on the bench and turned back to her. "Okay. First thing is that I'm putting in a request to transfer you to my department because I have no idea why they're wasting you as a NavComp."

"I'm not a NavComp, I'm a— Wait. Your department—to do what?"

"Look for planets." He studied the floor and his cheeks turned red. "Important and incredibly awkward question."

Imogene braced herself for another request for a date and how the hell was she going to turn him down without losing this shot? "Ask."

Jacob tugged his ear. "Miss Imogene . . . What's your last name? If you're going to author a paper while in my department, I feel like I ought to know."

She smiled and held out her hand. "I'm Imogene Braggs. Pilot and astronomer."

—AND THE MOON BE STILL AS BRIGHT

JOSÉ A. CABALLERO

ASTRONOMERS SEEK MOONS THAT ORBIT EXOPLANETS

CENTRO DE ASTROBIOLOGÍA, 24 February 2022 (Spain)—The astronomer who discovered the nearby transiting exoplanet GJ 486 b last May says moons will be found outside the solar system during the next few years, and possibly this year.

How to unpack all the themes in Mary Robinette Kowal's "Still as Bright"? As expected, mad science and engineering are of vital importance, but there are also allusions to languages, Arabic culture (including Islamic astronomy), African American discrimination, professional ethics or the lack thereof, and more. In 1965 in Imogene's alternate universe, the world has the technology to put overwhelmingly large structures into low Earth orbit, plans to build a Very Large Lunar Observatory, and even has the ability to send spacecraft to the icy giants! Imogene's universe diverged from ours in mid-20th century with the Meteor hit that led the world to pour resources into space flight. Fortunately, Imogene's universe and ours have some good things in common, such as The Marvelette's *Please Mr. Postman* (1961), the first number-one US *Billboard* single for Motown Records. *I've been standin' here waitin' Mister Postman . . .* Let's imagine that we are orbiting their 1965 Earth, heading toward the Orbital Telescope with the aim of discovering exoplanets. Do we have a chance to find any?

I will answer the question: *no, we don't.* But, luckily, *our* world is different . . . I'll be your guide to the 21st century exoplanetology in our universe. Buckle up in our metaphorical BusyBee: it's going to be a fast ride.

The idea of exoplanets, worlds orbiting stars other than our Sun, which may (not) resemble those in our solar system, has been discussed for millennia: Christiaan Huygens (1629-1695) and Isaac Newton (1643-1727), with their coarse telescopes, unsuccessfully looked for them; Giordano Bruno (1548-1600), the astronomers' martyr, and Epicurus (342-270 BC) speculated about their existence; and earlier, Democritus (460-370 BC), showing an intense clairvoyance, wrote: *"In some worlds there is no Sun and Moon, in others they are larger than in our world, and in others more numerous. In some parts there are more worlds, in others fewer [. . .]; in some parts they are arising, in others failing. There are some worlds devoid of living creatures or plants or any moisture."*

In our universe, my friends and colleagues Michel Mayor and Didier Queloz discovered 51 Pegasi b, the first exoplanet around a solar-like star, in 1995 [1], 30 years after Imogene's proposal. However, it was Otto Struve who proposed searching for exoplanet transits—planets passing in front of their stars from our point of view, causing regular dips in starlight—and for stellar radial velocity variations—regular shifts in the star's spectrum, based on the Doppler effect from motion caused by the planet's gravitational tug—in 1952 [2], 15 years before Imogene's idea. Actually, the vast majority of the almost 5,000 exoplanets discovered so far have been found with the two methods proposed by Struve. Furthermore, the measurement of light curves precise enough to detect transits by planets as small as mini-Neptunes around solar-like stars can be done with tiny telescopes of 10 cm or less. And, paraphrasing Dr. Benayoun's words, many of these measurements are indeed performed "for the love" by amateur astronomers!

Between Struve's proposal and Mayor & Queloz's discovery, there were also claims that took years to be confirmed or that are still debated, such as those: γ Cephei b in 1988 [3], confirmed a decade later; HD 114762 b in 1989 [4], which appears to be a low-mass star; and the two Earth-mass bodies in close orbit to the pulsar PSR 1257+12 in 1992, widely regarded as the first confirmed exoplanet discovery [5]. A pulsar is a neutron star, the dead corpse remnant after a supernova explosion, so the formation and evolution of such bodies must be very different from what we see in our solar system or in other thousands of exoplanetary systems.

There were also untrue claims. In our universe, van de Kamp claimed to have discovered a Jovian exoplanet around Barnard's star, the second closest star to the Sun after the α Centauri triple system, using astrometry in 1963 [5]. It took ten years to reject the claim. In Imogene's universe, he also claimed to have spotted this exoplanet, but it had been rejected already by 1965. When I write these lines, in February 2022, no uncontroversial astrometric exoplanet signal (using precision measurements of stellar movement with respect to background stars and galaxies, which can be caused by a planet's gravity) has been detected yet, but I am convinced that by the time you read this essay, the ESA *Gaia* mission would have indeed made a few of them public. Nonetheless, we may have to wait a bit longer for confirming or discarding a new Barnard's star exoplanet candidate, this time a cool exoearth found with the radial-velocity method, which was published in *Nature* by Ribas et al. in 2018 [6] and that I co-authored.

Searches for transits, radial-velocity variations and the astrometric wobble are indirect exoplanet detection methods. There is however a direct detection method: imaging. My PhD thesis at the Instituto de Astrofísica de Canarias (IAC!) was mainly focused on imaging exoplanets, both free-floating in star-forming regions [7] and as companions to nearby stars. In both cases, these planets must be (*i*) extremely young, of a dozen million years at most, because they are still contracting and emit their own light, rather than reflecting their stars', (*ii*) extremely distant from their stars, which shine hundreds of million times more brightly, and (*iii*) more massive than about three times the mass of Jupiter. For detecting Jupiter-like planets at Jupiter-like separations, i.e., about five times the Sun-Earth separation, we need spatial resolution (which implies the combination of a large telescope and an instrument with a specific optics design and a detector with a small pixel size), spatial and temporal stability (for the stars to always appear point-like), and suppression of the light of the host star. The latter is performed with complicated coronographs that "occult" the light of the star but let pass the light of the exoplanet outside the instrument's optical axis. On Earth, we must correct the effects of the atmosphere, which blurs our images, with even more complicated adaptive optics systems. In space, we do not need these, but the telescope pointing must be exquisite. We expect that the *James Webb Space Telescope*, on a halo orbit around L2 beyond the Moon, will be able to observe some of the indirectly discovered exoplanets, especially around the closest stars.

One way to circumvent the problem of host star light suppression is a stellar occulter or starshade, which flies in formation with the space telescope and works as Imogene described. The first time I heard of a stellar occulter was in 2006 from my Swedish friend Markus Janson. We are seriously considering using one for the *Nancy Grace Roman Space Telescope*, still under construction. While I don't doubt Imogene's piloting skills and the capacity of the mad engineers to adorn her BusyBee

B378 with an umbrella-like, sunflower-shaped structure that works as a coronograph, Dr. Benayoun's old-technology Orbital Telescope is far from being the right facility to carry out this study. For example, they use Kodak IIIa-J photographic plates that need to be exchanged by hand by a crew member, instead of the widely used (in our universe) charge-couple devices, commonly known as CCDs, which can be found in any smartphone. A large crewed orbital telescope, with its mechanical deformations, operating fans, and vibrations in the control room, corridors, and kitchen, would have a tremendous impact on the quality of the data, especially on the stability and spatial resolution, which would be much worse than what is needed for detecting exoplanets. If I were in the time allocation committee, I would not award time to their proposal. Good thing we have developed modern computers running on microchips . . .

If discovering exoplanets with their technology is difficult, if not impossible, discovering exomoons, moons around exoplanets, is beyond their imagination. However, it is tricky, but feasible, in our universe with 21st century technology. We would have been able to identify exomoons about two decades ago if HD 209458 b or HD 189733 b, the first transiting hot Jupiters around really bright stars, had them. For detecting exomoons, we would just need a stable space telescope with digital detectors (*Hubble, Spitzer, TESS, CHEOPS*), a bright star with a large transiting planet, and high signal-to-noise ratio data. However, exomoons appear to be rare, especially around hot Jupiters: planets of the mass of our Jovian gaseous giant, but with orbital periods of a few days (instead of years). Moons would have been lost, if formed at all, either during the exoplanet's migration toward its star in the protoplanetary disk during the early stages of formation, or afterwards due to the large amount of high-energy radiation at the short orbital separation of the hot Jupiter and its moon. But if there are moons in our solar system, why should they not exist around exoplanets?

Just before the COVID pandemic, I convinced two students of mine to investigate "Exomoons in the Habitable Zones of M Dwarfs." Red cool dwarfs of the M spectral type are the most common stars in the solar neighborhood [8] and, very likely, our galaxy. My team has discovered about half of the known exoplanets around the nearest M dwarfs, some of them in or near the habitable zone (HZ), where planets could host liquid water on their solid surfaces. However, while some M-dwarf exoplanets in the HZ probably have solid surfaces (e.g., Teegarden's b [9] is the exoplanet with the greatest Earth Similarity Index), others are likely mini-Neptunes—icy giants of deep ammonia atmospheres with no solid surface at all (e.g., HD 180617 b [10]). Either way, these exoplanets are tidally locked to their stars: they always offer the same scorched hemisphere to their stars, like the Moon does to Earth. What my students and I, with some help from the other side of the Atlantic, did was investigating the potential habitability, stability, and detectability of exomoons around exoplanets orbiting M dwarfs. What we found was very pessimistic: probably none of the M-dwarf planets found to date have exomoons based on long-term dynamical stability analyses and, if any do, they cannot be detected with current technology [11]. In spite of very recent claims (e.g., Kepler-1708 b-i [12]), no incontrovertible exomoon has been detected yet . . .

Perhaps, within a few decades, you or any other reader of *Life Beyond Us* will be able to study the atmosphere of a habitable exomoon with the Large Interferometer for Exoplanets, or *LIFE*.

REFERENCES

[1] Mayor, M. & Queloz, D. (1995). "A Jupiter-mass companion to a solar-like star." *Nature*, 378, 359.

[2] Struve, O. (1952). "Proposal for a project for high-precision stellar radial velocity work." *The Observatory*, 72, 199.

[3] Campbell, B; Walker, G. A. H.; Yang, S. (1988). "A search for substellar companions around solar-like stars." *The Astrophysical Journal*, 331, 992.

[4] Latham, D. W.; Mazeh, T.; Stefanik, R. P.; Mayor, M; Burki, G. (1989). "The unseen companion of HD 114762: a probable brown dwarf." *Nature*, 339, 38.

[5] Wolzscan, A. & Frail, D. A. (1992). "A planetary system around the millisecond pulsar PSR1257+12." *Nature*, 355, 145.

[6] Ribas, I.; Tuomi, M.; Reiners, A. et al. (2018). "A candidate super-Earth planet orbiting near the snow line of Barnard's star." *Nature*, 563, 365.

[7] Caballero, J. A.; Béjar, V. J. S.; Rebolo, R. et al. (2007). "The substellar mass function in σ Orionis. II. Optical, near-infrared and IRAC/ Spitzer photometry of young cluster brown dwarfs and planetary-mass objects." *Astronomy & Astrophysics*, 470, 903.

[8]   Reylé, C.; Jardine, K; Fouqué, P. et al. (2021). "The 10 parsec sample in the Gaia era." *Astronomy & Astrophysics*, 650, A201.

[9]   Zechmeister, M.; Dreizler, S.; Ribas, I. et al. (2019). "The CARMENES search for exoplanets around M dwarfs. Two temperate Earth-mass planet candidates around Teegarden's Star." *Astronomy & Astrophysics*, 627, A49.

[10] Kaminski, A.; Trifonov, T.; Caballero, J. A. et al. (2018). "The CARMENES search for exoplanets around M dwarfs. A Neptune-mass planet traversing the habitable zone around HD 180617." *Astronomy & Astrophysics*, 619, A115.

[11] Martínez-Rodríguez, H.; Caballero, J. A.; Cifuentes, C. et al. (2019). "Exomoons in the Habitable Zones of M Dwarfs." *The Astrophysical Journal*, 887, 261.

[12] Kipping, D.; Bryson, S.; Burke, C. et al. (2022). "An exomoon survey of 70 cool giant exoplanets and the new candidate Kepler-1708 b-i." *Nature Astronomy*, 6, 367. (arXiv:2201.04643)

DEVIL IN THE DEEP

Lucie Lukačovičová

My overshadowing Spirit and might with thee
I send along, ride forth, and bid the Deep
Within appointed bounds be Heav'n and Earth,
Boundless the Deep, because I am who fill
Infinitude, nor vacuous the space.

—*John Milton: Paradise Lost (Book 7)*

". . . ——— . . ." The sounds resonated through the mining tunnel. María de la Luz froze in her tracks.

"What was that?" she whispered.

". . . ——— . . ." The clanging repeated itself.

"It's them! We found them," shouted one of the miners' rescue team. "Somebody must have survived the cave-in! They found a tube of the cooling system and are signaling their position. The sounds carry through the metal."

The team moved as fast as possible in the claustrophobic tunnel; there was no time to lose. After a short while, the SOS in Morse code turned into wild and desperate banging.

Hang on! Hang on! We'll get you out! María de la Luz rushed into action together with the team. *Just hang on!*

Valerie's gaze seemed vacant and distant. The entrance to the mine was dark like the maw of a dragon. She watched the rescue team dragging out the saved miners, some of them injured, some unconscious, and two dead bodies with crushed limbs.

"Luz, are you okay?" Valerie livened up instantly as she saw her fellow scientist emerge from the deep.

María de la Luz smiled weakly, wiped the dust from her face, and took off her hard hat. "We found them, thanks to their foreman's idea to pound the SOS signal on the metal cooling tube that stretches through the tunnels."

"They should have a tracking device in each miner's lamp." Valerie frowned slightly.

"This is Bolivia."

"Worse conditions than at my last assignment in the Gulf of Mexico."

"What were you doing there?"

"Researching microbes in petroleum seeps on the ocean floor," Valerie muttered. She watched the survivors embracing their families. They were coughing, thanking God, cursing or swearing to get themselves drunk unconscious tonight. Three of the rescued miners were only teenage boys; one of them was weeping with fear and exhaustion in his mother's arms, tears leaving traces in the dust on his cheeks.

"They will have to go back to the mine tomorrow," María de la Luz said grimly, following Valerie's gaze.

"That's inhuman."

"It's their livelihood. Same as my family's."

The two dead miners were covered with blankets. Their wives' wailing was a thin, high, and somehow fragile sound, akin to the wind in the mountains.

As the scientists trudged by, Valerie wondered what the locals actually saw in them. *Strangers? Saviors? Exploiters? Although Luz—as she called María de la Luz—was practically one of them.*

Luz hailed from a miner family and looked like it: short, muscular, resilient. In her thirties, she was one of the best Bolivian experts on earthquakes and seismic waves.

Valerie was about the same age; she was of Czech origin, tall, thin, pale, and usually looked as if she had wandered to Earth from some other world by accident. Features in her long oval face gave the impression of something slightly alien. But she knew all there was to know about deep biosphere and rock mechanics.

I wish I could help them. Valerie suppressed a sigh. *Though they will probably always see me as an intruder.*

"The locals say the mine is stable now," María de la Luz stated. The morning after the accident, the two scientists were holed up in the tiny, cluttered room they'd been given in lieu of a proper lab. Valerie was sipping at her coffee, checking the seismograms from the time of the cave-in. "We can get in and continue with the work. Lay some transmission cables to be able to communicate better, and through them, we can use some tracking devices, at least for the two of us. Though it won't be easy at such depth."

"You trust the locals, Luz?"

"The rescue team didn't doubt my training and experience. They were reluctant to take me with them because if anything were to happen to a scientist who is supposed to find a way to make this hell pit safer, nobody would be happy."

"Except for the mining company?" Valerie suggested cynically. The absence of tracking devices and detectors obviously still bothered her.

"The Scientific Forum would sue their souls out of them," Luz grinned. "It's cheaper to keep us alive."

"True. The Scientific Forum is hungry for our results." Valerie put down the coffee and tapped at her tablet, lost in thought. "And I really hope we'll be able to deliver . . ."

"We will!" Luz was enthusiastic. "The mining company recently drilled deeper tunnels and shafts. And the earthquake gave us Archean rocks on a silver platter. Our mine makes Mponeng Gold Mine look shallow. We'll get our research, miners get more safety, and the world will get a look at the viscera of the Earth. Everybody wins."

"You have to bring offerings with you," the miner said slowly and clearly as if doubting that Valerie could comprehend his request. She took no offense, just nodded and showed him the coca leaves and a bottle of hard liquor Luz had given her in a hurry without proper explanation.

Valerie was entering the silver mine for the first time since their arrival. Luz had gone in before, with the rescue party, and that was a hurried descent. The main massive earthquake had occurred more than a week ago, but yesterday's accidental cave-in still took two lives.

Valerie would've been happier to have Luz with her, but there was too much work and only two of them. She wasn't afraid. She just felt Luz could better understand the language of the miners, regardless of the fact they all spoke Spanish.

"If you have a cross or rosary, leave it here," the foreman instructed her.

Valerie shook her head: "No worries. I don't wear any."

He looked surprised.

"I follow the tradition of my Czech ancestors," she stated with a bit of dry humor. "I'm an atheist."

The miner crossed himself quickly, and she wasn't entirely sure if he knew what the word "atheist" really meant.

"Come." He gestured. He had no choice but to take her with him anyway. The scientist, wearing working clothes and a hard hat, followed him through the entrance and to the mine shaft cage. She put on a respirator, got her gloves ready. With uneasiness, she realized that her guide wasn't wearing any. The rescued men yesterday also had had no protective gear except for the hard hats with headlamps.

"No kneeling before any statue, no crossing yourself, no uttering the names of saints," the miner said sternly as the cage whizzed into the darkness. The descent was like being swallowed by the mountain. The elevator rattled and clanked; the platform shook from time to time. The air she breathed through the respirator was strangely fusty.

It was a long ride into a black chasm—a journey almost an hour long, using a system of several elevators.

Finally, the last cage came to a halt. It was hot and Valerie started sweating immediately. The timbers supporting the walls and ceilings closer to the surface were replaced by flexible shotcrete reinforced with steel fibers and held in place by diamond-mesh netting—but only in some places, leaving the rock elsewhere bare. It was possible to see only what was directly in front of them, in the reach of the headlamps. Otherwise, they were enveloped by complete, unending darkness.

Why the hell had I come here? But she wouldn't change a thing. Not if it meant discovering life that had stayed hidden in the immense depths between grains of rock, persisting on the tiniest droplets of condensed water and low-energy chemistry, oblivious to the whole surface biosphere; microbes that metabolized with glacial pace and divided once every ten thousand years. The current generation could be older than agriculture. Some cells might have existed before modern humans spread out of Africa, and still lived their incredibly slow lives down here.

The miner led Valerie to the beginning of a tunnel where she stopped, surprised.

A tall statue of a horned man seemed to glare at her. It had an open mouth with sharp teeth and a wicked expression. It was made partly of rock, partly of clay, and was surrounded by heaps of coca leaves, cigarettes and empty bottles and cans.

Valerie and the miner added their own offerings.

"You . . . worship the devil?" she asked cautiously, her voice muffled by the mask.

"God rules the land above, the villages and cities, the sky," the foreman explained. "But here, below, is the realm of El Tío de la mina. There are many statues like this in different places in the mine."

El Tío de la mina. The Uncle of the mine. Valerie observed the statue. "You ask El Tío for safety and rich ore," she concluded.

"So, you know about El Tío."

She smiled faintly. *What else would they ask for?*

"All what lies beneath the surface belongs to him," the miner continued. "You don't want to anger him. He commands the darkness and the heat of the fires that burn in the deep. That's why it's so hot in the lowest parts of the mines. He doesn't like priests and women entering the mine. He gets violent."

"And . . . me?" she asked. She put on her infra-goggles, set with two thermal cameras to record and superimpose the infrared vision landscape over the normally visible one that she was perceiving with her own eyes. This way she could use her normal vision and thermal vision at the same time, controlling the device with a "command glove" with magnetic sensors at the joints to recognize how her hand moved and which fingers were bent or stretched.

The output went also to her tablet and was instantly saved in the cloud if possible. *Well, in the mines it was usually impossible.*

"You are a scientist." The foreman waved his hand. "That's something like a woman politician or the like. You do men's work and don't look after the wawas."

So, I'm something like a man and therefore, it doesn't count. Fascinating. Valerie followed the miner through the tunnel. *It was odd that he used the Quechua word "wawas" instead of Spanish "bebés" for babies.*

Luz wandered around the mining site, checking the aftermath of the earthquake and looking for the best locations to plant seismic sensors and electrodes to monitor the massive rock movements that took place in the mountain. The data collected so far were not precise enough.

In the distance, a pitiful wailing sound made a shiver run down her spine. She had heard something similar the day before and she knew it well. It was the sound of grieving.

Further down the dirt road under the merciless sun, through a landscape scorched and full of stones, dust, and gravel—nothing else— she came across a group of local women, relatives of the miners who perished during the earthquake. They weren't dressed in black, but in white blouses or colored t-shirts and jeans. They were in mourning, weeping loudly, carrying flowers and candles, on their way to the cemetery to pay respects to their dead.

"Lo siento mucho," she offered quietly.

"You are the big science lady. What could you know about our loss?" A young girl hissed. The others told her to hush up.

"Actually, I happen to know." Luz held the girl's gaze. "Both my uncles died in the mine. I sincerely hope I can come up with something to make the work safer. That's one of the main reasons I'm here."

"Only El Tío can protect us," somebody objected.

"If you offend him," another woman said, "what will become of us? And our poor wawas!"

"Does El Tío really want you to suffer so much?" Luz tilted her head. "He's been here since time immemorial. During past decades, the miners wore hard hats and used Davy lamps to prevent more deaths and injuries . . . he never objected, did he?"

"That's true," one of the women agreed. "El Tío is not so cruel. Yesterday I went to the mine entrance to bring him offerings, so he wouldn't take any more lives. I still have a brother in the mine, you know?" She gave a sob. "I wanted to appease El Tío and he consoled me."

"He . . . consoled you?" Luz asked, uncertain what to make of it.

"I embraced the cold wall and the rock turned hot."

"Isn't the rock warm by itself in the depths?"

"I didn't go that deep in the mine, Heaven forbid! And the rock wall became hot, hotter than a human body, as if the stone itself embraced me in return."

"You are distracted, Luz." It wasn't a question. Valerie looked at her colleague over a fresh cup of coffee. They were going through the resistivity tomography data monitoring movements in the rocky slope; the evening seemed to drag into eternity.

"I'm still thinking about what that local woman told me." Luz pointed at the chart she was completing. "There is no pattern to the sudden hot spots in the rock. The thermograph records them, but we have no idea what's their cause. I think there might be some connection to the woman's claim."

"It was a coincidence. She touched one of the hot spots, that's all." Valerie shook her head.

"I asked her about the details. She told me the hot surface traced the silhouette of her body perfectly. The wall all around was cold. It lasted only for a moment. Before the surrounding rock could properly absorb part of the warmth, el abrazo, the embrace, as she called it, ended and the whole stone returned to its former temperature. This happened just after the earthquake. You don't find it strange?"

"Are you sure she remembers it correctly?" Valerie asked. "She was desperate and grieving, looking for any comfort she could get. Their lives are so hard. It's natural they imagine things to make it easier. The men entering the mine wear no gloves, no masks, no protective goggles. What other option do they have than to be religious and superstitious?"

"The company didn't equip their people accordingly." Luz frowned. "We can mention it in our report and see what can be done."

Valerie just sighed. "We don't know if the hot spots have anything to do with the earthquake. They could have been here before. We simply haven't got enough data."

"None of the other women reported any similar experience before the earthquake." Luz turned back to her chart. "I know you found nothing unusual in the rock samples from the hot spots, but still . . . What could we find down here?"

"Archaea, Bacteria, and Eukarya?" Valerie suggested. "Perhaps some viruses present in the microbes that play a key role in the microbes' higher adaptability. Altering genetic content of their hosts . . . Luz? Are you listening?"

"Let's go for a drink," Luz suggested.

"There are only miners' pubs around here."

"Well, I don't mind. And if you don't like the idea, you don't have to go. You can stay here with your coffee."

Valerie sighed. She wasn't keen on going drinking at all. *Perhaps I'm a living cliché of the withdrawn scientist, but I just hate being around a lot of loud people.*

But she could see that Luz didn't feel well. They had worked together before and she was never like this. "All right," Valerie said, putting down her tablet. "I'll go with you."

Valerie watched her beer suspiciously as Luz drank a local hooch. The miners sometimes glanced at them, but that was all.

The Czech scientist let her mind wander, catching snatches of conversation here and there. The place was dark and full of cigarette smoke, which she was trying to ignore. Dust and the smell of sweat hung in the air.

She did her best not to stare at the miners' calloused and raw hands, and to ignore the loud coughing from many of them. Some had obvious difficulties in breathing or were suffering from chest pain. She knew symptoms of silicosis when she saw them. And she knew there was no cure; the men around her would continue to enter the mine, breathe the dust, and inevitably die.

In a corner sat a young man, an untouched drink in front of him. He was staring blankly at a piece of rope in his hands, its end visibly frayed. Valerie swallowed. *It must have snapped. Who fell to his death in a shaft when it did? His father? Brother? Uncle?*

Suddenly a few words from the other side of the room caught her attention. She averted her gaze from the rope.

"You sure she didn't touch anything?"

"Yeah, sure."

Valerie didn't think about eavesdropping—but that was exactly what she instantly started doing. There was a strange tension in both voices.

"Totally sure? I myself would double check. I would be afraid to take her to the mine. You know, nothing against them, but they know nothing about the mines. I know you had no choice. But I think they could . . . I don't know . . ."

Valerie didn't dare to turn around and look at them. She touched Luz's hand and signaled trouble with a glance in the direction of the talking miners.

"What could they do?" This was the foreman who took her to the mine speaking.

"I think . . ."

"Tell me!"

"Bring us bad luck. I think they already did." The other man lowered his voice. "They are women in the mine. They are outsiders. That's always bad, don't you think?"

To Valerie's shock, Luz stood up abruptly and went to their table. She slammed her empty glass on the scratched wooden surface. "You talking about me? You have a problem?"

"You brought us bad luck," the foreman shouted.

"Like you ever had any good luck to start with?" Luz snapped. "If you had any, you would have bought a lottery ticket, won a gazillion, and got the hell outta here!"

Ow. That was an ad hominem response. Valerie blinked. *She isn't exactly deescalating the situation . . .*

The people in the pub fell silent and turned to watch the confrontation. Someone laughed, obviously finding Luz's argument a good one.

"You should pack up and fuck off! You know nothing. You don't belong here," the man cried.

"I went to the mines and was part of rescue teams when you were still sucking at your mother's breast!" Luz didn't seem to be intimidated at all.

Valerie wished she could be invisible. Or somewhere far away from here. In the back of her mind, she realized the absurdity of Luz's statement—the foreman looked older than Luz. But nobody cared.

"You came here and almost instantly a roof fall happened. You angered El Tío! Zorra!"

"The trapped people were rescued! El Tío favors you still. So quit talking shit," Luz yelled.

"Two were crushed!"

Valerie thought of the hundreds of miners whose life ended in the mines long before any scientist had set a foot on this soil. *The statistics aren't exactly a helpful argument right now.*

"If there's another cave-in, it's all your fault," somebody from the crowd shouted.

It was a tall, ragged man and Valerie couldn't remember if she'd seen him before. *This is getting out of hand.* She felt a horrible urge to run. She tried to catch Luz's glance, to grab her attention, but their eyes didn't meet.

"If there's another cave-in?" Luz wasn't about to give up. "They happened before we came and will keep happening even if you chase us away!"

"It could be worse," the ragged man shouted.

"But it also could be better!" Luz jumped onto a table. "And damn it, that's why I'm here!"

The young man in the corner lifted his head. He stared at Luz, and she looked him directly in the eye.

"That's why I'm here," she repeated softly.

He let the rope fall from his hand.

"Does El Tío like cowards who do nothing, just mourn their fate?" she asked the crowd. But her gaze was fixed on only one listener.

"No," the young man responded.

"No! Of course not!" The miners echoed his words.

"Does he like brave people who fight for their lives? Who dare to do the impossible?" Luz continued.

"Yes!" The crowd cheered.

"So, give me a bottle and let's drink!" Luz said. "A drink for everyone! A toast to the impossible!"

"We won this one." Luz breathed as Valerie dragged her back to their quarters. Luz was an experienced drinker, but this evening was nearly too much, even for her.

"It's not the end," Valerie whispered. "When you started the party, I saw two people slip away: the ragged one and the man who was setting the foreman against you. I think those two are up to something."

Luz muttered curses in mixture of Spanish and Quechua.

"You escalated the conflict so fast," Valerie added. "I was . . . I was afraid they would come after us."

"I had to deal with it immediately." Luz's words were becoming slurred. "We don't want any sneaky rumors spreading behind our backs. If somebody talks shit about you here, you have to hit back and hit hard. Otherwise, you get no respect. And respect is more valuable than trust."

"This is so . . . alien to me." Valerie wanted to shrug but she had to support her staggering colleague. "I hope . . . I don't know . . . how to talk to them. It's as if they speak a different language."

Luz gave her a drunken smile: "Watch, learn, and use an interpreter."

The next morning was dull.

"I have a hangover . . . huge as this bloody mountain," Luz moaned.

Valerie was moving around as quietly as she could, bringing water, painkillers, and a bowl of soup. "Will you be able to work?" she asked.

"I'll have to, I guess? That's how life is."

"Good. Because I'm not setting foot in that mine," Valerie said. "Not in this tense situation. You know your way around this place. I'm an outsider and always will be."

María de la Luz sat down in the tunnel to rest and resisted the old urge to chew some coca leaves. Nobody protested when she went down the pit, and as soon as she gave the usual offerings to El Tío, she was left to her own devices.

She put down her equipment wearily, unclasping the infra-goggles and taking off her gloves. She still had a headache.

The darkness around her was absolute. There was nothing to see except what was straight ahead, in the beam of her headlamp. She tried not to think of the young boys she saw pushing carts filled with rocks from the underground. They reminded her of her nephews.

When she said she needed no assistance, the locals seemed happy. They had their work to do. The enthusiastic mood from last night seemed to linger. But she knew she had to come up with something fast. *That could be a problem. Science is slow. It's not like in the movies.*

A strange feeling touched her. The stone behind her back seemed a bit warmer. She stood up and touched it. *Probably just a sensory illusion. I'm still hungover.*

The air was warm and heavy. Only the pipes in which slurry ice was pumped made work at such a depth possible at all.

Luz hesitated. *Could it be El Tío? Is he trying to tell me something? To console me?* She watched the wall and felt stupid.

Then, on a gut feeling, Luz very slowly traced the word "wawa" with her finger on the wall. It was an easy word, simply the first that came to her mind.

Then she put her hand on the place, expecting nothing to happen really.

The letters were there, distinctly hot under her palm.

Luz jerked her hand away. She reached for her infra-goggles—but when she managed to do the reading, there was only a faint warmer spot.

Which proves exactly nothing.

A tremor ran through the earth like a huge animal shaking in anger.

The needle of the seismometer shook sharply, and the sound warning went off.

Valerie was instantly at the comm-station, sending the alarm signal to the miners and trying to reach Luz.

But the radio signal didn't carry into the deep, and the few transmission lines they'd managed to lay in the mine were interrupted.

"Luz? Luz . . . Do you copy?" Valerie repeated. "Luz!"

The communication line was dead. The tracking device was without signal.

Valerie tried to breathe. *An earthquake. Abrupt, not particularly strong, but who knows what it can set in motion in the mine?*

She hesitated only for a second. *I have to get some information from the locals. They will know what's happening—the rescue team will know.*

She put on a hard hat and grabbed her bag with field equipment and a bottle of liquor Luz had left behind.

The first thing she saw near the mine entrance was the ragged man from yesterday. He was in a heated discussion with a cleanly dressed white-collar worker who Valerie didn't know. The stranger passed a small package to the ragged man.

Money?

Valerie couldn't hear the words. *Either somebody is trying to persuade the miners to let us work in peace, or—more probably—to set them against us.* If the miners themselves protested and chased the scientist away, the company wouldn't have to invest any money in modern safety measures. In a way she had to admire the elegance of the solution.

She gritted her teeth and went to talk to the foreman who was with her the first time in the mine.

"Another cave-in. As far as we know it's sixteen men and your colleague missing," he said. "The rescue team is getting ready. The problem is we have no idea where they are. The affected area is quite large. And I doubt we'll be as lucky as last time with the pipe."

"See! I told you! It's because of those two women," the ragged man shouted to a group of desperate women who—perhaps when noticing the tremors—came looking for the trapped miners.

Valerie froze. *Can I tell them he took money from the white-collar person? Would they believe my word or his?* She had no interpreter—Luz was in the mine, perhaps injured, perhaps dead.

"Those two are bad luck," he cried again.

"Shut the fuck up," Valerie yelled. The strength of her own voice startled her. "Luz is also trapped down there so shut up or I'll beat you up with one my expensive gadgets and then make you pay for its repair!"

She turned on her heel and walked away toward the rescue team. She felt the fear, the helplessness she shared with the local women.

She really didn't know what to do. Or even worse, she knew there was nothing she could do.

She stopped in the shade of a nearby building, leaned with her back on the wall. Her mind was empty.

She reached into her backpack, put on her infra-goggles, and turned them on. The touch of the technical instruments calmed her. She ran her fingers over the endpiece and rim and put on the command glove.

She scanned people running and walking around, the temperature of their bodies giving away their stress. The colored silhouettes moving, the cold maw of the mine, the word "wawa" written in red paint—*near the entrance . . .*

What?

She looked again.

It was not written with paint. *It's heat! But that's impossible!*

Valerie remained motionless, staring at the rock. The inscription appeared again. Then there were three, five, ten words. Wawa, wawa, wawa . . . As if somebody was screaming the word in red color.

And then something else aside from the inscription appeared: a large spot flaring hot and disappearing in intervals.

". . . ——— . . ."

". . . ——— . . ."

". . . ——— . . ."

Valerie's mouth went dry. *There's something in that rock. And it's trying to communicate.*

She took her equipment and ran to the rescue team. "You have to take me with you."

"Are you crazy?" the leader answered dryly.

"No. I see infrared signaling." She fell silent at his uncomprehending gaze. *This doesn't work. What would Luz say?* She drew a deep breath. "El Tío has possessed one of my devices. It helps me see what others don't," she declared. "Look!"

She unclasped her goggles and held them in front of the man's eyes. *I hope I wasn't hallucinating and the signal is really there.*

"It's an SOS, isn't it? It's an SOS made by heat, by underground fire," she cried. "What else could it be?"

The man stared through the goggles.

"I can't give you the device because it takes time to learn to operate it. Take me with you and I will follow your command." She lowered the goggles. "We can find them. We can do the impossible!"

He turned to her as if waking from a trance and finally understood what she was trying to say. "You know you can die down there."

She looked at him directly in the eye. "Yes."

"Then get ready for the pit."

María de la Luz was in complete darkness, except for her headlamp.

She was well aware of the sixteen pairs of eyes, sixteen hearts beating fast behind her back.

Luz walked slowly, her hand on the wall. With the other hand, on which she had the command glove, she adjusted the projection in her goggles from time to time. It looked as if she was doing some mystical gestures in the air.

But I managed to persuade them it can help. Once they found each other in the tunnels, once they found out they were trapped, there was the question of where to move, where was the safest place, where was the greatest chance of getting help. No way how to tell. There were no pipes and no transmission lines connecting them to the surface.

Valerie. She knew Valerie could try to use the ground-penetrating radar or geodetic sonar. But their reach was limited. There could be many underground pockets and tens of meters of material in the way.

The miners followed her in silence, their steps and breaths—and water dripping in the distance—the only sounds in the dark narrow tunnel. They were saving the batteries in their lamps. The floor was uneven, and in some places, they had to wade in mud or dirty water. But they kept walking. It was like performing some strange ritual.

Does something bad happen whenever somebody touches the walls and feels the change of temperature? Luz pondered. *Or is it the other way round? Is it a warning?*

She walked on. Infrared spots appeared and disappeared on the wall, always a bit further ahead. They returned if she was too slow.

"... ——— ..."

The signal danced in front of her.

"... ——— ..."

Like a dog trying to show something to its master.

"... ——— ..."

Luz's vision blurred. Red spots began to float in front of her eyes.

It's the stress, thirst, alcohol residue, and concentrated staring through the goggles. It felt a bit like diagnosing somebody else, like it wasn't happening to her.

She stopped.

The way was blocked by fallen rocks. The signal disappeared. *What now? Are we where we are supposed to be? Or completely lost?*

They all tensed when a strange sound reached them, coming from somewhere beyond the collapsed ceiling.

"Another tremor," somebody gasped. And then: "It's rescue! They found us! They found us!"

Valerie and Luz stood aside in the tunnel as the rescue party extracted the remaining miners from behind the fallen boulders.

"The signal! The thermal spots," Valerie cried breathlessly. "Have you seen them? What do you think it was?"

Luz's wide smile gleamed from her dust-covered face as she embraced her. "What do *you* think it is?"

"Microbes," Valerie blurted. "I thought about it the whole way down here, the whole time before they were able to get you out. Colonies of microbes that produce unusual amount of heat at will. Metabolism *is* heat, in a way, and some microbes can control the temperature of their environment to suit their needs—but *this*? They must have some kind of intelligence. Don't ask me how it is possible. I don't know!"

"You think they were always here? Worshipped as El Tío?"

"No idea. Perhaps they came with the earthquake, stranded from their habitat—the hot depths, I think. I can imagine they caught and managed to imitate the SOS—but how on earth did they learn to spell the word wawa . . ."

"Actually, I think I taught them the word by tracing it on the rock," Luz whispered.

Valerie stared.

"Hey, you two, up we all go!" The rescue team leader interrupted. "You also need a medical check." He pointed at Luz.

"Of course," Valerie said quickly. "Just a moment for El Tío."

She set the bottle of liquor by the wall. *Now there will be no doubt that the spirit of the mountain favors us. The mining company won't be able to set the miners against us anymore.*

"You think the microbes consciously wanted to help us?" Luz shook her head in disbelief. Intelligent microbes from the viscera of the Earth—that was a lot to swallow.

"We don't know yet. We don't know what they are, it's just my guess," Valerie said.

Understanding each other without words, they both put on their infra-goggles on one more time.

They saw the darkness of the tunnel—and a human silhouette, shining bright red on the wall. Before it faded, they recognized the outstretched arms of the female figure. It was a copy of the miner's wife embracing the rock. El abrazo.

"We'll come back," Luz whispered. "And then we'll try to talk."

—to Avya, my guide in the garden of forking paths

SOME LIKE IT HOT

<section>NATUSCHKA LEE
& JULIE NOVÁKOVÁ</section>

"Wherever he saw a hole he always wanted to know the depth of it. To him this was important."

— Jules Verne, *Journey to the Center of the Earth*

All the trees rising toward heaven, millions of insect species crawling on the ground, cheetahs chasing gazelles, billions of bacteria and viruses almost everywhere—all the endless forms most beautiful, that make the Earth teem with life, inhabit only the tiniest fraction of it: a shell encompassing its surface, slightly above it and slightly below. But how far below can, in fact, life go? And is it possible life reaches much further down than we've been able to imagine so far, just as it reaches out much further up in the atmosphere than previously expected?

Life has a tendency to surprise us. Before 1969, few would have thought anything could live in temperatures hotter than 60 °C (140 °F). The discovery of *Thermus aquaticus* in Yellowstone hot springs changed that [1]. The year 1979 marked the discovery of living communities surrounding "black smokers," hot springs kilometers deep on the ocean's bottom [2]. Today, we know hyperthermophiles thriving in over 80 °C (~180 °F) [3], some even beyond 100 °C. Practically anywhere we look on Earth, there is life, no matter how extreme the conditions.

Regarding planetary depths, we have explored only a tiny fraction of our planet's interior. The deepest borehole, the now abandoned Kola Superdeep Borehole located on the Kola Peninsula in northwestern Russia, reaches over twelve kilometers deep, and throughout most of it, hydrocarbons were discovered. Could they have been produced by life? That's what astrophysicist Thomas Gold imagined in his seminal 1992 work, coining the term "deep hot biosphere" and drawing attention to subsurface life [4].

How deep *can* life go? Pressure doesn't seem to be a constraint, since bacteria have been shown to withstand pressures equivalent to

<section><section>LIFE BEYOND US </section></section>

over 30 kilometers deep in the Earth, in the deepest crust, or into the upper mantle, and they'll still be able to metabolize and likely reproduce as well [5-7]. Temperature, though, soon becomes a problem. Extreme cold seems to be less of an issue for life, as the molecular processes just seem to halt and "sleep" until they are brought back to active life by the kiss of a more optimal temperature. But as heat rises, organic molecules become less stable. Proteins, the building blocks and working machinery of life, begin to denature. Some more fragile ones start doing so at temperatures as low as 41 °C (105 °F); some very thermostable proteins can take nearly 140 °C (~280 °F) [8]. While we're not entirely sure what the exact upper limit is, heat certainly places huge constraints on the diversity of proteins that can work under high temperatures. Yet, if given enough time and opportunity, life can develop interesting adaptations—for example, it has been shown that viruses may aid plants in developing a tolerance for higher temperatures [9,10].

Hot caves and man-made deep mines such as the one described in Lucie Lukačovičová's "The Devil in the Deep" offer us useful glimpses of the amazing geological processes and life in the deep—both current life and fossils buried there long, long ago provide us with fantastic insights into what ancient life had once been like. We can also go deep in the thinner oceanic lithosphere—surprises are in store there. The Japanese drillship *Chikyu* managed to drill over a kilometer beneath the ocean bottom in the Nankai Trough (itself nearly 5 kilometers beneath the ocean surface), to a zone where temperatures reach 120 °C (248 °F)—around the maximum of what life as we know it can withstand—and found surprisingly rich microbial communities. Scientists have speculated that in order to keep constantly repairing the damage caused by heat, these microbes are forced to run on a rapid metabolism [11]—very much unlike the sluggish, barely-alive life discovered in deep, isolated sediments [12]. Both extreme speed and slowness can be key to survival in these inhospitable environments; ramped up repairs and thermostability can ensure survival hand in hand.

Thermostable proteins and the DNA sequences that code them, surprisingly ancient and widespread, also tell a story. They hint at ancient times when life was originating, or not long after, suggesting that life might have arisen in a high-temperature environment or at least might have spent an important part of its evolution there [13]. Are we all children of the stifling dark depths? We don't know if that's true on Earth (or elsewhere). However, we must not forget that Earth has periodically experienced cold periods ("snowball Earth" episodes) and that at least some of these periods seem to have triggered the evolution of life toward more complexity. The intriguing question is: how did life survive these cold periods? Some plausible hypotheses are based on ecological refuges such as deep hydrothermal vents.

Is there any way microbes could alter their temperature at will, though, like the suspected life-form in Lucie Lukačovičová's story? While communicating this way is probably going to remain in the realm of science fiction, some microorganisms can alter the temperature of their environment more than expected. All organisms produce heat as a by-product of their metabolism. For example, a bacterium can produce about 2 pW heat, or even more if stressed (e.g., when infected by a virus and thus getting a "bacteria-flu"). This may not sound like much, but microbial communities often consist of extremely high numbers of cells (e.g., the human body contains about 38 trillion bacteria), so they could therefore easily contribute to the heat production in their environment. Microbes in flower blossoms, when metabolizing sugar in the nectar, can slightly increase the temperature of the inner parts of the flower [14]. And some bacteria, such as *Pseudomonas putida*, can ramp up the temperature of a microbial colony to better suit its growth optimum [15].

Altering the temperature is almost trivial compared to the astonishing claim of the intelligence of microbes in the story. The normal assumption is that microbes are primitive and unintelligent, simply because they do not possess a brain or senses like ours. But perhaps our definition of intelligence is just as limited and anthropocentric as our definition of life. Microbe colonies are, in fact, in many ways superior to so-called complex life-forms with brains and various senses. Not only were microbes capable of turning the young Earth into the rich blue planet we live on today, but they are also much more metabolically flexible than more complex life-forms. Imagine eating arsenic or mercury compounds, breathing gold, immobilizing radioactive compounds, or simply turning into a spore when the life conditions turn bad—and then wake up later when things get better? Furthermore, microbes have developed ways to communicate other than vocally, for example, through chemical signals (quorum sensing). In fact, microbial intelligence is a new research field that is gaining more and more interest [16-18]. One famous model organism is the slime mold [19]. Not only is it capable of creating at least as efficient traffic networks as human traffic map managers, astronomers have recently been inspired by them to help them map the cosmic web [20]!

So far, we have been focusing on life as we know it. A whole other chapter is exotic life (such as non-carbon based), free of the physical obstacles imposed by pressure, gravity, or temperature. Clay minerals have long been thought to have played a role in the origin of life [21]— but could we expect something like a clay-based "shadow biosphere" to exist in the depths of Earth's lithosphere, reaching much further down than our own biosphere? Such a topic lends itself easily to science fiction—and indeed has served to inspire numerous stories!

What does all of this tell us about the chances of life beyond Earth? We need not be bound by "surface chauvinism." Even worlds with inhospitable surfaces could potentially host deep biospheres that don't depend, even indirectly, on sunlight. If there is water (or perhaps another solvent?), food and something to breathe (for instance hydrogen and nitrates, respectively)—how many noticeable traces would such life leave on the surface and in the atmosphere? It remains an important open question in astrobiology whether life, once it emerges, inevitably alters its whole planet (as James Lovelock, author of the "Gaia" concept, would have argued) or it could remain relatively isolated and difficult, if not impossible for us to notice. Is it possible that Mars even today has a hidden biosphere below ground—in some of its many lava tubes? The complicated thing is that both Lovelock and his opponents may be right because the extent of life's influence on a planet may simply reflect different stages of the cosmological evolution of the planet. After all, Earth was also once uninhabitable, and most likely, life developed first only on some selected locations. In the far future, it may be confined to a handful of places again.

Exploring the depths, to our continuous surprise, teaches us not to get too comfortable with what we've discovered so far and think "that's it, those are the limits." We have yet to scour the planet for more extremophiles, but when we do, we will no doubt discover novel kinds of metabolism. And we have barely explored, for instance, the world of viruses, which have also played an import role in the evolution of life on Earth, and which is now also starting to play a bigger role in astrobiology, leading to the new field astrovirology [22].

The Copernican revolution was pivotal for adjusting the position of Earth in a cosmological context. Do we need a similar revolution in biology—where we drop the definition of life on Earth as the center for the definition of life (and intelligence) in the universe? Probing the depths of our planet might not just help us discover "yet another exotic cellular species with some amazing extreme traits," but perhaps even help us gain more insights into intelligence as we don't know it.

Looking further out into the rest of the universe, we can imagine— just as Thomas Gold imagined thirty years ago [4]—that "subsurface life may be wide-spread among the planetary bodies of our solar system, since many of them have equally suitable conditions below, while having totally inhospitable surfaces. One may even speculate that such life may be widely disseminated in the universe."

Now it's up to us to find it and take the first step toward something even more exciting.

REFERENCES

[1] Brock, T. D., & Freeze, H. (1969). "Thermus aquaticus gen. n. and sp. n., a nonsporulating extreme thermophile." *Journal of bacteriology*, 98(1), 289-297.

[2] Corliss, J. B., Dymond, J., Gordon, L. I., Edmond, J. M., von Herzen, R. P., Ballard, R. D., . . . & van Andel, T. H. (1979). "Submarine thermal springs on the Galapagos Rift." *Science*, 203(4385), 1073-1083.

[3] Stetter, K. O. (2006). "Hyperthermophiles in the history of life." *Philosophical Transactions of the Royal Society B: Biological Sciences*, 361(1474), 1837-1843.

[4] Gold, T. (1992). "The deep, hot biosphere." *Proceedings of the National Academy of Sciences*, 89(13), 6045-6049.

[5] Sharma, A., Scott, J. H., Cody, G. D., Fogel, M. L., Hazen, R. M., Hemley, R. J., & Huntress, W. T. (2002). "Microbial activity at gigapascal pressures." *Science*, 295(5559), 1514-1516.

[6] Hazael, R., Foglia, F., Kardzhaliyska, L., Daniel, I., Meersman, F., & McMillan, P. (2014). "Laboratory investigation of high pressure survival in Shewanella oneidensis MR-1 into the gigapascal pressure range." *Frontiers in microbiology*, 5, 612.

[7] Vanlint, D., Mitchell, R., Bailey, E., Meersman, F., McMillan, P. F., Michiels, C. W., & Aertsen, A. (2011). "Rapid acquisition of gigapascal-high-pressure resistance by Escherichia coli." *Mbio*, 2(1), e00130-10.

[8] Matsuura, Y., Takehira, M., Joti, Y., Ogasahara, K., Tanaka, T., Ono, N., . . . & Yutani, K. (2015). "Thermodynamics of protein denaturation at temperatures over 100 C: CutA1 mutant proteins substituted with hydrophobic and charged residues." *Scientific reports*, 5(1), 1-9.

[9] Gorovits, R., Sobol, I., Altaleb, M. et al. (2019). "Taking advantage of a pathogen: understanding how a virus alleviates plant stress response." *Phytopathol Res* 1, 20. https://doi.org/10.1186/s42483-019-0028-4

[10] Tsai, W. A., Weng, S. H., Chen, M. C., Lin, J. S., & Tsai, W. S. (2019). "Priming of plant resistance to heat stress and tomato yellow leaf curl Thailand virus with plant-derived materials." *Frontiers in plant science*, 906.

[11] Beulig, F., Schubert, F., Adhikari, R. R., Glombitza, C., Heuer, V. B., Hinrichs, K. U., . . . & Treude, T. (2022). "Rapid metabolism fosters microbial survival in the deep, hot subseafloor biosphere." *Nature Communications*, 13(1), 1-9.

[12] Morono, Y., Ito, M., Hoshino, T., Terada, T., Hori, T., Ikehara, M., . . . & Inagaki, F. (2020). "Aerobic microbial life persists in oxic marine sediment as old as 101.5 million years." *Nature communications*, 11(1), 1-9.

[13] Akanuma, S., Nakajima, Y., Yokobori, S. I., Kimura, M., Nemoto, N., Mase, T., . . . & Yamagishi, A. (2013). "Experimental evidence for the thermophilicity of ancestral life." *Proceedings of the National Academy of Sciences*, 110(27), 11067-11072.

[14] Herrera CM, Pozo MI. "Nectar yeasts warm the flowers of a winter-blooming plant." *Proc Biol Sci.* 2010 Jun 22;277(1689):1827-34. doi: 10.1098/rspb.2009.2252. Epub 2010 Feb 10. PMID: 20147331; PMCID: PMC2871880.

[15] Tabata, K., Hida, F., Kiriyama, T., Ishizaki, N., Kamachi, T., & Okura, I. (2013). "Measurement of soil bacterial colony temperatures and isolation of a high heat-producing bacterium." *BMC microbiology*, 13(1), 1-7.

[16] Pinto, D., Mascher, T. (2016). "Bacterial 'intelligence': using comparative genomics to unravel the information processing capacity of microbes." *Current Genetics*, 62: 487-498.

[17] Tikariha H, Purohit HJ. "Unfolding microbial community intelligence in aerobic and an-aerobic biodegradation processes using metagenomics." *Arch Microbiol.* 2020 Aug;202(6):1269-1274. doi: 10.1007/s00203-020-01839-6. Epub 2020 Mar 4. PMID: 32130435.

[18] Westerhoff HV, Brooks AN, Simeonidis E, García-Contreras R, He F, Boogerd FC, Jackson VJ, Goncharuk V, Kolodkin A. "Macromolecular networks and intelligence in microorganisms." *Front Microbiol.* 2014 Jul 22; 5:379. doi: 10.3389/fmicb.2014.00379. PMID: 25101076; PMCID: PMC4106424.

[19] Jabr, F. (2012) "How brainless slime molds redefine intelligence." *Nature.*
https://doi.org/10.1038/nature.2012.11811

[20] Burchett, J. N., Elek, O., Tejos, N., Prochaska, J. X., Tripp, T. M., Bordoloi, R., & Forbes, A. G. (2020). "Revealing the dark threads of the cosmic web." *The Astrophysical Journal Letters*, 891(2), L35.

[21] Cairns-Smith, A. G. (1966). "The origin of life and the nature of the primitive gene." *Journal of Theoretical Biology*, 10(1), 53-88.

[22] Berliner AJ, Mochizuki T, Stedman KM. "Astrovirology: Viruses at Large in the Universe." *Astrobiology.* 2018 Feb;18(2):207-223. doi: 10.1089/ast.2017.1649. Epub 2018 Jan 10. PMID: 29319335.

DEEP BLUE NEON

JANA BIANCHI

Welcome to the Projeto Leviatã's Community Museum. I'm Mata Atlântica, but you can call me Tica. Today, we're celebrating the 25-year anniversary of the greatest scientific discovery of the 21ˢᵗ century, and I'll be your virtual assistant during your visit. Stay with me, for I will guide you through our amazing collection. Besides all the replicas, models, and specimens in our physical archive, you'll be able to browse through images, copies of important documents, and all kind of exclusive media produced by our team in commemoration of this milestone of a quarter century of history. Whenever you want to know more about an item, just let me know.

You want to browse: <u>"FOR A WHALE" CROWDFUNDING PROJECT | AS PER THE DATE IT WAS FUNDED (NOVEMBER 2022)</u>

FOR A WHALE
A sailing voyage to Tonga to prove the existence of an unknown species of beaked whale.
324 backers pledged US$18,789 to help bringing this project to life.

Story
Call me delusional, call me obsessed, call me whatever you want—the only thing nobody can call me is a quitter, and that's why I'm here. I'm Lis Boaventura, a marine biologist, and I used to be an oceanography postdoc at Rio de Janeiro State University. I say "used to be" because the Big Budget Cut came (if you're not aware of the deep shit we Brazilian researchers are in, read more about it <u>HERE</u>) and my scholarship was suspended. I was left with: a record of an unidentified acoustic signal captured in the Pacific Ocean, the old skull of a whale supposedly stranded in my Grandma's hometown in the year I was born (whose importance was totally neglected until I recovered it from the tiny local

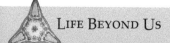

LIFE BEYOND US

museum), and a weird-although-promising story published years ago by a Tongan guy on his obscure personal blog.

But hey, this is all you need to look for a new species of whale out there, right?

Well, not quite. You also need . . . Yeah, money. I know, I know, but I don't make the rules. In my case, I need funds to acquire more sensitive equipment and sail to Tonga at the right time of the year so I can spot at least one of these little babies—and hopefully collect images, some DNA samples, and more acoustical records!

I'm not a sailor, but this problem was already addressed. If this project is successful (I'm counting on you!), not only one, but two dreams will become true—I'll go after my precious whales with none other than Joana Falcão, aboard the newest version of her fabled sailboat *Carcará*, which means she'll will be finally back to business after a too-long leave. If you don't know her (under which rock have you been hiding?), she was the first Brazilian woman, twenty years ago no less, to circumnavigate the world. Needless to say, she has inspired a lot of girls who loved the sea—me included. (Let's pretend I'm not freaking out because she accepted to be part of this!)

If you like science and also want to be part of this, check out how you can support us. Starting with US$5 pledges, you'll receive constant updates including what I know so far, details of the trip arrangements, and news about the journey itself—I promise a lot of amazing pictures and tidbits of our life on board, and you may even be able to vote for the name of the new species when I finally get to prove its existence.

Thank you, e bons ventos pra nós!

You want to browse: <u>HENRIQUE RUBIÃO'S STATEMENT | AS PER TODAY (JULY 2048)</u>

Contacted by the Museum team, Henrique Rubião, 61, Lis's fiancé at the time of her field trip to Tonga, didn't want to be interviewed—but he authorized the publication of the following note:

Life is made of priorities. A couple of things I've said were taken out of context, but I did state Lis was totally obsessed with her research, and I was not wrong, regardless of what happened next. We were in our late thirties and engaged, and I believed we should invest our time, money, and efforts in building our life together, not in going on adventures. She thought different, and that's fine. At the time, she said she expected me to support her. But I had supported her for a long time already. Too long, maybe. So we parted ways, simple as it is. More than two decades have passed, and I don't hold any grudges. I'm glad Lis lived her life. I did the same.

You want to browse: <u>THE SCRIPT OF THE PLAY "DEEP BLUE NEON",</u> <u>BY DIARA CORDEIRO DE SÁ | REHEARSAL EDITION (APRIL 2036)</u>

[read more]

ACT THREE, SCENE THIRTEEN
CARCARÁ'S DECK

SETTING: The sailboat is surrounded by darkness. It's a quiet, warm night. The sky, reflected in the sea surface, is strikingly starred. Instead of plain white, the stars sparkle in faint hues of pink, purple, and blue, evoking the bioluminescent life in the depths of the ocean. The prop of the boat stern is assembled on top of a hidden, high platform; there's a single spot illuminating the deck, so the blackness all around the boat makes it look like it's floating in deep space, the line where the sea meets the sky blurred. It's possible to hear the soft sound of the water splashing against the hull and a pleasant bossa nova coming from the cabin.

AT RISE: LIS and JOANA are laid on the deck, side by side, over a cozy blanket. They're looking up, the tops of their heads turned to the audience.

LIS: Do you miss your sons?

After a long silence, LIS props herself up on her elbow and looks at JOANA. JOANA sighs.

JOANA: I do, even though they're full-grown men now. But that's not the question you want to ask. Go ahead, Lis. After all these days traveling together, I think we can be honest with each other, right?

LIS stands up and leans on the railing, looking to the audience.

LIS: Okay. Here it goes: Do you regret it?

JOANA chuckles.

JOANA: You'll need to be more specific, dear. Are you talking about dropping out of university to sail the world? About quitting that life later to raise my kids? Or about being here now, a sexagenarian in a new journey, taking the chances of not being home when my first grandkid is born?

Now it's LIS who chuckles.

LIS: What about all of them?

JOANA: Well, it's not like the answer is different . . . No, I don't regret anything. Do you?

LIS scratches her head. JOANA stands up and joins her at the balustrade.

LIS: I don't think so. But I'm wondering if I should. Does it make sense?

JOANA: No, but I can't blame you. Listen, whenever I feel insecure, I try to remember that I believe in what I'm doing. Even when nobody else does. Especially when nobody else does.

LIS: Hmm. That's the point. I'm not sure if I do believe in what I'm doing.

JOANA: Don't fool yourself. You wouldn't be here if you didn't.

Sighing, LIS stretches her arms upwards. She stands on tiptoes, and for a moment it seems she's trying to reach the sky. She leans again on the railing.

LIS: But what if I did believe, but now I don't anymore? I mean, according to Pita's blog, we're at the right place and at the right time of the year. . . . But it's our fifth day without any sightings. And time is running out.

JOANA: It's not true. We saw things.

LIS: Oh, yeah, we've seen bioluminescent life behaving in a weird way—but my hydrophones are silent for whale songs and, when I try to dive, whatever is down there flees. It flees in a very weird way too, it's true, but I can't put that in a paper and call it a scientific discovery.

JOANA: You knew it wouldn't be easy. And if you don't believe in what you're doing anymore. . . . Well, then you can just stand down. It's fine. I'm entitled to talk about it, you know.

LIS rubs her face. She seems upset.

LIS: Argh! But is there a limit to how far I should go? A line I shouldn't cross? How do I know when it's time to retreat?

JOANA: You don't.

They don't say anything for a while. It seems JOANA is trying to suppress a smile. Finally, she turns to LIS.

JOANA (CONT'D):
Okay, go ahead. What do you have in mind?

LIS: Well, I'm about to ask you to take me to Pangai so I can search for an anonymous guy who, ten years ago, posted a delusional report on a personal blog about glowing whales who come to the surface only once a year. Hehe.

JOANA claps her hands once, excited. LIS startles.

JOANA: Now we're talking! I thought you would never ask me.

Seeming puzzled but suddenly excited as well, LIS grabs JOANA's shoulders.

LIS: Wait, really? Don't you think I'm crazy?

JOANA giggles.

JOANA: I never said I don't. And maybe that's the point.

The bossa nova gets gradually louder. JOANA leaves for the cabin, but before that she stops and observes LIS for a couple of seconds. LIS is smiling and looking up, dreamy.

[read more]

You want to browse: <u>*SCIENCE ACROSS*: INTERVIEW WITH LUKE AND LEIA TAKULUA | PUBLISHED IN JULY 2028</u>

AN UNEXPECTED LEGACY: WHAT CHANGED IN TONGA AFTER THE GREATEST SCIENTIFIC DISCOVERY OF THE CENTURY

Science Across visited Pangai to interview the twins Luke and Leia Takulua, 28, six years after their encounter with Lis Boaventura. They received us at the headquarters of the Takulua Community Center, inaugurated one year ago in memory of their father, Pita Takulua.

Science Across: Thank you for receiving us! Wow, this place is amazing. I want to start with a question you've probably answered a thousand times since the opening of the Community Center, but I really need to ask: What do you think your father would feel if he could be here?

Leia Takulua: You're welcome. We're very happy to have you. Well, I think we'll never tire of answering that one: Our father would be delighted. He was an inveterate dreamer. He loved both science and kids, so he would be in awe to know there's a place named after him dedicated to putting Tongan kids in contact with knowledge and nature.

Luke Takulua: He would also be a little bit surprised, if not disappointed, to see how our activities are more focused on marine life than on astronomy. Actually, he would be disappointed to know that humanity finally found intelligent life—but under the ocean's surface, and not in space. In case you didn't notice, he was a space aficionado. [*He points to a huge poster of the franchise which obviously inspired their names. We all laugh.*]

SA: I'm glad you mentioned this; my next question is about this subject. Do you think you father knew the leviatãs were sentient when he first got in touch with them?

Luke: Oh, no, we don't think so. He discovered a great number of things for someone who wasn't a scientist and didn't have the means to—

Leia: Yeah, for instance, the fact that they needed to breathe at an extremely slow rate, even when compared with other beaked whales, and that they came to the surface for special events, which we now know is a cultural pilgrimage.

Luke: Yeah, this. But no, I don't think he knew about their intelligence. This was Dr. Lis's and Projeto Leviatã's hypothesis only.

SA: Right, Dr. Lis Boaventura. Let's talk about her. By now, everyone knows how she found you because she read your father's blog posts.

Because she believed in them—so much, she sailed here. Would you mind talking about the first time you met?

Leia: Of course not. Well, it was. . . .

Luke: Unexpected.

Leia: Unexpected to say the least. We didn't even know one could still read Dad's blog; it had been offline for some time already, but somehow Dr. Lis managed to find it. She said she tried to contact us beforehand, but my dad had been dead for almost nine years, and the blog had no personal information which could lead to us. So, she just came to Pangai and tried her luck. It's a small place, plus our name is unmistakable, and that's how she ended up finding us.

Luke: At first, we thought Dr. Lis was joking. I mean, we did believe Dad was not crazy. We did believe he had found something noteworthy regarding his "glowing whales," but we had no idea it could interest a real scientist, from the other side of the world no less. And Dr. Lis . . . I don't know if you had the chance to meet her, but she had a shine in her eyes which made us believe she was not here to mock Dad. She was following his lead. She was acknowledging his discoveries and wanting to know more.

Leia: She was actually pretty emotional when she found out Dad was dead. She wept when we showed her all his journals, and she wept when we showed her his canoe. She only stopped weeping when we told her what had happened to Dad.

SA: You mean when you told her he died—

Leia: When we told her he had fallen very ill after physically contacting the whales for the first time. We told her everything we knew. We showed her the entries Dad had added to his journal when he was already sick. We thought it would make her give up, but she didn't.

Luke: Quite the opposite. When she read Dad believed the whales only approached when he was alone and rowing that specific canoe—all the sea moss on the hull included—she said, "That's why, then," and asked us to lend her the boat.

SA: Do you think she was afraid of also getting sick?

Luke: I think she was, but she didn't let it get in her way.

Leia: Yeah, she excused herself for a while and spent some time talking to her friend Joana. Then she came back and confirmed she would love to have the canoe for a couple of days. I don't think she and Joana argued, but they spent a long time pondering the ramifications, you know? She seemed determined to go ahead. She seemed to believe in what she was doing.

Luke: And well, we all know what came next.

Leia: She found them.

SA: And consequently . . .

Leia: And consequently, she fell ill.

Luke: Very ill. Just like Dad.

[read more]

You want to browse: <u>STATEMENT RELEASED ABOUT LIS BOAVENTURA'S MEDICAL CASE | AS PER HER ADMISSION AT THE ICU OF THE ROYAL BRISBANE AND WOMEN'S HOSPITAL (JULY 2023)</u>

Brisbane, July 23rd, 2023
Given all the buzz on social media and incomplete reports offered by irresponsible tabloids, we thought it was our duty to publish an official statement regarding the circumstances which brought Dr. Lis Boaventura, Brazilian, 35, to our care.

Dr. Boaventura was admitted on July 16th to our emergency room. She arrived accompanied by her friend Joana Falcão, reporting difficulty breathing and chest pain. Ms. Falcão also reported Dr. Boaventura had presented lethargy and an apparent, although not constant, delusional state. The medical team was informed that the symptoms started after Dr. Boaventura's direct contact with the spray blown by some specimens of a whale which was the subject of the patient's research.

As it has already been broadly shared, we discovered she had contracted a bacterial lung infection. Besides the presence of very common *Streptococcus pneumoniae*, the collected samples also presented a considerable amount of an unknown microorganism. In observance of our new isolation precautions protocols, improved after the 2019–2022 COVID-19 pandemic, both Dr. Boaventura and Ms. Falcão were immediately put under strict isolation, even though the latter presented no symptoms at all.

After extensive testing and observation, we can state that the new bacterium isn't likely to be transmitted from human to human through air. So far, given all evidence, testing, and both Dr. Boaventura and Ms. Falcão's accounts about the probable contamination event, the transmission is believed to only occur via liquid medium, after direct contact between a contaminated sample and human mucosa. Tests also showed the new bacterium is not resistant to regular antibiotics. Therefore, there is no reason for major concern—we have no knowledge of other contaminated humans besides Dr. Boaventura, who remains under strict isolation. Her condition is critical.

The Royal Brisbane and Women's Hospital commits to report any important developments in a timely manner.

You want to browse: <u>DR. LINA CHACON'S PERSONAL NOTES ABOUT DR. LIS BOAVENTURA'S MEDICAL CASE | AS PER DR. BOAVENTURA'S DISCHARGE FROM THE ROYAL BRISBANE AND WOMEN'S HOSPITAL (JULY 2023), PUBLICLY DISCLOSED IN AUGUST 2023</u>

20-07-23 | What a day. I talked to Dr. Boaventura earlier, and honestly? I'm bewildered. I mean, it's obviously not the first time I saw a person denying treatment, either for religious or other reasons, but she's clearly a woman of science! Also, she wasn't against being treated with antibiotics at first, but then something changed. The next day, she asked not to be medicated anymore—no, she begged, with such a passion I was even touched.

What is more curious: she said she would eventually accept the medicine, but she asked us to wait—what for, she wouldn't say. We considered administering the antibiotics anyway when she started to get worse, as she was in and out of delusional episodes since she had been admitted, and maybe we could claim she was not competent to make this decision. But then she asked to speak with Ms. Falcão and, after one hour or so of a private discussion, they both signed a statement officially denying treatment and taking responsibility for any consequences.

When I insisted on knowing why she was doing so, Dr. Boaventura just said to me: "Doctor, I really trust you and your team. But I need to trust myself too." When I said she could be risking a lot, including her life, she just shrugged and cracked the saddest, although the sincerest, smile I ever saw. I don't know what's going on, but I wish I could trust Dr. Boaventura as much as she trusts herself.

You want to browse: THE FIRST SCIENTIFIC ARTICLE ABOUT THE LEVIATÃS AND ITS SYMBIOTIC BACTERIA | PUBLISHED IN AUGUST 2024

Article | Open Access | Published: 13th August 2024
Symbiosis between *Ipupiatera vixii* and *Mashadonella gambialis*: Basis for non-asynchronous, complex interspecies communication
L. Boaventura, N. Ramos, A. F. Poker, R. Castro, T. B. M. Novello, & J. Falcão
New Nature, **392**, 62-66 (2024) | Cite this article

Abstract
Many parameters have been used to define animal sentience, such as the ability to feel certain emotions. However, there was no evidence so far of species capable of developing language and culture on par with humans and establishing complex non-asynchronous communication analogous to, for instance, human writing[1,2]. The recent discovery of a new genus and species of beaked whale (*Ipupiatera vixii*) and its symbiotic bacteria (*Mashadonella gambialis*) challenges this idea, establishing bases for complex communication—whale-whale, but also whale-human. This article describes both species and presents what is known so far about their biology and morphology. The exact biological mechanism responsible for allowing *M. gambialis* to facilitate complex interspecies communication is still unknown, but this work also provides the first complete report of a human experiencing the phenomenon—later evidenced by the consequent

discovery of the first leviatã settlement (currently known as Biotown) at the South Pacific Ocean seabed.

[read more]

You want to browse: <u>TRANSCRIPTION OF DR. LIS BOAVENTURA'S COMMEMORATIVE HOLO | AS PER TODAY (JULY 2048)</u>

Lis Boaventura, 60, is sitting on a blue armchair against a black background. She's wearing a black blouse and a light blue shawl over her shoulders. Her expression is serene.

You know, I wish I could say I never doubted myself. I wish I could say I always trusted my gut, and that it gave me the tranquility to keep going because I knew for sure I would be rewarded. But that would be a lie—it was a rough and uncertain road. Sometimes I did believe in myself, but most of the time I was risking important things—love, money, reputation . . . and, ultimately, my life, for something I had no guarantee would succeed.

Don't get me wrong: the first time I interacted with the leviatãs, I felt rewarded, with no regard to what would happen next. Pita had written something similar in his journals—from his deathbed, though, and I was very aware that the same fate could be waiting for me. But there, alone in a canoe under the night sky, surrounded by glowing whales . . . I knew I was on the right path. To where, I was not sure.

I took pictures, I recorded whale songs, and I collected samples, but I didn't need the results to know I had found the new species I was looking for. What I didn't know was what else my discovery would reveal—and what I would need to face to solidify those understandings. I mean, refusing treatment was the most frightening decision I've ever made. The only thing I had to support my choice were flashes of a blue neon town in the depths of the ocean. Not only the flashes, but the certainty that they were not a delirium—that *somebody* was trying to tell me *something*. That I needed to know more, and that the only way to do it was by not closing the communication channel opened between us—no matter how risky it could be.

I never told this to anyone, but that day was the first time Joana directly told me that maybe I was going too far. She said she would be there waiting for me if I ever got back, and she wouldn't judge me if I didn't—but she also said, "I think you're wrong. Maybe you're not, but I think it's not worth it this time." So yes, I was totally alone when I decided to refuse the antibiotics and wait for the next flashes, which could *possibly* give me more information about what we now know is the first non-human civilization we've met. [She laughs.] Isn't it ironic? That I needed to be totally alone so we could discover that we're not alone at all?

I now look back and have no regrets, of course. I didn't die—although I hung by a thread—and time brought back everything I'd risked and sacrificed. Yeah, I can say I couldn't be more fulfilled nowadays. Look at this museum. Look at how people are more concerned with the environment than ever. But the point is: it could have been different, right? Pita, for example. We made the same decisions, and time brought back his reputation, money for his family, good things for his country—but it didn't bring him back to life.

And speaking of time: I know we're celebrating twenty-five years of this story, so maybe you're expecting this statement of mine to be a conclusion, an ending. But you know, it's just a new beginning. Right now, while I'm here recording this, other researchers are making new sacrifices and risking everything, including their lives—at least, their lives as they know them—to learn more about the leviatãs. They're down there, at an unthinkably deep submarine station, trying to finally understand why our friends decided to talk to us in the first place. And that's the beauty of science: each reward is also an invitation to commit ourselves again and learn more.

[read more]

Thank you for visiting the Projeto Leviatã's Community Museum. If you want to know more about our project, access leviata.sci, *and consider being part of the biggest scientific initiative of the 21ˢᵗ century.*

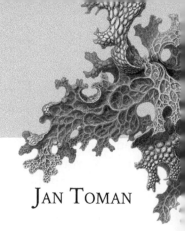

DESTINED FOR SYMBIOSIS

JAN TOMAN

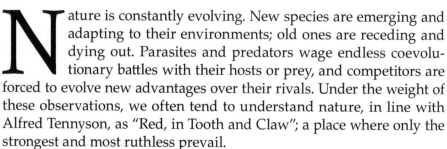

Nature is constantly evolving. New species are emerging and adapting to their environments; old ones are receding and dying out. Parasites and predators wage endless coevolutionary battles with their hosts or prey, and competitors are forced to evolve new advantages over their rivals. Under the weight of these observations, we often tend to understand nature, in line with Alfred Tennyson, as "Red, in Tooth and Claw"; a place where only the strongest and most ruthless prevail.

That is, however, largely nonsense. As Charles Darwin noted, the largest and strongest do not always "win" in natural selection, nor do those who have the largest teeth, claws, or venom glands. Those who best fit into their environment, that is, achieve the highest fitness, have the greatest success. The key component of fitness is, and always has been, the ability to closely cohabitate with members of other species. This ability—symbiosis—probably stood behind the emergence of life as we know it; behind complex cells; and behind many important processes in today's biosphere. Symbiotic organisms transmit, receive, and mediate signals, and the obstacles that symbiotic partners must overcome in communicating with each other can prepare them—and us—for the difficulties of interspecies communication.

Symbiosis can be defined simply as a close coexistence of two or more different organisms, mostly meaning organisms of distinct species and coexistence with a touch of cooperation. Strictly speaking, however, symbiotic relations include *mutualism*, from which all parties benefit, *commensalism*, which is advantageous only for one side, and even *parasitism*, in which one partner gains an advantage at the expense of others. Moreover, the advantages and disadvantages can shift over time; so many symbiotic relationships fall into a kind of gray area between all the processes mentioned above.

The partnership between unicellular algae (zooxanthellae of the genus *Symbiodinium*) and corals that make coral reefs possible has exactly this character. Depending on the species of algae and coral, water temperature, and other factors, their symbiosis oscillates between mutualism, commensalism, and parasitism. Therefore, we shouldn't succumb to naive notions of general harmony—as soon as there is a loophole through which one of the partners can get an "unfair" benefit, it will be exploited. After all, natural selection is not a wise planner. The short-term benefit usually outweighs any potential long-term gain. Finding long-term stability is thus not easy at all, which is one of the reasons why coral reefs have always been such a vulnerable ecosystem.

From this, it might seem that symbioses are a kind of icing on the cake; something only the most complex ecosystems have developed. However, the opposite is true. Several theories about the origin of life suggest that symbioses have been with us since the very beginning, just under four billion years ago. According to one group of theories of the origin of life, mutually interacting proteins which formed the basis of cellular metabolism constituted the first living organisms.

Theories summarized under the heading of the *RNA world concept*, on the other hand, emphasize the amazing properties of ribonucleic acid, which still plays a major role in translating DNA sequences into proteins. These theories argue that the first entities undergoing natural selection were short sections of RNA that gained the ability to copy themselves. However, without specialized enzymes of a protein nature, the process was very slow and inefficient. The first real organisms thus could have originated through a symbiosis of nucleic acid- and protein-based protoorganisms. Alternatively, several complementary protoorganisms—which used the products of their colleagues' metabolism and, conversely, produced substances that were used by other members of the association—joined forces to reproduce collectively. Such communities that incarnate symbiosis are called *hypercycles*.

Some two billion years later, symbiosis again determined the direction of evolution. A proliferation of photosynthetic organisms, specifically cyanobacteria, caused the oxygen concentration in the ocean and the atmosphere to rise. However, oxygen was a severe poison for life in this original, anoxic, environment. Fortunately, one group of bacteria could not only cope with oxygen, but even use it in a new type of energetically rich metabolism—*aerobic respiration*. It was these bacteria, specifically Alphaproteobacteria, with whom our direct unicellular predecessors, Archaea, established cooperation.

To this day, we don't know what form their union initially took. Perhaps the archaeon ate the bacterium but did not digest it completely.

Or maybe bacteria lived side by side with archaeons for a long time and slowly strengthened their cooperation, until finally they completely merged. Or possibly, further parties, such as viruses, participated in the entire process. What is certain is that alphaproteobacteria gradually evolved into organelles called *mitochondria* that remain inside cells and, in addition to aerobic respiration, mediate several other metabolic processes. The originally archaeal cell, with the help from its bacterial partner, was then able to enlarge, evolve new ways of movement, structure its interior, and gain a number of new functions.

The process of such an intimate and inseparable fusion of two originally independent partners is called *symbiogenesis*. In this case, it gave rise to a whole new domain of life—eukaryotes, which include all unicellular protists, as well as plants, fungi, and animals. Symbiogenesis has been repeated several more times in the history of life. For example, certain unicellular eukaryotic lineages engulfed living cyanobacteria to become photosynthetic. Green plants are distant descendants of these organisms. Other eukaryotic lineages, including the aforementioned zooxanthellae, have in turn engulfed their eukaryotic photosynthesizing "cousins." The early evolution of eukaryotic life on Earth can thus be described as a series of symbiogenetic events.

There is no doubt that symbiosis is a key process in the history of life on Earth. But can organisms exchange information through symbionts, like the whales do in Jana Bianchi's "Deep Blue Neon"? At first reflection, such a thought is almost hair-raising.

Nevertheless, recent findings place symbionts in a completely new light in terms of information transmission. These findings are based mainly on the study of the human *gut microbiome*, a complex ecosystem of various microbial species that inhabit our gastrointestinal tract. Relations between humans and their microbial symbionts range from parasitism (remember various intestinal infections, such as cholera) to mutualism, with the specific nature of symbiosis often depending on the individual's genetic makeup, diet, and other external factors. A substantial symbiosis with the gut microbiota is necessary for humans because it helps us, among other things, to synthesize several vitamins, to process fiber, sterols, or bile acids, and to metabolize several types of drugs.

Yet the intestinal microbiome is not only a passenger but, to some extent, also a driver. Indeed, studies show that various types of intestinal bacteria produce signaling molecules corresponding to human neurotransmitters. This would not be so interesting if the intestine wasn't surrounded by a dense neural network directly connected to the emotional and cognitive brain centers. Through this network, sometimes nicknamed "gut brain," a two-way communication between the center of our nervous system and symbionts takes place. We are just beginning to discover what they are talking about. However, it is clear that this information channel is of systemic importance—it fundamentally affects our development; affects settings of our nervous, immune, and hormonal systems; and affects our mental well-being and other aspects of health. Scientists have shown that, in addition to digestive system disorders such as Crohn's disease, it affects, among other things, our mood, the presence and depth of depression or anxiety states, the onset and progression of multiple sclerosis, and the severity of autism spectrum disorders.

However, even this is not the pinnacle of symbiont communication skills. The imaginary throne belongs to fungi. The fruiting bodies, so familiar as mushrooms, are just short-lived, above-ground protrusions of fungi, intended for spreading spores. The real fungus is a tangle of fibers residing underground called *mycelium*. Mycelia themselves do not live in isolation. They usually establish close symbiotic relationships with plants: *mycorrhiza*. Various types of mycorrhizae range from covering the root tip and ingrowing between its cells, to directly penetrating them and forming specialized cellular compartments. However, they all have in common that the plant supplies the fungus with energy-rich sugars produced in photosynthesis in exchange for water and minerals from the soil.

It is clear that fungi and plants had to establish communication channels between each other. More remarkable, however, is that mycelia usually connect many trees, shrubs, herbs, microbes, and fungal individuals[1]. They can grow for miles, and some of them are probably the oldest and largest living organisms on Earth. At the same time, they distribute water, minerals, and sugars among different individuals. In addition, this "wood wide web" transmits signaling molecules produced by plants under attack to warn others against parasites or herbivores. While it would be tempting to see an interconnected forest ecosystem as one big family where everyone helps each other, we should not forget the fickle nature of symbioses. Under certain conditions, plants tend to force their nutrients on fungi and take whatever

---

1 Editor's note: Looking back at previous stories, can you imagine Ondrej Bohatý from "Defective" talking to the ecosystem in "Forever the Forest"? Many stories converged on the strife for *communication*, and sometimes the hard-won *understanding*, so crucial for our hopes of ever making contact with life beyond us.

minerals they want. Conversely, many fungi have become parasitic in their evolution. We therefore encounter harmonious coexistence in the forest ecosystem, but it is a hard-won and constantly negotiated harmony.

Truly bizarre are discoveries suggesting that fungal fibers transmit information not only on a chemical but also on an electromagnetic basis. Specifically, the individual fibers generate and transmit electrical pulses. The characteristics of these pulses vary from species to species, but their duration is usually measured in hours and intensity in millivolts. Spikes of electrical activity follow each other in series and their distribution is highly non-random. They are remarkably similar to the electrical activity of nerve cells in animal brains. Of course, based on this similarity alone, we cannot claim that fungal mycelia *think*. The similarities can only be superficial. However, various evidence suggests that this may not be the case. The characteristics of spikes and trains of spikes change in response to chemical, optical, and mechanical stimulation. In addition, they play a role in the interaction with the plant root.

Recently, linguistic studies analyzing the complexity of the electrical activity of mycelia and comparing it with texts in Indo-European languages have gained attention. Their results showed that the electrical activity of fungi even exceeds human languages in several aspects of complexity. Fungi can use up to fifty different "words," i.e., typical series of spikes, and their length distribution is similar to human languages. Studied species differ in the characteristics of their electrical activity, but it seems that they could transmit a comparable amount of information. It is difficult to say whether we can talk about language or languages of fungi based on these findings. After all, we also do not describe the activity of nerve cells in the brain in linguistic terms. However, it is very likely that, in addition to the transfer of nutrients, fungal fibers also serve to transmit a considerable amount of information.

Can this help us in the search for alien life-forms? Surprisingly, yes! If we ever encounter extraterrestrial intelligence (or any other intelligence unknown to us), the basic problem will be mutual understanding. That is the same problem organisms encounter in the initial stages of symbiosis. A number of disciplines, from information theory to linguistics, deal with the difficulties of communication. However, try to decipher and translate, for example, one of the ancient Egyptian inscriptions. Although you will ideally identify individual symbols and be able to roughly assign them an English word or phrase, you will often miss the meaning of the whole message. That is because the key aspect of communication is mutual understanding, which results from sharing the meaning of individual signs (e.g., words).

This is the focus of semiotics, or biosemiotics. Many biosemioticians would argue that establishing and interpreting the meaning of individual signals, as well as creating adequate responses to them, are among the most basic aspects of being an organism. This includes their symbioses with other organisms.

At the same time, symbioses probably have their own biosemiotic rules. It is not surprising that closely related organisms "understand" each other's signals better than distantly related ones. However, studies show that the meaning of certain signs—such as hormones or proteins regulating development—remains very conservative for a long time after separation from a common ancestor. For example, the Pax6 gene, or rather its protein product, regulates the formation of eyes in almost all bilaterally symmetrical animals. If we switch Pax6 of fruit fly with Pax6 of mice, it works almost identically and leads to the formation of a fully functional insect eye: all despite fundamental differences in the structure of fly's and mouse's eyes, as well as hundreds of millions of years of separation from their common ancestor.

All these findings have a common denominator. The *meaning* depends on the *context*. The closer the contexts of two different sides—for example, language speakers or species—the greater the understanding between them. However, symbioses show that understanding can also be built. This may not be easy. There must be a willingness on both sides to sacrifice something for the joint venture. Nevertheless, evolution on our planet shows that joining into this effort through symbiosis is one of the few ways to create something genuinely new. We have no reason to doubt it will be the same elsewhere in the universe.

FURTHER READING

Adamatzky, A. (2022). "Language of fungi derived from their electrical spiking activity." *Royal Society Open Science*, 9(4), 211926.

Markoš, A., & Švorcová, J. (2019). *Epigenetic processes and the evolution of life*. CRC Press.

Schmidt, T. S., Raes, J., & Bork, P. (2018). "The human gut microbiome: from association to modulation." *Cell*, 172(6), 1198-1215.

AFTERWORD I

Forming A Bridge

WOLF D. GEPPERT

Astrobiology and its related scientific issues have always fascinated writers and artists. The questions the field deals with—*How did life originate on Earth?* and *Is there life on other celestial bodies?*—as well as the technological challenges and opportunities of space exploration, including those of missions searching for life elsewhere, have always captured human imagination.

This did not just begin with the Godfather of Science Fiction, Jules Verne. Earlier authors like Cyrano de Bergerac and philosophers such as Emanuel Swedenborg let their fantasy have a go at the possibility of extraterrestrial life. Many Greek philosophers like Democritus and Epicurus as well as Renaissance thinkers like Giordano Bruno also deemed it very likely that other planetary bodies would be inhabited.

Modern space research in the 20th century somewhat dampened the hopes of hitting upon life elsewhere in our solar system, but that neither deterred scientists from looking for traces and tracers of such life, nor did it quench the dreams of science fiction authors. Many subjects that capture the interest of scientists and the imagination of writers and artists are covered in the present anthology: the possibility of life on Mars and Venus, exploration of space by robots, the search for life on other planets, or life in extreme environments, to name just a few.

Science fiction is a great way to encourage people's interest in science—even those whose relationship with natural sciences and mathematics has been difficult. It has the potential to reach a wide sweep of audiences. However, there is one problem: the boundary between science and fiction is not completely clear for all readers—and taking fictional statements as facts can lead to misconceptions.

Therefore, anthologies like *Life Beyond Us* are very important. They offer the reader exciting and fascinating reading, but also illuminate concepts through authoritative essays covering the scientific background of the story. So, people get both—entertainment and scientific facts.

Moreover, science fiction can form a bridge between scientists and creative writers and artists. Relationships between these groups have not always been cordial; some scientists have frowned over the allegedly excessive fantasies of science fiction authors, while some writers and artists have mocked the dry style in which exciting new findings are presented by scientists. Increased cooperation between these two groups could benefit both—and most of all, benefit the scientifically-interested public. For instance, consider scientists, like Fred Hoyle, who count science fiction novels amongst their works.

Ultimately, science fiction needs a sound basis in science. Due to the vastness of the field of astrobiology and the multitude of scientific questions associated with the search for extraterrestrial life, national and local research communities alone will often be unable to muster the expertise to perform ground-breaking research in the area. This is something we hope the new European Astrobiology Institute (EAI) can achieve.

Life Beyond Us is the second anthology published since the inception of the EAI. I would like to express my utmost gratitude to the EAI Project Team "Science Fiction" and especially to Team Coordinator, Julie Nekola Nováková, who pulled off this project. Many thanks also to the publisher, co-editors, and authors of the different entries in the anthology—they ensured we included a wide and versatile collection of essays and stories. Last but not least, I want to thank all the backers of the crowdfunding project—without their generosity the publication of this anthology would not have been possible.

—Wolf D. Geppert, Chair of EAI, Stockholm, Sweden, 2023

AFTERWORD II

Don't Forget Earth

LUCAS K. LAW & SUSAN FOREST

What do artificial limbs, scratch-resistant lenses, and insulin pumps have in common? All were developed because of technology originally pioneered for space-flight. Add to that list: Lasik surgery, solar cells, water filtration, camera phones, CAT scans . . . and the list goes on and on. Space research has yielded unexpected advances in unlooked-for arenas—all applicable to our earthly lives.

A superficial survey of both current news headlines and life experience slaps us in the face with crises human life—and all life—on Earth is facing. The list is not pretty. Global warming and extreme weather conditions; habitat loss, pollution, and mass extinctions; food short-ages; war, displacement, and civil unrest; lack of affordable housing, personal safety, and food and energy security; and poor access to basic health care and eldercare, all threaten some or all of us.

Could the field of astrobiology be used to meet some of these current and future crises? In our view: a cautious and optimistic . . . *yes*.

We *may* be doomed, as speculated in many science fiction stories, to face a more hostile world than the one we were born into. Yet over the past two years, the world has looked on in awe as, during the COVID-19 pandemic, the world's governments came together in an unprecedented single mindedness and unity of political will, to bring vaccines on stream in record time. In the mid-twentieth century, humanity trans-formed from a non-spacefaring world to landing a man on the Moon in only ten years.

We've proved it. If—*when*—all branches of society, from public and private sectors, and from different faculties and resources and exper-tise, work together, we can do anything we truly set our minds to, including solving the world's most urgent problems.

There, of course, lies the rub: our will to set aside our petty desire for ego, profit, and greed. For our species to survive, people every-where need to feed their own curiosity, devour science, and access the educational opportunities available to them. Teachers everywhere need to allow the wonder of science to blossom for their students. Policy makers everywhere need to incorporate science into curricula, encourage its programming on all media, and fund research initiatives.

And writers—and publishers—need to continue to engage their readerships with enticing fiction, essays, or articles based on accurate scientific underpinnings so people everywhere will be empowered to engage their government representatives to fight for the survival of the human species.

Life on Earth—the only life in the universe we are truly aware of—is precious. Once our species has used up the resources we need to survive and poisoned the world for our own use, Earth and its living organisms will continue. But from a human perspective, to preserve our own kind, action is needed now. If we don't take care of life on Earth, if people are too busy dealing with one crisis after another or too burnt out to worry about tomorrow to have the capacity for creative and critical thinking, there will be fewer explorers and discoverers, dreamers and doers, space travellers, scientists, and researchers. Fewer options for survival and well-being.

So, take time when you step outside your door today. See the natural wonders beneath your feet, in the water, and in the air. Appreciate and respect the life on Earth. Maybe even look to the skies to discover a "life beyond us" from one of the stories or essays in this anthology.

—Lucas K. Law and Susan Forest, Calgary, Canada, 2023

ACKNOWLEDGMENTS

JULIE NOVÁKOVÁ

The book you're holding is a collective effort of over sixty people. All of them, and all the 691 backers on Kickstarter who enabled its existence in the first place, deserve thanks. I'm deeply grateful to my co-editors Lucas and Susan for giving the idea for *Life Beyond Us* a chance and embarking on such a massive and unusual (translation: commercially risky) project, and my colleagues from the European Astrobiology Institute for chiseling the idea and helping draft the whole project, writing some of the essays or finding the right person for a given topic, and spreading the word. Ultimately, I must thank all the people who inspired me and set me on my path: Writers, scientists and educators who lit the spark (Sagan, Grygar, Margulis, Dawkins, Zimmer, Clarke, Asimov, Lem . . . the list could go on and on) or steered me more directly. In the latter group, big thanks go to the Czech FameLab organizers, especially Dáša Sephton from the British Council and Jan Špulda from the Czech Centers (without them, I might never have gone to an astrobiology meeting in Sweden to later become part of the EAI from the very start), and to the people who gave me great inspiration at the Charles University (especially Jaroslav Flegr, Jelena Lenka Příplatová, Jan Votýpka and Daniel Frynta). We really are standing on the shoulders of giants.

LUCAS K. LAW

Many thanks go to Julie Nováková and Susan Forest for sharing the joy of co-editing, Jared D. Reid for his creativity and sharp attention to details in this anthology's interior layout, Veronica Annis for her cover graphic design, and Dan O'Driscoll for the cover art. And thank you to my partner, Tim, for his patience, understanding, and encouragement. Finally, a huge thank you to European Astrobiology Institute, our backers, and the authors; without you, there is no *"Life Beyond Us."*

SUSAN FOREST

Thank you to Julie Nováková and the European Astrobiology Institute for their confidence in me, and for the opportunity to team up again with the amazing Lucas Law of Laksa Media Groups on this inspiring anthology! I'd also like to thank the authors and artists for their gripping stories, insightful essays, and beautiful images, as well as our backers and all those who contributed to bringing out this classy book. Finally, and always, I'd like to thank my husband, Don, for his steadfast support.

ABOUT THE CONTRIBUTORS

Jacques Arnould was born a few days before Yuri Gagarin's flight and nourished by the exploits of Neil Armstrong and Buzz Aldrin. He was nevertheless interested in Heaven through the path of theology. Since 2001, he is the ethics advisor of the French Space Agency (CNES). Charles Darwin, Pierre Teilhard de Chardin and Giordano Bruno are giants of thought on whose shoulders he seeks to see beyond space and time.

Eugen Bacon is an African Australian—her books *Ivory's Story, Danged Black Thing* and *Saving Shadows* are finalists in the British Science Fiction Association Awards. Eugen is in the honor list of the 2022 Otherwise Fellowships for "doing exciting work in gender and speculative fiction." She's won or been commended in international awards including the World Fantasy Award, Foreword Indies, Bridport Prize, HWA Diversity Grant, Otherwise, Rhysling, Australian Shadows, Ditmar, and Nommo Awards for speculative fiction by Africans. Eugen's creative work has appeared in *Award Winning Australian Writing, Fantasy, Fantasy & Science Fiction*, and *Year's Best African Speculative Fiction*. In 2022: *Mage of Fools, Chasing Whispers* and *An Earnest Blackness*. Website: eugenbacon.com / Twitter: @EugenBacon

William Bains is a biochemist exploring the chemistry of potential life on other worlds as well as how the chemistry of life on this world breaks down with disease and aging. He has affiliations with the Massachusetts Institute of Technology (MIT) and Cardiff University, and is co-founder of Five Alarm Bio, a start-up company developing drugs to treat the diseases and disabilities of aging. He is author on numerous papers on subjects as diverse as corporate law, cosmic life, drug chemistry and sewage treatment, and five books. He is a lifelong science fiction fan but has so far stuck with writing fact.

Stephen Baxter was born in England in 1957. He worked as a teacher of maths and physics, and in information technology. He is a Chartered Engineer, a Fellow of the British Interplanetary Society, and a Vice-President of the HG Wells Society. Stephen has been a full-time author since 1995, and his science fiction novels have been published in the UK, the US, Germany, Japan, France, and elsewhere, and have won several awards. His non-fiction includes *Deep Future, Omegatropic, The Science of Avatar*, and *Revolutions in the Earth: James Hutton and the True Age of the World*.

Gregory Benford is a professor of physics emeritus at UC Irvine, a Fellow of the American Physical Society, winner of the Lord Prize in science, the Nebula and Asimov Prize for fiction and the UN Medal in Literature. His fiction and nonfiction have won many awards; he has published 32 novels, four volumes of nonfiction, over 200 short stories, and several hundred scientific papers in several fields.

Renan Bernardo is a SFF writer and computing engineer from Rio de Janeiro, Brazil. His fiction appeared or is forthcoming in *Apex Magazine, Podcastle, Escape Pod, Daily Science Fiction, Translunar Travelers Lounge, Solarpunk Magazine,* and others. He was one of the authors selected for the 2021 Imagine 2200 climate fiction contest with his story "When It's Time to Harvest". In Brazil, he was a finalist for two important SFF awards and published multiple stories. His fiction has also appeared in other languages. He can be found at Twitter (@RenanBernardo) and his website: www.renanbernardo.com.

Jana Bianchi is a Brazilian writer, translator, editor at Mafagafo magazine, and werewolf walker. Besides her novella *Lobo de Rua* (2016), her fiction has appeared, in Portuguese, in several Brazilian collections and magazines. In English, her work has been published at *Strange Horizons, Clarkesworld,* and *Fireside*. She also attended Clarion West in 2021. Find her online at @janapbianchi on Twitter/Instagram or at her website janabianchi.com.br/english.

Tobias S. Buckell is a New York Times bestselling author and World Fantasy Award winner born in the Caribbean. He grew up in Grenada and spent time in the British and US Virgin Islands, which influence much of his work. His novels and almost one hundred stories have been translated into twenty different languages. His work has been nominated for awards like the Hugo, Nebula, World Fantasy, and the Astounding Award for Best New Science Fiction Author. He currently lives in Bluffton, Ohio with his wife and two daughters, where he teaches Creative Writing at Bluffton University. He's online at www.TobiasBuckell.com and is also an instructor at the Stonecoast MFA in Creative Writing program.

José A. Caballero is a research astrophysicist at the Spanish Centro de Astrobiología (CSIC-INTA). He played a major role in the design and construction and now, in the scientific exploitation of CARMENES.

In addition to exoplanets, he is an expert in stellar multiplicity, astrophysical parameters and young stars, brown dwarfs and substellar objects below the deuterium burning limit, especially in open clusters. He has developed his career in a number of institutions in the Spanish mainland, the Canary Islands, and Germany. He will apply his expertise with current science missions (Gaia, TESS, CHEOPS) to the design of future spacecraft for the detection of biomarkers, such as the European Large Interferometer for Exoplanets.

Eric Choi is a Hong Kong born writer, editor, and aerospace engineer currently living in Toronto, Canada. He was the first recipient of the Isaac Asimov Award (now the Dell Magazines Award) for his novelette "Dedication", and he has twice won the Prix Aurora Award for his short story "Crimson Sky" and for the Chinese-themed speculative fiction anthology *The Dragon and the Stars* (DAW) co-edited with Derwin Mak. With Ben Bova, he co-edited the hard SF anthology *Carbide Tipped Pens* (Tor). His first short story collection *Just Like Being There* (Springer) was released in 2022.

Julie E. Czerneda has written 23 novels (and counting) published by DAW Books, as well as numerous short stories, and edited several anthologies over the past 25 years. She was inducted to the Canadian Science Fiction and Fantasy Hall of Fame in 2022. Her science fiction and fantasy combine her training and love of biology with a boundless curiosity and optimism, winning multiple awards. Out in August 2022 was Julie's first short story collection, *Imaginings*, followed in November by her standalone sf novel, *To Each This World*. For more visit czerneda. com. Julie is represented by Sara Megibow of KT Literary.

Dimitra Demertzi is a chemist, science communicator, and an aspiring writer. She is currently doing her Master's degree in Molecular Sciences, and wants to become a researcher, to help elucidate the origin of life. In her free time, she enjoys learning foreign languages, writing poetry and short stories, and traveling.

Martina Dimoska graduated from TMF, UKIM (Macedonia) with a Bachelor of Material Engineering and Nanotechnology. She is a Global UGRAD Program Alumna from Kent State University, a Commercial Space Studies Graduate Program Alumna from Florida Institute of Technology (Florida Tech) and a scholarship winner from the Aldrin

Family Foundation, as well as a Masters of Space Studies Scholarship Alumna from the International Space University and a NASA Space Apps Challenge Local Lead. Martina is a published research scholar; a talented, multifaceted engineer; a STEM and Space shaper; and a leader of many initiatives. She is a Top Rated Plus Freelancer on Upwork and an overall creative soul who innovates and influences her many prevalent communities.

Tessa Fisher is a PhD candidate and possibly the world's only openly trans lesbian astrobiologist. When she's not doing science, her hobbies include burlesque dancing, singing in her city's LGBT women's chorus, yoga, and writing LGBT-positive science fiction and fantasy. Her fiction has been featured in *Fireside, Baffling,* and *Analog,* among other venues. She currently resides in Tempe, AZ with her wife, along with a fairly aloof bearded dragon.

Ladon Gao comes from China and is now a PhD student in Cardiff University, researching the quality assessment of videogame localization. In his spare time, he works as a freelance translator, mainly from English to Chinese. His published translations include stories by sci-fi authors Andy Dudak and Julie Nováková. He has also published two poems: "Ghost Talk" in *Lux Lucet Zine* and "Crossing the River" on *Poetry Lab Shanghai.*

Wolf D. Geppert gained his PhD at the University of York, UK, and held postdoctoral positions in Bordeaux and Helsinki before joining the University of Stockholm, Sweden, where he was promoted to full professor in 2014. His research focuses on the following questions: "To which extent can biomolecules and their precursors be formed already in space and from which stage of the biochemical evolution are planetary conditions necessary?" and "How does interstellar chemistry influence the formation of planetary systems and habitable planets?" Complex organic molecules have been observed in the interstellar medium, but also in Titan's atmosphere and elsewhere. His interest is to elucidate the formation pathways and further reactions of these molecules. Since 2019, he has served as the Chair of the European Astrobiology Institute (EAI).

Simone Heller lives on an island in the river Danube in Regensburg, Germany. She has been working as a literary translator for 15 years. Her

first steps in writing in English were taken in 2016, after workshopping with a group of international writers in Munich, and her award-winning short fiction has since then appeared in several Year's Best volumes. She loves learning all kinds of things: words most of all, but also history, science, and everything about the strange creatures of Earth (and beyond?).

Dennis Höning is a planetary physicist researching the feedback processes that control the habitability of Earth and other planets, with a focus on the role of life in the coupled system. He received his PhD at the German Aerospace Center in Berlin in 2016 before moving to the Vrije Universiteit Amsterdam as an Origins Center Research Fellow. At the Potsdam-Institute for Climate Impact Research, he is currently also working toward understanding the consequences of global warming on Earth. Besides science, he enjoys paragliding and table soccer.

Valentin D. Ivanov is a professional astronomer. He was born in Bulgaria, where he got a M.S. in Physics. Valentin obtained a Ph.D. from University of Arizona, Tucson. He has been working at the European Southern Observatory for the last two decades. His research interests include star clusters, exoplanets, and astronomical instrumentation. Valentin has been a SciFi fan since his childhood. His stories and poetry appeared in *Letters to Tiptree, Star*Line, phantastisch!* and *Diamonds in the Sky*. He has published about thirty stories and scores of popular science articles in his native county.

Fabian Klenner is a Postdoctoral researcher in the research group of Planetary Sciences and Remote Sensing at Freie Universität Berlin in Germany. His astrobiology-focused work is associated with past and future space missions to icy moons in the outer solar system. He is active in outreach activities and member of various learned societies, such as NASA's Network for Life Detection (NfoLD). He is co-head of the ocean worlds and icy moons working group of the German Astrobiology Association (DAbG) as well as co-founder of the Astrobiology Network of Pakistan (ABNP).

Nina Kopacz is an astrobiologist. Currently a researcher at Utrecht University in the Netherlands, she is studying the potential for life in (sub)surface environments on Mars through laboratory simulation chambers. She is also part of the PELE team (Planetary Analogs &

Exobiology Lava Tube expedition), which investigates lava tubes as analog sites to possible strongholds of life on Mars.

Mary Robinette Kowal is the author of the Glamourist Histories series, *Talkers*, the Lady Astronaut Universe series, and *The Spare Man*. She is part of the award-winning podcast *Writing Excuses* and has received the Astounding Award for Best New Writer, four Hugo awards, the Nebula and Locus awards. Her stories appear in *Asimov's*, *Uncanny*, and several Year's Best anthologies. Mary Robinette, a professional puppeteer, also performs as a voice actor (SAG/AFTRA), recording fiction for authors including Seanan McGuire, Cory Doctorow, and John Scalzi. She lives in Nashville with her husband Rob and over a dozen manual typewriters. Visit maryrobinettekowal.com.

Lisa Jenny Krieg was born and raised in Germany, and has studied and lived in Heidelberg, Jerusalem, Amsterdam, and New York. She has a PhD in Anthropology and is interested in the relationships between humans, nature, and technology. Her academic research has explored German Holocaust memory and human-gecko relations (not in one project). Since 2020, she has lived in a small village in the Arava desert in Israel with her family, where she works as a painter of desert landscapes and writes speculative fiction.

Geoffrey A. Landis is a science-fiction writer and a scientist. He has won the Hugo and Nebula awards for science fiction and is the author of the novel *Mars Crossing* and the collection *Impact Parameter (& Other Quantum Realities)*. As a scientist, he works for NASA on developing advanced technologies for spaceflight. He was a member of the Pathfinder and Mars Exploration Rovers Science teams and is a fellow of the NASA Institute for Advanced Concepts. In his spare time, he goes to fencing tournaments to stab strangers with a sword. More on his web page: http://www.geoffreylandis.com.

Rich Larson (author of *Annex, Ymir,* and *Tomorrow Factory*) was born in Galmi, Niger, has lived in Spain and Czech Republic, and is currently based in Montreal, Canada. His fiction has been translated into over a dozen languages, among them Polish, French, Romanian, and Japanese, and was recently adapted into an Emmy-winning episode of *LOVE DEATH + ROBOTS*. Find free reads and support his work at patreon.com/richlarson.

Natuschka Lee has an MSc in biology and chemistry, PhD in environmental biotechnology from Lund University, Sweden. She was a guest research fellow at Aalborg University (Denmark) and Technische Universität in Munich (Germany), performing interdisciplinary research on microbial ecology, geomicrobiology, and astrobiology. Since 2015, she's been a research fellow at Umeå University, Sweden. Her research interests include astroecology and astrobiotechnology, ranging from subsurface and cave geomicrobiology, meteorite geobiology, phototrophs in space, symbiosis, and different types of extremophiles (e.g., tardigrades)—with the goal to explore the roles of microbes in different extreme ecosystems, and how this knowledge can be useful for novel sustainable biotechnological innovations for our health and environment.

Liu Yang has a PhD in physics and is a professor at Southern University of Science and Technology, Shenzhen, China. Since his first short story in 2012, he has published more than one million words of short stories in magazines such as *Sci-fi World*, and some of them have been translated into English and German. His first novel *The Orphans of Red Planet*, published in 2018, is now being adapted to movie and TV dramas. Additionally, as the chief world builder, he has deeply participated in the development of a variety of science fiction games.

Ania Losiak is a planetary geologist who studies impact craters on Earth and surficial processes on Mars. She is also involved in various outreach activities such as running the scientific part of the European Rover Challenge organized every year in Poland. She studied at the University of Warsaw (Poland), completed MS at the Michigan State University (USA), and a PhD at the University of Vienna (Austria). She was a summer intern at NASA's Lunar Planetary Institute in Houston. She worked at the University of Exeter (UK) and now she is a researcher at the Institute of Geological Sciences Polish Academy of Sciences. She received grants and fellowships from the Fulbright's Commission (Fulbrights' Graduate Fellowship), European Commission (Marie Sklodowska Curie Individual Fellowship), National Science Center Poland (research grants), and Foundation for Polish Science. She likes crocheting, making stained glass windows, copper smelting, and bronze casting.

Lucie Lukačovičová studied librarianship and cultural anthropology at the Charles University in Prague and has lived in Angola, Cuba, England,

Germany, and India. She has 6 published novels, co-authored 5 novels, and has more than 100 short stories published in various languages (Czech, English, Italian, Portuguese, Chinese, German, Romanian, Kannada). Her stories are often based on myths, urban legends, folktales, and on personal experience from journeys to various countries. She cooperates with Czech seismologists on a series of popular scientific comics about seismic waves, the geomagnetic field, and volcanism.

Stephen Francis Mann is a philosopher of science working primarily on cognitive science and biology. He answers questions about life, intelligence, communication, computation, information, representation, and a bunch of other -tion words that are occupying philosophers in the early 21st century. He lives in Leipzig with his wife Hedvig Skirgård, a linguist, where they argue about whether *Star Wars* is fantasy or science fiction. They have two cats, Cement and Sandy. Find more at stephenmann.isaphilosopher.com, philpeople.org/profiles/stephen-francis-mann and Twitter @stephenfmann.

Connor Martini is a PhD candidate in North American Religions at Columbia University, New York. Right now, Connor is thinking about science and situated enchantments, aliens and voices from the sky, ethnography and sensory and material cultures, science fictions and spiritual facts, and views of Earth from Mars. On good days, he is also an aspiring science fiction writer. On most other days, he's just a cat dad with too many books to read.

Tony Milligan is a Senior Researcher in the Philosophy of Ethics with the Cosmological Visionaries project based out of the Department of Theology and Religious Studies at King's College London. His work has a strong focus upon space ethics and the relationship between science and Indigenous Knowledge. His most recent book, *The Ethics of Political Dissent* (2022), focuses on how we respond to political opponents. Previous publications include the co-edited white paper on *Astrobiology and Society in Europe Today* (2018); the co-edited volume *The Ethics of Space Exploration* (2016); and *Nobody Owns the Moon: The Ethics of Space Exploitation* (2015).

Premee Mohamed is a Nebula award-winning Indo-Caribbean scientist and speculative fiction author based in Edmonton, Alberta. She is an Assistant Editor at the short fiction audio venue Escape Pod

and the author of the Beneath the Rising series of novels as well as several novellas. Her short fiction has appeared in many venues, and she can be found on Twitter at @premeesaurus and on her website at www.premeemohamed.com.

Philippe Nauny feels more European, despite being French. Trained in chemistry and biology, he worked as a research assistant before his interest in space exploration, the origin of life, and evolution led him later to do an astrobiology-themed PhD in Earth Sciences, studying biomarkers in environmental analogs for Mars. He is now a scientific consultant, which, sadly, doesn't involve doing any fieldwork anymore. Besides sciences, Philippe has other nerdy interests like board games and Star Trek. His essay in this anthology is his first written contribution outside the academic world.

G. David Nordley is the pen name of Gerald Nordley, a writer, consulting astronautical engineer, and retired USAF officer with experience in spacecraft operations and engineering. He has degrees in physics and systems management. His fiction writing has won four "Anlab" readers' awards, a Hugo and a Nebula nomination. His novels and story collections, available from Brief Candle Press, generally focus on human experience in scientifically plausible futures, often in astronomical settings. "Titan of Chaos," here, is his latest story. Gerald was born in Minneapolis and lives in Sunnyvale CA with his wife, Gayle Wiesner. See: www.gdnordley.com.

Malka Older is a writer, aid worker, and sociologist. Her science-fiction political thriller *Infomocracy* was named one of the best books of 2016 by Kirkus, Book Riot, and The Washington Post. She is the lead writer for the licensed *Orphan Black* audio sequel on Realm, and her acclaimed short story collection *And Other Disasters* came out in November 2019. Her novella *The Mimicking of Known Successes*, a murder mystery set on a gas giant, will be published in early 2023. She is a Faculty Associate at Arizona State University, where she teaches on humanitarian aid and predictive fictions, and hosts the Science Fiction Sparkle Salon. Her opinions can be found in The New York Times, The Nation, Foreign Policy, and NBC THINK, among other places.

Deji Bryce Olukotun is the author of two novels and his fiction has appeared in six different book collections. His novel *After the Flare* won the 2018 Philip K. Dick special citation and was chosen as one of the best books of 2017 by *The Guardian*, *The Washington Post*, *Tor.com*, and *Kirkus Reviews*, among others. His short story "Between the Dark and the Dark," published in *Lightspeed*, was selected by editor Diana Gabaldon for *Best American Science Fiction and Fantasy 2020* (Houghton Mifflin Harcourt). He currently works for the audio technology company Sonos, and he is a Future Tense Fellow at New America.

Erik Persson is an Associate Professor of Practical Philosophy at the Department of Philosophy, Lund University. His main research interest is applied philosophy, especially environmental philosophy and philosophical aspects of space exploration and emerging technologies. The philosophy of astrobiology makes for a perfect combination of all three. Presently he is involved in three major research projects dealing with the concept of invasive alien species, responsibility in relation to climate adaptation, and responsibility in relation to the development of Artificial Intelligence (AI). He's the coordinator for the European Astrobiology Institute's working group for the history and philosophy of astrobiology, and co-coordinator for Lund University's research platform for Space Humanities.

Tomáš Petrásek, born 1984, is a Czech neuroscientist, astronomy popularizer, and science-fiction writer. He has published two non-fiction books about astrobiological perspectives of the outer planets and icy moons, a science fiction novel *Lastwatch* (published in Czech in 2012, coming later in English), and multiple short stories.

Joanna Piotrowska is a PhD student in astrophysics, researching the influence of supermassive black holes on galaxy evolution. Born and raised in Warsaw, Poland, she moved to the UK to pursue an undergraduate degree in Natural Sciences, followed by a Master's in Astrophysics at the University of Cambridge, where she then stayed on to continue her doctoral research. She is a passionate public speaker and a strong advocate for accessibility in science, and in her work, Joanna frequently makes use of art to share knowledge with broad audiences. In October 2022, she begins her postdoctoral appointment at CALTECH to study accretion disks around supermassive black holes.

Giovanni Poggiali is an astrobiologist and planetary scientist with a PhD obtained from the University of Firenze (Italy). His main field of research is laboratory infrared spectroscopy in simulated planetary environments with the aim to support the interpretation of data collected by spacecraft. He is collaborating with several space mission teams: NASA OSIRIS-REx sample return mission, exploring and sampling the surface of asteroid Bennu; and NASA Mars2020 Perseverance, looking for signs of life in the Jezero crater, an ancient delta river on Mars. He is also the Co-Investigator of MIRS instrument on board the MMX mission from JAXA, the Japanese Space Agency, aiming to explore the moons of Mars.

Brian Rappatta, originally hails from the American Midwest, but currently resides in South Korea. His short fiction has appeared in *Analog, Baffling Magazine,* and *Amazing Stories;* in multiple anthologies such as *Writers of the Future, Gilded Glass,* and *Chilling Ghost Stories;* and in various podcasts such as *Curiosities, Tales to Terrify,* and *StarShip Sofa.*

Arula Ratnakar is an autistic, bisexual scientist, artist, and science fiction writer whose published stories can be found in *Clarkesworld Magazine.* She is interested in brain simulation science and the neuroscience of procedural and declarative memory, and she hopes to become an astronaut in the future. Twitter: @ArulaRatnakar.

Amedeo Romagnolo is an Italian astrophysicist currently doing his PhD in Warsaw, Poland. He works on the development of a theoretical environment to simulate the formation and evolution of binary black holes, binary neutron stars, and habitable exoplanet populations in the visible universe. He was a research assistant in the Nobel laureate Reinhard Genzel's team in 2019, and he has also worked in several space missions. LGBTQ+, polyamory and environmental activist, he is also a passionate Dungeons&Dragons player and video gamer, and he tries his best to be a half-decent amateur singer, writer, philosopher, and gallivanter.

Stefano Sandrelli, Primo Tecnologo at INAF (Milan), graduated in physics (Pisa), got a PhD in astronomy (Bologna) and a Master's in Science Communication (SISSA, Trieste), and is the Director of the IAU Office of Astronomy for Education Center Italy. He was the Head of the INAF Public Outreach and Education Office (2008-10; 2016-2020). As an adjunct professor, he holds science communication courses and story-telling in Milano and other universities. He wrote science and fiction books and won an Italian Andersen Prize (*Feltrinelli Kids*, best series 2010) and the "G. Dosi" Prize 2017 (*Nello spazio con Samantha*, written with the ESA astronaut Samantha Cristoforetti).

D.A. Xiaolin Spires steps into portals and reappears in sites such as Hawai'i, NY, various parts of Asia and elsewhere, with her keyboard appendage attached. Her work appears in publications such as *Clarkesworld, Analog, Nature, Terraform, Fireside, Star*Line, Liquid Imagination,* and anthologies such as *Make Shift, Ride the Star Wind, Sharp and Sugar Tooth, Deep Signal,* and *Battling in All Her Finery.* Select stories can be read in German, Spanish, Vietnamese, Estonian, French, and Japanese translation.

Bogi Takács (e/em/eir/emself or they pronouns) is a speculative fiction author, a developmental psycholinguist, a Hungarian Jewish immigrant to the US, and an agender trans person. E is a winner of the Lambda award for editing Transcendent 2: The Year's Best Transgender Speculative Fiction, the Hugo award for Best Fan Writer, and a finalist for other awards. Eir debut poetry collection *Algorithmic Shapeshifting* and eir debut short story collection *The Trans Space Octopus Congregation* were both released in 2019. You can find Bogi talking about books at http://www.bogireadstheworld.com, and on various social media like Twitter, Patreon, and Instagram as bogiperson.

Jan Toman is a postdoc at the Department of Philosophy and History of Sciences, Faculty of Science, Charles University in Prague. His special-ization is evolutionary and theoretical biology, focusing mostly on the questions related to macroevolution, evolutionary trends, and general features of the evolutionary process. The centerpiece of his research is Frozen Evolution Theory, an attempt to revise some of the basic assumptions of modern evolutionary biology. He is the author of two monographies and several scientific papers. Last but not least, he is a skilled popularizer of science—astrobiology included.

Floris van der Tak is a senior scientist at SRON Netherlands Institute for Space Research, and professor of astronomy at Groningen univer-sity. He is a Board member of the Netherlands Origins Center, and coordinator of an EU-funded interdisciplinary effort to investigate the

origin of life on Earth and other planets. Before his current position, he studied and worked in Bonn (Germany), Leiden (The Netherlands), and Berkeley (United States). His research focuses on the formation of stars from interstellar gas clouds, and the habitability of exoplanets. His students and postdocs use telescopes on Hawaii, in Chile, and in space. Besides astronomy, he enjoys playing cello in string quartets, baroque ensembles, and symphony orchestras.

Peter Watts is a former marine biologist, flesh-eating-disease survivor and felon/tewwowist whose novels—despite an unhealthy focus on space vampires—have become required texts for university courses ranging from Philosophy to Neuropsychology. His work is available in 24 languages, has appeared in 32 best-of-year anthologies, and been nominated for 59 awards. His (somewhat shorter) list of 22 actual wins includes the Hugo, the Shirley Jackson, and the Seiun. He seems disproportionately popular in countries with a history of Soviet occupation. He lives in Toronto with fantasy author Caitlin Sweet, five cats, a pugilistic rabbit, a *Plecostomus* the size of a school bus, and a gang of tough raccoons who shake him down for kibble on the porch every night.

Sheri Wells-Jensen (sheriwellsjensen.com) is a linguist and an associate professor in the Department of English at Bowling Green State University in Bowling Green, Ohio, USA. Along with xenolinguistics, her research interests include the relationship between language and thought, and between disability and space travel. She is on the leadership team of Mission: AstroAccess (astroaccess.org) and was absolutely delighted to have been chosen as a flyer on their inaugural Zero G parabolic flight in 2021 and to be an active part of their research plan for making outer space and the STEM fields accessible.

Raymond M. Wheeler is a plant physiologist at Kennedy Space Center where he has conducted research on plant growth in controlled environments for use in future life support systems in space. Ray has been co-investigator or collaborator for plant experiments on the Shuttle, the Russian Lada plant chamber, and NASA's Veggie and Advanced Plant Habitat on the International Space Station. He is the author or co-author of more than 270 scientific research papers and currently serves as Chief Scientist at NASA's Kennedy Space Center.

B. Zelkovich writes speculative fiction, anything from dragon hunting and space whales to demon-dealing and ghost tales. She likes to explore human emotions in very inhuman situations. When she isn't escaping through her imagination, she escapes into the wonders of the Pacific Northwest with her spouse and their four-legged son, Simon. Her fiction has appeared in *Luna Station Quarterly; City. River. Tree.;* and *Corvid Queen. The Lament of Kivu Lacus* is her first professional sale.

ABOUT THE EDITORS

Julie Nováková is an evolutionary biologist by study, active in science education and outreach, one of the many founding members of the EAI, and acclaimed author, editor and translator of speculative fiction. She has edited or co-edited four anthologies in three different languages (English: *Dreams From Beyond: Anthology of Czech Speculative Fiction*; *Strangest of All: Anthology of Astrobiological Science Fiction*; Czech: *Terra nullius*; Filipino: *Haka*, co-edited with Jaroslav Olša, Jr.). Her stories and translations appeared in *Clarkesworld, Asimov's, Analog, Tor.com, F&SF* and elsewhere, and she occasionally publishes nonfiction in *Clarkesworld, Analog* and other venues. Find more at www.julienovakova.com or Twitter @Julianne_SF.

Lucas K. Law is a Malaysian-born editor and author who divides his time and heart between Calgary and Qualicum Beach, Canada. He edits Laksa Media's award-winning anthology series (with Susan Forest—*Strangers Among Us, The Sum of Us, Shades Within Us, Seasons Between Us*—and with Derwin Mak, *Where the Stars Rise*). When he is not editing, writing, or reading, he is a corporate and non-profit organization consultant in business planning and development. Lucas is a life member of the Association of Professional Engineers and Geoscientists of Alberta.

Susan Forest is the author of dual Aurora Award-winners *Bursts of Fire* (2019) and *Flights of Marigold* (2020) as well as over 25 internationally published short stories (*Analog, Asimov's, Beneath Ceaseless Skies*, among others). She edits an award-winning anthology series for Laksa Media Groups and was the Editor Guest of Honor at Keycon in 2022. *Gathering of Ghosts*, the third novel of her Addicted to Heaven series (forthcoming, 2023) confronts issues of addictions in an epic fantasy world of intrigue and betrayal. More at http://speculative-fiction.ca/

COPYRIGHT ACKNOWLEDGMENTS

ABOUT EUROPEAN ASTROBIOLOGY INSTITUTE (EAI)

The European Astrobiology Institute (EAI) is a consortium of European research and higher education institutions and organizations as well as other stakeholders aiming to carry out research, training, outreach, and dissemination activities in astrobiology, to secure a leading role for the European Research Area in the field. Organizations as well as individual members (only in Working Groups or Project Teams) can join the institute.

To foster learning in astrobiology, we organize streamed seminars on topics ranging from prebiotic chemistry to the connection between space sciences and societal benefits, we collaborate on the organization of summer schools and conferences with European Astrobiology Network Association (EANA), Europlanet Society, and other partners, and we create science events and resources for the public. The book you're holding is part of our outreach efforts.

Our Biennial European Astrobiology Conference (BEACON) will take place on the island of La Palma, Spain, in spring 2023. The public program will include a science-themed concert and an exhibition, "Oceans on Earth and Beyond."

Find more at europeanastrobiology.eu.

ABOUT EUROPEAN SCIENCE FOUNDATION (ESF)

The European Science Foundation (ESF) is a non-governmental, internationally oriented, non-profit association established in France in 1974. ESF is committed to promoting the highest quality science in Europe to drive progress in research and innovation.

We work closely with our members and partners, sharing our expertise and offering solution-orientated scientific support aimed at increasing the quality and effectiveness of science and science-related activities in Europe.

We partner with diverse institutions by leading successful projects and facilitating informed decision-making through a broad range of science support partnerships: Research Project Grant Evaluation, the coordination of European projects, and funding programs and their hosting scientific platforms.

Find more at www.esf.org.

ABOUT LAKSA MEDIA GROUPS INC. (LMG)

Laksa Media Groups Inc. publishes issues-related general audience fiction and narrative non-fiction books. Our mission is to create opportunities to "pay forward" and "give back" through our publishing program. To know more about us and our award-winning books, visit laksamedia.com.

Also Available from Laksa Media Groups Inc.

LAKSA ANTHOLOGY SERIES: SPECULATIVE FICTION

This award-winning series has been recommended by *Publishers Weekly, Kirkus Reviews, Booklist, Library Journal, School Library Journal, Foreword Reviews, Locus, Quill & Quire, Lightspeed Magazine*, and many other venues.

STRANGERS AMONG US

Tales of the Underdogs and Outcasts
Edited by Susan Forest and Lucas K. Law
2017 (Canadian SF&F) Aurora Award winner
2017 Alberta Book Publishing Award winner

We are your fathers and mothers, brothers and sisters, sons and daughters, friends and lovers, invisible among you. We are your outcasts and underdogs, and often, your unsung heroes. Nineteen science fiction and fantasy authors tackle the delicate balance between mental health and mental illness.

THE SUM OF US

Tales of the Bonded and Bound
Edited by Susan Forest and Lucas K. Law
2018 (Canadian SF&F) Aurora Award winner
2018 Alberta Book Publishing Award finalist

What would your world be like without someone or something to care for or to care with? What if there are no front-line workers to support us? From the worlds of twenty-three science fiction and fantasy authors comes a gift that can be funny, heartwarming, strange, or sad. Or not what we expect.

WHERE THE STARS RISE
Asian Science Fiction and Fantasy
   Edited by Lucas K. Law and Derwin Mak
   2018 (Canadian SF&F) Aurora Award finalist
   2018 Alberta Book Publishing Award winner

Take a journey through Asia and beyond with twenty-three original thought-provoking and moving stories about identities, belonging, and choices—stories about where we come from and where we are going. Each wrestling between ghostly pasts and uncertain futures.

SHADES WITHIN US
Tales of Migrations and Fractured Borders
   Edited by Susan Forest and Lucas K. Law
   2019 (Canadian SF&F) Aurora Award finalist
   2019 Alberta Book Publishing Award winner

Join twenty-one speculative fiction authors to examine the dreams, struggles, and triumphs of those who choose or are forced to leave home and familiar places. Stories that transcend borders, generations, and cultures—to hold fast to home, to family—to strive for a better life.

SEASONS BETWEEN US
Tales of Identities and Memories
   Edited by Susan Forest and Lucas K. Law
   2022 (Canadian SF&F) Aurora Award finalist
   2022 Alberta Book Publishing Award finalist

What is a life well-lived? How should life be lived? What kind of stories will you leave behind? Travel with twenty-three speculative fiction authors through the seasons of life to capture the memories, identities, and moments of stepping through the portal of change, as they cope with their own journeys of growing older.

HELP US CHANGE THE WORLD, ONE BOOK AT A TIME

www.laksamedia.com